THE AUTHOR

BY

ROBERT BANFELDER

BB
~~
BROADWATER BOOKS
Riverhead, New York

Praise for *The Author*

"Banfelder is a very talented fiction writer who manages to weave his knowledge of the outdoors into his works. His novels are expertly crafted and positively compelling. Like *The Teacher*, *The Author* will have you sitting on the edge of your seat waiting for what comes next." Angelo Peluso, author, *Fly Fishing the Surf*

"Banfelder's descriptions are detailed, the novel well plotted, and his imagination without bounds. The book is well researched and has much to offer those interested in fishing and its gear, boats or environmental pollution. It gives the reader a peek into the world of police investigation and Mafia manipulation and control. Like the wonderful meal prepared at the Bella Sera restaurant, the thrills and chills just keep appearing, course after course after course." Donna Gestri, author, *Sweet Figs, Bitter Greens*

"If you're into *Criminal Minds* and *Dexter*, you are definitely going to enjoy *The Author*. The book will make you aware of your surroundings in the same way *Jaws* gave you that uneasy feeling in the water. The source of your fear is the character Malcolm Columba who is a vicious genius with no conscience. He is equal to Hannibal Lecter in his diabolical evil and twice as vengeful as the eco-terrorist in this contemporary suspense thriller." Eva Ercolani, New York

"As an avid reader of mystery, police and legal novels *The Author* is the most fascinating psychological thriller I have read since *The Silence of the Lambs*. Never has there been anything about a serial killer been so well written. The writer must have spent much time researching the material. All the details and descriptions of the characters and locations are very vivid leaving nothing to imagination." Edward Goodfield, Florida

The Buzz About *The Teacher*
Sequel to *The Author*

"*The Teacher* is a novel that really teaches as it entertains. It maintains an excellent flow and, being a very "visual" reader, I could easily see into the mind of Clarence (from the Latin word meaning "clear one") Emery. Very cleverly written." Betty B. Fitch, North Carolina

"This was a different genre for me to read but it kept me on the edge of my seat." Donna Hogan, Houston, Texas

"Ah, the master of suspense thrillers returns with a fast-paced and terrifying story that will chill you to the bone, even on the hottest day of the year." Patti Ann Bengen, author, *New Beginnings*

"If you like psychological thrillers or loved *Silence of the Lambs*, then *The Teacher* will prove to be a story that keeps you interested and reading until the very end. You will find yourself wanting to be a character in the book to actually help with the capturing and doing away with Clarence." Armchair Interviews

BOOKS BY ROBERT BANFELDER

Fiction

The Richard Geist Trilogy

Dicky, Richard, and I
The Signing
The Triumvirate

The Justin Barnes Four-Book Series

The Author
Winner "Best Suspense Thriller" ~ NewBookReviews

The Teacher
Winner "Best Suspense Thriller" ~ NewBookReviews

Knots
The Good Samaritans
***

Trace Evidence

Battered

Nonfiction

The Fishing Smart <u>Anywhere</u> Handbook for Salt Water & Fresh Water

The North American Small & Big Game Hunting Smart Handbook
Bonus Feature: Hunting Africa's & Australia's Most Dangerous Game

The Essential Guide to Writing and Getting Published
12 Color-Coded Lessons for Easy Comprehension
Bonus Feature
Making Decent Dollars ~ Plus Little-Known Reward-Reaping Benefits

This book is dedicated to

Jacqueline

Inspiration is the be-all and end-all.

Book I

Chapter 1

Eastern Long Island was enjoying a mild winter well into the middle of January. However, as the weatherman had warned, a steady cold spell suddenly swept the area, fathering freezing temperatures that would long be remembered to mark the new millennium.

Aboard a Sunrise Express bus bound for New York City, a young woman sat reading a current paperback novel. She was particularly pretty, casually but neatly dressed. The man sitting across the aisle from her duly noted that fact—as with the others he had pursued—although the newspapers throughout several states had used the word, *stalked*.

Wendy caught him staring and curled a corner of her mouth into a snide rebuff, lowering her dark eyes back to the thriller. The Suffolk Community College freshman first noticed him when she boarded in Aquebogue. That he noticed her, too, would be an understatement, for Malcolm had been watching her for months. It was the first time she had seen him en route—or elsewhere, for that matter. There was nothing out of the ordinary about the man, or she certainly would have moved toward the rear of the crowded coach. Complacently, she took the aisle seat alongside two middle-aged women: one in a state of semiconsciousness; the other, nearest the window, absorbed in her crossword puzzle.

Perfect, she thought. *To read and be left alone.*

Malcolm chastised himself, fighting off the urge to stare or even steal a tiny glance. *There will be plenty of time for that later, Wendy*, he absolutely thrilled at the event on the horizon. But first, the boat show at the Javits Center.

He knew her middle and last name, too. He could hardly wait to hear it on radio and TV—savor it in the local papers, as well as the Long Island edition of the mainstream press. Perhaps even stand before the student's headstone someday . . . her full name chiseled into the polished granite gravestone in the cemetery off of John Street in Riverhead. *Maybe even touch it!*

𝔚𝔢𝔫𝔡𝔶 𝔄𝔫𝔫𝔢 𝔏𝔦𝔫𝔡𝔢𝔫
1982–2000

Malcolm pictured it clearly in his tortured mind.

Yes.

Wendy's name engraved just beneath her maternal grandmother's.

But he was getting way ahead of himself.

God, how he wanted to sneak a single peek anew. He could barely contain himself, oblivious to the elderly man's head lolling against his right shoulder.

The bus driver had navigated the big machine toward the curb when the passenger seated next to Malcolm suddenly came alive, apologizing with embarrassment before turning his attention to the small group gathered along the sidewalk, forming a single line. The young men and women moved forward impatiently, shivering just beyond the cold, frosty window, which the octogenarian wiped clear with the back of a blue-wool gloved hand.

Malcolm kept his eyes dead ahead, momentarily rapt in the snake-like hiss as the driver applied the air brakes, bringing the bus to a full stop in front of a Hess station across from the Peconic Diner on Route 58. Several bundled-up teenage girls quickly boarded, immediately followed by their boyfriends. The driver's assistant asked one young man for a name and the number of people in his party, then checked them off the charter listing.

It was 8:15 a.m. The bus was already fifteen minutes behind schedule.

Malcolm returned his thoughts to Wendy. She was a slow but careful reader. She would take at least a month to finish a book, though he knew she had not another day left to finish anything, save her last meal. He had watched her several times in the New York Public Library, then once on a train—absorbed in a single passage upon the page. Focused. Turning the writer's words over carefully in her mind. Tunneling through his world . . . heedfully. *Yes.* Savoring the flavor of the author's state of mind. Smiling or furrowing her brow skeptically before moving ahead in the chapter. Of course, Malcolm could quote the novelist's prose chapter and verse, if pressed. Oh, she would be very impressed with him, he felt quite sure.

He had met many young women that way. First, by casually asking them what they thought of this book or that. How they either loved or loathed a particular character. If he spied a perspective *candidate* reading a novel that he had not devoured, and wanted to impress her next time out, he would plow through the tome in a single evening and be ready to discuss any aspect of the book; from the writer's style, to character development. And if he were talking to a dummy, he would home in on her limited interest concerning the passage that simply *grossed her out*, or the part that she found *positively groovy*; even *awesome*! But if he found a *truly* bright one, he would shyly offer commentary on structure, syntax, theme and underlying motifs.

Once, he invested two nights reading Nin, and was quite prepared to impress a pretty NYU student. The only problem was that he never saw the young woman again. He had observed her on the subway for two semesters before she suddenly disappeared. *Where?* He had been absolutely furious with both her and himself. For a nanosecond, Malcolm thought that his colleague, Clarence Emery, might have snatched her. But that would have been tantamount to the United States of America betraying Saudi Arabia.

Ludicrous.

Wendy, in many ways, reminded him of that graduate student. Aloof. Self-assured. Full of herself. *Oh, she'd soon curl and crease more than just a corner of her mouth in abrupt rejection if not repulsion,* he promised himself, for she would experience—firsthand —the means and methods the *author* literally employed in writing off *his* victims. Nonfiction at its finest.

Malcolm Columba looked up at one of the blank overhead TV monitors, projecting a movie of his own in his mind—excitedly envisioning several unspeakable scenes upon the screen. On it, Wendy Anne Linden was shivering hysterically, pleading with her abductor to simply end her torment, knowing that he would never let her go . . . grasping and understanding completely . . . gasping in the icy cold night air as she felt it firmly grip her entire being—until she could feel no more.

3

Numb.

Anything but dumb was the pretty young coed seated just across the aisle.

The mystery thriller Miss Wendy Anne Linden was engrossed in would not come close to the terror she would soon experience. Although, outsiders looking in—at first glance—might see the whole affair as anticlimactic.

Malcolm's mind tingled with anticipation.

Just one quick look.

No, he scolded himself.

Chapter 2

S elected from the commodious cellar, one of Evan Tamblin's servants carefully uncorked and poured from a fine bottle of 1947 Château Chevel Blanc. Value: $5,000. The rare vintage had reached its fifty-third year. The extraordinary industrialist was about to celebrate his sixty-second birthday. Without fanfare, the evening meal for the handsome couple was orchestrated around the splendid vin. Preparations began at 6 a.m. that morning by a staff of six; that is, three men and three women who knew their way around a kitchen as honeybees do a hive. Like busy little bees, Tamblin's hives of industry were composed of vast colonies of conscientious workers. Many were among the best and brightest in their diverse fields of endeavor.

Research and development in such areas as chemicals and pharmaceuticals were the crowning successes of Tamblin's empire. Evan's genius was highlighted by his marked ability to put and keep his people together. Tight-knit folks. People from all walks of life. From laborers to lobbyists. The man's corporations and concerns comprised well over twenty-five thousand employees within three dozen highly successful organizations, with distribution centers throughout fifty states and thirty-one foreign countries.

Needless to say, the entrepreneur could well afford the finer things in life. The irony being, of course, that Tamblin had precious little time to enjoy anything; hence, his selection of a fine wine to complement the fare—sheer enjoyment to be shared and consumed in a single, quiet evening at home with the light of his life.

Evan Tamblin sat at the head of the table. His second wife, Sally, thirty-three and lovely to look at, sat to his immediate left. If she were seated opposite him, as whenever the two entertained en masse, opera glasses would be required by half their guests, if only to define her shade of lipstick or catch a glimpse of her comely, youthful features. Precisely fifty cherry wood chairs bridged the expanse along but one side of the highly polished matching Queen Anne table. One hundred and two seats in all.

Tonight, however, Sally relaxed beside her lord and master in their modest waterfront mansion in South Jamesport, overlooking Flanders and Great Peconic Bays.

"Happy birthday, my love," Sally toasted her husband warmly.

Evan raised his Riedel goblet to hers with a gentle clink, then smiled handsomely. "Thank you, Sally. And I do wish myself many more," he declared immodestly. "With you by my side, of course," he added. "I cannot believe that God has been so good to me through the course of years."

"You are a man of goodness and vision, Evan Tamblin. It's no wonder that you're blessed." Sally brought the brim to her lips and took a sip. "Mmm. As fine a wine as the man beside me," she assured him, setting down her glass. "What is it, dear? Second time this evening. You look as though you're lost in thought, a good galaxy away. Preoccupied tonight?"

Evan took his eyes away from the setting January sun and fixed them on his attractive wife. "I was just thinking about Patricia, and how nice it would be if she were here with us tonight." He sighed sadly, the weight of his statement couched in undeniable disappointment.

"Well, she'll be flying in early for the weekend, dear. The question is, will you be here?"

"I've got to be in Boston by Thursday morning. But I'll be home for the weekend."

"Are you sure?" Sally took another sip.

"Absolutely, positively, and without a doubt," he assured her with a promising smile.

"Good, because Patricia and I are planning a little surprise for you."

Evan laughed heartily. "You've never planned anything *little* since I've known you, darling."

"I'm glad you note the obvious. So, I can count on your being here for the *entire* weekend." It was not a question.

"I'll be flying back Friday afternoon. Promise."

Sally was all smiles. She had the surprise of Evan's life in store for him.

The couple's eyes momentarily followed the flight of a single gray-white gull over the open body of water.

Chapter 3

Through a light snow, Malcolm Columba watched the easterly flow of the channel as it slowly sliced its way through the slushy ice-covered surface at the rate of approximately a foot every thirty minutes. However, daily back-to-back frigid temperatures in the twenties, teens, and single digits managed to keep the upper section of the Peconic River frozen solid as it had for a fortnight.

Bubble systems and de-icers barely eroded the four to six-inch thicknesses that imprisoned docks and watercraft held fast within the river's frozen death-like grip. Ice-eaters were impossible for immediate purchase, with waiting periods of up to a week for delivery at marine supply stores. Fistfights broke out over a first-come first-served policy, regardless of who ordered what, or when. Generators and compressors were on back order, so if the protective systems were not already in place, their purpose was moot. The damage was already done. Those unfortunates who did not have such equipment, found their fixed or floating platforms curved and twisted like the crest of a rogue wave, its frozen force uprooting pilings and laying piers out of the perpendicular, all in a matter of the first forty-eight hour freeze. Sledge hammers and chain saws flew out of hardware and retail stores.

The frozen body of Wendy Linden was found in the early morning hours, reposed on the snowy bow of an old wooden thirty-foot sportfisherman at a marina off East Main Street in Riverhead. The young woman lay clad in a black bikini. The captain of the vessel had discovered the stark frozen figure shortly after he arrived, explaining to the police that his purpose for being there was an attempt to free his hull from the tenacious cold hold of Mother Nature.

Suffolk County homicide detectives were busy trying to keep warm while investigating the area, interviewing residents who lived along or near the river. To say that the perpetrator's trail was cold would be a gross understatement—about as revealing and meaningful as the ambient temperature itself. That is, if there even was foul play suspected, Malcolm knew the authorities were sure to question.

Fourteen degrees Fahrenheit at 6:30 a.m.

Ground zero felt like minus zero.

No footprints in the fresh frozen snow leading to or from the boat, other than the captain's, were found. No additional tire tracks other than the owner's were discovered. No sign of a struggle. Not a single clue was found within the yellow-taped perimeter or beyond it.

Forensics would have anything but a field day, Malcolm grinned with certain satisfaction. They would work for what little they would get. But the getting was not going to be easy. Not like in that silly novel Wendy Anne Linden had been reading on the bus. The police would uncover very little trace evidence until the thaw. No apparent connection or conclusion could be drawn for the time being. He felt certain of that.

Fate would not fold him. God and country could not afford to let that happen. Each death scene *must* continue to prove dramatically different from the others, but with a common thread connecting each and every one. Every crime scene *had* to be a new one for the books.

In time, the only prediction the police would forecast with any assurance would be the impending nature of the killer's evolving violence. That, he could not help. It would take him by storm. To restrain his actions would be tantamount to attempting foreplay with an unbridled, licentious lover. And if the authorities thought him mad, so much the better. *They* would be the cocky and overconfident ones who would falter.

These were the tenets that Malcolm Columba held in his heart and mind and soul.

Returning to his cozy hideaway, Malcolm shivered and smiled happily while removing a pair of wet hockey skates from a beat-up black leather suitcase, wiping dry the blades before setting them aside. On the wall behind a narrow workbench hung a Peg-Board holding two new pair of skates suspended from silver hooks: figure skates and racers. Both ends of the speed skate blades were as pointed as a pin. To the right of the skates protruded full and empty plastic spools of monofilament fishing line, deep-trolling wire, a thick roll of duct tape, packages of amber-colored surgical tubing, and lengths of quarter-inch braided nylon line. Taking down one of the figure skates from the wall before putting on a pair of safety glasses, Malcolm started up the bench grinder and went to work on the single shiny blade, passing it back and forth across one of the whirling wheels. With deft precision, he began honing a keen edge that would soon rival that of a *samurai* sword.

Thirty minutes later, Malcolm switched off the machine. Tomorrow he would finish the pair by hand.

Chapter 4

The new trawler was scheduled for early morning delivery to the couple's home. The hauler had been instructed to drop both boat and trailer on Tamblin's property at the rear of the driveway. It would be sitting high and dry upon its shiny silver frame, well before Evan returned home from Boston. Sally planned the surprise right down to the tiniest detail: a giant sea-green bow fixed to the bow pulpit of the forty footer. The mild winter that held to the middle of the month and initially sparked the novel idea was not lost in the frigid moment. The first mate would present her captain with his little *ship* in a most befitting way. Evan, Sally and her beautiful stepdaughter, Patricia, would, weather permitting, take a shakedown cruise well east of the frozen waters of the Peconic River, if even for an hour; the trio would be well protected from the elements in the vessel's cozy pilothouse.

Therefore, when the boat hauler showed up later that morning from Maryland, Sally had new plans, along with a list of very specific demands. However, the man was insistent on leaving the trailer and trawler at the assigned address as directed by the Annapolis dealership. Period. He flatly refused to launch the vessel, even though the boat ramp was but a block away from the couple's private dock. Still, Sally had her mind made up, and that was that.

"But it's been winterized, ma'am," the hauler further explained. "Batteries are disconnected, manifolds and hoses have been drained and antifreeze—"

"And so she will have to be winterized again. My problem. Not yours."

"You've got *really* cold weather here, and—"

"And promising to break before the end of the week," Sally came back persistently. "Besides, re-winterizing can easily be done in the water. End of discussion."

"Look. I'm only the transporter, ma'am."

"Look." Sally revealed a hundred dollar bill. "All I'm asking you to do is haul this boat down to the ramp, which is literally around the bend. I'll hook up a battery myself, then pop in the stern plug. All you have to do is drop her in, and you can be on your way."

"This invoice says Scallop Lane."

Sally smiled indulgently. "You'll still be on Scallop Lane."

The man eyed the money. "Just around the bend from here?"

"Not a foot further."

"And you're gonna bring 'er around to your dock yourself, you said."

"Blindfolded, if I have to. Piece of cake. Wind is five knots. Tide is up. Current's a knot. I've single-handedly docked fifty-foot vessels in twenty-knot winds," Sally lied, although she had assisted her former husband in such sea conditions and knew she could do so if she had to. "Besides, our floating dock is well protected with fender-wheels and rubber guards all along the edge. It's really no big deal."

"Drivin' here, I saw the river's frozen over solid," he hedged. "Part of the bay as well."

"That's the Peconic River and Flanders Bay beyond it. Here, it's fine. I checked the launching ramp before you came. No problem." She subtly moved the money between her thumb and forefinger.

The boat hauler lightly stroked the tips of his fingers against a day-old growth of stubble.

"I don't know, ma'am."

"This would be for launching the boat," Sally said, putting the bill in his hand. "And this is a separate gratuity for bringing the boat north in one piece." Sally displayed another hundred.

"That's really not necessary, ma'am," the man said, staring down at the second crisp bill.

"But appreciated?" Sally questioned through a shrewd smile.

"Most certainly," the hauler answered wisely, gingerly plucking the second hundred from between her long, thin, gloved fingers.

"I'll go get us some tools," she offered.

"As a matter of fact, I have what we need in the truck." The man pocketed the money, then opened a narrow door to the extra-cab, getting his toolbox and other equipment.

Sally believed that if she had laid another hundred on the man, he would have gladly washed and waxed her new Mercedes sitting in the driveway. Hell, he might even have run out and bought a bottle of Champagne for the christening celebration, she entertained smugly.

As it turned out, Hank, the boat hauler, and Sally, the mariner, brought the boat around together. By late morning, they had the vessel secured to the private dock with lines and protective fenders.

There she sat, high in the water column. Clean and whisper white like the world around them—save the big green bow blowing in the snow-swept breeze.

It looked beautiful, berthed at their home port on the bay. Her lines were traditional—a downeast hull. She bore a workboat appearance outside, but with a luxurious interior: a full galley three steps down to port; a marine head with a separate shower stall to starboard, a well-appointed stateroom forward; guest accommodations aft. Come spring, it would serve as their little getaway; away from phones, faxes, and computers. Though she might first have to deep six Evan's cell phone and laptop, too, Sally considered. *Either that or Evan himself,* she reflected with delight.

Chapter 5

Detectives Brian Archer and Dean Nelson continued to supervise and work the crime scene that both Man and Mother Nature had preserved: the former with stakes, yellow tape and photographs; the latter with freezing temperatures that promised to retain a woolly mammoth, let alone the most minuscule clue that lay beneath the icy snow-capped banks of the Peconic River.

"He had to have come across the river from Southampton's side," Brian Archer maintained. "Probably used a sled of some sort."

"Unless he 'coptered or parachuted in," Nelson kidded.

"It just *had* to snow last night. Murphy's Law."

"Why do I have the feeling the perp counted on that?"

"If you were going to haul a body out here from the other side of the river, where would you begin?"

"Shortest distance between two points. Flanders." Dean Nelson pointed directly south across the river from the boat on which Wendy Ann Linden's body was found earlier that morning—now just a frozen imprint on the snow-covered foredeck . . . like an abandoned open coffin.

"Hennesey and the team found nothing over there but the cold," Brian bantered, facing back toward the boat. The sportfisher's stern displayed its name and origin in large, black, block lettering. **SEA~SHE**. Beneath it: **FORT LAUDERDALE**. "Maybe we'll get lucky; that is, if this stuff ever melts," he added pessimistically.

"Yeah, maybe we'll get to go to sunny Florida beforehand," Nelson said rather hopefully.

"Florida?"

"Sure. We could *plant* a palm leaf under all this white shit for forensics and tell Theo we want to pick up the trail in Orlando."

"Why Orlando?" Brian went along.

"Why? Because Doreen and Dawn took a flight out of Islip at eight-twenty this morning. Spirit. Spirited mother and daughter off to Orlando for the next three months. Embassy Suites. The beginning of our trial separation. Trial by ordeal. They'll be in fantasyland shortly, while I'm facing reality in fourteen-degree weather here with you."

"Well, it's more like in the thirties, now. Thank God for small favors."

"May be in the thirties, but that's without the wind chill factor, I can assure you."

"Spirit, you say?"

"Name of the airline.

"Never heard of it."

"Of the airline, or the wind chill factor?"

"Spirit," Brian managed through a yawn.

"Some budget *kamikaze* outfit out of a hole in the sky."

"That's an uplifting recommendation."

"Listen, you take your chances with any of them today. Me? I wouldn't fly commercial if a victim's life depended on it," he deadpanned.

"Department would love to hear that one."

"Fuck the department. I'd release that statement to the press."

"Public would love to hear that one," Brian ribbed.

"Listen. I've got six months, and I'm out of here. I'll have done my twenty, then it's *sayonara*, baby."

"What's with these Jap references this morning, Dean? Huh? *Kamikaze, sayonara.*"

"Slanted view on flying those unfriendly skies, I guess. Me? I'm gonna get me a go-anywhere fishin' machine like this one—" he declared, knocking appreciatively on the owner's hull with a sharp rap of glove-covered knuckles "—and then it's off to a blue horizon."

"And with your luck, one of those Spirit pilots will probably fall out of a hole in the sky and land right on top of you."

Dean Nelson looked at his partner curiously. "Whattaya some kind of jinx or somethin'? Tryin' to put the whammy on me, or what?"

Detective Lieutenant Theodore Groche hustled up a snowy embankment, down a shoveled frozen finger pier, then over to the pair. "Hey, know how cold it is in Washington, D.C. this morning, fellas?" the five-foot-seven figure and head of homicide questioned.

"No, Theo," Brian answered, playing straight man to their boss. "How cold is it?"

"It's so cold that the politicians have their hands in their *own*

14

pockets," the top cop delivered in deadpan. "Ever hear the one—"

"Ever hear of an airline called Spirit?" Dean interrupted, purposely cutting the commanding officer's routine short.

"Sure," Theo answered.

"See?" the short-timer said, addressing his partner with a smirk.

"Which reminds me. Your daughter just called and said to tell you they landed safely and not to worry," Theo relayed, funneling a single breath into a cupped pair of bony stark-white hands, capturing the ephemeral warmth within. "They're on their way to Epcot."

"Wonderful. She tell you to tell me the temperature in order to rub it in?"

"Seventy-two degrees."

Detective Brian Archer held a little smile in place until Nelson thought of something smart to say.

"And tell this guy standing next to me that it's no more than fourteen degrees out here; and that's in the fucking sun," Nelson complained bitterly, throwing up the collar of his coat for emphasis.

"It's thirty-two degrees," Theo corrected. "And that's with the wind chill factor. Put your long johns on, Dean, and get me a break in this dubious case."

"Why don't you get us some *real* help and pull Connolly out of retirement?" Dean balked. "He found that missing school principal in a block of ice when forensics couldn't even find their way to Laurel Lake. Right up Mick's alley. Cold-case files," the veteran detective chaffed half-jokingly.

"Can't," Theo said.

"Why not?"

"He's in Orlando—probably on the phone with your wife as we speak," the lieutenant teased.

"What the hell is he doing in Orlando, anyhow? I thought he was down in the Keys."

"Disney."

"So call 'im," he repeated.

"I don't think you understand."

"What don't I understand, Theo?"

"He's *with* Disney."

"With Disney?"

Theo nodded. "He works for them now. He's down there with his mistress and ready-made family."

"Call 'im anyhow."

"I did. Just to say hello."

"What did he say?"

"Nothing."

"Nothing? What do you mean, nothing?"

"He hung up on me."

"Why that ungrateful—"

"You'd never forget or fuck the department like that, would you Dean?" Brian asked with a smile. "Right?"

"Why, I should say not," Nelson declared emphatically, shooting a sneer at his partner. "Theo knows I'm a company man. Ain't that right, Theo?"

"True blue," Theo swore.

"Listen, Lieutenant."

The lieutenant stood looking up into the cold steel-blue eyes of the veteran detective. He was all ears. "Yes, Dean?"

"Maybe later you could ask the captain of this vessel if he'd be interested in getting rid of it since . . . well, you know."

"Since he found a dead body on his bow this morning?"

"Well, yeah. But for the right price, of course."

"You mean, for a song?"

"That would be music to my ears, Theo."

Theo shook his head.

"Why?"

"He won't go for it."

"How do you know that?"

"Because I already broached the subject," Theo tormented the man.

"You? You're a lake and small stream fly fisherman, Theo. This here's a blue water fishing vessel."

"I didn't mean for me, Dean."

"No? Then for who?"

"For you."

"Me?"

"Sure," Theo said with a straight face. "I was going to buy it, then sell it to you for ten percent more than *I* could steal it for."

Dean Nelson studied his lieutenant for a second before he opened his mouth. "And how did you even know that I'd be interested in *this* particular boat?" he emphasized, once again firmly and fondly knocking upon the solid wooden hull.

"How? Why, it was all over the department from the minute we started this investigation. That's all you've talked about, I'm hearing. As a matter of fact, if you had put half the amount of energy into this case as you did in surveying the boat, maybe we'd have something. What do you think?"

"What do I think? I think you're truly a ball-buster, buster," Dean Nelson retorted. "I really and truly do, Lieutenant."

Chapter 6

Twenty-one-year-old Patricia Tamblin flew into Gabreski Airport in Westhampton and was greeted by a smiley-faced driver with a shiny new vehicle that she had never seen before.

"Who are you?" the young woman asked cautiously, setting down one bag.

"Your driver, Miss Tamblin. Madison's car broke down, and your stepmother called me. He's out on the dock breaking up ice and trying to keep the new boat in one piece before your father gets back from his business trip and has a hemorrhage," he affirmed. "One of the ice-eaters broke, so she has Patrick trying to secure a couple of them from a marina in Connecticut. They're next to impossible to find anywhere here on the Island, and if you try and order them, it's a day or two to have them FedEx'd. You know your stepmom. She *wants* and *has* to have them *now*. And rightly so, because the ice is a killer," Malcolm reassured her with a warm smile.

Patricia knew her stepmother, all right. The problem was that she did not know this stranger. It was unlike Sally not to call with any change in plans. The young woman put her overnight bag down beside the other and was about to retrieve her cell phone.

"Truth is, Sally's in a frenzy right now. She's out there on the dock with Madison, making sure the ice is off those pilings; running the boat every now and again to ensure the engine block doesn't crack; inside making certain the kitchen crew is squared away; on the phone fighting with the florist; and giving the manager at the marina up in Connecticut a piece of her mind. Sally told me to tell you she's sorry the maiden voyage is off until the first thaw," he reported.

"Well, *I'm* sure as hell not. That woman is a bit eccentric, I'll have you know."

A sharp wind whipped across the airfield. Patricia and the man braced themselves against the force.

"Come on, Miss Tamblin. You can call her from the car if you think I'm Jack the Ripper." Malcolm grabbed up both bags in one arm, then gently placed a hand at the small of her back, guiding her toward the car. "It's too damn cold out here to think let alone hold a conversation."

Patricia stopped him cold. "What's your name?" she asked, before taking another step.

"Malcolm. Malcolm Columba, ma'am. I'm one of your father's employees. Overseas branch; Caracas. Bridgeport, Connecticut whenever I'm here in the States."

Malcolm knew she knew the name.

"Well, why didn't you say so, Malcolm? Dad's only mentioned you maybe a hundred million times," she declared, then smiled easily. "You got coffee in the car?"

"You rarely drink coffee, Miss Tamblin. Besides, Sally told me to make sure I brought a piping hot thermos of hot chocolate along for you."

"Well, did you?"

He opened the rear door for her. "Indeed I did, Miss Tamblin."

"Call me Patricia, Malcolm."

"Yes, ma'am."

Chapter 7

"It's a wonderful life, Patricia," Malcolm said rather morosely. "Anyhow, that's what your dad and stepmother would say anyway. At least that's what was quoted in the press. But you can't always believe what you read in the newspapers. True? Yet, when you read something over and over again—well, I guess you can lend some credence to it. No?"

Patricia could not muster a word or convey a single response—either by way of a nod, or the turn of her head. In fact, the once pretty woman could not move so much as a muscle at the moment. She wanted to scream but dared not make even a muffled moan, for he had warned her repeatedly from the moment she regained consciousness. Patricia simply shivered with her mouth silenced and sealed shut. Not with anything unimaginative like a strip of duct tape smacked across her face. For that would have been so crude and careless and ordinary. Malcolm was so much more selective and discriminating than that, having secured her silence with the aid of a hooked needle and length of fourteen-pound test fluorocarbon fishing line with which he had stitched and locked her full lips together firmly.

Yes . . . as if she were a sawdust doll whose gob could easily spill its packing, or reveal a dirty, dark secret, he mused merrily. *Maybe even yell for help. God help her.*

That he could not have.

Patricia lay on her back in bra and panties. Around a slim waist was a wide, well-worn man's leather belt. Her body rested within a cold, old-fashioned cast iron bathtub, set upon chipped and rusty metal claws. The young woman's mouth revealed a marvel of red that had bled, and then congealed about her chin like a crusty, crimson pirate's beard. A single length of one hundred-pound test monofilament line was threaded through the crossbar in the drain, up and around the industrialist's daughter's throat. Fastened firmly. Additionally, a stainless steel trolling wire, lashed through the bridge of her nose and across her eyes, held her head securely in place. She was not nearly as attractive as when he had picked her up at the airport that morning, Malcolm ruminated, imagining her as some sort of grotesque female adaptation of Lemuell Gulliver in the hands of the Lilliputians.

"Comfy?"

Patricia's dark blue eyes were two polluted pools of steaming hatred mixed abundantly with fear; hatred of the sordid smiley face looming just above her; sheer dread of the unknown—although she should have realized the situation by now. Not necessarily all the whys and wherefores that brought her to this point in time. Only the end result—that she was surely going to die. Just as surely as the sun would melt the icy Peconic shores before springtime. But for poor Patricia, so much the sooner, her tormentor thought and tarried, promising himself that she would first drown in her own sorrow.

Malcolm traced a finger along the section of titanium leader wire that bound Patricia's long and lithesome legs near the top of the tub . . . around her slim ankles, then over its edge—securely fastened to a vertical heating pipe running through the floor and ceiling of the prewar building. Coils of nickel-copper Monel held fast the captive's wrists as well, anchored at the small of her back by the belt.

Reaching across her, he turned on one of the cracked enameled faucets. Full blast. The icy-cold rusty water gurgled and splashed down in spurts before it forcefully hit her gory, hoary countenance. Fifty stitches suddenly tore a gap in the girl's supple, fleshy lips.

Malcolm quickly turned on the other faucet, along with a musical recording—loudly—drowning out her cry for help to the Mother of God. At least that is what he thought he heard from the mouth of Patricia Tamblin as the young woman writhed and thrashed violently within her bloody bath.

The floor of the tub was filling quickly, and Patricia's long black hair proved to be a hindrance as it snaked and coiled its way around and down into the open drain, clogging up the works as she struggled furiously to lift her head, fighting the futility of trying to raise or twist her body from one side or the other.

Again and again, Patricia fought to keep her head above the rising water. Fought to break the filaments that held her fast. But Patricia's ferocious fight was to be in vain. Dully, she heard her own muffled screams mingled with the crashing force of rushing water; the sanguineous liquid was quickly covering the lobes of her ears while the tears only added to the level of a watery grave . . . engulfing Patricia . . . the way her father and others like him were deliberately drowning the innocent, too . . . slowly—so that but a few would ever notice or even care, Malcolm mused.

The level of the water was up to Patricia's temples. And in all her anguish, she was taking in the frigid foul froth like a leaky hull sinking slowly in a lonely harbor.

Still, Patricia fought savagely to hold and keep her head up high . . . the unyielding loop of line cutting cleanly into her swan-like throat . . . the steady stream of water blasting away above the bloody bridge of her turned-up nose . . . wending its way and filling her nostrils completely.

In that chilling instant, Patricia's eyes seemed to comprehend the meaning of Malcolm's message. Oh, he so wanted her to fully understand without his having to explain or shout it out above the roar of the water and *The Best of Vivaldi*.

The tub was filling at a far greater rate than it was draining because of Patricia's lengthy coal-black eddying crop. She could not lift her head more than an inch or two off the tub's slippery surface. Try as she might, Patricia fought futilely to set herself free. Her lustrous inky mop continuously acted as a stopper that could not quite make up its mind whether to seal or send the vile solution southward.

Within several minutes, Patricia's eyes were deeply blanketed by the flow. Malcolm calmly shut off the water and recorder and watched the bloody tub drain ever so slowly.

Not a quarter of an hour later, dead eyes stared blankly up at the somewhat sad yet satisfied face that gazed down upon the distorted countenance of Patricia Tamblin.

Chapter 8

The police huddled just outside the four story walk-up in Flanders, located one block away from a boatyard. A young officer from Southampton Town P.D., who was the first to respond to the shocking scene twelve hours earlier, stood numb—not only from the cold but from the vision he carried around in his mind of the young Tamblin woman. The officer had been questioned thoroughly by several homicide detectives from Southampton, Riverhead, as well as the state police. The officer's handling of the crime scene, coupled with his verbal and written reports, was exemplary. He had taken the initiative and immediately sealed off the apartment to all civilians, allowing no one but seasoned detectives access. Not even fellow patrol officers would he allow entry. Thus, the integrity of the crime scene was maintained. Contamination, if any, was limited to two tenants who discovered the body and swore they touched nothing, having immediately called the police.

Forensics was thorough but unsuccessful, turning up nothing of consequence. Detectives Brian Archer and Dean Nelson were frustrated. Their lieutenant was furious.

"The D.A. and his brethren are breathing down our necks, fellas," Theo declared, sitting in the backseat of an unmarked gray sedan while delivering his harangue via a partially open window. Brian and Dean stood beside the vehicle and listened respectfully. "Not to mention the victims' families, who are trying to blow smoke up our asses. Especially, the Tamblins. To tell you the truth, I'm not sure which group to concern myself with more at the moment. Not even a week, and we've got ourselves two bodies. Zilch in both cases."

"Two bodies that are somehow connected," Dean Nelson insisted.

"There's nothing to connect them," Theo blew. "We've been over this a dozen times. At this point, we're not even sure the Linden woman was murdered."

"Come on, Lieutenant," Brian said through an impatient frown.

"You think she just wandered around and wound up on some guy's boat in a bikini in the middle of a freezing January night because she was lost? Or committed suicide by exposing herself to the elements and shivered to death?"

Theo shrugged. "Been known to happen."

"Not a trace of alcohol in her bloodstream, Theo," Dean reminded him. "No barbiturates. No drugs. No needle marks. No nothing."

"What about those tiny splinters on Linden's feet and hands?" Theo raised in question. "She could have been disoriented and crawled around looking for shelter."

Both Dean and Brian shook their heads in unison.

"Not from anywhere on the sportfisher, the lab boys assure us," Dean remarked.

"Just a hot dog with mustard, relish and sauerkraut in her gut, which she probably grabbed at the Javits Boat Show," Brian furthered, driving the point home to his boss.

"Before somebody *grabbed* her," Dean rejoined in support.

"Never boarded the bus back from Manhattan to Aquebogue, although she had a round-trip ticket, Theo."

"So why a sedative in the Tamblin woman's system and not Linden's?"

"Why?" Dean Nelson mocked. "Why did it snow in the Mideast this past week? First snow in fifty years. In the Negev Desert, can you believe? People there woke up in disbelief. White shit all over the backs of their camels and sheep."

"Where's the Negev Desert, Dean?" Theo asked with seeming interest.

"Israel."

"Where'd you learn this?"

"Newspapers. Why?"

"Because you seem more concerned about why it snowed in a goddamn desert than staying on track *here*, Dean. That's why. You've got nothing solid to link the two cases. Do you?"

"C'mon, Theo. We got boats for openers."

"Boats?" The head of homicide smirked. "You've got boats on the brain."

"You bet I do. Patricia Tamblin's body was found not a block away from a boatyard around the corner. Wendy Linden was found on the bow of a sportfisherman in a boatyard in Riverhead, accosted by someone after she left the boat show in Manhattan, I'm telling you."

"We don't know for a fact that she was even there, Dean."

"Yeah, well her mother said she wouldn't miss the show for the world. She had her eyes set on a day sailer. Guy selling one at a booth thinks he remembers her from the pix we showed him. Didn't speak to her directly. But he believes she picked up a brochure while he was busy with a couple. Said she was looking over its lines from fore to aft with the eye of a true admirer. By the time he finished his spiel, she was gone."

"And if that show was still running, I think you'd find an excuse to still be down there, Dean. Get my drift?" the lieutenant chided.

Dean Nelson smiled up at the dim and cloudy sky. "When I finally do get that boat, Theo, and I'm sitting in warm and sunny Florida, I'll remember days like today. And just in case there might be some confusion here, I'm talking about your vote of confidence. Not the fucking weather."

"Look. All I'm pointing out is that, ostensibly, we got ourselves a nonviolent death over there," he said, gesturing across the river to Riverhead. "No sign whatsoever of foul play. Strange as hell I'll admit, but backdropped against an overtly vicious, sadistic homicide, here."

"Both within days of each other; each within close proximity to one another as the crow flies," Brian added, bolstering his partner's theory. "This may or may not necessarily be connected to a marine environment or boats per se, but—"

"But unless you see the tub they found the Tamblin woman in as a kind of craft," the commander interrupted with a grin, "I'd begin with the basics, boys. Immediate family, domestic employees, relatives and friends, business associates, and *then* outsiders. Or did you forget good police procedure, fellas?"

Brian stood undaunted. "Still, I feel as Dean does, Lieutenant. Concerning those two bodies, I think we've got ourselves a sole killer out there."

"Well, Howard Mills and his brother are certainly out of commission, guys," Theo concluded, alluding to two noted serial killers—one dead, and the other might just as well be. "Anyhow, you're going to need something concrete to head in the direction you two want to move."

"How about a third body linked to a PWC?" Nelson forecasted. "Think that might do it for you?"

"What's a PWC?" Theo asked.

"Personal water craft," Brian answered with a smile on behalf of his partner.

The top cop scowled and sent up his window in disgust.

Chapter 9

Rita Linden stood staring out one of the upstairs windows off her daughter's bedroom. The modest seven-room colonial on Meetinghouse Creek in Aquebogue was but a stone's throw from the bay. The heartbroken mother ran her swollen red eyes past the row of homes that lined the inlet. A fine water view was afforded from those rooms sharing an easterly exposure when the deciduous shrubs and trees shed their leaves.

The distraught woman fixed a gaze on the dock in the distance where Wendy was to keep her new sailboat come spring. For the better part of nineteen years, her only child shunned piano lessons, ballet lessons, even acting lessons. *"I'm going to be a sailor when I grow up,"* she told her parents as early as her fifth birthday, Rita recalled through her tears, lowering her eyes to the family album she held open in her trembling hands. The couple's young daughter would continuously press her parents for sailing lessons until she finally got her way.

"Well," her father decided some fourteen years ago, *"first will come swimming lessons and, if you prove yourself, we'll see about sailing lessons. How does that sound?"*

"We'll see about swimming lessons when you and Mom promise me sailing lessons when I do prove myself. How does that sound, Daddy?"

"Just ducky, my precocious and precious little girl," her father agreed. *"Just ducky."*

"Mom?"

"Whatever your father says, dear."

And by the following season, at age six, Wendy was not only swimming like a fish, but also diving like a dipper duck. Before the close of summer, as promised, on her seventh birthday, their daughter received her first *Sailfish*: a nifty nine-foot fiberglass boat with a single sail. Wendy's instructor, a middle-aged widow, said by autumn's end that her young protégé was ready to venture the Seven Seas.

By age nine, Wendy had sailed solo all over Great Peconic Bay. At a tender ten years of age, she was navigating at night, with and without the stars to guide her.

"Sailing's a breeze," she would tease novice and seasoned sailors alike, showing off by running tight circles and figure eights around vessels on the hook in Dering Harbor, whose captains hailed her skills both with astonishment and sincere salutes.

A handsome teenager once handed her an ice-cold can of Coke from the swim platform of his parents' anchored yacht as she came cranking by at a good five knots. *"How old are you, cutie?"* the young man called out as she blew by the stern, returning after several minutes with an answer and the empty can.

"Thirteen going on twenty-one," she flirted shamelessly and truthfully. *"And I'll be back before sunset for the deposit,"* she promised, blowing past the transom and the tall, well-tanned lad sporting shoulder-length hair and cut-off jeans.

Both the boat and boy were gone by the time she returned from a sail around Robins Island, but she thought of that young man quite often, confiding in her mother some years later.

"He was the dreamiest in even my waking hours," she swooned. *"But I never saw him again. And it's not like I didn't look for him,"* she declared, then laughed lightheartedly.

Rita wondered if it could have been someone like that boy who took Wendy's life. Perhaps a passerby. Maybe a monster of a man who had been watching her daughter for days or even months . . . watching her mature into a beautiful young woman.

Angrily, Mrs. Linden turned away from the window and sank to her knees in a fit of sobbing. Cursing God. Cursing the police. Cursing Suffolk County. Cursing the boat show. Cursing her husband who had allowed their only daughter to get mixed up with boats to begin with. In a state of anguish and mixed emotions, Rita Linden closed, then brought and held the family album protectively to her breast.

Chapter 10

Sitting before her computer terminal in the Suffolk County homicide division in Yaphank, Detective Kim Booker spent the better part of a day processing information—feeding and retrieving data, keying in on behavioral modalities relating to violent crimes of a sadistic bent. She was particularly interested in crimes connected to or committed around boatyards, shipyards and marinas within the past five years. She covered several states. Kim assimilated her findings into a comprehensive listing, then passed it along to Detective Brian Archer. Brian spent the remainder of that day and part of the next on the phone.

"We got a call back from Maryland this morning," Brian announced with a note of excitement in his voice.

"Yeah?" Nelson said, unenthused.

"They've got themselves two unsolveds of a rather bizarre nature. Both female. One in '98. The other, September of last year."

"How's it concern us?"

"Laura Haynes. Black woman. Twenty-seven. Construction worker. Pretty. Found not so pretty hanging upside down, laced to a piling at a marina in Edgewater."

Dean Nelson suddenly grew interested. "Edgewater? That's in Florida."

"Well, apparently they've got one in Maryland, too. Pier Seven."

"Laced, you said?"

"Literally. Hands and feet tied with her own laces. Series of square knots. She was found in three feet of water as the tide was going out." Brian was excerpting a series of facts from his notes. "Actually, they were removed from her work boots. Forty-two inch pigskin laces. She was still alive at the time she was drowning."

"So was my neighbor's cat."

"Footwear still on both feet when they found her. No sign of any struggle. Nothing foreign in her system. But get this. A narrow-lipped, empty fishing line spool was jammed into her jaw. Standing on end. The hole in the center of the plastic cylinder flush with her face. Got the picture?"

"To ensure the passage of water."

"Which really didn't matter much because she was upside down and—"

"And the incoming tide would reach her nostrils first."

"So, she'd be sure to take her last breath through the hole in the middle of the spool."

"If not, the rising water would find its way around the edges of the spool anyway."

"We're dealing with a real sick fuck here, Dean. What do you think?"

"I think we need the pix and the full skinny on this one."

"I just got off the phone with a detective sergeant down there. Report and photos are being faxed."

"You said they had two cold cases. Who's the other?"

"Arlene Parker. Caucasian. Twenty. College student. Gorgeous. You're not going to believe this."

"Humor me."

"Found outdoors in a canoe in Annapolis. Tied facedown in a deep, upright canoe. Shallow watery grave."

"Hands tied behind her?"

"Like Patricia Tamblin and the Haynes woman."

"Same knots?"

Brian shook his head. "But secured behind her back with a *belt* —like Tamblin."

"Not Haynes?"

"Not exactly. Hers were laced behind the piling. Lashed like her feet. No belt."

"Maybe because Haynes wouldn't need the leverage that Tamblin needed to help keep her head above water—*faceup*—in a tub. Indoors. Where he felt more secure and could take his time with her. Enjoy the moment."

"That's good, Dean. Really."

"Anything else? Like the Parker woman couldn't rock herself free or something? Spill the water out?"

Brian shook his head sadly. "The canoe was secured on the top row of a cradle. Not how they're usually stored upside down on a rack so that water doesn't collect. This one was right side up and strapped in tight. It wasn't going anywhere. The water that collected was rain water."

"Jesus. What did he tie her with, Bri? Fishing line? Shoelaces? What?"

"Wire leader. Had her lashed and weighted down from her neck to her ankles. Drowned in less than eight inches of water. Recall the record rainfall they got last fall? Somehow, I bet he counted on that."

Dean nodded. "They find anything else?"

"Snorkel, alongside the body," Brian said solemnly.

"So, she panicked and probably spit it out."

The taller of the two nodded gravely. "As I said, it was a deep canoe. Given time, the water still would have risen above the top of the tube. Forensics says she didn't use it. Not for any duration anyhow —according to the depressions on the mouthpiece. They said it would have been bitten to smithereens in her fight for life if she had. Cheap plastic child's toy. A report's on its way from Cellmark. Kim should have it momentarily."

Detective Dean Nelson pulled a comb through a head of healthy jet-black hair. "They turn up anything that we can move on now?"

"Squat. Just like us, they're in the dark. They interviewed scores of folks."

"Well, we've got a few things goin' for us that those Merry-Land boys lack, partner."

"And what's that, Dean?" Brian questioned through a smile, knowing a wisecrack or two was headed his way.

"Tenacity tied to good looks, for openers—except for the obvious fact that only one of us still has all his hair, along with superior intellect . . . not to mention the fact that your partner has a vast knowledge of water, watercraft, weather patterns, and salty, sexy women."

"No argument there, short-timer."

"Didn't think so, Bri."

Chapter 11

S ally Tamblin had called Suffolk County homicide three times a
day, every day, for four days straight. Evan Tamblin was on the
phone with Maryland authorities, demanding that the man who had
delivered the trawler, dockside, to their home on Great Peconic Bay, be
picked up for questioning—the couple apparently nonplused that the
hauler was not even considered a suspect.

"You *haul* his goddamn ass in now, Sergeant, or yours is going
to be on the carpet for dereliction of duty. You got that?"

The desk sergeant in Annapolis was well-aware of the family's
situation, deciding to cut the grieving father a little slack. Otherwise,
the officer might have gotten his Irish up and told the big shot
industrialist how and exactly where to kiss his bloomin' arse.

"We have investigators in the field who believe the fella you're
accusing is in no way connected with the homicides down here, or up
there in New York, either, sir. And that's all I can say about it lest I'd
be compromising an ongoing investigation. Surely, you can appreciate
that, Mr. Tamblin."

"And surely, Sergeant, you can appreciate the fact that it was
my wife who first brought to your attention the connection between
the two murders that took place in your neck of the woods and my
daughter's murder—as well as another young woman up here."

"Sir. At this time we're not even sure there is a connection. We
have people looking into that possibility."

"Then I suggest, moron, that you tell those people to open up
their goddamn eyes."

"I'll be sure to pass that along, Mr. Tamblin," the cop assured
him, about to smash the phone onto its cradle until he heard the
whimpering on the other end of the line. "You still there, Mr.
Tamblin?"

There was a pause. "I'm sorry, Sergeant." Evan Tamblin's
voice quivered. "You didn't deserve that."

"I'm sorry, too, sir. Your daughter and the others didn't deserve what happened to them either. Believe me when I tell you that I empathize. All I can say is that we're doing everything we can down here. And I'll tell you something else. Those boys up there in Suffolk County. The very best. Believe me. Even a moron like me knows that," the cop proffered indulgently, a smile curving the corners of his lips against the mouthpiece.

"I'm really sorry." Tamblin wept.

"Forget it. Listen. If I hear anything that I *can* share with you, I'll call you personally. How's that?"

Evan was nodding and weeping bitterly. "Yes. Pl-please . . . and thank you." The man needed an ally. Not alienation. He was not used to being in a subordinate position. He was not used to taking orders. And that is what they were in effect. Orders. However nicely put. *Don't call us. We'll call you.*

"How is Mrs. Tamblin faring?" the sergeant asked sincerely.

"Not well."

"Be strong for her. She really needs you now, you know." Rarely had the sergeant become personal with a civilian in the course of police work. It felt strange, and he questioned his own judgment.

Evan was shaking his head. "She's the strong one, Sergeant. So much stronger than I. When I learned Patricia was gone, I wa-wanted to die myself."

"Have you two been approached for or sought counseling?"

"Yes."

"Going?"

There was another pause.

"Listen to me. Take my advice and go. Try and make the missus go, too. We didn't want to at first. But our daughter made us. It made things easier, if you can believe that."

Evan Tamblin wanted to ask the man a single question. Actually, a score of them. But he could not bring himself to do so. And the police officer, in turn, did not volunteer the information—not the cold fact that his son had been murdered by a carjacker.

"Anyhow, I gotta go. And like I said. If I hear anything—"

"That won't compromise the investigation—"

"I'll call you."

Evan forced a smile and set the receiver on the hook.

Sally was standing in the hallway.

"Sally. I didn't see you standing there."

"Anything?"

"Just a nice fella on the other end of the line who's trying to throw us a lifeline."

"Are they going to question the boat hauler?"

"It appears that he has a very good alibi, Sally."

"Did they say that?"

"Not in those words, dear."

Sally marched over to the telephone. "Give me that number."

He could have told her to hit redial, but did not. "It's on the table."

Sally Tamblin dialed the number for police headquarters in Annapolis. There was no stopping her, he knew. Her husband hoped she would get a different officer on the other end. Then again, maybe this would be the wake-up call she needed. For the time being, it was his.

Chapter 12

M alcolm found the little girl and her tiny pet about as happy as a child and her faithful companion could possibly be. He watched them on the ice together. Becky practiced a series of figure eights, while the pup tried in earnest to keep pace, attempting concentric rings around her gliding feet. Malcolm believed that if he could capture and contain her laughter in a bottle, it would serve as a stark reminder of pure innocence. But the planet and its people were way beyond saving —past the point of no return. All corners of the globe considered. Powerful people such as the industrialist had ruined it for the rest. People of position simply failed the population. And those people had to pay. Dearly. Not with their lives, dear God, but with the lives of their loved ones. It was the only lesson from which the polluters of their fragile planet would ever learn, for they had not heeded the early warnings: signs from the scientific community as big as billboards; caveats and admonishments as clear as crystal. Instead, those of position and power turned their backs and stuck their collective heads in the proverbial sand. About to exercise *his* power anew, Malcolm smiled sadly but soberly at the child and her dog.

Becky stood in her sister's old skates, bundled from head to foot and wearing a different colored mitten on each hand: one, blood red; the other forest green.

"Hi there."

Becky turned around abruptly and fell on her tiny padded tush. "Hey, you scared me!" the eight-year-old complained, climbing awkwardly to her feet on unsteady silvery blades.

"Better I should scare you than let you fall through the ice and drown."

Becky's little dog seemingly yapped away in disagreement.

"I can't fall through the ice, stu—silly, and drown." She almost called the perfect stranger *stupid*, but caught herself in the nick of time. "Shush, Suzie. Be quiet."

"How come you can't fall through the ice and drown?" the

happy-faced man wanted to know.

"Because it's only a few inches deep. That's how come. And that's why I'm allowed to come back here and ice-skate," she explained as if there might be a challenge that she was ready to defend.

"I see."

"Who are you? I'm not supposed to talk to strangers."

"I'm not a stranger," Malcolm replied. "You just don't recognize me is all." And with that the man contorted his face into a silly, sad frown.

Becky leaned back in laughter, then almost fell again, regaining her balance and skating over to a branch that extended outward over the ice like a friendly, long arm.

Suzie barked excitedly, and the little girl politely told her puppy to be quiet.

"You just don't remember me, I guess. But I remember you. You picked out all those colored candies from the big glass jars in Kmart, while your mother was busy shopping for a few things."

"And I dropped some of them. And *you're* the one who helped me pick them up! Right?"

"That's right. And your mother came over and told you to say . . . " Malcolm let the words hang somewhere beyond his frosty breath.

"'Say thank you to the man, Becky.'"

"And?"

"And you and mommy let me keep the candy that was wrapped but made me throw away the pieces that weren't."

"The Jujubes."

"But I got more."

"That you did, Becky."

"Uh-huh."

"So. I guess we're really not strangers."

"Guess not. What's your name?"

"Malcolm."

Becky thought it a funny name and smiled.

"Say, I got a great idea," the man said.

"What?"

"I know a bigger skating place right behind this one."

"Uh-uh." She shook her head. "That's the deep one. That's

where you can fall in. My brother fell in last year. He was lucky. He only went up to his knees playing hockey. And that's because the ice broke near the edge. It's a pretty deep pool. Mommy takes me to a real ice-skating rink sometimes. Only she's working now. But she's going to take me to the rink on Saturday."

"I know. I saw you at the rink with your mother. You wore a beautiful red outfit."

"Skirt," Becky clarified. "It's my ice-skating skirt. Mommy says when I get real good, she's going to buy me a brand-new one. These are my sister's skates. They don't fit her anymore. She's married now and lives in a *big* house on Long Island. That's in New York. Not in the city. But way out there away from it," she explained, waving an arm in illustration. "Have you ever been to New York? It's real nice."

"As a matter of fact, I just came from New York a little while ago. And it's not so nice. I mean, the ice-skating. You see, everything started to melt. Then they got a cold spell again, and everything froze up. But not enough to ice-skate safely outdoors. That's why I came up here. Here, it's nice and cold and everything is frozen thick. Why, I'll just bet that pool back there is frozen over at least a foot. Know how thick a foot is?"

Becky let go of the branch and showed Malcolm how thick she thought a foot was. "As long as my skate. Daddy measures feet by putting one foot in front of the other. Like this." Becky carefully placed the blade of one skate directly in front of the other. "See? That would be approx . . . uh . . . what's that word?"

"Approximately?"

"That's it. Approximately two feet."

"That's very good, Becky. I'll bet you're the smartest kid in your school."

"Smartest of the girls," Becky announced immodestly. "But Trevor Cassidy is the smartest in the class. In the whole school, I think. But that's not fair because he's a genis."

"Genius," Malcolm corrected.

"That's what I said."

Malcolm smiled. "Listen, Becky."

"Yeah?"

"I didn't come all the way up here from New York to stand around in the cold and chitchat."

"What's that mean?"

"Talk."

"Oh. So why *did* you come here?"

Malcolm smiled broadly. "I came up here, Miss Becky, to ice-skate," he answered, pointing to an old battered black leather suitcase on the path behind him. "And not on thin ice either," he assured her.

"Really?" she said with interest.

"Really. And if I could, I really would like to skate with you."

"Truly?" she questioned with genuine enthusiasm.

"Really and truly. But there's just one little problem, Becky."

"What?"

"We can't skate together on a little plate of ice like this. We need something bigger."

Becky thought for a moment. "Are you sure it's really safe back there?"

"Sure I'm sure. I was just back there."

"I know how to tell if it's really safe or not," Becky swore.

"How?"

"Well, if you see white ice along the edges you stay away from there. You look for the gray. Not the mushy looking gray. But the dark kind. You can tell. And then if you really want to be sure, you know what you do?"

Malcolm shrugged, bent low, and petted Suzie, who was busy sniffing away at the pair of olive rubber boots.

"You throw a big rock out on the ice."

"You certainly seem to know your way around the ice, Becky."

"I do because my brother showed me. C'mon. I'll show you."

"Okay, but let me grab my skates first."

Malcolm went to fetch his suitcase, and Becky started awkwardly down the path with Suzie running just ahead of her.

"C'mon," she called again. "I bet I can beat you there with my ice skates on," Becky declared, her arms held out at her sides for balance.

"Slow up there," he called out. "Wait up."

"Why? You sound just like my father."

"Didn't your father ever tell you you'll dull your blades by walking on the ground like that?"

"No, but my brother did. I don't walk on them until I get to the pond, which my brother calls a puddle. But it's only a little ways to the big pond if you take this shortcut. See? You can see it right from here."

"I see. But still you shouldn't walk on them at all." Malcolm put down his case. "Here, let me help you." And before Becky could say another word, she was up in the air, then down upon his broad shoulders. "There. How's that?"

Suzie made an about-face and started yapping in protest as the man stooped and swooped up his bag.

"Shush, Suzie," Becky insisted in a sharp tone, commanding the dog to silence with a downward wave of her red mitten.

Suzie went running off again, zigzagging through the brush adjacent to the pathway.

"Hey, this is really neat up here." Becky bent way forward from a narrow waist, craning her head until her eyes were inches from Malcolm's. "You in there?" she questioned with a giggle.

Malcolm tugged at and pulled up the hood of his coat, then nudged his neck fore and aft. "What kind of animal am I, Becky?"

"Uh . . .?"

"Hint, hint. Reptile."

"TURTLE!" Becky exclaimed with a shrill that sent Suzie into a frenzy.

"A deaf turtle," Malcolm complained, crossing his arms and locking both of Becky's spindly legs against his sides.

And with that, Becky fell backward in an entrusting descent that took the man completely by surprise. In an instant, she sprang back up and was happily taking in the wooded white world high above the ground as her new friend trudged and crunched along the frozen earth.

Suzie was circling the pair in a fit.

"I said, shush."

The blade of Becky's left skate chafed the corner of Malcolm's suitcase before he changed hands while plodding down the path.

"Well, here we are, Malcolm. Put me down. Are you sure that's really and truly your name?"

"Why? Don't I look like a Malcolm to you?" he asked, setting his suitcase on the snowy ground.

"No."

"Then what would you like to call me?"

"Charles."

"Charles?"

"Uh-huh."

"That's your daddy's name. Right?"

Becky kept her eyes frozen to the ground as he put her down.

"What's the matter, Becky?"

"Nothing."

"Then why the long face all of a sudden?"

"No reason."

"Gotta be a reason."

Becky said nothing.

"Gotta be a reason for everything we say and do. Right?"

"I guess."

"So, then there's a reason, but you just don't want to share it with me because we're not really friends yet. Am I right?"

Becky raised her eyes slowly from the ground, stretching her neck and staring up into the man's kind face.

"Well, am I?"

Becky nodded.

"I usually am right," he stated quite surely. "My parents would tell me that I take a very good read on people."

Becky was staring quizzically. "Huh?"

"Reading people."

"How can you read people?"

"Like you read a book, Becky. But instead of staring down at the words upon a page, you look into a person's eyes. They speak volumes without saying a single word. Then, when you really get good, you take in the entire face and body. Observing the way a person moves their lips. Even how they stand. What they do with their hands when they *are* speaking. You can tell so much about a person by studying them as you would a book."

Malcolm stooped and opened his suitcase.

Becky looked inside. "Wow!"

"Neat?"

"My brother would like them a lot. Racers. Right?"

"You're a very bright little girl, Becky."

"And so are you. Anyone who can read a person like they read a book has got to be smart."

"Thank you, Becky. That's a very nice thing to say."

"Well, it's true."

Malcolm gave up a queer little smile.

"What's in that paper bag," she asked, pointing with her green mitten.

"That? That's a little present I brought along especially for you."

"Me?"

"Yes, you." He handed her the plain brown bag, its top sealed closed in a series of folds.

Becky took and felt the weight of the package.

"Go ahead. Open it. It's a gift from me to you."

Becky thought she heard something jingling inside the second she received her present. She jiggled the bundle and heard the sound again, carefully opening the bag and taking a peek inside. She shook her head in disbelief, staring from the contents to the man.

Malcolm smiled broadly.

"Figure skates!" the girl cried. "With tiny little bells."

"And I believe they're exactly your size; that is, with a pair of heavy woolen socks like you're wearing."

"They're beautiful."

"White as falling snow."

"I know," she said and giggled excitedly, removing the pair as Malcolm retrieved the paper bag and returned it to his suitcase.

"Why don't you try them on?"

"Can I?"

"I don't see why not. They're yours. But I would like you to make me a promise."

"Sure." She would have promised just about anything.

"I want you to promise me that you won't do anything to dull the blades."

"Oh, I won't. I promise. Look. I'll even take a swear." Becky ran the green mitten of her right hand down, and then across her chest as she cradled her precious gift. Quick as a crippled bunny, she made her way over to a fallen log. "See? I can put these on right here. Then I'll only have . . . one . . . two . . . three . . . four . . . five feet to go in the snow," she measured meticulously, placing one skate directly in front of the other until she reached the very edge of the frozen pond.

"How's that, Malcolm?"

"Perfect, Becky."

Becky walked back and set her brand-new skates down alongside the log. Hurriedly, she pulled the pair of mittens off with her teeth, then sat and began undoing the laces of her sister's plain-Jane skates. When she finally freed herself from the well-worn hand-me-downs, she reached for the bell-tasseled beauties. All clean and shiny. Not a scuff or blemish anywhere.

It was as Becky finished lacing up and removing a protective rubber guard from one of the steel runners that she noticed something strange. The blade. It was different from anything she had seen before. Becky compared it the older pair. Examining them closely.

Malcolm was studying Becky. Reading her like a book.

"Hey, there's something funny here, Malcolm."

"What's that?" Malcolm was sitting on a rock, putting on his racers.

"The blade."

"What about it?" The man was racing with his laces.

"It's sharp."

"It's supposed to be sharp. Remember what I told you?"

"Yeah, but this is *really* sharp."

"Really and truly?" Malcolm inquired with a grin.

"It's supposed to be flat on the bottom. Like this." Becky held up one of her sister's old skates. "See?"

Suzie was staring up at the elevated skate as though it were a large treat. "*Woof!*" the terrier sounded.

"That, Becky dear, is supposed to be very sharp." The bearer of the gift got to his feet. "See? Like these." He lifted up his right leg and showed her his skate. And then the other.

"Like a knife?" she asked, her face all scrunched up in confusion.

"Like a razor," he replied, slashing his right leg out at nothing —holding it perfectly steady in the cold, still air.

Becky said nothing, Malcolm noted satisfactorily, setting his foot on the ground again.

Neither of them said a word for what seemed an eternity.

Finally, Malcolm spoke. "I think you're reading me perfectly, Becky. And I want you to know that I'm really and truly very proud of you," he said behind a smirk.

Becky began to cry.

"Now, get up! Take that other guard off." There was a sharp edge to his voice.

Becky immediately did as she was told.

"Good girl." Malcolm looked up at the gray-flannel sky. "Kind of dreary today. No?"

Becky uttered not a single word.

"Put your mittens back on, pet. The temperature is starting to drop."

Without taking her eyes off the man who she had thought was her friend, Becky reached down, picked up her mittens and put them back on. She dabbed the tears running down her angelic face.

"I'm cold, and I want to go home," Becky insisted.

"Not until we have our little skate first," Malcolm said flatly. "It'll get your blood flowing, and then you won't be so cold anymore," he promised. "Now, let me see you out there on the ice. And don't walk on those blades that I worked so hard to sharpen to perfection. All right? Use the toes of the blade. Those saw-toothed notches. That's what they're for. Go on now."

Becky moved forward clumsily on the toes of the blades, taking several steps toward the pond. Like a cockeyed inebriated ballerina, she swayed. As she reached the edge of the ice, the toes of the steel depressions dug cleanly into its surface.

Malcolm nodded approvingly. "Out to the center, Becky Lynn Dawson."

Becky suddenly wondered how he knew her full name. Was this some sort of punishment from God because she had lied by telling her mother that she finished all her homework so that she could go with Daddy when he came to pick her up on Sunday mornings? She promised God on the spot that she would never lie like that again . . . that she would have *all* her homework finished by Saturday afternoon. Even the math homework that she hated and would copy from Patty Mason on the Monday morning bus. Even if it meant *not* going to the skating rink with her mom. *Maybe that's it,* she somehow managed to sort out in her frightened mind. Maybe the *cheating* had finally caught up with her. But it really was not cheating. Patty was teaching her as well. Tutoring her. Sort of. *Yes. That has to be it.* God was really and truly mad.

Malcolm was racing toward her now.

Suzie was sliding on the ice, unable to get a firm hold beneath her clawing, pawing pads.

Malcolm stood before Becky, looking down at her unhappily. The man had gone from nice to mean in a matter of moments. She could see it plainly in his face. Becky dropped her eyes back to his skates—eyeing the sharp blades that protruded well beyond its heels and toes. They formed a point. A very sharp point. Like a butcher's knife minus its handle—the single blades pointing in both deadly directions.

"Let me see you skate," the mean man ordered.

Becky tried to push off . . . not so much to obey his instructions, but to instinctively move away. Her blades sliced into the ice and held fast.

"These are not right," Becky insisted. "They don't . . . glide."

Malcolm nodded. "These skates are not supposed to glide. They're meant for cutting and slicing. Mine have an added edge," he threw out with double meaning. "They're meant for piercing."

Becky tried to push off again. But the blades held fast. Her body shivered violently. "I can't skate with these."

Suzie was just coming up to Becky's unsteady ankles when Malcolm shot the point of a blade upward and into the dog's right side. The animal yelped in mid air, then fell forward in a ball of white fur that turned as red as a checker before Becky's disbelieving eyes.

Becky went clamoring for her pet.

"Oh, my God!" she wailed, knowing now that God had nothing to do with her homework or lack of it, or the cheating, or punishment of any kind. God was good and would not let a thing like this happen because she slipped a little every now and then. God would not punish an otherwise good little girl and her dog like this. *This* was about the bad men in the world who her mommy and daddy had warned her of time and time again.

Becky was on her knees, holding onto her little dog for dear life. She was trying to make Suzie's bleeding stop.

"Let that dog go now, Becky. I want to see you skate, I said."

Becky did not hear the man, only the sporadic whimpering of her little companion. She removed her woolen cap, pressing the

44

material against the dog's wound like she had seen actors do to wounded people in action movies. Violent videos that she was not supposed to watch.

Maybe it *was* all the lies and deceptions piled up on one another that had brought her and Suzie to this point, Becky thought again. Maybe *that* was the simple truth.

She felt a gentle tug on the collar of her coat, and Malcolm felt the sudden pull of defiance.

The next thing Becky saw—then felt—was a flash followed by the *whoosh* of a steel blade passing a fraction of an inch before her face. Another silvery streak grazed the outer fabric of her coat. A second later, she felt herself being dragged across the pond where the ice was milky-white and thin. She no longer had Suzie in her arms. Becky was screaming hysterically. All that could hear her were the squirrels that had stopped their scurrying just moments before . . . sitting motionless on their haunches upon naked limbs . . . others that suddenly buried themselves safely into their leafy nests in naked trees high above the ground. Too, the bevy of birds that had immediately taken wing, then disappeared when piercing screams sent them darting in all directions. The deer, also, hightailing it out from the edges of a dense woodland, which the herd pretty much sensed they had back to themselves after the last of the hunters abruptly ended the season many a moon ago. Suzie certainly heard Becky, too. Not more than fifty feet away. But neither of them could do anything for the other.

"Now shut up and get up, Beck, before I slice your fucking head off."

Becky clambered about, not quite able to make it to her feet. Suddenly, a blade tore through her insulated poly/cotton jacket, exposing a wisp of insulation. The girl scrambled in all directions upon the ice . . . sobbing bitterly, yet with hardly a sound.

"Okay, daughter of the Dawsons. Lie there on your lazy back and chop."

Malcolm got down on his back next to Becky and showed her how, slashing the backs of his tubular blades in a vicious semicircle all around them—the crisp sound of ice cracking as he moved clockwise in a furious arc. Icy water was spurting up onto the surface and soaking into the material at their backs.

Becky wept uncontrollably and made a halfhearted effort

purely out of fear.

Malcolm removed a thin leather belt from his pants, then looped the end back through its buckle and around Becky's tiny pair of trembling hands hidden in their mittens, tying off the prayerful package with a secure knot—right before her terrified eyes.

"See?" he asked excitedly. "Now, all you have to do to free yourself is cut through the leather strap with your new skates. That is, before the cold water chills you to the bone and covers you up like a blanket. It's about four feet deep right here, give or take an inch. But you must be very careful not to cut your wrists. Those blades are terribly, terribly sharp. I want you to have a fighting chance, Becky Dawson. That's more than your mother ever gave the public. And your dear father, *Charles*, who even fought *against* having the stream that feeds this very pond posted for pollution. *They're* not very nice people, Becky. I have zero tolerance for folks like that."

"Where's my Suzie?" Becky groaned.

"Where's Suzie? I'll show you where Suzie is."

On his back, Malcolm made his way along the dangerously thin gray-white ice until he reached the thicker, safer part of the frozen pond. Getting to his feet, then lifting one skate level with his knee, Malcolm brought the edge of the blade down like a guillotine upon the terrier's blood-splattered, wispy white body before calling out to its master.

"We'll be there in a minute, Beck. Don't you fret."

Down came another cut. And then another.

Becky was crawling around blindly on all fours, screaming mercilessly.

In less than thirty seconds, Malcolm knifed his way back to Becky. Between two gloved fingers, he held the dog's bloody head by one of its ears.

Becky was still screaming as the ice beneath her little body suddenly gave.

"Use your *blades*, Becky, to cut away the strap. Hold your breath when you go under, kid. Then stand when you need to catch your breath."

Becky was thrashing around in the chest-high water when the madman suddenly slid the head of her damaged dead dog into the dark watery hole alongside her as though he had successfully maneuvered a hockey puck across the goal line.

Becky bellowed bloody murder.

Malcolm walked to a safe corner of the pond and watched with fascination as Becky fought furiously between trying to cut away the strap and trying to stand erect.

On her fourth or fifth attempt, beneath the frigid water, Becky never found the surface.

Chapter 13

Detective Dean Nelson sat behind his desk at police headquarters in Yaphank. With a florid face buried in a travel atlas, a yellow highlighter in hand, he studied the state of Maine. Brian Archer entered the area and hung his hat and coat on a rack. He walked over, then took a seat alongside his partner's desk.

"Old Town," Dean said. "North of Brewer. Northeast of Bangor."

"Never heard of it."

"Old Town? You would have if you knew anything about canoes."

"I see we're back to boats again."

"Yep."

"Going to clue me in this morning?"

"It's where they build Old Town canoes. Pretty famous. Pretty nice canoes, in fact."

"What do you think is going on, Dean?"

"Haven't got a clue," the forty-four-year-old veteran answered quietly, reaching for his cup of cold coffee.

"Encouraging."

"One thing's for certain, though."

"That we should have become firemen instead of cops?"

The lead detective smiled without lifting his eyes from the atlas. "He's been workin' his way up the eastern seaboard, Bri. Been a bad and busy boy."

"I'm hearing the locals up there have very little to go on."

"But collectively, *we've* got plenty."

"Sure. Several bodies, one a child, and a decapitated dog. Impressions from three pair of ice skates."

"Two pair, which they at least recovered."

"Yeah, hers and her sister's."

"A set that they think the sick bastard gave her as a gift. With little silver bells. Blades honed to sword-like perfection on a professional grinder, then finished off by hand. So says their tool marks man."

"But where? In a machine shop? One of those itinerant trucks that do kitchen knives, lawn mower blades, hand tools and such? They don't even know where those new skates were purchased."

"No, but maybe now we have his approximate height and weight and build. And his waist size. Thirty-six."

"Yeah, well, suppose he used a different size belt to throw us off?"

"I don't think so, Bri."

"Why?"

"Just a feelin' I have about this guy."

"Like?"

"Like he doesn't go out of his way to leave deceptive clues. No staging. Doesn't bother to cover up important details. Yet, at the same time, he covers his trail pretty goddamn well. Still, he leaves behind those blatant signposts."

"Meaning?"

"An escalating degree of violence. He certainly wants us to take note of that."

"Maybe he's just totally out of control."

"I don't think so. Not yet, anyways."

"He didn't have to kill her dog like that, Dean."

"He didn't have to kick that little girl about the head and body with his skates in order to control her either. She weighed all of what? Fifty pounds, Bri. And I'm talking soakin' wet," he put forth sardonically.

"How do they figure he kicked her? Maybe he just used the blades of his skates as a knife and stabbed her repeatedly." *How do we even know he's a he?* Brian wanted to table but did not.

Dean shook his head. "Angles. Force of the blows. They're working with a criminalist out of Portland. Ullman. Knows his shit. Mick worked with him in '98 on the Vogel case before retiring. He was very impressed with him."

"With Vogel or the forensic guy?" Brian funned.

Dean laughed. "Both of 'em," he answered good-humoredly. "Mick said he didn't know which of the two was the looniest. Vogel, who the state committed, or Ullman. Anyhow, I think our perp's just

49

warming up. Thinks he's pretty safe at this point, working different states along the seaboard. Doesn't feel he has to be too careful. Pure arrogance, Bri," Dean concluded, lifting his eyes from the map. "You jus' get a haircut?"

"You can tell?"

Dean canted his head somewhere between the poles of mild disappointment and sheer deprecation. "I keep tellin' you to come with me to Joey's in Mattituck."

"I'm not going to lay out a sawbuck to have some guy cut a couple of snips off the sides," the younger, taller, light-haired balding detective complained, passing the tips of his fingers along a temple.

"It's not just the haircut, Bri. The guy's a personality. Nice young fella. Just bought the business from Gus on Love Lane. Kid's my shrink, food advisor and entertainment source. Moonlights, too, as a musician."

"Plays up at Giancarlos. Piano. Right?"

"Drums, to boot. And takin' singin' lessons as well."

"Used to live next-door to that artist in South Jamesport. Right?"

"So, ya writin' the kid's résumé, or you gonna give 'im a try next month?"

"Next month? I get this trimmed every eight weeks, my friend."

"In that case, take my advice and wait a year; then try combin' both sides over the top of your scalp. Maybe Joey can give it a style and a name," Dean teased.

Brian waved off the insult. "Theo still thinking these murders are unconnected?"

"If he does, he's got his head up his ass."

"Know what this could be, Dean?" Brian considered, passing a palm atop his balding pate.

"A sign that you're considering a visit to the Hair Club for Men?"

"That there're two or more of them working the coast separately but in concert," he posited, ignoring Dean's goading.

"I don't think that's the case."

"Why not?"

"We got boot prints at three crime scenes. Haynes, Tamblin and

Dawson. Right?"

"But different size imprints in Maryland and New York," Brian pointed out. "Heel and sole patterns, too."

"Bulletin, good buddy. Concerning the Dawson girl, they got the same boot size *and* pattern found around our Tamblin victim."

"Yeah? Says who?"

"Portland guy who examined copies of the pix I sent up."

Brian grew excited. Thinking. Passing both palms back across his oily scalp. "Okay, fine," he reflected aloud. "Then discounting the Linden woman, here, who wound up on the bow of that boat—"

"Whose footprints along with the perp's we couldn't find anyways because of the fucking snow."

"As well as the Parker scene down in Annapolis, where heavy rains washed away any trace—"

"Still leaves us with boot prints in all three states, as well as a match both here and in Maine."

"But that doesn't account for different *size* boots and *patterns* found down in Maryland, Dean."

"Unless you stop to consider why the perp might have worn a size smaller boot down south apart from the match we have here in Flanders and Old Town, Maine," Dean proposed, leaving a possible explanation up in the air for his cohort and partner in crime to grasp.

"Because of a warmer climate and the time of year the Maryland murders were committed, where our man wouldn't necessarily need a heavier boot," Brian declared. "He'd just grab another pair for up here."

"Are we a dynamic duo or what?"

"It's a good theory, Dean."

"It's more than a theory, Bri."

"How so?"

"The wear on the left instep taken from an impression at the pier in Edgewater, Maryland is consistent with that taken up in Old Town, Maine—*and* it's consistent with a homicide down in Florida a couple years ago. We got that confirmation handed to us on a silver platter from a Feebe friend of mine in sunny ol' Edgewater, Florida, where they found the body of a female floating along a canal. Sounded like our boy's handiwork."

"Edgewater, Florida. Edgewater, Maryland. Anything to that,

you think?"

"Don't know. Only thing we know for sure is that boats and water keep popping into the picture."

"How do the feds figure into this?"

"They don't. The SSRA's an old profiler pal of mine from that area, who just happened to be Johnny-on-the-spot—or close enough to the scene that someone connected with the case decided to call him in. I told 'im what we had up here."

"What's he think, Dean?"

"Believes we have a serial killer on our hands. That's singular. One and the same. Working the eastern seaboard from Florida to Maine."

"What's his take on this last episode?"

"Says the guy might suddenly draw a line and stop just south of the Canadian border. Or . . ."

"Or what?"

"Continue his travels, turning more violent than an erupting volcano. Anybody's guess. What's your forecast, Bri?"

Brian shook his head. "A lot more pessimistic than my wishful thinking might allow. I think we got our work cut out for us."

"I'm inclined to agree."

"So, where do we go from here?"

Dean put his face back in the book. "95 North, till we get to Bangor."

Brian smiled, leaning over the corner of the desk and staring down at the map of Maine. "But I see we're taking the scenic coastline part of the way."

"Before we grab 178 here, right into Old Town."

"How many boat places along the way?"

"Marinas, Bri. Marinas. How long ya been my partner?"

"Fine. How many marinas are we going to hit along the way?" he asked knowingly.

"Most of them are closed, ball-breaker. It's the 7th of February, and it's fucking cold right here. Imagine what it's like up there. Boating is a seasonal business, mate."

"When did *Closed for the Season* or the cold ever stop you from looking at boats, Dean?" Brian sparred.

"If our business leads us to boats, then we'll look at boats,"

Dean said defensively. "If our business leads us to flying model airplanes, indoors no less, we'll look at model airplanes. All right?"

"Why do you make fun of my hobby, Dean?"

"I don't make fun of your hobby, pal."

"Sure you do."

"No, I don't. I just don't see how a group of guys can get off on flyin' rubber band *p*owered *p*rop *p*lanes made of *p*aper. Flyin' them in hangars all across the country," he added, having popped his p's for the full effect. "That's all."

"See? You're poking fun."

"No, I'm not."

"You are."

"Look. I could see someone flyin' a real model airplane with those little gasoline engines, *outdoors*. That might be considered exciting to some. But a paper plane, Bri? C'mon."

"We use other materials, too."

"Like what?"

"Like balsa wood."

"Well, woop-de-doo! Or is it, loop-de-doo?"

"And microfilm."

"Microfilm?"

"Yes, microfilm."

"Your secret's safe with me, my boy."

"See, that's exactly what I mean."

"What? You want me to tell the fellas here you're flyin' *film*? Next thing you know, Theo will be sendin' you downtown for an evaluation." Dean smiled mischievously, screwing a finger within his ear. "How does that grab you?"

"Yeah, well you kid around all you like, but I'll tell you something right here and now, buddy. Building and flying a model made out of microfilm is one of the most challenging and demanding activities that I can think of, rivaling the *p*atience and *p*ersistence of the most ardent fly fisherman; like Theo pursuing his elusive trout," Brian countered. "Or worse yet, you and your single-minded, endless *p*ursuit of the *p*erfect *p*owerboat," he ranted, rocketing over his own set of p's in a game of one-upmanship.

Dean was staring at Brian as though his partner had a wasp on the end of his nose. "Does it have a rubber band for a motor?"

"Does what have a rubber band for a motor?" Brian asked with annoyance.

"Your microfilm plane."

"Of course it has a rubber band for a motor."

Dean slowly shook his head.

"You never saw one fly, Dean. It's . . . ethereal. Time takes on a whole other dimension. Like watching a graceful bird in flight."

"So, why don't you take up bird watching?"

"Why don't you come out with me to Lakehurst some weekend and see for yourself? You'll walk away with an entirely different view."

"Is there an immediate benefit? Like can I build up frequent flyer miles or something?" Dean kibitzed.

"You're thick, Dean. Like those inch-and-a-half raw steaks you devour."

"But tender, nonetheless, kid. Not unlike my new main squeeze."

"Stubborn, too."

"I'm stubborn? I'm thick? I'll tell you what. I'll go to that hangar with you in Jersey, if you come with me to my barber in Mattituck. How's that?"

Brian looked at Dean oddly. "What does one have to do with the other?"

"See. *You're* rigid."

"I'm rigid?"

"That's what I just said."

"You'll come with me to Lakehurst, if I go with you to your barber in Mattituck?"

"Didn't I just say that?"

"Fine."

"Good. You'll love Joey. He'll buzz his razor 'cross the top of your head like it was a landing strip. Make you feel right at home."

"You don't know when to stop, do you?"

"Sure I do." Dean stood and stuck the atlas under his arm. "We'll stop when we get to Old Town, Maine. Unless, of course, you tell me you gotta eat or take a piss along the way, like you usually do."

Brian got up, lost in a single thought. "Dean."

Dean was grabbing his coat.

"Dean, the canoe in Annapolis they found the Parker woman in?"

"Yeah, what about it?"

"Was it an Old Town, by any chance?"

"No. We·no·nah. Spelled and written phonetically."

"We who?"

"We·no·nah. The name of the manufacturer in Winona, Minnesota."

"Think there's a connection?"

"Absolutely."

"Well?"

"Well constructed and dependable," Dean responded. "We·no·nah, Mad River, Old Town. All built to go the distance. Like Olivia."

"And you wonder why your wife and daughter are in Orlando."

"Wonder and wait. But let's not be judgmental."

"No, of course not."

Chapter 14

Elizabeth Dawson lived alone in a large white Colonial surrounded by acres of woodland and streams. There was a remarkable resemblance between the mother and her two daughters as evidenced in many framed photographs that graced the highly polished surface of a Parsons table off the entranceway. Several expensive oil portraits of her son and ex-husband lined the dark stucco walls leading up the staircase. The boy unquestionably favored his father, both in terms of good looks and stature, Detective Brian Archer noted. Detective Dean Nelson could not help but discern the dichotomy between the two groupings, both in terms of gender as well as their spatial distance from one another: The three females displayed downstairs. The two male figures coldly exhibited along the staircase.

The single mother stood rigid, wearing a blue gingham housecoat, her arms folded across her thin frame. She and the two detectives finally stepped from Becky's tidy bedroom and headed back downstairs.

"So. That's about it. I told you everything I know like I told the chief of police, the state troopers, newspaper reporters, and on and on."

"I'd like to hear more about your ex-husband, Ms. Dawson," Dean put forth matter-of-factly.

"The only thing I failed to tell you about Charles and myself, Detective, is how we fought for Becky's time with our workaholic schedules. And now . . . " The heartbroken woman waved an angry hand through the air. "And now—" her voice quivered "—neither of us have her."

"Can we sit down and talk, ma'am?" Dean pressed.

"We're going to bury our youngest daughter on Friday morning, and you want to sit and talk. Maybe you'd like me to cook you two something to eat, too. How's that? Then we can all sit around here and have a fucking party. Talk about my husband?" she gritted angrily. "Want to hear about the separation and the toll it takes on an eight-year-old child? Well, I'm all talked out, guys. I said my piece in court. Besides. The whole town knows about the separation, the custody battle, and our less than amicable divorce. Just ask any of our neighbors down the road. Ask the local merchants. They'll tell you all you care to hear. Busybodies that they all are."

"We don't want to hear about your divorce, Ms. Dawson," Brian made clear. "We want to ask you a few questions about Charles and—"

"Look. He may have been a rotten husband. All right? Unfaithful right under my nose, and I didn't even know it. But he's still a wonderful father. He loves his daughters and son like he loves himself. He's not involved in any way with this—"

"Whoa! Time out," Dean interrupted. He was shaking his head and forming a T with two chubby hands. "I don't know what kind of trip the troops up here are puttin' you through. But we'll share a little secret with you. Your husband is not a suspect in this. I can tell you that simply because we had him, his friends, his acquaintances and all his business associates checked out seven ways to Sunday," he grossly exaggerated. "We want to talk to you about when you and your husband lived together on Long Island. That's why we drove all the way up here. Got it now?"

"Long Island?" Elizabeth stared over at the isolated photograph atop a bookcase in a far corner of the room. A family snapshot of the five of them on the front lawn of their former home in Manorville. An artificial houseplant obscured the cheap cardboard framed picture. Becky was just a baby. "We were a happy household then," she simpered.

"We know," Dean went along. "We know you worked for Brookhaven National Laboratory, and your husband worked for the DEC down there."

"Yes," she said as if recalling a distant dream.

"That's what we'd like to talk to you about."

Elizabeth squinted in confusion. "I don't understand what that has to do with Becky, Detective."

"Maybe nothing. Maybe everything," Dean put forth bluntly.

She sighed and directed them to the living room, reluctantly inviting them to take a seat on the sofa, sitting herself in a single matching chair. "It was five years ago that we left the Island and came up here."

"You were employed at the Lab from September of '92 until February, '95," Brian read from his notepad. "Is that accurate?"

"Yes, that's right. I started there shortly after Becky was born. But again, I don't see what this has—"

"Tell us what your primary responsibility was," Dean interrupted.

"Well, I had several responsibilities. But my primary duty had to do with monitoring toxic chemicals in the field; aldicarb as well as other compounds. Then submit reports. Follow-up information. Things like that."

"And what is aldicarb, Ms. Dawson?"

"Temik."

"You're referring to the chemical used on the East End of Long Island during the 70's and 80's to combat the potato beetle," Brian elaborated, more for the benefit of his colleague than for his own clarification.

"Combat is probably the perfect word, Detective Archer."

"Please call me Brian, ma'am," he said and smiled warmly.

"Fine, Brian. Call me Elizabeth," the woman capitulated, her mouth set in a pliable message of anguish. "It was an all-out war to protect the potato crop. The compound proved to be the chemists' as well as the farmers' panacea."

"Meaning the Temik?" Dean asked.

"Well, yes, Detective," Elizabeth answered Brian's partner with annoyance.

"And you found traces of this Temik and other compounds in your search," Dean questioned rhetorically.

Elizabeth glanced at Brian as though his partner's comment was nothing short of an understatement, which it was, and undeserving of a direct reply. "Traces would be an inadequate description, Detective Nelson," the young woman offered smugly, holding Brian's stare. "More along the lines of a plethora."

"Excuse me?" Dean remarked.

"An abundance," the woman elucidated with irritation, slowly moving her bleary blue eyes away from Brian's and setting them coldly on Detective Dean Nelson. "What does this have to do with Becky, Detective?"

"And where did you happen to find this abundance?" Dean pressed on.

"Wells."

"Underground wells?"

"Yes. And springs."

"Wells and springs."

"Yes. Lots of them."

"Where?"

"Throughout the East End."

Dean looked at Brian.

"Does a spring happen to feed those ponds in back of your home where Becky was found, Ms. Dawson?"

"Yes. Now, are you going to tell me what's going on, or not?"

"Can't at this point, ma'am," Dean stated flatly behind a frown.

"Can't or won't?" Elizabeth snapped through a scowl.

"Little bit of both, I'm afraid."

"This is an ongoing police investigation," Brian interjected.

Elizabeth was shaking her head.

"A very sensitive police matter," Brian added.

She shook her head angrily.

"It would compromise this investigation if—"

"If what?" she snapped. "If you would tell me where you're headed, then maybe I could help."

Dean ignored her and went on with his next question. "Who did you report this information to—about these compounds found in wells and springs?"

Elizabeth sat still as stone.

"Well?"

No response.

"How bad was this situation?" he pushed.

Elizabeth raised her eyes to the ceiling and said nothing.

"Did it endanger the health and well-being of the public? Answer me, please."

"I can't."

"Can't or won't?"

"A little bit of both, I'm afraid," she shot back, tit for tat.

"I'm afraid, too, Ms. Dawson. I'm afraid that lunatic out there is going to kill another woman or child. Soon. Now, we can't help

Becky, God knows. But maybe, just maybe, we can prevent the next killing. And if not, then maybe the next. And if not that one, then maybe—"

"Or maybe not at all," Elizabeth raised her voice. "The newspapers say that these killings are believed to be random and not part of any killing spree. All right? Becky's death is not connected with where I worked years ago. So, I don't see where any of this is leading."

It was now Dean's turn to differ, and he did so.

Dean looked at the woman rather mockingly. "Newspapers, she says. Give me a break."

Brian took up the talk.

"Look at me, Elizabeth. You and I both know that the media failed to furnish people with the truth about Temik till as late as the eighties because they simply didn't have the facts. Brookhaven Lab probably covered up certain information then, like I believe they did when you worked there. True? I think you learned certain facts early on in your short-lived career, Elizabeth. Facts that should have been disclosed by officials immediately but weren't. I don't think the public really received *all* the hard, cold facts. Not only about Temik, but about other harmful chemicals as well. Well, did they?"

"I can't talk about those things, Detective."

"Brian."

"I couldn't talk about those things then, and I can't now, Brian."

"Took a swear?" he questioned patiently.

Elizabeth nodded nervously.

"They had you sign something?"

"Their lawyers," she said, picking at the cuticle of her thumb with a forefinger.

"Look at me, Liz."

Elizabeth looked at Brian, then quickly looked away.

"Look right here."

The woman looked straight into Brian's fair-blue eyes. Several shades lighter than her own.

"Remember when you got a speeding ticket on the Long Island Expressway, Elizabeth?" Brian glanced down at his notes. "Nineteen ninety-two. No, I wasn't the officer then," he proffered. "But I'll bet you said to yourself, if not to him, 'Don't you have anything better to do? Why aren't you out looking for burglars or muggers or rapists?' I know I've had people say that to me when I was a traffic cop. And I thought the same thing when I was pulled over as a civilian. The point I'm trying to make here, Elizabeth, is that I'm no longer a civilian or a traffic cop. I *do* in fact have better things to do. I'm not looking for muggers or burglars or rapists unless they happened to have murdered someone in the act. I'm not out to write a report today or bring heat down on an agency that hid certain facts from the public more than a decade ago. Detective Nelson and I are out to nab a person who we believe to be a serial killer, acting alone, still at large, who will almost certainly kill again. We believe he has murdered six females, including your daughter and her dog.

"Now," Brian continued. "For the past few weeks, my partner and I have been focused in a direction other than where I think we should be looking. With me so far?"

Elizabeth nodded as if she were following an important lecture at a university.

"Good. Because at this very point in time, from the little bit you've told us, we're beginning to turn our heads in another direction. A direction in which the pieces of a puzzle are beginning to fit and make some sense to us. In a way, it's not much different from the way a scientist like yourself works. Of course, I can't intelligently discuss pesticides and other kinds of chemicals with you because I certainly don't have the proper training. Conversely, *you* can't—"

"Shut up," Elizabeth scrapped.

"I beg your pardon."

"I said, shut up, Brian. I get the picture. I'm not an imbecile. Just distraught."

"We understand."

"You understand nothing. Him? Maybe even less."

"I'm very fond of you, too, ma'am," Dean said evenly.

"Look, you two."

They were looking.

"This conversation can't ever leave this house. Understood?"

"We're not out to burn anyone at the stake, except this killer," Brian hedged.

"Understood, Detective?"

"Understood," Dean stated.

"Yeah, like I *really* believe what *you* have to say."

Dean shrugged indifferently.

"Why don't we do this," Brian suggested. "We may have to interview certain individuals. *May*," he emphasized. "I promise you that your name, as well as your ex-husband's, will not come up in connection with the Lab or the DEC."

"But if it ever goes to court . . ." Elizabeth said bitterly.

Brian started to say something, but the woman cut him short.

"I'll cooperate with you where I can, gentlemen. But I may have to draw a line in the sand. Let's see where this goes."

"All right," Brian agreed.

"Fair enough," Dean added, picking up exactly where he left off without missing a beat. "Who did you report this information to concerning abundant levels of toxic chemicals found in underground wells and springs?"

"Chief of Operations."

"Name."

"Kincade. Walter Kincade. He retired the year after I left."

"The name Sally Tamblin mean anything to you?"

Elizabeth Dawson thought for a second. "No."

"How about Sally Montgomery?"

"No."

"Three strikes and you're out, Ms. Dawson," the cop kidded. "How about Sally Pierce?"

"Sure. Sally Pierce. She was a supervisor at the Lab. Why?"

"We're asking the questions," Dean reminded her. "Remember how this works?"

"Don't make me sorry that I agreed to this."

"Don't let Becky have died in vain when you can help shed some light on these murders. All right?" the case detective continued, cutting to the quick.

Elizabeth nodded.

"Who did she supervise?"

"Sally headed up a small department. She had several people under her who analyzed soil fumigants."

"Don't make me beg the question," Dean said politely with the hint of a smile.

"Sorry," she apologized uneasily. "They're volatile compounds found in disinfectants and pesticides."

"She see your reports?"

"I don't really know."

"How come?"

"Well, I tested for these compounds in water supplies and wrote reports, and her people tested for similar compounds in the soil and wrote their reports. I don't know if mine ever crossed her desk or not."

"Do you know if her people's reports went directly to Kincade, or through an intermediary?"

Elizabeth shook her head. "No, I do not."

"But you worked in an office, also."

"Yes. But I spent most of my time in the field."

"All over the Island."

"All over the East End of Long Island."

"Both the North and South Fork?"

"Yes."

"And you handed your report directly to Walter Kincade. Head of operations."

"Yes, chief of operations."

"Know the name Evan Tamblin?"

Elizabeth's brow furrowed, but her mind just could not come up with the answer. Not immediately. "No . . . Wait! Isn't he that hotshot executive from the south or somewhere? Oh, my God! That's not the same Tamblin from Long Island whose daughter was murdered . . . is it?"

Brian looked over at Dean, and the case detective gave the go-ahead. It was just a matter of time before some hotshot reporter made the connection and had the full story anyhow. Elizabeth might just as well hear it firsthand, now, rather than read about it later—if, indeed, it was firsthand knowledge and not already a headline somewhere along the coast.

"Evan Tamblin remarried after his first wife passed away," Brian began explaining. "He married Mrs. Sally Montgomery. Formerly, Miss Sally Pierce."

"Then that . . . Jesus . . . that was Sally's daughter by . . ."

"Her stepdaughter, by marriage to *the* Evan Tamblin, originally from Atlanta."

"The industrialist."

"Correct. Chemicals and pharmaceuticals mostly."

Elizabeth Dawson's mind was spinning like a whirligig in a high wind.

A thought crept into Brian's brain. Maybe baseless. Maybe not. "Can you tell us why a man like Evan Tamblin would want to live on the water in South Jamesport?" Brian asked inquisitively. "What I'm getting at is that a man of Mr. Tamblin's means could have his pick of places anywhere along the North or South Shore of Long Island, or anywhere in the world for that matter. Yet, he picks South Jamesport. Not Nassau Point or some other opulent area. Not far from the Peconic River, no less. And as we all know, the Peconic River has certainly been the focus of controversy for quite some time, with strong claims that Brookhaven Lab is responsible for most of its pollution. The Radioactive River Route, it's been dubbed. Any thoughts?"

Elizabeth's mind gravitated from Sally, to Evan Tamblin's daughter, to Becky, then back to Brian's question.

"I don't know, Brian. I can't answer that one for you. What you say is absolutely true, though. Brookhaven Lab has been polluting the Peconic River for decades and doing a pretty good job of covering it up. Until the last few years, that is. I can't prove it, but I can tell you that the Suffolk County Health Department knew about it for quite some time but decided to look the other way. It's one of the reasons Charles and I got the hell out of there. There's a very good reason why the East End of Long Island has the highest rate of breast cancer in the country. One answer is in the water. And their Band-Aid approach of *'The solution to pollution is dilution'* is the slogan that they've carried into the new millennium."

"Dilution?" Dean questioned.

"Sure. Temik is the least of their problems now that it's done its damage, having had twenty years to move laterally off the potato fields where it was first sprayed, infiltrating the groundwater and poisoning the aquifer. There's a host of old and new chemicals out there that I'd be more concerned about. From carbofuran to radionuclides. I'll give you a glossary of terms and some articles before you leave. You want to round up a group of murderers, guys? Take a close look at Brookhaven National Laboratory, the Suffolk County Health

Department, and the Department of Environmental Conservation. You'll track homicides up the kazoo, tracing them back to the culprits just mentioned. Of course, the medical examiner's office has the smoking gun listed as having been fired from someplace else. So, I'd add him to the list as well."

"Where's the point where you draw the line in the sand, Elizabeth?" Brian asked with a straight face.

"Don't get me started on the *air* you two breathe out there in Suffolk County," she declared. "The *water* is only one of your problems, fellas."

"You're kidding, right?" Dean asked skeptically.

"What about the additives they put in gasoline to *improve* the air quality, boys?" Elizabeth raised. "That *additive* is another chemical that is tainting your water supplies all across the East End of Long Island. Of course, it doesn't stop there. But it's there that I'm going to draw the line," she declared with a somber expression.

The three of them sat in silence for a good fifteen seconds before Dean got back on track—backtracking into the conversation the trio held earlier, upstairs in Becky's room.

"Are you sure there's nothing else you can recall, like Becky ever talking to a stranger, or anything suspicious like that?"

Elizabeth shook her head. "No, I've told you every . . . no, hold it! There is something— Oh, it's probably nothing. He was such a nice man."

The two detectives leaned forward simultaneously and focused their full attention on the woman, giving her the distinct impression that if she were to so much as flinch, they would have her arrested for failing to preserve a Kodak moment.

"Who?" Dean sallied.

"What man?" Brian begged.

"At Kmart, down in Bangor. I had Becky with me, and she was talking to this man."

"What did they say?"

"Well, it's more like what I told her to say."

Brian looked confused. "I'm not following."

Elizabeth gathered up her thoughts, then quickly arranged them in a given order. "Sorry. I'm not making any sense. It happened so fast. He was picking up the candy she dropped on the floor."

"The guy Becky was talking to?"

"Yes. Another customer. And I told her to thank the nice man for picking them up. He threw out the pieces she dropped that weren't wrapped, then shoveled out new ones—putting them in the bag for her, along with the wrapped pieces."

"Shoveled out?"

"You know. With a scoop. Digging into those canisters that hold candy on the display counters?"

"Gloved hands?"

"I think so, but I'm not sure."

"When did this all happen?"

"Day before yesterday. After I got out of work."

"May I use your phone, Liz?" Brian asked, already heading up the hall.

"Yes, of course."

"What did this man look like?" Dean persisted.

Elizabeth shook her head. "His back was to me mostly."

"The whole time?"

"Yes, I think so. Busy bending down picking up the candy, like I said. Then scooping other pieces—"

Nelson shook his head and smiled. "Okay. Now, I want you to do something for me. I want you to think very carefully. Picture him meticulously in your mind. What can you tell me about him? His build. Picture him bending down and picking up the candy. Standing and scooping out the sweets."

"Sort of stocky. Not fat. Muscular, I'd say."

"Height?"

"Five-foot-eight . . . maybe nine," she said without hesitation.

"You're sure?"

"Pretty sure."

"The clothes he was wearing?"

"Dark. That's all I can remember."

"Color of his hair?"

She shook her head.

"His shoes?"

"He was wearing boots."

"You're doing fine. Tell me about his boots. Take it nice and slow."

"I can't remember." She was staring at the floor.

"Sure you can. And I'll tell you why. You're a scientist. And a damn good one, Ms. Dawson. Your powers of observation are better than most. You're back in that store now. And the man is picking up the candy. Close your eyes if it's easier, and tell me about those boots."

Elizabeth kept her eyes open and focused on the green carpet, staring at the space in front of the detective's feet.

"They were green. Olive green. Up to his calf, I think."

"So, his pants were tucked into his boots?"

"Yes."

"Anything else? Rubber? Leather?"

"Rubber. He might have had his laces tied around the tops, I think."

"Good. Can you see the color of those laces? How they're tied? Bowed or hanging loose?"

"No . . . not really sure they're laces. Peter had boots like that."

"Peter's your son."

"Yes. He's staying mostly with his father when he's home from school. Maybe I'm mixing up those boots."

"You're doing great. You stick with what you're sure of. Tell me about the man's pants."

Elizabeth curled her lips into a frown. "Can't."

"Wanna bet?" Dean coaxed. "Light? Dark? Whattaya see?"

"Definitely dark."

"Good. Baggy or tight?"

"Tight above the top of the boots, but I can't tell you anything beyond that."

"That's okay. You're doing fine. Now what about his jacket? Tell me what you see."

"Dark, too."

"Thin or thick material?"

"Parka. Yes! Definitely a hooded parka," she recalled excitedly. "I know because he pulled it out of the collar of the coat as he was heading out the store." Elizabeth suddenly started to cry and turned her head away sharply.

"Hey! You're going great guns, girl. You don't mind if I call you girl, do you? I mean, if my flunky partner can knock it down a notch from Elizabeth to Liz, surely I can get away with *girl*. I'm gonna tell ya what I tell my daughter when she wants to quit on me or her mother. And she's a lot younger than you, ya know. My daughter, I mean. My wife's an ol' coot, which makes me a fossil, I guess. Anyhow, I say, 'Hey, girl. You gonna let the ol' man and your mom down?' Know what she says to me? Are you ready for her punch line, girl?"

"Shut up," Elizabeth snapped, facing forward, staring back at the detective.

"What? You can't talk to a short-time, senior Suffolk County detective like that," he protested mildly, holding out his handkerchief at the ready.

"You're not in Suffolk County, now, Dean," she braved quietly through a sniffle, snatching the handkerchief and blowing her nose.

"So, it's Dean, now. Does this mean I get to call you Elizabeth, or what?"

"You can call me anything you like, Dean. Just get this *bastard* for me. Please."

Detective Dean Nelson studied the grieving woman before he opened his mouth. "I'm going to let you in on a little secret, then make you a promise, girl."

"Yeah, what's that?"

"I already got my paperwork started for retirement. But I'm going to stay on this case for however long it takes to get this scumbag. All right?"

Elizabeth nodded and wiped her eyes with a corner of the cloth, then blew her nose again.

"And you can keep that as a gift," he said with a grin.

Elizabeth smiled through a seeming stream of never-ending tears. "Thank you."

"On second thought, maybe you can wash it and send it back. Keep the old lady on her toes. Serve her right for taking my daughter off to sunny Florida, while I'm stuck up here in the boondocks with you."

Elizabeth could not help but surrender a little laugh. *He is certainly a strange man for a detective,* she thought. She was warming up to him.

"Say, how cold is it up here anyhow, girl?"

"You mean with or without the wind chill factor?" Elizabeth

asked vacantly.

"Forget it," he soured.

Brian came back into the room. "Couple of long shots," he said. "The store put out everything last night for early pickup."

"And the shovel or scoop?"

"They use two. Claims they're washed thoroughly with soap and water each night. Regardless, they're handled by scores of kids and adults each day. Anyhow, I told the manager they're not to be touched till the locals get down there. Containers, too. The boys are on their way."

"Long shot is right."

"How are we doing here?" Brian asked cautiously, taking in the woman's washed-out appearance, hating like hell to have left the two of them alone for two seconds, let alone those few minutes he was busy on the phone. "Making any headway?"

"Moving right along, Bri. She calls me, Dean; I call her, girl . . . even Elizabeth, if I wish. But we have Liz still reserved for you." Dean handed over his notebook to Brian.

Brian studied the notes from where he left off. "This is gold, Liz," he said after a pause. "This is absolutely fantastic."

"This girl good, or what?" Dean remarked, taking back his memo book as soon as Brian finished. "Think you're ready to continue?"

Elizabeth was sitting on the edge of her seat, unconsciously twisting several strands of straight long blonde hair between a thumb and forefinger. "Fire away, Dean."

"You said he pulled out his hood from the collar as he was leaving the store."

Elizabeth nodded anxiously.

"Note the color of his hair?"

"Just dark, I think."

"Short? Long? Dirty? Dull? What?"

She shook her head. "Sorry."

"Can you set an age on him? Twenty? Thirty? Older? Younger?"

Again, she shook her head.

"Color of his skin?"

"He was turned away from me mostly," she reiterated.

"When he scooped out the candy from the jar, Elizabeth, maybe it wasn't a glove. Maybe a bare hand? Black? White? Yellow? Try and see it, Liz."

"I really think he was wearing gloves, or mittens maybe. I can't be sure."

"How about the way he walked when he left the store? Anything unusual or unique? A strut, swagger? A stroll?"

"Now that you mention it . . ."

"What?"

"Like he was leaning."

"Like a limp?"

"No. Not like a limp. More like a . . . I don't know how to say it."

"Sure you do. Just think. Take your time and form a picture in your mind."

Dean did not want to put the words into her mouth, although he was tempted. He knew. So did Brian. But the questioning detective wanted it to be in Elizabeth Dawson's own words.

"Favoring."

Both Brian and Dean smiled inwardly.

"Favoring," Dean said flatly.

"Like he was giving support to his left foot or something. Not as pronounced as a lame leg. Very slight. I'm surprised I even noticed. Am I making any sense?"

"You're making perfect sense," Detective Dean Nelson assured her.

Brian placed a hand on her shoulder. "You're a tremendous help, Liz."

"Do you think he's the man that . . . killed my baby girl?" She was holding them both captive with her steely blue eyes.

Brian glanced at his partner.

"We think it's a good possibility," Dean offered truthfully. "And we're going to ask you to keep this conversation under your hat. Got that?"

Elizabeth Dawson nodded.

"Let me hear you say it," the case detective coaxed.

"None of what we said here this afternoon leaves this room," she said most seriously. "And that goes for the two of you, too."

"All agreed," Dean stated firmly. "Now, tell me what else you can remember. Anything at all. The smell of cologne? Garlic or liquor or mouthwash on his breath—although he never turned your way, you say. Put your five senses back in that store, girl."

Chapter 15

Detective Brian Archer was too quiet during the first leg of their journey back to Long Island. He sat behind the wheel of the gray sedan, clocking eighty while heading due south.

"Were we the dynamic duo back there or not?" Dean set forth unabashedly.

"We certainly were, Batman," Brian agreed passively.

"You tired?"

"No."

"Hungry?"

"No."

"Want me to drive?"

"No."

"Just gonna sit there and be piss poor company? Is that it?"

"I guess."

"Listen. You were smooth as silk with her. Loosened her up nicely, Bri. She was wound up like a coil spring. But you had her eatin' outta your hand."

"You didn't do too badly yourself."

"So why the long puss?"

"She's a nice lady, Dean."

"She is. No question about that, partner. She gave us our first important lead. Gold, as you said. And that it is! We've got threads of gold, partner. And do you know what we're gonna do with 'em? We're gonna spin them into an arrest and an indictment for murder one. Several counts. I can feel it. We're gonna nail this guy's ass but good."

"Yeah, nail him to the ice, you mean."

"Now, what the hell is that suppose'ta mean?"

"Slippery and slick. We're going to get him, Dean. Of this, I have no doubt. But it's a conviction I'm worried about."

"Worried? You kiddin' me or what?" the lead detective asked incredulously.

"Did you see what he did to them? What he did to that little girl?"

"Of course I saw what he did. To all of them. Saw the pix. Read the reports. We both saw two of the women he murdered up close and personal. The girl? Think I'll ever forget visiting Becky in the morgue?"

"Can you imagine how horrible her death was, Dean? Those self-inflicted slashes along her wrists in trying to free herself from the belt. Trapped alive under the ice like that. What kind of man does that to a little kid?"

"The kind we love to rein in and piss on, ol' chap."

"An innocent eight-year-old-girl. Her little dog."

"Listen to me, Bri. I made that woman a promise back there I'm gonna keep. I'm on this till we nab his ass. I don't care if it takes till the next century. We're gonna get him. And get him good. You and me."

"What about your retirement? What about promises to your family? Not to mention Olivia."

"What family? Those promises are moot now, good buddy. I lost Doreen and Dawn a long time ago, Bri. My own doing, or undoing as the case may be. They won't be coming back. Trial separation? Doreen had her mind made up a long time ago. As for Olivia, it's just a fling, kid. Anyhow, first things first. We're gonna wrap this up."

"I don't want this guy sitting in a loony bin, Dean."

Dean looked over at his partner oddly. "Hey. What you're suggesting definitely ain't cool. So can it. All right? Ain't your call. Ain't mine."

"Guy's a psycho. Psychos walk away in time. You know that better than anyone."

"Yeah, so is Manson, Berkowitz, Rifkin, Mills and many more before and after them. They ain't goin' nowheres, and neither is this perp."

"Some do. Some don't. But they still exist, meaning that they all have some kind of a life going for them. No picnic, I'll grant you. Yet, they're alive and breathing, while their victims rot for eternity and their families grieve forever. It's not right, Dean. It's not fair. Vertical. Horizontal. Note the difference?" Brian Archer demonstrated with the flip-flop of a hand. "And now *this* guy. Five women, a little kid and her dog to date—that we know about. How many more are there, or will there be? Tell me. Take a fucking guess."

"If it's any consolation, Howard Mills is gonna get the needle for what he did. Laws are changing for the better, Bri. Starting with Mills."

"I'll believe that when I see it. And if it does happen, it won't happen for a decade."

"Hey, I don't write the statutes, pal. We pick the pricks up and process them. Courts do the rest."

"Unsatisfactory, buddy. Un-fucking satisfactory."

Dean moved his eyes back and forth between his partner and the road.

"Let's stay focused here. All right? And slow it down a bit."

Brian kept the cruise control set where it was.

"Fine." Dean fixed the secondary seat belt across his lap. "Let's go over what we got. That is, if we don't get killed first."

Brian kept his eyes straight ahead and his mouth shut.

Dean broke out his notebook. "We got ourselves a male unsub. Race and age unknown. Stocky build. Five-foot-eight or nine. Maybe a hundred sixty, seventy pounds. Last seen in Kmart; Hogan Road in Bangor, wearing calf-high olive green rubber boots and a dark hooded parka and pants. Favoring his left foot when he walks that walk. We got matching boot prints at the Tamblin and Dawson scenes—although we don't know exactly how the other victims fit in just yet. But you can bet your ass it's all somehow connected with the environment; namely water and maybe the air we breathe."

"What happened to boats?"

"I never said this was *directly* connected to boats."

"You sure as hell did."

"What I said was that boats surround the crime scenes."

"So, what are you saying now? That boats are surrounded by water?" Brian goaded. "Not to mention the atmosphere," he pushed the envelope.

Dean looked over at his partner. "You think you're a funny man?"

"I'm not faulting you, Dean. You got boats and water on the brain," Brian kept up with a straight face.

"Listen, wise guy. Wherever a body turned up, there was always a boat directly or indirectly involved."

"The Linden and Parker women. Who else?"

"Who else?"

"Yeah, who else?"

"What about Patricia Tamblin?"

"She was found in a bathtub, for cryin' out loud. Or did you think the tub was U. S. Coast Guard approved?" Brian jabbed away good-humoredly.

"The building's one fucking block away from a boatyard, Bri." Dean shifted his weight in the passenger seat and glared out its window before turning back to face his partner. "And let me remind you of something else, Mister Wisenheimer. It just so happens that the Tamblin family took delivery of a new trawler the weekend before Patricia disappeared."

"So, what does that mean? She was last seen alive getting off a private plane at Gabreski Airport. Does that mean we should have started tearing through hangar bays and airfields throughout Long Island?"

"Whattaya talking about?"

"Well, you're the one who wanted to drive down to Maryland to the boat dealer—have yourself a look-see. Remember?"

"The dealership was in Edgewater, Maryland—then moved to Annapolis. Those two places ring a bell?"

"Sure. Where the Haynes woman was found laced to a piling, and the Parker woman was found wired and weighted down in a canoe. Edgewater and Annapolis, respectively. What's your point?"

"What's my point? You've got to be shittin' me, right?"

Brian said nothing.

"Two murders in two Maryland boating areas. One where the dealer has a vessel shipped to Sally Tamblin, shortly before Patricia Tamblin was kidnapped. You don't find that just a tad coincidental?"

"Dean. Those Maryland murders happened some time ago. You don't think the locals investigated? You think everyone's a hayseed south of the city line?"

"Jesus Christ, Bri. It was Sally Tamblin who actually made a connection and started callin' around."

"Yeah, to have an innocent boat hauler's butt hauled in. Maybe we should go back and have a talk with her again."

"We're gonna have Kim do a little checkin' for us first, just as soon as we get back, booby."

"And what about that homicide in Edgewater, Florida some years back? The one your Feebe friend got involved in. A boat figure into that one?"

"Workin' on it, kid. I'm workin' on it. Just keep in mind that she was found floating facedown in a canal."

Chapter 16

Malcolm Columba bought himself a brand new Mackinaw coat in Mackinaw City, Michigan. It was an expensive present to himself to help ward off the weather and celebrate the successful murder of the pretty coed from Lake Superior State University. *Talk about cold. Not the coed nor the college, but the city itself,* he shivered with delight, heading south on Interstate 75, keeping the vehicle five miles under the speed limit. Eight degrees Fahrenheit in the middle of freezing February.

". . . *the minimum normal low,*" a radio station out of Sault Ste. Marie broadcasted matter-of-factly as the serial killer listened for the news.

"Minimum normal low!" Malcolm exclaimed as if the announcer were a passenger seated next to him.

The young woman's body hung suspended from the Mackinac Bridge—one of the longest suspension bridges in the world. Seven thousand four hundred feet in length. It was as though she were waving goodbye to the world. Hanging there by a wrist. Twisting in the freezing wind from a single length of line. The news station had not picked up that report yet. But it was still early. *Maybe I should have given her more rope,* he thought giddily. But he certainly was not going back anytime soon.

"*Mo*nisha from Sault Ste. Marie," Malcolm sounded aloud. "S-t-e. for Saint, by God." He chuckled beneath his breath. "*Mo*nisha." He loved the way the m's smacked upon his lips—the way the tip of the tongue touched the alveolar ridge at the top of his teeth . . . enunciating the single n.

She had been a sultry sort. Fitted in tight, cotton-lined faded jeans and a white wool pullover sweater that accentuated her fabulous figure the very first time he saw her. Almost a year ago to the day. She radiated sexuality. He had observed her seated in the college cafeteria with her mouth around the edge of a seeded buttered roll. A steaming cup of coffee sat in front of her. Long, thin fingers turned the pages of a book. He could not see what she was reading at the time, but it had her full attention. Every sixty seconds or so she would brush away annoying strands of straight, blonde-streaked jet black hair that persistently fell across a corner of her striking light brown countenance. A face that belonged on the cover of a glamour magazine. *Ebony*, perhaps. Beneath the cheap Formica table rocked a thigh-high black leather designer boot; one atop the other.

Oh, he remembered every detail so well.

Malcolm turned up the heat and blower fan. The car swerved slightly from the force of the wind whipping across the Interstate. Immediately, he planted his right hand back upon the steering wheel and held it there firmly, trying to keep his mind on his driving, but thoughts of Monisha kept returning.

The evening before—just before he grabbed her—she wore coal-black tights beneath a thick beige terry cloth robe. It had been a very special day for her. Valentine cards and candy kept arriving at her door. And then came the special delivery that very same night. A large bouquet of long-stemmed red roses for the long-legged black beauty . . . *yes* . . . the serial killer played and replayed the scene excitedly through his mind:

"Yes, who is it?"

"1-800-Flowers, for Monisha Washington, ma'am."

Monisha had spied the prolific bouquet through the peephole in her door; the complement of baby's breath bordering at least two dozen American Beauties enveloped in clear plastic wrapping. The nice looking delivery fellow wore a winning smile written across his ruddy wind-beaten face. What Monisha could not see was the rolled up length of carpeting laying on the floor next to Malcolm's feet . . . just in case she would not come along quietly.

The flowers had to be from her Uncle Ed's next of kin on Long Island, she bet. Justin Barnes. He had not left her alone since the day he rediscovered that he had a sexpot for a cousin living alone in a remote corner of the north central United States. Actually, they had been an item off and on for years in New Haven and, since the time she went away to college to begin a new life, Justin had flown or driven up at least a dozen times a year to be with her, spending a few days at a clip shacked up in her rather large off-campus studio apartment. He loved her. Hated the cold. Made her promise to move in with him down in Mastic/Shirley, Long Island the minute she finished school. He promised her that he would be officially divorced by then. He and his wife had been separated for more than a year. The marriage had lasted about as long. Monisha found him to be generous and the relationship amusing, but she had no intention of moving in with him —no future plans that included Justin in her life for good.

Monisha opened the door against the chain that held it fast.

"Don't want to mash these, ma'am," was Malcolm's excuse for not handing the big bouquet of flowers through the narrow opening at the door.

"How come so late in the evening?" was the student's question as she partially closed, then fully opened the door after sliding the chain off its track.

"You should see what's waiting in the van," he answered. "You're getting yours early," he added, still smiling graciously.

He handed over the big bouquet.

"Hang on a second," she said.

Malcolm nodded politely.

Monisha laid the flowers on a table behind her, then stepped over to a highback wooden chair where her pocketbook was hanging by its strap. She took out her wallet and removed three singles.

"Here you go," she offered absently before looking up and realizing that the delivery man was standing just inside the doorway.

Malcolm smiled and shook his head.

"I didn't ask you in," the woman stated, startled as he took another step.

"Justin made me promise to catch your reaction when you open up and read the card," he outright lied, pointing to the small white envelope stapled to the wrapping.

"Justin made you promise what?" she asked, wide-eyed with surprise.

Malcolm kept smiling and, again, pointed to the card.

Without hesitation, Monisha stepped back, reached down and ripped off the tiny white envelope, opened it, then read. Her large brown eyes grew even wider.

"Downstairs?"

Malcolm nodded.

Monisha slowly shook her head in confusion. "Then why would he ask you for my reaction?" she reasoned aloud and quite suspiciously.

"Just in case you didn't come downstairs with me."

"Why didn't he come up with the flowers himself?"

"He wants to *really* surprise you, I guess."

Monisha was glancing from the delivery man back to the card.

"He write this, or you?" she tested.

"He told me what to write, ma'am. Said he didn't know how to. He said all he knew how to do was make money and look pretty. But not half as pretty as you. Those were *his* words," Malcolm added shyly. "He also told me not to take a tip from you." Malcolm pulled a twenty dollar bill from his pants pocket. "He gave me this." Malcolm waved the money. "If you're not going to come downstairs with me now, I have to go because I'm really running very late. I still got a lot of deliveries to make, ma'am."

Her *kissing* cousin *had* to be downstairs, she believed; for not too many folks knew that he never learned to read or write. Not well, anyhow. Not remotely, actually. She would be surprised if he could read or write more than two dozen two-syllable words. She also knew that he would never ever have told a single soul that information. Certainly, never a white person. But a delivery dude from Michigan, who he would never see again? No threat. No sweat.

"Let me grab my coat," she said, somewhat excitedly.

As they stepped out into the hallway, Monisha eyed the rolled up carpet on the floor beside her door. "What's that?" she questioned with a head gesture.

The man shrugged. "That was there when I got here," he lied again.

"Huh."

The carpet was part of Malcolm's back-up plan. If she had not come downstairs willingly, he would have carried her out bodily in that rolled up Berber rug.

Once outside, Monisha did not see a 1-800-Flowers delivery van. What she saw, instead, was a white Budget Carpet delivery truck parked along the quiet, dimly lit street.

"I'm not taking another step," the eighteen-year-old liberal arts student declared. "Not until I know what's going on here."

"What's going on here is that I think your boyfriend absconded with my van. I think I'm going to have to call the police . . . unless that's him hiding there in that truck."

"Where?"

"Back window, there!" Malcolm was pointing toward the rear doors of the truck. "He's probably the one who put that carpet upstairs. Playing some sort of stupid trick."

The last thing in the world that Monisha wanted was the cops. Not with the way in which Justin made his money. Not with what he could be carrying on his person. How could her cousin behave so stupidly? *Why would he take such a chance?* she wondered in anger. That's all she needed now, was to have her name linked with Justin's to some vehicle and carpet theft—or possession of a concealed weapon because she knew he almost always carried—or arrested for an illegal substance, like weed, or worse, good God. She bet herself that was it. Drugs, or maybe alcohol. She had seen him flying high on uppers before . . . before she bailed him out of a drunk tank on more than one occasion. "Shit!"

Monisha marched briskly up to the double doors of the stolen truck. She pulled them open wide. No Justin. Just several rolls of carpeting piled on top of one another, obscured in the hazy, cold crescent lighting cast from the distant lamppost. Monisha was getting madder by the moment, although it was but a few seconds before she lost consciousness as her head thrice crashed forward against the edge of a freezing steel-frame door.

Chapter 17

Detectives Nelson and Archer sat in Lieutenant Groche's office, listening patiently to their commanding officer tell them how they were to proceed from this point forward with regard to the Wendy Linden/Patricia Tamblin investigations. After Theo had his say, Brian tried to reason with the head of homicide.

"This guy's been working his way up the eastern seaboard from Florida to Maine, and now Michigan," Brian calmly but firmly reiterated his partner's concerns. "Let Dean and me fly up there for a week. Please," he practically begged. "We believe these murders are somehow *all* connected. We *more* than believe these murders are connected," Brian quickly emphasized. "Tell him, Dean."

"We more than believe these murders are connected," Dean echoed succinctly, which meant that he was not going to grovel once the lieutenant had his mind made up; what they had to go on was not enough to change their boss's thinking.

The pair would simply do what they usually did in such a situation. They would work the case together on their own time as they had worked others in the past—although time, for all intents and purposes, belonged to their full-time, real-time *god* . . . their earthly deity for whom they virtually worked around the clock whenever things suddenly turned devilishly hot.

God with a capital G.

Detective Lieutenant Theodore Groche.

Master of all he surveyed.

Apparently, matters remained cool in the lieutenant's mind at the moment. Standby, not time-and-travel, was presently the order of the day. One's *own time*, oftentimes could, in a heartbeat, become a distant memory. Not even time off for outstanding performance would be considered in such a situation. Certainly, not a second breath for the bleary-eyed. Downright *dead* tired might buy an hour's rest. Not a snore more. Not until the D.A.'s office had an indictment would Theo lighten up on his immortal angels.

But there was nothing *blazing hot* on the burner until the Linden/Tamblin murders. *So, why is Theo holding both of us at bay?* Brian wondered with concern.

Of course, all that could change in a nanosecond.

Flash point.

Does the lieutenant anticipate another murder close to home? Dean tossed the question around in his mind. *In which case, readiness is, indeed, next to Godliness.* It was the only reason the case detective could come up with to justify the man's actions.

It was not that Theo was pooh-poohing the out-of-state murders; he was merely limiting the scope of the investigation. *But why?* once again, the pair asked themselves.

"I know exactly what you two are thinking. However, comma, you're not going up to Michigan on a wing and a prayer," Theo stated flatly. "I can tell you that right now. You let your fingers do the walking, here. You work with the state police and the locals up there by phone. Call anywhere you like. I don't care if you call China during peak. Nobody's going to second-guess you. But you're not going to travel north again, let alone the Great Lakes, or down to Florida, like you wanted to earlier. Our perp obviously has or had a nest here on the Island in order for him to have gathered the information he did on the Linden and Tamblin women. This is not some transient. These murders were well-planned. Well thought out. Find his nest. If he's in it, roust him from it."

"My point," Brian stated steadfastly as he stood for one last stand before the lieutenant would surely oust them both from his office, "is that he's probably not *in* at the moment, but working his way along the northern border by now. We could stay hot on his trail until we caught up with him. And catch up with him we would. You know that, Theo. You know we'd uncover facts that—"

"That what? Facts those northern or southern boys would never put together for themselves? Maybe *yes* if you fail to share information. But what I'm telling you to do is share and share alike. All right? You do your investigating at this end. You don't see them running up or down here bothering us. Do you? No. Because they're handling things properly. Have they been cooperative with you guys to date? Well, have they?"

"Yes, sir," Brian answered in a deflated tone. "But—"

"Good. And I don't want to find out that you've held back anything that might help them get this fucking monster. This is not a pissing contest. Clear? You've got a lot to explore right here, because while you two were having your little outing up in Old Town, Maine, your teammates were busy churning up the mud. Literally. Either of you speak to Hennesey yet?"

"No, sir," Brian answered up.

Dean simply shook his head.

"Of course not. How about Young, Tucker or Gallo?"

The pair answered in the negative.

"I looked for them when I came in," Dean replied lamely. "They're out in the field. Figured you'd fill us in."

"'Out in the field,'" Theo parroted. "'Figured I'd fill you in,' you say."

"Yes, sir."

"All right. Here we go then. How's this for police work? While you two were touring the Town, and things were warming up here a bit from the thaw, Team Two uncovered steel and aluminum markings found on several rocks along the shore in Flanders, from where we believe our boy transported the Linden woman across the ice. Not on a sled, but on skates. Those steel markings are consistent with the alloy found along the pond up there in Old Town. Also, a scrape mark of aluminum from the tubular section where the blades are fused. See what Hennesey learned locally by picking up the phone and faxing information back and forth? And if we recover his skates, we'll probably find a good size scrape in the leather as well—along the lower or upper portion of the left skate—forensics tell us, although the leather particles found were degraded with all the rain and ice and snow. So, we might not be able to track a manufacturer so easily.

"When most of the snow melted along the bank," Theo continued, "Gallo went back and found a small brass corner-guard, like what you'd see protecting the corner of a piece of luggage. Lester says they'll eventually run it down but that it's definitely old. Could be nothing. Then again, it might belong to something he carried those skates around in. Like a valise or something, Gallo thinks.

"Oh, and we now have official COD confirmation on Wendy Linden. I'm sure it comes as no surprise. Hypothermia. She was exposed to temperatures in the low teens. Those tiny splinters in her feet and palms? Not from any defensive action, like warding off a blow. Quite the opposite, in fact. Purely aggressive. She tried to claw and kick her way out of some kind of wooden box. Forensics traced it to a hard wood. Seasoned oak. She wasn't going anywhere. Crate or cage of some kind, they think. Not much to go on with that, Hennesey tells me."

Brian slowly and sadly shook his head.

"He's got to be a powerful dude," Dean offered, getting to his feet. "Broad across the shoulders. 'Muscular,' the Dawson woman said."

"Had to be to carry Linden across the ice like that," Theo agreed. "Two hundred yards. On skates, no less."

"Anything new on the apartment?" Brian asked, referring to the Tamblin victim found in the bathtub in the Flanders tenement flat.

Theo shook his head. "No, the scoop you initially got from the Southampton Town Police was sound. It hasn't been rented out in six months. Not surprising, though. The whole building only houses ten families. No one wanted *that* apartment, nohow. No one saw or heard anyone come or go from there. Just that classical music, which one tenant identified as *trash*." The lieutenant could not help but smile. "Plebeian. The teams have been through that tenement and town with a fine-tooth comb and a lint brush. Nothing sticks."

"At least we're connecting the dots," Brian posited, alluding to the relationship between the Dawson and Tamblin families.

Again, Theo shook his head. "Too sketchy. Go connect some more; then come back and see me. If it forms a convincing picture, fellas, we'll talk further."

The two detectives were heading toward the door when Dean suddenly turned back to Theo. He just could not let go—could not let well enough alone.

"We've got the Tamblin victim linked to the Dawson child, via the perp's boot size and sole pattern. We got the mother's connection to past employment at Brookhaven National Laboratory, where Sally Tamblin worked. Elizabeth Dawson's job description? Reporting on the water and air quality into the early nineties. We got water-water everywhere flowing into crime scene photos going back two years to another woman found floating in a canal in Edgewater, Florida;

Noreen Walker. The Haynes woman, laced to a pier in Edgewater, Maryland. The Parker woman, tied inside a canoe in Annapolis. The Linden woman, found practically naked and frozen in Riverhead. Patricia Tamblin, fastened in a tub in Flanders. Becky Dawson, recovered under the ice in Old Town, Maine. And now, Monisha Washington from Sault Ste. Marie, Michigan—hanging off the Mackinac Bridge, high above a body of water. A body of water conjoining five of the Great Lakes. How's that for a connection, Lieutenant? Beginning to get the picture? Or do I have to draw you a goddamn map?"

Unruffled, Theo picked up their reports—which he had read and reread early that morning—then shook his head a final time. He set them back down on a pile near a corner of his desk. "See all these reports? Yours are just two of many, hotshots. Collectively, they tell me where I have to go and how to get there. Yours alone are about as enlightening as part of a treasure map without the X," Theo said banally. "What happened to your boat theory, Dean?"

Dean shot an exasperated look to Brian.

"First it was some connection between a sportfisherman and a trawler; then you included a canoe," Theo went on mercilessly. "You're up to your neck in water, Dean," he chided irritably. "It seems to me that you're trying to bail yourself out with a straw. Next, you're going to tell me that there's a connection between the two Edgewater names."

Brian glanced at Dean before staring quietly down at the floor.

"I want something solid, guys. We're not really sure half the homicides you're looking into were committed by the same perp. If you feel there's someone out there who has a grudge against those who worked for BNL, or whomever, find me the common denominator that connects the unknown to the death of these female victims. On the surface, with no pun intended, there's no apparent connection, meaning no one victim knew the other."

"We're not disputing that point, Theo," Brian rejoined. "What we're saying here is that there's got to be some kind of connection between the *families* of these victims."

"And what I'm saying is that when and if you find it, you let me know."

"We've already established a connection between two of the

86

victims' families and BNL."

"But not the others, Brian. Correct?"

"Not yet, sir. No."

"That's why I can't let you two go off half-cocked. That's why I'm not going to assign other members of the team to this just yet. That's why I want you working locally because you might be off on a wild goose chase in Michigan, or God knows where. You work here on Linden and Tamblin. The others, by phone from your desks. Got it?—and good morning."

Theo located a note on his desk that interested him, which meant that the meeting was over.

God had gotten through.

Ostensibly.

Chapter 18

Justin Barnes was about to leave on business when he received the shocking news. The news of Monisha's murder. The news that she was found dangling from a bridge in Michigan. Monisha's uncle from Hartford had been notified by the police, who in turn called Justin's uncle. The old man sadly told his nephew the gruesome details.
Justin was struck with grief.

The twenty-three-year-old wheeler-dealer immediately struck back by putting his fist through a plaster wall in the bedroom the second he hung up the phone. He paced the room like a caged animal before throwing open his suitcase on the bed. The business he had in the Carolinas could not be put on hold. He would see the man and close the deal—a deal that would put another twenty grand in one of his many bank accounts. He would then decide on a course of action concerning Monisha.

For now, he would just move his timetable up a bit . . . move his ass out of that apartment in a hurry before the police arrived with their list of questions. They would probably find good enough reason to haul his black butt in for questioning even if they were but standing on his doorstep collecting for the Police Athletic League. The reason being that his demeanor signaled a single message to the neighborhood boys in blue, who knew him well—well enough, at the very least, to read the maverick's eyes and body language, which hung like a conspicuous sign around his neck. It clearly conveyed a closemouthed, yet confirming, candid communication: *I hate cops!*

Cops, or anything or anybody to do with cops, would further curl the short kinky hair on Justin's scalp.

Cops were the bane of Barnes' everyday existence. Cops, in Justin's mind, were to blame for the fact that he had spent a good part of his youth languishing in the streets of Hartford and Harlem, in and out of parental homes and reform schools; then in later years, a two-year term in a Wyoming state prison.

Is what it is.

It was Justin's simple philosophy. A code to live by. His code. His creed. His breed. Nothing complicated. *Is what it is* was Justin's rationalization, along with his own set of rules and brand of justice, which he meted out whenever necessary.

Beginning life on the streets as a very young boy, Justin found it *necessary* to hand out justice on a daily basis in order to stay alive. By the time he was a teenager, he was something of an animal belonging to a pack. *Gangs* was the euphemism used by law enforcement and the media. As he entered his twenties, he went out on his own. Out of jail. Out of prison. Even out of sorts. But they could never nail him for the killing of a cop. They did, in fact, put his ass away for putting one in the hospital, though:

"No, I'm jus' a black motherfuckin' nigger who's gonna take you down a notch or two," was Justin's response to the cop who was *dissin'* him before putting a traffic ticket on the windshield of the black Cadillac parked in front of the Cotton Club on a hot summer's *nite* when he was fifteen going on fifty.

"Say what, nigger?" the huge black officer responded, then laughed. *"Don't make me spen' the evenin' fillin' out paperwork fo' lockin' up yo' ugly ass."*

"You take that ticket off my au·to·mo·bile, now, fuzz, or yo' gonna eat those words, 'long wif that piece of paper and my fist to push it down."

"This here your au·to·mo·bile, pimp?" the cop challenged, stepping up to and towering over Justin Barnes. The officer had the heel of his hand on his baton, figuring he would not need his gun.

Before the cop received Justin's answer, The Man received the teenager's fearless wrath, plummeting the blue uniform fast and furiously against the black macadam.

It was over before the policeman's white partner could respond . . . the ticketing Uncle Tom laying in a bloody mess on 125th Street between Broadway and Amsterdam Avenue . . . Justin's lightning fists having beaten the black officer senseless—but not the law.

One year in reform school. Not even a prayer of probation. Not after the white arresting officer told his story and showed the judge black and white photographs of his partner's face and the space of missing teeth that Justin had knocked out with the barrel of the *arresting* officer's handgun.

"*Arresting officer, my ass,*" Justin balked. "*I gave the honky bluecoat his peashooter back, empty. I let HIM go. He's lucky I didn't take his badge fo' a souvenir. Next time out, I damn well will,*" Justin promised all in attendance, exhaling a breath of disgust toward the vaulted ceiling sheltering family court.

"*You took the officer's gun!*" the judge declared angrily.

"*He had that thing stickin' in my ear,*" was Justin's only defense.

"*And the other officer,*" the judge resounded, "*can't even be here today because of serious . . . complications,*" he continued, staring down in disbelief at the report before the bench.

"*Fuck him! He called me ugly. It had little to do with the car, yo' honor. Christ, everyone knows I's the prettiest on the block. Maybe even the whole of Harlem,*" he declared through a wide grin, turning around to face his mother who was too busy crying into her kerchief.

. . . yo' honor . . .

It was the most respect that Justin would ever again show for a black robe or *white justice*, he swore. And the judge seemed to realize it in spite of the probation officer trying his damnedest to make a plea on the boy's behalf—to no avail.

"*It is the finding of this court . . . blah, blah, blah . . .*" or was it the ruling? Justin just could not remember. And on and on the judge blabbered . . . *Blah, blah, black sheep, have you any white wool?* the court might just as well have asked, for the family certainly did not have the necessary greenbacks for an adequate defense.

One year in an upstate reformatory was the prescribed sentence handed down by the judge. That was the long and the short of it.

"*Is what it is,*" Justin added to the proceedings. "*Jus' like to add one final thang fo' the record, flunky.*" Justin was being led out a side door in the courtroom by several burly servants of the state. "*When I get out of upstate, I's comin' back down here to finish the job. Meaning you and your asshole partner, flatfoot. Won't hold back next time. How does that please the fuckin' court?*"

Justin finished packing, then remembered his electric razor . . .

his Christmas gift from Monisha. She mailed it down because he could not make it up in time for the holidays. *Business being the reason.* In return, he sent her a belated gift. A full-length chinchilla coat—to *keep your pretty black ass warm,* he told her in a dictated note scribed by his uncle, save the signature:

Justin Barnes.

For Justin could, with a little effort, manage to sign his own name; legibly, if he took his sweet time. Maybe even a few dozen printed words. Short and sweet and to the point: *I lov u Monisha.* That was about the extent of it. Monisha would tease and tell him quite candidly that his signature looked like rat droppings on expensive stationery. She was about the only person in the entire country who could get away with such a comment. Joke or no joke. He could read a little, too. Mostly billboard advertisements when traveling back and forth from the *Ca·ro·li·nas* . . . mainly, by slowly sounding out the syllables. But there were not too many billboard signs in Mastic/Shirley. Traffic signs were a breeze, as he would breeze by them doing sixty in a thirty-mile-an-hour zone.

Once, when a town cop pulled the speeder over in the Hamptons and asked Justin Barnes if he knew what the area speed limit was, the motorist came back with an answer that cost him two hours, along with a one hundred fifty dollar fine.

"So, what did you say to this fine officer when he asked you that question?" the magistrate wanted to know by way of a quick-lipped, defiant frown.

"Why, I told this finely dressed peacekeeper that it depended on what area I be in," Justin replied.

"And do you happen to know what area you're in, Mr. Barnes?"

"Pretty sure that I do."

"Well?"

"That would be whitey's area. Less than five gallons away from Mastic/Shirley would be my guess," he answered smugly, giving the judge pause, along with the prettiest of smiles that, if you looked closely, showed all thirty-two of the black American's perfect bright-white teeth. Six more in number than there are letters in the alphabet, the maverick positively knew.

Numbers for Justin were a breeze. Letters and the law almost always spelled trouble.

Justin closed his suitcase and headed for the shower. He would drive down to Calabash, not even considering taking along his clubs for a round or two of golf with his *associates*. He would keep his mind on *business* . . . hunt for Monisha's killer just as soon as he got home, he decided, punching another hole along the hallway for good measure.

Chapter 19

The petite young detective sat in front of the mainframe, awaiting her instructions. She would not have to be told twice. She would not have to be pointed in a given direction once the situation was explained to her.

"So, we're looking for *anything* connected to polluting the environment, period," Brian elaborated.

Kim Booker tapped the keyboard and accessed a database in the District of Columbia. "You want me to start with the Potomac or Capitol Hill?" she kidded.

"Listen, don't laugh. That's as good a place to begin as any," he agreed encouragingly, scratching the back of his shiny scalp. "By the way. Know how cold it is in Washington, right now?"

Kim immediately hit several keys. "Fahrenheit, Celsius, or ambient temperature?"

"I'm trying to make a joke here," he said in mild frustration.

"Then I *am* in the right area of the United States," the pretty woman teased.

"Seems like everyone's a comedian around here but me," he pouted.

"All right, I'll bite," Kim surrendered. "How cold is it in Washington right now?"

"It's so cold—"

"That the politicians have their hands in their own pockets," Theo delivered the punch line with a smirk, passing through the annex with both hands stuck deep within his pants pockets. A Manila folder was tucked beneath an arm.

"That's twice you ruined my morning, boss," Brian complained to the man's back.

The lieutenant stopped dead in his tracks, then turned around abruptly. "Well, let me shoot for number three, Detective," the top cop challenged. "Kim told me that joke over a month ago; and I told it to you and Dean. She's just humoring you, kid. How's that for a laugh?"

he solicited sardonically, walking away with a degree of satisfaction splashed across his face.

"What's eating him?" Brian questioned.

"He just got a call from your partner. It seems Justin Barnes left town an hour before Dean got there. An uncle said he had business out of state. Didn't know when he would be back."

"Yeah, while Dean and I were sitting around arguing with Theo in his office," Brian stewed. "Wonderful."

"Maybe this will brighten your morning." The computer maven gestured toward the monitor.

Brian stooped and set his eyes on the screen as Kim scrolled down a long list of Evan Tamblin's companies and affiliations. She paused to highlight pertinent information. Brian fixed a gaze on the shaded bar, studying the information carefully.

> Oxygenated Fuels Assoc. Washington, D. C. 1990
> MTBE

"I know what MTBE is, basically. But what's it stand for, actually?"

Kim fired her fingers across the keyboard for further clarification. The information appeared most magically. MTBE: methyl tertiary-butyl ether.

Brian read the text aloud, scribbling notes in his memo book.

"'. . . additive used in gasoline to control vehicle emissions, so as to reduce air pollution concerns in the Eastern United States . . . .' Christ, that's one of Tamblin's companies?"

"Not one of his companies," Kim corrected, hitting a single command. "It's an association. See?" She gestured, boldfacing the abbreviation along the line item.

> Oxygenated Fuels **Assoc.** Washington, D. C. 1990   MTBE

"Sharp girl. I see, indeed. Can you tell me how he's . . . *associated*, Kim?" he questioned, wishing he had paid stricter attention to his business courses in college before becoming a cop. Companies. Corporations. Conglomerates. They all spelled out one and the same thing to him. Money. And now, *Associations*.

"It's going to cost you dearly, Brian," she stated firmly, her eyes glued to the monitor as a flash of polished red nails with tiny white hearts flew over the beige keyboard.

"How about a cup of coffee and a burger for lunch?"

"I said, dearly, dear."

"Whattaya typin' there, his biography?"

"More like a bibliography on this guy." More scrolling. "Here we go."

Brian read the title to himself and nodded. He could not take his eyes off the screen. "Another dot connected, Kim," he said in praise.

Oxygenated Fuels Association. Evan A. Tamblin; Board Chairman, Washington-based. 1990—

"Chairman of the board," Kim Booker affirmed.

"Detective Booker."

"Yes, Detective Archer."

"I want you to—"

"Rerun the victims' surnames and—"

"Their families surnames, Social Security numbers—"

"Then cross-reference—"

"Elements such as air, soil and water—"

"To related occupational titles—"

"Anything at all to do with pollution, and—"

"You'd like a printout on your desk, and . . ."

"*And* what?"

"And I guess that lunch today is out of the question," she balked.

"Dinner tonight," Brian promised, beaming as he walked away so happily that he could have kicked a can like a kid.

"Meaning, if I finish early enough," she said to his back as he exited.

"And produce the desired results."

"Then I'm changing the menu to a steak. Hear?" she practically shouted.

"Steakburger's fine by me, sweetheart."

"Black Angus, deary. Inch and three-quarters thick. Rare.

95

Steak-fries. And a Guinness Stout."

Detective Kim Booker stared down at her colorful nail art, wondering if he had even noticed the dyad of tiny white hand-painted hearts. Especially, the conterminous pair upon the tip of the bare ring finger that beheld the set of red initials: KB & BA. Finely detailed. The woman's downcast eyes gazed but glazed with uncertainty.

Yes? No? Maybe? Probably not, she figured, for Brian Archer had Evan Tamblin as well as several victims on his mind at the moment . . . *as well he should,* she sighed. *Maybe tonight.* Kim smiled, punching in a code which accessed RECORDS at Washington, D.C's Department of Justice – Quantico, Virginia's FBI headquarters – as well as a deep, covert California-based information/operations agency in Death Valley—that simply did not *exist* to those outside the loop.

An hour later, Kim re-booted Big Sister and its linkup to the states' departments of motor vehicles through a central satellite bank coalesced to a series of underground cables. The wizard, as the homicide teams called their beloved computer maven, connected her phone to a modem. Big Sister was simultaneously surfing the sea below Baltimore, along with the so-called protected airwaves. Big Sister was Kim's information highway that could not only bring up a person's last credit card purchase in an instant, or show how many points John and Jane Doe had on their driver's licenses, but if the two had ever bathed or showered together, and Listerined regularly as well.

If the general public only knew that privacy was a thing of the past.

The feds, of course, could zero in with pictorials that could count the hairs on a person's head at an undetermined distance, if need be, through satellite imaging. Big Eyes was everywhere. Another piece of equipment the feds were particularly fond of was Big Ears, which could record a conversation up to a quarter of a mile away. Big Eyes and Big Ears, working in unison with Big Sister, meant that Big Brother was watching and listening to some of the world's darkest secrets. And that's where Brian was headed, Kim surmised . . . to have an old friend help him do a little listening and snooping around. Detective Dean Nelson was not the only one in homicide with a Feebe in the *association* of law enforcement.

By late afternoon, Detective Kim Booker successfully cross-referenced six of the seven murder victims to families living in states well inland, in addition to those along the Eastern Seaboard. Families connected to associations, businesses, and concerns involving both the private and public sectors. Occupations and employment linking not only the pollution of air, soil and water, per se, but the fight to maintain their quality and purity as well. Kim's search led her to and through local, state and federal agencies and departments: Department of Energy (DOE); Department of Environmental Conservation (DEC); U.S. Nuclear Regulatory Commission (NRC). Her pursuit helped to formulate a list of over seventy suspects whose actions warranted scrutiny.

Kim Booker always went the extra mile, rarely looking for or expecting glory, for she already had the gold—her shield—which she prized like a piece of expensive jewelry. However, every now and again she would sour over her colleagues' lack of a little compliment, or even a simple thank you, feeling that she was being taken for granted. Occasionally, she was asked out for a burger and a beer; rarely, for a full course meal (for a job well-done) with her compatriots at Houlihan's—a favorite watering hole for the plainclothes crowd. More often than not, she would have to beat them over the head for the recognition she deserved—the cursory invite notwithstanding. Such was the plight of a woman cop in a man's cop world.

If she were a male, Kim knew, she would have been *número uno*, or damn near the top cop in the chain of command. Truly complain, or show any sort of bona fide bitterness, and she would have been at the top of the food chain, she learned early on in the game.

Through the information Brian had initially provided, she effortlessly linked Evan Tamblin, father of the deceased, to Oxygenated Fuels in D.C. Those were the easy dots to connect, for the industrialist's only daughter, Patricia Tamblin, was immediate family. Hence, the proximity of the dots easily formed a hopeful picture in her mind. Unfortunately, there were others that did not closely follow suit and fall neatly into place. Extended family members living throughout the United States expanded her search. Distant cousins, nieces, uncles and aunts. Stepbrothers and sisters. In-laws and divorcees. Et cetera, ad infinitum.

Kim concerned herself with *any* connection to air, soil and water pollution within the eastern states, especially along the coast.

Waste and sewage treatment plants. Chemical companies dealing in the manufacturing of pesticides and detergents. MTBE and other suspected carcinogens. Plutonium and twenty-two related radionuclides. Nuclear reactor sites. Licensed disposal areas.

The list went on.

The list was endless.

What we have done to this planet, was but one of her troubling thoughts.

By late afternoon, a clear picture was emerging in Detective Booker's ordered mind. Brian and Dean were certainly on track.

Kim worked away into the early evening without a break.

With the exception of the Walker woman from Edgewater, Florida, whose body had been found floating in a contaminated canal two years ago, Kim had connected all the dots:

Laura Haynes, whose inverted body was found fastened to a piling at a pier in Edgewater, Maryland, was stepsister to a woman executive at a waste management plant in Georgia.

Arlene Parker, whose body was discovered in a canoe in Annapolis, was the niece of a middle-aged executive who worked as a chemist for Dow Chemical Company in Baltimore, before starting his own company. Pesticides was the area of the man's expertise.

Wendy Linden, her body found on the bow of the sportfisherman in Riverhead, had been a protégé of a former director at the nuclear power plant in Shoreham, before it was dismantled. Rumor of a serious relationship between the two surfaced; the young student attended classes at Suffolk Community College, and her mentor taught Earth Science courses as an assistant professor.

Patricia Tamblin and Becky Dawson's dots were already connected and credited. Nonetheless, Kim ran a series of family surnames through the computer for further amplification. Nothing new or surprising surfaced.

Monisha Washington's dot took a bit longer to assimilate. Seemingly, no one in her family was remotely connected to a career or job that dealt with the elements for which the detectives were hunting. Kim duly noted that Justin Barnes' family and career were undoubtedly of the criminal kind. Mother and father deceased. One uncle—on the other hand—was as law-abiding as they come. The man had worked as a truck mechanic for most of his life before retiring with a modest pension. Separated from his wife and family, he lived to a ripe old age in Alabama.

Monisha's family hailed from Hartford, the majority of its members never having left the inner city . . . except for a distant cousin, Tyrone Phillips, who pulled down decent money working as a trucker for a toxic waste disposal plant in Kansas.

Kim Booker extrapolated that piece of information from halfway across the country. Topeka. That was the longest single line between connecting points.

"Blood certainly *is* thicker than water," she said quietly, analyzing and summarizing all the related dots.

Brian and Dean were *positively* on target, Kim knew. She sat forward and stared down at the printout she created for the team. Team Three. Of which she was a valued member. Kim felt proud to be a member of a fraternal family unit of dedicated cops. She was proud but at the same time *pissed* that they would not put her in the field on assignment. Just once. She would show them all that she could be a swinging dick, too, she ruminated before returning to her assignment, which she knew in her heart of hearts she was best qualified for: the garnering of pertinent information.

Back to the Walker woman.

What had she missed? What esoteric abbreviation, acronym or subcategory relating to the broader divisions of air, soil or water contamination did she fail to enter? Aero. Hydro. Waste management. What?

"Damn it," she said aloud to no one.

She plugged in scores of key words and phrases—working many variations.

Noreen Walker from Edgewater, Florida. No criminal record. No family connection under the umbrella of air, soil or water contamination dating back to antebellum days, she mused and stretched. The only connection she would find, for sure, would be to go back to the Flood, she frowned in fun.

Maybe there was no tie-in with the Floridian woman at all . . . found floating facedown on a raft of life jackets laced together. Not *in* one, but *upon* several of them—drifting along an oily canal. Maybe hers was an unrelated murder after all. But the crime scene pix and the fact that the life jackets were *laced* together bothered her.

In truth, that very morning, she first concluded that the young Michigan woman's murder, Monisha Washington, was a copycat homicide committed by a psycho with a flair for the dramatic—hanging Monisha high above a body of water from one of the longest suspension bridges in the world. After all, Michigan was way off the beaten track from the killer's linear path. Well off the Eastern Seaboard, she satisfied herself, measuring driving miles along a grid with a mileage pen. Then again, maybe their lunatic was leapfrogging his way along the central northern border. Also, the victim's connection to family did not seem to fit the geographical pattern.

Preconceived notions, she warned herself. As deadly a sin in deduction as ever there was. *Let the picture emerge before you, most magically, like in a developing tray*, she had been trained. *Stay away from preconceived notions*, she told herself again and again, about to give up on Tyrone Phillips before he emerged on the screen most magically. Kim had not connected his dot until she typed in the pertinent URL: departmentoftransportation.com—followed by a special access code. Seconds later, she had him pictured tooling across Topeka, transporting toxic waste in *his* own truck.

So then perhaps there is a missing element regarding the Walker woman, too, she worried and wondered. *Perhaps there is something more to the mystery. Perhaps Dean was onto something initially. Perhaps there is a possible link to boats as well,* she told herself.

Perhaps. Perhaps. Perhaps.
Patience. Patience. Patience.

Kim toyed with the idea of *oil* and *boats*, her fingers dancing intermittently across the keys.

In less than thirty minutes, Kim got her connection:

A shipyard on the Gulf, off the coast of Florida. A tanked up captain who tanked drums of oil around the Keys, and up the Intracoastal to Jacksonville—having had a *little* accident around the Daytona area several years back. Daytona. Just north of Edgewater. A *little* spill. A thousand gallons, exclusive of his liquor. The captain? The surrogate father of a beautiful five-year-old child, Noreen Walker, who he could never legally adopt because of his *little* problem with alcohol. But that did not stop the old salt, who simply "shanghaied" the girl from an orphanage in Washington state, authorities claimed.

"The two suddenly vanished—somewhere on the high seas," a spokeswoman for the FBI stated in an interview Kim was now reading.

Fact of the matter being that the man was basically a good soul who did a fine job raising his charge in a manner befitting a young lady of social class and bearing. Only he did so by schooling her while circumnavigating the globe in a sixty-five foot schooner, spending brief periods in foreign ports and picking up scores of books for Noreen, as well as necessary supplies.

He called her Nor. She called him Captain.

Kim learned that by the time Noreen Walker was fifteen, she spoke five languages; three of them fluently. From an early age, she simply looked upon her captain's moderate drinking as a mild affliction that came with the night's sea air shortly before bedtime, whereby she would maintain a steady course for several hours prior to his arising quite chipper and as fit as a replete sea bird—resuming command of the tall ship till all the stars retired with the night.

Never in all those years together did he ever utter a single profanity in front of the girl, unless it was beneath his breath. Never did he prove to be base or coarse. On the contrary. He was as gentle as the dolphins they saw running a course alongside them; those graceful mammals rising and falling in their endless world of water.

With a firm but gentle hand, he guided her through the years, Kim learned from a rather lengthy newspaper article. When Noreen was sixteen, he set her down on dry land. He told her she had the tools and wherewithal to make her own way in a new world, without ever having to worry about drowning in a sea of turmoil—"a sea that most landlubbers tread through out of sheer desperation in the course of their daily lives," he warned.

"The sea has been your classroom, Nor," her captain told her. "The continent is now your pearly oyster," he said before setting her ashore. "Find yourself a heap of happiness and share a slice with me from time to time, for I'll never be far away." The tortured soul wept openly during an interview, though he tried to lose his tears in a bushy beard, a female reporter wrote. And he truly never was very far from her. Even after her horrendous murder. For he had buried Noreen at sea —initially, against the wishes of her cherished husband, until the captain handed the handsome young man a page from Noreen's journal, which she had written in French, a year after he set her *free*. It was an excerpt from the published journal that Detective Kim Booker was now reading in translation:

> I am the steady sea,
> for it runs within me.
> Even upon solid stone,
> I float above it.
> Like a tall ship,
> I sense its surface.
> Marking fathoms
>   not years . . .
> till I will one day settle upon
>   its timeless floor.

A newspaper account went on to tell of the captain's excessive drinking after his surrogate daughter's death. It told of the oil spills and his other accidents that had occurred over the past two years. His hospitalization. His near escape from the hand of death. His recovery. His relapse.

Kim Booker was formulating a hypothesis of her own, based on what she had before her. Her head was swimming with information as she grabbed a cup of tea, then went outside the building for a bit of fresh air; to compose her thoughts and collect herself. It was 9:45 p.m.

Air, soil, and water. It all came down to that. Oil pollution and boats took Kim vicariously down the Eastern Seaboard to sunny Florida . . . to the captain of a tanker . . . coupling a caring sea captain to the Walker woman found floating on an oil-slicked canal.

Connection complete.

The common denominator between the respective dots? Mutual *love* and *affection* between two special souls, she realized. Not just in words themselves, but through the undying devotion and emotions that the sea captain and his surrogate daughter shared with one another.

Eternally.

That was the key, Kim knew as she wept quietly, hoping no one was around to see her tears. Noreen Walker was beloved.

Yes.

That has to be it!

The perp was killing off the worshipper as well. A little at a time. The actual victims suffered merciful deaths in the eyes of their killer—as compared to the dissolution their *so-called* survivors would endure. Their perpetual pain and interminable torment. The unbearable agony of it all. Eating away at the very fabric of their being. Like a slow and painful poisoning with no antidote. A diluted acid. Paradoxically, lethal nonetheless.

Not a *preconceived notion* on Detective Kim Booker's part any longer. Not remotely. Not now. For the pretty, dark-haired, light but thick-skinned black professional had a solid theory, by God.

Kim quickly wiped away her tears and went back inside the building.

"THEO!"

In addition to the lieutenant finally coming on board, Detectives Dean Nelson and Brian Archer already knew that Kim was totally on track, too, concerning the serial killer's *modus operandi*. After typing up and submitting her findings in an official report, the trio took the lady detective out for the best marinated burger and fries that time and petty cash would allow. It was well after midnight. Several other members from Team Three were approaching the foursome, pulling up chairs from surrounding tables.

Houlihan's was humming.

Kim was happy.

Kim was in her element.

Chapter 20

Thirty-five miles north of New York City, in the town of Buchanan, contaminated steam rose in the evening air from a nuclear reactor at the Indian Point Unit 2 power plant. It was a second-stage alert, which meant that no siren was sounded, so residents knew nothing of the situation until the following day. The Westchester Emergency Operations Center did, however, notify the Coast Guard, but not until two-and-a-half hours after the incident. The Coast Guard halted traffic on the Hudson River, until the area was deemed *safe*.

How ironic, thought Malcolm. *Water traffic is stalled, and the right of passage barred, while motorists sailed across the Tappan Zee Bridge. How ironic and irresponsible, indeed.*

It was later reported that Con Edison, who owns the nuclear power plant, did not notify the U.S. Nuclear Regulatory Commission of the leak until thirty-seven minutes after discovery. The utility's Vice President, Steve Oakman, passed out rhetoric like pabulum, detailing baseline levels and micro-rems per hour, downplaying the "minuscule" leak in one of the generator tubes.

"This event released about one point two micro-rems," Oakman said to several reporters standing in the crowd of protesters.

"Minuscule," echoed one of the pawns in support of the V.P.'s promulgation, explaining to the local gentry how a rem measured up. "Why, you get more radiation exposure working in your sunny garden," the plant manager declared, elaborating on how units of energy are absorbed by human tissue. "This event was nothing," he assured the group. "Forget about it. It's the first alert we've had in twenty-six years," he added proudly with a bright, sunny smile.

Nothing? Malcolm glowered. *Perhaps I'll expose the plant officials of Westchester to an event they'll absorb and that the town will long remember. There won't be anything minuscule about it,* he considered momentarily.

But the research and planning that would go into such an undertaking would certainly require a great deal of time and expense.

And many innocent folks would die as a result. More importantly, he learned that Oakman cared about nothing or no one in his miserable existence, except himself. And as for that callow plant manager, the sunshine boy, shielding himself behind company policy, Malcolm realized that the effort was not worth the risk at this point in time. Besides, there was important business at hand in the Adirondacks . . . a matter that took precedence, as considerable probing, planning and preparation over the course of many, many months had gone into the selection of the author's next victim.

Chapter 21

Justin Barnes took the loop around D.C. before picking up I-95 again, heading south to Calabash. He made the trip several months ago in thirteen hours flat. Today, however, he was fighting off the temptation to speed, reluctantly obeying all the traffic laws—stopping only to fill the gas tank and empty his bladder, denying himself even time for a cup of coffee. He was dog tired, not having slept very well after hearing the news of his cousin's murder.

After the drop, he would relax. Maybe arrange a score for the way back. Always a cache or a stash to be had. But for the time being, Justin concentrated on the immediate deal before he would involve himself in another.

It was impossible for him to cross a bridge without thinking of Monisha hanging from the one up in Michigan.

Fucking name of that bridge, he fidgeted and fought for silently, drumming his fingers anxiously upon the leather-covered steering wheel. "Mackinac!" the maverick suddenly resounded. "Mackin*aw*—like the coat and city. Mackin*ac*—like the name of the island and bridge. Yep. Fucker had to cross that span in order to get to her funky-ass *u·niv·er·si·ty*. Lake Superior State University. Not no *col·lege,* in and of itself, as Monisha explained on more than one occasion—but a kick-ass *u·niv·er·si·ty* . . . in—" the functional illiterate labored to recall "—Sue·saint·ma·re,"he blurted phonetically. "Had to be some motherfucking student who iced her. HAD TO BE!" he flared, hammering the heel of a hand against the padded leather dash.

He had been driving for approximately four hours, his thoughts continuously returning to her gorgeous face and foxy figure. Monisha's stunning features and body had not changed in all the years he knew her. She would turn heads and stop traffic two city blocks away, he fondly recollected, picturing her strolling along the busy boulevard in her Sunday best. He recalled the time some honky pulled his convertible to the curb and blared the horn, shouting racial slurs as she headed south along the walkway, right around the corner from her church. The clown sitting next to him suddenly stood up and onto the front seat, grabbing his crotch and hooting hilariously before shaking up a bottle of beer—a thumb covering its open mouth—then shooting the stream of foamy white liquid that caught her in the face.

Justin had been out jogging, rounding a playground and an abandoned building a block away from her home in Hartford, when he witnessed the scene. *Nailed that wigger—that white motherfuckin' nigger—smack in the back of the head with better than half a brick. Never knew a Corvair had that kind of pickup,* he roared, laughing and lauding over the remarkable shot that brought the rabble-rouser down. *Fucker completely vanished from view.* The maverick suddenly started tearing through a strange mix of emotion that momentarily took his breath away.

Justin was wiping his eyes as he replayed the scene over and over again in his mind. *Every nigger on the block had a laughing jack on . . . even the two old women who were hollering through their silly show of anger,* he reminisced.

"*Yo' gonna be the death of us yet, Justin Barnes,*" one of them railed.

"*Yo' uncle gonna kick yo' butt but good if the po·lice come lookin',*" the other bellowed.

Justin accelerated, signaled, then crossed two lanes of traffic, bringing the Cadillac up to the state's speed limit. Seventy. Partly to speed away from those memories of youth. Some fond. Some not so fond. Partly to shield his tears and move ahead of the nosy motorist in the middle lane, who, *ir·re·gard·less* of the Caddy's tinted windows, peered in on him. Tears of laughter. Tears from troubling times. Tears of mourning his precious Monisha.

The mergence of the two emotions was overwhelming.

The sentiment grabbed and held him in the center of a heavy heart.

For a split second, Justin wanted to put the Seville's hood ornament into the trunk of the Continental in front of him. But he finally calmed down, and his mind drifted back to *business*. Back to the contraband he was carrying in his trunk. Back to the goods he might be transporting on the return trip home. He signaled again and eased over to the middle lane, reducing his speed to sixty-five.

If only they'd raise the speed limit in New York, he thought. *That would surely save me a heap o' time and aggravation when conducting business, or jus' toolin' around. All those nasty-ass points on dat le·git·i·mate license . . . ohooo eee.* For he always drove fast when he was not wheeling and dealing. But New York was getting nuts. New York was confiscating cars! He could just imagine what would happen if a cop ever pulled him over and attempted to seize his car, along with the contraband he was carrying. He would, without question, seize the situation by sticking a pistol in the cop's puss and pulling the trigger quicker than a lizard could nail a fly.

Fuck Pataki. Fuck Giuliani. Fuck the Empire State. Still, New York was his *candy store. So, bro. Don't shit and dis nobody where it's oh, so sweet,* he reprimanded himself.

Another fucking bridge, by God! Another fucking toll.

Five hours into the trip, and Justin was getting antsy. Time for a lesson. He reached for the *Rand McNally, Easy-to-Read Travel Atlas,* flipping through the pages to the first enlarged-print map. Pausing to watch the road. Back to the book. Alabama began the section. He hunted for the circled star near the black, bold-lettered city, indicating its capital. Montgomery. *Fuck.* He thought the capital was Mobile, located in the lower left corner of the state. He knew a lot about that southwest city from his uncle's stories and how he grew up in poverty in a fire-ridden flat—realizing it was not pronounced as Justin was seeing it now, but as . . .

Mo· beal. Why isn't the fuckin' English language written like yo' hear it? he flustered. *Fo·ne·tik·ly. Why all those fucking exceptions to the rules?*

"How am I ever gonna learn all this shit anyhow?" he asked aloud.

"I be mobile, motherfucker. 'Cause I'm gonna moonwalk 'cross yo' fuckin' face," Justin once told the principal of the East Harlem elementary school he attended for a spell. The man told him he was suspended for a week. The following month he was expelled.

Justin saw a sign up ahead for Mobil gas and could not help but smile. "Now, I jus' know *dat's* pronounced Mo·bil, motherfucker." He had a quarter of a tank. He would fill up, then empty his bladder at the next rest area.

"The capital of Alabama is Mont·gom·er·y," he committed to

memory. "Located 'bout the center of the state. Not Mo·beal, cocksucker, which be tucked away in the southwest corner. Along the coast. At the mouth of the Mo·beal River." Maybe he would visit that city by the sea one day, he considered. "The capital of Alabama is Mont·gom·er·y, 'cause *y* is pronounced *e*," he repeated loftily, forming a picture of his uncle chewing gum—standing before a burnt out tenement—high upon a *mount*·ain, along the outskirts of the city where the old man had raised his family . . . standing there before the blackened monument.

All he had to do was switch the two cities around. *Seen one ghetto, you've seen them all,* he pretty much figured.

"Mount·gum·er·e. Whatever fucking works fo' ya, nigger."

Actually, the old man chewed tobacco . . . twenty-four hours a day. But gum was good enough. He would hold that picture in his mind for a lifetime, he knew.

"The capital of Alabama is Montgomery," Justin Barnes said confidently, making himself a promise that he would learn all fifty states and capitals by the time he arrived back in New York. Twenty-five down. And twenty-five back up.

Arithmetic was no problem.

The alphabet was another thing.

Monisha had reached a point where she had just about given up on him. But he did not give up on himself. He knew a little bit more than he let on so that she would not expect too much of him. That was his little game.

A fresh pool of tears welled up in his eyes as he thought about the surprise he was planning to mail out to Monisha in another month. His first full-page letter. Well, almost a full page, anyhow. But he wanted it to be perfect. All the uppercase and lowercase letters set where they belong. All the spelling correct. He had been working on it for quite some time. The grammar he knew he would never get down pat. Not even close. But no one who grew up in a ghetto would ever possibly care, he believed. Not even college-educated Monisha.

"Want to improve your vocabulary two hundred percent?" she had asked him with a straight face as the two of them were lounging around like lizards in her Michigan apartment.

"Sure," he responded sincerely.

"Remove the word 'motherfucker' from your limited list,

nigger."

"Shit, I do dat, da world'd think I be fuckin' dumb," he teased. *"Not stupid, but dumb,"* he added, covering his bright white smile with a large black hand. *"Dumb. You know. Like in Death and Dumb. Wouldn't have anythin' much left to say."*

Monisha studied him warily. *"But you are dumb,"* she finally said, staring down, face to face.

"Whattaya mean?" Justin was not smiling.

"What do I mean?"

"Yeah, whattaya, fuckin' death?"

"Deaf, nigger. Not death."

Justin noted the distinction immediately and flushed. He could feel the heat rising north of his neck. *"Guess I never heard that said quite correctly,"* he admitted freely, instead of the little dance he would usually do when they first started seriously dating. He could be himself around her. It hurt from time to time. More than he ever let on. *"Hey, maybe I am a little deaf,"* he said. *"But you gotta admit one thing; in death you're certainly deaf. Can't hear a motherfuckin' thing, nohow."*

Monisha rolled her naked body across the bed and was laughing toward the ceiling. *"Hopeless motherfuckin' nigger."*

"Yeah, look who's callin' the kettle black, bitch."

"You callin' me a black bitch?" Monisha teased.

"I didn't call you no black bitch, bitch. I just called you a bitch."

"I know." Monisha smiled handsomely. *"I just want to make sure you understand the importance in knowing where to place your commas, homeboy. Come on, time for another lesson."*

"Yeah, home in on this, bitch," Justin commanded, pointing to his semi-erect penis.

"Not until we cover tense," she teased.

"Tense?"

"Come on."

Justin recalled her yanking him up by the arm, pulling him from the bed, and over to the table where she did her homework.

"Hold on a second."

"What?"

"Guy goes to a psychiatrist and says, 'Doc, you jus' gotta help

me.' Doc says, 'Tell me what's bothering you.' Guy says, 'I'm a tepee, I'm a wigwam. I'm a tepee, I'm a wigwam. Can you tell me what my problem is?' The psychiatrist says, 'Sure, you're too tense.' Get it? Two tents. Too, tense," he clarified. Not as if the joke needed explaining, but only to show Monisha that *he* was not totally dumb.

Monisha was literally on the floor, laughing hysterically, still holding him by the arm. *"Come on, nigger. There's hope for you yet,"* she said encouragingly, when she finally caught her breath. *"Come with mama, baby."*

"The capital of Alaska is *June'a,"* he tried, rotating the cruise control counterclockwise, reducing his speed and holding the Cadillac at sixty while picturing a Jewish Eskimo standing in front of an igloo in the middle of June . . . melting right before him upon the ice.

Juneau.

He figured he was not pronouncing the capital properly, but what the hell. Few names were as simple and as neat as his own. Justin. *From some motherfuckin' Latin word meaning 'just.'* Justin grinned.

"You're just one motherfuckin' fair nigger; ain't you Justin Barnes," Monisha chastised him many a year ago, after he confessed to her that he once killed a cop.

The only person in the world he ever told.

"The capital of Hawaii is Honolulu," Justin read aloud off the adjacent page of the planner on his lap, wondering why the *motherfuckin'* state was out of alphabetical order, anyhow. "Alaska and Hawaii they just smack together. As if the *cocksuckin'* language ain't hard enough to follow, they gotta confuse you more."

Yet, he surely knew that his pronunciation of the state and capital in the Pacific Ocean was on the money, for he had missed very few episodes of *Hawaii Five-O*, while growing up—having killed that tall, white, cocky cop a million times over in his mind.

"'Book 'im, Danno.'" Justin laughed maniacally, unable to come up with the cop character's name. *Fuck 'im,* the 'businessman' said to himself in frustration, pushing aside the 11 x 15-inch copy of *Rand McNally. What the fuck is that cop's name, anyhow?* he wondered for the next two miles.

Justin learned the trick of associating names from Monisha and her memory book—introducing him to the method of framing pictures in his mind.

"The sillier the better—*"* she instructed *"*—*sad also works,"* he could picture her saying, smiling and frowning within her single, salient sentence. Sad. Like his uncle standing on a mountaintop in front of that burnt out tenement in . . . Mont·gom·er·y, Alabama. Chewing gum.

Oh, he would find Monisha's killer, all right! Even if he had to move to Sault Ste. Marie, Michigan, for a spell. Even if he had to impersonate a city cop—perish the thought.

Few people on the planet knew just how enterprising he could be.

Monisha knew, rest her soul.

Chapter 22

E van Tamblin sat at a table toward the rear of the uptown, upscale restaurant on East 76th Street in Manhattan. The Café Boulud. His three guests were greeted and immediately escorted to their table by the maître d'.

The exclusive establishment enjoyed a reputation of being ranked among the finest eateries in the city, second only to its sister restaurant, Daniel, owned and operated by Chef Daniel himself. The two restaurants were rated in the top five, more often than not, heading the list. The entrepreneur had the interior of the Café Boulud fashioned after a late thirties men's club, capturing the ambiance through the use of dark, masculine wood paneling and virile furnishings, along with a soothing, cool, complementing subdued salmon, copper, and blue cast. In contrast, occasional bursts of floral brightness splashed the corners of the room. Smaller bouquets of ginger and freesia sat at each end of the long wooden bar: its base a patina of hammered copper and bronze. The room could seat ninety patrons in a pinch.

Tamblin's guests were about to be treated to a *tasting*: a mini eleven course meal to tantalize their palates and whet their appetites— so as to do the industrialist's bidding; that being, ostensibly, the expeditious arrest and conviction of the killer or killers involved in his daughter's sadistic murder. Below the surface, in a dark recess of his brain, the man held a madness of his own . . . brewing within his troubled mind.

To Tamblin's right sat the reputed head of the Mafia crime family from Staten Island. Across from the burly man, the NYPD inspector settled into a comfortable chair. Directly in front of their host roosted the deputy mayor of New York.

The four men were tucked away in a corner toward the back of the room. The restaurant was officially closed for the evening. The business at hand surrounded details concerning the serial killer. Family business. And although neither Tamblin nor anyone else seated at the table were blood related, they were, nonetheless, considered a family of sorts.

A captain and his waiter approached the table with a bottle of champagne: *Verve Clicquot.* The server poured four glasses while Evan and the captain made small talk.

Afterward, the foursome spoke quietly of one Suffolk County homicide lieutenant's progress.

"Theo's a good man," the inspector said solemnly.

"No question," the city's deputy mayor affirmed.

Don Ciccio turned quiet, sipping from his glass and admiring the room: the rich cherry wood chairs; their comfortable, cushioned, salmon leather seats.

The deputy mayor took in the banquettes along the wall; taupe —the soft browns and grays lending a chiaroscuro effect against the muted fabric walls, bestowing an inviting, lighter, ethereal hue. The official's daughter was an interior decorator and, therefore, taught her father much about color and design.

The captain reappeared with two waiters. Evan Tamblin spoke French to the suited individual, politely instructing how several of the dual dishes, to be served shortly, were to be distributed.

A few pleasant minutes passed before individual plates of *Bluepoint oysters with Beluga Caviar* were set down simultaneously in front of the four gentlemen. Orchestration, choreography and precision were part of the fare, too. Presentation, not pretension, was purely practiced as an art.

More champagne, label up, was poured into their glasses.

The police inspector noted the way in which the waiter's fingers delicately balanced the bottle, the man's thumb neatly inserted into the inverted nipple at its base as he poured single-handedly, while a sommelier, standing alongside, explained the wines that were to be served through the course of the evening. The cop recalled the U-shaped depression as having something to do with pressure from fermentation, but refrained from raising the question out of sheer embarrassment, knowing full well that he was out of his element.

As soon as members of Daniel's staff left the table, Don Ciccio briefly explained how his family could and would be of service if sanctioned by the trio. In any event, he was sure to enjoy a good meal and drink.

"It would be a great honor for me to assist," the finely-dressed don said in all seriousness. "The only thing I ask in return is that I get all the carting contracts in all five boroughs over the next ten years," he jested with a grin.

"Don't even kid around like that," the deputy mayor balked.

"Whattaya think I'm wired for sound—" Vincent Ciccio teased "—that I'm gonna tell your boss we had a deal that you backed out on?" he taunted, knocking a meaty leg against the bony knee of the powerful man seated next to him while holding the stare of the nervous city official seated diagonally across the table.

"I'm not worried about any wire you may be wearing, Vincent. I'm just worried about that goddamn gun you carry around like a peashooter. You know how I hate guns at the table."

Although he had not expressed amusement in well over a month, Evan Tamblin could not help but smile.

"Hey, I'm licensed to carry, Lou. Tell 'im, Billy."

William Mattheson smiled but did not say a word.

"Say, you didn't forget to renew my paperwork, did you Billy?" Vincent kidded through a frown.

"Not at all. Just forgot to buy you a box of bullets," the cop bantered back playfully.

"Don't matter. I do my own reloading nowadays, anyway," he joked. "And talkin' about guns, Bill, here, is a collector. Right, Billy?"

"My father, actually."

The don turned his attention back to the young deputy mayor. "Whattsamadda? Afraid we're gonna order the veal tonight, Lou?" he taunted through a grimace, subtly clutching his throat but bulging his eyes in mock allusion to the restaurant scene in *The Godfather*.

"No ordering tonight, gentlemen," Evan reminded everyone. "This is a *tasting*. Little bit of this, and a little bit of that. Everything has already been decided."

"I hate guns, and I hate violence," Louis Penella stated firmly with a one-track mind, reinforcing his feelings so that no one would soon forget.

"Hey, ya know what Uncle Vincent's gonna buy his favorite nephew for his birthday comin' up?" the don continued to harass. "A Daisy Trainer. Every kid's gotta know how to handle a gun. Right, Billy?"

Louis' adopted son was of no relation to Vincent Ciccio, or any member of the man's family for that matter, yet the don and Louis' kid were extremely close. Too, Vincent's wife and Louis' were like sisters, fostered by the fact that their homes sat only several blocks apart. A first-time visitor to the Penella household might honestly confuse which family lived where, or wonder why Don Ciccio was almost always found sitting in Louis' favorite chair. At times the deputy mayor felt like a stranger in his own home.

Minding a more important matter was the grim reality that Vincent had been directly responsible for launching his protégé into public office, prior to the proverbial nod from the governor's office, which amounted to something along the lines of a wink. Moreover, the city official was secure in his knowledge that his underworld confidant was a man unquestionably true to his word. And when completely honest with himself, Louis knew, too, that Don Ciccio was a necessary evil in a righteous world of political bedlam. For Vincent had taught him very early on that there was no such thing as good government or bad government—simply government . . . in which the worlds of good and evil overlapped.

"Over my dead body," Louis replied in response to Vincent's offering his kid the gift of a BB gun, then washing down the last oyster with a sip of sparkling Pellegrino.

"What do you say we get down to business?" Evan asked evenly as several dishes and utensils were cleared from the table and selected silverware set anew. The words were not framed as a question so much as a direct request.

Louis nodded in agreement.

Plates of *Crisp Brandade Ravioli* were immediately brought out and placed before them.

The table grew quiet, and the inspector was not really sure whether Evan meant business in general, or the quiet business of indulging in the exquisite cuisine.

Vincent could not care either way, for he always talked with his mouth full anyway—about food or business or both.

The industrialist leaned over and lowered his voice. "There is no question that we need your help in this matter, Don Ciccio," Evan said with grave respect, using the man's title so that there was no question as to where the help was to be derived.

"Done," said the man, putting a finger to his lips, which meant *no further formality.* Looking up from his plate at everyone, he added, "These ravioli are fantastic." The man's mouth and hands were as busy as his brain, but he said nothing more for the moment.

"That's it?" Louis snapped. "You've got nothing else to say?"

"Talk's cheap. Action on the street's expensive. Got it covered. All right?" Vincent cut into another ravioli.

William smiled, turning the conversation back to the cuisine, knowing that the don's succinct statement said all that needed to be said—for now. "These ravs and sauce are fantastic. Probably prepared by some Frenchman, back there, Vincent," the cop needled, tilting his head toward the kitchen. "Right, Evan?"

Vincent swallowed abruptly, shook his head and waved his fork for emphasis, declaring in mid chew, " . . . Never—a defector or an impostor, maybe. But no Frenchman made this dish, 'less he deserted then repatriated; his mother, too. And just for the record, smart ass, this is a *gravy*, not a sauce. No self-respecting Italian would *dare* call such a robust, rich and zestful flavor such as this a *sauce*. And don't try to sound cosmopolitan neither—saying *ravs* for short. Ravioli, Billy. I hate it when you walk into my neighborhood deli and ask for a pound of *ravs* and a quarter pound *prosciut*. Ravioli and prosciutto. Say it."

"Just as soon as you say delicatessen instead of deli," William said sillily. "And stay the hell out of *my* neighborhood lest I sic the Irishman on ya."

"At least that Irishman knows how to behave himself, and not put on airs."

"Yeah, air this." William Mattheson grinned, gesturing to his groin from across the table.

Everyone, including Evan, surrendered a little laugh, then settled down.

"You'll coordinate with Lou's office, Bill," Evan stated evenly, "in setting up a task force."

"It's already in the works. By the end of the week, I can promise you half the country will be looking for this fuck," the inspector promised.

"Thanks, guys," Tamblin said warmly and sincerely. "Appreciated." The man truly looked relieved.

After some preliminary discussion, mostly between Louis and William, steaming hot cups of *French Onion Soup* and *Clam Chowder* arrived. William and Vincent received the latter, but the don made sure he got a taste of Louis'.

A white wine was poured moments before the *Nantucket Bay Scallops with Citrus and Celery Purée* arrived. *Meursault-Perrières Premier Cru '95*. Label up.

The night was young.

The inspector troubled himself over the strange looking utensil that was set down with the next course. On first glance, it appeared spoon-like, its face akin to that of a melted watch in a Dali painting, which he had seen in some uptown museum that his wife had dragged him off to for a full day crammed with culture.

He watched carefully as Evan used the funny-faced fish fork against the *Halibut Tail with Braised Veal Cheek*. Louis and Vincent seemed right at home, too. The cop wondered just how many late night meals he had missed, which both the don and the deputy mayor likely shared with the industrialist. Finally, he began to relax and was intent on savoring the delicate texture and flavor of the fish and veal when he caught the crime boss smiling and furtively gesturing toward his throat anew.

Vincent winked across at Louis. "How's your veal, *paisano?*"

La Croix de Beaucaillou, Saint-Julian '95 was the medium bodied blood red vin that was poured next, served along with the *Red Wine Risotto with Wild Mushrooms and Quail Egg* dish.

The men were at a halfway point that marked the lavish feast.

Evan and William were served slices of *Spice Roasted Duck Breast with Sweetbreads and Winter Root Vegetables*. Louis and Vincent were apportioned *Roasted Squab with Foie Gras and Endive Fondue*. Of course, everyone shared bites of the bounty. Aspects involving the prodigious network of operation were discussed at length, with William and Louis doing most of the talking. Vincent was quietly taking in all the information, sopping up most of the sauce and gravy, too, with a luscious assortment of breads.

Evan Tamblin's mind was almost entirely on his dearly departed darling daughter. Sweet Patricia. God, how he missed her. He had all he could do to keep from weeping in front of his guests. Her death. Its finality. Only now was it veritably creeping in. Like a boring corkscrew worm eating away at his brain.

Evan nodded at the waiter's invitation for another glass of fine red wine. Not nearly as fine as what he and Sally had stored in their cellar at home. But he really could not care. Evan truly believed that his undeniable thirst would alone be satiated by a single swill—sweet *Revenge*—quenched only after he would hold the killer down by the throat, underwater, until the lunatic drowned like his dear daughter, he fantasized . . . terminating the *animal*, or *animals*, who had viciously murdered his precious little girl.

Before Louis and William excused themselves to go to the men's room, Evan Tamblin made it abundantly clear that he wanted the mayor himself to announce a one hundred thousand dollar reward for information leading to the arrest and conviction of Patricia's killer —backed in full by a promissory note. And that would be for openers if nothing happened within the next two months. After that, he would up the ante, with no particular ceiling in mind. Both Louis and William told him, in so many words, not to jump the gun.

As the pair disappeared around the corner to the lavatory, Evan leaned forward and took Vincent into his confidence.

"Vinny."

It was as if he and the don were of the same mind. Vincent nodded knowingly before Evan ever made his appeal.

"Vinny, if your boys find him before the police do, I want you to bring him to me. Alive and kicking. One million dollars for his hide."

Vincent tapped the man's hand comfortingly. "Just the expenses, Evan," the big man stated. "Just the expenses."

"I'd be in your debt, Vinny."

When Louis and William returned to the table, *Exotic Fruit Soup with Assorted Sorbets* were served: *Apple, Blood Orange, Fromage Blanc and Ginger Vanilla Granité.*

Each man had a flavor to cleanse his palate.

If it were only that easy to cleanse one's soul, Don Ciccio reflected, taking in the large mirrors adorned and draped with folded fabric across the top and down its borders, spaced along an entire wall.

Louis lifted his eyes to the ceiling and noted that the fabric around the light fixtures matched the walls as well. The lush carpeting picked up the salmon, copper, and blue hues that were evident throughout the entire room.

Everyone but Evan took a taste of each other's scrumptious

sorbets. The man's was up for grabs.

"I'll just pick," Vincent insisted, relieving Evan of his plate.

"You've got company," William rejoined, taking a tiny amount upon his dessertspoon.

"Mmm. This is absolutely delicious," Louis delighted.

"The whole dinner was delicious," the inspector added.

"Wait till you try the desserts," Evan announced, trying to make some meaningful conversation. "To die for."

"Enough with the dying, Evan. I *live* for dessert," Vincent announced immodestly.

"You live for *food*, period, you fake," Louis teased. "You should see him over at the house. He's so busy with his hands and mouth, that he's eating out of *my* plate and drinking out of *my* glass. Yet, Nancy always sits him next to me no matter how many times I tell her, '*not*'. He's really on his best behavior with you guys tonight. Believe me, I know."

"You tell 'em I gotta come through the back of your house like I'm some sort of embarrassment, Louie?" Vincent complained. "And that I gotta take my shoes off in your mud room, no less? Can you imagine what it would've looked like my leaving that mob scene in Apalachin, in '57, if everyone took their goddamn shoes off?" he deadpanned. "Feds and the bloodhounds would've had a field day. Bad enough as it was. Me? I just made it out of there and through the woods in the nick of time. 'Course, Nicky never made it out, except in handcuffs."

William was smiling politely and slowly shaking his head.

As with every course, the plates were cleared and clean silverware reset. One of the waiters unobtrusively picked up Vincent's napkin from the floor, placed a fresh one in front of him, then disappeared.

Vincent glanced over his shoulder toward the kitchen, setting his steely dark eyes on the captain and his back waiters who served the fare, along with the front waiters who had brought the beverages and breads. The don faced back around and unfolded his napkin.

"You know, I'd love to have this laundry gig, Evan," Vincent confided with a wink. "If we can get Daniel to have the waiters change the linen napkins after every course, I think this could be a gold mine. We've been here, what? Four and a half hours? Figure another forty-five minutes to an hour for dessert and coffee and after-dinner drinks . . . times how many courses and tables in an evening? Hell, I'd clear a profit within a month. How's his other place doing downtown? I understand it's even classier than this joint."

"Joint? Are you complaining, Vinny?" Louis scolded. "You have absolutely no tact."

"It's the only decent place I could book last minute," Evan offered apologetically in feigned defense.

"Book?" Vincent questioned incredulously. "How many behind-closed-door tastings or dinners does this guy put together in a week?"

"You'd be surprised," Evan answered knowingly with a nod. "Anyhow, you remember the couple I introduced you to; my neighbors to the right of me?"

"Sure. Architect. Tall dude. Got that looker for a mate. Nice couple."

"Well, that looker is the reason we're sitting here tonight. She arranges all the parties for the upper crust."

"And whatta you? The bottom of a pie pan?"

Evan forced a smile. "Just a local yokel who made good about a million years ago, trying to keep these old bones aboveground and my head above water," he added, catching the cliché a little too late in the center of his throat. "Poor choice of words," he managed through a flood of uncontrollable tears he quickly dammed up with a handkerchief.

Vincent placed a comforting meaty claw upon his friend's nape. "All in good time, Evan. All in good time. Promise."

"We're gonna get this fucker for you, Evan. Believe me," the inspector affirmed, believing the sorbet had *been* the dessert and wondering if the man and Vincent were kidding about more food and drink en route. Remarkably, he was not at all bloated like when he would leave his neighborhood haunt in Queens. Then again, the man was learning a valuable lesson tonight. The difference between eating and dining. He looked up and could not believe what was coming their way.

The king of the kitchen was standing alongside his waiters, busy listing the sweet array. *Warm Bittersweet Chocolate Soufflé with Pistachio Ice Cream. Pineapple Napoleon with Rum Raisin Ice Cream.*

Raspberry Chocolate Mousse Cake with Vanilla Crème Brûlée. And *Almond Bavaroise with Orange Compote and Blood Orange Sorbet.*

William was shaking his head in disbelief as the desserts were being served.

"Monsieur Tamblin has selected a fine dessert wine for you this evening," the suited captain said, displaying the narrow, long-necked bottle.

Cave Springs Reisling; Late Harvest '98.

A waiter poured for everyone.

"*Santé*," the captain said in earnest. A moment later, both he and his servers took their leave.

Once again, sins were shared among the four men.

A single syllable . . . a word . . . a phrase—then finally, complete sentences sounded out among diminutive spoonfuls.

"Mmm."

"Delicious."

"To die for, as I said."

The three men glanced curiously at their host.

"Mikey likes it," Louis said of Vincent.

"John Gotti. Eat your fucking heart out."

"This wine is absolutely the end."

"Did someone say *the end*?"

"Not quite."

Coffee, Decaf and Tea.

"Five-and-a-half hours. I honestly don't know where the time went," William declared.

Petits Fours and Madeleines.

And then—the check.

Vincent insisted on leaving the tip, peeling off four one hundred dollar bills from a gold money clip. Louis and William made a noble gesture toward their wallets.

Evan was handed a cash receipt. Gratuity included. He waved off everyone's offer.

"Everything's been taken care of, gentlemen. Thank you for being my guests."

"I want to open an account here," Vincent insisted. "And I want the address of that party person of yours out East."

"You looking for a nightcap already, Vinny?" Louis teased.

"Can't get rid of him once he's got your number," the deputy mayor warned Evan playfully. "But you already know that."

"I want to wire a dozen roses to your neighbor in the morning, Evan," Vincent said sincerely, ignoring Louis' barrage of insinuations. "Anonymous, of course. You can say they're from a meeting you had with a prelate or a prince."

Again, Evan Tamblin was waving him off. "Not necessary, Vinny. Really. I'll pass along your thanks," he promised. "From all of us."

"Yeah, how's she going to explain a bouquet of flowers to her husband, Vinny?" Louis asked cuttingly, a little light-headed from all the wine. "Perhaps if you went out and bought the fella a diamond pinkie ring in the bargain, you'd pull it off," he slurred his words and tittered. "Maybe then, you'd come out smelling like a rose," he concluded through a guffaw.

"What's their names?" Vincent persisted. "Maybe a little note. I'll mail it to you, and you can pass it along," he persevered.

"Jerrold—with a j and two r's—and Mindy," Evan succumbed; for once Vincent had something in his mind—not unlike Sally—there was no way out.

"Their *last* name?"

"I didn't, nor wouldn't give them yours," the industrialist stated, smiled and yawned.

"Yeah, I noticed that right away, Evan," the don reminded him. "The very first and last time you introduced me. Their surname, please."

"Manfred," the host capitulated.

"Think they'll still remember me? It was awhile ago."

The inspector could not let the comment pass. "How about I send Evan the clipping from *Newsday* to pass along of when you tried to make Sammy 'The Bull' Gravano's bail?" he suggested, then tittered, too.

"You do that, Billy. And I'll send *your* wife a dozen roses, care of . . . what's the name of your brother-in-law's funeral home?"

"*Touché,*" the cop relented, raising his arms in mock surrender.

"Guess this would be a good time to call it a night," Louis suggested, pushing back his chair and glancing at his watch. "It's very late."

"Nah, it's still early," Don Ciccio insisted. "Gonna invite me over for a nightcap, Louie?"

"Yeah, one that you wear on your head," his protégé shot back impatiently.

"It's always nice to know that we all understand one another so clearly," Evan Tamblin said rather subtly and without expression.

Chapter 23

The lieutenant stepped up to the podium and was about to address a group of twenty homicide detectives assembled from three teams. Two stragglers entered the squad room. Theo waited until they were seated. Next door, four sleuths lay dead to the world—fast asleep.

"We've got an extremely difficult situation here, boys and girls. This guy doesn't sit still long enough to see his breath leave the shaving mirror." The squad room was completely silent as their commanding officer continued. "Florida. Maryland. New York. Maine and now Michigan. Five states. Seven victims. And those are only the ones we're sure about. I'd love to see his scorecard. Anyhow, we're talking a time frame covering twenty-seven months. Unquestionably, he's building up momentum, meaning shorter intervals between homicides. Our boy's developing an insatiable thirst for blood.

"Now. Dean, Brian and Kim have made impressive headway in this case. We didn't have anything solid to connect the victims until Team Three started nailing down blocks of information that made some kind of sense. From left, right and center field, Kim started connecting the dots. And things are beginning to take shape. We believe we have a motive to this guy's madness. Of course, we're not ruling out the possibility that there's more than one assailant working in concert. Though at this point, we think the perp's working solo, murdering attractive young females—one of them a child—all of them in some way associated with individuals in either the public or private sector whom he believes have contributed to the pollution of our environment. And from what we're learning about our air and soil and water quality on a daily basis, people," Theo stated unequiviocally, "he may be right to an extent—sad to say."

"Maybe we oughta pin a medal on the guy when we nail him," whispered one of the callous young detectives seated in the back of the room.

"Yeah, why's that?" breathed the seasoned cop seated next to him.

"Because I lay out over three hundred dollars a year for Poland Spring water. That's why," he declared through a scowl.

"You know how long those containers sit in some warehouse before they hit the shelf in a supermarket or beverage store?" the veteran offered quietly.

"You two back there got something to share with the rest of us?" Theo queried.

"Sorry, Lieutenant. Just sayin' what a unique case this is," the older, wiser detective covered.

"How so?" Theo inquired.

"Well, sir. Instead of the perp goin' after the person he holds responsible, he takes it out on some innocent whose death he believes will eventually destroy the one he deems accountable. In each case, it's a person who was fondly attached to the victims."

"Excellent, Sergeant. You read the reports, I see."

Hennesey smiled. "Yes, sir."

"Understand them well?"

"I believe so, sir."

"So, apparently you feel that your presence here is a waste of time."

"No sir, I—"

"What I'd like you to do, Detective Hennesey, is work with Robinson on the Carter case."

"Sir, with all due respect, that's a cold-case file."

"Well, go warm it up a bit. A man of your depth of understanding ought to come up with something that the rest of us have missed. I'd like you to get started on that right away," Theo put forth flatly.

"Yes, sir," the sergeant growled and glowered, crossing his legs, then folding his arms firmly across his chest.

"I mean, right this second, Sergeant."

Detective Sergeant Hennesey got up in a huff and started toward the door.

The young detective who was seated beside him rose, red-faced. "Sir?"

"Yes, Detective Miller."

"Sir, I was the one who initiated a dialogue with the sergeant."

"Thank you for sharing that with us, Detective."

Miller headed toward the door, too.

"And where do you think you're going?" Theo asked.

The young detective looked confused. "To help Detective Hennesey with the Carter case, sir."

"Sit–down–Detective." Theo took a breath. "You read the reports?"

"No, not all of them, sir." The man walked back, then sank into his seat.

"Then you'd agree you could benefit by paying strict attention to this meeting, I suspect."

"Yes, sir."

Theo picked up where he left off.

The young man frowned, fidgeted and found it rather difficult to concentrate, but concentrate he did.

"So, now we'll take a closer look at those relationships," Theo went on steadfastly. "The Edgewater, Florida victim. Noreen Walker. Surrogate daughter to a tanker pilot named Captain Isaac Fenton. Removed her from an orphanage at the age of five and raised her on a vessel that rarely saw port, according to authorities. Loved that girl more than life itself. And from what we learned from the Veteran's Administration Office down there, he's not doing too well since her death. Drinking very heavily. Paid for her college and bought her a brand new home when she graduated several years ago. Still a virgin when she met and married a professor of economics. We have updates coming in as I'm speaking. The intelligence we've gathered thus far tells us that Fenton's and Walker's relationship was on the up-and-up. Purely platonic and paternal. The kind of man any grown girl would be proud to call her father. His drinking was termed light to moderate back then. Today? He's not even considered a functioning alcoholic. Just a down-and-out drunk. Drinking himself to death. One too many accidents involving spills of the crude and hazardous kind—oil from tankers he was captaining, presenting some very serious damage to marine life and our environment." Theo turned a page of Kim's report and continued.

"Laura Haynes of Edgewater, Maryland. Kin to a devoted and doting stepsister, Curtisha Howard, who protected the younger girl from an abusive parent: the older girl's father. Seems Curtisha was the product of her mother's sexual abuse. Our sources tell us that Curtisha had designs on her younger stepsister that later developed into a full-blown relationship of the lesbian kind. Need I say more if you read the report? 'Course not, but I will. When Curtisha learned of her stepsister's murder, she went berserk, laying waste at a nearby waste management plant where she worked as a coordinator. That's past tense. She's recuperating in a *home* since the incident.

"Arlene Parker was also from Maryland," Theo reminded them, pleased that almost everyone was busy taking additional notes. "Annapolis. Her mother's brother's a hotshot chemist for a pesticide plant in Baltimore. He bought Arlene a new car every two years for maintaining good grades. 'Her favorite uncle,' Arlene's mother said. He'd be mine, too, if I got new wheels every time I made the grade."

Nods and smiles and light banter filled the windowless pale-green room.

"He loved that girl more than he loved his own daughter, who got herself pregnant at fourteen, quit school, married and divorced twice, and lives in California.

"I don't think I have to tell anyone here about our two Long Island cases. Wendy Linden and Patricia Tamblin. Wendy Linden's mother, Rita, sees her family doctor once a day. Every day. But not today. We have a report, here, that says the family's about ready to have her committed. She drove her husband's car into Merritt's Pond in Riverhead this morning after unsuccessfully trying to take her own life last night. Pills. And they're only *thinking* about hospitalizing her," Theo said as he sadly shook his head.

"Evan Tamblin? The man's coming apart at the seams. An exercise in quiet madness, if ever I saw. More money than green in a clover field. He had finally convinced his only child to give up acting and enter law school next year. 'Brightest of the whole *fam damily*; including her old man,' was what the father told me. Four point 0 through her first two years of college before she decided on a career that she believed her ol' man could exercise little or no control over. The three of them were planning to do some serious cruising this spring aboard their new boat: *Out There*. That is, Patricia—the captain of corporations, Evan Tamblin—and his second wife, Sally. The rumors I'm hearing are unsettling. The man wants to put a hundred thousand dollar *bounty* on the killer's head, for starters. I'm sure most of you are aware of the nuts who are bound to come out of the woodwork with that kind of moola being offered. He might just as well make it a million for the trouble it would cause. The mayor and the commissioner are begging him off, knocking it down to ten grand —for openers. Our only hope is that the crazies out there will be more interested in those two new reality shows on the boob tube, rather than stirring up a hornet's nest—starting with the crank calls." Knowing nods, smiles and light chatter carried through the ranks. "Then again, maybe we'll get lucky. Maybe someone who *really* knows something solid will drop a dime. Probably want it added to the proceeds." Theo waited for a laugh, or at least a line of polite smiles. "The dime— added to the ten grand. The reward money. No? Not funny, huh?" Theo frowned, recalling a well-received, tried-and-true joke he heard from an ADA. He figured he would throw it out for a bit of diversion. "All right, folks." Theo would not be deterred.

"A duck waddles into a pharmacy and asks for Chap Stick. The man behind the counter comes around and retrieves the item from the top shelf, asking the duck if he needs anything else. The duck politely replies, 'No, thank you, sir.' Returning behind the counter, then over to a register, the man asks the duck, 'Will that be cash or charge?' The duck looks up at the counterman and says, 'Just put it on my bill.'"

Nineteen wide grins and two guffaws. Theo seemed pleased.

"Becky Dawson's mother, Elizabeth, up in Old Town, Maine, is another lady who's taking her daughter's death pretty damn hard. She's blaming it on the divorce. So, of course she blames her ex. The divorcé, Charles Dawson, is the strong one in the broken family who's holding together what's left of their shattered world—but only by a thread. Becky was daddy's little girl. Elizabeth Dawson apparently wants him dead. She put a kitchen knife through his shoulder when he came around to pick up their son, who was home from school this weekend. Of course, you all know she worked for Brookhaven National Laboratory several years ago, along with Tamblin's new bride. Information concerning toxic waste was hidden from the public, then, as we suspect it is now. Just ask any member of the Peconic River Sportsman's Club in Manorville; downriver from the Lab. They've got a Catch and Release program in effect for one reason only. You *do not* eat those fish you catch there. Cleaning aluminum with arsenic at the Naval Weapons Industrial Reserve Plant, next-door, didn't help matters much, either.

"And now there's a Monisha Washington from Lake Superior State University, in Sault Ste. Marie, Michigan. At first we thought there might be a connection with her Mastic/Shirley cousin, Justin Barnes, because of his affections toward her through the years. That, and because of Barnes' *alleged* drug dealing and gun trafficking activities. But the rest of it didn't wash. Our narco boys, in addition to ATF affiliates, always came up dry. Slippery sort of chap. No formal education, but wily in his ways. Still, we figured, *pollution* of a sort. Directly or indirectly related—hooking young men and women by poisoning their bodies with his junk—something along those lines. We were far afield with that theory. But Kim, here, danced her magic fingers and turned up a more distant relative out in Kansas. Connecting *all* the dots. Tyrone Phillips. Truck driver associated with a toxic waste disposal plant in Topeka. Got his own rig. It seems Tyrone stashed away a lot of cash by dumping the stuff in illegal sites. Authorities out there heard rumors that Tyrone and Monisha had marriage plans when she finished college. Justin Barnes believed that *he* was in the running for her hand in marriage. Only those plans were solely in his head. Not hers. She had but one man in mind. Mister Tyrone Phillips. The rest of her admirers, of which she had many, were just 'playmates and supporters.' Her words, according to authorities up in Sault Ste. Marie, who interviewed her close friends and acquaintances. Lots of flings. One future plan. A master plan gone to pot.

"Oh, by the way. Tyrone quit his job and went back to Hartford. Staying with his sister. He paid for Monisha's funeral in full. Seeing a doctor for depression. Consuming lots of pills and alcohol. Got the picture?

"Now. What does all this tell us? It tells us that our perp is a master planner, too. He knows what victim to pick based on how much the person he *really* wants to punish is going to *hurt*, and hurt badly. Who would know this? A psychologist? A psychiatrist? A priest/confessor? Who in God's name would know? Maybe God himself," he proffered without so much as a smile. "Good a guess as any. Right? Because this fucker has to be *all knowing*," Theo underscored. "Any ideas?" he asked, opening his hands, palms up, as if he were offering them absolution. "Come on. Come on. The clocks a-tickin', troops. Some of the brightest people in the county are sitting on their asses in this very room."

One hand shot up.

Detective Miller's. The young detective who opened his mouth when he should have kept it shut.

"Yes, Detective?"

"Sir, one report of Detective Booker's, that I did go over, was on the first victim. The Walker woman from Florida."

"And?"

"And I think it's interesting to note Detective Booker's footnote regarding excerpts from Noreen Walker's published journal."

"You do?"

"Yes, sir. I—"

"Those passages were not included in her report."

"No, sir. But I—"

"But you felt compelled to locate and read them anyhow."

"Yes, sir."

"They weren't part of Detective Booker's report, but you felt it was important to read them anyhow," Theo repeated.

"Yes, sir. I . . ."

"You what? Spit it out."

I want to make sure you're not going to interrupt me anymore, is what the young man wished to say, and would have ordinarily, but refrained from doing so today. "It obviously illustrates the tanker captain's vulnerability—even more so than the victim's. The man had to be powerfully moved. After all, he was her mentor, the piece goes on to say. Someone else reading it would have come away with the same feeling."

Kim Booker was smiling and nodding her head in agreement.

"Go on, Detective."

"Well, if the killer read it—"

"Stop!" Theo ordered.

"Sir?"

"Say what you said again."

Detective Andrew Miller, on loan from another precinct, took a patient breath. "If the killer read it, well—"

"Stop!" Theo stated once again. "Freeze-frame that thought."

Everyone froze in their seats except Miller, who fashioned a bored expression as he threw a lifeless arm over the back of his chair.

"What if the killer lived somewhere here on Long Island, but wanted to know what was going on in, say, Florida, or Maryland, or Maine, or Michigan—or any state or city in the country, for that matter —where would he turn? Or more specifically, *what* might he turn to, Detective Miller?" Theo challenged.

"Business magazines from a decent size public library, or a newsstand that carries a good selection of out-of-state newspapers," Miller answered smugly. "Then again, he might surf the Internet."

Theo's opened-handed gesture made it clear that the discussion was now open to the floor.

"Headhunters!" a female blurted out from the center of the room.

"Newsletters profiling executives of major corporations," a suit seated in the second row answered.

"With emphasis on announcements and forthcoming events," an undercover cop in a ripped jacket and paint-stained pants offered, unconsciously trifling with a silver earring fixed between a stringy mat of dirty-blond hair and short curly whiskers.

Suggestions shot randomly around the room at a rate that would uplift the spirits of a burnt-out full professor. Methodically, Theo handed each and every member of all three teams their assignment. That is, all but one peon in the group.

"Detective Miller."

"Yes, sir?"

"Detective Miller. I want you to give Hennesey a hand—right now—with the Carter case."

"But—"

"But what?"

"But first I need the pages back from the journal that I lent Miller, Lieutenant," Kim Booker chimed in, "is what the detective was about to say. Isn't that right, Andrew?" Kim insisted, grabbing onto Miller's suit jacket by the shoulder and hauling him outside.

In the hallway, as everyone went about their business, Kim laced into the pup.

"You're still lucky you're a member of the team, buster. He's giving you a second chance because of how you handled yourself in there. He was about to have you transferred to First Squad Detectives in Babylon, after you first opened up your trap. Got it? Hennesey's on the cold-case file. But you were headed out the door. Believe me."

"For talking out of turn, teacher? Or are you the fucking acting principal?"

"No," Kim bristled. "I'm your saving grace, asshole. You owe me, fool."

"We got a problem, here?" Brian Archer asked, two full steps ahead of Dean Nelson, the pair coming up the back stairs, fresh from a meeting in Riverhead with an assistant D.A.

"And you two owe me, too. Big time! Cheapskates." She glared at Brian and his partner. "Cheeseburger and a cheap beer, for crying out loud," she bellyached. "Where's my *steak*?" she chastised the duo.

Pleased with herself, she left the three of them standing there as she sauntered off.

"I'll tell you right now, Miller," Archer warned. "That's a woman who always collects her debts."

"I can believe that," the man acknowledged, smoothing out the ruffled material of his silk Brooks Brothers suit jacket at the shoulder. "I truly can."

Chapter 24

The woman's frightened eyes followed the intruder as he removed several items from a scarred, black leather suitcase. He placed the paraphernalia in clear view upon the kitchen counter next to the sink.

"Why are you doing this?" the sultry young vixen demanded through her tears as she struggled fiercely against the restraints that held her securely to a heavy wooden chair. "I want you out, now!" she ordered, despite the fact that her ankles and wrists were already bound with lengths of clothesline. "Stop it!" she screamed as he reached for her.

"I want you to open your mouth wide, but to keep your trap shut. Hear me?"

Seeing the crazed look on her tormentor's face, in addition to the object Malcolm held in his hand, she suddenly shut her mouth tightly. A plaintive whimper accompanied the violent shake of her curly blonde head.

Grabbing a damp dishrag off the sink, along with a large stainless steel serving spoon from a drawer beneath the Formica countertop, Malcolm pried open Fern Rodman's mouth, then forcefully worked in an empty spool used to hold fishing line. Finally, he managed to jam the narrow object vertically between two rows of healthy, gnashing teeth—locking her jaw open wide. The woman pushed her tongue mightily against the solid plastic face before hyperventilating via the small hole at the object's center, through which Malcolm inserted a long, thick, stiff rubber amber tube, running it down her throat like a plumber's snake.

"Aughhh—augh," Fern retched and gagged and choked, trying desperately to dislodge the items by opening her jaw even wider than thought humanly possible, pressing futilely against the spool and tubing with a determined but powerless fleshy folded tongue.

"Ah, perfect fit," Malcolm said with certain satisfaction, securing the tube firmly in place by wrapping a wide gray band of sticky duct tape across her mouth and head like a big bandage.

Around and around.

Removing a small penknife from his pocket, he made two slits in the tape that covered her ears, tearing the strip back carefully so that she would not miss a single word.

"Hear me loud and clear?"

Fern gagged violently and shook her entire body, trying in vain to break loose from the solid wooden seat, its frame tied securely to the pipes in back of the open cabinet doors, just beneath the kitchen sink.

"'Why?' you wanted to know," Malcolm mimicked calmly. "Well, I was about to tell you why. But I can't tell you if you refuse to listen. Hollering and screaming and carrying on like you were wasn't going to help matters either. No one can help you out here because no one can hear you. Even the bears are asleep for the winter, Fern. Of course, they'll wake up soon enough since spring is just around the corner. Unfortunately, *you* will not, Goldilocks," the serial killer tormented.

It was the first inkling that Fern Rodman had of her imminent death. Rape and robbery were the acts that she initially believed the madman had foremost in mind—actually *prayed* he had—in lieu of killing her—then, *hopefully*, he would leave. She would have done anything to be free of this monster. Anything! She knew she was an attractive and *desirable* twenty-six year old vixen. She had teased men mercilessly since she was sweet sixteen, having her first sexual experience with a middle-aged man the very night of her *big* party—after her parents had gone to bed. The caterer. She allowed him to *think* that he was having his way with her. But they both knew better of it before the night was over.

Fern was choking uncontrollably before she somehow managed to catch a gasping breath—respiring forcefully through her partially taped nose. Why her mind was on the caterer now dumbfounded her.

She had been feverish for the handsome man throughout the evening of her sweet sixteen party, she recalled . . . even before that special day, in fact. She wanted to fuck him insanely and take him away from his priggish, puritanical wife. Fern wanted to be *catered* to. The two had sex in the finished basement for several hours. She did *things* to him and let him do *things* to her she was sure his wife would never entertain. Not that prissy little bitch. She did, indeed, in the end, take him away from her. But only until she tired of their sport. By then, the huntress had bigger and better game in mind.

Maybe this moment was her payback, she suddenly considered. A belated *hit for hire*, she cried so sorrowfully. A decade later to the date. For today was her birthday. The tears were streaming down her cheeks. Yet, she could clearly see the lunatic hooking up the other end of the hose to the kitchen faucet . . . amazed that she could even see or think or breathe at all through her violent retching . . . amazed that her illicit affair with a fucking caterer ten years ago kept cropping up in her crazed brain.

Please, God. Oh, please don't let him turn the water on. I'll be good. I'll be so good, Lord. I swear it. I won't disappoint You ever again.

As if in answer, Malcolm miraculously stepped away from the sink and stood staring down at her.

Fern shone a pair of pleading great green eyes. Eyes that had seductively said to her suitors through the years, 'Come to bed with me if you dare.' Eyes that could be read over a slinky shoulder as saying, '*Yes*, you can even put it up my *ass,*' as she traced the outline of her fine figure with a pair of ivory palms, past a trim waist—then down around the back of her shapely hips and buttocks. Fern's eyes now pled for bloody mercy. Eyes that simply told this monster that she surely did not want to die. Not now. Not at twenty-six years of age. Not on her fucking birthday! Not now or ever, in all God's honest truth.

Fern heaved and frightfully fought against the forces that brought her there. Her own evil, she was sure.

"It's not you, lamb," Malcolm lamented as if reading her thoughts. "It's your dear ol' dad who brought you to this juncture, pet," he revealed.

Fern was shaking her head in confusion, anger, and fear.

A disgruntled customer from her father's canoe and kayak rental company on the Peconic River back in Flanders? she suddenly wondered. *It has to be that!*

A booming business, but not without a glitch.

Rip this tubing from my throat, you fucking monster, and let me make it right! Dear God, I've more money than the local church. I'll feed you and fuck you and let you suckle my breasts while I transfer my funds via computer, then make you out a check for a quarter million. Don't take paper? Then take me with you to my bank. I'll close my savings account. Make an early withdrawal on my CDs. Even gladly pay the fucking penalties. Put a gun to my back under your new jacket you told me about before you boldly barged in. Waltz me up to the teller. I'll tell her to give you anything you want. Then, I'll call my broker and sell every fucking stock. I won't give you away. Dear God. Let me speak these words, she gagged.

But Fern was unable to utter even one intelligible syllable as the bile rose in her throat.

How could a man so handsome be so cruel? Why in God's name did I ever open the door to let him in?

Malcolm stepped back toward the sink, then lifted the single handle a little too sharply to the left. A blast of icy-cold water shot past the faucet, along and through the tubing and down into Fern Rodman's trachea. He was surprised the amber snake did not jump up and out of the woman's mouth.

Fern somehow elongated her entire body and retched.

Abruptly, he closed the spigot.

"Are you going to listen, now?"

Hawing, then heaving, Fern rapidly nodded her head up and down with the speed of an active rubber ball bounding off a child's paddle board.

"Good. First off, you know that the Peconic River is polluted with toxic waste from the Brookhaven National Lab. Yes?"

Fern, while choking violently, again flagged her understanding in the affirmative.

"Know what's in it? Twenty-three radionuclides. Plutonium being carried among them, can you believe? Good grief, Fern. How could they do that to people? Plus twenty-two heavy metals. You do know what heavy metal is. Yes? We're not talking rock music here. We're talking about the density of substances greater than five point zero. Metals like cadmium, copper, mercury, silver and such. Twenty-two of them, Fern," Malcolm repeated. "Twenty-two. All of them toxic to organisms. That includes you and me, kid. Even Lassie and the flowers and bushes he pissed on years ago."

Lassie had been Fern's collie as a child. A dog long dead.

"And yet, your father wants to *stop* the state and county from posting the Peconic River with warning signs. Warning people of its dangers. Just sit there for a moment and ponder that."

Malcolm lowered his head as though he himself were first considering the consequences of such an irresponsible act—weighing, as if for the very first time, how and why the government could allow industry and even small businesses to pollute the planet. How and why, indeed!

"Do you know why I chose you, my lamb?"

Fern shook her head frantically.

"Because your father had the audacity to stand before a group of legislators and drink from a cup of what he claimed was potable water from the Peconic River, attempting to prove that it was safe. Also, because he had the temerity to tell them that, at the next meeting, he would be bringing fish along to eat."

Fern was busy vomiting, but little was pushing past the spool.

"Fish, Fern! Filled with polychlorinated biphenyls or PCBs. Certainly you've heard of them. Still, the government wants to do *more* studies," Malcolm railed maniacally. "But both past and recent studies have already shown that the river *is* contaminated. At what point do they say, 'Yes, the Peconic River, and thousands like it, where we allow the dumping of sewage, the release of toxic waste, the use of pesticides and fertilizers, which leach into them, *are, indeed,* hazardous to your health?' At what point do they say, '*Enough?*'"

The young woman's body was convulsing.

"The answer? They *don't*, Fern. That's why there have to be people like me." He studied her. "I'm not here to punish you for your father's misdeeds, Fern. I'm here to punish *him*. Through *you*. You see, I know how much you mean to him. I've been watching the two of you for years."

Rodman's daughter thought she would lose her mind.

"I used to fish that river, Fern. Even rented one of your father's canoes. He seemed like a nice enough man, back then. But he got greedy. Granted, those signs today would hurt his business. But so what? He made millions. Not that that's any sort of criteria. Did you ever hear the expression, '*giving back*'?"

Fern was sending her head up and down. Up and down like a yo-yo.

"Well, I'm sure that *he* did, too. But he *didn't* give back. Not like he should and could have done. But only doing so when it benefited him. See, I know all about his business, Fern. To put it simply, he *never* did the right thing. But what he did at that meeting was unthinkable." Malcolm chuckled. "I almost said, *undrinkable*.

"Oh, but before you go—with the flow, that is—I've got to tell you a fish story. You've been cooped up in this cabin so long, I'll bet you didn't hear about the fish ladder that some Riverhead volunteers back home installed to assist alewives—you know, those twelve-inch or so silvery fish? I'm asking you a question, Fern."

Fern shook her head in the negative, although she knew all about the alewives, the new ladder, her father and the fact that he supported the effort.

"So, up and over the dam in Grangebel Park, in Riverhead, they leapt like salmon. Only much smaller in size, like I said. There, they'd spawn along the twelve-mile run to the headwaters of Brookhaven National Laboratory.

"Your father, among others in the town, did not want the river posted with signs warning people of the hazardous health issue concerning the taking of contaminated fish for human consumption. Yet, the town installs a *fish ladder* to encourage the migration of alewives to the very source of the Peconic River's pollution. What's wrong with that picture, Fern?" Malcolm asked politely and patiently.

Fern could only respond by shaking her head and making a gurgling sound.

"Of course, proponents of the program would argue that the alewives are not resident fish. But then again, neither are transient folks who consume contaminated fin and shellfish along the coast, who later develop cancer and die at home or in hospitals located several hundred miles inland. Get it, guys and gills?" Malcolm giggled. "This planet and its people are as polluted as their minds. Think about that, Fern. The world is three quarters water, like our bodies, and we've got a toxic sewer running through them both. Are you beginning to see the picture, now? To err is human, my lamb. But for your daddy, and others like him, not to correct those mistakes is to kiss your ass goodbye."

Fern fought a final battle to free herself of the restraints that held her fast.

"I mean, I could go on about the lobsters and other shellfish dying in abundance in Long Island Sound, partly and properly blamed on the dumping of toxic dredge from the Thames, as well as other Connecticut rivers feeding the Eastern Strait. A shell disease coined shellburn, in addition to a parasite called paramoeba, claimed upwards of ninety percent of the lobster catch last season. Ninety percent, Fern Rodman!

"Ninety-some Canada Geese, and over one hundred songbirds keeled over last week on farmland in Southold. I read it in a Long Island paper before leaving for this trip. Guess what? The cause of death was related to pesticide poisoning. Investigators from four law enforcement agencies swooped down on a farm stand in East Marion, but had to eat crow. Not a trace of evidence. Not with all the pre-publicity flap prior to the flop.

"I ask you, Fern. Who is really the monster, here? Me, or the monster with many heads? That is, the captains of industry, together with our local, state and federal governments who pollute or allow the pollution of our land, air and water, while those irresponsible companies and agencies hide their gargoyled faces in their hands."

Malcolm looked around the room.

"You know, it's almost like you are hiding out up here, Fern. I'll even bet you've got bottled water in the refrigerator," he swore. Wearing two pair of blue nitrile work gloves, the serial killer stepped over to the refrigerator and opened its door. Malcolm shook his head sadly. "Fern. Fern. Fern. Just as I suspected."

And with that closing remark, Malcolm stepped over to the sink and opened the faucet, steadily raising the single silver handle— all the way up toward the splashboard.

Like a miniature waterfall, a bubbly stream of blood and slaver tumbled from the woman's mouth and down the front of her pure white terry cotton robe. Desperately, Fern tried to close off the forceful passage of water with a pressure all her own, applied at the back of the throat with her helpless tongue. But the tubing was too thick and down so deep that it did not much matter anymore. Still, she sucked what little precious breath she could barely manage . . . until the deprivation of air, overpowered by the confluence of liquids, slowly ebbed away her life.

Minutes later, Malcolm shut off the water and left through the rear of the cabin, trudging across the deep snow-covered property of Adam Rodman's daughter's Adirondack retreat.

"Mission accomplished," he said quite satisfactorily, shivering from both the excitement and the cold.

Chapter 25

Justin Barnes awoke after dozing at a rest area in Virginia, *whose capital is Richmond*, he yawned and stretched, envisioning a rich man resting on a big front porch near Lake Anna, where he once vacationed with Monisha. She had told him she was still a virgin, which, indeed, she was—until their second night together . . . *a million years ago it seemed. It doesn't mean she didn't know a thing or three about sex,* he reminisced in mild amusement.

He glanced at his watch, then started up the engine, driving out of the area and onto the Interstate. Reaching for the travel atlas, he felt pretty confident that he knew his states and capitals from the A's up to the I's, having tested himself earlier. That was right before his catnap —a catnap that had lasted a little too long, to his consternation.

Since a New York State license plate, a late model Cadillac, and a black man sitting behind the wheel could raise a red flag south of D.C., Justin switched plates earlier as a precautionary measure. A phony Virginia driver's license, along with a bogus registration and insurance card were handy, too, in the event he was pulled over for whatever reason. The New York State Inspection sticker posed little problem, for he carried the fraudulent form letter of explanation in the glove compartment. Beneath the dashboard, clipped to a bracket, sat a .45 caliber Colt semiautomatic, just in case a cop had trouble with either the paperwork or his story.

"The capital of Idaho is Boise."

Hell, that was an easy one for Justin. For he knew a *ho* named *Ida,* who was a *noisy, bois*terous bitch, he recalled with less than fondness, realizing that this game of states and capitals could be fun and fitting.

After all, am I not a cap·i·tal offender . . . with a capital fucking C? He chuckled with satisfaction.

Only they never nailed his hide to the cross for his biggest sin of all, *thank God.* The killing of a cop. They never had the goods on him. Only their suspicions. He was surprised that the authorities never tried to frame him—though they did threaten him with violence from the onset. Actually, it had been more than just mere threatening. But he cheated death because he knew the law of the jungle. Survival of the fittest. *Positively.* For he was a black cat who knew how to count backwards from nine and was subtracting carefully. Superstition notwithstanding.

Drugs down to the Carolinas. Guns up to New York. A far cry from the contraband cigarettes and fireworks he used to run north and south as a teenager. That and numbers running in Harlem, too. But firearms and heroine carried some serious *hard time*. A lot more lucrative though, he learned early on. But *time* was something that Justin Barnes was not interested in doing. *Time* was a waste of time. Hard time, which was what he would be facing if he got caught dealing narcotics or weapons, was not an option. They would have to take him down for the final count. He was not going anywhere, except from this world into the next without an intermission curtain. *No state or federal prison for this boy,* he swore. *No way. Nohow. Not even a night in jail for pissin' in the park,* he promised himself.

"The capital of Illinois is Chicago—no wait! Shit," he declared after peeking at the page.

Got that one wrong before. Gotta picture Capone and his gang in that garage in Chicago, with Springfield *rifles. Never went down quite like that,* he knew from TV. But Monisha had said, "*The sillier the association the better, because the image stays in your mind.*"

"The capital of Illinois is Springfield," Justin said with confidence. "Can't jump the gun, guy. So, slow it down. Gotta sometimes stretch the image a bit to bring things into proper focus."

He remembered the time Monisha punched him in the arm when he pronounced Illinois with an s at the end.

"*The s is silent, stupid,*" she said with impatience. "*Il·e·noi.*"

Punched him hard, in fact.

And it's Feb roo er e. Not Feb yoo er e. Li brer e. Not li ber e, she had instructed him on more than one occasion.

"And now it's fucking Feb·roo·er·e. President's week. And my Monisha is stone-cold dead!" *What are folks sayin' 'bout 'er up in Sault Ste. Marie, Michigan?* he wondered. *They'll speak well of her, of course. Use their fancy fucking vocabularies with all the right pronunciations.* "Pre nun se a shens. Not pre noun se a shens.

Although, you *pre·nouns* your words distinctly." *Noun versus Verb*, Monisha explained over and over again, occasionally giving him a gentle smack atop his nappy pate.

"Shit." He was getting a splitting headache, but he forged ahead.

"The capital of *Indian*a is *Indian*apolis; so noted," he said with assurance, lumping together both state and capital, picturing two Indians sporting a pair of feathers.

"Fuck!" Justin spotted a state trooper's vehicle in the rearview mirror.

The car was closing on him fast.

Justin eased his foot off the accelerator. "Not too obvious, now," he mumbled under his breath. "Easy does it."

The trooper shot around him and went after a car in the far left lane—a quarter mile up ahead.

"The capital of Iowa is . . ."

Justin just could not think. He felt exhausted from the stress of his loss. Next exit, he would stop to hit the men's room and grab a cup of coffee.

"Should've done all that shit back there," he swore with absolute annoyance.

Chapter 26

The snowflakes were as large as Wheaties, and fell faster than if poured from a box.

Don Ciccio's crew had climbed and combed a two-mile radius in upstate New York's Adirondack Mountain region, in and around Fern Rodman's wintry cabin home on Long Lake. Like a morning fog, rumors and reports rose to a crescendo regarding a mob convention's goings-on throughout the otherwise bucolic town. Several *wise guys* had locked horns with the local authorities; two arrests were made.

In apparent retaliation, an inebriated county sheriff's wife was swept off a rural road and offered up in exchange for the immediate release of the crew captain's two *goombas*. A governor's aide was called on the scene posthaste, followed by a quick resolution that was reached moments before a federal hostage negotiator and his team were summoned forth.

Behind the scenes, however, the hostage rescue team was put on standby status—officially awaiting a green light.

Two factions, state and local law enforcement officials, fought for jurisdiction. The Hostage Rescue Team took command but was explicitly told to stand down by order of the attorney general himself. Several hours later, the female hostage was exchanged for two hoods in their late twenties who were released without incident, although the victim's husband, a sheriff from Blue Mountain Lake, turned in his gun and badge in protest after collecting his hysterical wife.

A gag order was issued by the governor. An *"unfortunate misunderstanding"* were the catchwords of the day so as to pacify an angry community before everyone finally went about their business. Reluctantly, at best.

No clues, no suspects; nothing of consequence was reported at the Rodman crime scene. At least that was the information given to the press. Everyone outside the official circle would await the coroner's report—as if one were really needed.

The residents of Long Lake were frightened and confused. The surreptitious behavior of law enforcement, on all levels, surrounding the murder of their young neighbor, shook the close-knit community to the core.

Detectives Brian Archer and Dean Nelson found it difficult to keep their frustration and tempers in check, finding a tad more cooperation and camaraderie among Don Ciccio's gang of street thugs in the Adirondack Park setting than with their brethren in "*Hayseed, USA,*" as Dean put forth bluntly to Theo over the phone late that evening.

The following morning, a larger-than-life figure brushed the falling snow from his shoulder-caped coat, throwing up its lamb's wool collar for added protection from the elements.

"We have instructions from Albany not to work at cross-purposes here, Detective Nelson," said the strikingly good-looking, well-spoken gentleman representing Don Ciccio's crew. "It seems the local boys got a bit bent out of shape when we started to grid the area, hunting for the unsub to the north of the cabin," the man explained.

Nelson smiled. "Grid the area? Unsub?"

"You seem amused," the dark, angular-jawed, clean-shaven fellow said with curiosity.

"Because that's police-speak," the detective explained straightaway.

"Well, I was a detective for nineteen years before they booted me off the force," the man clarified candidly and with indifference.

"Ask you why?"

"Sure. Go ahead and ask."

Nelson studied the man for an interminable moment before he spoke. "Okay, why?"

"You had to be there," the husky man replied with a smirk.

"I see. Maybe you'll share what happened with regard to the grid?"

"I had my crew assigned. Quarter mile up there," he said matter-of-factly, gesturing toward the inordinately steep mountain directly ahead of them.

"Up there?" Dean echoed in surprise.

"Yes."

"But why up there? Perp entered and left from the south road, if you want to call it that," he said decidedly, fully aware that every secondary road at the summit was buried in at least eighteen inches of snow, for it had been snowing on-again, off-again for the past sixteen hours.

The big fellow was shaking his head in the negative. "The guy came down here and exited back over there," he stated resolutely.

"How?" the cop pressed.

The man smiled knowingly. "You guys didn't pick up on it."

Dean looked perplexed. "Guess not. Gonna enlighten me?"

"Skis."

Dean looked toward the top of the formidable slope. "You shittin' me?"

"A big New York City homicide detective, like you, I'm going to kid?" the man kidded.

"Cut the crap. All right?"

"All right. But that's how he did it."

"You're serious?"

"Bet your boots," he said with a condescending smile, staring down pathetically at the detective's footwear.

"Locals know?"

"Locals, like the others, haven't got a clue."

"They screw things up for you up there?"

"Just about. But we managed to preserve the scene. Got what we wanted and got the hell out of there."

"How the hell did you manage that? And got what? I thought they were all over you guys."

"They were. So we created a little diversion for them."

"The sheriff's wife," Dean quietly voiced his realization. He was beginning to get the picture.

The crew boss stood there quietly in his impressive and obviously expensive full-length, umber, waxy oilskin coat, matching hat, and knee-high brown leather boots. He kept his face serious. A good half a minute passed between the pair before the big man spoke.

"I guess you'd like to have a look-see."

"Bear shit in the woods?" Dean rejoined, sweeping large flakes off the collar and shoulders of a flannel-lined waist jacket, borrowed at the last moment from the Carhartt collection—if he had to guess.

"Don't think you should be up there without *heavy* artillery if they're out and about," the stately figure cautioned, glancing at Nelson's weapon holstered at his hip.

"Who's they?"

"Bears," the fellow presupposed. "Unless you trust they're still in hibernation this close to spring," he added coolly. "Snow or no snow. Cold or not."

"Not me," Dean announced emphatically, wet snow finding its way into the tops of his ankle-high boots. "Whattaya packin'?"

"Come on. I'll back you up if Smokey wants a bite of your butt up there. Let's go take a walk on the wild side."

The two started up the snowy wooded mountain.

Dean had to widen his stride in order to keep up with the big man.

"Where's your partner?" Austin Izzo asked. "The one you introduced me to earlier."

"Either at the barracks or the cabin with the forensic team. Why?"

"He had on calf-high boots that you could have borrowed."

"Yeah, a full size smaller; or believe me, I'd have snatched 'em up in a heartbeat. Along with this coat."

"You really came prepared, I see."

"Grabbed what I could last minute and choppered in. It wasn't snowin' like this when we left."

"Wouldn't get *me* up in one of those eggbeaters."

"Why not?"

"You ask a lot of questions, Detective."

"I'm a fucking cop."

"If you say so."

"What the fuck is that supposed to mean?"

"Pretty testy, too."

"So, how'd *you* get here?"

"Four-wheel drive."

"From?"

"Westchester."

"And you think that's safer, I suppose?"

"I don't care to know, nor want to hear about statistics, Detective."

"Don't have any to give you. My partner, on the other hand,

could tell you plenty about air versus ground travel, though. Tells me all the time, but I never really pay attention. He's an aviation buff. Still, I don't think he ever mentioned anything about whirlybirds. Probably in a different category all together," Dean jabbered as they plodded along.

"He flies?"

"Yeah, you could say that." Nelson smiled at the man's back.

"Me? I wouldn't go near aircraft. Wings *or* beater-blades. I've got to have radials or both feet directly under me."

"Train?"

"Sure."

"Whatta 'bout by boat?"

"How the hell do you think I got here?"

"Whattaya talking about? I thought you just said—"

The crew boss turned and broke into a smile. "Ellis Island. Early forties."

"Fell into that one, didn't I? Little slow on the uptake. Uphill, along with the cold," he plodded upward with a heavy breath. "But I still don't get it. Not flying, I mean," deciding not to share his own trepidation with a perfect stranger, especially when it came to commercial aircraft.

"What's not to get?" Austin resumed his pace.

"Why you won't fly—at all."

"Phobia."

"You're afraid?"

"Deathly."

"A fuckin' mob boss who's afraid to fly. If that don't beat all."

"You got it."

"What if the big boss asked you to do a hit in Cleveland?" Nelson speculated for his own amusement.

"How'd you come up with that city?"

"Heard it in a movie."

"I'd drive."

"All the way to Cleveland?"

"Why not? Anyhow, I'm not in that end of the business."

"Hold on. I wanna write that down," he joked.

Austin stopped in his tracks. "Trouble keeping up?"

Dean was shaking his head while trying to catch his breath.

"See. I gotta go *where* my boss tells me. *When* he tells me. And *how* he tells me. So, tell me. What end of the business *are* you in? I won't say anything to anyone unless you sign-off on it," he bantered good-naturedly.

"Enforcement."

"Oh, enforcement." *Didn't know there's a difference* is what he really wanted to say, but thought better of it. "Now, isn't that a coincidence. I'm in enforcement, too," Dean continued playfully.

"Knew you'd find it amusing. Your feet cold yet?"

"How much fucking further, Izzo?"

"Just up and over this ridge," he answered as they entered a stand of dense white birches. "And call me Austin. Short for Augustus."

"And he did this on skis, you say, Austin? Or are you just luring me back here for a hit?"

"My back's been to you the whole time, Detective. Want to take the lead?"

"No, you're doin' just fine. Call me Dean. I'll watch your back for black bears. You cover the front," he half-kidded. "How do you know he was on skis? You don't ski out of here uphill." Dean clutched a heavy, snowy, springy branch that the man held back for him as they entered the tree line. "Nor even downhill, for that matter. Not through all these goddamn trees, you don't."

"You'll see soon enough."

From the top of the ridge, the pair gazed back across and through the wooded vista to the victim's cozy cabin.

"There's his course; a trail that runs right through here and down to the cabin," Izzo explained, directing a winding, planing palm to indicate the serpentine cut. If you look way to your right—over there—you'll see how he walked up and out of there, taking the more direct low-lying land that connects right back here to where he descended on skis."

"You mean *could* have come down on skis," Dean submitted. "And why the hell are we over here then?"

"*Did* in fact come down," the mob figure assured him. "Come."

Dean followed closely. The pair made their way across the

ridge and over to an endless row of power line poles running parallel to a sheer, narrow strip of land to the northeast, where the going was easier. Austin continued to lead the way along the rise.

"The county road is just beyond that berm where he parked his vehicle," the crew boss expounded. "He stepped out under the cover of darkness. Took his skis and put them on over there. Grabbed his poles and paraphernalia. And down he went on skis with hardly a sound. No sound or sight of a car coming up the narrow private roadway to alert Fern Rodman's distant neighbors or anyone. No long walk up from the lake where he or his vehicle might be spotted. He came down through these backwoods on skis, Dean. He walked up and out on foot where it's not as steep, over there."

"Interesting theory."

"Not a theory."

"Why's that?"

"Got the goods, fella." The man waved him ahead. "Right this way."

Austin led Dean over to a hollowed out section of a tall dead tree; at least a foot in diameter; seven feet in height and broken off at the top; barkless and brown. Most of it stood rotten to the core. A sharp blow from the Mafia man's shoulder might have toppled it, the detective entertained.

There, leaning in the niche, in plain view, stood a pair of short skis. In back of them were the poles.

"Jesus H. fucking Christ!" Detective Dean Nelson cursed the cold morning.

"Of course, he had some crap camouflaging them."

"What kind of crap?" the cop snapped.

"Don't get your bowels in an uproar. All right? Just some sticks and branches to break up the outline, so you'd miss it if you walked by. *I* missed it. But Barry picked up on it."

"Who's Barry?"

"My dog. You don't think I work alone, do you? I, too, have a partner, Dean," the man said with a wide grin.

"You were a fucking detective," Dean charged. "You remember COC?"

"Sure. Chain of custody."

"By the book, pal. A record of everyone who's handled

evidence from the time of collection to—"

"Everything by the book, huh?"

"Well?"

"Well, Barry's findings, along with mine, *are* a matter of record. Only we don't write up reports and stow files like you fellas. And if you investigate matters further, Dean, I'm sure you'll find both our *mugs* in a different kind of *book*," he needled. "Barry's the furry one on all fours."

"Listen—"

"Wrong. You listen and learn. Our forensic team—"

"*Your* forensic team?"

"You deaf *and* dumb?"

Dean pulled a cellular phone from his pocket and raised the tiny antenna.

"Better call Albany first, asshole, before you compromise this investigation," Austin Izzo clamored.

"*Me*, compromise? Who the *fuck* do you think you're talking to?" the cop blew, removing his gloves before punching in a set of numbers along with a lettered code.

Brian took his time in answering. "Yeah, Dean."

"You at the barracks?"

"Back at the scene."

"Listen. We've got a situation up here."

"Where are you?"

"Top of some mountain; just back of the cabin."

"You got the skis and poles?" Brian asked, lowering his voice and taking the conversation to a corner of the room.

"What? How in hell . . .? What the fuck is going on down there. I got—"

"Listen to me," Brian interrupted. "We're up to our necks in this neck of the woods. We might just as well go along with the program for now. You always wanted to do some downhill anyhow," he kidded.

"Brian."

"Yeah."

"You all right?"

"Never better, buddy."

Never better, buddy was their signal which meant that the

world around them had not turned into a pile of crap. *I'm fine*, denoted a heap of trouble. So, no one was holding a gun to Brian's head—literally speaking, that is.

"But you can't talk freely," he figured.

"Correct. But listen—"

"I'm listening."

"If that were the case, Dean, we wouldn't be having this conversation. Now would we?"

"Brian."

"Dean."

"Go fuck yourself."

"Never better, buddy," Brian repeated through a light yet seemingly frustrated laugh.

"Just remember who the case detective is on this one, fella."

"Yeah, I think it's the big guy you introduced me to in boots and breeches that you're courting favor to this snowy morning. The Marlboro Man in all his finery. I gotta go," Brian concluded, terminating the call.

Dean looked up bleakly at the big man. He wanted to engage the guy in a name-calling contest, starting with the word *wop*, but thought better of it.

"Ready for me to fill you in now, Dean?"

"Sure, Austin. Go right ahead."

Chapter 27

A three-way conference call was set for 4:00 p.m., linking Detective Dean Nelson at a motel on Long Lake, Detective Brian Archer at an Adirondack Park Police barracks, and an official speaking for the governor in Albany.

"The mob's not running this show!" Dean Nelson erupted like a volcano.

"Of course they're not running the show, Dean. Mr. Izzo and his people are *assisting*, is all," an assistant to the governor explained. "They're hoping that maybe the perp might return to the scene to collect his gear. This way, the skis and poles are there waiting for him —as I'm sure you will be, too."

"Assisting, my ass," Brian fumed in support of his partner. "They're taking over quietly, and someone's allowing it."

"And we want to know who that person is," Dean bellowed.

The three-way conversation was going nowhere.

"Look, boys. I can't make this any plainer. The evidence on the ridge was photographed, documented, collected and put back. You have the reports."

"Yeah, from Murder Incorporated!" Dean hissed into the receiver.

"Russ, listen to me," Brian tried to reason. "The local boys up here haven't got a clue on how to handle matters. Granted. But they're working *with* us now. Forensics got exemplars from the victim. They've scanned every inch of the cabin with ALS, brought in from —"

"Fine. But at the moment you got yourself a big fat goose egg. Even Advanced Light Source technology nets you nil until you find something or someone to compare those exemplars to. Therefore, it illuminates nothing but your egos. You're still in the dark, fellas," the governor's representative knew. "True?"

"We're not done here. And *you* shouldn't even know what we have and haven't got at this point."

"The point is—"

"No, I'll tell you what the point is, Russ," Dean cut in. "The point is that we need to move those hoods out of there, now, before the area turns any more contaminated than it already is."

"The area has been secured, Dean. Those skis and poles have been gone over for latent prints. Gone over thoroughly. Analysis, from what I understand, is complete. The vicinity has been searched."

"Not along the ridge it hasn't," Dean blasted. "There're samples to be taken."

"Samples?" the assistant asked and laughed incredulously. "From what I hear, you got yourselves a foot and a half of snow up there—and it's still coming down pretty heavily. Now, do you really think you're going to find anything in a snowstorm when you found zip in the cabin? Use you head, fellas. If you insist on traipsing through the snow though, do it outside the area. No one's going back up there, period. Not you. Not them. Let the locals handle it later. There's nothing further to be had. You're not going to type or match anything right now. And if you really want me to clue you in, gentlemen, no two snowflakes are alike," Russ promulgated through a boisterous laugh. "Now, I've got to get back to work."

"That's funny, Russ," Brian said. "And appreciated, too. But let me leave you with a little thought. If we didn't come up with a single thread inside the cabin, like you say—if the killer was that careful— why would he come back for those skis and poles? Why can't we just move ahead on this?"

"Because he probably doesn't know that we know how he came in on her. If and when he returns, they'll nail him. But with you guys setting up camp with your vans and microscopes and magnifying glasses, stirring up the works, you'll spook him. Is that so hard to understand?"

"I'll make you a deal, Russ," Dean said, putting his temper in check.

"No deals."

"Just hear me out."

"I'm very busy."

"We are, too. Just let us have the skis and poles so that we can run our own—"

"The evidence stays right where it is."

"Why, when we can easily have another pair of skis and poles put in their place if he does come back? We could make the switch tonight. Run our own tests. What's the fucking problem?

"Dean."

"What?"

"The forensic team who ran the tests is quite qualified. All right?"

"No, it's not all right."

"You just don't like it because they're not *your* boys. If they were—"

"They're mob boys, Russ," Dean interrupted. "Guys like Gotti. Gravano. Now they've got some Mafia crew boss named Izzo and his thugs running things up here."

"It's been sanctioned, Dean. Now, I've wasted enough time."

"One final question?" Brian pushed.

The man sighed heavily. "Sure. Why not?"

"Who's stonewalling this investigation, Russ? Tell us."

There was a moment's hesitation before the assistant answered. "No one is stonewalling, Brian. Now, I'm really very busy."

"Part B of the same question, Russell," Dean jumped in. "Doesn't your surname end in a vowel like the governor's?"

Russell Leone soughed irritably, then calmly hung up the phone.

Chapter 28

Team Three was reassembled with Theo riding roughshod over his troops, pulling manpower from the other teams. Men and women who had worked a sixteen-hour shift were about to work another eight.

"How the fuck does he expect us to keep going?" Detective Miller bellyached. "First we're on the case. Then he pulls us off. Now that he needs us, we're back on."

"You don't learn from your mistakes, do you?" Hennesey snarled. "Well, *I* do. That's the difference between us."

"The difference between us, old man, is twenty years."

"Not quite. But at least I'll see another two in homicide before retirement. You're lucky if you last the fucking week. Piss-poor attitude, kid. Piss-poor."

Detective Lieutenant Theodore Groche took to the podium, wasting no time in cutting to the chase. Though short of stature, the commanding officer stood tall before his men and women.

"We've got our work cut out for us, people. We can now add ski shops to our grocery list. Resorts. Lodges. Mail-order houses that sell Head Skis and accessories. Ski poles. Bindings. Hit those sporting goods stores hard, boys and girls. Department stores that sell those very skis and poles. Just like we did the skates. Maybe we'll have better luck this time around. As a matter of fact, go back and double-check yourselves as you're hunting down these new items."

Theo consulted a long list of distributors to whom the manufacturer sold the skis and poles in question.

"Now. We'll narrow the scope of this investigation to anyone who purchased those brand-name skies and equipment within the last twelve months—anyone who is or was a watchdog for any local, vocal groups concerned with conservation on Long Island. Conservation, that is, focusing in on the quality of our air and soil and water."

Theo paused, yawned, and forced a smile. "Bill Smith of Fish Unlimited comes first to mind. He'd find contamination on his kid's kite. But Dean, Brian and Kim checked him out seven ways to Sunday, and he's as straight and clean as an unspent arrow. The fact remains, he's Brookhaven National Laboratory's Public Enemy Number One. You've checked the Chapter's membership? You check it again. Past members. Present members. New Members. Charter members. People who pledged to give but didn't. People who gave a dollar or a dime.

"Keep your eyes and ears open for that band of bandits called ELF—acronym for Earth Liberation Front—although it's going to be difficult to get a handle on any of them because they're a loosely knit, yet well-organized nationwide extremist group whose press office is headquartered in Portland, Oregon. Their spokesperson recently claimed responsibility for a rash of arsons here in Suffolk County, targeting overexpansion of housing in the area. They're supposedly nonviolent—exercising extreme safety precautions by taking great care to ensure that no one is in proximity of a particular homesite before they burn it to the ground. Certainly doesn't sound like our guy. But then again, you never know. Could be a renegade eco-terrorist. The group's partner in activism is the ALF: Animal Liberation Front. It sets our guy, once again, far afield of these tree huggers and animal lovers, keeping in mind what that nut did to the Dawson girl's dog.

"Run down fishermen who work the bays for their livelihood. Anyone who has it in for the farmers. You all know the situation with the geese and other birds out at Peppy's Farm Stand in East Marion last week. You turn anyone you suspect is unhappy with the DEC, DOE, BNL, or the NRC—for any reason—upside down, then inside out," Theo went on. "Reinvestigate the Suffolk County Water Authority. I know the above may include members of your own family," he deadpanned. "But ask yourselves: do they ski—or skate— or rant and rave about our air, soil and water pollution situation? If so, then haul their asses in here for an *interview*."

Several smiles broke out, and a few sympathetic grumbles rippled through the room.

"I also want someone to look into the environmentalists and investors clash going on in the Hamptons, as we speak, regarding the preservation of groundwater recharge areas in the Pine Barrens. You know the first rule. Follow the money," Theo stated emphatically, rubbing his index and forefinger against the face of his thumb for emphasis.

"I know some of you have other assignments. And, now, you're going to be reassigned once more. And when you and your partner find time to breathe, I want you to overlap. What one misses, the other picks up." Theo took in the sea of tired faces. "Any questions?"

Miller's hand shot up

"Yes."

"Why would this guy take his skates from Maine, but leave behind a pair of skis and poles in the Adirondacks?"

"Why do I take my newspaper into the bathroom sometimes and sometimes not?" was Theo's immediate response.

"Maybe you were fresh out of toilet paper," Miller threw out sardonically.

"Maybe the skis and poles were too obvious or too cumbersome to carry around, whereas the skates were not," Theo suggested, ignoring Miller's ill-framed remark.

"Maybe that Mafia chieftain put that stuff up there himself for a reason you're overlooking."

Theo studied the rookie detective.

Hennesey, seated next to his junior partner, looked away as if he wanted no part.

"Detective Miller," Theo said.

"Sir?"

"You're aware that everyone in this room is a member of a team?"

"Absolutely."

"Then it's not something that *I* may or may not be overlooking. It's something that *we*, as a team, may be overlooking. Got it?"

"Got it."

"Good. Any ideas on that?" he asked, knowing full well that the man had something beating around in his brain, or he would not have raised the issue in the first place.

"Well, your idea—or should I say the team's looking into investors in the Hamptons clashing with environmentalists—makes me think, too, of the huge potential for profit here. And that kind of money makes me think about the mob. The two usually *do* go hand in hand, Lieutenant." Miller paused long enough to put on a wise-guy grin. "It's usually difficult to prove because of certain diversionary tactics they use. So. If the mob wanted to stop us from looking in one direction, they might set us off in another. Like with those skis and poles they're making such a big deal about upstate."

"Staging," Theo said.

"Come again?" Miller said, furrowing his brow.

"Tell him, Hennesey."

"It's when something's added, subtracted, or rearranged at a crime scene to make it look like someone other than the perp committed the act—or to even have it appear that no crime ever took place," Miller's partner addressed his charge, wondering if the young detective actually did not know . . . *or could he be playing games,* the detective sergeant considered.

"Ah, staging," Miller said, neither archly nor knowingly. "The point is that I think Nelson and Archer are taking Austin Izzo's bait—wasting their time trying to secure so-called evidence."

"You do?" Theo questioned, wondering how the man came to know so much so soon after pulling him off the cold-case file and putting him back in the loop.

Miller said nothing, sitting defensively with his arms folded across his chest.

"Well, then. Any idea on where to go from here regarding that theory, Detective Miller?"

"Sure. Send Hennesey and me up to Long Lake, and let us poke around."

Murmurs and snickers sounded up and down and back and forth across each and every row.

Hennesey's face turned ruby red, making it rather difficult to determine whether the sergeant's reaction was the result of sheer anger, or one of mere embarrassment for his charge. But if the lieutenant had to guess, it was probably a combination of mixed emotions.

"By the way. Any progress on the Carter case?" Theo asked, looking to rattle the rookie's cage—set a new example for the troops.

"Absolutely, Lieutenant."

Balls as big as blown up balloons about to burst, Kim Booker visualized.

Theo's eyebrows lifted. "Really? Care to share?"

Miller pulled a notepad from his pocket and turned a few pages. "You want this now, Lieutenant?"

Theo smiled condescendingly. "Sure."

Miller rose from his seat and was about to take a step.

"Right from there is fine, Detective."

"You want me to read this here?"

"If you don't mind."

"It's just my notes. I haven't written them up into a report yet."

Practically everyone in the squad room was grinning from ear to ear.

Hennesey was nibbling his bottom lip.

"Summarize it for us," Theo said, taking the detective's bait.

"Well, sir. First I contacted the victim's family. Spoke to the daughter who was seven at the time of her father's murder. I asked her if she still believed that the gardener, Ivan James, was the man responsible, and asked her if she'd mind coming out here to discuss it. Which she did. All the new evidence that was being gathered seemed to me to be misleading, pointing us in the wrong direction. So, I figured I'd put my money on the young woman with a very good memory for detail. I did some checking and learned that Mr. James, one of the initial suspects, was sitting upstate doing a dime for robbery. So, I got the D.A.'s office to follow through on the prisoner's DNA sample submission, then send the victim's T-shirt with the suspect's blood off to Cellmark. Then I had the findings run through the state's newly expanded DNA database and got a match. Bingo. Ivan James. I guarantee you he'll be doing twenty-five to life."

Theo was contemplating the ceiling. Maybe there was a God, the confirmed atheist ruminated, returning his eyes to the cocky kid. "How did you manage to expedite this business?" Theo remarked. "What I mean is . . . in such a short period of time?"

"Well, you were so busy, sir—with this other matter—that I just rubber-stamped the Carter file."

"Rubber-stamped it how?"

"Top Priority."

"And you're telling me a twenty-two-year-old murder case received top priority?"

Miller shrugged.

Theo thought carefully before he spoke. "Couldn't possibly be . . . no matter how preposterous this might sound, Miller . . . that the Suffolk County D.A.'s office, upstate corrections, Albany and Cellmark, all thought that the Carter case was somehow connected to the present case we're working on . . . could it?"

Again, Detective Miller shrugged. "Wouldn't know for sure, sir. But an ADA did ask me if I was on the serial killer case."

"And you said?"

"I *was*."

"Meaning past tense of course?"

"But of course."

"But you can easily see, of course, how that might have gotten turned around."

"I can, indeed, sir."

Hennesey was shaking his head in disbelief.

"And where were you all this time, Detective Hennesey?" Theo asked the older, supposedly wiser, man.

"Baby-sitting, sir. Holding the victim's daughter's hand."

"I see."

"I think we all do," Kim Booker offered, nodding her head in mild amusement and approval, attempting to defuse a potentially rash decision framing the lieutenant's face.

Theo released a breath. Took another. Then started assigning his troops.

Several minutes later, after everyone but Miller and Hennesey had left the room, their commanding officer eyed the seated pair. The senior man looked straight ahead uncomfortably, expecting the worse. His young partner was staring at the floor.

"Sergeant Hennesey," Theo spoke.

"Yes, sir?"

"You want to take this whippersnapper and copter up to Long Lake to give Dean and Brian a little support?" Theo inquired.

"Yes, sir," the man answered straightaway.

"You realize, of course, that we are out of our jurisdiction up there?"

"Of course." The sergeant grinned with satisfaction.

"And that you'll be taking your instructions from the locals?" he added, looking directly at Miller.

"Certainly," Miller agreed.

"And that Albany has the final say in this."

"Goes without saying," Hennesey affirmed.

"That is, unless . . . I can find a way to have the attorney general intervene on our behalf," the lieutenant thought aloud.

"Lieutenant, with all due respect, I'm sure the attorney general could have tied Don Ciccio's crew into knots up there if he was so inclined. Instead, it's like he gave 'em free rein," Hennesey offered.

"He?" Theo feigned surprise. "Oh, not the *state* attorney general, Detective Hennesey. I was referring to *she*; the Attorney General of the United States, Janet Reno. Have a safe trip, gentlemen," he concluded, then turned and left the room.

Chapter 29

Initially, the authorities were unable to reach the Rodmans or their immediate family. Adam and Audrey Rodman, parents of the deceased, were out of the country on holiday at the time of their daughter's murder. The Rodman's younger daughter was staying with an aunt in the Hamptons. Their older children, both boys, were stationed overseas. One was in the military; the other in the Peace Corps. Word of their sister's death reached the boys through the American Red Cross. However, the first mention of murder, in addition to the circumstances surrounding it, was revealed to Fern's parents by a callous CNN reporter who gave Adam and Audrey the shocking news as the two were deplaning at Kennedy Airport. The wife collapsed and was taken to a nearby hospital; her husband went into a severe state of shock.

Their eldest son had been given emergency leave and was en route home. The youngest boy just returned to the States. Their Uncle Hal had taken care of the funeral arrangements while his niece tended to her father as best she could.

Uncle Hal seemed to be the only functioning member of the family, as the others were forlorn and out of sorts—standing or sitting around in a trance. The group was gathered in the living room of Adam and Audrey's spacious home in Wading River. Adam Rodman sat alone in a corner. Hal Rodman spoke to the police in slow and deliberate phrases, as if what he had to say were to be translated by an inept interpreter.

"That man, sitting over there, my brother, is going to have a nervous breakdown," Hal avowed, stopping two detectives at the doorway.

Detective Amastate nodded sympathetically, yet tried to conduct official business. "We'd like to talk to him if we may."

"You may not!" Hal said definitively. "Not now. Not tomorrow. Maybe never," he reaffirmed. "Maybe my nephew, at some later date, vhen he returns home from the hospital vith his mother. But that figure, sitting in the corner by the *v*indow—" he stood waving a finger toward his brother sitting in a neutral corner "—that is a broken man. He belongs in the hospital *v*ith his *v*ife," the man declared, lowering his voice beneath a shaky whisper.

"Excuse me?" Amastate questioned. "I didn't quite catch that."

"I said . . . step over here," Hal directed, placing a firm hold on the detective's elbow and leading him across the threshold. "*V*hat I said *v*as, this is not a very good time."

"Has your brother received any threats; open or otherwise. Threats of any kind that you're aware of?" the detective asked politely, gently removing Hal's grip.

"Threats?"

"Maybe an argument over his opposition to posting signs along the Peconic River. Anything like that?"

"Open threats. Veiled threats." Hal pursed his lips and scratched the side of one leg. "I live in Oregon, mister. *V*hat *v*ould I know of threats or trespassing signs?"

"Warning signs. Not trespass— Never mind. Look," the detective said, trying to mask his frustration. "We need to speak to your brother. It will only take a minute."

Hal Rodman suddenly nodded in the affirmative. "All right. I'll tell you *v*hat. If you can get him to say more than *v*on *v*ord—*v*on *v*ord —mind you, you can ask him anything you like." Hal held up one finger. "Come. I'll even make this easy for you." He escorted the cop into the room before turning around abruptly. "That your partner there?"

"Yes, he is."

"He stays put."

"Fine," the detective replied, gesturing to his partner to just relax.

Hal made his way around and through the group, edging himself into the corner.

"Excuse me, please. Excuse me. Adam. Adam, this is Detective Amastacht."

"Amastate."

"*V*hatever."

"Detective Amastacht *v*ould like a *v*ord with you, Adam."

Adam Rodman was staring blankly past his brother and the

detective.

The young daughter scrambled over from a couch and took hold of her father's hand. "It's all right, Daddy. You don't have to say one word to the policeman if you don't want to. Does he, Uncle Hal?"

"Not *von*," Hal sided with the child, puffing out his chest like a proud peacock.

Tears started streaming down Adam Rodman's face while he continued staring off into space.

The detective nodded in surrender. "I can see this is not a good time," he conceded.

Hal smiled satisfactorily, leading the man back toward the front door. "And I can see that you're a very compassionate detective. A little thick at first, but mindful."

"How's his wife doing?" the cop inquired, ignoring the remark.

"Better than he. My sister-in-law is heavily sedated, lying in the hospital, like I said."

Detective Amastate bid the little man good day. "Take care."

Hal nodded his goodbye and opened the door abruptly for the pair.

"It's been a real pleasure, Hal," Amastate's partner said. "We'll try again later," he assured the man. The two detectives headed down the steps.

Hal shrugged and scratched his other leg, then quickly closed the door behind them.

Chapter 30

Justin Barnes finished up the first leg of *business* in the Carolinas, wiring money from the drug deal into one of several accounts. He thought about staying over and partying, but decided to head back home, making the necessary arrangements to pick up a shipment of handguns along the way to deliver north. He really was not much in a party mood anyhow, thinking about Monisha being put into the ground in that little cemetery up in Hartford, around the corner from her mama's home. He pictured their distant cousin, Tyrone Phillips, standing over her casket at graveside.

Justin knew that Tyrone and Monisha were an item on and off through the years. With all the fish in the sea, he and Tyrone had to hook into the likes of her. He and Tyrone and probably a dozen other guys, the maverick could well imagine. Still, Justin always believed that he would be the one to land her in his net. Maybe if he were not still *officially* married, things might have turned out differently, he rationalized. But Monisha had known his divorce was in the works. Perhaps if he were a bit more settled, like Tyrone, maybe—then—he could have had her *all* to himself, he figured. *Maybe she wouldn't be dead. Maybe this and maybe that. Maybe if I had simply put a bullet in Ty·rone's head.*

Always with the maybes.

Actually, Justin heard through the grapevine that Monisha came damn close to putting a bullet in Tyrone's chest several years back. She supposedly missed him by a foot from thirty feet away. Justin knew the incident had to be a warning. The fact of the matter was that Monisha would never miss a *moving* target at thirty yards. The fact was that she was deadly with a handgun as demonstrated at a town range while shooting at human silhouettes. The fact was that she had been trained by the very best. *"Bull's-eye Barnes,"* she would call him. *"Teacher extraordinaire."* He first trained Monisha with Lasergrips™ before teaching her proper sight alignment.

The travel atlas was back on his lap.

Now, where did I leave off? he thought for a moment.

"Iowa. The capital of Iowa is . . . Des Moines, or however the fuck you say it," Justin butchered the pronunciation badly.

That was the troublesome one. The one he kept missing. Des Moines. "I owe no one, *Desdemona*," he improvised out of context, recalling the wife of Othello in one of Shakespeare's plays. The only play he had ever seen in his entire life. The play that Monisha manipulated him into seeing. A play about a black nobleman. Monisha promised him lots of murder and intrigue during the performance, which it certainly had.

"You shittin' me or what?" Justin said just hours before curtain time. *"Ain't no noble nigger in any white man's play, else he be sportin' chains, woman."*

But Othello was, indeed, a black nobleman that evening. A Moor. With Muslim blood coursing through his veins.

Of course, Justin had to find criticism afterward, or he just could not be a critic.

"Ain't no body ever died like that," Justin challenged after the curtain fell for the final time that evening; he mercilessly charged the victims with overacting. *"Now, I can tell you how a body dies, and it ain't like anything you see on stage, Monisha. Tell you dat."*

That was the evening Justin confided in Monisha, telling her he killed a cop when he was young and foolish. She wished he had not told her. He could read it in her eyes. It was in that moment of weakness he realized both of them had seen *two* tragedies in a single night.

"Iowa. Des Moines. *Desdemona.*" His *own* Monisha, he would remember forever and a day, he swore.

Association. The trick Monisha drilled into his mind.

"Whatever makes you joyous, sad or angry," she had elaborated in a lesson.

"I·o·wa. I owe *no one*, motherfucker," Justin claimed emphatically as he had a million times. Famous last words. Repeated as far back in time as he could remember.

But of course he *owed* Monisha . . . knowing now that he could never pay her back. Or could he? He saw his own black body lying over Desdemona's . . . as at the end of Act V, Scene II.

He would never forget the capital of Iowa, he knew for certain. Des Moines for Desdemona. A bit of a stretch. He would never ever forget his first and last true love.

Monisha Washington.

Is that not an amazing thing? he realized.

He did not have to be up in Hartford standing graveside to prove to anyone that he loved her. He was feeling guilty nonetheless. Dead was dead. Yet, he felt a tugging at his heart.

"Shit."

He promised himself he would place flowers on her grave when he got back.

"Fuck!"

He would run a dagger through the killer's heart, he swore.

Justin turned on the car radio to barrage and bury his thoughts.

Five minutes later, he listened to a news report about a serial killer suspected in the murders of at least eight females; one of them a child. The latest killing was that of a young woman in her twenties, living alone in a remote cabin in the Adirondack Mountains in upstate New York.

"Their murders," the newscaster reported, "are believed to be related to the purported polluting of our planet. The victims range from the northern part of Michigan—down along the Eastern Seaboard to Florida. How the connection was first established is still unclear, although an unconfirmed report from a source in Albany tells us that members of the victims' families are presently, or have been in the recent past, affiliated with companies responsible for the safety of two of our most invaluable resources: the very air we breathe, and the water we drink," the commentator stated rather dramatically. "When asked if MTBE poisoning from shallow wells was in any way . . ."

Justin was staring at the radio instead of the road when two large tractor-trailers boxed him in: one to his immediate right; the other, passed, signaled and crossed in front of him from the left lane. He let up on the gas, then watched as the second rig flew by. He felt the force of turbulence catch and rouse the heavy automobile as it momentarily took command of the wheel.

What in the world does Monisha have to do with all of that pollution business? he wondered. *Serial killer? Air? Water?* No one in her family, who he could think of, worked for any power or water authority . . . although Monisha's stepbrother once worked as a meter reader; that is, whenever he worked, Justin recalled with a smirk. The young man was employed by Con Edison in the city—before getting himself fired—after which, he moved out east to Bellport, then took a job with LILCo, prior to the utility company becoming LIPA. Those two jobs lasted about a year.

But that did not jive at all because Monisha's stepbrother was doing hard time up in Attica for armed robbery. It made no sense. Maybe the commentator was not talking about *his* Monisha from the northern part of Michigan. Maybe he meant some other woman. Maybe it was all a mistake, he rationalized.

Of course, Justin knew the reporter *had* to be referring to Monisha—he fumed—first hearing the horrifying news from his Uncle Ed. Her body suspended from a bridge. Justin had flown or driven over that magnificent expanse many times. Lake Michigan to the west. Lake Huron to the east. Why did the newscaster fail to give details, or say *where* in northern Michigan the person was from? Was it Sault Ste. Marie? Had to be. That remote northern icebox of a city.

His thoughts returned to Tyrone Phillips. Living somewhere out in Kansas. *Yes.* Driving for a toxic waste company, last he heard. Caught up in all that controversy, he suddenly recalled. Justin heard the rumors from relatives. Tyrone was raking in the dough and had, once again, put the moves on Monisha. *Money motivated that girl more than any motherfucking university, or Shakespeare's Othello, for that matter.* He knew, too, that she wanted it all. Sex, security and a black knight in a shining suit of armor who would prove to be her savior.

A suspected serial killer of seven women and a child, Justin kept turning over in his mind.

Justin's wheels upstairs were spinning faster than the four below. How the hell was he going to find a serial killer moving through the eastern half of the United States, and as far west as Michigan? The question revolved in his mind.

Maybe he would see *Ty·rone*, his rival, back in Hartford. Maybe the man would be straight with him. Maybe with Monisha gone, they would not be rivals anymore. Maybe they would track the killer down together. *Yeah, right. Ty·rone couldn't track a black bear shittin' through fresh snow,* he mused. "Maybe an elephant in the zoo, though. Maybe one with diarrhea," he said and laughed aloud. "Just maybe."

Maybe. Maybe. Maybe.

"Damn."

Justin grew discouraged and disgusted, deciding to continue his game of capitals. He turned off the radio.

He was up to Kansas.

Now, isn't that ironic.

Kansas.

Smack in the middle of the nation.

He simply pictured a *can* sitting between *two peaks.*

"The capital of Kansas is Topeka."

That was where *Ty·rone* lived and worked. He would not forget.

A flashing red light in the rearview mirror caught Justin's attention. It was not a matter of the car closing in. The vehicle was directly behind him. Suddenly, the siren sounded with unnerving intermittent blasts.

"Oh, boy," Justin breathed uneasily, glad he was back in the state of bliss while traveling north through Virginia. Glad he still had the pair of southern plates displayed.

Where did the fucker come from? Out of nowhere, was Justin's assessment. *Out of no-fucking-where.*

The required paperwork was in the glove compartment, the handgun clipped directly below it—within easy reach. The cache of weapons was tucked away well within the trunk, beneath a lining. Covered with luggage.

Justin eased the full-size, luxury, 4-door DeVille D'elegance— with its weighty contraband—from the right lane onto a gravelly shoulder, praying it was not a soft-yielding surface in which he would find himself sinking, then stuck. It happened once before. Long ago. But the pebbly layer felt safe and solid. As solid as his story. God willing.

The trooper's car pulled up several yards behind him—then stopped.

Justin cut the engine and waited an eternity, wondering what was up. A broken taillight? A Cadillac doing under sixty, raising the cop's suspicion? Racial profiling . . . where The Man had spotted the back of his kinky head of hair? Or maybe it was a woman trooper, he considered. *Wouldn't that be a gas?* He wondered if he would have trouble pulling the trigger on a female officer if he had to. He did not give that idea a second thought. He would, in all truth, pull a gun on his own mother in the blink of an eye. Then again, that was not a fair example because he would have wasted her in *half* a heartbeat, he envisioned through an anxious, angry grin . . . like the night he found her with her own brother, masturbating him within her greedy money-making mouth. *Would've done them both right then and there,* he swore silently. But at age eleven, a gun was hard to come by.

By fourteen, he had an armory. Well, not exactly his. But he had his pick of the lot. And a lot of green was gotten for chancy but very little, lucrative, work.

What the fuck is taking so long? Maybe the fuzz was onto him, he worried. *Maybe there's a snitch.* Maybe the boys in the hood had decided to fuck him over once they had his money. Maybe he would just have a heart attack while waiting for the news.

Maybe. Maybe. Maybe.

But he remained cool.

Right.

Finally, the trooper stepped from the blue attention-getting marked vehicle. Flashlight in hand. Closing the door of the cruiser. Strutting toward the Caddy.

Male. Tall. Gussied up in gray and blue from top to bottom. Campaign hat saddling his close-cropped skull. Telltale yellow stripes bordering the trouser legs. The cop was right alongside the car.

Justin sent down his window without a word.

"License and registration."

There was no, *please.*

Justin reached across to the glove compartment.

"Hold it right there!" The cop had his hand on the butt of his revolver.

"Problem, officer?"

"Keep your hands where I can see them. Where's your license and registration?"

"Glove compartment. Along with the insurance card and some paperwork."

Justin's gun was already at his side. Just beneath his right leg.

If the cop asked him to step out of the car for any reason, there would be no turning back. It would all be over in an instant. The maverick was pleased the night was dark as dirt.

"Take them out with two fingers. Thumb and forefinger."

"Yes, sir."

Justin leaned over, feeling the solidness of the weapon beneath his thigh. He opened the glove compartment and carefully removed the items with two fingers as he was told.

"License, old and temporary registrations, insurance card, and paperwork from the state. I'm a new resident," Justin both lied and beamed brightly.

The trooper took the papers and stepped just forward of the windshield, shining a beam of light upon the lower left corner of tinted glass, scrutinizing the single sticker before stepping back and examining the items in his hand.

"Why isn't this temporary slip displayed on the driver's side of your windshield?" he snapped.

"Would you believe they didn't have any Scotch tape at motor vehicle? They told me to leave it on the dash. But when I put the window down, it almost blew out with the wind."

The state trooper looked back down at the paperwork before putting the light in Justin's eyes.

Justin put up a hand instinctively.

The beam of light roamed the interior of the car.

"You always carry your license and registration in the glove compartment instead of your wallet?" the trooper asked, shutting off the light.

"Yes, sir. Why?"

"Really not a good idea."

"Why's that?"

"If this car gets stolen, the thief has everything he needs."

Justin frowned sheepishly. "Never thought of that."

"I suggest you change your habit."

"I will, indeed, officer," Justin agreed in his best embarrassed yet appreciative expression.

The man handed back the papers.

"Thank you." Justin wedged the temporary registration in the corner between the windshield and the dash, putting the rest of the paperwork on the seat next to him. Inches from the handle of his gun. He was about to start the engine when the cop stopped him cold.

"Hold it."

"Sir?"

The trooper fixed his dark eyes on him suspiciously. "Aren't you curious why I stopped you?"

"A spot check, I guess," Justin offered lamely.

The officer shook his head.

"No? Then what?" he asked a little too abruptly.

"The way you swerved between those two trailer trucks back there—" he gestured "—I thought you might have had a drink or—"

"I don't drink, officer," was Justin's quick response, praying to God that the man would not ask him to step out and walk a straight line, or some crap like that.

"—or that, perhaps, you were a little tired," the officer amplified.

Justin shook his head. "No, I'm fine."

The trooper was staring at him if not through him. He seemed unsatisfied.

"To tell you the truth—" and Justin was about to, when another trooper's car pulled up directly in front of them, blocking Justin's vehicle.

An even taller, larger figure stepped out.

Two bullets—and he was sweating them—would take the troopers out in a flash . . . but only if he acted now . . . before it was too late.

"Graham."

"Evening, Brad."

Justin took in their every move.

Brad glanced at the out-of-state inspection sticker.

Graham turned back to Justin. "You were saying?"

"I was about to say that I heard a report about a serial killer on the news. It distracted me. Those two tractor-trailers locked me in, so I let up on the gas. Gust got me, I guess. I didn't realize I *swerved*, like you said," which he really had not, but went along for the ride, figuring that the trooper's car must have entered an on-ramp, or came off a divider . . . lights off . . . or whatever. "Sorry," was all he could think to say. Sorry that he had opened up his mouth at all. It was stupid. For it gave Graham a brand-new area to explore. Maybe the serial killer was black. Maybe they would want him for a lineup. Maybe he would just kill them . . . now!

"Guess what?" the trooper declared with a grin.

"What?"

"I heard that same report, too. Guess we both had the same station on."

"How about that."

"You take care, now."

"Will do."

"And don't forget what I told you about those papers."

"You bet."

Graham stepped forward of the car, and the two troopers talked for a good thirty seconds before heading toward their respective vehicles.

Graham brought the tips of his fingers to the brim of his hat in passing.

Justin politely returned the salute.

Chapter 31

A blue and white Bell Star out of MacArthur Airport—also known as Islip Airport—bladed down noisily but smoothly upon the helipad. Ten minutes later, Detectives Miller and Hennesey climbed aboard and were airlifted. With a headwind out of the north, ETA to Long Lake was an hour and a half. The two men put on a pair of headphones, resuming the conversation they were having on the ground.

"This guy could strike anytime or anywhere," Hennesey went on. "Kim's suspect list is endless. And the possible victims' printout sheet, too, goes on forever. I'd be an old man before we exhausted each and every name."

"Told you before. You *are* an old man. But not to worry. Our boy is not on any list," Detective Miller swore.

"Now, how in blazes could you possibly know a thing like that?"

The young detective smiled and pointed to his nose.

"You a bloodhound now, laddie?"

"Nope." Andrew Miller looked out the large starboard window, staring down at the miniature buildings and homes that dotted the land like Monopoly real estate pieces. He turned back to his partner. "But I'm going to turn myself into a water rat."

"How do you mean?"

"I'm going to get down into the sewer with him, Ed."

"Where?"

"Where it stinks to high heaven."

Ed Hennesey grinned and shook his head. "Give you a piece of advice, kid?"

"Yeah, give."

"I've seen a carload of guys like you come and go. Hotshots. Each and every one of 'em. Gonna take the world by storm, by God, instead of just keepin' a low profile and their traps shut. First, you gotta learn to listen before shootin' off your mouth. It's important to see the *big* picture, laddie. Not go off half-cocked."

"Better than half crocked," Miller replied, staring straight ahead.

"Hey! I never took a lick of liquor on the job," Ed Hennesey said defensively.

"Never said you did. I haven't been around long enough to note your habits."

"Never!" the cop repeated angrily.

"What about off the job, Ed?" Andrew Miller asked placidly, taking in the interior of the craft.

"A nip every now and then. What's your fuckin' point?"

"The point, Ed, is that it's been nipping at your body and soul for almost half a century. The point is that it impairs your performance as a cop. It impedes—"

"Now, hold on just a—"

"—your judgment. Your ability to react."

"I'm reacting right now, goddamn it."

"Precisely my point. In a rash and uncontrollable manner."

"Oh, I'm in control, all right."

"And I can see to what degree, like I can see a million thin and tiny red lines running through your face like cracked Depression glass, Ed. That's about the time you started nipping, would be my guess."

"Why you, you *little* son of a bitch," Hennesey flustered, twisting around in his seat until his face was an inch from Miller's headset. "I have guys like you for fucking breakfast, then spit them out," he flurried, forming an angry fist between them.

"Hell, I'd wager you'd throw an agreeable arm around those guys, then cry into your beer."

"You sayin' something queer here, Miller?"

"Not at all, Ed. I'm just giving you a sobering thought to consider. That's all. Why don't you chew on that awhile and let me get some rest. We've got a busy time ahead of us."

Detective Andrew Miller turned his face back toward the window and closed his eyes.

"Listen up, *partner*. Nobody speaks to me like that, then turns their back and goes to sleep."

"You picked me, *partner*. I didn't pick you."

"You know that's bullshit. Theo *stuck* me with you."

"Then I'd try to make the best of it if I were you."

"*Precisely* what I'm doing," Ed mumbled. "Fucking college squirt."

"Get some rest, Ed."

"Hey, Patrick!" Hennesey called out to the pilot. "You play any Irish lullabies up there?"

The pilot waved him off like he did not hear or want to.

"You know something, Andy?"

Andrew Miller was off in another world by himself.

"You remind me somewhat of my Irish water spaniel. Best dog I ever had. Great retriever." Ed Hennesey was nodding irritably in the affirmative. "He had long floppy ears that covered up his hearing. Lookin' kinda like you're lookin' now. You listenin', Andy? He didn't *haveta* hear me though. He watched my hand signals mostly. Operated mainly on instinct. I used him strictly for waterfowl. One mornin', he'd gone out too far after a downed duck, when suddenly the current caught him. Wouldn't listen to me. He had to get that goddamn bird. Just had to. The current became very strong. Took 'im with 'er. I couldn't get to 'im. No boat. I was pass shootin' on a peninsula. He wouldn't listen, Andy."

Andrew Miller was dead to the world.

"Hey, Pat! How about a wake-up call just before we land?"

The same wave of the pilot's hand.

In less than a minute, Hennesey was fast asleep alongside his partner.

Partner.

It was the name of the wing-shooter's water dog.

Partners thrown together.

For better or for worse.

Chapter 32

M alcolm was sitting in his motel room in the Adirondacks, watching the local evening news. His eyes were glued to the footage; ears listening intently to the incredulous report. He wondered how anything ever got done. Done right, that is. Here was some poor kid being escorted from what looked like a police or ranger's barracks in Adirondack Park. Donald somebody. A local handyman, a woman reporter said. Probably scared out of his gourd. Something about skis . . . frankly admitting that he had come by the cabin earlier and saw Fern Rodman inside . . . tied to a chair . . . claiming that she was dead before he ever got there.

Well, of course she was already dead. Are they that incredibly stupid?

Perhaps the report was all a ruse to flush him out, Malcolm considered . . . the cops maybe hoping he would suddenly call or come forward and *confess,* rather than see an innocent kid take the rap. He grinned. *Yeah, right. Fat chance of that happening, fellas.* If it were a staged performance, the young man certainly put on a good act . . . crying hysterically . . . yelling while telling a reporter holding a microphone that he was innocent of any wrongdoing. Three men led their prisoner from the building toward a car . . . carefully putting him into the backseat of an unmarked vehicle in full view of the TV cameras . . . some guy's hand atop Donald's head . . . so that the arrestee would not bump it . . . so that he could not sue the state or county or whoever the hell was ushering him away.

Maybe the person is not an actor after all, Malcolm frowned acerbically.

Maybe the young man is being used.
Scapegoat?
A nosy neighbor happening by?

Then back to *police plant?* Malcolm tossed the idea around in his mind before dismissing the notion altogether.

What in the hell happened?

Bad timing, kid, the killer finally reasoned. *Wrong place, wrong time. Tough luck.*

Still, Malcolm could not shake the feeling—a strange feeling of sincere sorrow for the poor fellow.

What to do?

Nothing.

Wait and see what happens next.

Malcolm paced the room but did not take his eyes off the tube.

A big man wearing an open, full-length coat stood off to the sidelines, taking in the scene. He looked more like a cattleman than a cop. Malcolm was amused. *Sheepherder, maybe, from the looks of the shearling lining. Nah. Too serious looking. Fearless fellow. A killer in his own right,* he thought as the camera moved in for a close-up, then swept across the crowd. Malcolm watched attentively as the *sacrifice* was led to slaughter. *An appropriate metaphor.* The real serial killer smiled sadly.

Surely, the prisoner is some local fellow who probably hasn't been out of the state park but maybe half a dozen times in all his— what—twenty-two years, tops, from the looks of him. Most certainly, the crybaby has to have an alibi for those other murders up and down the Eastern coast . . . and as far away as the northern part of Michigan. Yes? Inarguably, their suspect has to have an explanation and can prove his whereabouts at the time Monisha's body was meticulously lowered from the very middle of the mighty Mackinac Bridge, above the abysmal Straits. No? Five hundred plus miles away from Adirondack Park, as the crow flies.

Then again, what if the authorities eventually make the young fellow confess to one of the murders? Friendly Fern's demise, he frowned uncomfortably. *What if they believe the man has an accomplice?*

What if, later on, they say Donald confessed but that he never really confessed at all? Their word against his. Who would a jury believe? The police? Or a handyman accused of a most horrendous crime? Surely, my most spectacular event to date. Certainly not my most dramatic moment, for nothing could compare to the scene that occurred between the towers on that bridge. Dead center, mind you. Measured and rounded off to the nearest tenth of a mile on the vehicle's odometer—2.497 statute miles from one end of its entry to midpoint on a moonless night, where I put on the flashers, momentarily stopped the car and got out, threw up the hood and trunk —pretending to have engine problems—removed her body, then scurried over to the bridge rail and hung Monisha by her right wrist off the east side of the great expanse—carefully lowering her down to fifty feet before climbing back in the car and completing the 4.994 miles across the entire busy, span.

A most daring feat, indeed.

Who would have such complete and detailed information other than the police? It would certainly implicate a party privy to such particulars that had gone unreported in the press. Problem being, of course, that it would only point to one of several murders the police are keying in on. But certainly not the one for which the innocent young man is being held—most assuredly—without bail. Not if the accused is being charged with murder, which the newscaster says he surely is.

What to do? What to do? Malcolm wondered.

Perhaps I'll just have to give the police a detail or two of the earlier murders. One of the two in Suffolk County . . . informing them that it was a large and specially designed wooden oak-slatted lobster trap in which Wendy Anne Linden had to crawl through—a funnel-like access—in order to receive her last unrequested meal. One steaming frankfurter on a stale, ice-cold roll. But with all the fixings, mind you . . . before reposing her frozen body on the bow of that boat in Riverhead. Or I could simply reveal where they could find the cage, if they haven't already done so.

No.

He would have to give them something that would clear the alleged killer without question. But what? Nothing that Malcolm could think of, short of a written confession, would help the unfortunate soul if they were hellbent on persecuting him.

Maybe a few teeny details that only the actual killer knows might convince them they're holding the wrong guy. Yes! Like the bursting strength measured in psi of the surgical tubing snaked down Adam Rodman's daughter's throat. The inside diameter of the amber line. Even the thickness of its wall, gauged in fractions of an inch. How about that for openers? No. Too much information. Just enough to whet their appetites, he considered carefully. *Make them see the error of their ways.*

Who knew how it might play out?

Is it worth the risk?

Would Malcolm be opening Pandora's Box?

What to do? What to do? What to do?

Or should I just be a tough soldier and accept the fact that war has its casualties? Collateral damage. What, and be denied the credit? Absolutely not!

Maybe Malcolm would play the good guy.

A killer with a conscience.

Not for his victims or their families, certainly—but for a purely innocent soul.

Donald Bellport.

That's the kid's name.

Tough call, warrior.

Malcolm decided he would wait for an updated report before doing anything, as the authorities seemed to be moving fast. Maybe a little *too* fast for his liking.

Still and all . . . .

Chapter 33

The two were chatting away amicably.

"Naya."

"What are you talking about, Malcolm?"

"You've never heard of Naya?"

"Naya, who?"

"Not Naya, who? What you mean is, Naya what?"

"Okay then," she said cheerfully. "Naya, what?"

"Naya, Incorporated," he answered.

"Never heard of it." Diane Nash smiled magnificently. Her radiance outshined the sun.

"They're located at 2500 Naya Road."

"Where's that?"

"Mirabel, Québec."

"Canada? Would you mind handing me those, Malcolm?"

Malcolm Columba stooped, then handed over a flat of mixed pansies.

She held the plastic tray at arm's length. "Don't they have the prettiest of faces?" she said, staring down at the colorful array.

"*You* have the prettiest of faces," Malcolm said sincerely. "Even when you're sad."

Diane's face reddened. "Malcolm. You're making me blush," she declared, setting the gray tray down upon the edge of the planting table.

"Sorry."

"Don't be sorry. You just took me by surprise. You've never said anything to me quite like that before."

"Like what?"

"You know," she said, staring down at her lap. "Paying me that kind of compliment."

"Haven't I?"

The pretty woman shook her head. "No, you haven't. Not in all the years I've known you."

"Huh." Malcolm raised his eyes and took in the clear blue afternoon sky.

"Huh, what?" she asked in wonder.

Malcolm turned his full attention back to the young woman.

This time, Diane did not look away. She met and held his dark, mysterious stare. A look that beheld a thousand secrets, she believed. Eyes that she knew saw places far beyond the high stone walls that sheltered her through some terribly lonely years.

"Want to know a secret?" Malcolm asked innocently.

"One of many?" she teased.

"Oh, indeed."

"Tell me," she said invitingly. "Tell me, Malcolm."

"I've been waiting for you to grow up some."

"Some?"

"Some."

Diane wheeled her chair around and busied herself with the flats of assorted pansies and violas, carefully removing them from a series of miniature plastic cell packs, separating a network of dense, thin white roots at the base of each plant with a single decisive tear, arranging the host of exquisite faces in some semblance of size and color order.

He watched with interest as she grouped and set the small plants down upon a dark, rich plot of potting soil—piled high on the plywood sheet before her. After partially filling a medium-sized square pot with the mixture, Diane placed the larger-faced, leggier pansies toward the rear of the clay container. The smaller more delicate veils of viola were set in front. Arranging and rearranging the group, Diane dexterously produced a pleasing pattern, combining the annuals and perennials, composing an original potted prize. A splendiferous array was achieved.

Bingo Clear White, looming in the background. Sorbet Coconut, set low and over a little to the left. Imperial Beaconsfield, back a bit but infringing somewhat about the middle. Crystal Bowl Purple, just a tad to the other side. Yellow Delight, holding center stage, fixed firmly in the foreground—catching the eye of envy.

It was pure pleasure to watch her . . . create. For *work* was not nearly the proper word at all. Beauty accompanying beauty behind a bleak stone wall, which had virtually held the young woman prisoner over the course of fourteen out of her twenty-seven years. Her warden-watchdog? A devoted if not doting father; the wealthy lord and master of the manor, keeping a keen eye from a window high in the watchtower . . . like some sort of saddened sentinel . . . or so Malcolm entertained.

"So, Malcolm. Now that I've grown up before your very eyes, what do you propose to do about that?"

Malcolm stared down uncomfortably at the rich green grass. "Ask you out, I guess," he offered in answer.

Diane hid her smile behind four garden-gloved fingertips. "Are you asking me out on a *date*, Malcolm?" she questioned coyly, taking her hand away from her pretty oval mouth. "Or is it something you're *considering* asking?"

"I'm asking you out," Malcolm said awkwardly.

"And I'm accepting. Only you know that I can't leave these grounds."

Malcolm looked about the palatial gardens. "Who'd ever want to?" he responded in surprise.

"Me, from time to time. Most times, actually."

"Why? You have everything you could ever want right here. No?"

Diane wheeled herself back away from the planting table. "Look."

Malcolm looked up to where she was looking. "What?"

"The clouds."

"There are no clouds today, Diane."

"Exactly. But they were here yesterday and the day before. And they'll be here again by the end of the day. Free to drift along or disappear altogether." She craned her head a fraction, staring past him enviously. "I wish I were as carefree as the clouds, Malcolm. I wish I could drift along wherever I wanted. High above these walls. Then suddenly disappear."

"Your father gets you out and about every now and then. Right?"

"Oh, sure enough," she admitted sullenly. "A step or two in back or right alongside me. I can't move two feet by myself without him standing over me."

"He worries about you, Diane. You know that. Ever since the accident he—"

"I don't want to hear about the accident. Sometimes I even wonder if it *was* an accident."

"Diane! That's a horrible thing to say."

"I know, Malcolm. But it's the way I feel sometimes. Listen. Let's not talk about that, all right? I guess I'm just feeling sorry for myself today. At least I'm not as bad off as that stiff over there." She gestured.

Malcolm looked nervously over his shoulder before turning around completely. "Where?"

"Right there."

All Malcolm saw was the tall tree. "Behind that red maple?" he asked cautiously.

Diane laughed and shook her head of coal-black locks. Long and curly.

He hated curls on girls, except if they were babies.

"The tree itself, Malcolm. I call him Mister Maple. Leaves as red as wine in another two weeks or so. See all those buds already?"

Malcolm smiled and seemed to relax a little, yet he did not like the idea of Diane personifying the tree. Any tree for that matter. For trees were sacred to him. Especially, the magnificent elms that once lined Main Street in the town of Riverhead, over a half a century ago. Of course, he was not even born until the seventies, but he had read and seen beautiful pictures of them in old magazines. To Malcolm, trees stood the test of time—the line of demarcation between the water table and the atmosphere—rooted firmly in sand or clay or soil while symbolizing the purity of life's cycle. He grew sick when he learned that the town had cut down those magnificent ancient elms in the late fifties and early sixties. Better to have razed the buildings along the block than to fell those precious trees.

Mister Maple, indeed! Malcolm sneered inwardly. "You're such a silly goose, Diane. You know that," he said playfully.

"A silly grounded goose," she agreed. "At least I can move about some. Even if it is in this chair and behind these walls for the most part. But Mister Maple standing over there? He's fixed in one spot until the day he dies. Till he just rots away and topples over someday."

"Or unless someone comes along and chops him down prematurely," he offered gloomily.

"True. Still, do you know what he can do that I can't?"

Malcolm was standing quite still beside her as he slowly shook his head.

"He can see high over that wall. I can *hear* the world go by, Malcolm. But he can *see* it every day. Anyhow, I can see that I'm upsetting you with all this silly talk. Got a bug on the end of your nose," Diane jabbered.

Malcolm brushed the tip of his nose.

"April Fools'," she said behind a cupped hand that hid a giggle. "So, do we have a date, or what?"

Malcolm forced a smile. "Sure. But when?"

"Right now."

"Where?"

"Down by the boathouse. No one will bother us there."

"You sure? What about your father?" Malcolm asked, staring up at the window below the widow's walk.

"Sure, I'm sure. Daddy's away in town for the day. The gardeners are gone for the weekend. The housekeeper won't be here till tomorrow morning. And the servants won't be serving dinner until six o'clock. So, you have several hours to have your way with a cripple. How's that?" she asked, staring directly up at him.

"Please don't talk like that," Malcolm said, taking hold of her hand.

"How do you want me to talk, Malcolm?" She took off one of her gloves, pretending to wipe away an annoying piece of dirt while really holding back a tear or two. "What do you want me to say? For years I've waited for you to show me the slightest hint of affection. Since before I was a teenager, in fact. But all you'd talk about with Daddy is business. Like I wasn't even there. Bottled water company this, and bottled water company that. I thought you had water on the brain, just like Daddy. And now, today, you tell me I have a pretty face. Tell me, Malcolm. Tell me that I'm not one of April's fools."

Malcolm's heart felt heavy in that instant, filled with a curious mix of joy and sorrow. He wiped a tear or two away from his own eyes as he wheeled Diane Nash toward the boathouse.

The sky was the color of Sorbet Blue Buttercream. Her hair,

the likeness of coal at midnight.

Chapter 34

Detective Dean Nelson received a Manila envelope in the mail at his home during the early part of the afternoon. Inside was a map along with a cryptic message from the killer. No signature. No return address.

Dean scowled. *No shit, Sherlock.*

The envelope was postmarked March 31, 00; Riverhead, NY. The note was typed on an old manual machine with a notably light ribbon. The stationery was inexpensive, folded in thirds and found inside a newly published New York State Department of Health cancer map. The map depicted Queens, Nassau and Suffolk counties, noting the incident rate for most of the major types of cancer, ranking the three regions as being *"near the statewide average."* Across the face of each division was a neatly line-drawn letter,

L I E

which Dean knew had nothing to do with the Long Island Expressway, but everything to do with bold untold truths . . . at least in the mind of the killer.

Dean also knew, as did health care officials and watchdog committees, that the geographical representation was vague at best. A more detailed map by ZIP code was scheduled for release sometime around the middle of April—which, when translated, meant: Don't Hold Your Breath. Holding your breath, on the other hand—which, when taken literally, as Dean and Brian and the other members of Team Three were discovering daily through exhaustive research, would not be too bad an idea in light of what Elizabeth Dawson had revealed with regard to Long Island's poor air quality.

As if that was not a hard enough pill to swallow, members of the team learned early on in the course of their investigation that it would not be wise to drink the water, either, unless bottled from reputable, uncontaminated underground mineral springs from distant sources such as Vichy, France, or Poland Spring in southern Maine. At the very least, having one's own water supply outfitted with a state-of-the-art filtration and purification system, rather than simply accepting treated chlorinated liquid running through the tap, would not be too bad an idea either. Well water was, well, to put it mildly, risky business —even when tested regularly.

Team Three was well on their way to understanding the workings of the serial killer's mind.

Dean Nelson read, then reread the cryptic note. Cryptic, that is, to anyone who was not in the know. The detective deciphered most of the message in an instant.

MW: 13,186' on ctr. @ 50' descent
via 5/8" dbl.-braided nylon.
bridging the gap:
endoscopic termination @ 1' 1" pipe
insertion via CAT. # 203-323
1/2" x 3/16". Amber Latex Laboratory
Tubing; CMS Purged: FR.
DN Sfk. Co.: Dead-man's float. # 9

Dean immediately notified homicide. Within forty minutes, half of Team Three was assembled in a room down the hall and around the corner from Kim's area—a secured space off-limits to most civilians, including members of the press.

"I already faxed the locals up in Adirondack Park," Dean said before the troops as members from other teams were straggling into the windowless squad room. Several souls with less than two or three hours of sleep in the last few days had weariness written across their faces. "Thank God you're still here, Kim."

"I wasn't. I was home in bed when Theo called."

"Then thanks for getting here so fast," Dean stated with a warm smile of appreciation.

"Going to cost you, Dean," she swore through bleary eyes, setting her thin frame into the closest available seat.

"Landmark Cafe," Dean promised. "Any friggin' thing your heart desires."

"Where's my white prince, sport?" she asked absently.

Most everyone gave up an easy smile, privy to her feelings for Dean's partner, Brian.

"On his way. Already told 'im we'll split the check," the case detective bantered, bearing a row of crooked teeth modified by an overbite.

Theo walked into the room and took a seat beside Kim.

"Then again—" Dean half kidded, gesturing with an outstretched, palms-up hand toward their boss.

"Your show," the lieutenant instructed, missing the significance of the token acknowledgment; that is, the extending of an invitation to Houlihan's to help defray the cost of Kim's meal later that evening. Maybe.

More smiles. Stretches. A single loud yawn.

Detective Hennesey excused himself, then yawned again.

"That's all right, Ed," Theo said. "We're all running on empty. Get on with it, Dean."

"Right. Everyone have a copy of the note?" he asked, handing one to Kim and Theo. "Okay, then. Most of this is pretty straightforward. But we're all here to help fill in the blanks." Dean glanced down at his copy, ready to read and dissect the enigma one step at a time for anyone who may have missed a beat.

"'MW: 13,186 on ctr.' is pretty cut-and-dried," he began in a loud clear voice. "Monisha Washington was put out in the middle of the Mackinac Bridge; 13,186 feet from either end. The structure being 26,372 feet overall. The perp then lowered her body to 50 feet using 5/8 inch double-braided nylon line.

"'Bridging the gap' is his clever little way of letting us know that he went from the bridge murder—crime scene number seven—to the 'endoscopic termination' in the cabin where he terminated Fern Rodman by running a length of tubing down her throat—crime scene number eight. He goes on to accurately describe the item. The latex tube was found inserted exactly thirteen inches into her trachea. There's your one foot-one inch endoscopy: a medical term for an examination of the inside of the body using a much thinner tubular instrument. In the victim's case, the pipe the perp's referring to is, of course, her windpipe. Sick bastard.

"Catalogue number 203-323 corresponds precisely with the size tubing forensics reported; that is, half an inch in diameter overall with a 3/16th inch-thick wall. Made to withstand enormous pressure. And as sure as sin, it matched the manufacturer's labeling to a tee. Amber Latex Laboratory Tubing. Comes in twelve-foot lengths.

"CMS is the trademark for Curtain Matheson Scientific, Inc., which is a Coulter subsidiary company. We're looking into a list of distributors as we speak. Six feet of that twelve-foot section running from the sink is what he used to *purge* FR: Fern Rodman. In other words, cleansing her for her father's so-called sins." Dean Nelson looked over the sea of nodding, drowsy faces. "We all on the same page with this guy so far? Anybody see it differently? No? Fine."

A hand went up in the back of the room. A two-year tenderfoot on loan from Team Two.

"Olsen?"

"Who or what's 'DN Sfk. Co.'? And this 'Dead-man's float' business?" the detective asked impatiently.

"Any takers?" Detective Dean Nelson submitted for consideration.

Three hands shot straight up in the air. Most of the other detectives were pointing a finger directly at Dean Nelson.

"I was afraid of that," the case detective said uneasily. "Bo?"

"DN is *you*, baby," a well-dressed, light-skinned Latino interpreted from a corner of the room. "From good ol' Suffolk County. You to be victim number nine, amigo." The man held up nine fingers. "You top o' his hit parade, my man. He sees ya ass cheeks floatin' straight up, nose pointin' down. Driftin' 'long a lazy river, hombre. God only knows where," Bo concluded.

Bo-dacious, as the detective was monikered, gave his assessment in his usual dialectic delivery, rarely speaking the king's English, except when taking the stand as a witness for the state. In such undercover cases, Bo had successfully passed himself off as hit man for hire—ostensibly obliging either party in soliciting his services for a handsome fee; for example, business partner seeking *sole* proprietorship; perhaps an impatient mistress with *grave* concerns; a husband wanting the wife out of his life and her misery, *permanently*; or a wife wanting an unfaithful husband kept at *bay*, like in body of water. Et cetera, et cetera.

"I'm not so sure," Hennesey said, scratching his head.

"I'm not, either," Miller seconded, nodding in agreement.

"Yeah, you two did real good upstate, assisting Dean and Brian with those wise guys and Bellport's ski equipment," a voice from the other side of the room called out, shaking his head in exaggerated disappointment. "Pretty evident it was all *downhill* from there," the veteran funned, chuckling sleepily, lacing his fingers behind his shaven head.

"We're not the ones who had the guy arrested," Ed Hennesey blurted out defensively.

"Bellport could still be an accomplice," another detective offered. "Think about it. Why would the author of the note go through all this trouble if Bellport wasn't somehow involved? Huh? Tell me. Good Samaritan? Concerned citizen? Serial killers have no conscience, or so I'm told. But if one had the goods on the other . . ."

"Maybe the killer *has* a conscience," Kim Booker put on the table. "Doesn't want to see an innocent young man go down for some unexplainable reason."

"Yeah, that kid's no more guilty than the lieutenant here," Olsen added in support.

"Then why are they still holding him?" a female in the first row seated next to Kim asked, looking over at Theo for an answer.

"Maybe they'll release him when they digest this note," suggested a male detective in raggedy old clothes, twisting a hairy pinkie in his ear.

"I wouldn't be so sure. It doesn't mean he's not in some way involved," a stocky towhead grumbled.

"Your ass," the two-year tyro was willing to wager. "Twenty bucks."

"All right," Theo interjected, raising his hand from his seat for their full attention. "Glad to see some of you starting to come alive. But let's get back on track and focus on this last line. Any other possibilities? 'DN Sfk. Co. Dead-man's float. # 9.' The number nine I think we can all agree is pretty obvious. It either is or will be his next victim. Dead-man's float, too, doesn't leave much to the imagination. Bo could be on target with this. But maybe not exactly in the center of the bull's-eye. What else can we come up with? Let's hear it."

Hennesey and Miller's hands shot up simultaneously.

"Ed?"

"Well, unless Dean's been pissin' in the bays and macerating across Long Island Sound, it's probably another polluter that our sick fuck has in mind."

Nods of agreement and light laughter filled the room.

"What's macerating?" Detective Urusala asked.

"That's when you discharge body waste mixed with chemicals from a holding tank," someone explained. "Goes through a macerator."

The woman looked askance.

"Picture something like a blender in your kitchen," he elaborated.

"I *got* the picture. People *do* that?"

"Waste's supposed to go to a pump-out station," a rookie detective made clear.

"Jesus," she said quietly, staring up at Dean Nelson with disgust.

Dean was shaking his head defensively and waving his hands, assuring the troops that he only macerated when he was *miles* out in the ocean.

"How many miles 'at be, Cap'n?" Bo asked slyly, a boater himself and knowing full well that virtually every boater in the area who had a marine head with a Y-valve and/or a holding tank, discharged waste somewhere in the middle of Long Island Sound—if not the deeper, moving waters of the local bays. "Ya not a canyon runner, yet, far as I can see, Dean. I see ya fishin' mostly in the inlets and the back bays," he said convincingly. "I ain't ever seen no *ocean* flounder hit ya deck or dock, skipper. Seen ya hit the pier, though, once or twice," he rambled on through a snicker. "Bounced off *my* boat last season. You're lucky the wind was light."

Theo was getting annoyed. His veterans knew better than to digress from the normal course of inquiry. Excessive banter in the squad room had no place. His pet peeve. Bo certainly knew better. Hennesey, too, continued to badger Nelson, while Bo was really getting the case detective's goat. But it finally dawned on Theo that the pair was leading Dean Nelson down the straight and narrow, or its nautical equivalent thereof, having him come clean. *Had* the case detective, in fact, done anything on the water to provoke the killer as Bo and Ed were more than suggesting?

DN.

Jesus! Theo suddenly realized, taking a different tact. *What about Dean's wife and daughter, Doreen and Dawn?* he wondered. *Kind of farfetched? No, not Dean Nelson found floating facedown in the water like Bo depicted.* Theo plainly knew that there was no love lost between husband and wife, and that their so-called trial separation was practically a *fait accompli*, falling just short of any amicable divorce. *But what about Dawn?* The couple worshipped their daughter. DN.

Dead-man's float? Does it wash? Was he getting thick in the head? *Is everyone else who knows Dean's wife and daughter failing to note those two initials in another light?* he asked himself. A shiver shot through his body as he thought about his own family: his precious wife and three daughters. *God! The victims are all female. The Dead-**man's** float certainly isn't restricted to the male swimming population, for cryin' out loud. Are Dean's wife and daughter safe and sound down in Orlando? Will the killer resurface in Florida?*

"Dean!"

"Sorry, Lieutenant," he apologized, having finished fencing with both Bo and Ed.

Theo waved him off. "Where's Doreen and Dawn? I mean right now?"

Several in the group picked up on the top cop's drift.

"Soaking up the sun these last few months," Dean said blankly. "Why?"

"Jesus Christ!" Kim Booker said aloud.

"When did you speak to them last?" Theo pressed.

"Couple days ago." The bulb went off. "C'mon. You don't think—"

"Kim," Theo snapped.

Kim was already at the door. "I'll notify hotel security down there immediately. Embassy Suites, correct?"

Dean nodded in slow motion.

"Sheriff's office and chief of police, too," she went on. "Dean! Get ahold of that Feebe friend of yours. Now!"

Dean was heading for the door.

Theo stepped to the front of the room. "Kim, when you're finished there, you run those two initials for first and last names. Run them forwards, then backwards against the list of possibles you got. Run them through the eastern half of the United States, beginning with

Florida. How many warm bodies you need assisting you?" the lieutenant barked.

Detective Booker took in the entire room from the doorway. "None from this willing but weary bunch," she said quite seriously. "Zombies. Each and every one," she declared. "Listen. I'll patch it through Big Brother if you'll authorize clearance for me now. How's that?"

Big Brother was the Justice Department's equivalent of Interpol. Big Brother was big and fast—unquestionably on the cutting edge of technology, to which only the elite in law enforcement had access or even knew about. The United States had four such mainframes surreptitiously headquartered around the nation. One such computer stood alone in a room fifty feet away but was rarely used by the homicide squad. And with good reason. With a 40:25 murder-to-man ratio occurring yearly in Suffolk County, most felons fell into the non-career criminal-type category—such as crimes of passion, moment of rage sort of scenarios—with suspects disappearing no further than several states away. Georgia and North Carolina were apparently two favorites. Big Brother's overkill was usually not necessary. Big Sister could handle most anything; that is, with little sister Kim Booker sitting before her. But today was different. Today they needed warp speed on their side.

"Well?" Kim barked, snapping Theo out of his trance.

"Done. You know the access code, Kim? Of course you do. I'm telling you this woman's after my f'n job," Theo stated assuredly before the group, finding time enough to kid to keep his cool.

No one cracked so much as a smile.

"But first you need to call Doreen and Dawn, and make sure they're okay," Theo reiterated. "Tell them to stay put."

Kim disappeared around the corner.

The troops rose from their seats.

"Not just yet," Theo ordered. "Sit. We pick up right where we left off. Just in case we're off target here. Sergeant Hennesey, you were saying. DN Sfk. Co. Dead-man's float. What's on your and Miller's mind?"

"Well, DN could be anybody's initials, Lieutenant."

"Now tell me something I *don't* know," Theo said impatiently.

"Yes, sir. S-f-k., or Suffolk, doesn't necessarily have to stand for Suffolk County; I mean, here on Long Island."

"Go on."

"Well, a Suffolk sheep . . . " Ed looked around the room, then glanced over at his partner. "I'm going up and out on a limb with this one, sir."

"*Climb*, Detective. We'll let you know when you crack the branch," the lieutenant prodded.

"Well, a Suffolk is an English breed of sheep with a black face and legs. Rest of it is white, like regular sheep we're used to seein'. They're originally a cross between a Norfolk Horn ewe and a Southdown ram. That may or may not be important."

"What *is* important, Ed?" Theo pressed as patiently as he knew how.

"Donald Bellport."

Theo hid his surprise. "Gonna keep us in suspense?" he chided.

"Man's of mixed blood," Ed Hennesey answered soberly. "Black ancestry, actually."

"I'm missing something here, Ed."

"Detective Miller and myself . . . well, we're tryin' to put two and two together, and we think what the writer of that note is tellin' us is that Donald Bellport is innocent of the murder, any murder, and that like an innocent sheep, he's bein' led to slaughter," Hennesey finished, putting a tongue in the hollow of his cheek like a period at the end of a sentence.

Theo nodded slowly and deliberately. "Interesting, Ed. This Donald Bellport look black to you?"

"Well, not exactly, sir," Hennesey hedged. "Not on first appearance. And I was standin' pretty close to him. Detective Miller actually picked up on it. Then I noted certain features. Around the lips and nose. We checked it out. Light-skinned mother. Don't know anythin' about the father yet."

"Then this Sfk. Co. abbreviation could be referring to Suffolk County, England, and these Suffolk sheep."

"Could be," Hennesey said unsurely.

"And Dead-man's float? Any other ideas on that? Feel free to jump in here, Andrew. This is your brainchild as well, I take it."

It was the first time the lieutenant ever called Detective Miller solely by his given name.

"I know nothing about Suffolk sheep like Detective Sergeant Hennesey, Lieutenant," Miller admitted freely. "But it fits. And I do believe that whoever typed that note is sending Nelson precisely that message. Meaning that the kid is innocent. And that the killer works alone."

"Once again, this Dead-man's float?" Theo repeated.

Miller smiled. It was not a wise-guy smile that he often displayed in other meetings. It was a sad sort of smile. One of helplessness in the face of inevitability. "Simply, that whoever DN is, is going to be female and found floating facedown shortly; most likely in Suffolk County."

"Anything else?"

Miller thought for a moment before he opened his mouth. "She'll probably turn out to be mulatto, or something along those lines."

The troops surrounding the newest member of the team were staring at him as though he had two heads. Even Hennesey gave him a queer look.

"Why do you say that?" their commander questioned.

"Because the perp is somehow caught up in this black and white . . . mystique."

"Mystique?" Theo thought for a moment. "You mean like sheep being led to slaughter—suggesting Bellport's innocence?"

Miller nodded.

"And how do you think this business is all connected?"

"You mean the sheep?"

"Anything."

"I'd like to refer to my partner's notes if I may."

"Ed, give him what you got, man," Theo all but pleaded.

Hennesey padded his jacket for his most recent notes. "Don't have them with me, sir."

"Well, then give us the gist."

Ed glanced at Andrew. "I think Andy can do it justice, Lieutenant. What I mean is, he can put a face on things with the information I gave him."

"Put a face on things?"

"Yes, sir. To be honest, I thought Andy was all wet when he laid this profile on me earlier, but the more I think about it . . ."

"About what, Ed?"

"The metaphor," Ed said sheepishly.

"Metaphor?"

"Tell 'im, Andy."

"Well, Andy?" Theo pressed.

"Sure. Bellport's mother's the ewe," Detective Andrew Miller began. "His father's the ram. The killer's ninth victim is sure to be female and a passive figure like the rest. She'll most likely be of black ancestry. And like all his victims, she'll no doubt be connected to a person who the killer believes is responsible for polluting the environment."

Several in the group were taking down Miller's information as fast and as accurately as they could. Others were staring at the man in awe. One detective could not contain himself.

"I gotta go along with you on two things, Miller," he decided with a wide grin, passing his eyes over the rest of the teams. "I'll give anyone here ten-to-one odds the next victim ain't gonna be no stud, and that we'll connect her to a source responsible for pollution. But that's as far as I'd take it. This guy here," he declared, pointing an accusatory finger at Miller, "thinks he's Sigmund Freud, Carnak the Magnificent, and some kind of profiler all rolled into one!"

No one said a word or batted an eye, so Theo let the remark slide. "Let me ask you something, Andy."

"Sir?" Miller leaned forward in his seat.

"Are you suggesting that the perp is, in effect, killing off his mother when he commits these acts?"

"Yes, sir."

"I see." Theo stared down at the tiles, focusing on a single square. "Are you also suggesting that this killer sees *himself* in this young fellow that they arrested for the murder?"

"Could be, sir. But I'm not sure."

Theo nodded slowly. "And, are you further suggesting, Detective, that the person who sent this note to Nelson could possibly be of mixed blood?"

"I've strongly considered that possibility."

"Then you probably feel that this could be a turning point in the case for us. Would that be a fair assessment?"

"Yes, I believe it is, sir."

"Good. So. Here's what we're going to do rather than my handing out assignments for now. Sleep on it. Twenty minutes for those of you who are about to pass out anyhow. Not a second more. Then we're all going to come back into this room and pool our thoughts and pile on any and all new information to help land this guy in a net once and for all. Ed and Andy, hang tight. I need to talk to you."

The rest of the troops were out of their seats and heading for the door.

"Those of you who can stay high on coffee, or whatever you can cop from the narco boys next-door, more power to you. I want one of you—you," he said, pointing to the female detective, "to feed the information Ed and Andrew just shared with us into Kim's free ear while she's busy listening with the other to any fresh ideas that might surface. In the meantime, I'll call in the cavalry. Chop, chop!" he exclaimed, clapping loudly.

The woman blew by Theo like the wind.

The commanding officer turned toward Hennesey. "Ed, what's your gut telling you concerning Nelson and his family? I'd like you to speak frankly."

"Well, sir. I think the perp's after bigger fish than Dean dischargin' waste from his boat, if you want to know the truth. And that's if Dean even did the dirty deed," he clarified. "He goes out fishing, what? A dozen times a year? I don't think this fucker's standing around watchin' boats and shit drift by."

"Andrew?"

Andrew Miller looked up into the lieutenant's bloodshot eyes. The young detective shook his head. "Difficult to say, Lieutenant. Up until the Rodman woman, I'd have agreed with Ed. But killing her because Adam Rodman grandstanded before some legislators and argued against posting signs? How far behind or ahead of that action do you place polluting from a boat? I just don't know. Did Dean or his family in fact discharge overboard? Did or didn't the killer see it, if it even happened at all as Ed just said?" Miller shook his head again. "But you did the right thing erring on the side of caution, Lieutenant."

"Erring?" Theo questioned somewhat amusingly. "You mean my wasting valuable time by having Kim run down those initials and abbreviations."

Miller nodded.

"You would have handled things differently, I suppose?"

"Somewhat," Andrew Miller offered candidly.

"But not exactly."

"No, sir. Not exactly."

"You'd put the focal point on Suffolk County."

"Yes, sir."

"Suffolk County, New York? Correct? Not Suffolk County, England?" the commander half kidded.

"'Good ol' Suffolk County,' as Bo said," Miller clarified.

Theo went back to staring down at the tile. "Ed."

"Sir?"

"Ed, go tell Kim that Detective Miller would like her to shift the emphasis of her search concerning those initials and abbreviations to Suffolk County, New York, and that I concur; that is, of course, after she's sure Doreen and Dawn are safely tucked away for the night. Tomorrow I want them moved to a safe house as a precautionary measure. Andy, set it up with Dean. And tell him I said no back talk, which I don't think he'll give you 'cause he's spooked right now."

The two men left the room as Brian Archer entered it.

"Well, well, well," Theo mocked. "Glad you could finally make it, Bri. I was just going to call out the dogs. Sorry you missed—" The lieutenant suddenly reigned in the sarcasm.

Trouble deeply lined Brian's brow.

Chapter 35

McGarrett! Hawaii Five-O. That's the motherfucker's name and show, Justin recalled with a little help from an old issue of *TV Guide* found beneath a tidy stack of glossy-covered girly magazines piled high on the floor next to the toilet. *Po·lice Chief McGarrett.* The white cop stood tall—as if standing before the black figure seated on the porcelain throne.

"Caught me with my pants down, motherfucker," the cop hater cawed like a crow. *Steve McGarrett. How the fuck could I ever forget that name?* he wondered.

Log it down and lock it up forever in the memory bank, dude, 'cause ain't no nigger gonna help yo' ass out with that piece of trivia should you ever need it someday, say like on some silly-ass game show or somethin', the maverick guffawed.

'Book ' im, Danno' . . . you fuckin' fruitcake. He grinned in both cold remembrance and mild amusement, rehashing and rehearsing the story line from the dated series running through his restless mind, altering the script a bit for the sake of sheer *home* entertainment.

Well, if I be a fruitcake, Stevie, what kinda fruit do you take me for? Justin went on fatuously, summoning forth the tacit voices on command.

That's easy, Danno. I take you for a motherfucking pineapple 'cause you look like one. Justin laughed out loud.

Good Lord, Stevie. Denigrate me all you want, but you're still my Honolulu hunk. The maverick chuckled, playing out the dialogue in his head with utmost delight.

"Denigrate: to attack the reputation of," he proudly recited from memory.

Yet, Justin's favorite voice was the one he fondly called his 'second self'—his alter ego, as Monisha had termed it during her freshman year at college. Justin's voice of conscience, his mother aptly named it whenever she heard the whispers coming from his room.

Whatever people labeled it, that inner voice was truly his trusted friend.

Now, how in tarnation you ever gonna remember McGarrett's name? Huh, nigger?

"Shit, that's easy bro," Justin mused aloud, jawing away with his make-believe confidant. "I jus' think of all dem Mick cops hangin' 'round the precinct in the ol' neighborhood. Think cop, and nine outta ten of 'em's a fuckin' Mick. The one left over's a greasy wop. Irish and Italian, bro. With a token Tom thrown in the mix, nowadays," he jawed aloud with little satisfaction.

Fine! So you got Mick outta Mc, down pat. Whatchoo gonna do with Garrett, huh? I mean, what the fuck's a garrett, dude?

"Well, garrett's gotta mean somethin', bro. All names gotta mean somethin'."

Yeah? Then you tell me what, nigger.

Justin grabbed the thick, tattered paperback dictionary lying atop a white wicker hamper. "All right, but just remember that not every motherfucking word in the world is in this book, bro. Monisha showed me that for *all* the cocksuckin' words, you gotta go to one of them real fat fuckers. Thick as yo' neck. With the word *bridge* in the title. Wait. It's comin' back to me, man. Yeah, un·a·bridged. Dat be it."

Man, ya jus' can't go a fuckin' day without thinkin' or sayin' somethin' 'bout a bridge; can ya nigger?

"What's it to ya, motherfucker?"

Justin flipped through the text until he found the g's, noting the two bold lettered words serving as a guide at the top of the page in each corner, just like Monisha had taught him; then down the columns a single black digit ran, hunting for the sequence of letters until he found the word he was looking for. He had to concentrate very hard—failing first to note the second r in garret.

"Fuck. Ah, there they be: garr . . . Now for the letter e. Got it: garre . . . Almost there. There! Only one t in garret, though. But it *is* a word. I told you so, bro."

Justin double-checked the *TV Guide* to be sure there were two t's in McGarrett, just like there were two r's. Then back to and down the column his finger traveled.

"Garret. It's right here. Says, **gar·ret** (gar'it) *n.* for noun; garrret is an attic. That's it? Wait just a second, now." He looked up the word *attic* just to be sure. It took him a good minute. "Yep. A garret's an attic, all right. How about that, bro?"

Now, how're ya gonna make a picture in yo' mind, nigger, connecting McGarrett with a fucking attic?

"That's easy, motherfucker."

Yeah?

"Yeah."

So do it, nigger.

"Whenever I want to *conjure* up—howdaya like *that* five dollar word, bro?—McGarrett's name, all I hav'ta do is picture an Irish cop with a lot goin' for 'im *upstairs*. Get it?"

Oh, I get it, all right. You soundin' jus' like an Uncle Tom, boy. You paintin' some high and mighty picture-positive of a honky cop bringin' down those island boys. Hear what I'm saying, Justin Barnes?

"Oh, I hear you, bro. But I want you to hear this."

Go ahead. I's always listenin' to yo' shit. Well, ain't I, nigger?

"That's true. But you ain't heard nothin' yet."

Then lay it on me. Let's hear what you got to say.

Justin finished his business and flushed, washed his hands and reached for a razor, staring at his reflection in the mirror.

"I'm marchin' this black ass smack into Suffolk County homicide in Yaphank, and offerin' 'em my services. Maybe later on this afternoon."

Say what?

"You heard me."

Ya shitting me, or what?

"I ain't shittin' you."

Now, why you wanna go an' do a fool thing like that fo'?

"You *know* why."

Do I?

"I know you do."

So then let me hear ya say it.

"'Cause they're gonna help *me* find Monisha's killer, bro; and I'm gonna put that motherfucker down."

You bad, nigger. Badder than LeRoy Brown, Justin Barnes. Meaner than a junkyard dog, his other self sang in baritone.

"So true, bro. So fucking downright, motherfucking true."

Baddest cat in the whole damn town.

"Got that right, motherfucker."

Got but one question 'fore ya go.

"Shoot."

What 'bout that guy they got on network news? Donald Bellport. Some say he's the one.

"Scapegoat, sure as shootin'. *My* sources tell me he never left the sticks."

You jus' keep in mind what Monisha told you 'bout yo' mouth, nigger.

"What's that?"

You know damn well, what.

"So, remind me anyhow."

You want to improve yo' vocabulary two hundred percent, nigger? You want to make some kind of impression? You shit-can that trashy talk. You don't go 'round sayin' **motherfucker** *every other word, nigger.*

"How 'bout I just attach it to the end of my sentences, every now and then? Better than ending it with a *prep·o·si·tion*. No?"

No, nigger. That won't do at all.

"Well, I'm tryin', bro."

Yeah, you're tryin'.

"Well, I am, my man."

Yeah, like you was gonna know all yo' states and capitals by the time you got back home. Remember dat?

"Well, I was up to Kansas when that cop spooked me in Virginia, motherfucker."

That ain't even a third the list, nigger. You got thirty-four to go. So c'mon. Topeka for Kansas is where ya left off. You're up to Kentucky, now.

"Right, bro. Where horseshoes are lucky."

Well, go on.

"Where I picture two of 'em together—a pair of horseshoes—to form the letter m."

Might mix dat up with an upside down **m**, *nigger. Seeing it as a* **w.** *Maybe see it as a double* **uu**. *Jus' like you mix up the order of yo' other letters sometimes. You know. Reading* **ew** *backwards so you see* **we**.

"Oh, yeah?"

Yeah.

"But not upside down, bro. I'm not that fucked up."

No?

"No."

Yo' fo 'gettin' in school they labeled yo' ass dyslexic.

"Wasn't in school long enough for them to label shit."

Stop stallin', nigger. Capital of Kentucky.

"The capital of Kentucky is Frankfurt," Justin announced, reaching for and checking the atlas upon the pile of magazines.

Wow! How'd yo'do dat, nigger?

"Told ya. I put two horseshoes side by side to form the letter **m**."

What's the m stand fo?

"**Motherfuckers**, bro. Noun, plural. Besides cops, I hate horses, cops on horses, and motherfuckin' hot dogs. Hate dat motherfuckin' game of horseshoes, too. Therefore, the capital of Kentucky—where horseshoes are lucky, but only when shown with the heel calks pointed up, like a capital U or double UU you see hangin' over doorways in homes and barns, bro—be Frankfurt. Get it? Calks pointed downward, like a lowercase n or m for **n**o good **m**otherfucker, means yo' ass in fo' a world of shit," he jived and jawed, recalling fondly how Monisha had made him focus and concentrate, teaching him little tricks like that in order to keep those topsy-turvy uppercase and lowercase m's and n's and u's and w's somewhat orderly in his disordered brain.

You're incorrigible, nigger.

A queer sort of smile formed on Justin's lips, remembering the sexy, sassy college freshman and one of her many new ten-dollar words. *Incorrigible. Justin Barnes, you're incorrigible,* she'd say with an *at·ti·tude.*

In·cor·ri·gi·ble.

Justin counted the syllables in his head. He did not need five fingers. Not when it came to numbers. With numbers he was pretty damn good, he knew. Never did he transpose figures— only some of the letters of the alphabet, every now and then. Rarely did he invert those troublesome four characters; that is, if he concentrated with all his might. He may have been dyslexic, but he was not dumb like some of his teachers had told him to his face. Dumb like in stupid. Not like in *deaf* and *dumb* just because he never opened his mouth until the end of second grade.

Chapter 36

S taring uneasily at Archer, Theo knew from the detective's expression that whatever news Brian carried, it was not going to be good.

"What?" Theo barked.

"We've got ourselves a situation."

"What kind of situation?" he demanded.

"Broderick Nash of Sag Harbor," Brian began. "Nash Bottled Water Company on Route 25 in Riverhead."

"Never heard of it."

"His daughter's missing. Diane Nash."

"Jesus, Joseph and Mary. D.N.," Theo said quietly.

"I just spoke to Dean and Kim. Doreen and Dawn are fine."

"Why didn't we pick up on this earlier, Bri?" Theo asked angrily, starting to pace the squad room floor. "Tell me."

"Two reasons," Brian began in explanation. "One, they're a brand-new show in town. That's why you never heard of them. They're an offshoot of Pine Barren's Pure. Two, we're looking hard at polluters: companies, agencies and utilities that purportedly *contaminate* our air, land and water. Not necessarily those who are above suspicion because they *purify* the latter. Not a bottled water company, for Christ's sake." Brian dropped his exhausted body into a seat.

"We fucked up big time," Theo said.

Brian shook his head in the negative. "Even if we had plugged into bottled water companies sooner, we wouldn't have come up with Nash, his company, or his daughter. The company just hit the street, Theo," he reiterated. "Anyhow, Kim *had* run and just now ran Pine Barren's Pure for a lead. Nothing. Nothing negative on record regarding Nash Bottled Water Company. Off record, there's a rumor. Accident at the plant. Some contaminated bottles of water supposedly hit the shelves of a supermarket."

"Contaminated with what?"

"Hydraulic fluid from the bottle capping process. Kim's looking into it. So far, we got zip on confirmation."

"How long has the daughter been missing?"

"The father's not too sure. She was gone when he got back from town. Maybe several hours. He waited an hour before he reported her missing."

"What? That's ridicu—"

"She's a cripple, Theo. She couldn't walk from here to there."

"Who's got this, Bri?"

"At this point? Everyone. Feds, state, all the locals. We're pulling units from Nassau and Queens, as we speak. It's like the marines have landed. We've got people on land, in the air, and on the sea."

"Sea?"

"Well, at least the harbor area and bay. Father and daughter live on the water. We got a missing boat. Broderick's. A sixteen-foot canoe."

"Wonderful. You want to tell me who back there took charge in the few minutes I left you people alone? As if I couldn't guess."

Brian managed a weary smile. "Dean and Kim are at the helm. It's just a question of who's really second in command back there . . . but it certainly isn't you at the moment, Lieutenant. Not to worry, though."

"I'm telling you, that woman's after my job," Theo said absently. "We're going to get this prick, Bri," he swore. "Fifteen minutes, we all meet back here to coordinate our efforts."

"Gee, and I was going to ask you if I could grab some z's," Detective Brian Archer said half kiddingly.

"In your dreams, buddy," the lieutenant mumbled through a yawn. "In your dreams."

Chapter 37

The face of the wall clock displayed two types of time. Its pair of black hands displayed 6:00 p.m.—civilian time. A single red hand marked 1800 hours, indicating six hours past the noon hour—military-speak. The desk sergeant looked up at the man standing across from him.

"Help you?"

No, motherfucker. "I can help you."

The sergeant fixed his eyes on the strapping figure before him. "How's that?"

"Monisha Washington, man."

"She missing?"

"More 'long the line o' *bein'* missed," Justin Barnes said straight off, setting two closed fists like dark mugs down upon the counter in front of him.

The sergeant shook his head. "Not following you."

You followin' the motherfucking news, asshole? "Monisha Washington, man! Woman up in Michigan, who got herself murdered."

"Michigan?"

"Yeah, Michigan." *Capital be Lansing, cocksucker.* "Sault Ste. Marie, Michigan. College girl."

The cop looked at Justin as though he were *real* trouble. "Why are you asking about a woman murdered up in Michigan?"

"You don't know 'bout that, man?" Justin looked pissed.

The uniform slowly shook his head.

"A state trooper down in Virginia even knows 'bout the case. But you haven't got a clue 'bout what I'm sayin' here," he said in disbelief.

"What *is it* that you want, mister?"

"What I want is fo' yo' to find me one of dem suits that I can speak to 'bout all those murders."

"All what murders?"

The civilian's eyes burned deeply into the cop's. He considered yanking the man up and over the counter, thinking that he just might do it on GP—General Principle. Suddenly, Justin turned around as he heard footsteps coming down a flight of stairs. "Hey! Yo! Over here, Detective," he called out to a well-dressed figure passing through an open set of glass doors. "Got a minute?"

The man immediately marched up to the maverick, sizing him up and down, glancing across at the desk sergeant before turning his full attention back to the tall civilian.

"You a homicide detective?" Justin inquired politely.

"What is it?" the cop responded curtly, nodding arrogantly in the affirmative.

"Ooo. Got yo'self an at·ti·tude, I see."

"We're very busy. Got a name?"

"Got a mama, too. Can we sit down somewhere and talk?"

Detective Miller shot a second look back to the duty officer.

The uniform rolled his eyes at the ceiling and shook his head. "Something about a murder up in Michigan."

"State your business, sir," Detective Miller ordered.

"'Sir,' you say?" Justin liked that a lot. "State my business." He smiled and nodded, showing off two rows of pearly whites.

"He was rambling on about a state trooper down in Virginia," the desk sergeant elaborated.

"Why don't you start at the beginning?" Miller suggested impatiently.

"At the beginning," Justin echoed. "Sure. From the bottom up. Jus' fo' you, Mister Homicide Man: Florida, Maryland, New York, Maine and Michigan," he counted off on his fingers. *In another month, I'll give you the names and spellings of all of their capital cities, too.* "How's that?"

Miller nodded knowingly. "You're Justin Barnes, aren't you?"

Justin was only a little bit surprised. "That'd be me, my man. Understand you fellas was lookin' fo' me. So, now, I come 'round lookin' fo' you," he finished explaining with a wide grin.

"And what can we do for you, Mr. Barnes?"

"Well, sir. It's like I told the sergeant, here. It's what I can do fo' ya'all."

"You have certain information concerning your cousin's murder? Is that why you're here?"

Justin shook his head. "*You* have certain in·fo·ma·tion. I have the wherewithal."

Miller smiled condescendingly. "Wherewithal?"

Justin did not like the man's look or tone. "That's what I jus' fuckin' said."

"You watch your mouth."

"You watch yo' at·ti·tude."

Miller stood looking up at Barnes for an uncomfortable moment before walking over to the counter. "Sergeant," he said in a voice loud enough for the civilian to hear and hang on every word.

"Yes, Detective?"

"Let him log in, Nick. Then make him out a pass. If he gives you any lip, escort him the hell out of here. The slightest hint of trouble, lock his ass up." Andrew Miller gestured to a stocky colleague standing just outside the Pistol License Bureau across the hall. "Get Frohnhoefer over there to assist you if you have to," Miller instructed —although the detective instinctively knew that it would take a half a dozen Frohnhoefers to get Barnes out the door or into a cell if push ever came to shove. "I'll be back in a few minutes and take Mr. Barnes up," he concluded, leaving the lobby without so much as looking back at the black man.

"Mighty white of you, Detective," Justin called after him.

The public information officer faced an open black book before the civilian, grabbed a sheet of red and white peel-and-stick visitor passes, then handed over a pen. "Fill out the information in the log; I'll take care of the pass."

Justin looked down at the book, then over at the Visitor Pass sheet.

"You got a problem with this?" the sergeant asked huffily.

Justin shook his head. "I got me a problem with the world the way it is."

"Last name first."

"Barnes. No middle name. Justin. Like *just in* the nick of time, Nick."

"Spell Barnes."

"Ooo, I see you have trouble with spelling, too," Justin jawed, obliging the officer while very slowly and neatly printing his NAME and ADDRESS—silently sounding out while struggling with the syllables of the adjacent word: DESTINATION.

"Here. Stick this on your jacket," the man told him, handing Justin the pass.

Justin noted that above his name and date on the VISITOR PASS, the sergeant printed the word HOMICIDE. "Ah." He displayed the sticker-like badge above the breast pocket of his five-hundred-dollar plaid sports jacket before completing the information. "DES·TIN·A·TION, Ban·gor, Maine," he sang so sillily from the song, *King of the Road.* DESTINATION. Homicide, he printed carefully. TIME IN 6:05 p.m.

Off to Justin's right stood a small police museum, which was closed at that hour. The civilian was amused.

Now, who in their right mind would ever want to pay a visit to a place like this? he questioned thoughtfully, walking over to and placing his hands and nose against the dimly lit cold glass. He spied a police officer's badge and pen that had saved a cop's life in a shootout some years ago. Two of the three numbers on the silver shield were bent inward; the pen was cracked in the middle . . . just along its edge . . . before the days of Kevlar vests, Justin presupposed. It was one of the reasons why he would take point-blank aim at a cop's forehead, rather than the center of his chest or back . . . if the situation ever warranted itself again. Vest or no vest. Then again, it was simply the way the maverick had been trained when he was but ten. *Head shots almost always prove fatal. Heart and lung shots leave a margin for error.*

The Panther leader had taught him well.

Chapter 38

Diane Nash did not question why Malcolm wanted to leave the area of the boathouse. The paraplegic did not even object to his suggesting they borrow her father's canoe so that Malcolm and she could truly be alone and tour the bay together. As a matter of fact, she felt long overdue for an outing, as her father was far too busy with his new company to think or do much of anything else lately. Curiously, though, Diane could not understand why Malcolm was suddenly behaving so . . . differently. Then again, he never ever told her she had a pretty face—or anything else to indicate that he was the least bit interested. *Could it be that he is shy around girls?* she wondered. Perhaps she *had* grown up some since the last time he visited, Diane told herself. *How long has it been since his last visit? A little over a year.* Maybe she *was* maturing into a good-looking woman like her mother, God rest her soul, Diane smiled fondly.

Diane knew she would never be as beautiful as her mom. But she also knew that she had other fine attributes. A nice personality for one. Everyone told her that. Everyone who mattered, anyway. There was, of course, her dear grandmother; her mom's mom. A woman who always told it like it is. A feisty lady who spoke her mind. Veracity to a fault. Diane's overprotective father had trouble dealing with the candid and common-sense *advisements* the spunky eighty-six-year-old woman would invariably deliver at the dining room table on her weekly visitations. "*Wise up—*" was the woman's favorite expression, "*—and give that girl her space, Broderick.*"

Her tutors, too, told her she had a winning personality of the kindred kind. Miss Congeniality, she was labeled by both peers and professionals alike: her physical therapist; even her father-confessor— who would never ever tell a lie—she laughed inwardly. Not then; not now. Never ever. Not on his or her life, Diane smiled happily, having enjoyed Father K's visit earlier that morning. He had stopped by for tea and a little chat, leaving moments before Malcolm arrived unexpectedly.

Where was Malcolm taking her?

It was a beautiful afternoon with a light breeze coming out of the northwest. Diane was smiling at the world around her as the two of them glided through the water—like a lengthy, oddly colored swan, she mused gayly. She was sitting facing forward. Malcolm sat behind her in the center seat, paddling solo toward the east. Diane felt like an Indian princess . . . recalling one of her favorite epic poems: *The Song of Hiawatha*. Malcolm was her Ojibwa hero. The young woman brushed the hair away from her pretty face.

Diane knew she had lovely hair, too. Thick and long and shiny. A healthy crop. Shoulder length. She rarely wore it like the Indian women whose styles she most admired; that is, tied back or pinned up high in ornamental braids and combs. Diane refrained from doing so simply because she was very self-conscious of her tiny, pointed ears.

Still and all, Diane had another thing going for her. Something she did not flaunt. Her body. She was comfortable with it. At least from the waist up, anyhow. Diane did not just sit around in that upstairs room each night and ruminate. No way. Nohow. She worked out. Hard. Diligently. Dignifiedly. The determined paraplegic worked passionately at building herself *up*. And maybe one day, God willing, *up and out*. Out of that horrible wheelchair. Diane had good upper body strength. She was a cripple from the waist down. No denying that. "*You'll never walk again*," the doctors flatly told her. Then again, it was her own priest, Father K, who had twice administered last rites, which he went on to explain was nowadays called "*anointing the sick, Dee*," which she did not want or need to know at the time—regardless of just how sick she really was. Diane hated euphemisms, preferring the term *last rites* because of its ring of honesty and finality, having feebly, yet angrily, instructed Father K to get on with it—insisting that he perform the sacrament according to tradition, but with one exception. The dying teenager watched anxiously as the prelate literally touched her five senses with the oil: her eyelids, nostrils, lips, palms and elf-like ears—symbolically in the sign of the cross. Touching of the feet was part of the holy unction, too. However, as her ability to walk was taken from her—the legs therefore dead anyhow—she forbade it, determinedly showing sheer defiance in the face of God; for while still on Earth, she would make her own rules, she swore. Silly perhaps. But Diane Nash had her maternal grandmother's resolve.

On her second go-around with death, Diane merely told Father K, as she affectionately called him, to get on with the ritual. She did not really *tell* him, but sort of gestured because of her utterly weakened condition. And, of course, he did so. Ceremoniously, to be sure. First, the face, then down along the body to her palms. Finally, back up and over to her ears. *Down and across like a crossword puzzle,* the dying young girl vividly recalled . . . smiling peacefully . . . not actually seeing his hand touching her senses the last time out . . . but clearly feeling his fingers across her face and palms.

And by God's good grace, Diane miraculously bounced back. Not quickly. But rather like a ball being delivered in slow motion from the pitcher's mound . . . over the course of several seasons . . . her father's form of therapy . . . indefatigably lobbing a million missiles from fifteen feet away . . . across home plate: her ringed stump of a seat situated eighteen inches off the ground between two gorgeous perfumed gardens . . . spring, summer and fall . . . slamming softballs out to sixty yards . . . her father chasing after them tirelessly during a thousand afternoons . . . inevitably returning to the mound to deliver pitch after weariless pitch until his dear daughter was . . . *resurrected,* which the doctors and priest classified as nothing short of a miracle. Perhaps it was. Regardless, from that day forward, her body, or at least the upper half of it, became Diane's temple of worship.

From her waistline up, she had transformed herself into a powerful machine. Nothing grotesque or ungainly like rippling muscles seen on most women bodybuilders, but rather a trim and well-defined torso: firm stomach and lower back muscles, stalwart shoulders and neck. What rested upon it, she exercised, too. Outwardly, as well as from within. An organ of thought and reason that would have done Socrates proud. Looks? Certainly not a raving beauty by any stretch of the imagination, for no matter how often she exercised her facial muscles—contorting by elongating them before the mirror—could she rival those Indian maidens' features . . . women she considered the most beautiful in all the world. No, ma'am. For her tiny mouth would forever remain a perfect oval; an embouchure, she would giggle . . . much like a musician of a wind instrument readying one's lips before the mouthpiece.

Where in God's name was Malcolm taking her, she wondered anew, feeling the force from his powerful strokes across the bay, the paddle knifing through the water on a sharp turn to the south.

Carefree, she had allowed him to wheel her across the lovely manicured lawn and along the garden's path. Past her tree stump seat. Past a plot of blue star junipers that she alone had spaced and planted earlier in the week. Shunning and shooing away the burly gardener who insisted he at least dig the required two-and-a-half-foot hole for her. She being determined to do it all by herself from her wheelchair. Stretching and working forward from the waist. Moving the shovel through the earth with *shoulder power*. Making the necessary hole without anyone's aid. Setting the shrub's rootball solidly down into the earth. Filling it in with soil mix and mulch. Building in the basin. And, finally, the fun part. Watering her precious prize. She had planted a dozen such star-shaped evergreens in the course of several days without a stitch of assistance from anyone. Diane was proud of her achievement—pleased that the hard work was over and that she was not a sweaty mess when greeting her two visitors who happened by that morning.

Father K's visit was anything but a surprise, for he would manage to come by monthly for a chat. Malcolm's appearance, however, was totally unexpected—when she suddenly looked up and saw him standing there—truly overjoyed that she was already showered. All fresh and clean like a pretty perfumed flower—busy working on her pansies and violas in the shaded section of the prodigious property. Child's play.

Malcolm had parked her wheelchair alongside the boathouse and carried her down to the water's edge. Indian princess that she was, she pretended. Carefully setting his maiden into the canoe, facing forward, he helped her with a life vest for safety's sake. She was positively surprised and thrilled when he had given her a tender kiss upon the forehead. She could have died happily right then and there. With or without last rites, she entertained with a smile.

Malcolm covered a good distance before she realized where they were headed. To a stretch of beach across the harbor. Across and to the east.

Deserted.

Dead ahead.

Toward a tall stand of pretty pines.

She looked back over her shoulder. The high stone wall bordering her home had long since disappeared from sight.

"Malcolm."

Malcolm kept his mouth shut.

"Malcolm. By the time we get over there, it's going to be time to head back."

Malcolm was paddling and staring straight ahead as if looking past or clear through her.

Setting her palms flat upon the narrow gunnels, she carefully lifted her body off the edge of the cane seat, twisting herself and her dead legs completely around to face him—like a gymnast upon a vaulting or pommel horse—being exceedingly cautious not to rock and tip the canoe. Settled, she waved a hand three feet from his handsome face.

Malcolm began to smile.

"Well, that's an improvement," she said, smiling back winsomely. "Don't want me to help you paddle? All right. Don't want to talk? Okay. Then I'll just sit here and keep myself entertained by looking straight ahead at you. How's that?"

"Fine."

"How come you don't want me to paddle?"

"I want you to sit and enjoy."

"I meant to ask you earlier. Why are you wearing those gloves? The cap I can understand."

"Cold."

"Malcolm, it's sixty-some degrees. It's one of the nicest days we've had in quite awhile."

"I always feel cold when I'm on or near the water, Diane."

"You? A lobsterman?" she asked in disbelief.

"Yes." *But I'm so much more than that, you twit—as the world will one day learn.*

"Is that why your hands are usually in your pockets?" she asked with a scolding, playful grin. "Last time I saw you with Daddy, you were walking the grounds with your hands stuck in your pockets all afternoon. That was around this time of year, too. One year ago, in fact. The year before that was sometime in July," she let him know she was keeping track. "Shoulders scrunched up to your neck. Thin blood,

Malcolm?" she questioned warmly. "Poor circulation, probably. You *couldn't* have been cold then, were you?"

"You live on the water, Diane. You're used to it. I worked both on and in it for too many years, I guess."

"Then you must be freezing now, no? Or is it just your hands?"

Malcolm did not answer.

"Maybe if you put them in my pockets," she teased. "Bet they'd warm right up. What do you think?"

"Probably."

"Malcolm."

"What?"

"You've hardly said a word since we left. Is there something you'd like to talk about?"

Malcolm nodded.

"What then?"

"What I want to talk about, you really don't want to hear. Every time I talk about it, you change the subject."

Diane shook her head and smiled. "You mean the bottled water business?"

"That's exactly what I mean."

"Malcolm. Look at me."

Malcolm looked at her, then quickly looked away—putting more of a bite of the blade against the water. Alternating his strokes smoothly. Powerfully.

"I don't know a blessed thing about the bottled water industry. I truly don't. But if you want to talk about the bloody business, I'll listen. All right?"

"I was trying to tell you about Naya, before."

"The bottled water company in Québec."

"Mirabel."

"2500 Naya Road," she threw out.

"That's right!" Malcolm said, surprised.

"See? I listen, Malcolm. It's just that I don't have very much to say on the subject. Gardening I can talk about. Flowers and shrubs. Water? That's what I shower my little prizes with to make them grow strong and healthy," she let follow with a pleasing smile. "That and organic food. No chemicals."

"That's very good, Diane."

"Especially living on the water."

"It's a very delicate ecosystem we have."

"I absolutely agree."

"But most people don't seem to care."

"Some people do."

"Like who?"

"Well, like my father for one."

Malcolm wanted to throw up.

"Malcolm! What's the matter?"

"YOUR FATHER'S A FAKE, PHONY, FRAUD, Diane." The veins along Malcolm's neck stuck out like vines strangling an upright bough.

Diane brought the tips of ten fingers to her frightened face.

"Your father couldn't give a good goddamn about pure water, the environment, or his dead wife."

"What are you talking about, Malcolm?" Two tears started down her pretty face, paralleling her button nose and full lips. "What are you saying?"

"What am I saying? I'm saying that your mother died of breast cancer and that people like your father are to be held responsible and accountable. That's what I'm saying."

Malcolm picked up speed and propelled the canoe through the water like a torpedo targeted for a beachhead—dead reckoning—shooting the vessel expertly between two protruding slick black rocks before running it up onto the pebbly, sandy strand.

Diane flew back off the hickory-framed cane seat like a headpin.

Malcolm got out and pulled her roughly from the bow.

"Want to hear what he did at the company and tried to cover up?"

Diane was shaking her head for a different reason. Disbelieving his behavior and sudden cruelty.

"Well, you're *going* to hear it; like it or not. You're going to hear what the head of Nash Bottled Water Company did that Naya would never do. He lied to the health department when a customer complained about his quart of water tasting and even feeling slippery. Slippery, Diane. So, of course, the department ran tests and discovered that the bottle of water contained hydraulic fluid. Your father claimed that the customer added the fluid himself in order to ruin him overnight. Your daddy wasn't even in the new place a month. Know how the hydraulic fluid happened to get in there? Every time one of his machines put a cap on the bottle, it received a shot of oil. Your father, Diane, corrected the problem, of course, but denied that there ever was a problem to begin with—surreptitiously ordering a new part from the manufacturer before the sleuths arrived—hoping everything would be hunky-dory and that the trouble would go away. But it didn't. The cover-up backfired. The authorities knew that the new part had recently been replaced. But Broderick fought and *bought* his way back. The following week they found the toxic chemical in his wonderful water once again. What do you think about that?"

"If what you're saying is true, which I don't know that it is, do you think my father did it on purpose? Do you?" she decried.

"Diane! That's not the point. The point is he lied and tried to cover up his mistakes. And the government let him buy his way out. Twice. To make matters even worse, the bottled water that he's selling under his own label is the exact same water as Pine Barren's Pure, bottled in Riverhead, too—tapped from one of the wells owned by the Suffolk County Water Authority, which is spitting distance from Suffolk County Community College. What's wrong with this picture, Diane? Tell me."

"What do you have in that suitcase you brought, Malcolm?" she demanded, pointing aft of the seat in the canoe, knowing that something was terribly wrong.

Malcolm reached for and held up the black leather case. "In this?"

She nodded from her helpless position upon the cold, wet, pebble-strewn beach.

"Some rope. Duct tape. An empty spool of fish line. A few yards of surgical tubing. Disposable gloves. Oh, and a gallon of hydraulic fluid. Brake fluid, actually. Why?"

Diane was crying and planting an angry fist in the sand. "You're him. Aren't you?"

"Him? Who?"

Diane could just about get her words out. "The one . . . who's . . . ." She was sobbing uncontrollably, now. ". . . who's been . . . *murdering* all those women. Oh, Malcolm."

"Yes, I'm sorry for you that I am that person," he said so sadly. "Now, please. Don't make this any harder than it has to be."

"*Has to be?*" she questioned, practically mixing in a laugh.

Malcolm nodded. "Come on, now." He started to help her up.

Diane gave her hand, but then suddenly grabbed for and toppled the canoe. A paddle came flying out of its cavity; its handle only inches away. In one swift, fluid motion, she lifted and swung the implement as Malcolm scrambled toward her. She caught him squarely and solidly across the bridge of the nose with the edge of the wooden blade.

Malcolm let out a horrifying scream.

From a sitting position, Diane deftly drew back the bladed board as she would a baseball bat, intent on delivering a devastating blow. But as the batter was about to execute the blow to end all blows on that dimming afternoon, the pitcher released a handful of sand that caught the cripple full in the face, blinding her as she swung wildly, missing her target by a foot.

Diane immediately rolled away, then came up pivoting on her rump. Her weapon held out defensively. She could barely see.

He came from behind and brutally bludgeoned the back of her head with the flat part of the shorter, laminated cherry and ash paddle, splitting the blade in two before he stopped. Down she went. Flat on her face. He could have used its broken edge like a hatchet, or the handle as a hammer. But he didn't want to finish her off just yet. Not like that. In the end, he wanted her daddy to know that she had suffered greatly. To visualize the moment of her death. Malcolm would get that message across perfectly. Broderick Nash would think twice before ever acting irresponsibly again, the madman promised himself.

He dragged Diane's limp form from the shoreline, pulling her by a bloody fistful length of crimson coal-black curly hair. Into the cool, tall pines he hauled her, pitching the unconscious cripple down like a rag doll—upon a strip of barren earth—then returned to the canoe.

Malcolm tossed his belongings and the one good paddle back into the Kevlar shell, along with the larger broken pieces of wood. Next, he dragged the craft back toward the pines no differently than he had trailed her body across the sand and stone. Eerily, with each step, the tapered end of the canoe sounded steadily, scoring the stone and sand as it scraped along the scarred bottom before he removed and hid the whole of the yellow aramid frame from sight. Breathlessly, Malcolm turned and saw that the tide was ebbing and would soon take with it the smaller pieces of debris, covering any and all telltale signs.

The serial killer smiled satisfactorily.

Chapter 39

"Let me see if I understand you correctly," Detective Andrew Miller said, leaning back in his seat, arms folded across a long-sleeved linen shirt and matching tie. "You want us to use you as *bait*? Is that what you're saying?"

Justin Barnes nodded. "Yes."

"How?"

"You da Man. *How* is up to you."

Miller smiled appreciatively but shook his head. "First off, I'm not the case detective. Secondly—"

"So why da fuck am I wastin' my time witchoo?" Barnes blurted out angrily.

"I told you about that mouth of yours, *boy*," Miller warned, unfolding his arms and sitting forward in his seat.

"Yeah, an' I tol' you 'bout yo' *at·ti·tude*. So we even. Now, let's cut da bullshit an' figure this thing out together, else I'm gonna do dis *thang* alone."

"You won't be doing anything from a cell, Mr. Barnes."

"Yeah? You keep threatenin' me wit' dis cell. And who gonna put me in there, motherfucker? You?" Justin gave a little laugh. "You tell me the charge. *Pro·fan·i·ty*, Mister *Po·lice·man*? What's 'at carry? One to five? You gonna tell the judge I came in here to offer my services, or you gonna trump up some phony fuckin' charge? Huh?"

Miller remained as cool as the weather outside. He even smiled. "So, then. Let me talk *your* kind of language, P.I. *Spade*," the cop said calmly. "So that you'll understand exactly."

Justin leaned into Miller's desk and formed two upright fists like bookends, placing them at each corner of the detective's desk. "Say what, whitey?"

"That late model Cadillac parked out front. Blue. That be yours? License plate number, AXE 113. Huh?"

"So?"

"So, I got a sawbuck says you're in *pos·ses·sion*, Mr. Barnes. Not on your person. But in that trunk."

Barnes laughed. "You blowin' smoke." No drugs. No guns. He had delivered everything. The car was clean, he knew.

Miller shook his head. "I took Lance with me for a short walk over to your vehicle before. He lit his front paws and nose on the back of that trunk like he'd found liver. Either you have or had contraband in that trunk, or a sawbuck's yours." Miller reached back into his pants pocket, withdrew his wallet, removed a ten dollar bill, then slid it across the desk between Justin's two big mitts. "Narco boys can tell us what's what in a matter of minutes. I'm apologizing for them and the dog beforehand if they just happen to cause any damage—make any scratches or chip the paint. Your recourse is to sue the department if we're careless or wrong."

Bluffin' motherfucker. But Barnes did not want to take the chance. Maybe a packet *had* fallen behind the spare and disappeared into the well on the last delivery, although he strongly doubted it.

Justin grinned confidently. "And who's gonna open up the trunk? Not me, motherfucker. Less you got a warrant, which I know you don't."

"Emergency Services will open up your trunk, Barnes. You see, Lance does double-duty around here. Narcotics and bombs. Never know how his tail's a-waggin' means what," Miller explained with a straight face. "Can't fuck around wasting time if Lance thinks there are explosives in that trunk of yours. Your call, Mr. Barnes."

Manipulatin' bluff-ass motherfucker, he fumed.

I tol' you so, nigger. It's dat motherfuckin' mouth o' yours gonna be yo' downfall. Don't say I didn't warn ya.

"Whatchoo want, Miller?"

"What I want, Barnes, is for you to take your civilian ass the hell out of that chair and leave police work to us. I'll pass along your offer to the detective handling this, but I wouldn't hold my breath. That about wraps it up." Miller made a head gesture to two detectives, three desks over.

Justin pushed back his chair, then slowly got up. "Better be no motherfuckin' scratches on that car. Hear?"

"Good day, Mr. Barnes. Oh, and I do like your do-rag. Looks good on you."

Justin reached up and peeled the sheer-black nylon cap from his skull, tossing it on the detective's desk. "Souvenir, chump."

"Thanks. I'll be sure to toss it to Lance so he gets to know you a little better. Never know what he'll turn up."

"You do that."

"And don't bother signing out, stud. Fellas here will escort you to the door."

Two husky undercover narcotics cops stood before the maverick.

Justin Barnes turned and sashayed down the stairs and out of the building with his tail between his legs.

Yo' lucky ya even walkin' upright. Hear me, nigger?

"Mo' than one way o' skinnin' a cat, bro," Justin said to no one present. "Mistake was I be talkin' to da flunky instead o' The Man. Quote. 'You got to talk to the head, not the feet, if you want to move mountains.' Unquote. Monisha Washington. Forgot one of her most important lessons, is all. Won't happen again."

Don't know when to quit. Do ya?

"Quit? Word ain't part of my *vo·cab·u·lary*, bro."

Chapter 40

As the sun was setting, Diane Nash lay playing possum. Praying to God Almighty that Malcolm would leave her for dead. What else could she do? Scream? No one would hear her, she knew.

"Sit up, Diane. Do it, now!"

Diane lay as still as stone, locking her breath tightly in her lungs.

Malcolm came over with his suitcase and gave her a hard boot in the ribs through the orange padded life jacket.

The frightened young woman expelled a sudden burst of air and started crying again.

"I said, sit *up*."

She sat up shivering.

"Cold? Maybe you want to put your hands in *my* pockets," he tormented, giving birth to a hideous grin.

"Why do you wa-want to hurt me like this, Malcolm? I had a cr-crush on you ever since I was a kid." She was sobbing bitterly. "I thought you li-liked me."

"Oh, I like you well enough, I guess. It's your father that I don't particularly care for. It's your father who has to pay."

Diane shook her head. "No, Mal-Malcolm. You don't like w-women. That's why you're doing all this. Who hurt you so ba-badly in life? Tell me. Some old girlfriend? Your mother? A teacher in s-school, or an aunt? Who? Because that's what this is all about. Isn't it?"

Malcolm shook his head. "It's all about the pollution of our air and water and the devastation in between, Diane. It's all about our planet. The planet's dying, bitch." Malcolm kept touching the bridge of his nose. "You hurt me. Good thing for you I'm not bleeding, you fucking cunt."

"Malcolm. You're sick." She touched the back of her head and showed him her bloody hand. "*I'm* bleeding. Do you s-see what you did to me? Do you know what you did to that little girl in Maine? Why would you do that to a child if you weren't sick?"

"Shut up."

Malcolm started removing the items from his bag.

"It's about your mother. Isn't it, Malcolm?"

"I said, shut up!"

"You already sh-shut me up once when I asked you about her last summer. When you *really* stuck your hands deep down into your pockets. Remember that? Bet you were *freezing* then. Weren't you?" Diane was starting to get a grip on herself and the situation.

Malcolm came over to her with tape and rope. "Put out your hands."

Diane shook her head. "No."

He wanted to kick her teeth in right then and there. But he needed them to lock the spool tightly into place.

"Listen to me, Malcolm!" She knew that reasoning was her only chance. She eyed the plastic gallon container of dark pink fluid, the length of pale yellow tubing and the empty spool. "Please. Listen to me good."

Malcolm put down the rope and peeled off a section of tape.

"You can find and get help. I can help you if you let me. Please, Malcolm. The police are going to fi-find you. You can't get away with this forever. If you give yourself up—"

"Why would I want to give myself up?"

"Let me finish. Please. I have a plan."

"I have a plan, too, Diane."

"Not like mine. I can *save* you."

Malcolm smiled.

"No, I can! I know a lot about the criminal courts. Our judicial system. I read everything, Malcolm. I know how things work."

"You do?"

"I honestly and truly do. Just hear me out. Okay?"

Malcolm removed the cap from the container and screwed on another through which he partly inserted the tubing, sealing it off with the tape. He turned the plastic bottle around so that the label was facing her.

She stared at it for what seemed an eternity.

NASH BOTTLED WATER COMPANY.

"Think he'll get the message, Diane?"

"If you're found guilty by reason of insanity, Malcolm— Are you listening to me?"

"I'm listening."

Diane began her plea again. "If you're found guilty by reason of insanity, they'll put you in a—" don't say *mental* "—hospital until you're better. And you will be better, Malcolm. I promise. I'll write and come to see you as often as I can. I swear it!" she lied. "On my mother's grave." *Please forgive me, Mom.* "Once you're better, they *have* to let you go. It's the *law*, Malcolm. I read about it all the time. I can quote you passage and verse. They've *got* to let you *go*." That part was certainly true enough, she shivered. "I'll stand by you every step of the way. I give you my word."

"You can't *stand* at all, Diane. You're a cripple. Remember?" he said so cruelly.

Diane wept bitterly. "I'll testify in court how I saw the br-breakdown coming, yet refused to s-see the signs. I'll tell them you came to me when it was too late. How morose and remorseful you were and *are*. How you couldn't help yourself and pleaded with me to help you—telling me that you would take your own life rather than take another soul."

"I killed eight females, Diane. I'm afraid you're number nine."

"It doesn't ha-have to be this way," she bawled. "We can get through this thing together. You and me. You told me I was pretty, Malcolm. That I had a pretty face. Why do y-you want to hurt me? I would love you and make us a happy home. We were this far away," she showed him, spacing her hands but a foot apart.

Malcolm reached down, then roughly took and placed her trembling hands together, wrapping the wrists with tape.

She was crying hysterically.

Had God led her to His threshold not once but twice only to be struck down, *now*, by this lunatic? Had He? Was it not enough for Him to take her legs out from under her as she was approaching puberty— putting her at death's door for a third time just for the *fun* of it? Was He as sick and sadistic as Malcolm? Or was this His *ultimate* test? To look down upon a cripple and see how she would and *did* perform in the penultimate hour with a paddle in her hand before a final go-around? Is that what He wanted from her? Was *this* His grand design? Was that the *true* test for this child of God? To defend her precious life with her own two bare *taped* hands?

She was never so frightened or furious.

"I still have sand in my eyes, Malcolm," she cried, bringing the tips of her fingers to the tearing corners along her broken nose. "They burn so badly," she swore, wiping the grit away. "Oh, my God! You *are* bleeding," she fibbed, pointing with prayerful hands to a spot before his nose.

Malcolm tore his hands away from hers and brought them to his face as Diane shot quarter-inch long fingernails like little daggers into his dark brown eyes.

"FUCKING BITCH!" he reeled and raved. "You fucking, fucking cunt." Malcolm was *indeed* bleeding, now.

She had reached for, but could not quite grab his ear. She bit the tape between her teeth while trying frantically to unwrap the dangling roll—rolling away from his fierce and ferocious kicks.

Savagely, he kicked her with all his might—striking the back of her bloodied head with a pair of steel-toed leather boots. Landing one foot unmercifully. And then the other. Painfully enjoying her horrifying screams of terror. He booted her lower spine for good measure. With the thick, padded life jacket she wore, he seriously considered whether or not he could break her back.

"Whore!"

If she were conscious and up to conversing, she might have challenged him by asking how she could be a whore and a vestal virgin at the very same time. But she was knocked senseless.

Malcolm finally stopped. He could barely see—frantically wiping away the blood on his jacket sleeve. The madman took a deep breath before immediately setting to work.

First, he finished wrapping her wrists with the tape, making positively sure that they were secure. He turned Diane over and onto her back. Opening her jaw effortlessly, he snapped the plastic spool solidly into place with the dexterity of a fight trainer putting in a mouthpiece for his champ.

"I'm in your corner, Diane," he declared through a nervous laugh. "Gotta stay *focused*," he gritted mercurially for lack of a better word—trying desperately to put aside his bloody pain. "Round three at the sound of the bell. Ready, you goddamn bitch," he wailed, shaking like a leaf.

But why was he shaking? Pain, he had certainly dealt with before. Far worse pain, to be sure. It was certainly not for lack of confidence concerning the spool and tube procedure that had initially failed with regard to the Haynes woman from Maryland, having succumbed too quickly. Of course, he had painstakingly told her beforehand that the two items were all part of an underwater breathing apparatus she would be needing for when the tide came in. It was not his fault that she somehow pushed the tube out through the opening in the spool. Probably panicking. She could have bought herself a good ten minutes in the way he had rigged the tubing up through her clothing, securing the length at her ankles. But by the time he got to the top of the pier from where she was laced, upside down to a piling, the plastic tube was gone—most likely washed ashore by the incoming tide, for the flow was quickly carried forward by a strong wind. He had told her at least half a dozen times *not* to move her head, that the tube could easily be pulled out if she did not follow his instructions and stay perfectly still. Which, obviously, she did not do. That is when he promised himself next time out that the tubing was going to be made of rubber and most assuredly *in*. Not just a few inches or so. But down deep. Different application altogether. Fern Rodman had been his second pick for the spool trick. Diane Nash? An entirely different operation altogether. No one could say he was not original.

Malcolm began to calm down some.

He lifted Diane's body and, with quarter-inch double-braided nylon mooring line, suspended her arms heavenward, fastening her wrists to a thick pine limb well above her head, hands taped and solemnly tied together in *prayer*, or so it seemed.

Diane was coming to her senses.

"Comfy?"

Her mouth was no longer a pretty little oval, but rather a large and perfect circle—displaying a bright white plastic wheel. Grotesque, if not surreal. A tiny hole smack in the center of the spool . . . its edges around her lips now being sealed with strips of tape for good measure.

"Gosh, Diane! You look a fright. And that's coming from someone who can hardly see, bitch."

Her sand-crusted eyes traced the tube Malcolm was holding firmly in his fist, following the amber line to the gallon of fluid hanging upside down, set high above her like an intravenous bottle—

the plastic container held securely in place by its handle through which several wraps of tape fastened it to a branch of the tree.

Why, Malcolm? she wanted to utter but could not. To God, she simply continued to cry.

The end of the tube within the bottle bubbled as Malcolm gravity-fed the fluid through the aperture at the face of the spool, sending the liquid down and around the loop of line like a lazy but colorful snake.

Diane's fearful eyes met Malcolm's bloody pair. He stared at her with unadulterated hatred, there in the fading light—the crimson liquid filling her throat and entering her body blindly as it found its way within. She could feel the slippery snake traveling steadily down her plumbing as she fought mightily to close off the passageway, applying a fierce and ferocious pressure with the back of her tongue.

Malcolm forced and ran the tubing deeper, getting the action going good as evidenced by the liquid leaving the living, breathing, buckling container as it glugged.

Diane was gagging . . . choking . . . retching—swiveling her head wildly about.

Malcolm grinned. He smacked her face silly with an open hand just to hear the sound— feeding in another foot.

Diane could not close off the line—her gag-reflex giving up against the thickness of the tubing's wall. After a full and agonizing minute, she gave way to the fluid flowing freely through her body, now entering her lungs as well.

Malcolm ran his fingers across the slithery oozing mess pooling around the spool fixed firmly in her mouth. His sick grin gradually changed into a sympathetic smile before her wide and terrified eyes.

In one continuous downward motion, with oily fingers knitted neatly together, Malcolm gently touched her senses: the palms of both hands; the pair of frightened dark brown teary eyes; her broken button nose; the corner of a malleable mouth; then finally, pushing back her coal-black curls—the tips of those funny little elf-like ears. Seconds before convulsing, Diane shut her eyes tightly—tacitly cursing both God and her familial priest. Ironically, Malcolm Columba was the farthest from her thoughts.

"Oh, by the way, Diane. You were absolutely right. That was

no accident fourteen years ago. The very day you became a teenager."

Chapter 41

It was pitch-black all around them, except for the artificial light.

"We found her, Lieutenant."

"Where?"

"Across Sag Harbor Cove. North Haven Peninsula. On the point," Detective Sergeant Hennesey spoke into his cell phone, practically out of breath. "You won't believe what this fucking guy did to 'er," his voice raced ahead in a spurt.

"Sure I would, Ed. Just lay it out for me. Nice and slow."

"He fed her a gallon of brake fluid—down her throat. Used a spool to hold the tube in place like he done on the Rodman dame."

"Woman, Ed. Victim, in this case." *Show a little professionalism and respect*, he wanted to add but did not.

"Oh, right. Sorry, Lieutenant. Listen. We got blood. How's that for news? Hers as well as *his*."

Theo smiled against the mouthpiece. "Maybe, there is a God, Ed. Both Dean and Brian with you?"

"You bet. And the lab boys 'n that shrew. I mean, Carla, sir," he censored himself through a smile.

Detective Carla Crenshaw was busy with the body.

"The team brought in what they needed by boat," Hennesey explained. "It's faster from the Nash home and across the water than trying to get wheels down here, believe it or not. Got 'er in a secluded spot. Can't get down with a vehicle. We came in on foot. And get this. Carla thinks she's got a partial from the perp. Thumbprint."

"Why does she *think* that, Ed? Why doesn't she *know* for sure?"

"Because she doesn't think Diane Nash ever touched the tubing. Not with 'er hands tied high above her head, she didn't. We *all* believe it's *his* print—" Hennesey said excitedly "—at the point where he stopped feeding the tubing through the spool. Print's the size of half a thumbnail. 'Along the ventral surface,' she's telling me to tell you.

Anyhow, Bri and Dean think one of the gloves he was wearing must have ripped. And I'll tell you something else, Lieutenant. The young woman put up a pretty good fight for a cripple. We're not sure whose blood is whose, right now. But there's a good deal of it. Sure glad we got here before the storm, though. He cracked 'er back of the head with an oar. I mean paddle. We got some splinters from her hair and scalp. This whole area shows signs of a struggle. Both here and where he pulled the canoe up on the beach. The tide probably washed away most of the broken pieces. He dragged her and the canoe into the pines behind me. Left the same way he came in—only under the cover of darkness, Carla said," he elaborated, gesturing to the second divergent depression in the sand as if Theo were presently standing beside him viewing the crime scene.

In his mind, Theo could do just that. It was always quite amazing to the troops how quickly the lieutenant could piece together details with very few facts, either when physically present at a crime scene, or from miles away while sitting behind his desk. Some claimed he had a sixth sense.

"What about that container of fluid? Siphoned from the ground up or gravity-fed from a level above her head? I'd put my money on the latter."

"Yep. Well above her body, Lieutenant. Duct taped to a branch. But it's clean, 'cept for the tubing on the end—like I told you—where we found the partial print."

"What else you got?"

"Little streaks of fluid on the palms of her hands. On each eyelid. And her nose." Hennesey was looking at Nelson's notes with a penlight. "Had it running down her mouth of course."

"How did you guys find her so fast?" Theo asked calmly, yet absolutely thrilled by the report he was hearing.

"Kid with binoculars happened by. He saw them cross the harbor heading east in a canoe. Saw them hit the beach. Hard and fast, in fact. Yellowish canoe like we was lookin' for. Said he saw the woman fall backward."

"Give you a description of the guy?"

"Nope. Kid said he had the glasses pretty much glued to the woman the whole time. Said she was pretty."

"He see anything else?"

"Nothing. When she fell, he got scared 'cause the guy got out and looked around. The kid didn't wanna be seen spyin' on 'er, so he left immediately." Hennesey laughed. "He was afraid we were goin' to arrest 'im for bein' a Peeping Tom. I told 'im if he saw that yellow canoe again to give us a call and that we'd buy 'im a good pair of field glasses for scopin' out broads. Broads is what *he* called 'em, Lieutenant," Hennesey caught himself and fibbed. "Of course, if I get that call, I'll be sure to correct 'im an' have 'im mind his manners, sir," he added with a grin.

Theo smiled. "You get that call, Sergeant, and I'll buy *you* the biggest and best bottle of Irish malt whisky money can buy."

"Oh, I can see that the keeper of the coffers will be goin' on the dole if those two promises 're ever kept," Hennesey replied happily, laughing like a leprechaun.

"We nail this guy as a result of that call, I'll pay for both gifts out of my personal savings," Theo swore. "But I'm afraid that kid's going to phone you for a week straight when he sees *anything* yellow," he remarked pessimistically. "*Any* yellow watercraft, for openers. Later, it'll be school buses and taxis," the lieutenant exaggerated to make his point.

"Oh, I don't think so, sir."

"Why's that?"

"Well, for one thing, the kid's pretty knowledgeable about boats. Especially canoes."

"Don't let Dean get anywhere near him," Theo joked.

"He already did. That's how we know the kid knows what he's talkin' 'bout."

"Meaning?"

"Well, the canoe the perp took from Nash's place is made of Kevlar. Like our vests. Oh, 'fore I forget. Guess what the life vest she was wearing said?"

"Said?"

"The make, I mean. Dead Man's Float, Inc., would you believe?"

"Manufacturer has a sick sense of humor."

"So does our killer. Anyhow, that Kevlar canoe? Natural skin. Unpainted. Yellowy. Kid knew all that. Knew, also, that there aren't too many of them around. Close to two thousand bucks a pop with tax, he told us. It's gonna surface, sir."

"Not if the killer sank it, it won't," Theo pointed out.

"Good point, Lieutenant. Hadn't really thought of that. Guess that's why you get the big bucks," he kidded. "So, if he sank the canoe, it will most likely be sittin' in shallow water. Just so long as it's out of sight. I mean, he's not gonna submerge it in ten feet of water and swim back to shore. Not in this weather he's not. Water's still as cold as you know what."

"Know what I'm thinking?"

Hennesey smiled. "Sure I know. You're gonna grab Patrick and run a chopper 'long the shoreline to see what you can see. Maybe grab a late night dinner on Shelter Island while you're at it. Privileges of rank, or some crap like that, you'll tell me later on. Right?"

"You know, that's a damn good idea, Sergeant."

"Glad I thought of it," the Irishman bantered laughingly.

"Any place to put down?"

"Hold on a sec." Hennesey called over to a technician some fifty yards away, then signaled by whirling a finger high above his head.

The man gave him the high sign and pointed north.

"Affirmative, Lieutenant. They're just finishing up here, but they want you landin' north of the scene. I'll have someone florescent in an X and give Patrick a call with coordinates. But you better do it before the sky opens up, which it's gonna do pretty damn soon."

"I think we've got this guy in the bag, Ed."

Ed Hennesey stepped away from the group. "Body-bag this guy, Theo," he declared gravely, lowering his voice to whisper. Formalities were over. "Red-light his farkin' arse."

"Is that an order, soldier?" Theo countered good-naturedly.

"Friggin' A it is." He looked back at Carla, still down on her hands and knees. "And a dame is still a dame, boss."

"Just so long as you remember *who's* the boss."

"See you in a bit."

"Before you go. That fellow upstate? Donald Bellport? They just released him."

"About time. Hope his lawyer sues their pants off."

"He doesn't have a lawyer from what I hear."

"Then I'm surprised they let him go at all," Hennesey

considered quite seriously.

"I'll tell you something, Ed. I'm not so sure that was a good move just yet."

"C'mon, Lieutenant. Guy's no angel. But he's no more connected to this business than you or me."

"Might be a good thing for him if he were. *Connected* I mean. Connected but protected."

"Mob connected?"

"They're the ones who got him locked up in the first place. True? From what I'm hearing now, one of them pushed hard to get him out."

"Jesus."

"There's a couple of loose cannons still hanging around up there running that show. Something really stinks, Ed."

"You're tellin' me. Thought Dean and Brian were gonna have a kitten. I have to say, though, that Miller helped calm things down a bit."

"Good man, Miller."

"Still . . . behind the . . ."

"Come again, Ed. You're breaking up."

"I said, he's still wet behind the ears."

"Copy that. Listen. Speaking of ears, this Nash woman have a trace of fluid on either?"

"Ears? I don't know. Let me find out right now. Hold on."

Hennesey called over to Carla.

The lieutenant waited patiently on the line.

Seconds later, the sergeant was back. "You're right, Lieutenant! Both ears. Just like on her eyelids. Little oily streaks . . . wait a second."

Theo could hear Carla in the background.

"She told me to tell you, 'tragus and antitragus, above the globe,' lieutenant. Hold on another second. What, Carla?" Hennesey cupped an ear to catch what Carla was saying; against the other, he pressed the phone. "Oh, above the *lobe*. Thought she said globe."

"I get the picture, Ed," Theo said knowingly.

Carla was holding back Diane's coal black shoulder-length curly hair with a lighted probe.

"How'd you know, Lieutenant?" Hennesey asked with a mix of

admiration and amazement.

Theo was seeing something from miles away that the homicide team and forensics were missing up close and personal.

"The palms of her hand, you said, Ed. Eyes and nose and ears. Brake fluid coming out of her mouth. Correct?"

"Correct," Hennesey answered, at a loss for an explanation, although his mind was racing away in fifth gear. "What do you make of it?"

"Good Irish Catholic boy like you? Come on. Think, man."

"I'm thinking, sir."

"Extreme unction."

"Extreme what?"

"He *touched* her five senses, Ed."

"Jesus," Ed said, suddenly realizing what Theo was getting at. "Last rites."

"Also called 'anointing of the sick'. Today, they just do the palms and forehead and leave it at that."

"Yeah, I heard the term. Been so long, Theo. Guess I'm out of touch. God would have a field day if I showed my puss in church. That's after the roof caved in," he swore.

"Maybe our boy administered the sacrament to Fern Rodman and the others before he wasted them, too."

"Using water instead of oil."

"Unholy, in either case."

"Or maybe he just wants to point us in another direction."

"Then again, there's that spool."

"A circle."

"Symbolizing the circle of life and death, perhaps."

"Christ!"

"What?"

"I just thought of something Broderick Nash told me earlier."

"I'm listening, Ed."

"Their family priest was by this morning. Father Kerrigan."

"Mother of God," Theo stated solemnly.

"No, no; he checks out, Theo. Frail fellow. He's a monsignor. Pushing eighty and couldn't propel a wheelchair, let alone paddle a canoe. What I'm thinking is maybe he's got some idea. Maybe he knows some sick fuck with a calling. Maybe a colleague with his own fucking cross to bear. Hell, who knows? Worth a try."

"Think maybe you could put it to him a bit more tactfully, Sergeant?" Theo suggested politely behind a big smile.

"Nah. I'm just gonna come right out and ask 'im if he's figured out God's mysterious ways in all his seventy-some years and perhaps, together, we can shed some light on who of all God's children might have murdered nine innocent human beings with the good Lord's fucking blessing."

"Knew I could count on you, Ed," Theo surrendered through a highly audible sigh. "Call me the second you have something. But don't bother if you've been excommunicated and need a shoulder to cry on."

"Wouldn't think of it, Lieutenant. Not in this fucking lifetime," Hennesey swore beneath his breath.

Chapter 42

Malcolm was studying himself in the mirror. He was not so handsome now. Diane, *that bitch*, he bawled inwardly, *that fucking cunt*, had caused injury to his eyes. Real and perhaps permanent damage. If he had the power to bring her back from the dead, he would—only to kill her all over again, he swore.

Malcolm's eyes were afire with fright, hatred, and pain. Emotional pain he had learned to deal with early on in life, but the physical pain he now suffered was unbearable. He hurt badly. His vision was impaired. He wanted to scream and shatter the entire mirror before him with his fists. No one had ever hurt him like that. Never! Certainly not the beatings across his backside from a strap wielded by his father. Nowhere near the face. Surely, his mother's words wounded him more than her sudden, cat-like swipes and swats. But he had learned to handle her. It only took him twenty years. She simply refused to understand, listen, believe, or come to trust her only child— right up until the very day she died. Very much like her namby-pamby pussycat that she kitty-sat and kept all cozy in the kitchen, until the day he rolled it up in a carpet and made it disappear. It never listened, either. Alive or dead. He hated it as much as her. If that loathsome woman were somehow the reincarnation of her miserable cat, she would positively be out of lives by now. *All fucking_nine of them*, he clawed the counter before blotting his eyes with gauze pads and ointment. Maybe that was finally the end of that. Her and her miserable cat. *She* was surely the one who had tried to poke his eyes out only hours earlier in the guise of Broderick Nash's daughter, he firmly believed.

Dogs he did not much care for, either. Specifically, little yapping, snapping types. But unlike that crafty cat, at least dogs did not skulk around both day and night. Dogs he could cope with because dogs stayed dead when you delivered them from one world to the next. Like the little poodle that lived next-door to them when they lived abroad. That little mongrel, which kept barking night and day whenever the neighbors were away—and always while he was busy with his studies. Rarely were the owners around. Both the husband and wife worked full time during the day, then went out drinking virtually every evening, visiting their friends and relatives, of which they must have had a million. It went on like that for years.

Yap Yap Yap.

But the authorities would not do a thing about it.

Malcolm's mother had been officially informed that the only way to handle the matter was for her to file a complaint in civil court, which he knew she would never do.

Malcolm's mother.

A mousy woman who was truly a fraidy-cat.

Except when it came to Malcolm.

Him, she would push around.

Not so much with muscle, but with her whining, maw-like mouth—ordering him to do her bidding after the divorce. *All* the work both in and outside the house. From the cooking to the cleaning. From the front yard, *all* the way back to her precious perfumed gardens—while she sat quietly by in her chair, beside Kittylina, and read voraciously.

The barking dog never seemed to bother her, although he knew it did.

Yap Yap Yap Yap Yap.

Day and night.

Night and day.

Till *someone* took matters into their own hands.

Till *someone* put a good size portion of marinated chopped steak into the small dog's outdoor bowl.

The neighbors never suspected that the young religious scholar living next-door would ever do such a horrible thing like poisoning a poor defenseless little pup. Nor would they even think for a moment that the mother of such a fine young man would do such a dastardly deed as soaking half a pound of prime in antifreeze and slip it to that *mutt*, Malcolm summed up in a single word.

No one thought that for a moment.

The two were surely above suspicion.

Perhaps it was simply because the handsome mother and son did not have ethylene and diethylene glycol lying about the house or yard. And why would they? They did not own or operate a car—or any equipment that required such toxic chemicals—now that his father was gone for good.

Plainly put, she could just about put food on the table. She certainly could not afford the half a pound of prime for such a crime when she only purchased chuck with food stamps and discount coupons. Yet, she could continue to feed that devious cat of hers.

It *had* to be those neighbors who lived on the *other* side of poor little Princess, everyone believed; or the ones in back, who had lots of property and insisted on their privacy. It just *had* to be one of *them*.

Therefore, he did not turn out the way he had because of a mousy-mouthy mother, or because there was no father figure in or about the house. He did not buy into any of that broken home nonsense. Nor was he the product of poor potty training, drugs, alcohol, inferior genes, TV violence, a devilish barking dog, a spoiled kitchen kitty cat, or any kind of crap like that, he ruminated before the mirror. *No.* He turned into a stone-cold serial killer purely by his own choosing, simply because he and millions of innocent people were slowly being *poisoned* by the environment . . . no matter what that bitch on the beach, Diane Nash, had to say on the subject.

End of discussion.

Literally.

The people of a great nation needed a true leader. A man who came up the hard way. One of the downtrodden like themselves. Not merely a boy who was physically abused with a belt by his civil servant father in another land. Not some lad who was more emotionally than physically mistreated by his mousy mother. But a young man who had been persecuted by two superior powers.

One secular. The other spiritual.

Oppressed and blasphemed, respectively.

State government and the Catholic Church.

Malcolm vowed that he would someday worm himself into their very ranks and take matters into his own hands.

Malcolm pledged that he would one day *seize* that power.

And a charismatic Malcolm Columba truly became that person to those who knew him *well*. Of this, there was no doubt. Malcolm was indispensable. Few men in the world were.

His manuscript would certainly prove that very point.

The tome, if ever read and decoded, could seal the fate of thousands—like a tomb.

The book, if ever published, would mean the fall of America.

The cryptic document woven throughout his prose was positively the serial killer's insurance policy.

As far as Malcolm was concerned, industry was the root of all evil. Industry was polluting the planet. World politics was purely a game of three-dimensional chess. A game he played so well. It was as plain as putrid apple pie.

Malcolm simply murdered certain individuals because he wanted to punish those who held the position of power, yet failed to act accordingly in the areas concerning our environment—whose only real interests were ultimately motivated and governed by infernal greed—be it in the form of a fat company paycheck, profit sharing, stock options, or the most insidious sin of all in Malcolm's mind: the deficit found in misplaced pride.

Pride goeth before the fall.

But to merely murder the man or the woman held accountable would have sent a sorrowful message. Malcolm's communication had to be so much more . . . *telling.* It had to destroy the very soul and bury the spirit within its *living* shell—putting it through an *emotional* and *everlasting* hell.

Malcolm knew how to pull their chains, all right. First, to find the chink in their armor; the weak link in their vulnerable being. Finally, to finish off and flush *not* the flesh of the fiend—but the very essence of selflessness—mirrored in the image of a loved one. Not the doer of the deed would he deceive and corporally destroy, but their little darlings. Surely, success would follow.

Malcolm studied his reflection in the fogged glass.

What he saw would, indeed, be considered strange. A kaleidoscopic collage of faceted faces:

Noreen Walker, Laura Haynes, Arlene Parker, Wendy Anne Linden, Patricia Tamblin, Becky Dawson, Monisha Washington, Fern Rodman and Diane Nash.

All those females inarguably had one thing in common. They were surely loved and would be sorely missed.

That was his genius, he knew. It stood apart from Malcolm's momentous governmental task and sole undertaking. The undercover assignment of the century—covertly and, oh, so cleverly concealed—overtly portraying a poor lobsterman—his penchant for murder protected by officials at the highest levels of government. Fall guys and scapegoats at the ready if need be. Namely, Malcolm's protégé. Clarence Emery. Diabolically in league with the devil himself and arguably one of the most prolific serial killers in American history. Although Columba and Emery never worked in concert, the pair were most definitely keeping score. Who would ever suspect Columba's true calling? Who, aside from the few within the intelligence community, would ever know that he was the Father of the Federation, a man solely responsible for secretly and, therefore, safely placing operatives in countries around the globe?

In any event, Malcolm, alone, had created a living hell for his enemies of the planet.

Polluters.

Federal agents, who followed Malcolm Columba's formula for success, kept America safe and sound.

Ironic.

But if the police did catch him in their web, perhaps they *would* set aside the death penalty and put him in a cage for the rest of his natural life. Or, like Diane Nash had said, indirectly, a rubber room, whereby, over a period of time, he could bounce back after being treated and cured. Whatever. For Malcolm knew that the prisons people create for themselves within their own minds and of their own making are far more confining than the four walls of any cell one might possibly imagine. This he considered quietly, studying the victims' composition there in the misty mirror. Two dark bloody pools peered back at him from behind their ghostly image . . . staring back monstrously.

He listened to the steady pounding of wind and rain upon the rooftop, praying that the high tide and perpetual spring downpour would wash away all traces of blood back in North Haven. He was sure it would.

But Malcolm knew the *real* reason he was scared.

A latent fingerprint.

He had not discovered the tear atop the gloved thumb until the moment he got back out of the canoe after leaving the beach.

Too late to return to the scene.

He prayed to God that the authorities would not find her until the elements had a chance to work their wonders. Among those tall pines, in that minimal afternoon light, Malcolm felt confident that he had done a thorough job of cleaning under Diane's nails so that there would not be any trace of his skin or blood beneath them—nails that had bloodied his eyes less than two hours earlier.

"Bitch," he brayed anew. "How could I not have *seen* or *felt* the thumb-tear in that goddamn glove? Two layers, in fact!"

The bloody beach, of course, he could not *really* clean completely, tidying up as best he could after clobbering her with the paddle before dragging her off toward the cone-bearing evergreens— concerned mainly that the area would not be discovered until after the deed was done and he was safely away. But all forensics would need was a single unadulterated drop of his own blood, he shuddered knowingly. And now, he had to worry about a latent thumbprint, too. All that was supposed to be *evident* was Broderick's daughter's body —along with the pertinent items of death so that his final message would be crystal clear.

"Vicious bitch!"

Chapter 43

The figure slipped on a pair of dark prescription sunglasses as he headed toward the young boy skittering backward while dragging an inverted horseshoe crab by its tail across a strip of debris-strewn beach. The result of the recent storm.

The man stuck his hands deep within the pockets of his baggy pants. "Hi, there," the stranger called out as he approached the ten year old.

The lad looked up but said nothing in reply.

"What on God's good green earth do you have there, son?"

"Horseshoe crab," the boy answered quietly.

"Horseshoe crab? Well, I'll be darned. I didn't recognize it upside down like that," he said, tilting his head and smiling in mild amusement.

The kid turned the shell back over with a twist of its tail.

"Ah, sure enough. Horseshoe crab it is, indeed. Is it alive?"

The boy shook his head.

"How do you know?"

The youngster picked up a nearby stick, squatted, and poked the slick brown carapace to make his point. The shell remained motionless.

"Huh. But suppose it's just playing possum?"

The boy stood and stuck the toe of his shoe beneath the marine creature, then put it on its back once again. "It's all dried out and dead. See?"

Malcolm stooped low. "I see. What are you going to do with it?"

The boy shrugged.

"Hmm. Say, have you had lunch?"

The lad glanced up but said nothing.

"Because I'm starving." Malcolm stood. "You like peanut butter and jelly sandwiches and milk?"

The boy nodded his head.

"Creamy or the crunchy kind?"

"Creamy."

"Me, too. The crunchy kind gets stuck in my teeth." Malcolm made a funny face and bared his teeth.

The boy cracked a smile.

"You like milk or lemonade?" Malcolm asked.

"Chocolate milk."

"With peanut butter and jelly sandwiches?" the funny man asked in horror, pulling his hands from his pockets and covering up his face.

The boy laughed.

"What's your name?" Malcolm asked.

"Freddie Dupree."

"Mine's Malcolm." Malcolm extended his hand.

The boy took it, and the two shook hands.

"Well, what say the two of us have some lunch?"

"Where?"

Malcolm glanced over his shoulder. "Right back there over that dune. I got a creamy peanut butter and jelly sandwich we can share along with a thermos full of milk. Got me two fishing rods, too. After lunch, maybe you and I could do a little fishing. I know a spot where we can catch fish this long," Malcolm swore and spaced his hands better than a foot apart.

"Where's that?" Freddie asked suspiciously.

Malcolm glanced back over his shoulder. "Same place. Not far from the car where I have the sandwich, milk and rods."

"Got any bait?"

"I got lures. Know what they are?"

"Sure. But what are we gonna catch with lures around here now?"

"Weakfish."

"My dad says weakfishin' ain't for another month."

"Well, your dad's right, son—for where *he* fishes. But he doesn't know about my secret spot."

"You know where my dad fishes?"

Malcolm smiled handsomely. "Freddie. I know where your father fishes, on what tide, his favorite fishing grounds come the middle of May, what color lures he uses on cloudy days. I even know what he did for a living up until this year, and how he's breaking his back raking clams right this minute. How do you like them oysters?"

Freddie Dupree seemed impressed. "How do you know all that?"

"I worked pretty much the same waters as your father. Only a bit west of here. I'm a lobsterman, too. Or was. I'm sure you know the whole sad story."

The boy nodded his head. "Sure do." But there was still a note of suspicion on Freddie's face. "Wait a minute! If you're a lobsterman, or *was*, like you said, how come you didn't know what a horseshoe crab was?"

Malcolm grinned. "Just funnin' with you, Freddie. I wanted to make sure I was talking to Harold Dupree's boy. Not some other kid walking the beach this morning."

"You don't sound like a lobsterman to me."

"No?"

"No."

"And how is a lobsterman supposed to sound?" he said in challenge. "Huh?"

"Tough."

"Tough?"

Freddie nodded his head.

Malcolm stuck his hands back into his pockets and lowered his head. Thinking. Staring down at the horseshoe crab. Suddenly, he withdrew two fists, then opened them with fingers spread to their max, palms inward, rotating both hands in opposite directions a foot away from his face. Malcolm tightened his lips for the delivery. "Ready, Freddie?"

The boy stood in a trance.

"You dirty arthropod," Malcolm said in a tough-guy, nasal Cagney tone. He was talking to the shell. "You big overgrown arachnid." He was referring to the marine creature as being a descendent of the spider family, which indeed it was. Then with a swift boot from the toe of a rubber bottom, laced-up moccasin, Malcolm sent the pseudo crab sailing along the beach. "How's that, Freddie? Tough enough? Or do you want to see *mean*?" he questioned, slipping back into his former role of Mister Nice.

Freddie went running after the skeletal shell and gave it a boot of his own with his sneaker, sending it several yards ahead of him. "Did you know that they're related to spiders?"

"I sure do. That's why I called it an arachnid. Hey, I bet you saw—"

"*Arachnid Avenger!*" Freddie said excitedly. "I definitely saw the movie! It was awesome."

I know you did, Freddie. I saw you in the video store with your stepmother when you picked it out all by yourself. I was watching you from a corner of the room. "Then you know that lobsters are in the insect family. Right?"

"Sure I know. I know a lot about lobsters from my dad."

"Still don't think I'm a lobsterman?"

"I guess so."

"Want to give me a test, just to be sure?"

"Okay."

"Go ahead," Malcolm said confidently. "Ask me anything."

"All right. If you're a lobsterman, tell me what's causing the die-off in Long Island Sound."

"The pesticides that the government sprayed last fall that ringed the waters."

Freddie nodded and scratched his head. "All right. Now. If you're *really* a lobsterman, tell me what happened when you pulled your traps with the lobsters that had the shell disease."

"There was slime all over them and had the smell of rotten eggs."

Freddie smiled. "You're a lobsterman all right, Malcolm."

"So, we gonna have lunch together and do a little fishing?" Malcolm looked at his watch. "You know, it's almost noon. You've got be hungry. What do you say?"

"Sure. But I gotta be back by three. Mom and Dad think I'm in school. But I'm really playing hooky."

Malcolm grinned. "I play hockey, too."

"Not *hockey*, man. I said hooky. I cut school today."

Malcolm smiled.

"You were only kidding, right? Right," Freddie asked and answered his own question.

"Right, you are, Freddie."

"What kind of boat do you have?"

"A thirty-five foot open-sided pilot. Downeaster style. Pretty much along the lines of your dad's. Only we're both working out of skiffs right now. Digging up clams for a living to rake in a few bucks," he punned.

Freddie smiled. "My dad says it's not only the bug spray that's killing the lobsters off, but the dredging, too."

"Your dad's absolutely right. Lobstermen like him and me look at Long Island Sound as our very own farm. Industry has turned it into a sewer by dumping their toxic wastes and polluting the Sound, bays, and rivers. What settles in gets stirred up with those dredging projects. The contaminated mud containing toxins spreads out everywhere. Marine life can tolerate just so much, Freddie, before it takes its toll. The spraying last September, combined with some other factors, did those lobsters in."

"Dad says they sprayed because of the mosquitoes that carry the . . . a . . . whatchamacallit?"

"West Nile virus."

"That's it. We talked about that in school, too. My teacher says they *had* to spray."

"Your teacher's dead wrong."

"That's what my dad says, too."

"The government is supposed to be a system of rule 'by the people and for the people.' But in truth, most of government is a body of greedy folks that does what's good for government. The government represents the *few*, not the *many*."

"You sound just like my dad."

Malcolm looked down at the lad and fondly mussed his crop of stringy blond hair. "You see, Freddie, we have enough things to worry about just with Mother Nature doing what it normally does to us."

"Huh?"

"You know. Like storms. Flooding. Severe winters like we had this year."

"Right."

"That certainly adds to the problems the creatures of the sea are having. But like us, they're pretty adaptable. But when we heap problem after problem on top of them, and us, there comes a point that our systems," Malcolm reached down and poked a firm finger against the boy's belly for emphasis, "can't take it any longer."

Freddie giggled. "And that's what happened to the lobsters. Right?"

"Right. Years and years of dumping poisons into our waters, then giving them a final shot. Like the methoprene they sprayed last fall to kill the mosquitoes. Anything that kills a mosquito is going to kill a lobster because, Freddie—?" he quizzed.

"Because a lobster is related to a mosquito that's in the insect family. Just like a horseshoe crab is a big spider and not really a crab at all. Right?"

"Right you are, Freddie my boy. They're distant cousins, actually. A lobster undergoes a larval stage just like mosquitoes and other insects. It sees the same as insects see. Smells the same as insects smell. Feels its way along like insects feel." Malcolm wiggled two fingers across the front of the boy's light-blue Windbreaker. "They even have outside skeletons, depending on their stage of life, just like insects."

"Just like insects," Freddie echoed.

"Would you spray bug poison on a caterpillar that was about to change into a beautiful butterfly, Freddie?"

"No, sir."

"Well, that's what the government did when they sprayed that larval pesticide along the waters, making those creatures— " he was going to use the word vulnerable or susceptible but decided to keep his language on the boy's level so that he would fully understand the situation "—*weakened* so that they'd be likely to catch diseases."

"Like I could catch a cold if I go outside without my hat and gloves and coat in the middle of winter. Right?"

"And a school chum comes along and sneezes on you to help the cold bug along."

Freddie nodded emphatically. "I like the way you explain things. I bet you'd make a good teacher."

Malcolm smiled modestly. "Anyhow, the government's responsible for killing off millions of lobsters."

Freddie bent down and picked up a flat stone, skimming it over the calm body of water. "Well, when I grow up, I'm going to do something about it."

Malcolm held his tongue.

Freddie skimmed another stone.

Malcolm pointed across the Long Island Sound to Connecticut. "Both sides of the shore are responsible, Freddie. Industry on both sides of the Sound are criminals. But it's not just here and over there, son. It's all around the globe."

"Let's go get that lunch and do some fishin'," the boy decided.

"A fishin' we will go," Malcolm merrily sang aloud, gently placing an arm across the boy's shoulders, guiding him in the direction of the car.

Chapter 44

Too busy to assemble his people in the squad room, Theo conducted business at one end of the hallway. Like a four-star general preparing for an imminent siege, their commanding officer gathered his troops before him. Other plain-clothes detectives and uniforms moved swiftly along the second floor with purpose.

Detective emeritus Michael Connolly had been called out of retirement. The well-tanned veteran stood veritably tall, although he was of average height and noticeably overweight, too. For the past few years, he lived 'the good life' down in Florida—which was, in fact, far removed from anything favoring a *healthy* lifestyle. Too many sumptuous dishes blanketed with splendid sauces. Too many rum drinks served in the cockpit of his sportfisherman. Still, his swan song played sweetly in Yaphank's hallowed halls that morning, redolent of the Howard Mills serial killer case and trial. Connolly had been the lead detective, having tracked the postal worker to his one-room apartment in Hicksville (described as a slaughterhouse in the press), making the arrest several blocks away from the killer's home on Easter Sunday, April the 7th, 1996. Four years ago to the day. It had been the first death penalty case on Long Island in twenty-one years. Connolly helped the state win a conviction, having spent a month on the stand as a witness for the prosecution. Battling daily with the defense. His length of testimony was unprecedented.

Victory *was* and *is*, indeed, sweet.

Detective Michael Connolly's reappearance that morning was looked upon by all as an encore performance.

Bob Fowler, canine handler extraordinaire, stood by just outside the building with his dogs: German Shepherds trained in cadaver work. Max, everyone's favorite pup, was the pooch who alerted Connolly's team that there either was or had been a body or bodies in Mills' car trunk.

But that was yesteryear.

To Michael Connolly, it seemed like only yesterday, as though he had never left the job.

Team Two's supervisor, Detective Sergeant Seth Mason, was busy handing out Department of Motor Vehicle photos of their suspect —Malcolm Columba—along with a comprehensive report to the Magnificent Seven who had handled the notable Mills case. Detectives Gary York, Otis and John Bailey, Vic Posteraro, Ken Zanetti, Eric Bokina, Troy Anderson and Michael Connolly were being given last minute instructions by Team Three's lead, Dean Nelson.

Detectives Brian Archer, Ed Hennesey, Andrew Miller, Kim Booker and several others were busy discussing the devil in the details.

Teams One, Two and Three were closing in on their man.

Their supreme suspect was being sought.

"All right!" Theo announced, raising his arm for silence. It took a good thirty seconds to bring everyone to order. Theo's teams were pumped. "Listen up, and listen up good. We're pretty damn positive we know who this guy is. We've got his blood, and we've got a partial print. In 1998, the man was stopped in his boat on the Intracoastal along New Smyrna Beach, Florida, for a violation. Just north of Edgewater. Same time frame that the Walker victim was found. No summons was issued. The man was traveling north, according to the officer who issued him a warning for a No Wake Zone. Our suspect is a twenty-nine-year-old male Caucasian. Malcolm M. Columba. Dark brown hair and eyes. Five-foot-nine. Two-inch scar between the thumb and forefinger of his right hand. Favors his left leg —ever so slightly. Lobsterman from here on Long Island. That's his seasonal daytime job. Sources close to this investigation tell us he's a powerbroker—confidant of, and consultant to, Evan Tamblin.

"In the late eighties, Columba purportedly ingratiated himself among the industrialist's powerful inner circle of friends and acquaintances, making new contacts around the globe who were more interested in making quick deals and *truly* big money. Dealers and distributors of the illegal sort. Columba, together with a man known as The Teacher, Clarence Emery, allegedly helped build a criminal network, trafficking in heroine and cocaine. However, it's Emery who is under the microscope of late. For some very strange reason, it seems that a certain faction of the federal government keeps Columba on a veritably short leash—either unable or unwilling to rein him in. Reliable sources suspect the latter. This surreptitious player of ours maintains a POB in Port Jefferson. He hasn't picked up his mail in over two weeks, which an official there tells us is not unusual for this guy. It sometimes piles up for a month or more before he comes around. That tells us this fellow probably moves around a lot. We know that he parks his vehicle by his workboat docked at Orient By The Sea Marina. Car's gone. APB is out. No new leads as to where he might be holed up."

Theo held up an enlargement of the DMV photo.

"So, we know what he looks like, which fits the physical description the Dawson woman gave Dean and Brian—as best she could. The manager at the marina tells us Mr. Columba has plans to sell his boat to a family who wants to convert it into a pleasure craft. Manager got Carla and her crew aboard for a look-see. Pine needles and some sand found in the cockpit and around the helm area are consistent with samples collected at the last crime scene on the beach at North Haven Peninsula. That tells us that he's probably been back to the boat since then. Stakeout's turned up nothing. Boat hasn't moved, or we'd certainly have. We have to find him before he kills again.

"First off, we have—" The lieutenant spotted two civilians as they appeared in the middle of the hallway. He caught the eye of one of the duty officers and gestured while snatching up the phone from a nearby desk. Theo spoke briefly to the uniform before hanging up the receiver. In less time than it took to swallow a mouthful of black coffee, two attorneys were being escorted off the floor.

Theo resumed.

"We have a missing ten-year-old boy out east in Orient Point, last seen by a neighbor talking to a man who fits our suspect's description. The two were observed leaving the beach off Land's End Road, getting into a vehicle that matches Columba's. We believe he has Frederick Dupree. Son of Harold and Virginia Dupree of Orient Point. Interracial marriage. Stepmother's a homemaker. Like Columba, the father's a lobsterman. Father before him was a lobsterman. The man told me his son wants to be a marine biologist when he grows up. I want to see this kid grow up to be whatever he wants to be. You want to see that, too. Not because I tell you so, but because most of you have children of your own. I don't need to tell you Dupree and his wife are hurting. What I do need to remind you of is that we have very little time. Malcolm Columba starts his killing process almost immediately. Some of his victims take little time to die. Others take awhile. We know that grabbing this Dupree boy doesn't fit his M.O.

"Now. What we may have going for us is that he probably doesn't know we're onto him. We hope. Freddie Dupree hasn't got a prayer if he does. A ten-year-old *boy*, boys and girls. And in that may lie the answer to his whereabouts. There has *got* to be a good reason for his snatching a male instead of a female this time around. I want you to find it. I want you to find that kid. Fast. That's it."

Detective Miller's hand shot up.

"We don't have time now to start brainstorming this, Andrew," Theo snapped, uncharacteristically on edge.

"You don't have time not to, Lieutenant," Andrew Miller barked back, ignoring Theo and addressing the gathered teams. "What we're looking for is something that the father is holding back."

"Here we go again," a team player blew sky high. "This is the same guy who told us victim number nine was gonna be black and that the killer had mixed blood streamin' through his veins, if you recall."

"I said, possibly."

"You also said——"

"All right, enough," Theo commanded.

"I just want to set this dickhead straight."

"One more word, Falco," Theo challenged. "Just one."

The irate detective shut his mouth and swept his eyes across the ceiling before setting them, once again, on Miller.

"Look," Theo reasoned, addressing Miller with a glare. "Dupree's not going to put his son's life on the line, Detective. He told us *everything*," Theo stated firmly.

"Who's *us*?" Miller snapped.

"Dean, Brian, and myself."

"Told *me* squat. Of course, I wasn't part of any interview. I'd like to interview him now."

"You don't go near that home, hear?"

"Then send someone else." Several heads turned toward Detective Gary York. "We're missing an important piece," Miller insisted.

Theo's face was red. "We're wasting valuable time here, people."

Detective Michael Connolly received a solid jab in the ribs

from Detective Kim Booker. The Mick, as he was fondly monikered, looked over with an annoying frown. He was about to receive another poke.

"Sir?"

"Mick. Nice to have you back for this inning," Theo said cordially. "Make it quick."

"Thank you, sir. I was just thinking. This young detective here's way out of line, but I feel he could be right."

What Mick felt in the past carried significant weight. Most everyone present recognized that fact. Despite the sudden challenge, Mick knew that Theo would not dare send him packing.

"Who the hell was it called you back here, Mick?" Theo barked.

"You did, sir," Mick said, wearing a lopsided grin.

More than several smiles lined the faces of the troops.

"Guess I'm getting desperate," Theo lowered, furrowing his brow.

All smiles vanished.

"Yeah, so I guess I'll just grab a flight back to Disney and tell Goofy I met his match," Mick said flatly.

"Hold on there," Dean Nelson said, pulling and dramatically waving a handkerchief from his pocket, calling for a truce. "You're not going anywhere just yet, Mick. Lieutenant, respectfully, cool your jets." He blew his nose before continuing. "Fact is, I didn't walk away from that interview with Dupree feeling that we'd gotten everything. Truth is, we didn't walk away at all. We ran—like we're running now —knowing time is running out for that boy."

"He's right," Brian said in support. "I felt—"

"All right," Theo snapped. "The teams are teaming up on me, I can see. Maybe we did move a little fast back there." He caught Kim's eye. "What is it, Kim?"

Kim Booker flashed her eyes from Theo to Gary York, then back to Theo. She did not have to say anything. Theo did not need to hear it. He knew.

"You want Gary to follow this up, I suppose," Theo relented.

All three teams were nodding in agreement.

Gary York was staring down at the tips of his highly spit-shined shoes.

Theo looked up at the ceiling tile.

Kim gave Mick another stab in the ribs.

"Why not give him a shot, boss?" Connolly cajoled.

Theo laughed. "Boss now, huh?"

"Yep." *Soft soap and a little tap dance,* he figured This was no time for his usually stouthearted self. *Lay it on thick.* "You'll always be my boss, boss. As a matter of fact, you'll always be my god."

My God! Don't over do it, Kim told herself.

Everyone knew that Theo was tough but fair-minded. Theo knew he was not infallible. Certainly not omniscient. He simply wanted every warm body out looking for Freddie Dupree. Now! Not rehashing what had already been covered in an extensive interview with the boy's parents by himself and two of his seasoned detectives. But maybe they *had* missed something. Or maybe Harold Dupree *was* hiding something. Yet, Theo firmly believed that the father was not going to hold back anything that would put his son in further jeopardy. That would make no sense at all. Harold Dupree was a strong, caring and loving father. Maybe the man *inadvertently* held back some important piece of information. But what? Back and forth between the poles of uncertainty, the lieutenant vacillated. Debating himself. Wasting valuable time. Should he send his man in for round two of questioning? York was the very best when it came to interrogation tactics and techniques.

Detective Gary York could discern lies from half-truths, separate appearances from reality, glean facts from a narrator's fiction, find truth in advertising and self-deception in the Pope's own heart. He achieved this very simply and completely by fully believing in a maxim of his own coinage: The truth, the whole truth, and nothing but the truth was a myth. Man could no more attain pure truth than he could salvage his soul. That conviction, in and of itself, was the closest to an absolute truth a human being would ever come to realize; that is, in the mind of the veteran homicide detective.

No one could argue with the detective's past and present success; it was Gary York who had secured a full confession from Howard Mills—trickery and deceit deemed fully justifiable—as all was fair with what had transpired behind the walls of the 8 x 8 foot interrogation room in Yaphank's homicide unit four years earlier, both in the mind and heart of every detective assigned to the case.

The sign still hanging above the doorway leading to that claustrophobic space said it all: 𝕿𝖍𝖔𝖚 𝕾𝖍𝖆𝖑𝖙 𝕹𝖔𝖙 𝕶𝖎𝖑𝖑

York had been sent in as the closer.

Their last bastion of hope.

He alone had succeeded where three separate interrogations, led by four skilled detectives, covering thirty-six hours, had netted less than the desired result.

Gary York did not threaten or beat his suspect. He did not have to. For he was brilliant at what he did. Armed with a pad and pen and the gift of gab, Gary York had passed himself off as Howard Mills' attorney.

Most everyone within the close-knit community of cops believed that York could manipulate the very devil himself. The few who reserved judgment did so solely on the grounds that they neither believed in a Supreme deity, nor the dark demon of a fiery pit. For those folks, both heaven and hell existed right here on earth. Like Gary, they did not conceive of gods or devils. For them, there were only the truly wicked who walked the face of the planet until the day they were apprehended and led beneath the Gothic-like lettered sign, then into the eerie realm known to very few as The Kingdom of Confession—held within a state of limbo for a spell.

The Suffolk County Homicide Squad enjoyed a ninety-eight percent conviction rate based on signed, sealed and delivered admissions of guilt.

"All right," the lieutenant finally said. "Handle it, Gary. Dean. Brian. Brief him. But be brief about it. Time is killing us all. Let's rock-'n'-roll."

Detective Kim Booker gave Mick an affectionate pinch in the middle of his cheek. The right one. Just below his love-handle, right above the thigh.

"Good to be back," he said with a wink and a nod. And he meant it, for he missed the team terribly. He followed Kim down the hall and around the corner to her area.

"You really going back down there when this is over?" she asked as they went to work, knowing full well where his head and heart belonged.

Mick surrendered an ambiguous grin. "Got to. Long fishing season. No fucking snow. Broads galore in bikinis. Boat's found itself a little harbor we both call home. Although, admittedly, an expensive and thirsty son of a bitch to support."

"I thought boats were thought of fondly as female," she needled, booting up the system.

"At fifty gallons an hour? No dame ever drained me like that in me life. Whore-ass that she be," he elaborated in a solemn Irish accent. "But, yes, she's *all* mine," he minced with a brogue.

"You're sounding more like Hennesey as time goes by," she assured him with a laugh, hurrying the machine along with an impatient gesture.

The truth was that Mick was no more Irish than a rabbi, but loved the lilt.

"You got something good for me, Kim?"

"For you, Mick, I've got gold."

She did indeed.

It was an important lead.

Kim moved over and led him closer to the computer screen, hit several keys, then scrolled the mouse down along the pad.

"Dean's handing you a plum." She tapped the screen with one of her festively painted nails: a tiny yellow chick surrounded with the teeniest of brightly colored eggs. "Note the obvious," she said with irritation. "It's the reason why Columba's name didn't pop up when we plugged in New York licenses for commercial lobsterman at the start of this investigation," she lamented.

With large paws planted on both knees, Detective Michael Connolly bent forward and looked over a list of surnames beginning with C-o-l—searching for Columba, Malcolm. "Don't see it."

"And you won't. I messed up," she explained quietly. Her fingers flew over a series of keys, and a new list appeared in its place. She pointed to the second set of names registered in Connecticut, homing in and highlighting their prime suspect toward the bottom of the screen.

Mick was nodding with understanding. "I see," he said, immediately realizing what had happened.

"Sure. Obvious for a brilliant detective such as yourself," she offered, anxiously biting and marring a fingernail painted with a diminutive white bunny surrounded by several bright blue eggs.

Mick deftly removed the digit from between her gnawing teeth, then took and placed her hand into a gentle claw-like grip. Depending on how he held her ring finger, there either stood or lay a single golden egg with four finely scripted, wee, white initials within—*KB&BA*.

"The obvious *is*, is that you're still carrying a torch for that baldheaded prick."

"Pay attention to the list, Detective," she scolded.

"All I know is that I'd take Brian off mine if I had a figure like yours—a body that just doesn't quit."

Kim took her hand from his and stared him up and down. "Now, that's as chauvinistic a compliment as ever I've heard."

"Without prejudice, I might add," he offered coyly.

"The lists, Mick." Again, she tapped the screen.

"All right, so you didn't find Columba's name initially, because the list for New York licensed commercial lobstermen is different from the list of Connecticut licensees—is different from recreational licensing, et cetera, et cetera. And you're blaming yourself because Albany didn't—"

"I fucked up, Mick."

"Now stop it! You did no such thing. New York and Connecticut have a reciprocal agreement, whereby a licensed commercial lobsterman working the middle of Long Island Sound can apply for a nonresident license and operate both sides of the water. Columba, for whatever reason, canceled one and kept the other. It's not your fault Albany took him out of the computer." Mick straightened up and groaned. "This fucking back of mine."

Kim ignored his discomfort, shaking her head despondently. "I failed to connect the dots, Mick. I should have known—"

"Fuck those dots. All right? I'm gonna tell you a little story. When I was working a case with some of those numskulls from narco next-door, I ran an idea by the Coast Guard, DEC, et cetera. It was a long shot. I had this notion that the perp we were hunting for was a local fisherman. The agencies ran a cross-check through their computers; like what you're doing now. Narco hunted through their system. Me, through ours. No name with a prior *anything* turned up that pointed to drugs and/or murder. Then I thought to myself. Self? Right church, wrong pew. I was looking for a possible *commercial* fisherman. But what about the *recreational* type? Like Theo fishing for his freshwater trout. Or like Dean and me—saltwater fishermen who don't need a license for the brine. Not yet, anyhow. But it's coming," he said knowingly. "Well, I ran it back through Albany. Once again, no suspect. At least no one who wasn't already sitting behind bars or resting in the ground. As it turned out, the guy I was searching for *was* a recreational fisherman. But his name never popped out of any computer, either. Not everything's in the computer, Kim."

"So, this guy didn't have a fishing license. So what? Not your fault. Not something you *missed*."

"Ah, but I did because the guy *had*, in essence, a fucking fishing license, Kim, me dear," he said most assuredly. "But I missed it all together."

"I don't understand."

"The guy was an American Indian who didn't need no fucking fishing license. They're *exempt*! That's what I fucking missed. I blamed myself for a month before I realized the agency should have had it in the computer and not on some separate sheet."

"But Malcolm Columba's name *is* in the computer." She poked the screen at the bottom with a gun-finger. "See? Right there. Connecticut!"

"Yeah, but not in New York, sweetheart. Albany should've had Columba cross-referenced somewhere with the state of Connecticut. You had no way of knowing."

Kim was shaking her head. "It's not the same thing, Mick. I should have known about *reciprocal arrangements* between the states."

Mick put up his hands in surrender. "Fine. Then I should have thought of the *exception* to the rule. Okay? So then we're both a couple of fuck ups. Is that what you want to hear? Feel better now?"

"No," she gritted. "I might have saved that child, or one of those women."

"Oh, really?"

Kim nodded.

"And I might have saved a government official and his wife. Try living with that one. My rationalization is that she was just as guilty as him. That half-breed blew them both away. It was a contract killing involving national security. The buying and selling of nuclear secrets. I shouldn't be talking about it even now. But my advice to you is to put the dead in the back of the closet where they belong and get on with cleaning up the rest of the house."

Kim sat staring at the screen. Nodding. Realizing that Mick was probably right.

"So, where's my gold, girl? I don't want you to have another body on your conscience."

Kim Booker sighed and shut down the computer. "Right here. Carla got it off Columba's boat; found wedged between the folds of the helm seat." She handed Mick a thin strip of cardboard packaging, sealed in a transparent evidence bag.

Mick looked at, then took the seemingly innocuous piece of evidence. "You are and always will be my golden girl. With a body— never mind."

Kim smiled. "Good lead?" she asked brightly.

"Seems good, indeed."

"Happy Easter, Mick." She kissed and pinched his chubby cheek affectionately—just below the ear, this time. "And thanks."

Mick smiled happily, then disappeared around the corner.

Chapter 45

Freddie Dupree believed he would never catch his breath again. The boy's tears were uncontrollable. They streamed down his freckled face like tiny rivers. The sides of his body and stomach actually ached. He never laughed so hard in all his ten years. Malcolm had to be the funniest man on the planet. Funnier than anyone he had ever seen on television or in the movies. Funnier than the Marx Brothers, although some of the one-liners flew well above his head. Funnier than Eddie Murphy. Funnier than the Three Stooges. Bill Cosby. Robin Williams. Funnier than all of them put together, he would wager anyone. He would even bet his bike. His mounting collection of stamps. Even his most valued possession—a thousand dollar microscope. Well, almost a grand, anyhow. And if he owned his father's thirty-six footer, he would have gambled that, too.

Malcolm was a madman. Freddie had never seen a grown-up man act so . . . outrageously. *Yes.*

That was the word he wanted.

Outrageously.

Freddie loved words. Words were his secret friends. Like his collection of old but *powerful* bronze toy soldiers. The problem was that the words were never really there when he needed them. They always came to him when it was just a little too late. Never ever would they come immediately on command, nor in the heat of battle—unlike Malcolm's ready arsenal. Still, the boy held a small army of nouns, adjectives and verbs in abeyance . . . off in a distant corner of his mind. They would serve his purpose later in the form of prose. Perhaps a short story or a poem that he would diligently compose.

Malcolm had words at the ready.

A battalion of them.

Port arms.

Snapping and wagging that verbal weapon smartly at will.

Present arms.

Warding off *any* enemy without warning.

Parry to the right or left.

Ready to slash his opponent to the quick.

Fix bayonets.

Moving in swiftly for the kill.

Thrust!

Yes. Just like Malcolm had done to that snippy, portly waitress who took their supper order only an hour earlier, providing them with less than adequate service in that silvery, greasy spoon that someone had the nerve to call a diner.

Reduced the woman to tears, Malcolm surely did.

Not the kind that Freddie was now shedding. Quite the opposite, in fact. But the kind that made a person wish that they were already dead.

Malcolm could do that in a heartbeat. Malcolm could also make you laugh until your sides burst with breathlessness as he was doing now while the two tooled past nurseries and acres and acres of farmland.

"Fat cow. I should have pushed her puss into that miserable, watery pumpkin pie. For a minute there, I thought her face *was* the filling from which it oozed," Malcolm mocked. "Some crust. Standing there ticking off a list of desserts with about as much enthusiasm as a clock."

"And then you asked her if—" Freddie could just about get the words out "—asked her if it was left over from last Thanksgiving," he roared, balled up in the middle of the front seat of Malcolm's *borrowed* car. He would never ever forget the expression on the waitress's pimply face.

"And that little crop of gray-green hair bunched atop her greasy gourd? It even *looked* like the handle of a pumpkin. Didn't it?"

Freddie was nodding and laughing hysterically that, indeed, it did.

"And that oversized orange getup she had on? I thought she was the carriage that left the prince's palace after the costume ball," the comic continued, creating hysterical pictures in the young boy's impressionable mind.

"A *carriage*," Freddie pealed, unable to contain himself—feeling the urge to pee.

"And did you catch the look when I called her a pumpkin-head? She had absolutely no idea what a western omelet was because her brain was scrambled eggs."

Freddie's head was buried somewhere between Malcolm's shoulder and the back of the leather seat. The whole of his upper body shook. He squeezed his skinny legs together to keep from urinating in his jeans.

"I should have given her a tip she'd remember. I should have told her to find herself a factory job. She was about as popular with the public as venereal disease."

The boy lost his breath entirely.

"Oh, so you know what venereal disease is?"

Freddie bobbed his head.

"How old are you?" Malcolm asked, although he already knew the answer.

Freddie put up all ten fingers.

"Ten going on twenty-one?"

"Ten-and-a-half," Freddie howled.

"I think that waitress back there *is* a venereal disease. I think whatever hauled that carriage, suddenly pooped and hit her smack in the middle of the face before it finally festered."

Freddie's face was as red as the leather upholstery.

"A pus-puss like that, handling food." Malcolm shook his head. "Imagine. What a disgusting human being. How was your meat loaf, Freddie? I hope she didn't *leak* that fluid and call it gravy. Did you stop eating long enough to look down at her shoes? They're supposed to be white. I'd say she swept out a stable before she ever arrived at work. Or maybe they were clean before she stepped into the kitchen. Probably a veritable grease pit back there. That's why I always order eggs out in a place like that. Can't be too careful. Eggs they can't screw up too badly. Can you picture anyone ever eating tongue there, Freddie? Could you puke? Then again, you know where an egg comes from. Yes?"

Freddie was getting grossed out but could not stop laughing, tapping his behind to show that he understood.

"So, you see? Nothing's perfect, my little man."

Malcolm signaled and turned off the main road, then headed up a long dusty drive, giving the boy time to settle down.

"Where are we going?" Freddie finally asked.

"What's the matter? Not having a good time?"

"I'm having a *great* time. But I don't want them to be worried about me."

"I told you before. They both know you're here with me," he assured the boy with a smile. "323-2913. That's your number, right?"

"Right."

"So, relax. You're not going to get in any trouble, I told you. Everything's going to work out fine. But first I've got to pick up a few things at that home just up ahead. And if we have time, we'll pick up some flowers for your mom before I take you back."

"Stepmom," the boy corrected.

"She nice?"

Freddie hesitated. "She's all right, I guess."

"You guess?"

"She's pretty," Freddie offered. "And she's a pretty good cook, too."

"Do you remember your real mom at all?"

Freddie shook his head. "But I've got a picture of her in my stamp collection."

Malcolm smiled understandingly.

"Whose is *that*?" Freddie asked, leaning forward and peering through the windshield.

"That old shack?" he asked with a grin.

An enormous mansion came into view and grew steadily in size before the boy's wide eyes. The estate sat high on an impressive landscaped hill. It looked more like a castle than any home Freddie ever saw. A place where a prince might summon Cinderella to a ball. A palace. A palace out of a fairy tale. The kind of place where a royal coach could most magically turn into a pumpkin after the stroke of midnight . . . a coach drawn by a draft of magnificent white horses in one instant—then a team of mighty mice harnessed together in the next, the youngster envisioned.

"Wow! That place yours?"

"It is for the spring and summer. I rent it. It overlooks the Sound."

"Do you have a wife and kids?"

"I did. A wife and kid," he clarified.

Freddie waited for Malcolm to explain, but he did not.

"That's a pretty big place. I bet you could get lost in there."

"That's why I keep all the lights on at night."

"Are you afraid of the dark?"

"I'm afraid of everything, Freddie."

"Really?"

Malcolm nodded. "Well, here we are."

"I'm not afraid of nothin'. I mean anything."

"Nothing?"

"Maybe snakes, but only the poisonous kind."

Then have I got a surprise for you, Malcolm thought.

"Malcolm?"

"What, Freddie, my boy?"

"If you're afraid of the dark, how come you wear those sunglasses?"

Malcolm removed his glasses and showed Freddie his eyes.

"Wow! What happened?"

"Cat."

Chapter 46

Detective Gary York was seated directly across from Harold Dupree in the den of the family's modest home in Orient. Mr. Dupree was a big man. Six-foot-three in stocking feet. Dark complexion. Lobsterman turned clam digger out of necessity. Father. Husband. Moose and Yacht Club member, too. In good standing, to be sure.

"And that's all I really know about Malcolm Columba, Detective," Harold Dupree said. "Just like I told the other detectives," he concluded, looking the interrogator in the eyes.

The nearest Moose Lodge was on the Peconic River, in Riverhead. As a point of interest to the homicide detectives working the Columba case, the fraternal organization was the only establishment in the entire country to boast a marina. The Loyal Order of Moose. Lodge #1742. *Loyal. To what or whom was Harold being loyal?* Gary York wondered. Country, cause, or perhaps a friend? Harold was a man of some principle and conviction, Gary was about to learn. A man with purpose written across his brow.

Virginia Dupree, Harold's second wife, was serving the two men a second cup of coffee. She wore a nervous smile upon her pretty face. The homemaker refilled, then carefully slid the floral creamer and matching sugar bowl across the rough-hewn lobster trap coffee table toward the cop. Gary admired the hand-painted tiny flowers on beige porcelain: green and yellow and blue, with matching cups and saucers.

"We're running low on half-and-half, so I added a little milk. I hope that's all right," she said politely.

Gary lowered his eyes to the little pitcher. When last he looked it was nearly empty.

"Three-to-one ratio," the cop commented casually, setting Harold up for a tactical give-and-take. "It's fine," he added, seeing that Virginia looked perplexed at his arcane comment.

It took a moment for her to reply. "Oh, yes, well, there's

certainly more milk than cream, now. I mean half-and-half—which I guess makes it three-to-one, if you say so," she said uncomfortably. "Sugar's right there."

"Thanks."

Virginia ran a pair of moist palms down along the fringed borders of her apron.

Harold seemed preoccupied.

"It's an interesting ratio, Harold," Gary threw out casually, adding cream and sugar and stirring the mixture with a tarnished silver teaspoon.

"Excuse me?" The man leaned forward, coming back into the conversation.

"I mean, as it applies to boats," the detective said.

"Boats?"

"Three-to-one ratio. Length-to-beam."

"Sorry, I was thinking of something else. I thought you two were talking about milk and cream or something," he replied with a forced smile.

"We were. And then I thought about the three-to-one ratio I often hear of from a colleague of mine. It seems to be the magic formula in selecting a vessel, and I was just wondering if you subscribe to that thinking."

"Well, it depends on what you want to use a boat for. For fishing offshore waters, I certainly would. But you've got to be careful with what you mean by length-to-beam," the man professed.

"Not sure I follow," Gary muddled.

"Well, first there's the overall length of a craft, and then there's its waterline length. In other words, the length that's actually sitting in the water."

"Is that significant?" What was considerably significant to Gary was that the man was willing to talk a blue streak about anything except Malcolm Columba.

Harold smiled. "It is if you're trying to determine a workable ratio."

"What I mean is—aren't they pretty close? Overall length and waterline length?"

"Could be like night and day. Give you an example." Harold used his hands for demonstration. "Take a boat that's say thirty feet in length with a ten-foot beam. What's the true length-to-beam ratio?"

"Three-to-one," Gary answered straightaway.

Harold shrugged.

"No?" the cop questioned.

"Could be. But I asked for the *true* length-to-beam ratio. That you can't determine till you know the LWL. Length at the waterline. Not the LOA. Length overall."

Gary was nodding, but still seemed a bit puzzled.

"Now, we take this same thirty-foot boat and find that its length at the waterline is only eighteen feet," the captain continued. "What happened to that ideal three-to-one ratio?"

"It just became less than two-to-one," Gary caught on *knowingly.*

"Exactly. You'd need another twelve feet at the waterline to make that boat perform well offshore, if that was your intent. If you have eighteen feet LWL, but only *thought* you had thirty feet sitting in the brine, that could wind up being an eighty thousand dollar mistake, or better. There's a lot of things to consider in the purchase of a boat."

"I'm beginning to see that."

"Well, you're not the only one with boat questions, Detective York."

"No?"

Harold shook his head. "Detective Nelson and his partner were here with your lieutenant."

"Ah. Dean loves to talk boats."

"Indeed, he does. He had a lot of questions after the lieutenant left."

Gary smiled. "Boat questions, I'll bet"

"Yep."

"Well, I can't speak for Detective Nelson, because I wasn't here for the first interview, but this whole business concerning Malcolm Columba has been surrounded by boats and water."

Harold nodded and clammed up once again, lifting the cup of coffee promptly to his lips.

"What I'm getting at is, well, that I hope you don't feel we're not paying enough attention to this case with a lot of questions that seem unrelated. It's just that we can sometimes ask a question seemingly out of left field, and then suddenly it sparks something that could be significant."

"Oh, no. Not at all, Detective," Virginia chimed in. "Please. Feel free to ask us anything you like."

"That's much appreciated because, unlike Detective Nelson, I don't know a blessed thing about boats, except what's rubbed off on me. So, again, please excuse me if I seem to be going off on a tangent."

"If you weren't interested in this case, you wouldn't be back out here," Virginia said sincerely. "And you did ask a hundred questions about the organizations that Harold belongs to before you even asked about boats," she offered appreciatively. "Right, dear?"

Harold put down his cup and nodded.

"And I'm sure you're going to go back and look over a list of members who might also be suspect, Detective. Am I right?" she pressed.

Gary York smiled. "You're very perceptive, Mrs. Dupree. Fact is, we already checked." Gary put a hand inside his jacket pocket and came up with a thin, narrow maroon directory.

"What's that if I may ask?" Virginia asked anxiously.

"It's a Directory of Lodges for the Loyal Order of Moose." Gary noted her surprise and Harold's immediate recognition when identifying the little book.

"Oh, I didn't know they had one. Did you, dear?"

Harold said nothing.

"It's a handy little book, Mr. and Mrs. Dupree."

"Harold. Please call me Harold," Harold said uneasily.

"Ever use it, Harold? In traveling, I mean."

"Oh, I guess maybe once or twice."

"It's got lodges listed all over the United States. Once or twice you say. Huh?" Gary pulled out a notepad about the same size as the directory, turning over several pages. "I never realized they had so many places. You ever *visit* any of these lodges?" he rephrased the question.

"Maybe a few times," Harold expanded, kneading an earlobe between a thumb and forefinger. "You remember that trip down to the Carolinas, sweetheart? We stopped at one of those places along the way. Had a few drinks and a nice dinner. Not *too* many drinks," he bantered, winking across the table at the cop. "Recall, honey?"

"Yes, I do, Harold," Virginia brightened. "It was in Myrtle Beach, South Carolina. Just across the state line from Shallotte. We were on our way to your sister's. March of '92, I do believe. In fact, I'd make a bet."

"Let's see here," Gary said, placing the notepad adjacent to the directory before thumbing through several more pages. "Ah, here it is. South Carolina, Myrtle Beach. 1959."

"Oh, no, Detective! You're mistaken, because I didn't even know Harold until 1990." Virginia leaned in close to the detective and forced a frown. "I wasn't even born till 1969; you're making me older than I really am," she scolded playfully.

"Mrs. Dupree, I—"

"Virginia."

"Virginia. I was referring to Lodge number 1959."

Virginia's hands went up slowly to her face, covering her mouth like a mask—the tips of all ten fingers stopping just below the bridge of her nose. She held them there for a second before she spoke. "My God, but you must think me a moron."

Gary smiled and shook his head. "Not at all. Not in the slightest. How anyone can remember details eight years back is remarkable. I commend you. Really."

Virginia dropped her hands down into her lap. "Mean it?" she questioned, her expression gradually turning into an appreciative smile.

"Absolutely. As a matter of fact, I think you're going to be quite a help to us here."

"Oh, I hope so. I really do."

The homicide detective turned his attention back to the husband. "Well, what we find interesting are the Moose Lodges where you selected to have your meals and drinks, Harold," he stated, careful to shield his notes from view, for Gary York was flying by the seat of his pants—maybe with a prayer thrown in for good measure. Just maybe.

"Interesting in what way?" the lobsterman/clammer asked gruffly, whose change in tone even took Virginia by surprise.

"Let me review my notes, here, Harold. You took a trip to New Smyrna Beach, Florida—February of '98."

"So? They have a lodge there."

"I know. And you spent some time at that lodge."

"Yes."

That's what Gary needed to know. Records showed that Harold Dupree used his credit card all over Edgewater and New Smyrna Beach, that February. What the homicide detective did not know was whether or not Harold had gone to that lodge. Now, he knew. The lodges dealt in cash, which, of course, could not be traced.

"And you stayed five nights in Edgewater, just south of New Smyrna Beach."

"Yes. I took the boy to Epcot and Disney."

"But you stayed a week in Edgewater. Why not in Kissimmee, or Cocoa Beach? Port Orange or Saint Cloud? Or Indian River, in Titusville; they all have lodges, too. Why stay at a hotel in Edgewater? Why visit the lodge in New Smyrna Beach?"

Harold smiled nervously but maintained his cool. "Listen, Detective."

Gary leaned forward, transferring his notes beneath the directory in hand. He picked up his coffee. Took a sip. Put the cup back down. Pen poised. "I'm listening, Harold."

"In case you don't know, those lodges don't provide lodging. We stopped to rest. Stretched our legs. Walked around. Had a meal. You must understand that you've got to hit them just right. The meals, I mean. It's not like a regular restaurant. They're not open for dinner every night of the week, you know."

"I understand that, Harold. I just want to know why you picked the lodge in New Smyrna Beach, and spent a week in Edgewater— especially, if you were taking the family to Epcot and Disney."

"I wasn't on that trip, Detective," Virginia made perfectly clear. "Harold and Freddie went down—"

Harold Dupree raised his hand like a cop directing traffic. The palm facing Virginia meant, *STOP!* "Do you know what it's like to get a place around Disney and Epcot during President's Week? Any idea?"

"Well, Harold. I'd imagine it's quite busy."

"Damn right. Every kid and his cousin is down there that time of year."

"But you booked accommodations well in advance. Why Edgewater?"

"Well, if you really want to know the truth, Detective—"

"Oh, I do, Harold. Just like that *true* length-to-beam ratio you explained so aptly—if I'm to have a meaningful picture. Truth versus tall tales," he elaborated by way of a simple demonstration of his own, illustrating a scale in motion through the use of upright open palms—moving them up and down proportionately.

Harold Dupree studied the man and the situation before he opened his mouth. "It was too expensive to stay anywheres near Orlando or Kissimmee. It was cheaper to the north."

It was the answer Gary expected. And a good one at that. Yet, he pressed on. "And those other lodges that I mentioned? Apart from Kissimmee and Saint Cloud, which is in the heart of kiddy land, I'll grant you. Even the one in Titusville is close. But what about the others, Harold? Hum? Cocoa Beach, Melbourne, Palm Bay? They *all* have Moose Lodges."

"They're further south, I believe. Why would I want to travel further south?"

Another good answer. Made sense. Why travel out of the way? Harold seemed to know the Eastern coast of Florida fairly well. "Then why not Port Orange instead of New Smyrna Beach? That's the first Moose Lodge you would have hit in that area. Right above New Smyrna Beach . . . where you could have stopped and stretched your legs . . . looked around. Maybe gotten a bite to eat with the boy."

Harold had his answer ready. "Because it's a free fucking country! That's how come." The lobsterman's neck and face were as red as the prodigious lobster on the paneled wall above his head.

"Harold!" Virginia said in alarm.

Harold put out his hand again for silence.

Gary took his eyes off the lobster and fixed them on the angry man. He sat quietly, letting Harold know that his answer was unacceptable.

"Look."

Gary was looking.

"I had reservations in Edgewater. So, I stopped at the Moose Lodge in New Smyrna Beach, first. Is that a crime? Didn't you ever drive to the furthest point before continuing on to your destination? Yes, I could have stopped at the Moose Lodge in Port Orange. I could have stopped at a Rest Area. Or a Cracker Barrel. But I didn't. What's the point?"

"We're getting to the point, Harold. Slowly. But I assure you we'll arrive there together. Now. You've had a lot of downtime lately. Business being off for you like it is."

"Yeah?" Harold leaned back into his lounging chair. "So?"

Gary looked back at his notes. "Been doing quite a bit of traveling lately."

Harold was beginning to sweat.

Not a good sign to set upon the scale of truth.

Gary wondered where to hit him next. It had to be a glancing blow, otherwise Harold might run for cover early. *Keep it in the past*, Gary told himself. *Nothing current. Not just yet.* He put away his notes, then opened up the directory once again. "I see they've got a lodge in Annapolis."

Harold kept his mouth shut and shot a telling look over to Virginia, who sat statue-like with her hands placed squarely on her lap.

"Last year you stayed at a Ramada Inn, nearby."

"We were at the Annapolis Boat Show."

"Who's we?"

"Freddie always wanted to see the show, so we went."

"Virginia?"

"She stayed home," he answered abruptly.

Gary gave her a little smile that, apparently, she was afraid to return. "Visit the Moose Lodge there in Annapolis?" he questioned, staring back across at Harold.

"May have."

"Yes or no?" York asked sternly.

"I think so, yes."

"I think so, too, Harold." Gary nodded like he knew.

The time frame surrounding the murders in and around the Riverhead area was moot at this point. Further inquiry, there, would only serve to antagonize the man—giving him too much time to think. Gary was dealing in distances for the moment. The more miles the merrier. Orient, to where the North and South Forks of Long Island meet in Riverhead, was merely a throw. But what the homicide detective wanted to do—now—was drop a boulder on the shell fisherman's skull. And then he would hone his sword and home in for the kill. He would have nothing to lose at that point. So. Where should he swing and lower the boom? Over Adirondack Park in upstate New

York? Maine? Michigan?

Seeing as Harold had (and maybe *had* was the operative word) a young child of his own, perhaps Gary could get through to the man via Becky Dawson. Deceased.

"We know you've been to Maine recently, too, Harold. The timing there is interesting. The same week Becky Dawson and her dog disappeared. But not for long. They both turned up dead. Her dog was decapitated with surgically sharpened skates. Malcolm Columba came down on the animal's neck like it was a loaf of headcheese. Then he went to work on the girl. Becky was found in a pond in back of her house in Old Town. Drowned before she bled to death. That's only after Malcolm kicked her around a bit with those blades. Their points and edges honed to perfection. They found Becky's hands bound in front of her with Malcolm's belt." He could hear Virginia weeping, but did not dare turn his head a fraction away from Harold's face. "We found slashes along the inside of her wrists from the skates he had given her as a gift. Sharpened like razor blades. She was trying to free herself in four feet of water surrounded by ice. Flesh and leather. Get the picture, Harold? We figure he helped her in. The ice was chopped up all around her. Thin ice. Like you're skating on right now. That was Malcolm's little game. He probably told her he'd let her go if she could cut herself free, knowing she'd cut her wrists to ribbons in the act. Either bleed to death or drown. Whichever came first. Hey, Virginia, I'd bet big bucks Malcolm even watched poor Becky Dawson die. That's how he *really* gets his kicks." Gary still did not move a muscle, keeping his eyes fixed on Harold's. "Eight years old, Dupree."

"I was nowhere near Old Town," Harold finally said.

"I didn't even know where Old Town was, Harold. I had to look for it on the map. So, *where* in Maine were you that you knew you were nowhere near Old Town the day Becky and her little dog were butchered? Another Moose Lodge?"

"Why don't *you* tell *me*," Harold challenged.

"Sure. Why not?" There were only two lodges in all of Maine: Scarborough, a city in the southwest corner of the state; and Portland, maybe ten miles further north along the coast. Two lodges. A fifty-fifty shot—unlike Florida, that had well over two hundred branches alone. The detective had no credit card record for Harold Dupree anywhere in Maine. He figured the man knew it. *Roll the dice, Gary,* he told himself. *Take the gamble. Throw in a taradiddle, too. What the hell. Put the money on the biggest city of the two.* "You bypassed Scarborough, Harold. And went on to Portland. We have two witnesses who can place you there during the time in question," he outright lied. *Spread the icing across the cake. Put it on nice and thick. Go for broke. There's a pattern here, and you know it. You're the **closer**, buddy. Do it!* "You had Freddie with you, too."

Harold took a deep breath through his nostrils and looked over at Virginia, then quickly looked away—expelling a forceful stream of air in absolute anguish.

"Wherever you stayed in your travels with Freddie, there was always a Moose Lodge nearby."

Harold nodded, averting the detective's eyes. He hung his head sorrowfully.

"Where did you stay in Adirondack Park?"

No answer.

"Bet it was close to Fern Rodman's cabin on Long Lake," the cop said cocksurely.

Harold gave the detective a rueful look. "I . . . Freddie and I stayed at Raquette Lake."

"Less than twenty miles to the south."

Harold nodded. "I suppose."

"And?"

"And the next morning we headed up to Tupper Lake."

Gary consulted the small directory in conjunction with his notes. "Just north of Long Lake; along Highway Thirty."

"Yes."

Gary noted that there were two Moose Lodges in the vicinity. One in Tupper Lake. The other in Saranac Lake, approximately another six miles further north.

Detective Andrew Miller and a certain civilian had done a good job researching all the Moose Lodges and their distances in proximity to where the murders occurred. But it was Brian Archer's fine eye for detail, together with Dean Nelson's brainstorming, that netted the pair their golden lead. It was Brian who spotted the Moose cap hanging from the back of the costumer in Freddie's room. It was Dean who went on forever about boats and marinas in general. And, of course, it was Theo's doing to allow the man with a felony record to participate in a multiple murder investigation after Justin Barnes had proven himself worthy of invaluable information. Information unrelated to the case. Yet, information that had saved the Riverhead correctional facility quite an embarrassment, if not a life or two or more in the bargain.

"And you had business at the lodge in Tupper Lake," Gary deduced. Business that Harold Dupree did not want anyone to know about. Including his wife.

"I didn't kill nobody." Harold's voice quivered.

"Anybody," Virginia said and stood immediately, correcting her husband's English as she had her stepson's a thousand times before. "What is this all about, Harold?" she demanded.

"Sit down!" Captain Dupree commanded his wife.

Virginia walked right up to him. "This is our home, Harold. Not your boat. You don't order me around in here. I'm your soul mate —not your shipmate. What have you gotten yourself and Freddie into? Please tell me and this detective. We have a right to know." Tears welled up in the corners of her blue-green eyes. "Please, Harold. He's my stepson, and I love him dearly. But he's your only flesh and blood."

Harold put his face in his hands and his elbows on his knees, then slowly shook his head.

Virginia put the tips of her fingers on a broad shoulder. "Harold, please. For the love of God."

Harold lifted his arm and brushed her hand away. "I didn't kill nobody," he repeated.

"I know you didn't, Harold," Gary interjected. "But I wouldn't have a lick of trouble naming you as an accomplice. Now, would I?"

"I didn't know he killed anybody. Not in the beginning. Up until now, I wasn't even sure."

"I suppose it was just a coincidence that these bodies started turning up in proximity to where you and the boy stayed and the lodges you visited," the detective put forth caustically.

"I didn't even know about the murder in the Adirondacks until I saw it in the local papers when they ran a story about a serial killer."

"What about the Riverhead and Flanders murders? What about the young woman over in North Haven? A cripple. Not near enough to home for you to have realized, Harold? Live under a rock, man? Long

Lake, maybe I can understand. Know how far that is from Dannemora as the crow flies? Less than sixty miles. Dannemora, Harold. That's where our killers and their accomplices sit. Right near the Canadian border. Closest Moose Lodge there is Plattsburgh," he mocked. "But once we stick you in Dannemora, Captain, you forfeit your membership to the human race. Got it, fella?"

"Now, you just mind your manners, Detective," Virginia cautioned carefully. "Talking tough to this man only makes him close up tighter than a clam. You let me handle this."

Gary was seeing another side to the woman. Beneath her softness was a tough interior.

She stood rigidly beside her man. "When you went on these little trips of yours, Harry, I thought there might have been another woman."

Harold reached up and took his woman's hand. He shook his head.

"But I said to myself. Why would he insist on taking Freddie along if he was fooling around? It didn't make too much sense to me. So, I chalked it up to this male bonding thing you guys have. Father and son and the freedom of the road, I guess. I know that Freddie has no idea what this business is all about, but as we sit here apart from our little boy—" Virginia swallowed several sobs "—a murderer is holding him who means to do him harm."

Harold shook his head. "He won't hurt him, honey. I swear."

Virginia pulled her hand out from her husband's. "What do you *mean*, he won't hurt him? I'm just hearing he killed a lot of young women and a little girl. Even her dog."

"He won't hurt him," Harold insisted. "You've got to trust me."

"Trust you. I'm appealing to your sense of reason, but I can see that maybe the detective's right." And with that remark, Virginia slapped her husband hard across his face.

Harold shot up from his seat like a jack-in-the-box.

York came around the table and stood between them.

"This is my house," the keeper of his castle stated heatedly before the cop.

"And you're about to swap it for a cell. Now, sit back down there and listen to your wife."

Harold remained standing where he stood.

"I said, sit."

Harold sat.

"Michigan. You've been to that state recently." It was not presented as a question, although it could have been, but Detective Gary York knew that he was on solid ground. "Middle of February." It was a sure bet. "Left your lovely wife all alone on Valentine's Day. Well, she might be alone for a long, long while, Harold."

"Leave my wife out of it," the burly man warned.

Gary smiled sarcastically. He was almost there. "Aiding and abetting. Carries a stiff sentence in a homicide case. Imagine what it will carry—are you counting—in assisting nine, possibly ten murders?" Gary held up nine fingers in front of the man's face before adding then subtracting a thumb. The cop finally dropped his hands and brushed aside the bottom of his expensive light-gray cashmere sports jacket, reaching past his holstered revolver and revealing a pair of shiny handcuffs.

"I didn't aid or abet nobody," he seethed.

"Aid and abet, *anyone*," Virginia corrected inanely. "You better talk."

"I didn't aid or abet anyone." Harold stood corrected. Sitting calmly. Changing his tone. A bit more civil and bridled. Relinquishing a mounting rage as York unsnapped the pair of silver bracelets. "I didn't," he repeated.

"What exactly *did* you do, Harold? It's your last chance," the detective promised him. "Michigan."

Harold was trapped like one of tens of thousands of lobsters he had taken through the years. His livelihood was over. Maybe even his life. He was fifty-two years old and did not want to spend the remainder of his days in prison—let alone a single night.

"I want to call my lawyer."

A homicide cop's worst nightmare. The cry of last resort. Defense attorneys. They were the bane of the detective's existence. Gary York could slip into the role of counselor just as surely as a chameleon could change the color of its skin, just as he had done on the Howard Mills serial-killer case. Passing himself off as the postal worker's savior—having the suspect confess to a series of murders that he may or may not have committed but who was, nevertheless, fully involved. However, that was then. York could walk the walk and talk the talk. He was that good. He could play the sympathetic mouthpiece to perfection. Even crawl under a *client's* skin if need be. Build them up or tear them down as he was about to do now. Not as an attorney, but rather as a doomsday cop.

"Gonna get real expensive, Harold. You're gonna need lots of clams for a good criminal lawyer. Gonna break the bank, I promise you. And then you're still gonna wind up in the slammer anyhow. For openers, you're not even going to make bail. This house is only half paid for. True? Your boat, you can kiss goodbye. On the bright side, we both know a cop who's about to retire who will be happy to give you ten cents on the dollar. Then, when I finish telling the district attorney's office just how uncooperative you are, he's gonna go for the maximum sentence. And if anything happens to your boy, it's going to be on your head. I'm personally going to see to it that it's handed over to the D.A. on a silver platter. Now, let's go. I'm through talking to you. I'm not wasting anymore time here. You can make your call from headquarters."

Detective York stood the man up, grabbed a wrist, then snapped on one of the cuffs.

"What is *wrong* with you, Harry?" Virginia wept. "What are you hiding? How can you play around with Freddie's life like this? Answer me, goddamn you!"

"I told you. Nothin's gonna happen to him, Virginia."

"How can you say that?" she screamed, scrambling over to him.

Gary turned the man halfway around and slapped on the other manacle. "Move!"

"He's killed *nine* people, Harry," she stated. "Why won't he hurt Freddie? Please tell me," she begged, dropping to her knees and wrapping her arms around her husband's legs, hanging on to him for dear life. Her life as well as his. The life of their little boy. "Why, why, why?" she whined, then wailed. "Oh, God, please tell me why."

Harold Dupree resisted the detective's tug, remaining fixed in the corner of the family den—like a large African cat. A black panther with wild, wide-open eyes. The prisoner looked down at his pathetic wife and slowly shook his head.

"Why?" she repeated.

Harold drew a deep breath. "Because Freddie is Malcolm's

son."

Virginia Dupree took her tearful eyes off her husband and cast them in confusion from floor to ceiling. Detective Gary York roughly set the man back down in his easy chair.

It was the hardest hour in Harold's life.

"Where is he?" Gary demanded.

Harold shook his head. "I don't know. That's the honest to God truth."

Gary York was a human polygraph machine. He believed Harold plainly was not lying. Had not been, in fact. Just not forthcoming with information, up until now. *Now* was a new moment. Now, Harold would spill his guts.

"One little white lie from you, one single fib, and I put you in that car outside. It will be the last trip you take for a week before you're arraigned in front of a District Court judge, then transferred to Riverhead Jail, where you'll rot for a year before you ever go to trial. Are you a doubting Thomas, Harold?"

With his arms pinned behind his back, Harold shook his head. Still, it looked to Gary as though the man was more afraid of his wife than he was of him.

"Talk."

Harold Dupree unfolded a story while his wife and Gary listened to a tale too bizarre, too outlandish, to be a work of fiction. The cop took copious notes. Virginia wept quietly and chewed her cuticles until they bled.

BOOK II

Chapter 47

Donald Bellport cleaned, waxed, then stored his set of Head Skis and accessories, evidence that had been returned by the police to the handyman following his release. From the back of a hall closet, he removed a pair of aluminum storage tubes. Each cylinder protected two sections of the finest graphite fly rods made by Sage and G. Loomis: one six-weight, with which to work the larger lakes and streams; a second, shorter, four-weight, in order to make a delicate presentation upon the small ponds and rivulets. He was surprised the items were still there, for the authorities had gone through his cabin like a wrecking ball—to the point of tearing up floorboards. The two fly rods were among his prize possessions.

If Donald had money to burn, he would own lots of fly rods, reels and skis. The man had to have the very best sporting equipment that he could afford, and he took good care of his toys. He loved to ski Adirondack Park, but trout fishing for brookies, rainbows and browns was his passion. His mother taught him, very early on in life, precisely how to work the *magic wand*. And that is exactly what it was to the boy back then. A mystical length of pure unadulterated magic. But only in the hands of sorcerers, he once believed.

Actually, it had not been that difficult a skill to master. Practice and patience were the keys; that and a loving mother's drive and determination to set her boy apart from the rest. The young colored boys growing up in the back country learned to fish the ponds, lakes and lazy rivers, using their pithy cane poles and lengths of cotton line, not to mention those ridiculous red and white cork or plastic bobbers, both mother and son would smugly smile.

"Those setups are strictly for 'porch monkeys,'" his mother would call those *other* folk, until the day she died. Not so for a boy of color whose skin was as light as coffee and cream, drunk from the cup of circumstance, determining complexion as well as social station. Certainly not for the purist who could lay down a light cahill quieter than the very fly itself, skittering the imitation across a glassy surface as if it were about to suddenly take to the air before enticing and battling a wary four-pound brown or rainbow rising to the occasion. Donald would almost always intimidate a dozen small brookies before running home in order to prepare for school.

During spring recess, he would wade the ice-cold mountain streams in sneakers and shorts. Hunting up food for the table. A.M. to P.M. Productiveness in lieu of sport. Wet flies weighted with wraps of thread-like lead wire and an intermediate shooting line to plumb the depths of rapid streams and rivers—whisking a host of hackle and hairs through the deeper pockets and pools. Along seams and riffles, too—where slow-moving water met the faster flow. Donald was proud of his deadly hand-tied artificials. Woolly buggers, muddler minnows, and dun-colored streamers to begin the season. When the wicker creel was weighed to match the appetites of his mom and several friends and neighbors, he would simply play. Catch and release. As the season progressed, dozens of patterns of pupae, nymphs, gnats, and caddisflies were employed to match the hatch and lure the leery. He loved to experiment. Innovation was the hallmark of a good fly tier.

Each night, young Donald would say his prayers, thanking God profusely for all the good and beautiful wonders in life. The clean mountain air. The crystal clear waters of the many lakes, streams, rivers, ponds, brooks and pools. He knew them all. Life was truly fine. He did not have a Sage or a Loomis—or even a girlfriend back then. But that would come later, he supposed. In the interim, he thanked God again and again for the inexpensive but effective Four Star glass Garcia that his mom had bought for him with her baby-sitting and housecleaning money. Good-paying jobs around the neighborhood and town. A weekly *salary*. Not the low, daily wage associated with the back country deprivation which surrounded them.

Of course, his notorious mother kept the expensive, custom, split bamboo rod all to herself, carrying her magic wand through the region *wherever* she cared to roam—freely—as only white folk dare walk the neighborhood and town, while the colored folk slinked along its outskirts between dusk and dawn. Although his mother was a light-skinned black, she was accepted because she positively passed for white. That and the fact that she was beautiful. However, there was no mistaking, upon close examination, the dominant features of her race. Still, her beauty belied as well as masked such subtle traits—

particularly through the eyes of the predominantly white population.

Donald's likeness was not as telling. His so-called father, who left them both when he was three and she nineteen, was as black as coal. Father in name only, Donald knew. He knew, too, secretly of course, that he was the bastard son of a man who presently sat in an ivory tower down in Albany. A man whose father before him also occupied a seat in the citadel as lieutenant governor. Hiding under a dome of darkness was how the Adirondack handyman pictured his biological father. Not that Donald ever expected or even wanted the man to surface in the *back country.*

Donald got even, though. Quite recently, in fact—immediately following his release from jail. Or if not *quite* even, then at least he felt somewhat satisfied after sending off a package to the capitol building, enclosing a fresh Polaroid of himself—giving the finger to any and all who cared to take a look. Accompanying the picture was an old snapshot of his comely, pregnant mother. The parcel, void of any return address, also contained a brand-new DNA testing kit. Donald believed that he had gotten his message across:

I know who you are, and I really don't give a good goddamn is what it amounted to, although no correspondence accompanied the bundle of frustration. Not one word.

Donald Bellport was mad at the bureaucratic world, and with good reason.

Donald was busy arranging a series of interchangeable spools for his Abel fly reel when he heard a knock. It was 8 a.m. The handyman sauntered toward the front porch of the modest cabin and opened the door wide. His heart skipped a beat. *What a nice looking gal,* he thought.

"Hi, there," came the sultry voice, followed by a seductive smile.

"Hi, there, yourself," he said cordially.

"Got a minute?"

Donald lifted a lazy hand, yawned, looked at his watch, then smiled. "For you, sweetheart, I've got till tomorrow morning. And then maybe we could do some fishing together, if you like. Fly-fishing, that is. If you've never handled a fly rod, I can teach you in a heartbeat."

The pretty woman laughed. "They warned me about you—"

"Who warned you?" he snapped, exhibiting a degree of irritation—perhaps a remnant or two of animosity left over after weeks of confinement and a steady dose of jailhouse food.

"Just about everyone in town I asked who I might find to fix a chiffonier," she answered evenly, realizing she had hit a nerve.

"A chiffonier?"

"I'm sorry, it's a—"

"I know what a chiffonier is, darlin'. I just didn't know that anyone this side of the mountains used that word. Especially, out here in the boondocks."

"Well, it's been in my family for generations. And I don't care what it costs to fix. I just want someone to repair it, and repair it right. They say that you're the best in the area—that you can fix anything."

"The area? You sure they didn't say the *back country*?" he funned behind a feigned frown.

"Did I say something wrong?" she asked in confusion.

Donald laughed easily. "Nah. It's just that I've been tryin' to fix a busted bureaucracy, but failed miserably."

"But can you fix my chiffonier?"

"Sweetheart, I can fix practically anything but a decent cup of coffee. Care to come in and lend a helping hand?" he offered invitingly.

"Oh, no, really, but thanks. I have the piece with me in the van. Could you come out and take a look? If you can fix it, I'll give you a deposit, and I'll even help you carry it inside, or wherever it is you do your work. It's rather heavy."

"I have my shop out back." He looked over her shoulder at the blue van. "Why don't you pull around, and we'll have a look."

"My name's Charlotte." She put out her hand.

"My mother's name was Charlotte," he flat out fibbed. It was a silly thing to say, but he said it.

"I heard it was Macon."

Donald looked oddly at the woman. "And just *who* have you been talking to, Charlotte?" Donald demanded with a pout, hands placed squarely upon on his skinny hips, standing there like his mother used to stand in that very spot whenever she scolded him for a thousand different reasons.

"I told you. Lots of folks." She jingled her keys before him like little bells, then walked off the porch in tightly-fitted jeans toward the vehicle.

Zing went the strings of his heart.

He sized her up immediately. Spoiled, white, rich bitch. But seemingly nice. He pictured her in his bed. He enjoyed women even more than expensive graphite fishing rods, reels, and skis . . . though he had not thought about another woman in weeks—not since Fern Rodman. Some kind of a record. Maybe it was time.

Charlotte looked as though she might have been in her early to mid-thirties. A bit older than he. She had a few miles on her. But all of them were highway from the looks of that chassis, he figured with a satisfying sigh.

Things were looking up.

He figured she had heard about his recent *ordeal*. How could she not? Long Lake was a gossipy little community like many lakefront resort areas throughout Adirondack Park, especially during late fall through early spring when life slowed down and gradually grew quiet. Not like the summer months when the townsfolk were too busy making money hand over fist from tourists.

Nothing out of the ordinary ever really happened in Long Lake. So happenings had to be invented. Everyday occurrences were somewhat embellished upon; otherwise, they held little merit in the local meeting spots. But Donald's arrest had and would keep the locals talking for years to come, he knew.

It did not matter that he was totally innocent of *any* wrongdoing. His arrest gave everyone a chance to put their own spin on the facts concerning Miss Rodman and her local handyman. Donald Bellport had been held without bail, and that had to account for some measure of guilt. The fact that he had some black blood flowing through his veins took on a certain *je ne sais quoi* in the fertile minds and imaginations of young and old alike. After his release, it afforded everyone the opportunity to express their *deepest* regrets and sorrows. Yet, while he had been sitting in a cell, not one person, black or white, made any attempt to contact him or show any kind of support. When he got home, there was not one letter, note, or phone message. Not even after he was settled back into his routine. It was only when Donald bumped into a person on the street, or popped into a store to do some shopping, did he receive their condolences and/or *outrage* over his false arrest.

Donald would simply furl his lips and nod his head, agreeing with whatever it was they had to say. Repay a perfunctory politeness. Pay the bill. Then be gone.

A week later, though, opportunity knocked. Like it had a moment ago with Charlotte somebody, standing on his porch.

Now, suddenly, he was in demand.

Hey, Donald, my man. Can you fix this or that? Mrs. So-And-So said that you were pretty good with your hands. Me, I'm all thumbs.

Say, Donald. I hear you can do a little 'lectric.

Mr. Bellport. My sink won't stop leakin'. Can you come by an' havalook 'fore the bucket overflows?

Sir, I have my own lawn equipment. Can you come around once a week and cut our grass?

Got a project for you, Bellport. Need a deck. But I want a good price.

Can you build and install kitchen cabinets? Pay you the going rate.

It was the town's way of finally saying: *Sorry some of the others thought you were guilty. But let us make it up to you.*

Donald had never been so busy.

He quickly ran a toothbrush across and up and down his teeth and gums, then promptly pulled a comb through his wavy black hair.

He headed out the back door.

"You're not from around here, Charlotte."

"No. Well, yes. But not this area."

Donald smiled. "What area *are* you from?"

The woman stood off to the side of the vehicle. She was smiling, too. "Albany."

"This unlocked?"

"Yes, but you have to give it a good shove. It gets stuck sometimes. I don't have the strength."

Donald put his shoulder to the sliding side door panel and gave it a good push.

"Hi, Donald. Step aboard," the man seated inside the vehicle said.

"Do exactly as he says," Charlotte instructed, holding a small caliber handgun an inch away from the back of Donald's head.

"Get in," the big man insisted.

Donald recognized him from the police barracks. The guy with the long heavy coat and cowboy hat—reminding him of The Marlboro Man. The one who stood close to reporters and watched as the cops ushered him off to a waiting vehicle for arraignment. Scary bastard then, and twice as scary now. Only this time, the man wore an open leather jacket with a large gun slung across his chest.

"What do you want?" Donald demanded.

"My reward money," Austin Izzo answered with a snarl. Then, with a single motion, Donald was snatched up in the man's powerful grip and hurled violently across the van's interior. Don Ciccio's thug reached over and slid the door closed with a thud.

Charlotte headed the vehicle out the drive.

Donald saw no chiffonier inside the darkened box. However, toward the front of the van, standing on gargoyled legs, stood an old-fashioned bathtub, oddly rigged with shiny new plumbing—fixed to the floor. The same type of tub in which Patricia Tamblin's body had been found. Drowned. The same design, except for the fact that the fixture was porcelain instead of cast iron. He recognized the outdated monstrosity from the crime scene photos the police had stuck beneath his nose.

Donald's nose was bleeding profusely. He pulled out the front of his shirt to stop it. "The police let me go. I'm not the one you're looking for."

"You shut your fucking face."

"I won't. You have no right—"

Once again, Donald was slammed against the steel frame. A large fist found the center of his face and did the job the metal panel failed to do. The handyman's nose was flattened. Broken beyond repair.

Donald's pain was unbearable, and his screams filled Izzo's ears.

More fists went flying.

Two of Donald's struck the air.

In an instant, Donald felt the cold enameled floor of the tub smack up against his face.

"You skinny little cocksuckin' nigger," Izzo swore.

Austin Izzo lifted Bellport's head a foot off the floor of the tub before smashing it cruelly against the pitted porcelain surface several times. Next, he forced the young man's arm up into a hammerlock. Forced it further along the back of Bellport's body until he heard and felt it crack.

Donald Bellport let out a final cry before he lost all consciousness.

"Fucking nerve!" the Mafia figure blew.

"Everything all right back there?" Charlotte barked, keeping her eyes peeled straight ahead, fully focused on the winding mountain road.

"Fucking guy tried to take a swipe at me." The big man massaged the knuckles of his right hand. "Fuckin' punk."

"Be cool, now. We got a lot riding on this guy. Gotta stretch this out—"

"Shut the fuck up and drive."

Charlotte smiled in the rearview mirror. "Whatever you say, shithead."

From a large canvas boat bag, Austin removed a length of ribbon-like steel wire—threaded through a long curved needle.

Chapter 48

Malcolm Columba took Freddie's hand as they entered a room off the dimly lit foyer. With his free hand, the killer immediately hit the lights.

Freddie stepped forward excitedly, pressing his palms and nose against the glass. "Wow! I never saw so many snakes."

"I thought you were afraid of snakes."

"Not stuffed ones, I'm not."

"That's called taxidermy."

"I know that," Freddie said defensively. It was another word that Freddie knew but did not have handy on the tip of his tongue. "They're taxidermied."

"No such word," Malcolm said with a smile.

"Oh."

"Taxidermal, taxidermic, taxidermist."

"Then they're taxi . . . taxied what?"

Malcolm shrugged.

"Tell me," Freddie insisted.

"They're stuffed. Just like you said."

Freddie Dupree looked up at Malcolm before they both broke into laughter. The boy nuzzled his nose against Malcolm's side.

"You're so funny." He turned his head around and went back to peering at the snakes.

Thick snakes and skinny snakes. Snakes hanging from limbs. Snakes coiled in front and on top of rocks. A snake with a rodent frozen a fraction of an inch away from the reptile's fanged-mouth. Snakes in the grass.

"Know what these showcases are called, Freddie?"

"Sure. Dioramas." Freddie was very pleased with himself for remembering the word. "Mom and Dad took me to the Metropolitan Museum of Natural History in Manhattan. They've got everything taxiderm . . . *stuffed* in there," he underscored with a grin. "Like it was really real. Just like in there."

"Go to many places like that with your mom and dad, do you?"

Freddie scrunched his face up into a weighty thought. "More with Mom than my dad. But my dad and I take some really neat trips. Places very far away from here. Like Disney World and Epcot Center. And we did stop at the Adirondack Museum in Blue Mountain Lake, but it was closed."

"That's when you went upstate to Raquette Lake, then on to the Moose Lodge at Tupper Lake."

"Right. How'd you know that?"

"I have a crystal ball."

"Yeah, right."

"No, really I do, Freddie. I can show it to you. Would you like to see it?"

"Sure. But I'll tell you right now that there ain't—excuse me—isn't no—isn't *any* such thing as magic. I mean there is, but it's all fake."

"Trickery."

"Right."

"And may I ask who told you that?"

"Dad. He tells me the truth about everything."

"Does he, now."

"You bet. Like where babies come from and stuff like that."

"Think he tells you *absolutely* everything?"

"Everything I ask him about. But not always in front of Mom."

"He ever tell you about us?"

"Us?"

"Yes, us."

"You mean what you told me about you and him being lobstermen?"

"Things beyond that."

Freddie shook his head. "Can I call home now?"

"In a little while. First, I want to show you that crystal ball."

"All right," the boy said skeptically. "But then I really got to call."

"Right you are."

Malcolm led the boy out of the room and down a hallway, guiding him into a huge white space that was sparsely furnished. He switched on another light.

Freddie looked around, then up at the vaulted ceiling. "Wow! This is the largest room I've ever been in, except for the museum I told you about. Ask you something?"

"Of course."

"Why do you have all those stuffed snakes back there?"

"Well. Because."

"Because why?"

"Just because."

"Mom says because is not a reason why."

"Does she, now?"

"Uh-huh."

"Maybe I'll explain it to you later. But right now I want you to take a look at my crystal ball."

Malcolm pointed toward a glass table in front of a long white couch. On its top sat a small crystal—a many faceted sphere about the size of a Ping-Pong ball.

"That's not a crystal ball, Malcolm."

"But of course it is."

"Is not." The boy looked disappointed.

"Is, too."

Freddie shook his head.

"Why do you insist it isn't?"

"Because a crystal ball is bigger. Perfectly round and smooth. It doesn't have all

those . . ."

"Facets, like a gem."

"If you say so." Facets. Freddie stored away the word.

"That's what it is, Freddie. A crystal ball," Malcolm said most assuredly.

"Show me."

"Show you what?"

"The future. If that's a crystal ball, it's supposed to tell the future."

"Oh, the future is easy, Freddie. This crystal ball is a little bit different."

"I knew it."

"Knew what?"

"That that's a fake."

Malcolm shook his head. "This crystal ball tells the past."

Freddie giggled.

"What's so funny?"

"It's the *past* that's easy to tell."

"It is?" Malcolm said with some surprise.

"Sure."

"How easy?"

Freddie thought. "As easy as picking up yesterday's newspaper," he said smartly. "As easy as reading the encyclopedia. Or a history book." *Let Malcolm try and argue that.* He grinned from ear to ear.

"But not everything that's happened in the past is in newspapers, encyclopedias, or history books."

"Everything that's important is," the boy came back like a champ.

"Really?"

Freddie nodded. "Yep."

"Are you and I important?"

"Well, sure. I guess."

"Well, are we or aren't we?"

"Yes," Freddie said decisively.

"Then how come *we're* not in the newspapers, encyclopedias, or history books? Huh?"

Freddie had to think hard. "Because . . . because we're not as important as the president of the United States, or the pope."

"Ah, but we are, Freddie. You just don't know that yet. That's why it's important to *see* into the past to know who you really are."

Freddie was getting a little confused, like in school, but he remained focused. He concentrated very hard on the last part of Malcolm's statement. He took it nice and slow. Malcolm was a patient listener.

"I *know* my past. And—"

"No, you don't."

Freddie was thrown. "Don't what?"

"Know your past."

"Sure I do."

"Prove it. Take an important event that happened in your life, then start to tell me about it."

"All right. Let me think. Oh, Epcot!"

"Wait!" Malcolm went over to the crystal and swooped it up, examining it closely before he spoke. "Science exhibit. Marine biology. You couldn't get enough. So you stayed for a week in Edgewater, but before all that . . . wait . . . wait . . . wait—you stopped at the Moose Lodge in New Smyrna Beach and ordered a lobster, but they didn't have any. So you settled for grouper, which you thought was great. Your dad told you to take your hat off at the table, which he's told you a million times before . . . wait . . . scratch that—make that a million and one."

Freddie stared in amazement and started to say something.

"Hold it. Hold it." Malcolm brought the crystal closer to his face. "You were wearing a New York Rangers jacket."

Freddie stepped closer to Malcolm, wanting to peek into the crystal glass.

The boy gazed upward.

Malcolm looked down.

"And you had on those same sneakers you're wearing now."

Nothing further was said for several seconds.

Freddie was the first to break the silence. "How'd you do that?"

"Believe in the power of this crystal now?"

Freddie nodded slowly.

Malcolm handed him the orb.

The boy held it between prayerful hands. The crystal reflected brilliantly in the downcast light from one of the high hats in the ceiling. Freddie studied his own multifaceted image.

Malcolm stooped and gazed—viewing a series of shifting forms and faces. Victims. Nine . . . no, *ten* contorted countenances changing within a colorless kaleidoscopic-like pattern.

"I've seen you in all those faraway places that you traveled to with your dad. Florida. Maryland. Maine. Michigan. Upstate New York in the Adirondack Mountains. Even close to home."

Freddie raised his eyes to meet Malcolm's. The boy carefully studied the small, yet heavy lead glass object in his hand.

"Now. Do you really want to know about *our* past?"

Freddie seemed a bit uneasy. But he nodded a yes.

"Sure?"

"Yes."

"No turning the hands of the clock ahead once we go back in time."

"I understand," the boy said cautiously.

"You will shortly," Malcolm said enigmatically. "You will, indeed."

Chapter 49

Homicide detective work, in round figures, habitually totaled out to approximately ninety percent tenacity and tedium—about ten percent sheer excitement, combining pure horror along with occasional traces of terror. For the most part, the horror scene usually occurred at the beginning of a case; that being, the discovery of the body, which might include anything from a fatal bullet found lodged inside the skull of the victim, to a lethal shotgun blast making mincemeat out of some rival member's mind and/or midsection. Just as abhorring, though not seemingly so upon first glance, might be a victim's virtually bloodless bludgeoning—ending in ventricular fibrillation; that is, cardiac arrest, brought about by the pummeling of pulpy portions of the body. Examples of such savagery were mortal blows delivered to the kidneys, frontal assaults inflicted upon the abdomen of pregnant women as the target of pugilistic punishment or, quite commonly, the complete and merciless battering of a child. The end result? Massive internal bleeding followed by a painful, dilatory death. Down along a lengthy list of foul play might be found a poisoning or two. Multiple stab wounds seemed to be the latest *rage*: ninety plus puncture marks per torso is not an uncommon sight. But unlike a seemingly merciful gun blast to the back of the head, or a single knife blade thrust clean through the heart, the formidable *coup de grâce* of murder that would unnerve even an inured veteran cop, was the act of pure unadulterated torture of an innocent victim—unimaginable in the mind of most civilized men. That was the truly horrifying and terrifying part.

In kind, the veritable Reign of Terror the police customarily unleashed upon a perpetrator, once apprehended, was tantamount to torture, too. Case in point: Howard Mills, convicted serial killer—four years earlier. The Suffolk County homicide detectives had the make, model and color of their suspect's vehicle, so noted by the press; namely, *The New York Post*. Mills' favorite newspaper. The headlines, accompanying a series of articles, struck fear into the heart of the purported killer. He knew the cops were gradually closing in. When the police finally apprehended Howard and his brother, *terror* was the catchword associated with the 8 x 8 foot interrogation room in which the pair were *questioned*, unmercifully, until a full confession was finally taken from and signed by Howard Mills. The authority's methods, simply put, were that the end *positively* justifies the means. Both brothers were guilty; however, it was somewhat unclear who did what to which victim. But in the minds of the homicide detectives, the point remained moot. Both were guilty as sin itself.

In retrospect, the Mills brothers were choirboys as compared to others that the homicide boys and girls played host to over the course of years. Torturing the mind, many times, far outweighed bodily punishment in obtaining the desired result—at which Theo's Teams were pros.

But in all their years of police work, *never* had the veterans of homicide *ever* witnessed anything quite like Malcolm Columba's deeds. Never ever. His acts went far beyond what any of them had ever experienced. Light-years, in fact; across the span of time of *sick* and *sicker*—with a capital S for the superlative: The *Sickest* they had ever seen.

Detective Michael Connolly–emeritus–was thrilled to be back on the job—even if it was a one-shot deal—even if it was a temporary arrangement among Theo and the other earthly gods. In truth, Connolly had always wanted Theo's position . . . to sit in the seat of power and wield away at will. But toward the end of his career, he saw the handwriting on the wall. The rulers of his universe had other plans for him; that is, unprecedented overtime in the Howard Mills serial-killer case, both before and during trial. Conviction at any and all cost. Thereupon, Mick was quietly put out to pasture, but with an unbeatable retirement package. The staggering amount of overtime he accumulated in finding the killer of prostitutes, then assisting the district attorney's office in bringing the man to justice in a trial to end all trials on Long Island, had, relatively speaking, made the retiring detective *rich*—notwithstanding his heavy mortgage and high property taxes with which Suffolk County had metaphorically murdered Mick in the north before saluting and sending him south to play in the sun.

Along the southern Atlantic coast, Mick fished to his heart's content. Twelve months out of the year, if he wanted. He worked the part-time job that Disney offered, for which he received a full-time paycheck as head of security. Thirty minutes away from his boat and home. It had all been arranged. *Fuck the seat of power. Fuck the politics,* he swore off with not a hint of resentment. He fished and forgot about the sick world all around him—until he got the call. Two in fact. He had hung up on Theo at the beginning of round one, before the case turned red hot.

So. Here he was back in New York for a final fling with madness.

Ambivalence at its best.

What the fuck.

He was feeling great.

He was sensing those sensational vibes once again.

God bless America.

Kim had given him something solid. That precious strip of printed cardboard taken from the killer's boat. It was up to Mick to spin and weave the finding into a net that would help nab the murderer.

God willing.

Mick's sixth sense was kicking in mightily.

Oh, he was damn good, and he knew it. God was *not* pissed off at him like he initially believed He was. And even if He *had* been, it was now clear to The Mick that God had forgiven him for his sins— for floundering in a sea of infidelity. Once again, he promised himself and God that he would be as good as gold.

Whereas Gary York wagged the gift of a facile tongue, tied with the knots of trickery and deceit in order to obtain truth and justice as a servant for the state, Mick Connolly relied on the nuts and bolts operation of good old-fashioned gumshoe detective work. Pounding the pavement. Taking to the Tarmac, streets, sidewalks, and trails. Trudging through fields and forests. Rooftops and alleyways. Subways and sewers. There was not a place he had not walked or crawled in his long career as a cop; frazzling the heels and soles of his footwear along with his arthritic joints . . . in search of a single solitary clue. And when he found one . . . just *one* . . . which inevitably lead to another, the culprit had better run for cover because The Mick was somewhere close behind, on all fours if necessary. Like the predator he was.

Uncanniness, unsavoriness, and a dash of viciousness were the three nouns which best described Detective Michael Connolly to a tee; the latter of which The Mick enjoyed administering whenever he had such a monster in his midst . . . whether it was during the arrest, or shortly thereafter—that is, within the confines of the infamous 8 x 8 foot interrogation room back at headquarters. *"Confession time, guy"* or *"gal,"* he would growl and gloat. *"Good for the soul,"* he would *convince* the suspect. Sick or slick, his or her ass was grass, and Mick was the proverbial lawn mower.

Detective Michael Connolly was busy sharpening his double-edged blade.

Chapter 50

Freddie Dupree had a gift that some might consider a deficit and not at all a prize. The ten-year-old had the ability to tell when people were lying. At five, Freddie suffered a brain disorder resulting in language difficulty, clinically diagnosed as mild aphasia. A dysfunction occurring in the left side of the brain, symptomatic of impaired speaking, reading, and/or writing skills, usually brought on by a stroke, head injury, or disease.

The boy treasured words, but had great difficulty expressing himself verbally, from kindergarten right up through the third grade. *Freddie the Freak* was the cruel nickname affixed to the youngster, as if it were actually printed smack across the middle of his forehead. He frequently heard the reference from other children on his block, as well as in school. Several adults referred to his condition as retarded.

Then a remarkable thing happened. Freddie, with a lot of help, learned to put aside his fear, frustration, and embarrassment. He learned to fully focus and work on his handicap. By the end of fourth grade, the boy comprehended and spoke far better than anyone could ever have hoped for or imagined. The transformation was absolutely amazing to everyone except his stepmother, who worked with Freddie daily—until they both had splitting headaches, whereas, only two years earlier, there had been nothing but heartache. Now, in fifth grade, he was considered well above average in both reading and writing.

While aphasics have an extraordinary ability to detect untruths, scientists are uncertain as to how the skill is developed, but believe that a compensatory mechanism comes into play. Whereas cues of prevarication are often camouflaged by language, the aphasic is somehow able to set aside a person's speech, per se, focusing in on the individual's facial expressions in relation to intonation.

An aphasic's preternatural skill with respect to lie detection was noted more than seventy years ago, but only recently had it been scientifically studied, tested, and deemed seventy-five percent accurate. However, Freddie's ability exceeded ninety-eight percent, failing only when the person he was questioning actually lied to one's self and, therefore, believed *his* or *her* own untruths—as when Harold Dupree, Freddie's presumed father, told him, unequivocally, that he was the proudest father in the whole wide world to have, for a son, such a loving boy as he.

Harold Dupree *was not* Freddie's biological father, the boy had learned from Malcolm. Moreover, the man who pretended for all these years to be his father was a fraud.

An out-and-out liar.

How could Freddie ever forgive such . . . *deceit*?

Every word that Malcolm had told the boy, Freddie *knew* to be true.

His so-called father had been living a lie. Freddie wondered if his stepmom knew the truth and never told him. It would not surprise him in the least. He hated both of them in that moment.

"So. Do you want to make that phone call now, Freddie? Or do you need time to digest everything I've told you over the last two hours? Hum?"

Freddie did not answer his newfound friend who had, most magically, become his father. His *real* father. For he was mad at him, too, trying desperately to understand. Trying to act . . . act . . . *mature*. That single, solitary word was in the vocabulary of every responsible adult he knew . . . observed from firsthand experience. *Maturity*. Freddie felt like he was twenty years old. He might just as well have been a hundred or a thousand, he seethed.

"Malcolm?"

"Yes, son?"

Son.

Freddie posed a different question than the one he had intended . . .the truth being that he forgot the one he had in mind only a second ago. Forgot, too, why he was even mad at Malcolm.

"Do you want me to call you Dad or Father?" Freddie faltered.

Malcolm smiled magnificently. "Call me anything but late to supper."

Freddie and Malcolm looked at one another briefly before they both broke out in laughter once again.

And laughed and laughed and laughed.

It felt *good*, yet at the same time *strange*, to be *home* with his *father.*

His real *honest-to-goodness* dad.

Chapter 51

Like the staggering series of cumulonimbus clouds covering and uncovering the face of the luminous moon above, Donald Bellport drifted in and out of consciousness. Time wore on pitilessly. Brief periods of obscurity were as welcome to Donald as death itself would be to a terminally ill cancer patient being deprived the benefit of powerful painkillers. The young man knew the end was near and tried to draw the curtain early through a litany of prayers and pleas that proved futile.

Don Ciccio's orders down through the chain of command seemed relatively simple. Austin Izzo was to slowly and methodically torture the Adirondack handyman as inhumanly as possible for a period of eighteen hours. Death by drowning in his own slather would probably be the final wave of resolution, but not before Donald Bellport suffered extraordinary pain through every nerve ending in his body, which began with the soles of his feet.

Polaroid pictures in living color were taken as proof positive of the moribund punishment. Additionally, a written record was kept of every ghastly hour the man endured, listing the method and means of torture employed as a kind of scorecard so as to document the poor soul's implorable cries and pleas of mercy, for which there would be no earthly redemption. Apart from the handyman's incorrigible philandering, God's forgiveness was a given, for Bellport never hurt anyone in his entire life. But a path to heaven would first have to follow a rocky route to perdition, a bumpy off-road terrestrial terrain better suited for four-footed creatures, or all-wheel drive vehicles. Only then would Bellport's body come to rest in a bath of sulfuric acid, devouring all flesh while savoring stubborn bone matter.

It was well after midnight. Donald had been mercilessly tortured for the better part of sixteen hours. Austin was tiring of the game. His associate, Charlotte, sat engaged in keeping records as if she were a busy bookkeeper at a bank. The account was kept in columns within a thin green and red threaded ledger that would be burned along with the Polaroids, as promised, soon after delivery to Don Ciccio's patron later that afternoon. Additionally, an incriminating piece of planted evidence would accompany the package, so-called proof that pointed to both Bellport and Columba as partners in crime. Accomplices *extraordinaire*.

For Austin's and Charlotte's laborious task, they would each receive fifty thousand dollars in cash. Less than the price of two cases of fine vin lying in a corner of the client's wine cellar in South Jamesport.

Charlotte was exasperated, anxiously awaiting the moment that their bloody business would be over and done with. She ran an inverted pen down the page of horror. Their mark, D.B., so noted, had suffered greatly. Soon, Donald Bellport would be dead. Don Ciccio would be pleased. Evan Tamblin would be somewhat satisfied.

The blue van sat momentarily bathed in an eerie light filtering through the tops of tall trees before the vehicle was swallowed up whole by the darkness once again. In and out of consciousness their prisoner traveled, gazing up blankly at the metal ceiling while lying motionless in the tub. A temporary coffin for the nearly departed soul.

Donald's bare feet flaunted eight sticky-stubbed black candles fused between each fleshy taloned toe. His soles were both black and purple from where the pointed flame of propane had flashed and singed them until they stunk like foul meat. The smell of burnt flesh still reeked and rose through the stench of feces, blood and urine that had not quite completely drained from the tub through a fitted pipe in the floor of the van and out onto a secluded rocky beach.

An interminable battering of wind and waves had roared and crashed against a distant jetty for a period of many hours, assaulting the craggy shoreline less than fifty feet from where the party of three was parked. Only within the last thirty minutes, and not unlike their captive, did the weather abate into a state of contrary calm.

The needle Austin now injected into the man's left eye elicited but a whimper. One of sorrow rather than any pule of pain.

Donald never even saw the flash from Charlotte's camera.

"I'm famished," she swore, snapping another series of pictures as Austin stuck a second needle into Donald's other eye.

"Right."

"I mean it. We've been at this since eight o'clock this morning.

It's now after one a.m."

"You had coffee and a sandwich. So shut your mouth."

"*Half* a sandwich."

"Be glad you had that."

Charlotte made another entry in the log. It had been a grueling, gruesome task. The first few hours had been fun for both of them—watching the handsome lanky fellow squirm and scream and beg shamelessly for his life. But after several hours, it had become a bore for her.

Austin, on the other hand, was actually fascinated, although he, too, was worn. He had tortured scores of people through the years, but never a single one over such a span of time. And never in so many different ways. But those were the instructions he had been given, and that was exactly what was being carried out to the letter. The fact that he could be creative was a rewarding experience laden with lessons that would undoubtedly prove invaluable in future assignments.

It was truly amazing to him what punishment a human being could endure. If God had indeed spawned the shell and soul of man, Austin Izzo reasoned that the Creator would be equally proud of the ways in which he, the family enforcer, chose to divide and conquer the body, mind, and spirit of this handyman.

Donald Bellport had unquestionably gone mad sometime around the eleventh a.m. hour. Quite insane before he ever saw the setting sun. As the moon came out, Donald disappeared somewhere deep inside himself. An occasional cry. An incoherent mumbling. Rumbling noises emanating from his bowels. Blood and mucus congealed around his broken nose and busted jaw.

Through all the initial unpleasantness, Donald's agony carried clear as a bell tolling from its tower, Charlotte mused as she looked over the timetable of events. Still, it remained remarkable to her how the pounding ocean could muffle the horrific howling of a man clawing his way hopelessly toward the heavens. Too, why he even fought to get there. For the single, flat, razor-sharp concertina wire, which Austin had threaded like a catheter along the length of Donald's sinewy light-skinned body, certainly ensured that their prisoner was not going anywhere.

One end of the wire, protruding from the mixed-breed's neck, ran to the top of the tub, over its edge, then underneath—wrapped around the single plumbing pipe passing through the vehicle's floor. The other end exited Bellport's right ankle and, like a coiled thin snake stretched to its limit, was fixed to a post within the skeletal metal framework of the gutted van's interior.

Charlotte had taken the gruesome yet dramatic high-angle, color, close-up shots of Bellport's features from the front seat of the vehicle. The ghastly, full-length figure photos, which she somehow managed to fit and focus in her viewfinder, were sharp and fascinatingly surreal. Most of the snapshots morosely resembled those of the crime scene photos taken of Patricia Tamblin, flat on her back within her cast iron coffin.

Austin smiled wearily. "I think he's finally going bye-bye."

Charlotte scowled. "You could've pulled the plug on this guy hours ago, and no one would be the wiser."

"We do this right. Hear me? The boss said eighteen hours—or until he croaks—we do eighteen hours before we pull the plug. Look at him. He's not gonna last another fifteen minutes. So quit your bellyaching."

"What are you, some kind of know-it-all? You said that a half hour ago. I say we fill the tub now, drown the sucker in his misery, drain it, pour in the chemical, and be done with it."

"You say?"

"Yeah. You know how much work we have ahead of us after we lay his fucking ass in acid? The client wants pictures in progress of that procedure, too, I'll remind you."

"How do you know they're for the client? Maybe the boss wants them for his scrapbook," he bantered. "Just remember that you're getting fifty G's for a day's work. Not bad."

"You mean a *full* day's work and well into the morning of the next. We're lucky if we finish up by this afternoon."

"Tax free," Charlotte was reminded.

Charlotte laughed good-naturedly. "Guy wasn't even guilty."

"*Isn't* guilty," Austin stated testily. "You're speaking about him like he's already dead. I told you; we take this right down to the wire." And with that pronouncement, the enforcer lifted the razor-sharp ribbon but an inch with a canvas gloved-covered hand, cutting further through Bellport's flesh like a knife through hot butter. Their patsy remained as still as stone.

310

Charlotte sighed with impatience. "Sorry, Donald," she apologized, waving goodbye by opening and closing her hand like a little claw, calling over to a barely breathing *corpse*. "Please forgive me if you aren't dead yet." She stared back at Austin and smiled. "Guy *isn't* even guilty. Better?"

"Better."

"So why are we doing this?"

"Fifty thousand apiece. Did you forget?"

"Seriously, Austin. I mean, why him?"

"I guess the client wants all bases covered."

"How do you mean?"

"The client feels that the connection between Bellport and Columba was too coincidental."

"Who's the client?" she tested.

Austin shook his head. "You know better than to ask me a question like that."

"Think maybe they really are connected? Or perhaps they just knew each other casually."

Austin shook his head. "No. Not at all."

"Think he told us the truth, the whole truth, and nothing but the truth?" she questioned sardonically, looking down at Donald.

"I do."

"How come?"

"Because."

"Because why?"

"Because, baby, I'm the best in the business. That's why. The guy had nothing to do with Columba."

"So then why didn't you just report back to the boss and tell him Bellport's bell had the ring of truth to it? Why kill an innocent man?"

"Because you don't question orders. That's why."

"This isn't the Nazi army, you know. I need a better answer," she pressed.

"Because this came from the top. Need a better reason?"

"Don Ciccio?"

Austin simply shrugged.

"Maybe Inspector Mattheson?" she probed.

Austin's face showed no expression whatsoever. "Where did

you come up with that name?" he asked after an uncomfortable moment.

The moment in which Donald Bellport quietly died.

"Figures."

"Figures how?"

"Well, it's certainly not Lou Penella, is it?" Charlotte pressed.

"Deputy mayor? Some folks think the mayor himself plays an integral part," he suggested slyly, steering her onto another track.

"Part of what?"

"Part of day-to-day operations."

Charlotte shook her head and smiled wearily. "Mayor's just a puppet."

"Think so?"

"Know so. Lacks the brass."

"Brass balls?"

"That, too. But you know what I mean."

"I do?"

"You and I both know that it's Mattheson who's second in command."

"An NYPD inspector? I think that honor could go to the first deputy commissioner," Austin dodged, ascending the chain of command.

Charlotte laughed loudly and shook her head. "Yeah, the first under fire to head for the hills. Ciccio runs the entire show through Bill Mattheson. And I think you know that."

It was Izzo's turn to laugh; and he actually roared. "You kidding me or what?"

Charlotte surrendered another sigh, about to present Austin with a startling piece of news. "And now, I'm going to let you in on a little secret."

"Oh, yeah?"

"Yeah." Charlotte walked over to the tub and took Donald's hand in hers, feminine fingers pressing firmly upon the inner wrist. No pulse. "I'm number three in command. *I* picked *you* for this assignment."

Austin looked at her with a blank expression, then laughed. "You? You're fucking daft."

Charlotte nodded and dropped the hand. "We're done here.

Let's go."

"What the fuck are you talking about?"

Charlotte did an about-face and whipped out her cell phone. She plugged in several numbers, having to wait but several seconds. "It's me," she said. "We're done here, and we need a crew." . . . "That's correct." . . . "That'll be fine." . . . "He's right here." Charlotte held out the phone for Austin. "Take it."

Austin snatched the cellular from Charlotte's hand and looked at her like she had lost her mind.

"Go on. It's a secure line," she assured him, moving to the corner to collect her records and pictures, putting the entire contents into a large Manila envelope. The camera, she put into a leather bag.

"Hello?"

"Congratulations, fella."

"Who's this?"

"You know who it is."

Austin recognized the voice but did not quite know how to respond. "I'm listening."

"That's good because I have some good news and some bad news for you."

"Yes, sir?"

"Which should I give you first?"

"Any way you like, sir."

"Well, the good news is you don't have to clean up anybody's mess anymore. You're to quarterback *all* crews from this day on. The bad news is that you're to report directly to Charlotte," he added. "How do you feel about working for a woman?"

Austin Izzo did not know what to make of anything and decided to keep his tongue in check. "Listen, I'd like to do this face to face. I don't—"

"What you have to *face* is the music. She's your immediate. Got it?"

"Got it."

"Good. Now, we all have important work to do. So let's get at it."

"Yes, sir."

"But before you go, somebody here wants to say hello. Hold on a sec."

Austin held his breath.

"Hey, Aussie! Congratulations, kid. How the hell are you?"

The man himself. Don Ciccio.

"Fine, sir."

"Well, you should be fine, I mean to tell ya. You just moved from a number twenty-two spot on the hit parade to number four. Now, you get along with number three, or I'm gonna kick your butt. What do you think about that, Aussie? Think I can't do it? Huh? Tell me right now."

"Maybe with a crew you might," the big man stated through a smile.

If Austin could see the don's fist waving through the air, he would have laughed.

"I don't need no fuckin' crew to clean your clock, Aussie baby. Just you and me. One on one. Think not?"

Austin heard a thud on the other end of the line. It was the bottom of the big boss's fist meeting the top of a wooden desk.

"Well, maybe if you lost sixty fuckin' pounds and stayed out of gourmet restaurants for a year, you might get a lick or two in before I'd pulverized your ass," Austin affirmed with a pleased grin.

"Do you hear the way he talks to the boss?" Vincent Ciccio addressed the inspector. "THE BOSS, you fucking moron," he denounced his newly promoted henchman. "I feel like Rodney Dangerfield. What kind of a boss like me gets no respect? Makes no fuckin' sense. You, you piece of dog shit. You there?"

"Yeah, I'm still here."

"He do it?"

"Who did what?"

"Bellport. Whattaya been doing the last eighteen hours? Charlotte? Ya better not 'ave. 'Cause I want you to know she's my favorite piece of ass."

"He didn't do it."

"Ah, too bad. But what the hell. We take on shitty assignments like this to fill the war chest. Right, Aussie?"

"Right."

"Listen."

"Sir?"

"Behave yourself."

"Thanks for the vote."

"Don't thank me. Thank Charlotte. She's been watching and studying you like a hawk. Today was your final test. You do good work. And just as importantly, you know how to keep your trap shut. Know what that means, kid?"

"What?"

"It means I'll see you two later tonight to celebrate and drink to your health. *Salute*," Don Ciccio toasted, tossing down a shot of Sambovca before terminating the conversation.

Austin closed and handed back the cell phone.

"Congratulations," Charlotte said evenly.

"Thanks. I would have never guessed."

"That's how we do things around here. You never know who's looking over your shoulder." The pretty woman smiled, moving toward the door with the envelope and bag.

"What about him?"

"Like I told you. We're done here. Someone else's mess. They're dispatching a crew immediately. They'll dissolve and resolve this business for us," she quipped cannily. "They'll also take the rest of the necessary pictures, et cetera."

"So where do we go from here?"

"Well, I was going to take us out to breakfast when we got back. Won't be anything open till then. But to tell you the truth, I don't think I could hold a fork. We'll get some rest first. If you behave yourself, I'll buy you lunch later on. But first you've got to beg. Just a little," she trifled through a stifled laugh. "Or I could just shut my fucking mouth altogether and watch you choke down a slice of pizza with a beer," she tormented. "Come. A car's waiting for us at the top of the ridge."

It felt strange suddenly taking Charlotte's lead. Two minutes ago, it was the other way around. He thought about how badly he had treated her from the time they started out early yesterday morning. Now, *she* was *his* fucking boss, he stewed, realizing that you never knew what awaited you around the next corner. *Another day in the life of the mob*, he soured.

Austin slid open the door for the woman, wanting to give her one good swift kick in the ass.

Chapter 52

"The capital of Louisiana is . . ." *C'mon, think, motherfucker.*
Think! You know you know it, Justin forgot but fought to remember.
"Nope. Don't know no motherfuckin' Louie," he resounded in utter
frustration, setting down his razor and massaging his temples to help
coax along the answer. "Louisa! Yes. Good ol' Louisa. How the fuck
could I have forgotten her?" he chastised himself unmercifully.
    Cut it close that time, nigger.
    "Yes. Louisa was that mama's name," he declared as he poured
himself a cup of coffee. "That be the bitch sure as brown sugar
contains molasses."
    His homely baby-sitter.
    "Ug·ly."
    Just how ugly?
    "So damn ugly that the tide wouldn't take her out, bro."
    That's pretty damn ugly.
    "Woman was so ugly she made Uncle Ed's glass eye tear.
Hideous lookin' woman. Always battin' me 'round the house with the
wrong end of a broom when I was just knee-high to the festering
tumor on her leg," he said with sheer disgust.
    Battin' yo ass wif 'at broomstick, 'cause you deserved it most
times, nigger.
    "Wretched woman. Cajun broad with some French blood
runnin' through her varicose veins. High cheek bones that she caked
with rouge. Tryin' to make herself look more human than she really
was. Baton Rouge! That's it. The capital of Louisiana is Baton
Rouge," he grounded out satisfactorily, batting a thousand.
    Bit of a reach, nigger. But you pulled it off.
    "But, of course."
    Association being the key to Monisha's crash memory course.

Detective Brian Archer, to whom Justin was temporarily

assigned, was quite impressed at how the civilian, without the aid of any notes, could remember all the Moose Lodges in relationship to the cities and towns that so concerned the teams, having logged their respective distances to the crime scenes in preparation for York's interview with Harold Dupree.

Archer proved to be a decent sort of chap—*for a cop, that is*—the maverick entertained. A little square, but still tolerable. It was the lead detective, Dean Nelson, who fought to keep him at bay and away from the case. Ironically, Detective Andrew Miller had gone to bat for Barnes.

Of course, Justin first had to convince their lieutenant that he had information worthy of a seat and an assignment in homicide. As it turned out, it was solid intelligence that prevented a truly violent inmate from murdering someone—maybe even thwarting the career criminal's escape from Riverhead Jail. Justin simply told them how Nicholson Fitch, the third runner-up for the death penalty on Long Island, would casually walk out of his cell and quite possibly through the gate of the correctional facility itself. In any event, Fitch was sure to take a life or two in the process. That was a given, Justin knew, now that the career criminal was being held for the rape and murder of a supermarket employee.

Initially, Theo and several other detectives had a good laugh listening to the maverick's story, but afterward got on the phone with the head of security at the jail as a precautionary measure. What the corrections officers found twenty minutes later was unbelievable. Fitch had used toothpaste to glue several Scrabble tiles in the tracks of his sliding cell door, giving the appearance that it was locked when, in fact, it was merely closed. Justin knew the man and his antics well, having served time with the killer upstate years ago.

"How in all hell did you know that?" Theo had demanded of Justin, with Nelson and Archer looking on in disbelief.

"We got a deal?" Justin asked and smiled slyly.

"We don't make deals with felons," Dean squawked.

"Sure you do," Justin summarily corrected. "You make them all the time. They're called *flea* bargains. I scratch your back; you scratch mine. And I just scratched your fuckin' back, fellas, but mine's still itchin'," *motherfucker*, was the twelve-letter word he had in mind but held in check.

"I said, we'd consider it," Theo set forth.

"Yeah? Then consider this. Fitch got himself several shivs planted in and around lockup for when he does or doesn't do his *ex·o·dus*. So, I'll jus' *think* about whether or not I'm gonna clue you in as to their whereabouts. Dig?"

The head of homicide dug, all right. Deep into Barnes' criminal record as well as Fitch's. Their past—right up to the present. There was not much of a gap between releases and resentencings for the latter. Barnes, on the other hand, had some brains and managed to sidestep the law in several instances. Fitch, sitting on the other side of the fence, was a two-time loser. The lieutenant also learned that the two did a little time together up in Attica. It was probably how Barnes knew about the Scrabble tile and toothpaste ploy, the cop figured. Theo further learned that Fitch recently stabbed an inmate in the neck with a weapon fashioned from a ballpoint pen. Another man he knifed in the shoulder—a trustee—with a blade sharpened from a spoon handle. Seven guards had gone after him in the bathroom following that incident, and all seven took a spill when the six-foot-five fellow threw down a pail of soapy water and washed away their pride. Five wound up in the hospital from a beating. Another, crippled in a corner, wore a bucket for a helmet, while the other officer fled. Two hundred seventy-five pounds of pure muscle went after the single soul until the prisoner was finally corralled and threatened by a team of no less than thirty zookeepers brandishing batons. Fitch had calmly put up his hands and smiled knowingly:

"I surrender, man," Fitch had declared with a smirk. "But lay one o' 'dose sticks on me now, and I'll break e'ry one o' yo' punk-ass fuckin' necks later, I swear."

No one stepped within a foot of the gorilla-like monster as he coolly strode back to his cell.

"All right," Theo finally said, folding uncharacteristically before the cagey felon. "You probably saved us all a headache."

"No 'bout a-doubt it," Justin swore. "Man's a mean killin' machine."

"Now, about those knives he may or may not have planted 'in and around lockup,' you said."

The deal was that Justin Barnes had to be mindful of his place, do exactly as he was told, and not question or second-guess any member on the team in exchange for the privilege of working an *important* aspect of the case. The two men shook hands. Justin was leery that the lieutenant might be giving him a snow job—maybe have him fetch coffee or doughnuts for the squad—or tell him it was *important* that the detectives all had sharpened pencils. *Some shit like that,* he figured. But Theo was true to his word. Justin Barnes was *still* working on an important facet of the case . . . following a trail that the serial killer just might be keeping to, God willing.

Amazing, dude!

Justin Barnes, cop killer as a kid, became something of a deputized assistant *hom·o·cide* detective. Monisha Washington was surely spinning in her grave.

"Doin' this for you, kid," he said to the sexy snapshot taped to the upper corner of the refrigerator. He also carried a photo of the pretty coed in his wallet. "Well, maybe a little bit for me in the bargain." He threw her a kiss as he closed the light and exited the kitchen, promising to visit her grave just as soon as this business was settled. "Bye fo' now, girl."

Justin headed for the living room then returned to the listing of Moose Lodges and his travel atlas.

"The capital of Maine is Augusta."

He pictured the state of Maine and what it clearly stood for in his mind. The *main* attraction—noting that in all his years of travel, he found very few blacks residing north of Portsmouth. Particularly, in the colder upper corner of that state. Maine. Vacationland. Stamped on each and every license plate. Justin thought of that northerly territory as a white man's playground. Honky Heaven. A tourist's outdoor paradise until around the first of September, *when any self-respecting black knows enough to beat feet south of the Mason-Dixon line. Not as any line of demarcation between the slave and free states of days gone by, but rather as freedom from the godforsaken motherfucking cold.* Justin shivered at the thought.

August was his favorite month of all.

"Talk 'bout a lazy nigger," he announced to no one in the room.

For Justin, August symbolized true freedom. Vacation time. Drug and gunrunning were put on hold. It was a time to *rec·re·ate.* Fishing in Lincoln (of all places), on the Penobscot, was the way he and Monisha spent a summer together before she returned to school. A remote cabin on the river where he became a predominantly freshwater fishing fool. A three hundred fifty mile river running past Old Town, on its way to Penobscot Bay.

Only two Moose Lodges in the entire state. Strange. Scarborough and Portland. So very close together. A distance of less than ten miles. How weird.

Justin closed his travel atlas and the Moose Lodge directory, set the alarm to wake him in an hour, switched off the light, then lay down upon the sofa. He would be back at police headquarters in Yaphank shortly. Maybe they would cut him loose tomorrow. He already finished up one assignment. Then again, maybe they would keep him on. Either way, he could not say that Theo did not keep his promise.

Justin needed just one more piece of the puzzle to keep him on the killer's path.

Chapter 53

Detective Michael Connolly, technically a civilian with a terrific pension and a temporary license to kill, was making headway, closing in on Columba. Hunting for killer sharks along the Atlantic would have rated a top spot, too, for the seasoned cop. But shark fishing was an expensive sport. Tracking down killers at the government's expense, Mick had to admit, gave him a far greater thrill.

The moldy, musty scrap of cardboard that Kim had handed Mick, leapfrogged from one steppingstone to the next. The investigation revealed that the narrow end strip came from fly line packaging, which fell into a Saltwater Series category; that is, a heavier more durable line than the freshwater type—made to stand up to the harsher elements as explained by the manufacturer during a phone conversation. Further inquiry made it clear that the pasteboard packaging contained a premium 10-Weight line, generally used for inshore saltwater fly-fishing, identified by a product specialist as Prestige Plus No-Vis, an item recently sent out C.O.D. to a Connecticut post-office box from a Cabela's mail-order house in Owatonna, Minnesota. On back order was an expensive graphite saltwater fly rod and reel combination—addressed to Donald Bellport. A customer service manager for Cabela's explained to Connolly that the balance of the order had been placed on hold because the company would not mail oversized items to a P.O.B. The person who placed the order said he would call back shortly with a suitable mailing address. To date, no one had done so. But apparently, someone signed for and picked up the fly line in Bridgeport. *Who?* the veteran detective tossed around in his mind.

Although the lead, with regard to the fly line and saltwater rod and reel outfit, pointed to the coastal waterways, scores of detectives and investigators on loan from other units and jurisdictions, in addition to those procured from the private sector, scoured the popular trout streams and rivers throughout Adirondack Park, looking to question the handyman who appeared to have vanished into thin air.

Mick, however, homed in on the homes and businesses along a Connecticut waterfront. He walked the wharves and docks with simply a hunch, a two-year-old photo of Malcolm Columba, a more recent one of Freddie Dupree, along with a copy of a signature card from a post office in Bridgeport: Box 872; in C/o ISFCWS&A.

Initials standing for what?

Mick bet himself a bacon cheeseburger that the last three letters stood for Water, Soil and Air. Clearly, the seven initials was not an acronym. ISFC could stand for anything. It could be that Connolly was wasting valuable time in the armpit of a city, period. However, he noted that the signature card named a subscriber whose handwriting appeared questionable—penmanship notwithstanding.

Mick was suddenly struck by an idea. He dialed his colleague's cell phone number. Gary York answered immediately.

"Yeah."

"Gary?"

"Micky?"

"No, Donald Duck. Can you talk?"

"I could quack, or I could step outside."

"Just stay put and listen. I take it you're still baby-sitting Dupree and his wife?"

"As we speak. Still hoping maybe Columba or the kid might call. We're all set up here if they do."

"Any new news?"

Gary smiled sadly and shook his head. " Nothing aside from Columba being the kid's biological father, I assume you heard."

"Yeah, Kim left a message earlier. Didn't get all the details, though."

"Dupree and the boy would visit those Moose Lodges during periods the victims' bodies turned up. Columba would be somewhere close by to observe his son, but kept his distance— according to Harold, here. Says he only caught a glimpse of Malcolm once or twice."

"No other contact?"

"He claims not. Except for a fat check Harold'd pick up twice a year."

"Where?"

"Columba's P.O. box in Port Jeff."

"Interesting. I got one I'm looking into here in Bridgeport, Connecticut. Ask them if the letters I-S-F-C-W-S-A ring a bell."

"Once again; you're breaking up."

"I-S-F-C-W-S–ampersand–A."

"Hold on."

Mick was looking out over the Sound toward Port Jefferson from the Connecticut side. It was a nasty morning.

"They both say no. Whattaya got?"

"Nothin' yet. Gary. Do me a favor. Find an excuse to have this guy write something down. Script, not print. Something with l's and h's in it. Both lowercase and capital letters. Not a person's name, though, because he might catch on. You and I are gonna check a signature after you call me back."

"Got it."

"Call me soon as you can."

"Will do, buddy." Gary York closed his cell phone and stared keenly at the anxious couple.

Virginia was on her third cup of coffee. Harold was a wreck.

"I'd like you two to do something for me," Gary said calmly.

"Sure," Virginia agreed freely.

"You have some paper and a couple of pens?"

Virginia got up and went over to a small antique secretary, lowering the leaf that converted to a desktop. She returned with a few sheets of typing paper and two pens.

"Great. Now. I'd like both of you to write down Freddie's favorite flavor of ice cream; next, the flavors he would settle for if they were put in front of him; lastly, those he wouldn't touch at all—even if it meant going to bed early without dessert, " he added with a smile.

"This is ridiculous," Harold Dupree said.

Virginia had already started writing.

"Well, Harold. There're many things we do in the course of a police investigation that might seem ridiculous to you. And I guess this is one of them. But it might serve a useful purpose. So. If you'll just cooperate. All right?"

Harold snatched up the pen and sheet of paper from the table in front of him, then sat down on the couch next to his wife, glancing over at her list.

"Hold it right there, Harold," Gary ordered.

Harold looked up with annoyance. "What?"

"It's got to be spontaneous. Straight from you. No help from Virginia," he instructed ceremoniously.

"Never heard of anything so asinine."

"Just do like the detective says, dear. There's probably a very good reason behind this," she said encouragingly. "Just write."

Harold frowned. "Howda ya spell chocolate?"

"C-h-o-c-o-l-a-t-e," Virginia spelled. "Oh, dear. I hope that's all right, Detective. I didn't mean to—"

"That's fine, Mrs. Dupree. Don't worry about spelling," Gary said to Harold.

"He's a horrible speller," the wife whispered as though Harold could not hear a word.

"I spell good enough," the lobsterman said testily.

Virginia shook her head in contradiction. "Just write," she repeated. "He doesn't write too neatly either," she persisted, staring directly at the detective.

"You just mind your own business and write," her captain/husband snapped.

"I'm finished," Virginia stated, handing her sheet over to the cop.

"Hold on to that for a second," York said politely.

"Yeah, he wants all the homework passed up front and collected at the same time," Dupree blathered belligerently.

"You, I'm holding after class," the cop threw back playfully.

"There. Done." Harold set his paper faceup, then stuck the pen behind his ear with a peevish gesture.

"We're not finished yet," Gary stated, satisfied that Harold was writing in script.

"Why not?"

"Because I need to know the make and model of every boat docked at the marina where you keep your own."

"That's over twenty boats!" Harold protested.

"Both big and small," the detective pressed. "Please jot them down."

"I can name a few," Virginia volunteered.

"That'll be fine," Gary told her.

"Harold knows his boats like Freddie knows his plants and animals," she assured him with a labored smile, wiping a tear or two from the corner of her eye.

Harold was busy writing out a list. At least this made some sense to him. But Freddie's favorite ice cream flavors? Was the cop kidding them, or what?

It was a small marina. Twenty-two slips to be exact. The captain listed most of the boats. He probably could have scribbled down their respective horsepower, fuel consumption and length-to-beam ratio as well, if pressed, Detective Gary York smiled inwardly.

Gary collected what he needed and made the call back to Connolly.

"Mick? Gary."

"Got it?"

"Got it." Harold's list was placed on top.

"All right. I'll do the talking, and you just answer yes or no. Don't want to spook him unless we have to."

"Right."

"You got a capital script L to look at?"

Gary went down Harold's list of makes and models over in the right-hand column, each beginning with a capital letter—thank goodness. Larivee. He had never heard of such a boat, but that was hardly the point.

"Got it."

"Okay. Now follow me closely. I'll try and put this in plain English. Does the top of his L have a tight loop to it? In other words, it doesn't start over from the left, but looks almost like a squeezed-in capital P."

"That's correct."

"Yet, the bottom of the letter *does* loop way over to the right to form the next lowercase letter."

"Yes."

"All right. Let's move to a lowercase script *l*. Got one of those for me?"

The detective's eyes shot to the word at the top left column: *chocolate*. Favorite ice-cream flavors was the first listing he thought when Mick requested l's and h's. However, the category might have proved somewhat limited in scope, he also realized. But by having

Howard list the good, the bad and the ugly—he smiled to himself—how could he go wrong? Gary even reviewed Virginia's sheet to make the farce seem comprehensive.

"Got it, Mick."

"Does his little *l* have a wide-open loop to it, like a tied shoelace, rather than a normal narrow shape?"

"That's right."

"I'm talking wide, Gary."

"I understand."

"Like a . . . almost childlike scrawl."

Gary wanted to tell him that he could pass a bullet through it in order to make his point; but he simply answered, "Yes."

"Great. Now, let's do a capital H. Please tell me you got one of them."

"Hatteras."

Harold and Virginia exchanged questioning glances.

Mick smiled. "You had him list boats?"

"And their models. Got everything you asked for."

"Dean will be very proud of you, Gary," he assured him with a laugh. "So, tell me his capital H is like printing, but then follows into script."

"Can you be a bit more specific?"

"Gettin' there, kid." Mick fixed his eyes on the copy of the signature card he was holding. "The crossbar to his capital H is what drops to connect the lowercase letters."

"On the money, honey."

"Are we a fucking team or what?" Mick said with mixed emotions, punching a hole of happiness through the misty morning fog that rose up before him; pissed, too, because he could not be there in person for the finale when his teammate sweated the guy. "One more, and you're on your way, Gary."

"Give it to me." He had no idea what Mick had, but he knew it was hot. The two could feel each other's excitement mounting across the wireless.

Detective Michael Connoly gave it to him succinctly. "His lowercase script h is seated like a chair."

That said it all.

"It looks like you got this nailed down, Micky. But what

exactly's fastened?" Gary York was staring at the couple as he spoke. He smiled and winked at Virginia.

"Harold there with you now?"

"Sitting right across from me."

"Good. Look him dead in the eyes when you ask him who Lola Heather is."

"Who is she, Mick?"

"Haven't got a clue. But Harold Dupree took out and signed that name for P.O. Box 872 here in Bridgeport. A week before Donald Bellport was arrested. I don't know who actually came by and picked up that package of fly line. I tend to doubt it was Columba. It might have actually *been* a Lola Heather. Who knows? Might be someone using a phony name. Might have been Harold himself. But let's take this one step at a time. Hit him with the fly-fishing line package pick up and the back order from Cabela's. Then, beat him over the head with the name Donald Bellport."

"I hear you."

"I just can't figure why anyone would want to send Bellport saltwater equipment when he fishes strictly fresh. Anyhow, have him in your sights when you hit him with the broad's name, then watch Dupree's eyeballs do a little dance. Lola Heather. Sounds like a stripper," Mick said decidedly through an infectious laugh. "Probably fictitious. You know how these perps and their accomplices just love P.O. boxes and aliases. I figured it wasn't a woman's signature because I got a ninety-three-year-old Irish grandmother with arthritis in both hands who writes neater than this."

Detective Michael Connolly had no such grandmother. Mick was orphaned at an early age and had no knowledge of his parents. No record existed, whatsoever. Mick could find blood under a two-ton boulder. He could find trace evidence in a teeming sewer. But he could not trace his roots. After the age of eighteen, he finally gave up searching, concocting fabulous stories instead—fantastic accounts of a predominantly Irish family upbringing—chronicling and confounding German, Polish, and Italian ancestry. He could be, and was, anyone he chose at any given moment. That was his fiction. But the fact remained that he was a damn good detective. One of Suffolk County's finest.

"Damn good work, *mouseketeer*," Detective York offered in advance. It was the new moniker Gary added to the other on the day

327

Mick retired and went to work for Disney World.

"Listen. I'll probably be ferrying back and forth between Bridgeport and Port Jeff. You might want to grill him on that, too. Port Jefferson to Bridgeport. Bridgeport and back. It's probably how he traveled. Anyhow, I got a call in to Kim to fax me a photo that I'll show around."

"I thought you *had* a copy of Columba's puss."

"I'm talkin' about that shithead you got sittin' there."

"Aha."

"Well, before I run, laddie, throw that name in his face. I want the satisfaction of at least *hearing* his eyes pop out."

"Hang on, buddy." Gary looked across to Harold. "Say, Harold?"

Harold was all ears. "Yeah?"

"Got a colleague on the other end who says your charade is about to end. I asked you if you were leveling with me, and you told me, yes."

"I am," Harold stated.

"Then tell me who Lola Heather is."

"Who?"

"Lola Heather."

"I don't know no Lola Heather."

"No?"

"No."

"Well, he says you do." Gary held up the cell like a microphone.

"Your colleague's an asshole," Harold sparred.

Virginia stood up and left the room.

"You hear that, Mick? Mr. Dupree, here, says you're all wet," Gary reported with a humorless smirk.

"Lean on him, Gary. Paint a picture for the fuck. One brush stroke at a time."

Gary glared at the man. "Been to Port Jefferson lately, Captain?"

No reaction.

"How about Bridgeport, Connecticut, Harry?"

Harold's eyes went wide.

"Post office there in particular?"

Harold dropped his eyes to the wide-planked pegged floor.

"Box number 872?"

The liar shook his head.

"You took it out using the name Lola Heather."

Still in denial, Harold raked his gnarly fingers through his hair.

"Someone picked up a package of fly line that we traced back to your buddy, Malcolm. Like the kind used in the murder of one of his victims. Want to be that close to the fire, Harold? It's practically right under your ass. That someone back-orders some items for Donald Bellport up in Long Lake. Remember the fellow in the Adirondacks who the police arrested up there then released?"

No response.

"You ferry back and forth from Port Jeff to Bridgeport, Captain?" Gary glanced toward the doorway to the bedroom where Virginia had disappeared. He set his voice just low enough for Harold and Mick to hear. "If you're not Lola Heather, Harold—or whatever her fuckin' name is—you humpin' her? Huh?" Gary waited for a reply. "Doesn't want to talk to me, Mick. You got that signature from the post office in front of you?"

Mick was smiling as he approached the ferry with a purposeful gait. "Yeah, right here in my hot little hand."

The pair had played a similar version of the game that was about to unfold. Played it several times, in fact. Once they had a piece of silver in their hands, the two knew how to turn it into gold. Both of them felt pretty damn confident that Harold Dupree had signed that post-office box request form in Connecticut.

"You deny signing such a card in Bridgeport, Harold?" Gary asked calmly.

"Ask him if he was wearing a dress," Mick threw out for giggles.

"My partner's going straight to the D.A. with the form he says matches your signature on file with motor vehicles and your bank. He says there's no mistake."

"No mistake at all, motherfucker!" Mick raised his voice for the full effect.

Although Harold could not hear the words precisely, he heard the cop's angry tone.

"Right. I'll bring him straight there now," Gary stated firmly.

"Where?" Harold demanded to know.

"The D.A. just loves it when you call him on the weekend," Gary swore, speaking directly into the mouthpiece, although the message was particularly for Harold's ears.

The Suffolk County District Attorney had a reputation that preceded him. Rumor, well- founded, marked him as one vindictive son of a bitch. The irony being that Harold would be in far safer hands standing before the D.A., than if one of the homicide detectives had the suspect sequestered in their 8 x 8 foot interrogation room back at police headquarters in Yaphank.

Even Nicholson Fitch would have conceded that point.

The mere mention of the D.A. sent shivers through Harold's body. The big man was folding right before Detective York's eyes. Eyes that pled for another chance.

"I'm gonna tell you everything I know," Harold promised sincerely. "I swear it."

"Heard all that before, Harold. You chose to be loyal to this guy who's going to help put you away for a long, long time. You made your bed, and now you're going to sleep in it."

"But I want to sleep in it here," he whined and wept like a two-year-old child. "I—" Harold looked up and saw his wife standing in the hallway with a suitcase. "Where are you going, V? You have to be here for Freddie's call. I need you here."

Virginia shook her head. "Freddie's not going to call, Harold. Malcolm Columba won't let him. And you're responsible."

"Yes, he will! I know it. I need you here with me. Please," he repeated anxiously.

"You don't need anybody, Harold," she said rather sadly.

Harold got up to stop her, but Gary stood in his path.

"Let her go, Harold. If you really want to talk, it's probably better this way. I'm going to give you one more chance to tell me the whole story." He turned to Virginia and handed her his card. "Call me."

"V, please stay. I'm gonna tell 'im everything. Honestly."

"I don't want to hear any of it."

"Gonna stay with Charlotte?" Harold snipped bitterly.

Virginia did not answer. She turned away sharply, heading for the front door with car keys in hand. In the next instant, she was gone.

"You there?" Mick asked.

"Right here."

"Well, that was quite a touching scene. Got most of it. Time for me to bow out while you do the thing that you do so well."

"Please tell your partner not to make that call to the D.A.," Harold whined.

"Now, don't dick me around, Harold! Hear?" Detective Gary York bellowed.

"I won't."

Gary and Harold heard the car door close.

"You don't have that pretty wife around to witness me kick your ass if you bullshit me. Understand?"

Dupree's cold brown eyes locked onto York's steel-blue stare.

The two men listened to the engine start and the vehicle pull out of the driveway.

"I understand."

All kindness and understanding left York's being as he transformed himself into one ruthless truth-gathering cop. "Sit down, Harold." The detective put a finger in the man's massive, heaving chest before putting the cell phone back to his ear. "Hold that call unless you hear from me."

"I think you're home free with this turkey, Gary. Listen, before I take my leave, you call me back with anything you got. I'm on this to the very end."

"I hear you loud and clear, partner."

"That's music to my ear, pal."

"This guy lays down on me again, you roust Patterson and his people up pronto. I'll deliver Harold's ass from Orient Point to Riverhead Jail in fifteen minutes flat—clockin' ninety."

Mick laughed at the embellishment and folded the flap of his cell phone.

Gary placed the instrument down in the center of the table between them as a constant reminder.

"All right, Harry. Let's hear it from the beginning."

Chapter 54

"Hey! That hurt." Malcolm rubbed his right shoulder, letting go of the steering wheel momentarily.

"Punch-buggy don't punch back," Freddie vocalized through a fit of uncontrollable laughter, glancing over his own shoulder at the vehicle that just blew by them.

"What are you talking about?"

Freddie caught his breath. "Whenever you see one of them new Volkswagen Beetles, whoever sees it first gets to punch the other person in the arm. But first you gotta say, punch-buggy don't punch back," Freddie explained. "And I didn't punch you very hard."

"You did."

Freddie shook his head. "Did not."

"Yes, you did."

"Didn't."

"Did, too. My arm's going to be all black-and-blue."

"It will not." The boy was smiling.

"It will, too. I can feel it swelling already."

"You *can* not."

"Can, too." Malcolm quickly peeked inside his shirt. "I can see it changing color right now."

"Can not."

"No, I can. It's turning into one gigantic bruise. Look."

"No, it's not. I can tell when people are lying."

"You can?"

"Sure."

"How?"

"It's a secret."

"You can't have secrets from your father."

"Why not?"

"Well, because."

"Because is not an answer." Freddie suddenly grinned. "And,

punch-buggy don't punch back," the boy barked, delivering several jabs in quick succession against Malcolm's upper arm.

"Hey! What was that for?"

"Well, look."

"Where?"

"Over there." Freddie pointed across the road.

Malcolm made a disgusted look at the long line of brightly colored cars parked under a well-lit canopy. "That's not fair, Freddie."

"Why not?"

"Because that's a Volkswagen *dealership*. That's why not."

"I know!" Freddie pealed and practically peed.

"I think my arm's going to fall off."

Freddie shook his head.

"Yeah, you won't think it's so funny when I club you with my amputated arm immediately after the operation," Malcolm declared.

Freddie's head shot forward in hysterics and practically hit the dash. "Oh, yeah?" he rejoined when he finally caught his breath. "If I really wanted to give you a wallop, believe me, it would hurt."

"That a fact?"

"Uh-huh."

"Well, I've got a bulletin for you, squirt."

"Oh, yeah?"

"Bet I can make you jump out of your skin."

"Bet you can't."

"Open that glove compartment."

Freddie looked at the little compartment door with the silver button in its center.

"Go ahead. *If you dare,*" Malcolm added in a spooky voice.

"You don't scare me."

"No?"

The boy shook his head without taking his eyes off the glove box.

"Then open it. I double-dare you," the killer droned in a ghostly tone.

Freddie cautiously opened the tiny door, then pulled his hand back quickly. "Just maps. Cassette tapes. And a lot of junk."

"Behind those maps and tapes, Freddie my boy," his father intoned.

"You don't scare me with that . . . phony . . ."

"Chant?"

Freddie nodded quickly. "How come you always know the right words?"

"Because I'm an author."

"I thought you were a lobsterman like—"

"Like what?"

"You know what I was going to say."

Malcolm shook his head.

"Yes, you do. Like my phony father."

"Well, let's not be too hard on him, son. Why don't you refer to him as Dad, like you did before, and call *me* Father?"

"All right. So, how can you be an author if you're a lobsterman?"

"Why not? I'm not lobstering right now. Right? And even when I was, I was still writing."

"Writing what?"

"About air, soil and water pollution."

"Really?"

"Yep."

"Can I read it?"

"Maybe I'll read it to you one day. Everything but the ending."

"How come?"

"Because I want it to be a surprise. Besides, I think you're too young."

"No, I'm not. I'm ten-and-a-half, and I'm above grade level. Ask my teacher."

"I will. But I think she's going to tell me that you have a poor attention span."

"No, she won't," Freddie said defensively.

"Sure, she will."

"Why do you say that when you really don't know?"

"But I do know."

"How?"

Malcolm pointed to the open door of the glove compartment. "You forget?"

Freddie frowned. "Boy, oh boy. Give a guy a break, will you?" He reached behind the pile of folded maps and audiotapes—touching something strange. Smooth. Long and rubbery. He pulled out whatever it was, then laughed. "It's a rubber snake."

"Huh. I thought you'd go right through the roof."

"Nope. But if this was the convertible we had before, I'd toss it at one of the girls back there in town," the boy swore.

"Would you now?"

"Sure. Why not? Afraid we'd get in trouble?"

"*We'd* get in trouble? *You'd* toss it at some girl in town, and *we'd* get in trouble?"

Freddie laughed. "Uh-huh. You're the driver."

"Yeah, but this isn't even my car."

"But you'd still get the ticket. And why did we switch cars anyhow?"

"Why, don't you like this one?"

"Not as much as the convertible. But it's all right, I guess."

Malcolm smiled and mussed the boy's hair playfully.

Freddie held the toy snake upside down and wiggled it by its tail.

"Maybe we should go back and find that ugly waitress. Stick that in her apron."

Freddie swung around abruptly in his seat. "Want to?"

Malcolm laughed wholeheartedly. "Nah. We're too far away from there, now."

"Where're we going anyways?"

"Running away."

"Away where?"

"Wherever fate leads us."

"What about school?"

"I'll tutor you."

"In what?"

"All subjects."

"You don't know all subjects."

"Sure I do."

"Do not."

"What does your teacher teach you? Only one subject?"

"Most subjects," Freddie conceded. "But you're not a teacher."

"Sure I am. Didn't you even tell me when we met on the beach that I should be a teacher?"

"Well, yeah. But saying you should be a teacher and being a teacher are two different things."

Malcolm looked over at his son fondly. "Tell you what, Freddie."

"What?"

"I've given up the idea of becoming your teacher."

"You have?" the boy said with a degree of disappointment.

"Yep."

"Well, then *you* have a very short . . . *interest* span," Freddie said mischievously.

"Attention span. Instead, I've decided to become your professor."

Freddie and Malcolm drove themselves silly before the driver suddenly turned off the secondary road and onto a pitch-black stretch of macadam.

"Better watch where you're going," Freddie warned through genuine tears of laughter.

"I told you before that *I don't* know where we're going," he reminded the boy. "See, you don't listen."

"I *do*."

"How am I going to teach you anything if you don't listen?"

Freddie cupped his left ear and leaned in close to his father. "What did you say?"

"I said, punch-buggy don't punch back, you little bugger," Malcolm answered with a grin as he planted a closed fist firmly against his son's shoulder.

"Hey!"

"Hey, what?"

"That *really* hurt."

Malcolm was still grinning as he tromped down upon the accelerator and brought the vehicle up to eighty.

Freddie glared. "I know what you're trying to do. You're trying to scare me. But it's not going to work. And besides. You're going to get yourself a speeding ticket."

"There are no cops out this way, fearless Freddie."

Freddie folded his scrawny arms across his skinny chest.

"Got your seat belt on, son of mine?"

No answer.

"Huh! Our first fight, Freddie." Malcolm grinned and brought the coupe up to eighty-five—then ninety miles an hour.

"I thought you were afraid of everything. Your words, oh, father of mine."

"Not when I'm in control, oh, son of mine."

Freddie watched the speedometer's needle climb steadily to ninety-five miles per hour as the Porsche rocketed over the pavement.

Chapter 55

The Bella Sera Restaurant, located in West Tiana, was considered by most South Fork residents to be one of the finest Italian eateries on the East End of Long Island, open year-round for lunch and dinner, seven days a week. Pizzeria in front. Restaurant in back. The recent addition of a second dining room accommodated another twenty-four tables. Forty-five tables in all. Apart from a common surname, the thirty-year-old family business, owned and operated by Phil Cancilla, bore no relation to the notorious Cancilla mob family of New York. No connection to organized crime whatsoever, despite the fact that Don Ciccio and his cronies could be seen dining there frequently. Then again, on any given evening, one might see Cindy Crawford, Michael J. Fox, Adam Sandler, or Jerry Seinfeld and entourage.

Dominic Cancilla, Phil's older brother, had just returned from Palermo to visit family and friends and to help run the successful establishment—now that spring was finally in the air and the place was turning quite busy. Dominic would tease and attest to the fact, without exaggeration, that his younger, single brother, Phil, was married to the kitchen. A jealous mistress who knew no mercy. Three times a year, for a fortnight, Dominic would come to lend a helping hand.

Phil Cancilla, a good-looking forty-four-year-old no-nonsense hardworking Sicilian, not only oversaw the entire day-to-day operation, but shared in all the chores, politely and patiently instructing his amicable staff—setting a fine example for everyone— from busboy to chef. A hands-on individual who was not too proud to shop, chop, slice, dice, cook, serve and clean. He could be found planning or reciting the evening specials, chatting easily and pleasantly among his customers, or acting as sommelier or sous-chef. When the pressure was on, the man would work indefatigably alongside his crew of at least four chefs, six line cooks, a sea of waiters and waitresses, busboys and girls. It was how Phil had learned the business from his brother, Dominic. From the ground up.

Don Vincent Ciccio, Charlotte Magni and Austin Izzo were just pulling into the crowded parking lot filled with upscale vehicles. Everything from SUV's to stretch limos.

Friday, Saturday and Sunday evenings from Memorial Day through Labor Day at the restaurant were organized chaos at its best. Webster's would do themselves proud to include Phil Cancilla's picture next to the words 'omnipresent' and 'ubiquitous,' for the man was seemingly everywhere at once. Mondays through Thursdays, the pace was somewhat abated but still busy, giving Phil a chance to catch his breath before the weekend madness began anew. The owner-operator had been at it virtually every day since the day he first arrived from Sicily, thirty years ago, at age fourteen.

One of the so-called secret ingredients to Phil's success became evident after a single visit, for nothing was hidden from the eye. The ever-present power of family pervaded the thriving operation.

Nieces, nephews, cousins, uncles and in-laws paraded the fare, cleared the tables, unfolded and laid down clean white linen, set the tables with spotless plates, utensils and glasses, popped the wine corks, swept and mopped the imported Italian ceramic tile floors, watered all the indoor and outdoor plants, cut and arranged fresh flowers, scrubbed and scoured pots and pans, then wiped clean the kitchen's stations of stainless steel surfaces and tiled walls at the end of a very long day. Together, Phil and his nephew-in-law, Tomas, portioned out ingredients in grams and milligrams for a tasty and truly healthy low-fat menu. Several chefs and cooks traditionally prepared the more popular dishes, as sixty-plus percent of Bella Sera's patrons ordered from the facing-page—no matter what health conscious and concerned loved ones had to say on the subject of a sensible diet. Regardless, the very best of both worlds was always offered.

Ordering the traditional bill of fare included an assortment of appealing appetizers, mouth-watering meat dishes, sumptuous seafood, and a wide variety of pastas and sauces served in most imaginative ways. Their famous thin-crust pizza—along with a long list of sandwiches, beer, wine and a host of other hot and cold beverages—was always available as well.

Don Ciccio ate what, and when, and where he wanted, regardless of his doctor's orders. The big man tipped the Toledo at two hundred and sixty-five pounds, claiming his enormous consumption of wine, garlic and onions cleaned his arteries—making it perfectly clear that aggravation, not cholesterol, was the killer of man. "*Family* feuds notwithstanding," he would tack on in conclusion.

The second component of the Cancilla family's ill-kept secret of success read like an open book. It was Phil's insistence on using a plethora of fresh ingredients; a welcome assault upon the senses. The enticing aroma of sautéed vegetables, fruits and herbs, such as broccoli rabe, basil, oregano, asparagus, eggplant, escarole, spinach, peas, beans and tomatoes—prepared with the proper amount of garlic and cold pressed extra virgin olive oil—wafted from the kitchen through a system of well-ventilated ductwork. Up and out the single-story stucco, the pleasing aromatic odors swirled—across the ample parking lot to the fringes of Montauk Highway.

In point of fact, it was how Don Ciccio came to discover the restaurant, driving by one sunny fall afternoon some twenty years ago.

"My first drive-by," Vincent kidded, shooting off his mouth as the trio stepped from Austin Izzo's green Mercedes. "I made an immediate U-turn in front of oncoming traffic," the don bellowed, relating the story for the hundredth time. "A nose for business and fine food, Aussie. Wait till you taste this chow," the gangster said excitedly. "Right, Charl?"

"*Chow*, Vincent?" Charlotte chided as they headed toward the entrance.

The artistry of presentation at the table was always a sight to behold. Plump mussels, jumbo shrimps, shimmering clams, delicately golden-battered calamari—all beautifully arranged on freshly made beds of al dente pasta and blanketed with sheets of savory sauces: tomato marinara (red), clam sauce (white), pesto (green)—served as an attribution, subtly incorporating the symbol of a nation, unfurling the promise of a banner banquet.

It became quite apparent, rather quickly, that Phil Cancilla was a genius at what he did.

Austin Izzo held the front door open for Vincent and Charlotte. The don stepped foot inside the bustling establishment and immediately took in his surroundings.

The pleasant sounds of laughter and language encompassed the entire area, with Sicilian spoken in and just off the kitchen as waiters, waitresses, busboys and busgirls moved busily back and forth. Vincent deftly reached for and picked a lightly crusted, delicately seasoned buttery garlic knot from a fast-moving platter, tore the delectable morsel open, popped half into his mouth—then the other half.

The appreciative oohs and aahs from customers complimenting the spectacular array of savory dishes arriving at their tables enhanced the friendly family ambiance.

Grabbing a fresh white linen napkin from a table being set by a busgirl at the head of the front dining room, Vincent wiped his stubby, filmy fingertips upon the cloth, raising it to his lips as the threesome headed toward the hostess. The don felt and made himself right at home. The irony was, of course, that he and his cohorts were never *really* welcome at the restaurant.

But what am I gonna do? was the look that Phil shot to Dominic in passing.

And what bounty would be complete without the celebration of fine wine? Reds. Whites. Rosés. Nectar of the gods.

Austin cradled two bottles of Vincent's wine, as the mob boss was more than happy to pay Phil the handsome corking fee for carrying in his own. The bottles were an expensive gift from the renowned industrialist, Evan Tamblin. 1947 Château Chevel Blanc.

Wine and food aplenty. The signature of Bella Sera's prosperity. A cornucopia of satisfaction. Vin and fare. The latter was served in prodigious portions and encouraged beyond the boundary of the building in the form of a fancy foil-lined doggy bag, for the establishment was truly a family-oriented restaurant. Parents and children with their nannies were a permanent fixture; a mainstay. The bread and butter of the business.

Hence, the hallmark and certainly no secret to the establishment's *true* success. Abundance.

"*Abbondanza!*" Vincent waved and blew kisses to anyone who cast their looks his way.

Abundance?

Absolutely.

Intemperance?

No.

For Phil and Dominic Cancilla despised intemperance and was one of the reasons why they so detested the customer now crossing the threshold to the back dining room with his two associates. It was the likes of Don Ciccio and his kind that had motivated the good and God-fearing Cancilla family to leave Palermo and immigrate to the United States in 1970. It was only within the last decade that Dominic had returned to Palermo after an amicable divorce.

Don Ciccio was evil personified. Gargantuan. Greedy. Guileful.

"Hey, Philip, my good fellow!" the mob figure blustered as he stopped before the front bar, handing over hat and coat to his henchman, taking and covetously clutching the costly bottles of wine in his claw-like mitts. He sat them gingerly down upon the counter. "Protect these with your life, Phil. They probably cost more than you rake in in a week," he boasted, affectionately pinching the owner's cheek.

Austin helped Charlotte off with her coat.

Rarely did the don showcase Charlotte Magni.

Charlotte took her boss's arm, giving Phil a quick, curt smile, turning her attention to the attractive hostess behind the counter. "Table twenty-nine, reserved under Ciccio," Charlotte announced. "Eight o'clock sharp," she snapped, coolly showing the friendly woman the face of her expensive bejeweled watch.

A minute to the hour.

Like the service, the hostess was snappy. "Please follow me," the woman replied pleasantly as she led her party to a corner table reserved along the far wall at the rear of the new dining room.

"It's a great country, Philip," Vincent Ciccio went on rather loudly as Cancilla trailed close behind. "Plenty to go around for everyone. Food for thought," he added none too subtly, alluding to a still standing offer to smoothly pave the way for Phil's eldest brother, Raymond—who owned the new sister restaurant, La Siciliana, in Noyack, along the bay—to import olive oil from Sciacca, Sicily.

Phil smiled ceremoniously as Vincent Ciccio faced back around.

"Vincent, Vincent," the proprietor said politely, glancing down at one of the pale yellow and green labeled bottles sitting in the center of every table throughout the two dining rooms. "Next month, the labels are being changed from Bono, to read La Siciliana. It's a done deal, and without your help, I'm happy to say."

"Hey, that's great, Philip," Vincent said with some surprise.

"But you and Raymond could've had all that business settled and done with years ago if you guys would've listened to me. With considerably less red tape—and, at a fraction of the cost," he added, nodding most assuredly.

Phil shook his head knowingly. "Doing business with you, or through you, Vincent, would be *considerably* more costly in the long run."

Don Ciccio briskly waved away the comment. "Have it your way, Philip. One day, you may need a friend."

"*Buòn appetito, signori e signora,*" Phil said, tipping his head politely to the pretty woman.

Charlotte acknowledged the courtesy with a nod.

"And send Jackie over here to take our order, Philip," Vincent ordered.

Phil said nothing in reply but cordially took his leave.

"Ya gonna love the food here," Vincent said to Austin. "Him, ya don't 'ave ta deal with," he threw out dismissively with a flagging gesture of annoyance at Phil's back.

"Aren't you afraid he might poison you?" Charlotte questioned with a sobering grin, gesturing toward the kitchen.

Vincent frowned. "Nah. Bad for business. Might try and have me shot in the parking lot after hours, though. *That* I wouldn't put past him," he kidded. "But let's fuhgetabout murder for a moment and see what we're gonna 'ave. I think you two had enough killing for one day —no?" he whispered quietly and winked. "Let's eat."

As if on cue, a busgirl brought out a plate of mini-bruschetta (a tangy medley of diced tomatoes, garlic and basil on lightly toasted slices of Italian bread) in addition to half a dozen buttery garlic knots. Gratis. Compliments of the house. Delivered to each and every table with a winning smile.

One young woman's smile was special. Winsome, warm and wonderful. Her God-given emerald-green eyes were set like precious stones, unveiling and revealing His masterpiece in Vincent's own mind's eye. He credited the Creator a Supreme jeweler; a ruler of the ordinary and extraordinary until that magic hour when He far surpassed the superlative and blessed Jacqueline Rubino—Dominic's youngest married daughter—with exquisite beauty, bearing, and charm. She was His *tour de force*. The Savior's *magum opus*.

Jacqueline appeared before Don Ciccio's table just as the busgirl made her way back through the seated crowd.

"Hey, Jackie," Don Ciccio beamed. "How ya been, kid?"

"Fine, Mr. Ciccio," the waitress answered and smiled good-naturedly.

"How many times I gotta tell ya to call me *Zu* Vincent? I'm like an uncle to you, no? Charlotte, I'm sure you remember Jackie. And this big lug, Jackie, is my associate, Mister Izzo."

Jacqueline curved the corners of her mouth most magically into a magnificent smile. "Can I get you something to drink?" she addressed the three politely. Big smile. Bright eyes. All business.

"Your top shelf Scotch; neat, for me, kid. Charl? Aussie? Whattaya gonna 'ave to whet your whistle before we crack that wine?"

"Glass of champagne," Charlotte answered crisply.

"I'll have Jack Daniel's—rocks," Austin ordered, drinking in the green-eyed, goddess-like creature standing at his side.

Jacqueline wrote down the drink order and was gone.

Vincent poured a generous amount of the green-tinged olive oil onto his plate, ground a black shower of peppercorns above the bath, then turned quiet, absorbed in thought, dipping both the crusty bread and knotted dough simultaneously—a morsel in each hand. In two bites, the knot was gone. Another, and the bruschetta disappeared.

Austin and Charlotte ate deliberately.

"She's lovely," Charlotte commented between nibbles.

"A rare beauty," Austin Izzo agreed. "Um, this bruschetta is delicious."

"She's Phil's niece, Aussie," Ciccio clarified as he chewed another garlic knot. "Dominic's daughter," he elaborated, pointing a fat, stubby gun-finger at the serious man in a red shirt standing near the back bar off the entranceway. "Hey, Dominic!" Vincent called out obnoxiously from across the crowded room.

Dominic Cancilla nodded gravely.

"Jackie's husband, Tomas, is back there cookin' up a storm. Frankie—Phil's other nephew-in-law—you saw out front making pizza," Vincent yakked away. "Jackie's sister-in-law's over at La Siciliana; she keeps the books. You could chart the family tree just by taking a walk through the kitchen," he swore and chomped and swallowed.

"A regular dynasty, I hear," Austin rejoined.

"Nepotism in its strictest sense," the don stated emphatically. "They keep this up, the government's gonna declare them a monopoly," he jested.

"A classic beauty," Charlotte stated, her mind still on the handsome woman. "Poised. Flawless features. Perfect nose, cheeks, lips, hair and skin. And those eyes!"

"You're a classic too, Charl. Ain't that right, Aussie? See, another woman would be criticizing. Finding fault. But not Charlotte. I hate them catty broads. Full of spite and jealousy. Anyone can see you appreciate real beauty, Charl."

"I was thinking more along the lines of recruiting her, Vincent. Who'd ever figure her to whack a target? Not in a million years. She'd be perfect," the hit woman remarked.

"Hey! Don't even fuckin' kid like that 'fore I whack *you*," Vincent whispered. "Poison me, hell. I wouldn't even make it to the back door. You believe this broad? You wanna recruit somethin', recruit this," Vincent sneered, making an obscene gesture toward his crotch. "Tallest member of the lot."

Austin Izzo laughed. "Cool it. Here she comes."

Jacqueline carried over their drinks. After serving the threesome, she asked if they would like to hear the evening specials, which they did, indeed. Phil's niece went through an extensive list of specially prepared delights, stating that she would be back to take their order whenever they were ready.

"I'm ready for some more bruschetta and those garlic knots," Don Ciccio instantly decided. "How about you guys?"

"I'm saving my appetite," Charlotte begged off.

"Ditto, but thanks," Austin agreed.

"I'll have another plate brought out right away."

"You do that, kid," the don said, smiling up happily.

Jacqueline smiled back in such a manner that could have melted butter if not a bar of steel.

"He practically ate that whole plate by himself," Austin revealed to the waitress.

"Mikey likes it," Jacqueline joked, laughing lightly as she cleared away the empty plates—signaling a busboy while speaking Sicilian to a nearby waitress.

"That girl just loves to see me eat," Vincent managed through a mouthful.

"Loves the way you tip, you mean," Charlotte suggested.

The big man shook his head. "I leave a straight twenty percent. Period. I don't spoil nobody. Doesn't pay."

Charlotte giggled and shook her head. "I meant *tip* the scale," she teased, lifting the glass of champagne to her lips. "*Salute.*"

Vincent glared at her.

Austin took a mouthful of bourbon and let it burn smoothly down his throat before he said another word. It had been a long and tortuous time. "*Salute.*"

Vincent took a swallow of the expensive Scotch and turned his attention to the menu. The appetizers in particular.

Before a second round of drinks was brought to the table, Vincent ordered a fine bottle of wine for his guests. Solaia, Antinori. One hundred and sixty dollars a pop. The two bottles of 1947 Château Chevel Blanc were his and his alone. He was not sharing. One was to be opened, aired, and brought out with the first course.

After cocktails, Jacqueline appeared, and Vincent took the liberty of ordering appetizers for everyone.

"Got enough ink in that pen, Jackie?" Vincent questioned. "I don't want you stopping my flow of concentration before I finish."

"I'm all set," she assured the man.

"Good. We'll start with an order of Insalata di Mare for *three*. Not *two* like it says here: scungilli, calamari, mussels, shrimp, and octopus. And don't tell me you're out of one or the other, or we'll go across the street."

"Okay, I won't tell you," Jacqueline teased.

"Better not," Vincent bantered back. "And do up a nice Gorgonzola salad. Half a dozen clams on the half shell—and tell 'em I want topnecks this time, or I'll go back there and pick 'em out myself. Two orders of baked stuffed clams. We'll sit with that, and you can bring the wine."

"Be right back," she promised.

"Tell 'em topnecks," Vincent reminded her when she was halfway across the room. He turned to his guests. "Last time they brought me the smallest littlenecks they could dig up. I sent them back; so the smart ass over there," he whined, pointing to Phil, "comes out with cherrystones about the size of chowders. A person couldn't get those suckers down a toilet with a plunger, let alone your throat. Always specify topnecks. They're the perfect size. In between a littleneck and a cherrystone."

Austin swallowed, smiled and shook his head. "The reason he brought you out clams a little larger than cherrystones is that's what a topneck is, only immature."

"What the fuck are you talkin' 'bout—larger and immature?"

"Topnecks," Austin said. "They're actually larger than cherrystones. In Massachusetts, the seedlings—"

"The fuck they are."

Charlotte put a finger to the don's lips. "Keep your voice down, Vincent. This is a respectable family restaurant. There are children over there."

"Yeah, but this guy's tryin' to tell me that a topneck is larger than a cherrystone. Hey! How can anything that's larger be immature? Answer me that, wise guy."

Charlotte leaned over and affectionately tapped Don Ciccio's stomach. "I rest my case," she ruled, laughing like a little girl.

Austin smiled and shook his head. "Vincent, they're all quahogs. *Venus mercenaria.* My family's been clammers for years. Maine to Massachusetts. Here on Long Island, too. Bonackers to boot; five generations back."

"Bonackers! What's a fuckin' Bonacker?" he asked quietly. "I thought you were a renegade cop. Hey! You're not one of them born-agains, are ya?"

Austin laughed and shook his head. "All I'm saying is that I know my clams." He took a final sip of bourbon before he touched his wine.

"You know your clams?"

"That's what I said."

"How many I pay you last year?"

"Well, I guess the real question is how many more you gonna shell out, now that you promoted me?" Austin Izzo put forth directly.

Charlotte gave her accomplice a little kick under the table.

"You know what your problem is, Aussie?" the don blustered in question. "You don't know how or when or where to negotiate a deal. That's your problem."

Austin shrugged indifferently. "I didn't know it was open to negotiation. I just thought it was something that I either accepted or rejected."

The man received another kick under the table from Charlotte —only, a bit harder this time.

"Accept or reject?" Don Ciccio gave a hardy laugh. "You kiddin' me or what? There's no rejectin' *anythin'* I put on the table, for your information."

Austin grinned. "Really? Then how does '*negotiate a deal*' fit in? Your words, Vincent. Not mine."

"It don't," Don Ciccio automatically decided. "Just like no topneck could ever follow a cherrystone in size order. Littleneck. Topneck. Cherrystone. Chowder. You see, Aussie, like or unlike the policy of this restaurant, the *boss* is always right. Right, Charlotte?"

"Right you are, Vincent."

Two young men carrying large trays came up to the table as Jacqueline stepped around and carefully set down platters and plates of baked and raw clams. Another waiter poured the wine.

"Take note, Aussie." The huge man smiled. "Not too big, and not too small. But just right. Jackie, would you please tell this lady and gentleman what kind of clams these are."

Jacqueline delivered her disarming smile. "I believe *you* call them topnecks," she replied politely.

"You see?" Vincent beamed brightly. "The customer's always right. Right, Jackie?"

Jacqueline put down a mountainous Gorgonzola salad that could have fed a hungry family of six; next, an enormous sumptuous seafood salad that looked like it contained gems from the Seven Seas.

"Hey! Where's the octopus, Jackie?" Vincent searched the platter with fork in hand.

"We ran out," she answered quietly.

"Well, run out and get some more," Vincent ordered.

"I gave you extra calamari and shrimp," she said so sweetly.

Vincent Ciccio nodded and looked up into the angelic face. "Extra's good," the don decided.

"Can I get anyone anything else right now?"

"Yeah, later. Two hand trucks." Austin winked. "One for the leftovers. And the other to wheel Vincent out to the car."

"This is nothin'," the boss affirmed. "Just a little somethin' to tide us over till the next course. I think we're fine for now, Jackie."

Jacqueline collected and temporarily set aside the menus, telling the trio to relax and enjoy as she took her leave.

"Wait till you see what Vincent orders for entrées," Charlotte warned. She held up three fingers, then put up a forth for good measure.

"Whattaya talkin' 'bout," Vincent said with a mouthful. "I eat one big meal a day. Big guy next to you? I've seen him put away some chow."

"Yeah, one meal a day, but he snacks hourly," she gave away with a smirk.

"Couple chips and pretzels," Vincent chomped.

"Couple bags, you mean," Charlotte tattled.

"Hey! I'd bet good money that if we totaled the amount of calories I consume in the course of a day, measured against the three meals and snacks this gorilla puts away, my intake would be considerably less. Two-to-one odds. Any takers?"

"Not in the last thirty-six hours, it wouldn't," Austin Izzo challenged. "And would that be a gorilla, like in ape? Or guerrilla, like in soldier and warfare? Careful how you answer that, fella," the don's hatchet man added with a straight face.

"Well, *I'd* sure take a piece of that action," Charlotte jumped in, tactfully turning the conversation back to the bet, cheerfully raising her glass of red to her ruby lips. "Because all Aussie and I had since yesterday morning was a half a sandwich, cup of coffee, and a couple slices of pizza before we came here," she elaborated.

"You–had–pizza before you came here?" Vincent asked as though the two had committed a mortal sin.

"I had *one* slice," Charlotte snapped. "A late lunch. Neither of us had a thing to eat before that, except an egg salad sandwich we shared, along with a thermos of black coffee."

"First you complain that *I* ate all the bruschetta and garlic knots —"

"I didn't complain. He complained."

"And, now, I find out that the two of you had pizza before you came here. You don't come to the Bella Sera unless you plan to *eat*."

"We'll eat. We'll eat, for Christ's sake," she pledged. "I told you before, I'm famished. I could eat a goddamn horse. All right?"

Phil Cancilla walked up to their table. "Everything okay over here?"

"Just great, Philip," Vincent answered, slurping down his fourth raw clam with lemon and cocktail sauce. "Charlotte wants to know if you have horse on the menu," he deadpanned.

"Please don't pay him any mind," she insisted. "Listen, these baked clams are absolutely the best. I mean that. Oh, and I also mean to tell you your niece is every bit as gorgeous as I remember. It's been awhile, but she gets lovelier with age. If she ever needs a change of pace, I'm sure Vincent could find her a cover girl spot. I'm serious."

Phil nodded gratefully. "I'm sure you are. And I'm sure Jackie would appreciate the compliment. But if my niece ever decided on the glamour world, or any world for that matter, it would be on her own terms, and she would make her own way," Phil said just as politely as he knew how.

"Still, it's always nice to have friends nearby to help pave the way," Don Ciccio interjected.

"Jackie will always have her family close by, Vincent."

"I could do so much for this family," Vincent said through a sigh. "So much, my friend."

"You do," Phil Cancilla assured the man. "You pay the bill and always leave a nice gratuity."

"You're thick, Philip."

"Enjoy the rest of your meal."

Phil walked over to a table of good friends and warmly shook the gentlemen's hands, graciously planting dual kisses upon each woman's cheeks.

"You eatin' that other clam?" Vincent asked Charlotte.

"Take mine. I had enough clams on the half shell to last me a lifetime," Austin swore.

With heavy dark-cast eyes, Vincent followed Phil's back. "He hurts me, Charlotte," the don confessed.

"Phil?"

Vincent nodded.

"So why do you bother to come here?"

Vincent looked at her as if she had two heads. "For the food, you idiot. Next question."

"Why do I put up with you? Maybe Phil would take me on as a hostess here. *Then* what would you do?"

"Go back to my first or second wife, I suppose."

Austin put aside his drink and helped himself to salad and calamari. "This squid is absolutely fantastic," the underworld associate declared after an uncomfortable lull.

"All right, let's get down to business," Charlotte suggested.

"Let's," Vincent agreed.

"What am I going to do about the kid's mother, Virginia Dupree?"

"Stepmother," the don corrected.

"Whatever."

"You befriended her. You make her disappear."

"Fine. Now that business is settled, can we all enjoy the rest of this meal?"

"Not a problem," Don Ciccio reassured Charlotte. "Not a problem."

Chapter 56

Donald Bellport's remains were reduced to a residue. All that a group of hikers discovered off a well-worn timber trail was an abandoned blue van with an old-fashioned bathtub stashed away inside the vehicle. A short length of pipe running from the bottom of the tub through the metal floor had drained the last drop of Donald's being into Lake Champlain, near Ausable Chasm. Depending on the flow of water, Bellport's aftermath was somewhere between New York and Vermont. Perhaps a bit northward toward the Canadian border.

The skeletal frame and other remnants of the Adirondack handyman, which did not succumb to acid, had apparently been carted off by a professional clean-up crew long before the police arrived. Upstate and local authorities out of Burlington had little to go on. But Evan Tamblin, sitting in his comfortable home on Long Island, believed he knew all he needed to know concerning the likes and whereabouts of Donald Bellport.

He held a series of Polaroid pictures taken of the light-skinned young man. One of two men he deemed responsible for his daughter's death. *One culprit down. One to go,* the industrialist envisioned.

Don Ciccio told Tamblin that his people were still several steps ahead of the police, but if he wished the desired result—a fate similar to what Donald Bellport had suffered—the price of *criminal justice* would now be costly. And with no guarantee or rebate in the bargain. The police might beat them to the punch. Justice would then be meted out in a court of law . . . the chips to fall where they may.

But Evan had already made his decision. He was committed at all cost. He focused on the revolting stack of Polaroid pictures in living color—of Bellport being tortured in the tub. One of the shots showed the bloody face with a clear, thin line running through the victim's tongue, stretched to its maximum. The subtlety of the empty spool of Prestige Plus No-Vis fly line, sitting in plain view on the edge of the bathtub, was not lost on the avenger—line supposedly sent by Malcolm Columba to his alleged accomplice. Evan held that very item in his hand, clearly labeled a WF-10-I—indicating a weight-forward, intermediate sink rate. One photo in particular was a representation not at all unlike that of his darling daughter found murdered in the Flanders flat.

And then there was the wire.

Wire that could slice through skin and tissue like a stick of butter.

Razor wire.

It was certainly an imaginative and sadistic step-up from the trolling wire Columba had used on poor Patricia. But the shiny razor ribbon Don Ciccio's man had threaded through the length of Bellport's body did nothing to alleviate Evan's suffering.

The industrialist could not shake the feeling of pain and fear Patricia had to have endured in her final hour. It was as if he himself had gone through her entire ordeal. A thousand times over in his mind and heart. He felt totally justified in that Bellport should die a thousand deaths had the handyman but merely been an onlooker who watched his daughter fade. Columba, who was the central figure in this string of serial killings, would pay quite dearly for his horrific deeds. He did not know how more cruel a punishment Don Ciccio's people could administer if and when they caught up to the madman, but Evan Tamblin was willing to satisfy *any* price. Forget a finder's fee. A fixed fortune he would gladly hand over to Vincent for Malcolm Columba's head. Additionally, he would turn over the bulk of his company stock as a bonus in order to double the time and trouble it took to terminate Donald Bellport. In doing so, he would want a guarantee. Twice the pain and terror the Adirondack playboy had endured for almost eighteen hours.

Don Ciccio threw out a ballpark figure of two million dollars to continue looking for the madman. Evan Tamblin was prepared to put five million down and another five million for the delivery of a live body. Columba's. An additional ten million on top of that to ensure the man's pain and suffering, using the standard he had just outlined in his mind:

Thirty-six hours of sheer unadulterated torture.

Twenty million dollars for peace of mind so that his own tortured soul might rest.

One fiftieth of a billion bucks.

That ought to create the incentive needed to find Malcolm Columba before the police laid their hands on him.

No?

He would request—no he would demand—the same people who had performed and recorded the horror shown in more than two dozen of the photographs he was holding on his lap. The Nazis employed within their infamous death camps had nothing over Ciccio's crew. As a Jew, Evan was daunted by how he himself could come to loathe a human being so—having always been *astonished* at how much hatred Hitler and his henchmen had in their hearts for a race of people. Yet, the loathing Evan felt toward Columba, this monster who had claimed his only child through such an unfathomable act, clearly overshadowed the evil carried out by the Nazis and their supporters.

Amazed and appalled by this self-admission, frozen in the forefront of his mind, but with no intention of withdrawing from his resolution, he knew what he must also do in that final hour, should it come to full fruition. A coward's way out, perhaps . . . like Hitler himself in that ultimate hour of madness.

The renowned and affluent magnate would not have any need for millions of dollars any more than a pigeon would have need of a penny. And Sally would still be well-provided for in the end.

Both funny and strange . . . how a man that he had always hated most passionately in all the world, a long dead military dictator at that, was not so far removed from the Godless soul he himself was turning into. For he knew that if he had to pay handsomely to exterminate six million Malcolm Columbas and Donald Bellports, so as to avenge his daughter's death and quell his tortured soul, he would, indeed.

Evan Tamblin knew, too, that he was on the fringe of madness.

He reviewed the pictures in a pair of trembling hands. There was a single *pose* of some person pouring a bath of acid into the enameled tub. Evan could not see the stooping figure's face—only the shadowy shoulder and arm of a specter. In the final photo, the influential mogul could plainly see what was left of Donald Bellport's skeletal remains.

It was a rather chilly late May night, especially with a wrathful southeast wind whipping across the water. Consequently, there was nothing at all odd about smoke billowing from a chimney top. A roaring blaze was crackling in the fireplace when the stranger arrived at Tamblin's door. Sally escorted the man into the commodious, comfortable library. The figure stood by and watched as Evan tossed all twenty-four photographs into the fire, along with the telling book; that being, the timetable of Bellport's ordeal.

Thirty minutes later, the man left the industrialist's home with what appeared to be a pair of leather saddlebags with which the foreigner first entered. The only difference being, they were filled with cash when the two gentlemen finally said good night.

Sally Tamblin closed and locked the heavy wooden door behind Don Ciccio's emissary.

Malcolm Columba was truly one of the industrialist's most trusted and well-paid people in his employ. Why in the world would he sadistically murder his beloved Patricia? Evan wondered—having received only sketchy details from his two contacts: Vincent Ciccio and William Mattheson. Why would Columba, his revered Middle East as well as East Coast powerbroker here in the United States, be mixed up with an Adirondack handyman?

"Why?" he questioned and wept bitterly in Sally's lap. "Why, dear God?"

Chapter 57

Harold Dupree had not heard from his wife in well over a week. Nor had Malcolm or Freddie phoned the house. The police were still standing by to trace the call in the unlikely event of contact. It did not surprise Gary York in the least that word was not forthcoming. What did surprise the detective, though, was that Virginia Dupree had not bothered to call him to learn of any development concerning her stepson.

Rarely, did he read people wrong.

The detective gave Harold Dupree a call at home.

Harold picked up on the first ring. "Yeah?"

"Dupree, it's Detective York."

"You hear anything?"

"No. Have you heard from Virginia?"

"No, and I'm plenty worried about her. Not that I don't have enough to worry about with Freddie still gone. But it's not like her not to call. We had our ups and downs before, you know. She'd go off to her mother's in Shirley, or stay overnight at a friend's house. Nothing ever like this."

"Well, she was pretty upset with you when she left," the cop reminded him, trying to mollify the man.

"She's been mad before. Believe me."

"You call her mother's house and friends?"

"Sure, I called. No one's heard a word from her. I even called *you* a couple times and left messages, remembering you gave her your card. Thought maybe she contacted you. You don't get your messages, Detective?"

"I've been very busy. One of the reasons I'm calling now," he hedged. "Listen, there's a good chance she might have told her mother and friends not to let you know where she is. Happens all the time. Want to give me their names and numbers? I'll make a few inquiries."

"I'll give them to you, but it won't do any good."

"And why's that?"

There was a slight hesitation. "Because I already told them I was calling on your behalf. I said that you said it was very important that I speak to her."

Gary just smiled and shook his head. "You *lied*, Harold?" he asked sternly.

"No, I'm through lying. To you, I mean. I told you that, and I mean it. It's just that I'm worried sick about them. I haven't eaten or slept since she left—'cept for catnaps in this chair."

Gary pictured the big man in his overstuffed vinyl recliner. He believed Harold about not sleeping well. But not eating was another story—like in fiction.

"Harold. Just before Virginia left the house, you asked her if she was going to stay with Charlotte somebody."

"Yeah, that's right."

"Charlotte who?"

"Never asked."

"You never asked?"

"If I did, I don't recall."

"You don't recall?"

"No, I'm tellin' you the truth. If I knew, I'd tell you."

"You figured Virginia was going to stay with this Charlotte somebody, and you don't have any idea who she is, or where they might be staying? No phone number? No address? No nothing?"

There was another hesitation. "This Charlotte moves around a lot."

"What do you mean, moves around a lot?"

"Just what I said. Moves around. Last I heard, she was back in Connecticut."

"Connecticut?" Gary's mind was racing. "Listen, Harold. I asked you about Bridgeport and this Lola Heather, whose name you signed when you took out that P.O. box."

"Yeah? And I told you that's the name Malcolm's go-between told me to use."

"Some woman called and told you to take out a box in Lola Heather's name, you said. Whose name you didn't even bother to ask. She could be anyone. Maybe even this Charlotte."

"No, because this Charlotte has a very distinctive voice. Low.

Sexy. I told you the woman who called on Columba's behalf sounded rather sophisticated. Like she had a broomstick up her ass."

Gary's mind was locked on Lola. "How about, Lolita?"

"Lolita. Lola. I'm telling you I don't know no one by that name."

"How about a Dolores, Harold? Know anyone by that name?"

Harold considered the name. "Yeah, I think so. Let me think. Think I heard of someone by that name. Some time ago, though."

"Well, *think* out loud, man. Tell me what you remember. And no bullshit this time, or I'm gonna have to take you in. The district attorney isn't going to be as patient as I've been with you. Believe me."

"I know, I know. And I want you to know that I've been straight with you from the second Virginia walked out. I've told you *everything*, Detective."

"Except who this Dolores is."

"She was the girlfriend of some big Mafia guy from the city. Maybe Staten Island. I'm not sure."

"Mafia guy? Who?"

"I don't know his name. All I know is that a fella I once knew said he saw Malcolm and this Mafia guy talking."

"Talking about what?"

"I don't know for sure. I think it was something about his crew trying to muscle in on Malcolm's turf. Something like that."

"Turf?"

"Territory. Waters he was working for years—for lobsters."

"Muscle in, how?"

"Cutting and stealing traps, before Malcolm put a stop to it. All I know is that the fella recognized him from the newspapers and TV news. Big shot. Up-and-coming hood. Some time ago. Said the guy was bad news. Underboss, or something like that. Politically connected, too. The girl he had on his arm was Dolores somebody."

"Who's this fellow you knew?"

"Lobsterman, like myself and Malcolm."

"Gotta name?"

"Rick somebody. Don't remember."

"You don't remember dick, do you?"

"I told you; it was a long time ago. We was in some bar."

"Think you could find this Rick?"

"He retired and moved to Florida. Last I heard, he passed away."

"Swell. Ever hear of this Dolores referred to by any other name?"

"Don't think so. Like what?"

"Like Lola, Lolita or Charlotte?" Gary snapped impatiently.

"No. Why?"

"Because Lola, Lolita, and Dolores are all forms of the name Charlotte. That's why."

It was now Harold Dupree's turn to speculate. And speculate he did. Hard. Certain things were falling into place for him. Fast. Matters concerning his wife and her newfound friend, Charlotte. His mind was turning into a whirlwind. Furiously. A storm was raging between his ears.

"Earth to Harold."

"You've got to find her, Detective York. I think Virginia's in serious trouble."

"And so is Freddie. And so are you if you're not telling me *everything*. Big trouble. With a capital T."

"I think that woman Dolores and Charlotte might be the same person."

"And so do I, Harold. It's just a hunch, is all. But I think *you* have something more telling, I'm sure. So tell me."

"This Dolores woman, who was with the Mafia guy I just told you about, is very pretty, my friend said. Only she made herself look . . . different."

"How do you mean, different?"

"You know, like less attractive than what she really is. Pants instead of a skirt or dress. Hair pulled back and stuck under a baseball cap. Stuff like that. Only she couldn't really hide the fact that she was damn good-looking. Made herself look, you know, tough."

"Tomboy type?"

"Yeah, that's the word. Like a tomboy."

"And?"

"And so, when Virginia told me about this new girlfriend of hers, Charlotte, well, she described her pretty much the same way. No lipstick, perfume, jewelry, or any of that woman stuff. She said her boyfriend didn't like it. It seemed like he'd only let her doll herself up when she went out with *him*. Jealous type, Virginia said. He wouldn't let her wear clothes that were too tight or too flashy. No high heels neither."

"How did Virginia and this Charlotte meet?"

"At some gym out here. I don't know the name. Can't be too many. In Cutchogue, I think. They worked out together. Took a dance class where they all exercise to music. Jazz-a-something. Then they'd swim and sit in the sauna and bullcrap. They became pretty good friends. Virginia would visit some big fancy estate in Connecticut whenever I took Freddie on the road. Horse farm, she said. Charlotte also had a rental out here somewhere. Boyfriend paid for everything. That's all I know."

"Did Virginia say anything about what line of work the boyfriend was in?"

"Yeah." Harold gave a nervous laugh. "Extermination. We both had a chuckle over that."

Chapter 58

Detective Gary York passed the baton to Detective Andrew Miller, while the veteran cop went to work hunting for a Charlotte *somebody* in Connecticut, supposedly connected to an anonymous mob figure. The proverbial needle in a haystack. Miller and his charge, Justin Barnes, paid a visit to Virginia Dupree's mother in Shirley. However, the maverick reluctantly waited in the vehicle as he was told, while the rookie detective went inside to conduct an interview with the elderly widow. Still and all, the civilian considered himself lucky that he was on the case.

"Hey! I'm still a motherfuckin' *Dick*, Monisha," he lauded and laughed aloud as he stretched his arms and tickled the cushiony overhead liner of the detective's personal set of wheels. "Whitey even has me sittin' up front in his snazzy-ass SUV. Now ain't dat somethin'? We closin' in on the fucker that did you in, baby. And if I get my two hands on him fo' these hotshots do, I'm gonna make him bleed, Monisha. He gonna die slower than Othello did at the end of that dumb-ass play you took me to."

Justin spotted someone inside the house peeking out at him from behind a set of curtains.

"Guess that motherfuckin' hotshot figures I can't do what I'm told," he griped, believing it was Miller near the window. "Got a little surprise fo' dat white boy. Hey, you gonna split a gut when I tell ya I picked up an audiotape of *Hamlet* the other day. He's as wacky as I am, sittin' here talkin' to a ghost. At least you ain't talkin' back to me jus' yet. Jus' doin' all the listenin' like you suppose' ta be doin'. Day I start hearin' yo' voice is the day I go—" Justin fanned his forefinger up and down his lips, making the sound of a babbling idiot "—an' commit myself to one of dem homes fo' the *de·ranged.*

"Anyhow, I gotta get back to my states and capitals, woman. Wanted to have all fifty committed to memory weeks ago, but they had me busy lookin' up Moose Lodges from Florida to Maine, then up by you in Michigan." Justin reached for his travel atlas that he toted around in a Book of the Month Club canvas bag. Purely for show. "Got me this bag in a bookstore when I bought that audiotape. Cool?

"Let's see now. Where did I leave off last? Here we go. Maryland. The capital of Maryland is Annapolis. That's where yo' murderer snuffed out Arlene Parker's life in a canoe. Sick fuckin' dude. Don't need no *as·so·ci·ation* trick to stay that state an' capital in my mind, Monisha. Been studying *all* the homicide cases. All nine o' 'em to date. Night and day. Inside and out. They thought they had all the files locked up safe and sound from this here nigger. Closed but unlocked is how I found them, girl." Justin grinned. "Imagine that? Inside *in·fo·ma·tion* is what I have upstairs, woman." Justin tapped his head with a knuckle. "*In·fo·ma·tion* that gonna help me find Malcolm Columba and take him down. And when this all be over, girl, I'm gonna take a chunk of money I been savin' and build a big-ass monument in yo' memory. Won't anybody need no *as·so·ci·ation* game to remember the likes of Monisha Washington when I'm finished, 'cause I gonna erect a statue the size of Lady Liberty up there in Sault Ste. Marie, fo' a foxy lady, such as yo'self.

"Uh-oh. Here come that hotshot," Justin said, looking up from the map. "Wasn't much of an interview if you ask me. Seems grandma got rid of his white ass real fuckin' fast."

Miller marched right up to the window. "Come on," the detective snapped.

"What's up, hotshot?"

"She saw you sitting out here jabbering to yourself. Doesn't want to talk to me. Said she'll talk to you. Now, here's how I want you to conduct yourself in there. First I want you—"

"Whoa! Time out." Justin made the sign of a T as he stepped from the vehicle. "This is my case, too, partner. See, this be my neighborhood, man. And these are my people. Even purchased this new suit fo' the occasion. Cheap, unlike yours, so I'd look da part. But you slick-ass stick me in the corner like I'm some kind of funky-ass broom. But I told ya I was gonna come in handy, partner. Now, we're gonna walk in there together, and *I'm* gonna con·duct this in·ter·view. That's how I'm gonna conduct myself, hotshot partner o' mine."

"Listen to me, lamebrain."

"Oh, now yo' gonna call me names."

"You don't know what to ask or how to ask it. Got it? You're gonna listen to me in there. I'll lead off with a statement. And you'll pick it up from that point. Rephrase it. Turn it into *your* question, and let her answer. I'll take notes of what she says. Understand?"

"Yeah, I understand we gonna sound like a couple of morons. *Tongue* and his partner, *Tied*. You think black folks are stupid? Huh?"

"There's no time or room for discussion. Don't make me sorry I took you along. All right?"

"Listen—"

"No, you listen. I want—"

"I know more about this case than you think I do. Okay?" Justin hinted.

"No, it's not okay. Now get in there before the old bag takes a nap and we come away with nothing."

Justin put up his hands in mock surrender. "You da man, hotshot."

Back inside the woman's home, Detective Miller began again with a vague introduction, not wishing to offer too much information should future questions arise concerning their so-called *unofficial* visit. "This gentleman is an associate of mine, Mrs. Johnson."

"His name?" the old woman demanded.

"Barnes," Miller furnished with a frown.

"And I'm Viola," she brightened, putting out a thin gnarled arthritic hand, which Justin took as though he were handling fine china.

"I'm delighted to meet you, Mrs. Johnson," Justin said just as charmingly as he knew how—and with decent diction when the situation warranted it. "I'm just so sorry it has to be under such circumstances. But we do have to ask you several questions concerning Virginia's whereabouts."

Viola Johnson studied the man as one would a pedigree. "You're not a detective, are you, Mr. Barnes?"

"No, ma'am. I'm surely not," Justin admitted freely. "Actually, I'm a neighborhood buck, here on assignment."

"But this detective led me to believe that you were his partner. 'My partner's in the car,' he said."

"Well, *that* I can assure you I really and truly am, ma'am. But it's only a temporary assignment because his regular partner is home in bed with the flu," he fibbed.

"So then you're *assisting* Detective Miller," she declared.

"Yes, ma'am."

The woman tried to snap her fingers. "You're a fed!" she said wisely.

"Mrs. Johnson," Miller interrupted. "I—"

The widow turned around abruptly on a pair of black, scuffed old-lady shoes and almost lost her balance. Justin put a hand out to support her.

"*You*, I don't like," she said to the detective. She looked up appreciatively at Justin. "He gave me one of them holier-than-thou looks when I asked to see his identification. Anybody can procure a badge."

"That's Andy for you," Justin said with a big, wide grin.

Detective Andrew Miller rolled his eyes.

Viola caught the look and glared. "You don't think I know what's going on here?" she said to the detective. "Well, I do," she affirmed with a satisfying stare. "You don't like it when the *Federal* boys take over. Do you, Detective Miller? And a neighborhood brother to boot."

"Mrs. Johnson, please—"

"Now it's, *please*," she continued with derision. "Two minutes ago, he was trying to push me around in my own home. I looked out the window and saw a black man sitting in the car and said to myself, here's another one of us that the establishment is holdin' down. But you made it all the way to the top," she said proudly, as if Justin were family, which in a sense he was. "How long you live 'round here, Agent Barnes?"

"Long as I can remember, ma'am," he exaggerated. "Over where Parkwood joins William Floyd."

"Ain't that a kick. Neighborhood boy made good. Your mama must be *very* proud of you," the old lady jawed.

"Yes, ma'am. But I'm afraid we're not here to talk about me and Ma. I have some questions to ask you about your daughter, Virginia. Detective Miller is going to take notes. Think we might sit down?"

Viola Johnson looked over rather disconcertingly at the detective, as if he might soil her couch if she invited him to sit.

"Please," she said, more to Justin than Miller. "But before we get started, I wish to make something perfectly clear."

"Yes, ma'am," Justin said with alacrity.

"I-don't-like-cops."

There was not a split second of hesitation on Justin Barnes' behalf as he launched into laughter that filled the small but immaculately kept home. He landed softly in a comfortable chair the moment the old woman took a seat upon the sofa. Justin slapped his knees and could not stop laughing.

Detective Andrew Miller sat down quietly and kept his tongue.

Justin looked up and over at the woman, then slapped his knees again and shook his head.

"I'm sorry, but I just *don't!*" the old woman stated firmly. "Never did. Nohow," she concluded.

Justin was still shaking his head while trying to regain composure.

Miller was fuming.

"Listen," Justin said after quieting down. "I don't either. And that's the God's honest truth." He bit down hard upon his bottom lip to keep from bursting apart at the seams. "It's the reason I became a *special agent.*"

Andy Miller rolled his eyes a second time, but knew better than to open his mouth. He was outnumbered, outgunned, and on the home team's playing field. Besides, he could plainly see, though somewhat paradoxically, that Justin had complete control of the situation.

The woman beamed. "I like you, Agent Barnes."

"And I like you, ol' woman. So. You gonna help us out here by tellin' me some things we need to know about Virginia?" Justin was slipping back into the role of his former self. Toning down the degree of formality. Fine tuning his down-home dialect. "Like where your daughter might be fo' openers? Don't have to let that ol' bastard, Harold, know anything. All we want to know is that she's safe. Don't have any other business with her. Cops, nor the FBI. Look on over here, sister. C'mon, now. Right into these baby browns."

The old lady looked up solemnly.

"On my honor, ma'am."

"You're a smooth talker, Agent Barnes."

"Jus' a nigger in a ninety-nine dollar suit with a mission to keep yo' daughter safe and sound, ol' woman. God strike me dead 'f I don't."

Viola nodded and wiped away a tear. "She's staying with her girlfriend, Charlotte Smithe, with an e."

"White woman?"

"Dark of heart but as white as any woman could be without callin' her a spook," the wise old woman spoke through a savvy grin. "Young. Ambitious. Ruthless."

"Italian? Spanish?"

"Sicilian, if I had to guess."

"So, what you're sayin' is, she ain't no *contessa*—lest she be lookin' fo' a meal ticket—attached to a marriage of mockery."

Viola Johnson nodded her head in agreement. "The only design that woman has is to remain mistress to *número uno* who's married to the mob. Just as sure as God made little green apples. This vixen's rotten to the core, Agent Barnes. She's not in bed with him for a night on the town and a few bucks. I'd wager you she's an earner."

"Running somewhere above rank-and-file?"

"I'd bet you dollars to doughnuts," Viola asserted.

"Ma'am?"

"Viola, if you please."

"Viola, can you tell us where we'd find Charlotte and her prize?"

"Would if I could, but I can't. Just don't know. Everything was always a big secret with Virginia. I can tell you that Charlotte has a big farm somewhere in Connecticut. Not a working farm from what I gather. But a gentleman's farm. You know. Horses and stables. A white man's spread. That's where she and my daughter go to ride."

"Charlotte's fella have a name?"

"She called him Vincent. Vincent this and Vincent that. She was always trying to get him to go on a diet, I recall. Said that he was overweight. Virginia told me in confidence that he was just plain fat."

"So you never met him."

"Never did. Met her just once. Few months back."

Andrew and Justin exchanged glances.

"Where?"

"I dropped in unexpectedly on my daughter out in Orient. My son-in-law and grandson were traveling at the time."

"Tell me what she looks like," Justin pressed.

"That's easy. Mid-thirties. Made herself up to look ten years older. Ve*rrr*y pretty woman. A knockout if she had a mind to be. Long dark hair. Big brown eyes. Expressive. Tall. Thin frame. Stand 'er at 'bout five foot eight in flats. Got some figure beneath her blouse and those breeches."

"Breeches?"

"Riding breeches tucked into her boots. Small but full breasts. Nice tight butt, too. The kind all you men would like to mount," she said and smiled mischievously.

"Would that be saddle or bareback?" Justin asked unphased.

Viola Johnson let out a hoot. "Can you just picture Andy over there doing this Q and A? Look at 'im! Why, he's redder than a head on a pecker," she roared. "That'd be a woodpecker, Andy, 'case you're wondering," the woman howled.

"I'll just bet his bird's as hard as balsa wood, Viola."

"I think Andy's very, very shy," she teased.

Detective Andrew Miller stood, figuring that the interview was over anyway. He had a decent lead or two and believed that the woman was being truthful, that she had told Justin everything she knew about her daughter in connection with Charlotte and her crime boss boyfriend.

"Excuse me," Miller said somewhat irritably, heading for the front door. "I'll be waiting in the car," he stated without bothering to look back at either of them.

Viola and Justin watched him close the door behind himself and head toward the vehicle.

The old woman smiled slyly. "How'd I do?"

"You were sensational, Viola. I really mean that."

"You going to find my daughter for me?" The old woman brushed away a tear. "You know she's all I got."

"I'm going to try just as hard as I know how." It was obvious that she knew nothing about Freddie's kidnapping.

The woman nodded her gray head.

"I promise you, Viola."

"Can you tell me your real name, now?" she asked, looking up with sad, wet eyes.

Justin stepped forward and took the old woman in his arms.

"Barnes *is* my real name. Justin Barnes."

"Why couldn't you tell me that on the phone?"

"I didn't want you to slip in front of him before any introduction was made. And just for your information, I don't think Detective Miller wants either of us to know too much."

"Why didn't you just come over here by yourself?"

"Because they're watching me like a hawk."

"And you mean to tell me they're not monitoring the phones?"

Justin gently pushed her shoulders out to arm's length and reached inside his jacket pocket for his cellular. "Not this phone they're not." He held her there for a moment before he spoke again. "Viola?"

"Justin?"

"Do you trust me?"

Viola Johnson nodded a rapid yes.

"Want to tell me where she is?"

"Told you on the phone I would if I trusted you. Wouldn't if I didn't."

"Well?"

"Try and bring her back safely?"

"I will."

"Stables."

"Whose?"

"Charlotte's people."

"Run by this Vincent guy?"

"Yes."

"Stables where they keep horses?"

Viola shook her head and wiped her eyes on the sleeve of her housedress.

"Then, what?"

"Stables where they keep young girls."

Justin nodded. "Where?"

A horn blared just outside the woman's home.

"Where?" he repeated.

"Just a little north of Bridgeport. In a place called Redding Ridge. Locals call it the Okay Corral, because the police and politicians up there make everything okay." Viola took a deep breath. "Virginia started going there back in January. Charlotte helicopters her in and back once a week. This week, she didn't come back at all."

"Who told you all this?"

"My daughter. In the strictest of confidence."

Justin nodded.

The horn blasted again, then the two of them heard the engine start.

"Gotta go," Justin said, giving the woman a final hug.

"Did I do the right thing in telling you all this, Justin Barnes? Or should I have told the police?"

"I think you did the right thing telling me, ol' woman. But we really won't know that till I find 'er and bring 'er home to you. It won't be into headquarters for further questioning. All right?"

The woman shaped her lips in understanding and approval. "I don't care what she's done, Justin. She's still my baby girl."

"That's why folks like us gotta stick together," Justin offered. "For better or for worse."

"You tell her mamma's always here for her." The old woman forced a smile.

"I will."

"You better go now."

Chapter 59

"**I** w-want—want—to go h-home—now, F-father," a frightened Freddie Dupree stammered and wept. "Pl-please," he begged.

"You do-*ooo*?" the serial killer tormented.

"Y-y-yes," the boy stuttered.

"Ever hear of Thomas Wolfe?" Malcolm questioned and shivered excitedly in the dark.

Freddie sobbed instead of answering up.

"What, son? I can't hear you."

"Nooooo," he barely uttered.

"No, what?"

". . . No, Father."

"Well, if you did, you'd know that *you 'can't go home again.*'"

Freddie's mind was a pit of blackness that suddenly lit with both fear and hatred as the lights came on in the diorama. The boy immediately recognized his surroundings; for a little more than a week ago, he stood on the viewing side of the glass. Now, he found himself within it. Trapped. Strapped grotesquely to the base of a fairly good-sized gnarly tree—holding center stage. Its contorted branches and twisted twigs pointed helter-skelter.

"The tree is called Harry Lauder's Walking Stick, Freddie. Latin name: *Corylus avellana* 'Contorta.' Striking, I'm sure you would agree. A living sculpture."

A soft bed of dried yellow catkins covered the floor beneath the boy's bare feet.

The snakes were all around him.

None were stuffed as before.

One lay less than several feet away.

Freddie's heaves and shivers covered most of his interminable wailing. The boy pled for his mom between gasps.

"Pleeease," was the single ululating syllable accentuated at the end of each immeasurable wail. "Pleeease," followed by a breathy pause.

Malcolm Columba would positively gush with excitement whenever he heard his victims plead for their lives or, at the very least, beg for dear mercy—meaning nothing more or less than a speedy delivery from their pain and suffering. Yet, with his very own flesh and blood, he felt nothing but disappointment. Not that he had expected heroics from his young son. Good heavens, no. The boy was only ten. But Malcolm surely expected something more than what he saw and heard at present. So ordinary an appeal. Just like all the others.

"Can you tell the poisonous snakes from your garden-variety kind?" Malcolm asked quite seriously.

"I want my mo-mommy!" Freddie cried out.

"Even Becky Dawson put up a better front," he said through a sheer sigh of disappointment. "She had a hell of a lot more spunk than you. And the girl was only eight."

Freddie's whole body trembled.

"Remember when I asked you how you liked your stepmom, Freddie my boy? Well, do you?"

Freddie nodded as he blubbered.

"'She's all right,' is what you said. Remember saying that?"

No reply. Just a scrunched up face that could make you puke, his captor simpered.

"She was very good to you, Freddie. Only you were too ashamed of her because she's part black. Am I right? Do you know what an octoroon is, Freddie? Pay attention when I'm speaking to you, son," Malcolm said over the intercom. "Stop looking over there. Do you know what an octoroon is?" he repeated.

Freddie shuddered as he shook his head.

"It's a person who's one-eighth black. That's what your stepmom, Virginia, is. One-eighth black ancestry. Black blood coursing through her veins. She's the daughter of a quadroon. Are you paying attention to me, you little shit?"

Freddie lowered his eyes to the pencil-thin banded snake that wound its way along the grassy, yellow-green leafy floor, less than a foot in front of him. The boy nodded, confirming the gesture with a high-pitched, "Yesss!"

"Yes, what?"

"Yes, Father!"

"That's better. But I still don't like your tone. You sound a might miffed." Malcolm smiled. "Now, as I was saying. Your stepmom is the daughter of a quadroon. Oct is a prefix for eight. Quad is for four. So, a quadroon is a person who is one-quarter black. With me so far, son o' mine?"

Freddie nodded rapidly, although his mind was keenly on the viper sliding inches from his bare toes. One of the most lethal serpents in the world for its size, the boy positively knew.

"Very good. Because this is where you and I come in. Listening?"

"Yes, Father . . . yesss," Freddie hissed.

"Your *real* mother was a mulatto. Know what a mulatto is?"

Freddie was staring down at the venomous black, red, and yellow-ringed coral snake.

"I'm talking to you! You say you're so interested in biology and all, I'd think that you'd be interested in your own biological mother."

Freddie was not concerned about his stepmother, his biological mother, or even the deadly coral snake alongside his foot at that moment. The boy assessed his immediate danger as coming from the arboreal creature entwining itself around one of the scores of spiral snake-like limbs that encompassed him—a single serpent suspended half a foot above his head. The venomous eyelash viper hung there like a question mark. A fraction of an inch from his face.

"Do you know what a mulatto is?" his father repeated impatiently.

"No," Freddie whispered without moving a muscle.

The coral-colored body, with its triangular-shaped head, drew back, then darted forward a centimeter from the ten-year-old's right cheek.

Malcolm was amazed that Freddie did not scream, although the boy did jerk his head sharply to the left and held it there.

"A mulatto is a person with one white parent and one black parent."

Freddie could not care if both of them were blue.

"My mother was white, son o' mine. My father, too. But my wife—your biological mother—may her soul rest in everlasting peace, was mulatto. Know what that makes you? It makes *you* a quadroon.

One-quarter black. Twice the amount of black blood in your body than your stepmom, who you're so ashamed of. Now, don't you feel bad?"

The tree viper was nearing Freddie's neck.

"Okay. Let's try it another way," the madman offered patiently.

Freddie shivered. "I'm scared."

"What's larger?" he insisted, ignoring his son's fear. "A quarter or a half?"

No answer.

"Better tell me," Malcolm warned. "Unless you want more venom than black blood flowing through those youthful veins. What's the greater fraction? Quarter or a half?"

"Half," Freddie barely breathed as the two-foot long snake slithered down and coiled itself tenuously around a thin lower branch, level with the boy's right arm.

"Good for you! Now. Tell me. What's the smallest fraction? One-half? One-eighth? Or a quarter? Concentrate," Columba insisted.

"Eighth." The boy wept.

"Excellent. Excellent."

"Plea*se, Father.*"

The banded snake by Freddie's foot slipped across a naked ankle. The thicker and more elegant viper slithered close to the youngster's shoulder, then traveled out of view. Behind the eight-foot tree, a four-foot cottonmouth slid along the edge of a dry brook.

Freddie could not have moved his body if his life depended on it. The lad lowered his eyes fearfully as he urinated in his last clean pair of underwear.

What was clearly the result of sheer terror on the young boy's behalf was construed as newfound guilt in the mind of the serial killer.

Both father and son were terribly tired. Freddie was now completely drained. Neither of them saw the timber rattler closing in steadily from behind a moss-covered rock.

"Don't you want to know all about your real mother, Freddie? Aren't you the least bit curious about her life? She was a warm and wonderful young woman, my boy. Very beautiful, too. But neither my mother nor my father ever accepted her as my wife. So, your mother and I went off together. All across Europe—finally settling in the United States. We were never really welcome as a couple in our land. Wherever we traveled, people had their snake eyes open *wide*. Then, without warning, they would strike.

"To make a long story short, we disappeared into the back country and leased a home with lots and lots of land. Acres upon acres. One day, we found and combed the woods for wild blackberries. The two of us loved the fresh, natural fruit—just as we loved the lakes and streams and rivers we fished. The air and soil and waters were clean, Freddie. Every square inch of it. And the trees . . . the trees were magnificent. In short order, we cleared a space and cultivated a garden. Vegetables and fruits and flowers abounded—plants, and bushes and stalks and vines—perennials and annuals that would rival an English garden. The following year we had our *own* blackberries, along with huckleberries, raspberries, and strawberries. Rhubarb took a second season. You name it; we picked and ate them all. Amber would make delicious pies and jams. What we didn't eat then, we canned. Amber was your mother's namesake, Freddie. Same given name as her mom. Only, you weren't Freddie then. You weren't even born. Just a gleam in your father's eye. When you did arrive, we named you Tabor."

With little warning, the sidewinder suddenly sounded and struck the back of Freddie's left leg, just below the knee.

The author tried to continue the story. But who could catch a word above the welter of hysterics? Malcolm positively could not hear his own voice above the terrible uproar. Hence, there was no point in resuming the account of Amber's and Tabor's roots. A shame. However, it was not as though the world would fail to come to know and understand the truth, because Malcolm had recorded everything right up to the very moment. It was all set down in a journal started a little more than a decade ago.

A history rich in detail.

Beginning with the killings.

Continuing with a thorough examination of ancestry—diffused throughout the middle of the manuscript . . .

. . . Then recommencing with the poison spreading through his son's body as the author penned away feverishly, realizing his own mortality and urgency to begin the conclusion at once:

Tabor's true father was the boy's talisman, the serial killer wrote. *But the dormant resurrection of evil raised its ugly head and struck.*

Chapter 60

Working from Detective Miller's information regarding the interview with Viola Johnson, homicide detectives from three teams, in conjunction with other state and local jurisdictions, scoured the East End of Long Island, in addition to the Bridgeport area, for further leads that might steer them to the elderly woman's missing daughter—and, hopefully, Freddie Dupree. Although Gary York's initial curiosity and concern had been for Virginia's safety and whereabouts, having sent Miller and Barnes out to Shirley to speak with the widow, the authorities now believed that Viola's daughter held the key to several important but unanswered questions. The great irony being, of course, in that Justin was now privy to sensitive information that literally put him miles ahead of the police. Information that would place him in imminent danger if he were not careful.

Justin considered that it might have been pure Providence that prompted Detective Miller to cut him loose immediately following their interview with Viola, for now he was free to investigate the matter on his own. A free *agent*, so to speak. The maverick could not help but laugh aloud. He could not help but think that he might have made a damn good detective if circumstances in his life had been different . . . maybe to have one day made the grade of *ho·mi·cide*. The cream of the crop and a far cry from your everyday run-of-the-mill cop, Justin had to admit. It felt both strange and positively exciting to be working the case, in spite of the fact that Miller—supposedly speaking for Theo—officially let him go. Therefore, the maverick was not beholding to any of them any longer. He would simply work the lead alone.

"The capital of Mississippi is . . . *Jesse* . . . Jackson!" Justin exclaimed, proudly recalling the time he shook the civil rights leader's hand, right before the man delivered an important speech in that capital city. Justin was just a kid, but what an impression the man made on him. The way the reverend had with words.

"Can you imagine me a *po·lice·man* or a politician, Monisha?

Boys in the hood would flip their lids." Justin flipped through the pages of the travel atlas. "We headin' north on Route 58 to a place called Redding Ridge, girl. Got me a couple of handguns hidden in the trunk that could take down a polar bear nasty as any white-ass motherfucker. But I'm gonna tell yo' somethin', Monisha. I got this queer feelin' I'm gonna need more than bullets where I'm goin'. Gonna need a lot o' luck. Gonna need a guardian angel on my shoulder. So, that's where you sit in," he punned, putting on a pearly grin for himself in the rearview mirror. "Need you right here," he declared, driving a thumb firmly atop his shoulder. "We gonna try and pull a woman out o' there by the name of Virginia Dupree. Haven't quite figured out how to do dat yet, but we sure as hell gonna try. Hell, I don't even know where this place be at, 'cept it's called the Okay Corral. Local knowledge of the area is what we need to know. Gotta first get the lay o' da land."

Justin glanced up and down between the map and the road, keeping his distance from the car ahead of him.

"Accordin' to this map, we ain't got far to go. So, hear this, girl. Remember what I said to you outside the ol' lady's house in Shirley? 'Bout *you* talkin' to *me* an' all? Well, I got this funny feelin' I ain't gonna be able to pull this off by my lonesome. Understand what I'm sayin' here? So, if I'm in some kinda trouble up there, and you really *are* sittin' on my shoulder, well, you sure as shit better say somethin', 'cause nuts or not, I ain't ready to meet my Maker jus' yet. I probably first gotta fuck with some mob boss, his bitch, and maybe even his crew in order to get to Virginia, then maybe the serial killer who hung yo' pretty ass from that bridge up in Michigan, Monisha. And I ain't even had my Wheaties yet, let alone a cup o' coffee. So, you better be by my side, on my shoulder, or wherever the hell it is you angels hang or hover. See, I know somethin' else I didn't know before 'bout your murder. I know you was still alive when Malcolm Columba lowered you from that center span over the Straits of Mackinac that night. Certain *in·fo·ma·tion* the *po·lice* almost always hold back from the press. But I read the full report. Saw yo' white-gloved hand and naked body from every conceivable angle, angel. Gonna take that fucker down fo' you and me, Monisha." Justin wiped a teary eye. "Fo' all them other folks who lost their loved ones, too. Whatever color they be. Tall order, Monisha. Need yo' help, baby."

Justin wiped his other eye.

"Christ. So, here I be talkin' to a ghost again and expectin' answers and action. All right. Listen up, spook. If yo' real and really wif me, 'at's real cool. But if yo' jus' one o' dem figments of my imagination, well, then butt on out. I'll handle this show alone. Hear? Jus' don't *ma·terial·ize* all of a sudden like a real ghost and scare the shit out o' me as I'm sneakin' 'round some stable, 'cause I'll probably slip in horseshit and break my motherfuckin' neck."

Justin rounded a bend when he saw a figure up ahead.

"Well, lookie, lookie, lookie. What *have* we here, Monisha? Fine lookin' momma pushin' a shoppin' cart filled with fruits and vegetables and bags of groceries. Let's see what the townsfolk know 'bout this Redding Ridge and the Okay Corral."

Justin sent down the passenger side window.

"Hey, Momma. Where you goin' wif 'at supermarket cart any ol' how? Huh? 'Cause dat be a prime example o' shopliftin' as I ever done see. Fruits and vegetables look to me like they fresh off some tractor-trailer."

The young black woman smiled without turning her head. She kept right on walking as Justin kept pace alongside her.

"Say, baby. I caught ya red-handed wif da goods, but dat don't mean we can't strike a deal. Like say maybe you open up dat big ol' bag o' tater chips you got sittin' on top dat grocery bag. Maybe find us a soda pop, too, to share."

The woman said nothing, pushing the cart dead ahead.

"Man, I ain't never saw so much *pro·duce* in one basket in all my born days. Now, da checkout man I jus' knows don't pack up all dem fruits and vegetables wif'out a grocery bag; now do he? He jus' don't dump 'em in da cart like dat and say, 'Now, 'ave a nice day there, missy.' And it's way too early in da growin' season to 'ave picked 'em from the fields I seen back there. So. Yo' know what I think? I think you wheeled dat cart 'round da back o' dat big- ass store after you grabbed and paid fo' some chips and soda pop. Maybe a six-pack fo' the ol' man sittin' home in front o' da TV, while his lady's out doin' what she do bes'. Huntin' and gatherin', honey. Yep. I think you found yo'self an admirer back o' the sto' who handed yo' a shitload o' dem fruits and vegetables in exchange fo' one of yo' movie star smiles," Justin jawed.

The woman stopped in her tracks and made a sour puss.

"Oooo. You ugly, girl, when yo' make a face like dat. I wouldn't even give ya a *rotten* banana fo' such a mean-ass look."

The thin woman tried to cover up her laugh with the back of her hand. Without a word, she reached into the cart and withdrew the large bag of potato chips.

Justin winked. "Wise move, woman."

"Who says they're for you?" the Connecticut shrew groused, grabbing both sides of the bag below the seam and tearing open the seal. She took a single chip and slipped it snappily into her fresh mouth, studying him intently before making an offering.

Justin put the car in Park, scooted across the seat, and helped himself to a handful.

Reaching into one of the other grocery bags, she came up with a can of Coke.

"Coke is cool," Justin tested.

The young woman stooped before the window. "This one's still warm," she sallied, popping open its top as a rush of gas escaped and brown foam fizzed, cascading down the side of the can and car like a mini, muddy waterfall.

"Hey! Don't get that shit in here," Justin scolded.

"My, my, my. A neat-freak nigger with New York plates."

"Not nice," he grumbled, grabbing a couple of paper napkins from the glove compartment before wiping clean the leather and chrome strip at the base of the window.

She threw her dark head back and drank thirstily, draining half the cola. Drying the sides of the can with the hem of her gingham blouse, she handed over the rest of the beverage. "Here."

Justin hesitated.

For good measure, she brought a knee up and passed the bottom of the can along the edge of her cut-off jeans. "There. That ought to do it, Mr. Fusspot."

He took the drink and washed down several chips, handing her back the empty. "Thanks for breakfast. What's your name? Now that you know mine," he said with a friendly smile.

"Ms. Slopbucket," she answered with a straight face.

"Well, Ms. Slopbucket. Now that we've been *in*formally introduced, would you like me to put your groceries and goods in the trunk and take you to where you're goin'? Which I'm sure is home sweet home."

The lanky woman shook her head. "You're headed thataway. I'm turning off up there," she told him with a simple gesture of her narrow chin as she moved the cart ahead.

"Can't be too far out o' my way," he said decidedly, listening to the noisy, rusty, wobbly shopping cart roll along next to his own set of wheels. Ms. Slopbucket and Mr. Fusspot continued forward at a snail's pace.

"No, thank you."

"Any particular reason why?"

"Several."

"Name them."

Ms. Slopbucket stopped abruptly, canted her head back at an odd angle, then folded her arms across her chest for the challenge. "Sure. I don't get into cars with strangers. I don't ride around in no pimpmobile. And—" she reached down deep into the bag, then came up with a can of Budweiser "—this one is *not* for you. It's fo' my ol' man sittin' home in front o' da TV," she mocked. "Got 'im two six-packs, in fact."

Justin shrugged. "I see. But before we continue on our separate paths, I'd like to ask you for directions."

"Sure."

"Redding Ridge?"

"Straight ahead. Can't miss it."

"Ever hear of the Okay Corral?"

The woman bristled before turning briskly away, wrapping two fists firmly around the handle of the cart and pushing it ahead without saying a single word.

"Hey! Did I say somethin' wrong?"

"I figured that's where you were headed the second I saw this pimpmobile."

"Listen. You've got it all wrong."

"No, you've got it all wrong. You got it wrong when you came across the river. Go back to where you came from, buster."

"I guess you wouldn't believe me if I told you I was a New York homicide detective working an important serial-killer case, would ya?"

"No."

"Cool, because now I know you ain't gonna blow my cover."

Ms. Slopbucket could not help but laugh again. "Why don't you just blow away."

"And leave you out here all alone with a serial killer on the loose?"

"You're a sick puppy, Mr. Fusspot."

"A lovesick puppy, Ms. Slopbucket. 'Cause the fucker killed my Monisha up there in Michigan." Another tear or two was about to form in Justin's eyes.

It was the timbre of Justin's voice that made the woman stop and stare. "*Oh*, you're good, you are. You one of them off-Broadway actors?"

"No, it's the God's honest truth," he swore. "You know the rash of killings that's been going on?"

"The what?"

"Spree of murders."

"Man, you talkin' like a white boy, now."

"You haven't heard 'bout the bunch of murders on Long Island, and up and down the coast?"

"Nope."

"You live in a fuckin' cave or somethin?"

"Or somethin'," she agreed.

"Seriously. You don't read the papers or watch TV?"

"Never learned to read. 'Cept for labels like Coke and Wise and Budweiser," she explained with a smile. "But if I *had* a TV or a radio, I might just look and listen," she went on.

Justin stopped to look and listen before he opened his mouth again. "You tryin' to hustle me, woman?"

"You eat *my* chips and drink *my* Coke, and then ask me if *I'm* tryin' to hustle *you*?"

Justin sighed and shook his head. "You're the one who's good, girl. You ain't no ravin' beauty like my Monisha. But you got yo'self some fine-ass figure, woman. Bet you get just about anything you want. Fruits and vegetables included."

"And with that pimpmobile of yours, I bet you get all the action you can handle in *New York City*. So, why you got to come over here and pay for it at the Corral?"

"Number one, this ain't no pimpmobile. If you was ever uptown, girl, you'd know what a pimpmobile looks like. This is a bought-and-paid-for late model *Cad·il·lac*. I buy one every three years. That's how I spend my money. Not on whores. Number two. You ain't got no ol' man sittin' home, 'less he be yo' granddaddy—which I kinda doubt. Although I am curious who the beer's for. Number three. I'm goin' up to this Okay Corral in Redding Ridge to find and bring back a woman who got herself into a heap o' trouble. Then I'm goin' off to find this serial killer, who I know you believe I'm lying 'bout, but I'm not. But before I get started up in Redding, I'm goin' to need a place to crash. Maybe stash this car. Pick me up another. 'Cause I don't need to advertise I'm coming jus' yet. I can pay you cash." Justin flashed and unfolded a wad of bills. "Fifty a night and no funny business. Two nights in advance—even if I stay fo' one." He peeled off a hundred dollar bill. "Another fifty to keep yo' mouth shut." The maverick pulled that denomination from the bottom of the roll. "Keep you in groceries for a while. Whattaya say?"

He handed her the money.

She stared wide-eyed at the bills. "No funny business?"

"No funny business."

"The beer's for Spanky," she said matter-of-factly.

"Who's Spanky?"

"My dog."

"Is beer good for a dog?"

"Lived this long."

"And how long's that?"

"Pushin' twenty-one."

"You're kidding."

"Huckleberry lived to eighteen plus."

"Whattaya feed 'im?"

"Dry dog food. Chicken once a month. Table scraps every now and then."

"You a good cook?"

"Spanky never complains."

Justin laughed and withdrew another fifty. "What's for dinner tonight?"

The woman laughed, too, and took the money. "Chicken."

"What will Spanky get?"

"A little less bird."

"A little more beer?"

She shrugged sadly. "I can't afford his arthritis medicine like I used to. That's why I give him a little beer."

"Damn, you *are* good," he swore, peeling off another fifty.

The woman smiled and shook her head. "He prefers the Bud," she explained.

"Come on. I'll drive you home."

Justin opened the trunk lock from inside and started to get out of the car to help her with the groceries, but the woman told him no and shut the shiny lid.

"First left between the fields after you round the bend. But give me at least an hour to tidy up some. I wasn't expecting company. You're a stone's throw from Redding, the way you're headed. Not much there. If you don't want folks to know your business, I wouldn't ask about the Okay Corral. They probably wouldn't tell you anyhow. Head on past the ridge into Arleneel and grab yourself a cup of coffee to kill some time. I'll tell you what you need to know when you come back. First left between those fields," she repeated. "Can't miss it. Only shack off the beaten track."

"Arleneel," he said, wondering about the two hundred bucks and if he would ever see her again.

"If you want, you can bring back a newspaper."

"Why? I thought you couldn't read."

"Can't. But it's never too late to learn," she said with a sincere smile.

"You want tutoring lessons, too?" he asked with some surprise.

She nodded her head excitedly.

"It cost *me* for food and lodging and *you* want readin' lessons? How 'bout a quick lesson in addition and subtraction?"

"Not in arithmetic. In reading. I can pay you," she decided with a grin, holding up one of his bills.

"I get twenty-five bucks an hour. Two hour minimum."

"Agreed."

"In advance."

She shook her head. "This is my security that you'll come back."

"I'll be back. You just make damn sure that *you're* where you say you're gonna be."

"I will," she promised.

"What's your name, girl?"

"Later." And with that announcement, she pushed, then forcefully shoved the rusty, silvery cart forward until the stuck left rear wheel broke free and shimmied forward like the others.

Justin drove off and watched her in the rearview mirror until she disappeared from sight.

Chapter 61

"We've been to farms and ranches below Bridgeport, all the way up to Waterbury and beyond," Detective Dean Nelson reported to his commanding officer via cell phone. "We've been on a wild-goose chase since early this morning. Boys in Stratford tell us there's a large spread just outside of West Hartford. Tremendous operation. Brian and I are headed up that way. The family checks out fine, but we're told they might be able to point us in the right direction. The foreman says he'll talk to us when we arrive, but not over the phone."

"Interesting," Theo replied.

"I'm sure you know that Vincent Ciccio has no holdings, whatsoever, in Connecticut. He has no real interest in horses or horseracing, either, from what I understand. He goes to the track maybe once a year like he goes to Atlantic City and Vegas. Takes in the shows and all the fancy restaurants. Up here, he bets a yard on a long shot at the tracks in Westchester and Bellmore, whenever he does play. Never wins. Never bets a second race. But friends of his have acres of property and horses in Jersey. However, he never goes near those places. Personally, I think this Virginia Dupree woman was handing her mother a lot of crap."

"Speak to Mick?" Theo asked, as though he had not been listening, whatsoever, to his detective.

"Yeah. Gary's with him now. They're both back on the other side of the Sound, working another angle."

"What about Miller?"

"Haven't heard from him since he phoned us with all this happy horseshit."

"Stay with it, Dean," Theo said evenly.

"If you ask me, I think this Miller's full of crap, too. Sure as hell's full of himself."

"I'll tell you something, Dean."

"Yeah?"

"This kid's uncanny. As I said before, I'm not saying he hits the bull's-eye every time. But he's pretty much on target. You know that mixed-race business he was theorizing about?"

"Yeah, the fellas all had a field day with that one," Dean reminded Theo. "He thought the next victim was gonna be part black. Columba's next victim was Diane Nash. Recall? No black blood in that family. I don't care if you went as far back as Thomas Jefferson," he joked. "So what that he picked up on Donald Bellport's features after the Rodman killing. Miller even believed the *killer* could be partly black when you asked him what he thought. Well, we now know that Malcolm Columba is as white as a picket fence. Miller shoots from the hip, Theo. Smart kid. But he's too quick to shoot off his mouth."

"You finished shooting off yours?"

"Yeah, I'm finished," Dean concluded in an exasperated breath.

"Kim's been doing some digging."

"And?"

"And she's come up with something that's a tad more than coincidental."

"I'm listening, Theo."

"Columba's other half was half black."

There was a pause. "I thought he didn't have a wife."

"Common-law. Going back a decade. About the time he started killing, as far as we can determine."

"You said '*was*'. She dead?"

"Missing."

"Sick bastard probably did her, too. Whattaya got on her?"

"Not much. Their time together is sketchy, at best. Moved around a lot. Kim's delving into the history, surrounded by mystery. Coming up with muddy water. We're trying to sort things out. But now we have some interesting developments."

"Yeah." Nelson's mind was churning. "Like who's who in this mix of total madness. So, the kid's part black. Freddie Dupree."

"One-quarter."

"Which means his real mother is or was mulatto?"

"Right."

"And Freddie's stepmother, Virginia? Who's really not related

385

at all. Not even by marriage."

"One-eighth black."

Nelson's mind was reeling. "Then Virginia's mother, this Viola Johnson, is half—no, I guess a quarter black . . . just like Freddie Dupree.

"You got it."

"Freddie's biological mother got a name?"

"First name, Amber. Like in amber fields of grain. Like the color of the latex tubing Columba ran down Fern Rodman's throat."

"Jesus. Amber what?"

"That's all we know right now."

"Nobody wants to talk?"

"I don't think too many people know their story, Dean. No records. No nothing."

"But somebody's gotta know something."

Theo did not say anything.

"Theo."

"Yeah."

"Listen, I'm not too good with fractions, but if you want to find the common denominator in all of this, I'd send a black and white— like in police car—back out to Viola Johnson's house and have someone read her the riot act."

The lieutenant smiled ambivalently. "Don't you think I already did that, Dean?"

"And?"

"And she's gone."

"How do you mean, gone?"

"Like the wind. Didn't pack. Left no note. Food left out on the counter. Full cup of tea sitting in the center of it. No sign of a struggle. No sign of anything. Just gone."

"Christ."

"Find the daughter, and my guess is we'll probably find the mother. It's important that we find them both—and fast," Theo added solemnly. "Something tells me this whole business is somehow all connected. Virginia Dupree. Her mother, Viola Johnson. Freddie and Malcolm Columba. This Charlotte woman."

Dean gave a grunt.

"Do you still think you're being sent on a wild-goose chase,

Detective?"

"No, Theo."

"Good man. Have Miller call me the second you hear from him."

"Yes, sir."

Chapter 62

"**Y**ES!" the computer maven cried out with excitement and satisfaction, hanging up the phone before tapping away madly upon her keyboard.

"What's up?" Theo asked in passing, backpedaling to a stop.

"Not so much *what* as *who*," Detective Kim Booker voiced and smiled radiantly.

"Then *who,* rather than *what,* gives?" the lieutenant questioned impatiently, standing fast in his tracks.

"I just finished connecting and confirming two intriguing dots," the woman declared, bracing herself in her chair, hands wrapped tightly around its arms as if she were about to either land or take off.

Detective Lieutenant Theodore Groche stepped over to Kim and her massive mainframe: Big Sister. It served as the department's brain trust, entrusted to the woman who knew how to push its buttons and come away with jackpots like a percentage player at a casino—but with better odds. There were a million leads connected to a billion unsolved crimes, if one only knew how and where to retrieve them. Kim was among the very best in her field—a single solitary soul sitting off in her remote corner of the world in Yaphank, tapping into a warehouse of classified information. Information compiled and stored by scores of similar brainy individuals doing their own specialized share of daily brainwork, such as designing unique software systems and writing unparalleled programs. Others, like Brian and Dean and Mick and Gary, were out in the field gathering all the glory and the gold, while obscure wizards like Kim were in-house having downloads of *fun*, oftentimes infused with freight loads of frustration.

"You going to keep this to yourself?"

"This is *big*, Theo."

"Bigger than your bulging eyes that look like they're about to pop?"

"Bigger than those twin, two-pound lobsters the team's taking me out for after this is over."

"Now it's lobsters instead of steak?"

"With giant claws and tails and melted butter on the side."

"I'll even crack them open for you if we crack this case."

"Which case?" she asked.

Theo looked askance. "What do you mean, which case? The only case you should be working on right now. The Malcolm Columba Serial-Killer Case. That's which one."

"I got news for you. Like an amoeba, this case is dividing before my eyes."

"I'm not sure I like the sound of what I'm hearing."

Theo was standing over Kim's shoulder. Stooping. Staring eye-level with the screen.

"Believe me. You won't. Not when you have to pick up and pay the check."

"Who's Russell Leone, my little genie."

"Rub my shoulders, and I'll show you more."

"Sounds promising."

Theo began to massage a tangle of tight unyielding muscles in the maven's neck and shoulders.

Kim hit a single key. "Albany bureaucrat. Assistant to the governor. His daddy was a director before he retired."

Theo nodded. "I thought the name sounded familiar."

"Leone is the one Brian and Dean locked horns with over the Adirondack evidence. Remember? Those skis and poles."

"Oh, do I remember, all right. The guy ran interference for Austin Izzo's crew up there. One of Ciccio's men."

"Ouch! Not so hard."

"Relax. Your neck and shoulders feel like bands of steel."

"What do you expect? I've been at this day and night for months."

"So, what skeletons are lurking in Mr. Leone's closet?"

"I think the last one got dissolved in Lake Champlain."

"Donald Bellport?"

"Daddy's oldest boy. Only the guy's in denial."

"Donald Bellport is, or rather was, Russ Leone's son?"

Detective Booker nodded solemnly. "And that's not all."

"I'm all ears."

Kim suddenly clammed up.

"Well, are you going to tell me, or do I have to guess?"

"Well, are you going to keep massaging, or do I find another masseur?"

"You want fine dining and massages, too?"

"Lower, please."

"Just don't ask me to do your feet. Not here, anyway."

"When I show you what I got, you might want to bow down and kiss them." Kim hit a dozen keys before the screen flashed from boxes within boxes to a page of prose. "Read," she ordered with a grin about as wide as a set of handlebars.

Theo read through the text, pausing for a millisecond as a name grabbed his full attention.

Macon Emanon.

"Macon Emanon," Theo read aloud.

"No birth certificate. No Social Security number. No kept records of the any kind. Yet, she's all mine. Finders keepers," Kim said with certain satisfaction. "Found abandoned at birth in the middle of Georgia. Literally. Macon, Georgia. Center of the state. Raised by several families, hand-to-mouth, who could barely feed their own. Macon was passed back-and-forth among shanty homes, depending on who had what going on in their lives at the moment. The truth is, newborns like that usually don't make it through the first year. What Macon had going for her was a strong constitution and beautiful features. People in the area named her Black Beauty—though she was light-skinned. When she was twelve, she headed north on her own. Guess where she eventually wound up?"

Theo read the subtext. "Adirondack Park. Somewhere above Long Lake."

"Yep. She was legendary throughout the region for her skill with a fly rod."

Theo was smiling, nodding and kneading the detective's neck, shoulders, and aching back muscles as he listened and read.

"Seems she took up with this white dude. She was about sixteen then. Russ Leone was twenty-nine. Macon became pregnant. He became very, very miffed. Tried to persuade her to have an abortion. Threatened all kinds of horrible things if she didn't. Well, she didn't. Leone's old man stepped into the picture, paid her off and told her not to come back. She went off to have the baby, then returned two years later with little Donald in one arm; a fly fishing rod in the other. This part you're going to love. She adopted the name Bellport, taken from the cul-de-sac the Leone family lived on. Bellport Terrace."

Theo guffawed.

"It gets better."

"The old man sold the house six months later at a considerable loss. Six months after that, he had Bellport Terrace renamed Knoll Court."

"Maybe he should have gone that route earlier, before he sold the house," he said decidedly through a snicker.

"A retired real estate person I just spoke with, who wishes to remain anonymous, said the whole business haunted the Leone family from the day Macon returned with little Donald in her arms. Moving really hadn't solved anything for the Leone's. Rumors still flew about like pesky flies. People still talked behind their backs. Changing the name of the street only reconfirmed what the gossipmongers had on the tip of their wagging tongues anyway. Even after Macon died, the stories didn't go away. Neither did Donald. He was watched. Tested. Never caused any trouble by bringing up the past. Until his arrest and release, that is. And I have good information that Donald Bellport tried to contact his alleged biological father shortly before the handyman was murdered."

"You for real?"

"A little over to the right, please. Ah, that's good."

"What's this business all about, Kim?"

Kim rolled her head in a circle. "We're getting there, Theo. Slowly. A few clicks at a time. Anyway, Bellport sent him a package, which was returned—purportedly unopened. That's where it ends for now."

"Dean and Brian would just love to show up quietly in Leone's office with subpoena in hand—just in case he decides to go the reticent route."

"I think you'd better check that out, *thoroughly*, with our law department."

"How so?"

"Iffy."

"Why iffy?"

"Well, what are we going to say to Mr. Leone? Chastise him for refusing to accept a package that was sent back to Bellport, supposedly still sealed?"

"Something like that."

Kim shook her head. "I don't think so. Why alert him to anything just yet?"

"Was the package delivered and returned by regular mail?"

"Yes, indeedy."

"Any idea of its contents?"

"None."

"And of course you checked with the illustrious post office up there."

"Signed for and apparently sent back the day after it arrived."

"Not that it means anything, Kim. But I used to send books back to the Book of the Month Club after I opened them. You weren't supposed to, of course. And the fellow picking up the return would always examine the seal to make sure it wasn't broken," Theo explained mischievously. "He'd turn the package upside down and all around. This went on month after month."

"How did you manage it?"

"Steam iron to loosen the glue; mucilage to seal the box back up again."

Kim laughed. "Read any of them?"

"That was the whole idea. In those days, I had no money to buy a single title. Nearest library was thirty miles away. I'd start with those stupid stamps they have you cut out and stick on a return card. Ten books for a buck, or something like that."

Kim nodded. "And you were obligated to take four a year, I think."

"Didn't matter. I never sent in the notice telling them to cancel next month's selection, so like clockwork, the book of the month would arrive. I'd scrub my hands super clean and place it carefully on the kitchen table so that the spine wouldn't even crack, read the book from cover to cover, then send it back."

Kim leaned back in her chair and smiled up into Theo's intense and thinly-framed inverted countenance. "I know there has to be a point in you telling me all this."

"Of course, there is. To let you know that I know that Leone opened up that package before he sent it back."

"Well, maybe he did, Theo. Proving it, however, is another story. Knowing its contents is something we'll never know if we flat out ask him."

The lieutenant nodded his disappointment. "I just wish we knew if this business is relevant to the case or not."

"What's important is that we know for *certain* that contact was attempted by Bellport, shortly before his death. So, I'd leave that one on the back burner for now, or we might get burnt."

Theo considered the dilemma. "Tough call."

"Tell you what. Let me work on this some more."

"All right. By the way. The name Macon, I understand. But how did she first come up with Emanon?"

Kim smiled and lightly hit six keys, putting Donald Bellport's mother's pseudonym back up on the screen:

Emanon

Next, she typed the last name backwards.

Noname

Then, once again, with a revealing space.

No name

"She assigned herself that anonym after using B.B. for many years—so far as I can tell. A guess as good as any as to when and where she dropped it altogether was probably just before she returned to the Adirondack Mountains with her son as sort of a reminder that she would no longer be a nonentity. So, she went from a virtual nobody, or a *no name*, to Macon Bellport. Couldn't very well go through life being called Black Beauty," Kim said with a smile. "Although she was precisely that."

Kim hit a few more keys, and a picture of the very attractive woman began to fill the screen from the top of the monitor down.

"Wow! Reminds me of that old but familiar saying."

"Which is?"

"Once you go black—"

"Never mind, Theo. *My* saying is that you men are all alike. Except maybe for Brian. Then again, I'll probably never really know," she concluded rather ruefully.

Chapter 63

The desk sergeant at police headquarters in Yaphank switched the call upstairs to Detective Amastate's extension.

"Detective Ives," the man answered wearily.

"If I vanted a Detective Ives, I vould have asked for a Detective Ives. I asked for Detective Amastacht."

"Amastate," the cop corrected, knowing immediately who was on the other end of the line. "He's my partner. Is there anything that I can help you with?"

"Bevare of partners. I had a partner for tventy years."

"What happened?" Ives humored the man.

"Vhat happened? I'll tell you vhat happened. He dropped dead owing me tventy thousand dollars. That's vhat happened. Von thousand dollars for every year the bastard vas in business. His vife? She vouldn't turn over von nickel. Vhere's Amastacht?"

"Out of the office. Tell me what's on your mind, Mr. Rodman. I'll pass it along just as soon as he comes in."

"Ah, you remember me. That's very good, Detective."

"Yes, it's been awhile. How are your brother and sister-in-law doing?"

"You might just as vell have ripped their hearts out. Audrey's still taking it very hard. But at least she's getting help. Adam? Vell, he's not doing too vell at all. The reason I'm calling is because Audrey and me, ve had this little chat. She remembers something she feels could be important."

"I'm listening, Mr. Rodman."

"If I tell you, you going to remember to tell Amastacht? Or you going to forget to tell your partner?"

"I can *assure* you that I'm going to tell my partner," Ives emphasized as well as empathized.

"Vell, all right then. It may be nothing, but Audrey said that a friend of Fern's up in Long Lake told her of this voman, Lolita something—Audrey can't remember vhat her last name vas—who vas asking lots of qvestions about this Donald Bellport. The von they arrested for my niece's murder, and then let go."

Detective Ives immediately straightened up in his chair. "Go on."

"That's it. Like I said, it may be nothing. But Audrey thought you might vant to know."

"When did this Lolita woman come around asking these questions?"

"Shortly before Fern was murdered."

"Did she say what the woman looked like?"

"A fairly attractive voman. Driving an old, beat-up blue van. That's all she said. Oh, and that she vas looking for a good carpenter."

"Why did you wait till now to tell us this, Mr. Rodman?"

"Vhy? Because it just popped into my sister-in-law's head. That's vhy. Is there a law for vhen it should and shouldn't pop?"

"Do you happen to have Fern's friend's phone number handy?"

"Audrey doesn't know who she is exactly. Just that she vas her daughter's friend. She called Audrey shortly after the funeral to offer her condolences. Vanted to know if she could do anything."

"Where can my partner and I reach you if we need to, Mr. Rodman?"

"I'm returning to Oregon end of next veek sometime. Until then, I'm staying here vith my brother and his vife, like a good brother should."

"We appreciate the call, sir. And if anything else pops into anyone else's head concerning this Lolita, please call us right away."

"Right avay. But be sure and tell your partner."

"I will."

"And von more thing."

"Yes?"

"Remember vhat I told you about partners."

"How could I forget?"

"I'm surprised that you remember me," Hal Rodman repeated. "I vouldn't tell them who I vas vhen I called."

"You're unforgettable, Mr. Rodman. Let's just leave it at that," Detective Ives responded ambivalently, smiling into the mouthpiece.

The two men hung up.

What the detective would remember most about Hallah

Rodman was how rudely he and his partner had been ushered toward the front door of the younger brother's home. That aside, he liked the little man and felt quite sorry for the entire family.

Chapter 64

Charlotte Magni (alias Charlotte Conte, Dolores Manno, Dolores Smithe, Lola Heather—a.k.a. Lolita or Lolet—ad infinitum to a growing list of assumed names that would fill a small-town phone directory) paraded back and forth across a checkered black and white tiled floor. The area was off-limits. The space was casually called the *Drilling Room*, which connoted a machine shop of sorts to those who had heard mention of it.

"It doesn't matter what Virginia told her mother, Austin. Does it? They're both here now, and they're both leaving in body bags. What's important is that neither of them said anything to anyone that could possibly connect us to our base of operation here in Redding Ridge. We know that it's in Virginia's best interest not to have said anything incriminating to anyone. Right?"

"That was before her stepson was grabbed by that lunatic, Columba, and consequently got the police involved."

"That lunatic is going to make us a fucking fortune when we find him. Evan Tamblin is buying and paying dearly for his revenge. And when we find and deliver this madman's head, like we did Bellport's, we can all write our own ticket. As for the police, you let Vincent and me worry about them. All right?"

"You're forgetting that I was once one of them, Charlotte. We're not dealing with a bunch of choir boys. This is not the eighties."

"Now, tell me something I don't know."

"What you don't know? How about if that whore in there you groomed said anything to her mother, who in turn said something incriminating to the police. *That's* something you don't really know."

Charlotte studied her accomplice carefully, wondering how much she should tell him. Both Vincent and she knew he could be trusted. Of that, there was no doubt. He had proven himself many times over—over the course of years. Fearless. Smart. Loyal. The question was, did Austin Izzo really *need* to know? She decided to share a small but important piece of information so as to put his mind at ease.

"The police *were* at Virginia's mother's door," she confided.

"You see!"

"More clearly than you do right now."

"The old lady come right out and tell you this? Or did you have to pull it from her?"

"She admitted it right off the bat, but she didn't have to."

"What does that mean? You don't know what she really told them. She could have told them anything."

"What she told me earlier is what she told them. Period."

Austin looked at Charlotte scornfully. "You have a crystal ball or something?"

"Something more reliable," she said, sending her tongue into a corner cheek.

"Yeah?"

"Yeah."

"What?"

"A snitch."

"Who?"

"You don't need to know that right now. But this person is well-placed."

"Well-placed where?"

"Never mind where."

"Reliable, you say?" Izzo smirked.

"Like the rising sun."

"Come on, Charlotte. We're in this thing together."

Charlotte shook her head. "I'll just add that this person's power is paramount."

"You kidding me?"

"Ever know me to kid around like this?"

Austin Izzo put up his hands in a sign of exasperation. "I don't know what to tell you, Charlotte."

"You don't need to tell me anything," she vaunted. "You're not forgetting who works for who around here, now are you?"

Austin smiled shrewdly. "No, but I think I do need to remind you that I've seen these types of relationships blow up in people's faces before. So, you got yourself a snitch. Top gun, who can be bought by the highest bidder. Or maybe a plant put in place by the police. Maybe let you operate under an umbrella of protection for a while. Make a few successful scores. And then, BOOM!" The man's hand hit the wall like a hammer. "Instant diarrhea. You wouldn't even see the shit hit the fan."

Charlotte nodded appreciatively. "So. This person *we* have placed, and *not* the other way around, would have to be as trustworthy as yourself in order for you to feel secure. Right?"

Austin Izzo shook his head. "Trustworthy," he scoffed. "Poor choice of a word in the business we're in, Charlotte. Trust is a word that doesn't even apply in most marriages. It's what I've got on the next guy that I can use against him is how I'm able to sleep at night."

Charlotte Magni nodded knowingly. "And so that you won't lose any sleep tonight, I'll share this much with you. A rookie detective was sent over to Viola Johnson's house, asking about her daughter's whereabouts. A rookie," she emphasized. "He asked the old woman if she knew of anyone Virginia might be staying with, and Viola told him about this friend of her daughter's who she met when Viola dropped by unexpectedly for a visit out in Orient Point. *Moi.* Charlotte Smithe with an e. That's exactly how Virginia remembered me. To the letter." Charlotte laughed. "Anyhow, the old lady told the detective that Virginia goes horseback riding with me in Connecticut, and sometimes stays over. She didn't know where. The cop's visit was an *unofficial* call, Austin. He even had some civilian he's working with wait for him in the car."

"Nothing homicide does is ever unofficial. *Trust* me on that. They file a report, and it gets handed out to every member of the team. On a case such as this? Believe me when I tell you that more than one team, along with other jurisdictions, are working in concert. And that includes the feds."

"Oh, the detective did, indeed, file a report," Charlotte assured him. "And Vincent has a copy of it. That's why I'm telling you that what the old lady told me inside is what she told the cop and nothing beyond that."

"Christ, they even know what state we're in."

"It's a good size state, Austin. Sixty-seven hundred square miles. Lots of farms and ranches, dude," she quipped gleefully.

"Did Viola tell them where in Connecticut?" Austin pressed, still unsure. "North? East? South? West, maybe?"

"She said she didn't know where. And that's confirmed in the detective's report. These guys are running blindly all over Connecticut as we speak."

"How can you be sure Virginia Dupree didn't blab this to other detectives—like the ones who visited her and her husband's home?"

Charlotte stuck the tip of her tongue in her other cheek. "I'm sure," she said quite seriously. "You see, Vincent has copies of those reports, too."

Austin Izzo stared at Charlotte for a good ten seconds before he spoke.

"Let's just say for argument's sake that they home in on this area," he posited.

"Several Suffolk County detectives have been through Bridgeport for a second time," she disclosed, "and are now north of Waterbury, on a wild-goose chase. We've been posted. And our contacts are on full alert. So just relax."

"Contacts?"

"Contacts."

"In all the right places, I suppose?"

"Right. High. And *Mighty*."

"Cities' police departments?"

"All I'll give you at this point is a reminder that you were given a green light in Adirondack Park. True? Murder investigation or no murder investigation, you were protected. You virtually ran the show with your crew and the local boys up there. The Long Island bunch tried to throw their weight around, but they didn't get too far. Did they, Austin?"

"No, they didn't."

"So now, buddy. Are you secure in your knowledge that those two women in there are going to go to their graves without either of them having said a *damaging* word to the police or anyone?"

"Let me throw another monkey wrench into the works."

"Hurl away."

"What about Virginia's husband, Harold?"

"What about him?"

"Isn't there a possibility she might have told him something . . . something that could lead them to us?"

Charlotte laughed wholeheartedly. "If that asshole had an

inkling about what his sorry-ass wifey was engaged in up here, well, we'd only be whacking one member of the family tonight—because he'd have fucked Virginia ten times over and put her body in the bay."

Austin nodded compliantly. "All right. I get the picture, Charlotte."

"Amen to that."

Chapter 65

It was, of course, tragic but still fascinating in that Freddie had, *indeed*, been able to tell whether or not his father was lying to him or speaking the God's honest truth, as the boy did not fall for the story about the snake antidote: the remedy in exchange for the simple telling of what it was like to linger there—*dying* in a diorama—tied to a *living* sculpture. All Freddie could do was plead and whine and weep . . . before he finally went to sleep . . . before his father ultimately moved him to his final resting place.

Malcolm Columba finished digging a long, deep, narrow cut in the land behind his rental home before hitting the water table. At least a good six feet down, by two feet across, by twelve feet in length. He had to deal with lots of clay and stony earth. It proved to be arduous and torturous work.

At least it was to be an eternal sleep for the boy, among the wormy limbless creatures of the earth, far removed from the scaly, fanged vipers venturing behind the hallway glass less than a hundred yards away.

Columba blessed the boy before he rolled him within a tarp, then carefully lowered his body into the ground via an old length of rope that suddenly broke. The dull *thump* resounded in Malcolm's ears, and at the same time clutched his heavy heart. The brownish-yellow claybank was the color the author duly noted and would later record in his journal—turning about abruptly at the sound of footsteps coming up behind him. He reached for the spade and shovel.

"Here. You can help me fill this end in," Malcolm ordered, handing over one of the implements.

"I can help you do what?" the woman laughed, standing off to the side of the grave.

"You can help me fill this end," he repeated. "I've been at this for hours. The ground is like a bed of rock. I'm tired."

"You're tired? Frankly, we're all tired, Malcolm. We've all been working like demons now for months."

"No. I'm the only demon. None of you even come close. Here, I said."

Sally Tamblin snatched up the spade. "Just remember who put this all together. All right?"

"Just *you* remember the sacrifice I made. He's my own flesh and blood." Malcolm threw the first shovelful of stony clay-earth down upon the boy's shrouded body.

"Well, dear. It's like my late husband used to say. 'Cash is king and thicker than both blood *and* water,'" she stated solemnly, pushing in a pile of dirt with the side of the blackened blade.

"Our bodies are three-quarters water. Did you know that, Sally?"

"So's the planet earth. What's your point?"

"The point is the entire world's polluted."

The two worked together covering Freddie's body. Dust rose in the ditch as the rocky earth fell in on the boy.

Sally gave a little laugh. "Funny what sets us off in life, Malcolm. Isn't it? You've got water on the brain. And I've got money on my mind. We're not so terribly different though, really. Are we? We've both been hurt and disappointed in much the same way. You had a woman whom you loved and loved you in return, but the Lord took her away. He took my loved one, too. I had a man who worshipped the ground I walked on, but he didn't have a pot to piss in. He died penniless. So, I had to go back to work. Then along came Evan who lost his wife to cancer and wanted a younger woman on his arm once again. Only he wounded me severely when he asked me to sign a prenuptial agreement. Sure, I would have spent his money. I do now to a degree. But I never would have left him or hurt him in any way. Not until he *made* me sign that paper. Not until the ink was dry. I stood to inherit a paltry sum." Sally stopped and wiped her brow before continuing. "Patricia, however, would receive virtually everything. I didn't have to wait to see the handwriting on the wall. It was there on the page in front of me. Along with his Last Will and Testament. He sealed his fate with that stroke of poor judgment, poor dear. But even my signature on that piece of paper didn't satisfy his daughter. His darling Patricia never said anything, but I could see the resentment and jealousy in her eyes. She saw me as a gold-digger,

Malcolm. Patricia Tamblin. Daddy's precious little girl. Now Daddy's dead little darling."

"Actually, you and I are quite different, Sally. Like night and day, if you want to know the truth. You *need* someone to do your killing for you. Me? I *need* to kill."

Sally smirked. "So, then Freddie isn't really much of a sacrifice after all. Is he, Malcolm?"

Like a spear, Malcolm planted the rounded blade of the shovel solidly into the pile of dirt. "Let me explain something to you, Mrs. Sally, know-it-all, Tamblin. My boy lost his mother at a very early age. He barely remembered her. I tried to bring a few things back to him through some photographs I kept. It was pretty painful for the boy. Learning, for instance, that his maternal grandmother was as black as the ace of spades; his biological mother a mulatto; the fact that he was one-quarter black; his stepmother an eighth. And as we stand here discussing this, Virginia Dupree and her mother are probably dead by now. So. Do you think that I wanted to send my boy back to a motherless living hell with Harold Dupree? He's better off this way."

Malcolm lifted a shovelful of earth and angrily sent it into the trench.

Sally laughed again, only louder. "Now *that's* a rationalization if ever I've heard one."

Malcolm did not say a word, but kept right on shoveling.

"Why such a deep hole, Malcolm? No one's ever going to find him back here."

"Animals," he muttered.

"Why so long? I mean you could pile a heap of bodies in half that space. One on top of the other. No?"

"No."

"How come?"

"Because I don't want another soul crowding him. That's how come."

"What other soul? It's over, Malcolm."

Malcolm looked at Sally and smiled. "One more, Sally."

Sally looked at Malcolm queerly.

Malcolm held her stare.

"You touch me and you won't see a dime. You know that, don't you?"

"I'm not looking for a dollar, Sally. More like fifty cents."

"Fifty cents?"

"Sure. Two pieces of silver to cover both your eyes. Now watch me telegraph this message so that you fully understand."

Malcolm Columba drew back the shovel and in one swift motion whirled the implement about, knocking Sally's defensive hands away—catching the woman squarely in the face as she slipped and reeled rearward.

"NO!" she screamed.

Malcolm threw down the shovel and picked up Sally's spade.

Sally was on her back as the next blow split her skull open just above an ear.

Malcolm smiled down satisfactorily with a heavy breath. "See, you didn't even notice how nice and sharp I've honed these edges, Sally. Just before you came. Machined to razor-like precision—courtesy of your first husband's workshop over there," he blared, pointing with the bloody blade to the outbuilding.

Sally arched her back and held up both hands weakly to deflect the forthcoming blow, but Malcolm put the spade down and shook his head.

"No, Sally. I'm not going to put you out of your misery just yet. I'd rather just stand here and watch you bleed to death. On second thought, I'll sit." Malcolm sat down quietly by the graveside and stretched. "You didn't believe me when I told you I was tired. I've had very little sleep. A ten-year-old can *really* run you ragged."

The blood was pouring out of Sally Tamblin's head like a mini-fountain.

Sally dropped her hands and fell back silently.

"Never was about money, honey. It was and still is about ridding the world of pollution. You and others like you are part of the problem. I'm simply the solution." Malcolm rolled his head and stretched his neck. "I'm sure I know what the others have in store for me. But I'm quite prepared. Are you, Sally? Are you prepared to meet your Maker? He's only several shovelfuls away."

Columba rested his weary bones, rubbing two quarters together in a pants pocket. "What's the matter, Sally? The fight and sarcasm all out of you? Huh? Punch buggy don't punch back?" he managed through an outrageous chortle.

Malcolm laced his hands behind his head and studied her pleading eyes.

It was a good ten minutes before the killer withdrew two coins, leaned forward leisurely, then placed them, heads up, upon the vacant stare.

"There. Who ever said that you can't take it with you, Sally?" Malcolm smiled down handsomely.

Chapter 66

Detective Kim Booker was smacking the heel of her hand against her forehead with increasing force until it actually hurt. "Stupid! So stupid." Suddenly, she stopped hitting herself and started striking keys. "Damn. Come on. Come on. Come on," she said to Big Sister. "Please be a good girl and give your Kim some gold. Come on, you great big bitch. Little sister here is so close, baby, that she can actually taste those twin, two-pound, buttery, lemony lobsters—tails and claws and all." Kim ran her fingers across the keyboard, then downloaded the information as her mind raced miles ahead. "Shit!"

Two detectives sitting just outside her area smiled at one another and shook their heads.

Ten tiny bouquets of brightly colored spring and summery flowers tap-danced their way about the plastic keyboard, clicking away persistently with the sound of serious business at hand.

Suddenly, Kim Booker stopped typing, ran the mouse across the pad and shot the cursor to a corner of the screen. The detective clicked the icon, cackled, then started scrolling the information while her mind unraveled several threads that unlocked and beheld the mystery. "I got it!" Kim yelled. "Got you. Got you. Got you!" she screamed, stamping her feet beneath her seat in sheer excitement.

Several chairs rolled and raked nosily backwards from messy desks piled high or strewn with papers as half a dozen detectives hurried forth.

Kim punched a button on the printer. Stood. Did a little dance with the detective standing nearest her. Leading. Leaning. Twirling him around before planting a kiss on the tip of his nose. "Theo!" she shouted, releasing the man from her arms. The startled detective stifled the ring in his ear with a pinkie.

"THEO!" she shouted again. Louder.

Theo appeared behind the group. "What's all this?"

"I want witnesses!" Kim whooped.

"We all want witnesses," Theo agreed calmly.

With eyes closed tightly, chin up, fists directed downward and fixed rigidly at her side, Kim Booker announced in a loud, clear voice for all those in earshot to hear: "I want all those assembled here this morning to bear witness that our demanding, commanding officer, namely one Detective Lieutenant Theodore Groche, along with our illustrious homicide squad, owes one Detective Kim Booker a lobster and champagne dinner."

Theo stood excited but kept his cool. "Tell us why, Detective," the top cop commanded.

"Because Big Sister and I have just completed connecting *all* the dots. We have this *whole* thing figured out. Therefore, we have *things* to do. *People* to see. And *places* to go. And I do mean, now!" Kim turned abruptly away from her commanding officer. "Get some able-bodied bodies immediately out to 112 Sunny Line Drive in Calverton. Rental home of Mrs. Sally Tamblin, under her maiden name, Pierce. I'll bet dollars to doughnuts she rented it to Mr. Malcolm Columba. There's a good possibility that's where you'll find Freddie Dupree."

A dozen detectives looked pleadingly at Theo.

Theo gestured to several of them. "Amastate. Ives. Hennesey. Posteraro. Bokina. Go! We'll radio SWAT and maintain Code Two," he called after them. "Zanetti, you find Judge Vesey and have him back-issue an a.m. warrant—like in this morning—for the house, property, garage, dog house and a wishing well—whether there is or isn't any."

"Sir—"

"I want full discretionary power, complete autonomy—"

Sir."

"—unconditional–unlimited authority. I don't want any stone unturned. Clear?"

"Sir."

"Zanetti."

"Sir, Judge Vesey is either at the Nissequogue or Connetquot River fishing for trout. He does *not* answer his page or cell on Wednesdays. He could be on any beat between site two and—"

"Zanetti."

"Lieutenant?"

"That is precisely why I told *you* to go find him. If it were a

Monday evening, you'd be hunting for *two* fishing fools. Yes?"

"Yes, sir."

"And you be sure to tell him this ain't no fishing expedition."

"Yes, sir."

A file of men and two women followed Theo over to a wall map. Kim was one of them. The lieutenant raced and placed his finger on the grid. "Over here on County Road 25, across from the Naval Weapons Industrial Reserve Plant." Theo did some finger tapping of his own. "We'll set up a command post, here. Southeast corner off Old Stone Road. I want men on foot on each side of Fresh Pond Avenue leading into South Path. Timber and Penny Drive empties onto the County Road. That'll take care of vehicle traffic. To the north and northwest is all government land. We'll figure out something when we get out there."

"Theo."

Theo turned to Kim.

"Those stables up in Connecticut our team is hunting for?"

"What about them?"

Kim took in her lips in hesitation.

"Come on," Theo coaxed.

"I think we're looking for the wrong kind of stables. I think we're looking for young colts on two legs, and their johns who help pay the operating costs. That's what I think."

"Don Ciccio's secondary source of income," a rookie detective acknowledged. "Prostitution."

Theo drove the flat of his fist into the palm of the other hand. "Thick. Of course, that's it!" He turned to his people. "Fendricks. Get me Nelson on the phone. Anybody hear from Miller yet?"

No one had a clue.

Theo shook his head in frustration. "All right, troops. Time to rock-'n'-roll."

"**Y**ou! Stop right where you are."

Justin Barnes turned around, looked about, and pointed a questioning finger at the center of his chest.

"Yeah, you. Hold it right there."

"Yes'am," he obeyed politely, touching the brim of a faded gray and white striped railroad cap on loan from a veritable stranger, Ms. Slopbucket, who had provided him with the rest of the outfit as well. The trespasser wore a well-worn, long sleeved, wrinkled pin-striped shirt—two sizes too big—draped like a nightshirt over clean, baggy charcoal denim pants.

A rather large yet short-legged woman waddled over like a penguin. "What the fuck are you doing up here?" she demanded.

Justin's mouth fell open in mock surprise, as if he were quite unaccustomed to hearing such language, especially coming from a female in such *rich* surroundings. He immediately removed the cap and dropped his chin to his collarbone before slowly raising a pair of big brown eyes to meet her aggravated stare.

"Well, speak up, man."

"Yes, ma'am. Mr. Tooly, he takes me up dis way sayin' dat ya folks gots lots n' lots o' work 'round here. He tol' me ta tell ya-all dat I's a human workhorse; dat I can do da work o' four good men in a fraction o' da time fo' half da pay n' a little somethin' to eat, like it say here in my letter of *in·tro·duc·tion.*" Justin tapped his right front pocket over the badly wrinkled shirt. "It say dat he . . . a . . . *vouch* fo' me. Dat's what he done write down," Justin affirmed just as proudly as he could.

"I don't know any Mr. Tooly; and besides, all the work around here is assigned by the foreman. How did you get onto this property?"

"I jus' walk right in from o' dere." Justin pointed to a field over the woman's right shoulder. "Mr. Tooly, he drop me off dat side o' da woods. Says dere be lots o' work 'round here. Maybe I be at da wrong farm, ma'am."

"Farm?" The woman frowned. "This is a ranch. Not a farm. What kind of work you looking for?"

Justin put his cap back on and lowered his head in submission. "Did mos'ly field work, ma'am. But I's do jus' 'bout anythin'. Do da work o' four good men in a fraction o' da time fo' half da pay plus a little somethin' to eat. Not much, mind ya. Maybe a place to put my head down fo' da night." He looked back up into her unpleasant eyes. "Could work a day o' stay on jus' as long as da boss allow. Ain't got no place special to go."

She studied his eyes carefully as she spoke. "You in trouble with the law? Any kind of trouble whatsoever? Recent, or going back in time?"

"Oh, no, ma'am. No trouble wif da law o' anyone. Patrol car stop me 'bout a month ago as I makin' my way no'th. Called me ah . . . *vagrant* till I shows him my billfold wif a hundred bucks, 'long wif a note fo' a promise of a job wif Mr. Tooly up 'ere." Justin pulled an envelope from under the shirt, handing it over.

The woman opened it, removed and read the referral. "Worked in Norwalk for a full month?"

"Yes, ma'am. If he had mo' work, Mr. Tooly would 'ave kept me on. He say I's be da bes' worker he ever sees."

The big woman spoke without lifting her eyes from the paper. "Jerome Slowey?" the woman read.

"Das me." Justin smiled brightly. "Only dere ain't one thin' 'bout me ya gonna finds slow, ma'am. No, siree. 'Cause I can do da work o'—"

"—four good men in a fraction of the time for half the pay; yada, yada, yada," she recited curtly.

"Plus a little somethin' to eat. Not much, mind ya. Maybe a place to put my head down fo' da night," Justin repeated earnestly, nodding affirmatively at the end of his delivery.

"Just a little slow upstairs, Mr. Slowey," the woman said sarcastically.

"But dere ain't one thin' ya gonna finds 'bout me dat's slow. No, siree," he declared solemnly.

"Jerome."

"Yes, ma'am?"

"Shut up."

Justin hung his head back down sorrowfully.

"You ever work in a kitchen, Jerome?"

The maverick's eyes lit like a Christmas tree. "Yes, ma'am. Sure did. In da Navy. Worked in da scullery peelin' taters n' onions; cleaning pots n' pans. Worked da chow line, too, from time to time. Even did a little cookin'."

"Well, we certainly don't need any cooks right now, Jerome. But we might be able to use a hand in the kitchen. Cleaning. Mopping up. Maybe husking corn and cutting string beans. Peeling onions and potatoes, like you said. Beats working in the fields, I'd think."

Justin grew all excited, rubbing his hands together in earnest before holding up two black meaty mitts. "Fastest hands ya gonna sees this side o' heaven, ma'am. I can husk a large bucket 'o corn in sixty seconds flat. Peel a large pot o' taters in twenty minutes flat. Onions in no time a'tall. Do da work o' five good men in less time—"

"Now it's five men, Jerome?"

"Yes, ma'am. 'Cause when it comes to da kitchen, I's be a tornado."

"Would that be a white tornado, Mr. Jerome Slowey?"

Justin thought hard for a moment, then suddenly laughed. "I get it!"

"Good boy," the woman said condescendingly.

Justin beamed and showed his bright-white perfect teeth.

"Follow me. I'm going to introduce you to the foreman. His name is Mr. Jones."

"Mr. Jones," Justin said contemplatively.

"Jerome."

"Ma'am?"

"When you meet Mr. Jones, I want you to be quiet and let me do the talking. Understand?"

"Yes, ma'am."

"If he asks you something, I want you to answer him in as few words as possible. Got that?"

"Got it."

"He doesn't like anyone who goes on and on about themselves. I'll tell him what you've done and show him this letter. You just act polite."

"Act polite."

"Right. And tuck your shirt in."

"Yes, ma'am."

Justin followed a step behind the big woman waddling toward a huge red barn. He tucked the front of his crumpled shirt into his puffy pants. The shirttail he let hang loose, for it covered two semiautomatic handguns holstered at the small of his back: one, a Taurus Millennium Pro 9-millimeter pistol packed with enough power at close range to rival a small canon; the second, an AMT Backup 9-millimeter Kurz, fitted with a silencer that could whisper the deadliest of sins.

Justin was ever as good as he said he was with his hands. Better than a few good men—with handguns as well as his fists. He could move from Sambo to Rambo in a flash.

"I wantcha ta know how much I 'preciate dis . . . ah . . . op·por·tun·ity, ma'am. I really and truly do. God bless ya, ma'am."

Chapter 68

Within the spacious two-story structure situated on a hilltop along Redding Ridge Ranch, Viola Johnson and her daughter, Virginia Dupree, were brought from separate quarters. The pair were led into the center of the commodious *drilling room* and told to kneel down upon a large white, plastic-covered canvas tarp. Viola and Virginia huddled together, the latter trembling in pure panic, clinging to her mother as she wept bitterly.

"Oh, God. Plea-se don't hurt us," Virginia begged. "Please."

"Shut up," a short, hideous-looking fellow in his early twenties snapped. He held a small caliber pistol a foot away from the back of Virginia's skull.

Seconds later, Charlotte Magni and Austin Izzo stepped into the room, then closed and locked the heavy set of double doors behind them. She wore a black buckskin jacket over a white silk blouse, leather jodhpurs and matching ankle-high boots fitted with silver buckles at their sides. In her right hand, she held a riding crop. Austin sported a light-brown suede jacket with a caramel-colored shirt opened at the throat. A pale-yellow bolo tie threaded through the button-down collar defined his brawny chest. A pair of tan linen trousers and mocha Loafers completed the outfit.

Viola cradled her daughter's head. "You may kill us before the feds ever get here, woman, but they're gonna hunt you down like the animals you are."

"Feds?" Charlotte smiled in amusement.

"Yes, the feds. I told an agent where to find you up here in Redding Ridge. I told him about the Okay Corral. I told him all about this filthy business that you're involved in. I told him *everything*, Charlotte Smithe with an e, or whatever in hell your name is."

"Oh, I don't see how. A little while ago, you told me exactly what you told a detective who came to your home. Therefore, there was no FBI man out to visit you, Mrs. Johnson. None whatsoever. You're telling us a little fib, which is perfectly natural and even forgivable under these circumstances," she declared confidently.

"Oh, but you're so wrong, woman. Terribly wrong. Agent Justin Barnes was waiting in the detective's car when I insisted he come in. Barnes took over and conducted the interview while the detective took some notes, then went to his car. That's when I told the FBI man everything I know about you, bitch," Viola averred, spitting in defiance upon the stark white tarp, designated as her and her daughter's burial shroud as such.

Austin Izzo stood beside his boss, staring at her uneasily.

"That's a very flimsy story, old woman," Charlotte insisted. "But I credit you with trying to save your butts. See, it wasn't a total loss. I think you bought you and your daughter a precious minute," she goaded. "And just so you don't go to your grave with any misplaced satisfaction, it doesn't matter whether the police or feds know about this place or not. It wouldn't even matter much if they wound up suspecting that Austin and I kidnapped you and signed your death warrant. They'd have to *prove* it. At worst, it would prove an inconvenience. So. We'll just let my young nephew here make his bones by blasting yours. Oh, and for your information, we have feds in our corner, too. Not too many, mind you. But we're making inroads every day." Charlotte smiled haughtily.

"And for *your* information, *my* FBI man is a friend of mine who made me certain promises," Viola said with strong conviction through her wrathful tears. "He won't rest until he finds us," she added reassuringly.

"Then I'm sure he'll be doubly disappointed if both your bodies turn up, which I doubt they ever will. And as for you, my little harlot," Charlotte spouted, raising Virginia's chin with the tip of the riding crop, their eyes locked together like radar, "you're going to be especially missed."

Virginia's upper body shook violently in her mother's arms as she bawled so loudly that Charlotte had to speak over her in order to be heard.

"You were certainly an earner, my dear. I'll bet you brought in more dollars in a single evening than that poor excuse of a husband of yours did in his best month on the water pulling lobster traps. Your mother should be extremely proud of you. Tell her how proud you are of her, old woman."

Viola Johnson did not take her hateful eyes off the procurer. "I'll tell you this, bitch," she said forthrightly. "God does not like ugly."

Charlotte nodded. Not in acknowledgment of the remark but rather as a gesture for her nephew to execute the pair. She and Austin stepped aside.

The miserable soul standing over Virginia, his face covered with acne, the muzzle of the silencer pointed inches from her head, flew back in a single instant—the instant he received the verbal command from the madam of the house. The wretched little fellow lay still as stone. Austin Izzo immediately had his gun out, but that was as far as it got before he received a bullet that traversed the bridge of his nose and exited the back of his skull.

Charlotte stood transfixed, dropping the black leather crop lest it be taken for a handgun.

Virginia was crawling and bawling, making her way to a set of double doors.

"Stay right there," Justin Barnes ordered, speaking directly to the daughter. "Don't move."

But Virginia was clawing before the threshold, fighting with its golden pair of locked handles.

"Stay put like he says!" her mother commanded.

"Put those hands up real high," Justin ordered Charlotte. He trained the smaller of his two handguns on the center of her chest. The larger weapon was pointed toward the doors above Virginia's head—the doors from where they heard voices and footsteps coming at the other end of the hall. "How many hired hands in the house?" Justin demanded of Charlotte.

Charlotte shrugged. "Too many to shoot your way out of here, cowboy, if that's what you have in mind. If I scream, it's all over, mister."

"If you scream, lady, *you'll* take the next bullet between the eyes fo' you even blink." Without taking his eyes off Charlotte, he addressed the old woman. "How many?" he asked her in a gentle voice.

Viola shook her head and struggled to her feet. "Just these three is all I seen, Justin," she lowered her voice as she went over to comfort and coax her daughter away from the doors. "But there were quite a few around the property when they brought us in."

Justin patted Charlotte down.

"Listen to me, Justin," Charlotte demanded. "I'll make you a deal. I—"

Charlotte was interrupted by a knock at the door.

Justin waved Viola and Virginia out of the way with the handgun and set the muzzle of the semiautomatic's silencer forward of Charlotte's ear.

"Send them off without a worry," Justin whispered, "or you'll wish you had but never know it."

Charlotte looked down at her twenty-three-year-old nephew. The blood was oozing from his temple—off the tarp and onto the black and white tile floor. The young man did not move a muscle, lying there as quiet as the afternoon. Out of the corner of her eye, she caught Austin. Faceup. The big man slowly formed a fist, which suddenly unfolded like the petals of a pan-sized flower.

Justin pressed the cold, steel-blue barrel against her skull.

"What is it?" Charlotte shouted to her people behind the door.

"Vincent's on the phone for you," a male voice answered.

"Tell him I'm busy in here. I'll call him back."

"Everything okey-dokey in there?" another asked.

"Everything's fine."

"You ready for us then?"

"Not just yet."

"Thought I heard a couple of pops and that you'd want the place spick-and-span."

"You heard a couple of pops, all right. The old woman has a few more things she wants to tell us before I kiss her ass goodbye. Isn't that right, Viola?"

Justin looked at Viola and gave her the high sign.

Virginia held her breath.

"I ain't tellin' you a goddamn' thing, bitch!" Viola swore on cue.

"Maybe a bullet in her belly instead of both her legs might change her mind. Right, Ronnie?" Charlotte chanced.

Justin figured that Ronnie was the one bleeding from his temple, so the maverick gave an affirmative grunt and moved the muzzle of his firearm firmly against Charlotte's evil eye.

"Tell Vincent I'll call him back soon as this is over," she surrendered.

"Will do."

"Hey, Aussie. There's only two of us here and Carol," the other said. "So stick around. Two bodies, dead weight, ain't no fucking picnic, buddy. I hired me a nigger for the kitchen. Dumb as dirt. He's almost as big as you, my man. If you don't help us out, I'll probably haveta use 'im. Then where am I gonna be? I'll haveta kill 'im an' find me another *melanzana* to do all the work we got around here. Vincent's expecting an early dinner tonight. Carol didn't know and sent The Greek and Tony home early. Hey. You hearin' me? I'm asking for a little help. Or are you too much a big shot now that you got yourself promoted?"

"Big shot's busy with our newest filly in the back room, Gino," Charlotte wisely invented on the spot. "He's riding her ass to the very last mile. Now, beat it. We'll work things out later."

"Hey, Aussie baby. Ride 'er cowboy!" Gino hollered. "See that, Danny? I told you so. 'Cause Dan, here, thought you was a big queer —big guy," he managed through uncontrollable laughter.

"I said, beat it," Charlotte repeated.

"I bet Charlotte's with her camera snapping away pictures," Danny's voice trailed off, following Gino back to the kitchen phone.

"Nah, that's evidence, asshole."

"Who you callin' an asshole?"

"I'm callin' you an asshole, asshole. Vincent's comin' in less than two hours with some important friends to feed, and we got a zillion things to do."

"You just watch your smart mouth. All right?"

"Hey. Who the fuck invited you into this family anyhow?"

"Nobody invited me. I married into it, putz."

"Whattaya, a regular wise guy?"

"No. You're a wise guy. Your whole side of the family is wise guys. Me? I'm just tryin' to make a living."

"Living? I'd be more worried about dyin' if I was you. If Vincent gets here and we ain't ready with the fixin's, somebody might be digging *our* graves."

"Then who's gonna bury us. Carol?"

"*You* got the smart mouth, fella. You just give Carol a hand in the kitchen like I tell ya. Me and Aussie will take care of those two dames," the foreman instructed.

Chapter 69

"How in hell are we going to get out of here?" Virginia Dupree trembled.

"Same way I came in," Justin explained calmly. "Out the back."

"You're not going to get off this property alive, I'm telling you," Charlotte warned. "And if you do, the police will pick you up within minutes. Pick you up in pieces, that is," she promised knowingly.

"Uh-uh," Justin countered. "You're our ticket out of here, Miss Fancy-Pants. But just in case we don't make it, you don't make it either."

"You won't get through security, I'm telling you. And the old lady's not going to make it through those fields and woods, which is the way you had to have come in. Now, I was starting to offer you a deal."

"FBI doesn't deal, woman," Viola Johnson told Charlotte straightaway. "And if they do, Agent Barnes, sure as there's a hell, don't. Tell 'er. You goin' to jail, woman."

Charlotte laughed. "FBI. If he's FBI, then I'm Mother Theresa."

"You're a mother, all right, you white piece of trash," Viola lambasted. "You gonna rot in prison, or worse, bitch. Tell 'er, Justin."

"What's your deal?" Justin asked calmly.

Viola Johnson slowly shook her head.

"Austin Izzo's share," Charlotte offered. "Half a million greenbacks."

Justin laughed. "Who do I gotta murder?"

Charlotte glared at the two women. "A pair of liabilities."

"Just like that?"

"Just like that."

Virginia Dupree's shoulders shuddered. "She'll kill us all," the daughter swore.

Justin faced the female crew boss directly, taking her deep brown eyes into his. "I want to know the score here," he demanded. "I want you to tell me where to find Malcolm Columba."

"We haven't got time for that," Charlotte barked.

"You better find time to tell me. Now. I want his sorry-ass hide."

Charlotte sighed in exasperation. "You and half the country. He's our key to a fortune, Justin. He's worth more than his weight in eighteen carat gold; that is, if we can find him before the police do and bring him in alive—for openers," she clarified.

"Bring him to who?" he asked decisively.

"A wealthy client who's willing to pay dearly for undamaged goods. Just like we did with Donald Bellport before we *dissolved* the relationship," she confessed. "Got the picture, Justin Barnes? Client wants us back."

"You can find Columba?"

"I can find him, and I can get you out of here alive. But we've got to move fast. Half a million bucks, Justin. That's your share for starters. And let me sweeten the pot. When we do find him and turn him inside out, literally, you'll pick up another half a mil. That's what you're really after, fella. Isn't it? It's either got to be reward money or revenge. Wouldn't it be nice to have both? One million bucks and his hide. If Columba lands in the hands of the authorities, which I can guarantee you he won't, if we move now, you'll still walk away with half a million dollars and your head."

Justin smiled at the offer and nodded in satisfaction.

"We have a deal?" Charlotte pressed.

"Why not let these two walk?" he asked curiously.

"Simple. They know too much. You want them around to testify that they just saw you commit a double homicide? That you impersonated a federal agent—being the least of it? A black man in America? Get real, fella. Besides. You have no idea who you're dealing with here, Mr. Barnes."

"Oh, I have a pretty good idea 'bout that. And to tell you the truth, it doesn't really bother me at all. Just like the police don't seem to bother you."

"Well, it should."

"Let me tell you what does bother me, though."

"You're wasting valuable time here."

"What bothers me is that I think you enjoy killin' as much as that Columba nut. Would I be wrong?"

"You'd be wrong not to accept my offer. That's where you'd be terribly wrong."

Justin shifted an eye to Virginia. "Virginia," he said softly.

Virginia was still shaking but held his stare.

"This is the time for you to be totally honest with yourself, girl. Hear me?"

Virginia nodded quickly.

"I read all the police reports concernin' Malcolm Columba. All of them," he repeated. "You held back certain information from Detective Gary York when he came to your home. Didn't you?"

Without hesitation, Virginia nodded in the affirmative.

"Information that would point the police in a certain direction. Columba's."

Once again, she nodded.

"Information as to his whereabouts."

Virginia held her tongue.

"You know where he is. Don't you?"

Virginia's silence tightened the tension.

"Virginia. We're talkin' lives, here. Mine, your mother's, yours and maybe your stepson's—if we're not too late. Gonna help yourself by helping me?"

"He rents the old Pierce place in Calverton."

"Shut up!" Charlotte demanded.

"Sally Tamblin's former home," Virginia finished.

"You're making a big mistake," Don Ciccio's mistress and gun moll threatened Virginia Dupree directly.

"I made many of them up to now." Virginia wept and shivered with fear and hatred scrawled across her face. "I thought you were my friend, Charlotte. I trusted you. You told me Freddie was safe."

"Where in Calverton?" Justin demanded.

Virginia shook her head. "I don't know where. All I know is that it's near a big cemetery."

"Fitting," Justin said with a frown. "Calverton National Cemetery?"

Virginia thought hard. "Yes, I think that's the one."

"Just north of 25. Near the Naval Reserve Plant." He studied Charlotte's eyes as he spoke.

"You're playing with fire," Charlotte cautioned.

Justin tightened his finger around the crescent-shaped trigger. "I'm about to put that fire out," he swore.

"Don't flatter yourself, mister. I'm your ticket out of here, I told you. You said so yourself."

"And you just about wore out your usefulness, lady. Now get undressed."

"What?"

"Boots. Pants. Jacket. Do it."

Charlotte shook her head.

"I'll count to one."

Charlotte kicked off her riding boots.

"You do the same, Virginia," Justin instructed.

Virginia looked at her mother.

Viola nodded.

Charlotte was down to her underwear. The boots and garments lay at her feet.

"Step back," he told Charlotte.

Charlotte Magni took two steps backward.

With his foot, Justin swept the small pile over to Virginia.

"Put those on," he told her.

Virginia stood in bra and panties, reached down and picked up Charlotte's clothing.

"And I guess you want me to put on her clothes," Charlotte said with a bored expression.

Justin shook his head.

"No?" she said with some surprise.

"Uh-uh."

"Huh. Want to have your way with me before we leave?" she questioned seductively, tracing her shapely figure with cool cupped palms and long fingers.

"No time," Justin said.

"No?" she cooed. "How come?" she purred.

"'Cause you're checking out of here right now."

"Oh, really?"

"Really." Justin squeezed the trigger and sent a round into the center of Charlotte's forehead. He read her eyes and lips clearly before she fell backward in front of him. They seemed to whisper . . .

. . . *Why????*

Justin quickly collected two handguns off the floor near the bodies of Ronnie and Austin. With a foot-sweep, he sent Charlotte's riding crop across the tiles and tarp toward Virginia. "Pick it up," he instructed the woman as she quickly finished getting dressed. "You'll lead us the hell out of here."

Chapter 70

Rarely was Detective Kim Booker invited to a crime scene. Each member of the team had an area of expertise, and Kim's was clearly accessing, analyzing and processing information through a series of sophisticated computers; mainframes like Big Sister, housed internally like she. Today, however, she would accompany Theo. It was time for a breath of fresh air, even if the atmosphere around the back of the old Pierce property in Calverton was already laden with death.

Kim brought along her laptop for added company and peace of mind. The computer maven sat beside the lieutenant in the backseat of a shiny black sedan, speeding east at eighty miles an hour along the Long Island Expressway, crossing from Brookhaven into Riverhead Township.

Immediately after the command post became fully operational and a SWAT team swept the area, several unmarked cars as well as black and whites blew into 112 Sunny Line Drive in Calverton. Two hours later, earthmoving machinery uncovered the graves of Freddie Dupree and Sally Tamblin. Except for a few articles of the serial killer's clothing, along with a collection of both live and mounted snakes, Malcolm Columba was nowhere to be found.

Kim and Theo shook their heads simultaneously, sighed in sheer frustration, and argued at cross-purposes with one another.

"Stop blaming yourself," Theo demanded. "We're not that far behind him now."

"Wrong. He could be out of the country. Sailing the Seven Seas. God only knows where," she said with outright disgust. "Damn my stupidity. Sally Tamblin had roots in Georgia. Right outside of Macon, for Christ's sake. I should have picked up on that piece of information earlier and explored it to the nth degree. It was staring me right in the face. Shit." She kicked a small stone several feet away from Sally Tamblin's freshly exhumed body.

"I said, stop it, Kim! You did a fine job. Their prenup read that she wouldn't collect a dime. That's what put us all off track concerning any involvement."

"Yeah. Not until Evan Tamblin's *natural* death."

"And he's alive and kicking. So stop beating up on yourself."

"Sure, but the man's this close to closing the lid on his own coffin, Theo." She held her thumb and forefinger a fraction of an inch apart. "I just know it. Once he learns that he's been had, that Donald Bellport was completely innocent, that his daughter's death was part of an elaborate scheme put together by his *loving* wife, along with Don Ciccio and his crew, it'll kill him—or he'll wind up killing himself. Mark my words. If we can prove that he paid out big bucks for the revenge killing of an innocent man, not to mention a multimillion dollar contract for Columba's head, our industrialist will be facing some serious jail time. Frankly, I think the truth of Bellport's innocence alone would do him in. He's unstable, Theo. Hanging by a thread. I think Sally knew that, too, and was what she counted on."

Theo shook his head. "I don't think so, Kim. For the simple reason that suicide isn't a *natural* death. How would she collect?"

"She wouldn't, ostensibly. Instead, she'd *control* his business and his fortune. Spend his money where she saw fit. It'd be the next best thing. His daughter was to receive virtually everything in the event of his death. The estate is set up so that if Sally survived Patricia, she'd gain control of his corporations. We're talking billions of dollars. I traced a large cash withdrawal from one of his offshore accounts," she explained. "The paper transfer is in limbo in a bank in Belgium, slated for a holding company owned and operated by Don Ciccio's ex."

Theo smiled. "Which ex? I think I lost count."

"His first. Apparently they agreed on and exchanged a marital partnership for a business relationship. Fifty-fifty. Rumor is she funnels back percentages into his companies as business expenses. All legal. Nice tax benefits, too, from what I understand. Both parties benefit. What I'm seeing here, Theo, is that the mob is out looking for Malcolm Columba, same as us. But as we're looking to serve justice, Ciccio and his crew are looking to line their pockets with a *big* score. Bellport was merely chump change. Malcolm's head on a silver platter would summon forth the gold. And I'm sure Sally's share alone would have proven a tidy sum. I think Ciccio's people were going to furnish us anonymously with proof of Tamblin's involvement in the Bellport murder, putting the screws to him real good. I'm sure Sally figured that if her husband only went to prison instead of taking his life, she'd still gain control. Who knows? What we do know for sure is what she got for all her trouble."

The two of them looked over at Sally Tamblin's bagged body.

"An early grave."

"Amen to that," Kim said with some degree of satisfaction.

"Anything on that I-S-F-C-W-S and A?"

"I'll take a shot," she offered.

"Take it."

"I Stand For Clean Water, Soil and Air."

Theo considered it for a moment. "Good a guess as any. How'd you come up with it?"

"Had a little help," she admitted.

"Big Sister?"

"Actually, Mick and Andrew had a hand."

"Speaking of Detective Miller, I'm getting a bit concerned. I haven't heard a word. And neither has anyone else."

Kim shook her head unknowingly. "Can't help you out there, Theo."

Chapter 71

The trio stealthily made their way down the stairs, then out and around the back of the house, heading toward a new, shiny silver Mercedes. Justin clenched Austin Izzo's keyless-entry remote in his fist as if he were holding onto dear life itself.

"Slow down and walk straight ahead as if you own the place," Justin told Virginia. "And keep that gun pointed at your mother's back. Prod her along with that crop. You look a lot like Charlotte from a distance. If we're approached, you push the safety off like I showed you. You know what to say. If they're armed and continue coming, turn, aim for the center of their bodies, and *squeeze* off rounds till the gun is empty. Even if you miss, they'll scatter. I *won't* miss. I promise you."

"I want a gun, too," Viola said in a low drawl. "We got four," she reminded him. "You got two. You took two more from those dead men. Virginia got one. So you give me the other," the old woman insisted.

"Behave yourself and just keep walking toward that silver car," Justin instructed.

"Think I'm gonna shoot myself in the foot, don't you?" Viola complained.

"How do you know that's his car?" Virginia questioned, stopping and staring at the eighty thousand dollar Mercedes parked in the lot a good fifty yards ahead of them.

"This was in his pocket," Justin explained, displaying the dead man's door opener. "See? Mercedes symbol. That's his car in the corner. Now, let's move."

"What about that one over there?" she questioned, gesturing toward another Mercedes parked in a distant lot to the left of them.

Justin stopped dead in his tracks, turned obliquely and looked at the adjacent lot. "Shit."

"Head toward that one," Viola ordered.

"Which one?" Justin asked in confusion.

"The green one. Out there."

"Why?"

"More his color; earth tone, like his clothes. The green one's his."

"Izzo's?"

"Yep," the old woman answered with assurance.

"What were they driving when they snatched you?" Justin snapped.

Virginia pointed. "That Chevy wagon right there. Belongs to the foreman. Charlotte took the keys with her."

"Well, we sure as hell ain't goin' back to that house. Still, I think the silver-gray one is his," Justin proffered, weighed and wondered, although really quite unsure, pointing and pressing the remote toward the two Mercedes, neither of which unlocked the doors at their overwhelming distances. "I don't want us headin' into that open area if we don't have to. Besides, the color green's more for girls and flashy niggers," Justin concluded in frustration.

But the old woman stood her ground. "Dark beige shirt and brown suede jacket; tan trousers and chocolate brown shoes. Goes with that light green Mercedes coupe. Trust me. Those are his colors, and that's his car," she persisted. "Silver Mercedes's hers."

"So what the fuck did you two tool and pal around in?" he asked Virginia directly.

"SUV. Range Rover."

"Swell. Well, we just can't stand here arguing forever," Justin said decidedly, heading toward the silver four-door.

Viola refused to take another step, pointing to her daughter's borrowed outfit. "Black buckskin jacket; black pants and boots with silver buckles go with that silver four-door sedan. The silver one's Charlotte's," she insisted. "Or was. Big machine to match her ego. Key thing you're holdin' ain't gonna open or start her car, Justin Barnes."

In the old days, Justin could have ripped off *any* vehicle in less than two minutes. But this was a new era. The age of high-tech. This was not the Nicholas Cage movie, *Gone in Sixty Seconds*, either.

This was do or die.

"Green it is then, Viola," he conceded. "Let's go, girls. Thataway."

The three of them turned and headed toward the sage-green Mercedes coupe parked alone in the middle of the far lot.

Sitting ducks was all that Justin could think of as they left the relative safety of the bushes and tall trees that had concealed them to a degree.

"Ms. Magni! Jerome!" a woman's voice rang out.

It was Carol, waddling toward them like a penguin—the woman honcho who had brought Justin to the foreman.

"Later," Virginia managed, raising the handgun to her mother's head, glancing over her shoulder at the heavyset woman with short legs.

Carol was still coming toward the three of them.

"We's gots to take da ol' woman fo' a ride," Justin hollered. "Be right back," he said, walking backwards before facing about, heading toward the coupe.

"Well, where's the fucking daughter? Where's Mr. Izzo?" Carol demanded, closing the distance between them. "Say, wait a second. That's not—"

Virginia spun around and waved the gun in Carol's direction. "Here's the fucking daughter. Now, back up bitch before I fuck you up real good!" Virginia screamed. "Stay the hell away from us!" she shouted while shedding a bucketful of tears.

"Jesus H. Christ," Carol said, picking up the pace, heading straight toward them as quickly as the woman's short, thick legs could carry her hefty upper body weight. "You're not Charlotte Magni."

"NO!" Justin shouted as Virginia unlocked the safety and leveled the gun at the center of Carol's body.

A sharp report sounded throughout the area as the stocky woman took a bullet in the chest. And then another. Four more tore through her shoulder, stomach and neck. A near miss nicked the side of her head as she dropped dead before them.

Back at the house, two faces appeared in each corner of a kitchen window: Danny's and the foreman's.

Justin, Virginia and Viola moved quickly toward the coupe.

Danny was on the phone with security in seconds.

Gino's cheek rested solidly against a highly-polished rifle stock, locked securely in the man's shoulder, his forearm supported by the windowsill. His right eye aligned the cross hairs of the telescopic sight with the moving target—leading the body by half a foot. The foreman touched off a round, and Justin heard the *thwack*.

Viola took the bullet in her back from a hundred fifty yards away. The old woman went down on her knees as she reached the curb.

"Oh, my God!" Virginia screamed. "Oh, my God—Noooo."

"Yes!" Gino grinned as he slapped the bolt up and back. Ejecting the spent cartridge. Slamming another round into the chamber.

Justin and Virginia were at the woman's side. Pulling her off the pavement and back toward the trees.

"Stay low," Justin commanded.

A lead missile whizzed past the top of Justin's left shoulder.

"Missed, 'cause Monisha's on my right, you motherfucker," Barnes mocked quietly, pushing Virginia down.

Another bullet hit the surface and ricocheted.

Virginia was moaning and holding her mother tightly.

Justin moved the two of them out of the line of fire, behind a giant red leaf maple. He put three fingers against the old woman's neck and slowly shook his head.

"NOOOOoooo," Virginia groaned, burying her head in her mother's bosom. "Dear God, no."

A massive hand clamped down on Virginia's nape.

"Get up. We gotta go," Justin ordered.

Virginia shook her head in a series of shivers.

Justin stood her up roughly and smacked her mask-like face.

"I said, we gotta go. She's dead. We'll come back for her." He spun her around abruptly and harshly to the right. "See that tree line over there?" Justin did not wait for an answer. "On the count of three, we go. Three!"

And the two were off and running for their lives.

Two shots rang out over the next four seconds: a near miss and a streak of lead that grazed Justin's left leg just as they made it into an island of trees that bordered the second parking lot.

"All right, now." Justin caught his breath. "Hold onto these." He handed over two weapons, then reloaded the one she had emptied into Carol. "Here. I'm going for the car. You stay put."

Virginia wailed. "No, don't leave me!"

For all her trouble, she received another slap in the face. Only, harder this time.

"Now, I want you to quit your fuckin' bawlin'. Understand?"

Virginia nodded and quickly wiped away her tears with a hand full of hardware.

"I'm not gonna leave you unless you don't do as you're told."

"You're bleeding," she said, looking down at the ground, then toward the top of his bloody leg.

He took her by the shoulders and shook her hard. "It's nothing. Pay attention. You stay right here while I get the fucking car."

"Why can't I come with you?"

"Because you don't know how to run."

And with that explanation, he released her and was off and running, zigzagging his way toward the green Mercedes.

One shot flew inches past his upper body. Another creased his trousers just as he reached the car.

Gino was out of the ranch house and shooting wildly, making his way toward the lot.

"You there, Monisha? I need you now, girl. Mean motherfucker's gonna take us out if I don't move fast."

Justin pushed the left button on the triangular black remote. Nothing. Again. Same result. "Shit." Next, he hit the button to the right. The trunk flew open. "Motherfucker," he managed, slamming the trunk lid shut. Finally, he gnashed the button at its tip. *Click.* The locks snapped closed—closed because they had been open in the first place. Justin hit the button once again. The locks snapped up, like his heart into his throat.

"Thank you, Viola Johnson. Monisha Washington, I'm still waitin' fo' a fuckin' miracle, woman. Don't let me down."

Justin climbed into the coupe, kept his head low, then started up the mean green machine as a bullet crashed through the windshield, creating a web-like world before him.

Keeping down, Justin slammed the shift into reverse and spun the car around wildly.

Another bullet took out a rear tire. Then the other.

"I'm in a world of shit out here, Monisha. I'm doin' this fo' you as much as fo' me, girl. So, help me out here if yo' hearin' me. All right?"

"All right," a voice answered.

Justin whirled around as a fourth bullet splintered the rear window and continued through the passenger side windshield.

"Keep your head down, jerk, if you want to keep it at all," Miller barked from the backseat.

"Miller?"

"No, your mother."

"Jesus fucking Christ, Andy. What the fuck you doin' here?"

"Watching your black ass from the moment we left Viola Johnson back in Shirley."

"Well, you're not doing a very good job, Andrew. Where are the police? Where's your backup, buddy? Don't you watch any fucking cop shows or movies? Even John Wayne knows when to call in the cavalry, sucker. Where's your cell phone?"

"Can't do that, partner."

"Oh, now I'm your fucking partner again."

A sudden thud took out the right front tire, and the coupe sank several inches, like a cripple dropping to one knee.

"Mother*fucker*." Justin put the car in forward gear and hit the gas. The coupe sprawled forward in a spin. "Shit."

"Where the fuck you going?" Miller snapped.

"I got Virginia Dupree back there. Her mother's dead." Justin tromped down on the accelerator once more; the car screeched and bucked forward like a wagon with half a wheel, heading bumpily toward the tree line—when suddenly he saw Virginia in the distance, running for her life.

"Stop this fucking car now!" Miller commanded.

"Well, that's easy, *partner*." Justin hit the brakes hard, and Miller went flying forward.

"Now, you listen to me, and you listen up real good," Miller thundered, raising himself to the seat.

"No, you listen! I'm a civilian, motherfucker," Justin reminded the man. "You done fired my ass. You. Remember? I be *un*deputized. Recall?" The maverick adjusted the remote side mirror to keep his assailant in view.

The foreman was in the first tree line, nestled against a birch.

"Shit." Justin worried for Virginia's safety.

"Listen to me. In a matter of minutes, security is going to be on us like stink on shit," Andrew said angrily. "Now. They don't know I'm here. Just you. And we're going to use that to our advantage."

"How?"

"You're going to surrender."

"Am like hell."

"Take a peek back here. But keep your head down."

Justin glanced behind the seats and saw a Heckler & Koch submachine gun on the floor. He looked up and spied a vehicle coming toward them in the distance. Several figures sprinted behind it.

"They got themselves a big-ass truck back there," Justin said unhappily, feeling about as deflated as the tires beneath him. "Three hundred yards and closing in. Gotta be six or seven warm bodies, hot to trot."

"Gonna listen, now?"

"I ain't surrendering. They'll cut me down the second I step outta here. I just took out three of Ciccio's soldiers. They were gonna shoot Virginia and her mother. I wasted the triggerman, Charlotte and Austin. Virginia panicked and killed an unarmed broad."

"They won't shoot you if you tell them what I tell you to say."

"Oh, yeah? Can I get that in writing, chump?"

"Sure. I'm gonna write their epitaph across their bodies as they step forward."

"Really?" Justin smirked.

"Really. What are you packin' there, junior?" Miller mocked.

"AMT Backup and a Taurus Millennium. 9-millimeters. Two full clips each."

"Street junk, Justin. You'll throw them out one at a time when they tell you to."

"Say what?"

"I'll dispose of them later. Meanwhile, I'm gonna cut those bastards to ribbons with this." Miller's H & K MP5 / 10-mm was set for full automatic. "Two magazines. On top of that, I got two SIG SAUER Classic pistols for backup. You'll surrender yourself and both your guns."

"*Fuck* I will. And what *about* backup? Theo or anybody know we're here?"

"Just you and me, partner. Didn't tell a soul."

"Now, that was fuckin' dumb. You're supposed to be so fuckin' smart. What gives?"

"They got a couple moles in their midst. A snitch. A traitor in their ranks."

"Who's they?"

"Suffolk boys and NYPD's finest. They got a pipeline into Theo's pact. Hindering the Columba investigation from the start."

"Who? Why?"

"Don't know yet, but I will."

"How do I know that mole ain't you?"

"Because I don't belong to either side."

"Whatchoo mean?"

"I'm FBI. Special Agent Andrew Miller. Out of the Savanna office."

"Yeah, right. I already did the dress rehearsal with Viola Johnson. Recall?"

"I am, Justin. For real. If I had called this into Theo, or the locals up here, I'd be dead by now. You're practically history unless you listen to me carefully."

Justin thought hard. "Ciccio's woman said she had a few FBI men in her corner, Andy."

"If I were one of the renegades, I'd 'ave put a bullet in your brain the second you stepped into this car."

Justin stole another peek just above the line of fire. "Christ."

"What?"

"They got another vehicle comin' up on us fast."

"So's our funeral if you don't listen up."

"What do I gotta say?"

"You had orders from Don Ciccio to waste Charlotte Magni, Austin Izzo, and any witnesses to the act. That will give you an excuse for taking out their triggermen."

"What about Viola and Virginia?"

"You were to bring them back alive."

"Back where?"

"To Don Ciccio."

"Why?"

"Soldiers don't ask questions. They simply follow orders. That's your answer, if it even gets that far."

"And then?"

"And then they're dead meat."

The two of them heard several doors open and slam shut.

"Hey, nigger. Game's over."

It was Gino, the foreman. The one who hired and fired him up.

"Yo, whitey. Whatchoo want, motherfucker?"

Gino laughed like a hyena. "Your motherfuckin' black ass, cocksucker. You got ten seconds to come outta there with your hands up. High over your steel wool pad."

"Got a message fo' you, Mr. Fo'man. Don Ciccio is real pissed and hired me to take out two double-crossers. The kid just got in the way. Vincent's gonna be real upset that you took out the mother, asshole, 'cause I was suppose' to bring 'em both back alive. The mother fo' a chitchat. The daughter fo' a *ho*edown. Know what a hoedown be in the figurative sense, prick-face?"

"Yeah, I know what a hoedown is, you hillbilly coon."

"Don't think ya do, stable breath."

"Your ten seconds are up, dickweed. Out! Now!"

Justin sat up in his seat and laced his hands on top of his head where they could clearly be seen, slowly pushing open the car door with a bloody foot. A half a dozen handguns were trained on his upper body. Two men from the second vehicle stood ready.

Gino's Weatherby was aimed at Justin's head. "Give it up, sambo. By the barrel. Nice and easy."

Justin handled the AMT 9-millimeter by its muzzle, dropping it to the ground.

"Now the other," the foreman ordered.

"Ain't got no other weapon, bossman," Justin drawled.

"A hit man totin' one gun? I don't think so, spear-chucker. Let's have it. Or you're fuckin' dead."

"The *ho* has it." Justin gestured in the general direction of the trees, figuring and praying that Virginia was clear of the area by now, hoping she was holed up safely for the time being. "Jus' put a bullet in my head and be done with it so that Vincent can really ram it up yo' ass. The *big* bossman can't 'ave no *ho*edown, nohow, without no *ho*; now can he, Gino? And now that Charlotte's gone . . . well, he told me Virginia's the best piece of ass that money can buy and that he'd make me a present when he got finished with her for all the trouble she caused," he concluded, abandoning his 'dumb nigger' routine in exchange for the king's English, along with nerves of solid steel.

Justin was out of the car and standing tall before the group of deadly men—his hands back on top of his head.

"I said hands *high* over your head, Mau Mau."

"All of them as prejudiced as you, Gino? See, when Vincent gets here, oh, say in about an hour, maybe less, he's gonna kick some butt. He's gonna kick yours especially hard when I tell him some of the things you said. 'Cause guess who's comin' to dinner, too, white boy. No, not Sidney Poitier. But me! That's who," Justin claimed with a wide, white smile. "I'm supposed to meet him at the docks in Bridgeport, then ride back up here. He told me we were havin' fettuccine with butter-and-sausage sauce. His favorite. Call him and see."

Gino's eyes seemed to widen as he slowly lowered his rifle. The foreman stood nonplused. He really was not sure.

"Lower your fucking weapons," Gino ordered everyone.

Six security figures pointed their weapons toward the ground as they were told, moving forward cautiously behind and alongside Gino.

The foreman took out his cell phone to call the don for confirmation.

"Oh, lookie! Here comes Danny boy with his tail between his legs," Justin said distractively.

The cook came out of hiding, believing everything was under control.

Three security guards faced obliquely as Danny came loping along. The other three, along with Gino, had their eyes set dead ahead as Agent Andrew Miller suddenly came up firing long bursts from a short yet menacing weapon—first, laterally across the middle of their bodies, then back again—working his way higher, catching them fully in the chest and neck and head.

Justin made a grab for the AMT, coming forward fast and furiously with the Taurus holstered at his back, sending several bullets into the bodies of two men—the first who foolishly rushed forward— while the second turned to flee.

Danny was down on the ground with hands and arms wrapped protectively around his head, screaming bloody murder as the slaughter came to a standstill. "I'm only the cook," Danny blubbered as Agent Miller handcuffed him and pulled him to his feet. "Tell him, Jerome. I'm the one you spoke to earlier in the kitchen. Remember? I'm the one who told you what we were having for dinner when you asked. Tell him." Danny wept bitterly. "Tell him!"

"Book 'im, Andrew," Justin quipped satisfactorily. "Maybe we can turn him over to the Board of Health or something," he joked joyously, happy to be alive, moving from body to body—making sure all the bad guys were doubtlessly dead.

Chapter 72

The sun was setting at the end of East Point in Rampasture. The wealthy Eyler family would not be moving into their new twenty-two room waterfront mansion until the end of the month. Malcolm Columba was busy preparing a cozy spot for Evan Tamblin, within the claustrophobic crawlspace, amidst the plumbing and wiring. The plumbing fed an enormous kitchen in addition to ten-and-a-half tastefully tiled bathrooms: showers, sinks, tubs, basins and a sole bidet. The wiring and tubing heated, cooled, lit, dimmed or darkened the private world in and around a spectacular 360 degree water vista, encompassing Smith Creek, Tiana and Shinnecock Bays—situated on the East End of Long Island's south shore.

From *any* room within the imposing residence, owners and guests would be afforded a most magnificent view of the water. It was the perfect place to lay Evan Tamblin to rest, Malcolm smiled. He was very, very pleased with his selection. The carpenters were certain to return after the weekend to complete the decking surrounding the home. The electrician's crew had pretty much finished the work they had to do. Most likely, it would be the two plumbers who would soon discover the CEO's body, for the men were running a bit behind schedule and would surely return to the crawlspace first thing Monday morning. Malcolm had literally bumped into the pair earlier in the week—the three of them chatting for a spell—flat on their backs on flatbed carts set upon pneumatic wheels, as the two brothers happened by unexpectedly one afternoon.

Fortunately, for Malcolm, he was able to pass himself off to the plumbers as the building foreman's nephew, who had purportedly been given permission for a peek around the place. Malcolm almost made the mistake of claiming to be an inspector, but figured that most of the work crew knew everyone connected with the job. At least by face. Luckily, too, the impostor was covered with soot, casually explaining that he had just come off a job cleaning out a chimney and fireplace that morning. A true enough story in part, for it was in a blackened chimney that he had ensconced the executive, gagged and bound within a carpet, standing upright inside a huge outdoor fireplace/barbecue pit located in a nearby park's playing field.

With more than a degree of admiration, Malcolm had complimented both brothers on their fine craftsmanship, which was not an exaggeration by any stretch, because the men's installation was sheer artistry—the solder work alone having been carefully applied and meticulously brushed along the copper pipes at each joint with the precision of a portrait painter. Malcolm appreciated perfection. He could only hope that the authorities would appreciate the attempt of *his* workmanship as well. However rude.

Malcolm Columba and Evan Tamblin shared a corner within the four-foot high crawlspace. No more than half a foot of clearance remained above the killer's head. He sat placidly on his own cart, alongside the naked soul strapped flat on his back upon the narrow steel platform. Its six-inch wheels were securely locked in place, for the man was not going anywhere. The terrified figure lay motionless. Dirty and sooty. Frightened beyond comprehension. Tamblin knew that he was going to die a most horrible death. The mere grasp of his hopeless situation sent the man's heart into overdrive.

"Imagine, Evan! Just imagine how Donald Bellport must have felt. How many hours was it before Don Ciccio's people put him out of his misery? I tried to intervene. Innocence never knew such cruelty. Maybe Satan will deduct the time you spend with me from your eternity in hell," he offered as a comforting acknowledgment toward sin itself.

Malcolm had never witnessed such a display of mixed emotions from any of his victims, so he savored and nurtured Evan Tamblin's every plea and promise, knowing full well that those precious moments would not last forever. The author began by reading excerpts from his massive manuscript, starting with Noreen Walker, then working his way through Wendy Anne Linden's murder—the young woman he had killed with kindness and then the cold—shortly before drowning Evan's darling daughter, Patricia.

Next, he read a page he scribed from the industrialist's industrious life. He read quietly and deliberately from the thick journal, while Evan stared vacantly at the overhead, refusing to listen to the madman's account.

Malcolm read on:

"And so, when Patricia Tamblin was born into the world, the planet stopped spinning on its axis and ceased its orbit around the Sun. From that moment forward, the sphere, known as mother earth, radiated a new energy from within. The man who thought himself a master of the universe, put his own spin upon the natural order of the cosmos. With unabashed pride, the corporate giant emitted what he believed to be a brighter light than the light that lit the heavens, challenging the very center of the solar system: its fixed and brightest star; his fiercest competition. In short order, the very Sun hung its downcast face in shadows, whilst the industrialist greedily gobbled up the whole of all he surveyed, bathing in profits amassed from mergers and acquisitions, universal takeovers, conglomerates cradling and lulling infant enterprises . . . before extinguishing the breath of babes."

Malcolm paused, lifted the prodigious tome, and shooed a daddy-longlegs away. "And *now* look at you, Evan. You're as poor as the most ragged beggar found in any ghetto or slum in corporate America. Bargaining shamelessly for the darkness because you know the light is very low. Haggling when you should be listening closely so that you'll understand exactly how you got yourself into the fix you're in. Then, when you meet your Maker, you'll be able to explain it all without tripping over your tongue. For example, how you wanted to pay certain people millions for my remnants like you paid out tens of thousands for proof of Donald Bellport's remains." Malcolm stroked one forefinger against the other. "Shame, shame, shame, Evan.

"And like a self-deluding slave master, you say to me, 'But look at the thousands of people I put to work, Malcolm.'" Malcolm laughed. "Refusing to listen to me unless I insist, time and time again. Big shot. The man who consumes five thousand dollar bottles of wine. Five thousand dollars, Evan! That's more than a thousand dollars a glass. You have the gall to swill such drink. You have the guile to pollute the planet and pretend that you are God's gift to commerce. With the law behind you. The law that your bloody body of legal eagles bend as easily as one's knee. I see right through you, Evan. *You're* evil personified. That's why your precious daughter, Patricia, had to die. I never killed *any* of you luminaries before this day, Evan.

Instead, I allow your kind to suffer through their natural but miserable little lives. But you're so different from the rest, Evan. *You* had the gumption to come after *me*. Actually, you had the *resources*, you lucky devil, you," Malcolm tormented the man.

"Please," Evan Tamblin swallowed dryly. "Please."

"*Please*, he says. How positively mundane. You so disappoint me, Evan. From a man of your magnitude, I'd have expected lofty threats or pledges lasting through the night. Promises both positive and negative of a kingly kind. Not a whiny, *please*. You gave up so easily, E.T. As alien as that might sound to others," the madman goaded. "But it's all recorded right here." Malcolm tapped the journal.

"I'll give you anything you want," Evan said halfheartedly, knowing the futility of his situation.

"In exchange for what?"

"For end-*ending* this right *now*," Evan Tamblin choked.

Malcolm smiled benignly. "I'll tell you what." He paused for the full effect. "You listen to exactly how I killed your daughter," the writer declared, holding up the heavy bound book. "Every detail. Her gruesome chapter is but a mere twenty pages. And at the end, I'll pull the plug. How's that? I need to know—and see—if I truly broke your heart."

Evan Tamblin prayed he would have a massive stroke, but God was not in a charitable mood that morning. "You're a very bright but disturbed young man, Malcolm Columba," Evan offered weakly. "My people trusted you, putting you in touch with giants of industry for the betterment of mankind—not for your perverted misdirected goals. Had I only known it was you beforehand—you malcontent. What could have happened in your miserable life that brought you to do these things you do to people? That's what I'd like to hear about. I have the power to save you from the death penalty; to have you committed, instead, to a mental hospital where you could get the help you need."

"Think they'd cure me, Evan?" Malcolm questioned with a grisly grin. "Then they'd have to let me go. That's the law. Isn't that a rip? It's the very point Diane Nash maintained in order to save her own hide. Poor dear."

The naked man said nothing.

"Are you so powerful as to get those who'd be assigned to me to say that I'd never ever do anything like this again? The psychiatrists, I mean. Maybe they'd let me out in twenty years. It happens, you know. I'd be a year shy of fifty if we got started right away," he offered mischievously. "Think I'd stand a chance?"

"Anything's possible," Evan answered hopelessly.

"So, how come you didn't want to help me like this before you put a price on my head? Suddenly have a change of heart?"

Evan turned silent once again.

"I see. How about I tell you a few things that made me quite *mad* over the course of years. I mean, aside from the serious pollution of our planet. It started with little things, Evan. You might not even understand how they could bother me so. But those molehills eventually manifested themselves into mountains. Like a young person spitting on a sidewalk, for example. Or a sweet old lady littering in the park. Then there are those who refuse to clean up after their dogs. I'd even take the trouble to show them how to put the feces in a plastic bag and turn it inside out so they shouldn't get their hands all shitty. All to no avail. There are disgusting people out there, Evan. Cities disgust me. Garbage along the shoreline positively drives me nuts. I go ballistic when people in authority, who are supposed to police such action, turn their backs. Those are just some of the *little* things.

"Imagine how angry I become when companies and corporations dump toxic chemicals into our waters, ignoring both the law and a sense of public responsibility—depositing huge profits into their personal accounts—yet are held unaccountable for those dastardly deeds. Then, when occasionally cited, they're slapped with a mere pittance of a fine in the final *scheme* of things. I go wacko, Evan. Just imagine how enraged I become when industry releases carcinogens into our atmosphere. Into the very air we breathe! The world has become a cesspool, fella. Below its canopy and beneath our rivers and seas." Malcolm took a meaningful breath. "You know that I know just how successful your corporate lawyers are in burying the bulk of all those summonses and lawsuits. It's unarguably criminal, Evan."

Evan scrunched a tightening muscle between his neck and shoulder. He could barely move.

"So. Are you going to listen while I read of Patricia's demise? It was really quite extraordinary. She fought very hard for each and every breath. Finally, drowning in her own diluted tears by adding to the level of the bath water, would you believe?" the madman pressed. "There just wasn't enough strength left in her frail body to break the line or wire, poor wretch."

Evan Tamblin's chest rose and fell involuntarily. "I'm so sorry."

"*Please* and *sorry*. Sorry that you're here? Or sorry for your deeds?"

"Sorry f-for ev-erything." He coughed and wept. "Sorry for what you did to my little girl. Sorry you're so sick and twisted."

"And I'm sorry, too, Evan. Sorry that you're not getting it." Malcolm slowly shook his head before launching into song. "*Sor-ry. Sor-ry. Sor-eeee. I didn't meeean to make you cry. Let's make a-mends, after all, we're more than frien-en-en-en-ends.* Of course, we're really not friends, E.T. We're actually fiends. Both you and I. Only you, and others like you, made me what I am. Not the other way around. I didn't make you what you are. But I'm going to tell you something right here and now. I'm doing you a favor by killing you for the simple reason that you will no longer suffer Patricia's death. I know how it eats at you like a cancer. So, in just a little while, I'll operate. But first the reading. All right?"

Chapter 73

Wearing a knitted camo cap, Malcolm sat upright on the cart, his head but several inches below the overhead. He reached for the can of insect repellent, spraying the front and back of his hands, applying the chemical to his neck and face as well.

"See what you've subjected me to, Evan? You ought to be ashamed."

Four wide canvas straps encircling Evan's body secured the industrialist to the cart next to Malcolm's. Evan stared blankly at the shallow ceiling, serving as a panoramic canopy to his open-sided coffin. Eight thousand square feet of virtually dead space surrounded the two of them. Nine blow-in type storm windows off to the southeast corner, facing East Point, dimly lit the crawlspace. The special windows were installed to protect the home's foundation in case of severe flooding arising from hurricane force winds should the waters build across the creek or bays or both. Evan could no longer see the outside world through the filmy tempered glass. Not clearly, anyhow. There were no pairs of work boots parading back and forth like he had seen earlier, nor the men's long-handled aluminum landscaper rakes with which to spread and level the gravel bed for the spacious circular drive. No longer did he see the endless rotation of man-size dull-black rubber wheels moving along the perimeter, nor hear the eruption of heavy machinery crawling past those windows—not after Saturday's skeleton crew had left suddenly. All he could see now was the mud and grime that had splashed and collected upon the panes shortly after the torrential downpour.

The morning remained as still and as silent as Evan's impending death. Even the songbirds were absent from the scene.

Malcolm looked over at the mosquito bitten man lying on the cart a foot away. Marked by a million big and tiny bites.

"Now, this is what I call an *open* casket," the sadistic killer deadpanned, exhibiting the plastered-on-puss of a practiced mortician. "Be funny if you died of the West Nile virus before I had a chance to properly say goodbye," he added mercurially, curling up the corners of his mouth in a sickening grin.

Evan could not have commented if he wanted to, in that his mouth was sealed shut with broad strips of duct tape. Gray and as telling as the gun-metal sky itself.

"A perfect morning for a funeral, chief." Malcolm smashed a mosquito on the back of his neck. "Overcast. God will not smile down on you today, Mr. Evan A. Tamblin; born 1938; soon to die on this cloudy day in May, year 2000. My only prayer is that the owners of this mansion have flood insurance at this Point. East Point, if you'll pardon the pun. I don't know if you have any idea the damage that water can do to a home. I'm glad the man's a multimillionaire. Not quite as wealthy as you, Evan. But he never did anything to hurt the environment. As a matter of fact, he not only complied with all the rules and regulations in building this magnificent home, but he saw potential problems and, without anyone having to tell him, spent an extra million on protecting the beach from erosion by planting precious grasses and putting in additional bulkheading. Hence, the aquatic creatures that inhabit the shoreline will have a happy home. He actually second-guessed the DEC, the Army Corps of Engineers, and the town. He's my hero, Evan. I wouldn't harm one hair on his family's head. Therefore, it's not the loss of any monies he'll incur that bothers me, so much as it is the cost of inconvenience—because the Eylers have to be out of their old home shortly. Where will he and his family go, Evan?" The killer raised his eyebrows. "I guess maybe they'll just have to live out of the second story. Oh, well."

On his back, with hacksaw in hand, Malcolm wheeled himself over to one of three main valves, then began cutting a copper pipe just beneath the juncture. The new blue blade immediately scored and marked the beginning of the ceremony.

Black-green flies buzzed around the middle of Evan's naked body where the corporate giant had unavoidably defecated and urinated upon the steel cart.

Water from the severed pipe quickly entered the space.

Malcolm was halfway through a second tube. "Of course, I could accomplish the same thing by turning a few of these valves. See?" Malcolm flashed his penlight across a section of the plumber's chase. "But now there's positively no *turning* back," he taunted.

"Oh, I've just got to tell you all about this house before I go, Evan. Sorry you didn't get to see it for yourself. It's not to be believed. Man knows how to spend his money. Thick, solid oak floors. The construction crew had to put on special paper booties at the entrances so as not to track in dirt or mar the wood. Next, imagine riding an elevator to the second floor." Malcolm raised his eyes. "For luggage and stuff like that, I suppose. But let me walk you through it, so to speak. Okay? A little tour through the first floor first; and then the second. Maybe around the grounds if we have time. Vicariously, of course.

"We'll start at the point where I carried you in from the side entrance. You bumped your head. Hard. I'm sure you remember that. Anyhow, the laundry room is off to the left. A wine closet to the right. Nothing elaborate, mind you. Room for one hundred fifty-two bottles. A curious number, to be sure. Well, I wasn't—sure, that is. So, I counted the spaces again. Thirty-two, top left. Ninety-two below that. And when you face about, there's another fourteen off to each side, for a grand total of one hundred and fifty-two bottles of wine. Of course, the racks are empty now. But I'll wager that family would never fill them with five thousand dollar bottles of wine. Ever! Last I looked, you had an even dozen bottles of Chateau Chevel Blanc, 1947, in your cellar. Five thousand dollars a crack. Sixty thousand dollars for those dozen bottles alone. That goes way past *ostentatious*, Evan. *Obscene*, is all I can think to say."

Water was rushing steadily from two of the two-inch copper pipes, gushing upon the concrete floor, covering the soles of Malcolm's rubber boots, licking the wheels of both their weighty, narrow platforms. Platforms unlike the buoyant craft in which he had kidnapped and placed Evan Tamblin—the two of them cruising the North and South Fork waters from South Jamesport to Rampasture. *Certainly not the seaworthy craft Sally Tamblin had ordered for her captain and never got to use,* Malcolm mused, before continuing the so-called tour.

"Bathroom, next. Then a large pantry with two separate entrances before you step into the kitchen. And what a kitchen, Evan. With a commercial six burner stove: four off to one side, two on the other, and a grill between them. A wall oven. Stainless steel sinks with an 'out-of-sight shelf' to hide sponges and such. Corian countertops. A microwave. Two big stainless steel drawers for keeping food warm." Malcolm waved away a persistent fly and smacked the back of his hand on the overhead. "Bastard. And instead of all those ugly visible appliances you see in virtually every home, everything is built-in and covered in wood. Cherry. With matching cabinets lined in maple, I think."

A sudden sound sent shivers up and down Malcolm's spine. For Evan, it was the announcement of hope. But the noise was nothing more than a sump pump kicking on that Malcolm had not unplugged.

Malcolm hid his anger at the oversight. "Be right back, buddy." He laid flat upon the cart, then wheeled himself rapidly away through the ascending water, heading over to a far dark corner of the foundation, moving and steering the cart with oar-like sweeping feet.

Less than a minute later, the pump stopped.

Evan wished it was his own heart that had ceased.

Malcolm hurried back in reverse.

"I think we were heading for the formal dining room. Yes. Seating for fourteen. Done up in dark blue." Malcolm spoke anxiously. "Off to the side, a beautiful refurbished safe. On first glance, you'd think it was a serving piece." He shook his head knowingly. "A steel repository for money, jewels and important papers. Good thing I'm not a thief, Evan. I even know where the tumbler is. But I'll never tell a soul. Let's see, now. Ah, yes. Another dining room. Antique table and ten chairs brought over from Italy. Wood and floral fabric. More to my liking. And my favorite piece? A counting table. Very old. Ever see one? Round. Waist high. Thirteen pie-shaped—alphabetically lettered in pairs, of course—sections. A through Z. Used by landlords to account for and collect their tenants' monthly rent.

"Seventeenth and eighteenth century fireplaces shipped over from Ireland and Italy. Three hearths and chimneys in all. I wouldn't be surprised if one of them had *Angela's Ashes* on the mantel," he joked joyously. "Be thankful I don't cremate and stick you in an urn for all eternity." Malcolm killed another mosquito. "Little bastards just won't quit. Oh, the one fireplace has bunches of beautifully hand painted grapes bordering its jet-black top and sides. And get this. High above the entryway, there's a crystal chandelier that you can raise and lower with a key, hung from a beautiful vaulted ceiling. The chandelier, not the key, Evan, lest you accuse me of a misplaced modifier." The author chuckled. "I toyed with the idea of suspending you from it, but I didn't want to shock the missis when she first walked in. Could you just imagine?"

The stream of water was ankle-deep as Malcolm sat back up. The carts' wheels were practically covered.

"Pocket doors separate a game room from a twelve-seat movie theater. Cushioned in red velvet. Off to the right, an antique pool table holds stage center. A bedroom for the handicapped, thereabouts—with bath. And every bedroom has a bathroom surrounded in expensive, imported tile. What else can I tell you before we head upstairs? Oh, yes. The hallways have niches and recessed cabinets for displaying *objets d'art*. As a matter of fact, the couple just brought over a magnificent shell collection that they're beginning to showcase in the hallway. Several hundred shells, I'd say. All carefully wrapped and carted over in pillow cases, would you believe. Real down-to-earth-folks. Truly not pretentious. I'll bet she even bought her expensive linens during a white sale. Ah, the hardware on all the doors is ornate: gilded gold hinges, doorknobs and keyholes set in fair-sized rectangular plates."

Malcolm looked at his captive with a bit of irritation. "You know, I can't tell whether you're lying there in total fascination or just plain fright." He rolled the cart back a bit, reached for the hacksaw, then cut completely through a third and final copper pipe. There were additional pipes he could have cut, but there was no need to now, for the space was filling up very quickly. The water was rising to the top of the two carts.

"I think I better run us through the upstairs. And fast, fella."

Evan Tamblin seemed to be studying a length of black overhead pipe.

"The plumbers call that a future, Evan. Hooked up to nothing at all. It's just there for a future date. You don't have a future, mister." Malcolm smiled maniacally.

The cold water actually felt sensational against the prisoner's back. He would have given a cool billion in a hot second if he could have turned completely around to immerse his insect-bitten body. And in the bargain, the seemingly facedown folly would have ensured a quicker death—as if anything really mattered anymore, Tamblin entertained. *Nothing* was of consequence any longer. Patricia would be there to greet him on the other side, he wished to believe. Or, would he go straight to hell as Malcolm had assured him he would? His body burned and ached and itched severely. His face was entirely swollen. The eyes, moist and puffy. A sweaty hairy chest and pubic area proved a veritable nest; a haven for anything minuscule that flew, then vanished . . . mosquitoes and gnats especially . . . venturing in from the beach but a hundred and fifty yards away . . . first, mercilessly attacking his torso, legs, and toes, too. It was amazing to him that his brain still functioned with some sense of sanity. It was *normal* to want to die immediately, if not sooner. *Wasn't it?* he wondered. It was certainly right to curse God and all creation for giving him the exemplary life he led, and then to suddenly snatch it away via a madman of His own making. *Correct?* He would give everything he owned on the planet to know the reason *why*. Why God did these things.

"Off the other staircase, the man has his office."

Malcolm's tongue was really racing now. Words shot out of the author's mouth like flying lead.

The sounding water played along the edge of Evan's ears.

"Bedrooms and baths for the grandchildren. Around a border of the boys' bathroom are tiles spaced every so often with salamanders, frogs, lizards, dragonflies, one monarch butterfly—along with some other creatures I'm really not sure of. Maybe a toad or two. The girls' bathroom is tiled in light yellow and blue. And then there's a baby's room. An exercise room with a large mirror. I noticed that I've aged a bit in preparing myself for you. You? You look a fright."

Evan could barely hear the killer's voice . . . he struggled mightily against the straps that bound his body tightly . . . so strange to him as to why he even bothered.

"The other end of the upstairs is set aside entirely for the masters of the mansion. Closets within closets for all Mrs. Eyler's clothes and shoes. Salvatore Ferragamo; 7 ½ B, according to the shoeboxes in the master bedroom. A sitting room off to the side. And this you'll love, Evan. The master bath has showerheads opposite each other, set at different heights after measurements were taken of the couple in their stocking feet. Or so the plumbers told me. Neat? I like that touch a lot. Golden fixtures against green marble. Exquisite. Additional sprays to hit the entire body."

Evan fought fiercely but in vain to raise his head above the flowing water.

"You, you'll take a bath and like it."

The industrialist choked and sucked what precious air he could through the tape across his mouth. The water was entering his nostrils.

"The plumber and his son did all the tile work as well. The men are, indeed, artisans. Can you appreciate with what precision these pipes are all laid out? Straight as an arrow. Check out the hangers, Evan. Those two take great pride in what they do. Anyhow, I hope you liked my little tour. I'm no Robin Leach, but at least you got to see the other side of paradise."

The killer ripped the strip of tape from Tamblin's mouth.

A stream of air and water suddenly shot upward like a whale.

Malcolm stared down smugly. "I guess that's your way of saying goodbye, Evan."

Chapter 74

Outside the Eyler home, Malcolm took a casual stroll around the property. All alone. Along the lovely gardens west to south. He stretched and smiled complacently, taking in the grand flash of forced late spring color. Fleshy purple sedum. The black-eyed-Susans; their dark-centered disks reminding him of Evan's pleading eyes as the clear, cold water covered them completely—not five minutes before— before a torrent flooded the entire space.

A water view to end all water views. No? Malcolm mused, glancing over his shoulder. Making sure there were no trailing ghosts.

The killer continued along a garden path.

Yellow daylilies: *Stella de Oro* for the longest bloom. Purple and white coneflowers. Coreopsis: moonbeam yellow. Lavender: with their pale-blue purplish fragrant flowers. Ornamental grasses. Phlox: spent like the decedent. Bloodgrass: to give the place an added boost.

Between the creek and mansion was an Olympic-size swimming pool, with a wading area at one end for the kiddies. Kiddies who would one day grow up to be kings and queens of a kind. A circular hot tub sat several yards away.

Malcolm made his way past a brick, horseshoe-shaped bread and pizza oven with a flamboyant chimney. A pile of wood stood stacked and ready by its side. He continued along quite merrily, traipsing toward the pool house before going into a silly little dance, passing a hand atop a cool, gray granite countertop.

Once inside the outbuilding, the serial killer immediately quit his clowning, stopping dead in his tracks and looking up at the image in the right-hand corner along the back wall. He turned stone-cold serious, falling into a trance-like state, staring fixedly at the thirty-six tiles that composed the large mural made up of one-foot squares. It was a nautical setting depicting a young, barefoot fisherman throwing a seine into a crystal clear body of water near the shoreline. Malcolm remained as still as the figure itself. He stood there for every bit of five minutes, studying each and every block as though they were pieces to an intricate puzzle—abstracted by the past.

The boy's blue hat, pyramid-shaped and truncated at its top, was similar to the one Malcolm had worn as a lad growing up in Scotland and Ireland. Even the young fellow's boots looked familiar, too. A mere youth of about ten or eleven. Freddie's age. He shivered.

Malcolm rocked his head carelessly from side to side . . . traveling back in time across two distant shores. Across the North Channel. Ballycastle to the Mull of Kintyre. Across the span of years. Off to visit or live. Live or visit. Unsure about anything and everything in life. Being shuttled back and forth between two dysfunctional parents . . . while drifting interminably on a sea of sadness with his baggage. Not the kind one would necessarily hold in hand. But the sort he would store away in some murky corner of his mind. Intellectual baggage, which he would try and off-load just before a crisis . . . of which there were many. Emotional baggage that the boy somehow managed to disguise, or quickly fling down some darkened corridor of madness building deep inside.

Malcolm's ordeal was in some strange way both mentally and physically tied to that beat-up piece of leather luggage, found almost always close at hand—filled with tangible items he so often packed and unpacked at a moment's notice—although, like the clutter in his mind—its contents no longer latent or repressed—once emptied, never quite fit back compactly. Not even after squishing down squarely upon an unyielding lid to lock it—trying desperately to press and hold both sides in simultaneously—even pouncing upon, then sitting determinedly down on the billowing surface so as to at least, momentarily, hold its contents intact—finally, stamping and stomping maniacally and repeatedly upon its outer shell—caring little if the bag burst apart at the seams in the process.

Ever and anon.

The struggle with the baggage, Malcolm one day realized a little too late, was analogous to the rage building up inside him, flooding his entire being, raising him to the rafters, pushing out the very walls and windows of reason—no dearth of demons lacking anywhere within his solitary house of horrors.

Malcolm Columba had simply drowned . . . much like the body of Evan Tamblin . . . now moving freely through the current . . .moving within the crawlspace from behind confining walls . . . the industrialist's body still strapped securely to the metal cart, though drifting buoyantly in spite of its prominent weight . . . unbeknownst to the serial killer . . . the powerful wall of rushing water carrying the corpse where it may.

Malcolm left the pool house and walked along the eastern side of the home, heading back, stepping from the newly lain sod to the dusty earth, then onto the circular stone drive—marching backwards, back to frolicking as the cart and body of Evan Tamblin somehow came crashing forward of the foundation on a small but persistent wave—hanging up halfway through an Andersen blow-out basement window.

Malcolm instantly quit his nonsense and went over to the soul. The cart sat like a seesaw, teetering upon the sill.

"Can't keep a good man down is what I think God is trying to tell me, Evan." The killer fixed his angry eyes on the large plank of scrap lumber that had somehow lodged itself lengthwise beneath the wheels. Malcolm put two fingers to the man's carotid artery, glaring into the pair of dead watery eyes. "Just double checking, E.T. I don't need any surprises from you or from Him," he said decidedly.

"How about from me?" a voice behind Malcolm questioned. "I'm just full of surprises, Mal. Mal means bad, motherfucker. That's what the fuck *I* am. One bad-ass motherfucker, as you're about to learn real soon. Now move."

Justin gestured in the direction from which Malcolm had initially come. The two men walked past a boathouse and headed toward the water. Justin trained a SIG Classic just left of center of the serial killer's back.

"You're Monisha Washington's cousin, aren't you?" Malcolm asked politely.

"I'm her avenging angel, asshole," Justin swore. "Keep moving. Faster, fuck-face. Like you was on the wing."

Malcolm smiled and picked up the pace.

Captor and captive quickly made their way along the new wooden pier, down its shiny aluminum ramp, then out to a pair of floating docks off a T.

Malcolm turned left, heading for the bigger of the two boats, in which he had arrived with Evan Tamblin.

"Not that way, dickhead." Justin gestured to the right. "This way. We're goin' out in the open boat. In open waters. You can think of it as an up-and-coming burial at sea. Here. Put these on."

Justin handed his prisoner a pair of beige latex gloves.

Chapter 75

During the late fifties and early sixties, the trees along Main Street in Riverhead were mostly elm. Old, if not ancient. Magnificent trees. By late fall, a capacious cover of leaves would blanket the streets and walkways, leaving a colorful matted swath. Unfortunately, the accumulation was looked upon by the town as a hazard, a nuisance, or simply a general mess. As a result, those stately shade trees were cut to the ground, their stumps uprooted from fertile soil with chain and rope and muscle, for there were no stump grinders in those days. The elms were replaced mostly with unimpressive European mountain ash.

Malcolm first read about the history of those beautiful trees in local newspapers and magazines many years ago. Angst turned to anger, manifesting itself into a blind rage as he further researched the plunder of those majestic giants. It tore at his heart, then, as it did now —on a spiritless ride out to nowhere with Justin Barnes.

Nowhere were there trees or rich black earth where the two were headed.

A decided curse, Malcolm fathomed.

But there was surely water.

Water, water, everywhere.

Water, along with the crisp sea air.

Even from beneath the confining canvas boat cover that hid his nearly naked body, Malcolm could smell the brine. He could certainly feel and hear the vibration of the fiberglass hull beneath him, too, from his cramped position in the bow of the boat where Justin had rudely stashed him.

The maverick kept a keen eye peeled from behind the helm of the twenty-two foot center console.

The serial killer stirred.

Justin demanded that he remain as still as stone.

Malcolm cursed the nonskid. It chafed his knees and then his elbows as he turned from his stomach onto his back, for the man's body was stripped down to a pair of skivvies; latex-covered hands locked behind him; lower limbs secured with line. He was cold and felt like a brittle bundle of mid-winter boughs.

"I said, stay the fuck still."

The boat passed beneath the Ponquogue Bridge, heading toward the Shinnecock Inlet.

When they were completely through the bight, Justin left the wheel just long enough to lift the cover and rip the strip of sticky gray tape from Malcolm's mouth—pulling with it, a pair of the serial killer's socks that the maverick had stuffed into the madman's gob.

Malcolm was considering his situation, held captive by a man hellbent on revenge—a dark-skinned novice navigator traveling better than thirty knots. The small craft flew toward the gradually deeper waters of the ocean. The sea was a silvery sheet of glass. The prisoner's perspective, however, was a tentative look toward the patchy gray-white sky.

"*Boy 'n' Sea*. You like 'er, Mal?"

"What?" Malcolm questioned, rolling out of thought and toward the Igloo seat/cooler fastened to the deck before the helm.

"Name of the boat," Justin explained, raising his voice above the roar of the engine, easing the control lever forward, taking her up another several knots. "*Boy 'n' Sea*," he repeated. "Buoyancy. Get it?"

"What?" he asked again, raising his voice and head before the black man.

Justin smiled down and spoke up clearly. "I said, I'm going to enjoy watching you sink or swim out there." The maverick swept a hand before the face of the Atlantic Ocean. "I'm going to deep-six you solo very shortly, Mal. So low that the sand eels are going to clean the wax out from between your ears. Hear me now, paleface?"

Malcolm shrugged off the threat as utter nonsense.

"Know what I like most about the gear on board, Mal? The anchor's got four feet of five sixteenths-inch chain attached to two hundred feet of rope, marked off in twenty-five foot sections."

"You're not at a rodeo, dude," Malcolm offered priggishly. "It's called *line* when you're talking salty, sailor," he said, yawning rather boorishly.

"Oh, yeah? Well, this line you're gonna like a lot. It's gonna be your lifeline between here and the great beyond. One end's tied off to a stainless steel doohickey in the anchor box."

Malcolm laughed. "Called a well, skipper. The line is secured to an eye bolt in the anchor well."

"The other end to a thingamabob fixed to the last link of heavy chain," Justin expanded, ignoring Malcolm's curt remarks.

"That's a shackle, swabby."

"Guess where you fit in, motherfucker?"

"You got murder on your mind, Mister Mariner?" Malcolm smoldered.

"Of the coldest kind," Justin assured him. "Of the coldest kind."

"I wouldn't hold my breath," the man said confidently.

"Won't have to. You're the one who's going to need a healthy pair of lungs. 'Cause I'm gonna find us a nice deep hole out there, Mal."

"Just be careful *you* don't fall in."

Justin continued to toy with Malcolm, like he believed the serial killer must have tormented Monisha and the others. "I'm gonna suspend you down there like you suspended Monisha Washington from the Mackinac Bridge, Mal. Only you'll be hanging around in a couple hundred feet of water instead of the sea air up here. Four feet of chain and that heavy anchor ought to take you down at the speed of a locomotive. Head first would be my guess. Unless you tangle up. I'll let you dangle there a spell. Check on you every thirty seconds or so. A little bit longer each time you revisit your watery hell. Air and water, Mal. Down and back up again you'll come and go. Over and over until I tire of hauling your ass up, cocksucker. Till I decide you sleep with the crabs. My only regret will be if a shark gets you before you take enough water into your lungs and drown. Whattaya think? Any sharks out there today, badass? If I come up with half your body, I'm gonna go fishin' with the rest of you. Use whatever parts are left over for chum. That the right word, Mal, ol' pal o' mine?"

Malcolm gave a giddy little giggle.

"We'll see if you're still laughing on your rocket ride to hell, you piece of dog shit." Justin glanced over his shoulder at the wake he was leaving behind, then fixed his attention on the anchor buoy at the stern. "See that big-ass orange ball in back, Mal? I saw something like that in a fishing video once—and how they pulled up the anchor using a ring gismo." Justin dipped into his jacket pocket and withdrew a stainless steel ring twice the size of his palm. "It's supposed to help free and lift the anchor right on up to the surface when you're ready to leave the spot. I was thinking I could rig it so you'd have some *buoyancy* when *you* come bobbin' up—spent and gasping for your motherfuckin' breath.

"Another feature, *creature*, is that it's designed for tuna fishing, from what I understand. Release and Chase is what they call it. When the fisherman hooks into a big game fish, he releases the anchor, and the ball acts like a buoy marker, then he's free to chase the sucker. But you probably know all about that stuff, Barnacle Bill. Anyhow, that got me to thinking some more. What if I was to attach *you* to the ball somewhere out there. Then I come around with the boat like *Miami Vice* and smash your motherfuckin' face in with the bow. Hitting you head-on so that the propeller mixes up your brains and churns the rest of you into little pieces would give me a great deal of satisfaction. The only problem with that idea is that it's too merciful, 'cause it's over too fuckin' fast. I want to do this nice and slow, Mal. That's how you did most of your victims. Right? Nice and slow, sicko. So, that's how I'm gonna do you. I want you down there knowing that I'm gonna string this out as long as I can, Mal. I want you to fight for your life like I know Monisha fought for hers—that's if you even gave her half a chance." Justin was growing madder by the moment and breathing heavily.

"Sounds to me like *you're* the one who's going to be out of breath before you even get started," Malcolm stated through a smirk. "You're going to run out of gas before you ever get going, mate."

Justin shot a glance at the fuel gauge. It read three quarters of a tank.

Malcolm smirked again. "Poor excuse for a seaman, if you ask me," he mocked. "I wouldn't be a bit surprised if you capsized us before you ever got to your destination, blackie."

Justin spun the wheel hard to starboard.

Malcolm's body smashed face-first against a bulkhead. A trickle of blood started at the corner of the madman's mouth.

"I'm gonna hav'ta insist that you call me Captain, Mal. 'Cause for better or worse, I'm the one who's in charge of this vessel. Understand?"

Malcolm twisted his body and craned his head around to look

459

up at the man in charge. "Before this little excursion of yours is over and done with, skipper," the author preambled with a sinister sneer, "I'm going to take *you* on a voyage you'll remember for the rest of your days. A journey that shall prove to be your last," he promised. "Up until that moment, I'll insist that *you* refer and, hereafter, think of me as Father. Tit for tat."

"Father?" Justin had to laugh.

"Forever and always. You'll see soon enough, Justin Barnes. You'll soon see," he repeated brazenly.

"What I'm gonna see is your body sinking to the bottom of a deep hole I pick out for you." Justin peered at the depth sounder atop the console. "Thirty-four feet right here, Mal. Gee, I wonder if I sent your sorry ass all the way down to the bottom on a single ride, then suddenly hauled you back up real fast, if you'd get the bends," he thought out loud. "Wouldn't that be fun? Nah, on second thought, you might black out. It wouldn't be any fun because I want you fully alert. Like I told ya, you're gonna die nice and slow, then be gone forever."

Malcolm Columba shook his head. "Not just yet."

"And why is that, fuck-face?"

"Because I have a tale to tell."

"Is that right?"

"Absolutely."

"And how does it begin?"

"With a beautiful young and vibrant black woman receiving a bouquet of long-stemmed roses on Valentine's Day."

Justin reeled the craft sharply to port. The back of Malcolm's head crashed solidly against the hull.

"1-800-Flowers," Malcolm elaborated with a hearty laugh.

Justin pushed the control all the way forward as the boat came out of its sweep.

"I lured Monisha out of her apartment by saying you were waiting downstairs, Justin Barnes," Malcolm shouted over the roar of the screaming single outboard engine. "I even scribbled down a few flowery words in a little note as if the phrasing came from you. You see, I know you don't know how to read or write too well. True?" the killer railed. "But you're moving in the right direction from what my sources tell me. Looking up a new word or two each and every day. Commendable. Still practicing your states and capitals?"

Unnerved, Justin looked down at the prostrate figure, gradually cutting back on the throttle.

Malcolm, in kind, lowered his tone to a melodic lure. "Oh, I know lots about you, buddy," the author assured him. "Maybe you could use a tutor. What do you think? I am the very best. When I was studying for the priesthood, under another name, of course, all the other seminarians came to *me*. *Me*, fella. Not only did I fix their prose, I taught them how to *think*! Not all of them agreed with my beliefs, to my chagrin. That's when I knew I had a mission. To convert those who were truly being led astray.

"But first I had to point an accusatory finger—not at—but rather directly into their sordid souls. You see, a good many were either latent or out-and-out homosexuals, Barnes. The priesthood, for a number of reasons, draws those unfortunates to the light like a moth. Some of them were so far back in the closet that you had to sweep them out with a bristly broom before standing them in the glorious light of truth. Of course, most ran the hurdles of outright denial, self-doubt, or acceptance of self under the guise of goodness and godliness and crap like that. I showed those tortured beings that their affliction was nothing more than an imperfection and asked them *what*, if anything, was indeed perfect in all the world? Those who told me and truly believed that God was the exception, suddenly disappeared. Just like that." Malcolm snapped a rubbery thumb and forefinger behind his back for emphasis. "One by one they vanished. It wasn't a year later that the head of the seminary asked me to leave the grounds for good. He couldn't prove anything, of course, but he *knew*. So, instead of my kicking up a fuss, which is what I'm sure he expected, I left quietly. But not without taking a few good soldiers with me. Those ripe young fellows eventually recruited several more; and before I knew it, I had a following, J," Malcolm divulged most divinely. "Hundreds eventually. And then thousands. They're all out there, Mr. Barnes. God's most imperfect, *perfect* creatures. When they come for you, and I can assure you that they will, I shan't be able to protect you if one of them wants to put it up your ass. I don't think Cl— Good God!" Malcolm took a single deep breath. "I almost slipped and said *his* name. I don't think he's ever had a slave before." Malcolm rattled the pair of handcuffs for effect, then giggled once again. "I don't think he's ever had such a brute," he swore before he absolutely roared.

461

When Malcolm stopped laughing, and Justin's heart slowed to a normal beat, the captain of the borrowed vessel spoke.

"Mal?"

"Yes, Justin?"

"You really are fucking nuts. Aren't you?"

"Let's just say for the sake of argument that you'll be calling me *Father* before long. And if you're smart—"

"Farther along the *line* than you'd care to imagine is where I'm going to send you, Mal," Justin trifled.

Malcolm grinned. "Sounds spooky, cap'n."

"I'm going to enjoy this, shit-for-brains."

"As much as you enjoyed killing a cop?"

Justin studied the stone-faced serial killer for a good moment before bringing the machine back up to cruising speed. "More so, motherfucker. So much more so."

The Whaler moved along at a thirty-knot clip for a good ten minutes before either of the men spoke again.

Justin was heading southeast, away from any and all boat traffic. "A hundred and three feet here, Mal. Tell me you're not the least bit concerned."

Malcolm smiled. "How did you find me?" he finally asked.

Justin said nothing.

"Tell me. You said I'm going to die anyway."

"Got that right, Mal."

"So then tell me, Captain."

"The boat you came in back there gave you away."

"How? Come on. Tell me how you actually found me. It can't matter now."

"You're predictable."

"That so?"

"You're an open book, in fact."

"Give. It's my dying wish to know," he said quite seriously.

"The *name* of the boat you borrowed."

"*The Author.*" Malcolm understood in part. "But how did you know—"

"A boat was reported stolen from a marina in South Jamesport. Right around the corner from Evan Tamblin's home, asshole. Tamblin was missing, too. I figured you took him away by water. Not too difficult to fathom. You like that word, Mal? Got a double meaning. Guess which one applies particularly to you?" Justin grinned demonically. "You broke into the mechanic's garage and removed a set of keys. You had your choice of any boat out there, but you selected *The Author*. So. You fancy yourself a writer, do you, Mal?"

"There has to be more to it than that, Mr. Barnes. You just don't hear that a boat and man are missing and assume that *I* stole them—or that *The Author* holds any significance."

Justin winked. "Two little birds of a feather carelessly dropped a hint in the heat of battle."

"Who?"

"Whooo," the captain mocked evasively. "Unlucky for you, but lucky for me, they weren't very wise."

"You followed me to East Point."

"Nope. If I did, I might have saved Evan Tamblin in time. I just kept radioing people on the water, asking them if they saw *The Author*. Some time later, a cruiser out here came back to me with a radio check. Guy told me he passed you early this morning on Great Peconic Bay as it was getting light. He said it looked to him as though you were traveling toward the Shinnecock Canal. Another boat spotted you heading west in Shinnecock Bay. I spotted *The Author* with those binoculars," Justin clarified, "docked along East Point. A needle in a haystack. But I found you, Malcolm."

"You got lucky, Justin. That's all there is to it."

"Gee. And I thought it was a pretty good piece of detective work."

"Do your police buddies know what you know?"

"Do you really think I'd pass along that information and miss out on all the fun I'm gonna have out here with you?" he asked rhetorically. "I don't think I'd have no better time than if I went deep sea fishin' for Jaws."

"Double negative, fella. *Any* better time is what you mean to say. I'm telling you, you need a tutor, fella," the author solicited good-humoredly.

"Fuck you, jerk-off."

"Just trying to help you improve your grammar, J.B. Make you think. I know how hard you're working to improve yourself."

"I am thinking, Mal. I'm thinking that this is as good a spot as any. A hundred and sixty-three feet."

Malcolm feigned a shudder.

"What do you think, Mal? Huh?"

"I think you're in way over your head. I really do."

"That a fact?"

With expressionless dark dead eyes, Malcolm stared up at Justin.

The captain slowed the vessel, then shifted into neutral. The boat bobbed about upon a two-foot chop. Justin cut the engine and stepped forward of the helm. All business. He was through talking for the time being. The coast was clear as was the body of water all around them. Not a single boat in sight. From his pants pocket, he withdrew a pair of pelican clips attached to both ends of a short, braided length of quarter-inch nylon line. Justin stepped forward and snapped one of the spring-loaded stainless steel items through a link of anchor chain, connecting the other clip to the handcuffs at the killer's back. "Get up," Justin ordered.

Malcolm stiffened his body in resistance.

"I said, get up!"

With bound feet, Malcolm kicked out at his captor.

Justin moved toward the anchor roller and unwrapped the section of chain from around a five-inch cleat.

The author tried to scramble past the console toward the stern, struggling to get away as Justin lifted the galvanized anchor and chain from its shiny, narrow metal frame along the bow pulpit—the fiberglass lid of the well-cover rattling violently against the links before the line tore freely from its locker.

Malcolm fought viciously, kicking out at the captain for all it was worth. But Justin easily pulled the man to his feet again, double-checking the connection at his back and along the stark, steel snake.

"There! All set for travel, Malcolm. How does it feel to know you're about to leave the atmosphere? Tell me. Don't you wish that you had gills, motherfucker? 'Course I'd rip them out of your head in a heartbeat," Justin menaced. "Still want to tell me more about Monisha while I whet my appetite?"

Suddenly, in one furious motion, Malcolm was airborne—past the safety of the Boston Whaler's freeboard—free as a bird for a fraction of a second before the prisoner began his plunge into sixty degree waters at the edge of the Atlantic Ocean—the vessel's ground tackle striking then raking the gel coat across the gunwale—following forward before immediately overtaking the denizen of the deep—Danforth anchor and chain finishing first and foremost.

Justin yanked the line, felt the load, then drew the scope taut, quickly tying it off on the starboard midship cleat. Immediately, the rope swung inward against the v-hull; it hung there obliquely at a ten-degree angle.

Captain Barnes beamed joyously. "You're not nearly at the end of your rope yet," he vowed. "You're only fifteen to sixteen feet down. Farther, Father? Maybe we'll go another . . . nah. Let's see how you're doing first."

Justin prayed that the man was still conscious. Maybe he would work him down five feet at a time, he considered. Ten, if the author *really* pissed him off. He pulled on the line. "Christ. I thought things were supposed to be lighter in the water. Feels like I'm pulling up a fucking ship." *Dead weight*, he panicked. "Where's the fun and fight in this?" Hand-over-hand, Justin hauled in the line. Serious black muscles bulged beneath his long-sleeved, buttoned-down collar shirt.

Back.
Neck.
Shoulders.
Forearms.

Malcolm hit the surface. Thrashing and gasping frantically for air.

The sound and desperate motion actually startled the punisher.

Justin thought it funny as Malcolm actually tried to grab the dangling rope and chain with chattering teeth before descending once again—the weighty streak of silver leading and clearly winning the way downward for the second race.

Justin let out another couple of yards for good measure, then yanked at the length of line, pulling it up gradually this time, holding the top end of the chain against the cleat.

Malcolm Columba hung helplessly against the bright white hull.

"Please!" Malcolm pleaded frantically. "PLEASE," he cried aloud.

"You pulling my chain, or what?" Justin asked in fascination.

"THROW ME THE MARKER BUOY," Malcolm screamed.

"The what?"

"The fucking ball, you ignoramus."

"Oh, I's don't no nothin' 'bout no ball, mister," Justin drawled in a lazy fashion, raking a free hand through his kinky jet black hair. "I's jus' a dumbshit nigger," he taunted. "Dumber than dirt. Still wet behind da ears." He stopped his hand in the middle of a second pass and scratched his scalp. "Ah, did I's jus' use one o' dem double negatives, mas'er Columba?"

"Orange ball!" Malcolm choked and wept.

"Oh, dat. I don't think I's gonna use dat—*whoops*—" Malcolm sank like a lead balloon as Justin let loose the chain from around the cleat, then stepped aside. "One Mississippi. Two Mississippi. Three Mississippi," the captain counted, watching the instant downward passage of bubbles as the anchor, chain, body and line rushed away before Justin secured the latter with a loop around the cleat, and then another.

The boat gave a sudden jerk and listed to starboard.

Justin raised his eyes to a patch of slate-gray sky set between two massive anvil-shaped clouds. He massaged his temples, lost in a single thought, suddenly remembering where he had left off alphabetically from the long list of states and seats of government.

"Ah, yes. The capital of Missouri is Jefferson City. The capital of Montana is Helena. The capital of Nebraska is Lincoln," he recited loudly and proudly.

Justin paused satisfactorily and undid the line, taking his time in lifting his trophy carefully from the waters.

Malcolm grew mad as a hatter.

Insane, to say the least.

Justin wondered what had happened to the man's arrogance. Where did it go? Did it just wash away with the current? Was this the real Malcolm Columba? The face that the rest of the world would never get to see? He suspended the lunatic's handcuffed and foot-bound body half in and half out of the water, having trouble keeping the killer upright.

"Stay still," Justin ordered.

But the man was busy twisting and thrashing and cursing and making his own set of waves that were breaking angrily upon the surface. "Ma-manuscript," Malcolm muttered, swallowing a good mouthful of sea water. "Leather suitcase—Rampasture Park Beach House—behind the out-outdoor fi-fireplace," he sputtered. "In the rafters. Pl-please."

"What?"

"MY MANUSCRIPT—YOU FUCKING MORON," Malcolm managed, choking and wiggling his body like a worm. "Journal. Tells you . . ." the author fought for the words and the breath with which to push them out ". . . all about Monisha," he barely breathed.

Justin glanced at his right shoulder, then stared back at the sea creature tangled in the line.

"You see him there, Monisha?" Justin said in question just as calmly as he could. "He's goin' down for the count, baby. Didn't I promise you, girl?"

"Kill you . . . cocksucker . . . kill your fucking swarthy kind . . . You-you'll love it! Read my journal . . . For you and . . . all the world to see."

Justin looked over at the depth sounder flashing a series of intermittent numbers. 164 ft. 164.5 ft. 165 ft. Back to 164 ft.

"Have a nice journey, Mal," Justin said evenly.

"No, listen son of—"

Justin listened to the clunk of chain followed by the line paying out smoothly over the gunwale as he fed it freely, until there was no resistance whatsoever. Quickly, he gave the rope a tug to be certain dead weight was felt.

Undoubtedly, there was.

For the next full minute, Justin was left with the distinct impression that the creature on the other end of the line was surely a killer fish, swimming and pulling outrageously for its life—before the fight was finally out of it.

Defeated.

For the good of God.

Justin withdrew a jackknife from his pants pocket and put it to the line. "Cuttin' you some slack, Jack," said the captain to the man missing in action who hung suspended no more than a foot off the bottom of the salty sea's sandy floor. "Consider my act a merciful one, motherfucker."

Just for giggles, Justin pressed the MOB (Man Overboard)

button on the GPS (Global Positioning System), then waited a solid six minutes lest his shanghaied passenger should summarily surface. Finally, the counterfeit captain fired up the engine.

Or am I to be considered a predator pirate? the maverick wondered and grinned.

A salty sea dog.

A swarthy buccaneer.

"Blackbeard!" Justin exclaimed, then stroked his chin with a certain satisfaction.

Chapter 76

The maverick was cruising along close to forty knots. The stretch of shoreline ran east to west. When Justin reached the point where he believed the cut to Shinnecock Inlet lay, guesstimating the run be a good ten miles due north, the navigator aligned the needle on the compass card to 360°.

The wind started picking up considerably, causing the sea to kick up its heels, forcing Justin to reduce his speed.

"Piece of cake—so long as no fucking fog rolls in."

A healthy respect for the sea and seamanship he was fast developing while keeping a sharp lookout for any creature, monster, demon, or any denizen of the deep that might suddenly rise out of the choppy waters and swallow the boat and boatman whole. For Malcolm's words had indeed spooked him; that being, the madman's threats to take him on a voyage—one that he would supposedly remember for the rest of his days. *Who* exactly would be coming for him? he wondered. Who were *they*? Were *they* truly Columba's followers? *Yeah, right. Just a lot of lunatic talk. Tryin' to scare off a superstitious nigger with a lot of mumbo jumbo,* Justin swore. *Last-ditch effort. That's all that is,* he told himself.

"The big fuckin' stall, was all. Before I sank his honky ass down deep fo' good," Justin mulled aloud in his unsettled mind.

The swells were three feet high and building.

Malcolm was at the bottom of his game.

It was over.

The serial killer was gone forever.

Dead was dead, and Malcolm Columba was surely dead.

No sea monster would rear its ugly head.

No hand would rise up out of the water to grab him bodily—or wave a farewell warning.

No body alongside the borrowed bobbing boat would rise upward to tip the plastic tub.

"Only happens in the movies. Right, Monisha?" Justin

questioned. "Right as rain, J.B.," he answered for her with a big wide grin.

A bevy of birds was circling off his port bow.

Gulls and terns and gannets.

Justin made slow progress back toward the inlet, quickly learning to cut the waves at an angle so as to avoid taking on water over the bow.

He no longer feared Malcolm and his idle threats.

Justin's immediate concern was the law.

Undercover FBI Special Agent Andrew Miller, to name but one —if that was even his name. Perhaps an alias. The lawman was no dope. And the guy was sure to be pissed, Justin positively knew. For he had cold-cocked him after the shootout up at Redding Ridge— somehow sensing that Miller would have prevented him from pursuing Columba. It was something he read in the man's eyes that told him as much. The maverick felt that there was a whole lot more to the case than met the eye. What, exactly, was above and beyond his comprehension. He did what he felt he had to do in order to get away from the federal agent without being followed. Not like before. There was little choice in the matter, he firmly believed. Time was his enemy. He had searched in vain for Virginia before returning to the home of the woman who helped him. Ms. Slopbucket. He left her that evening —then went to hunt down Malcolm Columba.

Justin readjusted and anchored one of the federal agent's personal handguns firmly forward of his right hip, behind a wide leather belt. The SIG felt solid. Comforting, too. About as comforting as the knowledge that the heavy metal anchor and chain that carried the serial killer down to Davy Jones's locker, held him fast—no more than four feet above the sea floor. The pirate peered down over the console.

Consoled.

Suddenly, not fifty yards in front of him, the surface of the sea started bubbling like a boiling cauldron. Instinctively, Justin pulled the semiautomatic weapon from his waist and leveled it at the center of the disturbance, off the starboard bow. Baitfish flew in every direction before him. Pure mayhem and bedlam surrounded him. He half expected a monstrous head to appear in the center of the turmoil and claim vengeance.

Maybe a sea of horn-like heads or a single figure brandishing a pitchfork, his disordered mind warned him as he gripped the pistol, prepared to menace any emerging beasts or phantoms ready to do battle: zombies or goblins or ghosts or sea devils. *Maybe the sole ivory skull and skeletal remains of a hard-nosed cop looking for and finding trouble anew from days of long ago. Maybe a horde of Don Ciccio's soldiers—executed twenty-four hours earlier at the ranch in Redding Ridge. Maybe, just maybe, the rising impatience and reprisal of a lone madman sunk in a hundred and sixty-four feet of water no more than thirty minutes ago.*

Maybe. Maybe. Maybe.

Is this Malcolm's master counterblow? he wondered.

"I don't think so," Justin told the angry sea as at least two dozen elongated bodies broke the surface with the breakneck speed of torpedoes, their silvery blue-bowed forms chasing, thrashing and tearing into their targets. A school of menhaden, a.k.a. mossbunker, succumbed to the much larger school of ten to twelve-pound bluefish, of which the Sunday sailor at that moment had little clue, having fished mostly freshwater ponds and lakes and rivers. They were all just fish with flashing fins to this tyro who had cruised along the Penobscot with Monisha, never having really ventured into its bay to bear witness to large schools of choppers in full pursuit of the smaller pods of baitfish.

Justin's heart raced as he fought to recover his footing and sense of sanity, sticking the agent's weapon back behind the belt. He stood mesmerized, maneuvering the boat to-and-fro as the feeding frenzy lasted a murderous five minutes.

"Fucker had the nerve to call me a moron," he suddenly remembered, wondering what Malcolm's last thoughts were as the serial murderer took his final plunge toward a watery hell, fighting the line that ultimately offered no resistance or assistance . . . no chance of ever being pulled back up and into earth's precious atmosphere.

No hope whatsoever.

Justin would have paid a handsome price to see Malcolm's terrified expression as the severed line snaked limply and finally sank along with the madman's expectation of being hauled safely from the sea.

The murderous pirate took a deep breath through rather large nostrils and fully appreciated filling his lungs to their capacity. A luxury Malcolm Columba would never ever again enjoy.

The captain of the borrowed craft could clearly smell the murder of the menhaden upon the rough whitecapped surface. The pungent rich fish oil of mixed solidly with the salty thick sea air. Justin desperately sought to catch and hold a melody in mind. He hummed awkwardly, trying to recollect the tune, shaking his head in frustration. Fought for it, then tried again . . . finally remembering the silly song from early childhood.

"Oh, the big, big fish,
eat the little, little fish.
And the little, little fish,
eat the littler fish.
And the littler fish,
eat the littlest fish—
'cause that's the way it goes.
That's the way it goes.
Everybody knows.
That's the way it's always been
and how it's gonna be."

Justin felt neither like a big fish nor a little fish. What he felt was . . . *drained*.

Repositioning the bow back into the wind, he navigated the vessel steadily through a three-and-a-half-foot chop, heading slowly and carefully toward the inlet. Up and down the boat pounded, making very little headway.

Although he tried to shake the eerie daymare from his mind with a soothing lullaby, apropos of nothing save his weariness, the avenger just could not stop envisioning a grotesque figure suspended several feet above a dark, sandy sea bottom . . . pulling, twisting, turning . . . fighting furiously for his life before the single, sinking snake-like bleached white *rope*.

As Justin approached the shoreline, the brisk wind out of the northwest abated somewhat, and its gentle breeze had a calming effect upon the captain's feverish face and body. Heading back through the inlet, he thought about the woman he had met on the road in

Connecticut yesterday morning. Her modest clapboard dwelling. Heated in late fall through early spring with a small rusty aboveground oil tank. To call it a shack would have been an accurate description had anyone else lived there but that precious lady. To refer to its immaculate housekeeper as Ms. Slopbucket could not be further from fact, as Justin had realized the moment he first pulled into the neatly flower-lined drive.

He had not even taken the time to properly say goodbye. He had just time enough to return the borrowed clothes and gas up his car. No time for excuses, explanations, compliments, thanks, or small talk. Hardly enough time to tell her all about the massacre up at Redding Ridge, let alone the details concerning Malcolm and Monisha. For Justin knew he had to find the serial killer *fast*, before the law succeeded—or the vigilante would never ever have had the opportunity to ensure and mete out his own brand of justice.

A quick kiss upon the stranger's forehead, and he was gone with the wind.

Justin promised himself that when things got settled, he would at least drop by and pay the special woman a visit. Bring her flowers and a gift. He could not call her, as she had no phone. He did not even know her mailing address, which he comically figured could be Rural Road, Anywhere, U.S.A. Most incredibly, he had not even taken the time to learn her proper name: first or last. Absolutely amazing, he laughed with annoyance.

And now that Malcolm Columba surely slept with the crabs and fishes, Justin would simply clean up his act, cruise *Boy 'n' Sea* back to the dock at East Point, then notify the police. And depending on whether or not someone had already found Evan Tamblin's body, he would fashion his story to fit the situation. If no one had happened upon the scene, he would merely call and tell the authorities that he just arrived by boat, found Tamblin, then hunted about the property for the killer, on foot, to no avail. Why raise speculation to the possibility that he had caught up with the madman and took him out to sea for all eternity?

If on the other hand, workmen, police or anyone else had already discovered the industrialist, he would have another story handy to end all stories. About how he had given chase in *Boy 'n' Sea* after a fictitious boat in which the serial killer and a phantom accomplice made good their escape.

In any event, he first had to be sure to thoroughly wash all traces of blood that fell from Malcolm's mouth earlier, along with any other evidence the killer might have left behind in the Whaler, reminding himself to cut the remaining length of rope completely off the eye bolt in the anchor well. He would have to go over the stories very carefully in his head.

Murder was a relatively simple act to commit.

Most difficult to cover up completely, Justin knew—most assuredly.

The so-called perfect murder was as deceiving as the devil and the deep blue sea, Justin fathomed nervously as he finally brought the vessel through the inlet and over to a distant dock, far enough away from East Point and the adjacent creek. Not even from the raised bungalow set on stilts behind a barrier of ten to twelve-foot reeds could anyone see him helping himself to the hose hooked up to dockside water. He prayed that no one had found Evan Tamblin's body yet. It would make things so much easier. He could not just abandon the craft and leave it at that, for there were boaters who had seen him on the bays, or heard him on the marine radio earlier. Fishermen, too, had spotted him from those banks and nearby jetties—along with the lockmaster, situated in his steel perch atop the Shinnecock Canal. A man with a birds-eye view who had clearly seen Justin earlier as the maverick waited patiently for the lock gates to open. Justin Barnes. A black man with purpose of mind and clearly on a mission, the police would quickly surmise. He had to cover all bases.

Justin worked quickly.

His story would have to be anchored solidly. There was a good chance that folks along the inlet would recall seeing him as well. A big, black dude standing behind the helm of the *borrowed* boat, heading southeast toward the open waters of the ocean, then back again. It was the main reason why he decided to return to East Point and hand the police a particular story to fit either event. Lady luck and an angel on *each* shoulder were sorely needed. He had to get his *facts* straight. He could not afford to contradict himself with regard to one story or the other, whereby he was either looking for the killer on *land*, or in hot pursuit of Columba and a fictitious accomplice in a fanciful boat at *sea*, so as to account for *The Author* still tied to the private dock at Rampasture's East Point estate.

Yes. One if by land; two if by sea. He giggled anxiously, remembering at least *that* much of a history lesson from a million years ago, or so it seemed. He had to return to the scene of the crime, he told himself. Not his, but Malcolm's. Hated, but had to. He prayed no one was there. It would prove the lesser of the evils and give him more than ample time to get his story straight in his mind. The homicide cops were pros at confusing the issue as a means to try and trip a suspect up, he positively knew—firsthand. Hopefully, he would be believed. Hopefully, Agent Miller would not make a federal case out of the fact that Justin had knocked him unconscious, *borrowing* the man's pistol and handcuffs, just as the maverick had borrowed *Boy 'n' Sea*.

Hopefully.

Chapter 77

The woman wept bitterly. "Business. Honestly. That's all he said. I didn't ask where."

"Then I want you to tell me where you *think* he might be, Miss Sloop," the furious man shouted, ripping one of the flimsy foam cushions from the back of the upholstered couch.

Thelma Sloop sobbed, shivered, then shook her head, cowering against the hardwood frame. "I tr-truly don't know. He left immediately after dinner," she fibbed. "Around eight, like I told you. He said he had business to do. That's all I know. I have no idea where he is. Please go now. I don't want any trouble."

Agent Andrew Miller reached inside his jacket pocket and withdrew one of Justin's handguns. With his other hand, he rested the sandwich-thin bolster against the side of the woman's head for more of a shield against blood splatter than any cushion of comfort or sound deadener. He pressed the business end of the semiautomatic weapon, fixed with a silencer, against the material above her right temple.

"I'll count to three. You'll tell me where he is and what you know, or you'll be lying in the morgue in a matter of hours. I won't ask you again."

"You're not a fed-federal agent like you said you were—are you?"

"Oh, I assure you that I am, ma'am. *One*."

"I can't tell you what I don't know. Pl-please."

"*Two*."

"He said he had business on Long Island. I don't know where," the woman insisted, wiping her eyes with the back of her hand. "That's it," she concluded, covering her face with a trembling forearm.

"*Three*."

"Ple—"

Three shots rifled through the cotton-duck fabric and foam, drilling the side of Thelma Sloop's skull. The innocent young woman sloped to a corner of the couch, a bare shoulder dropping upon an upholstered arm. The similitude between the woman's surname and her pitched position upon the sofa was not lost on the lawman as he smiled down in amusement before turning his attention to her old dog.

"Well, that about winds things up here, ol' boy. Spanky, is it? I'm sure someone will find you a good home, fella," Miller bothered to mention, tossing the powder-burned bolster onto the floor, patting and rubbing the animal's head and ears affectionately with a pair of black, Ice Bay neoprene glove-covered hands before heading out the door.

Chapter 78

Suffolk County crime scene personnel were busy searching the deluged home and property at the East Point Eyler estate in Rampasture, scouring every square foot of living space and acreage for a clue. Evidentiary, or otherwise. The pursuit included two outbuildings as well as the pair of purloined vessels tied to the T dock: *The Author*, a Stamas Express, reported stolen from the angry novelist's marina slip in South Jamesport, near Tamblin's home. *Boy 'n' Sea*, a Boston Whaler, *borrowed* from the same location, as the culprit freely confessed.

"Yes, borrowed," Justin insisted. "The keys were in it—" whereby the maverick related how he had hunted for, then allegedly spotted the serial killer coming down the ramp and onto Eyler's dock "—right before Columba quickly boarded another boat—" by God "—before I gave chase," or so Justin's story unfolded.

"So, what you're telling us," Homicide Detective Brian Archer questioned, "is that you were heading toward the dock as Malcolm Columba was heading out?"

"Speeding away was more like it," Justin fabricated.

"In another boat?"

"How many times do I have to say it?"

Brian looked down the aluminum ramp toward his partner.

Detective Dean Nelson was busy going over *Boy 'n' Sea* with the patience and practiced eye of a marine surveyor from the moment the forensic team finished giving the boat its due.

Brian kept Justin focused on his tale while the latter looked on anxiously.

Detective Nelson continued his examination. He stepped just aft of the console. Stopped. Stooped. Stood. Scratched his wavy, dark head of hair. Scribble-scrabbled notes. Paced the deck fore and aft. Passed a palm along a gunwale. Stooped again, then ran the tips of his fingers across the padded white combing.

"What's he doing down there?" Justin asked uneasily.

"Detective work," Brian stated flatly.

"Really? You'd think he was figuring to buy the fucking boat," Justin said kiddingly, trying to seem at ease.

"May be," Archer agreed with a smile.

"Forty minutes he's been dickin' around down there," Justin added with a degree of annoyance. "He should be on the *other* boat lookin' 'round."

"The boat you saw Columba come in on."

"I told you. I didn't see him come in. Saw the boat. That boat. *The Author.* Next thing I see is Columba coming along the pier and down the ramp, and he gets into another boat that pulls alongside the dock and picks him up."

"And you couldn't see this other person in the boat, you're saying."

"That's right. He was facing away from me."

"Then how do you know he was a he?"

"I don't," Justin swallowed anxiously. "Just assume."

"But you saw Columba, you say."

"Clear as day."

"And they just sped away."

"In one of them fancy racing boats."

"Cigarette type boats."

"Long and sleek."

"Red, you said."

"Red as a ruby."

"No other markings."

"I told you. Gold scalping, I think."

"You think."

"Yeah, I fuckin' think. I was concentrating on the two of 'em."

"But you can't tell us one thing about the person driving the speedboat."

"They flew out of there like lightnin'."

"And no name or anything on the boat."

"Not that I saw."

"And you called out to them."

"That's what I said, Brian. 'Hey, motherfuckers!' I hollered. And I followed them for about a mile before they disappeared."

"East."

"Yes, east." Justin gestured. "Till they was a tiny dot and were gone."

"And you didn't bother to report the craft. A person aboard who you knew to be Malcolm Columba."

Justin just nodded, then shook his head.

"You had a marine radio aboard, but you didn't bother to notify anyone."

"Concentrated on following them as long as I could."

"Not the Coast Guard or anybody."

"Told you before—"

"—that you called other boats earlier, asking if they saw *The Author* on the water."

"That's right."

"Makes no sense, Justin."

"Makes perfect sense to me."

"How's that?"

Justin said nothing but shook his head again and peered out over the body of water in the general direction that he swore the fanciful, fast red boat had disappeared.

The day was heating up quickly. The maverick felt the temperature rising from the moment he reached the point of no return: East Point . . . pulling up to the dock before the assembled crew of fact finders and interrogators. Their suspicions mounting by the moment.

Can this motherfuckin' nigger moron pull it off? Justin asked himself. *Do they know about the shootout up in Redding Ridge, yet? Have to. No?* Should he even broach the subject? he considered. *Fuck no! Maybe later. Have to convince them it was self-defense. Have to think things through one step at a time. Yes. Why haven't they asked about Connecticut? Just as well.* Agent Andrew Miller would back him up, he knew. *At least about the scene that went down in the parking lot. Right? Christ! Where the hell is Miller anyhow? Do they even know the man is a fed, by now? Keep your mouth shut, nigger,* he told himself. *Strange that they haven't mentioned him.* Justin had handed over Miller's gun to Brian earlier. Surrendered it, actually. Along with his pocketknife. *Yes, surrendered.* He wondered. *Will they be arresting me? What are they holding back?*

Finally, Dean Nelson came up the ramp and along the pier with an object in his hand. "Know what this is?" Brian's partner asked.

The question was directed at Justin.

Justin shrugged and shook his head.

"It's an anchor ring," Dean said. The detective hooked and unhooked the stainless steel ends of the circular item.

Both Justin and Brian stared at it blankly.

"Any idea where the anchor is for that boat you *borrowed*?" Dean asked curiously.

Again, Justin shrugged, running a forefinger around the buttoned up collar of his flannel shirt.

"Aren't you hot like that?" Brian remarked.

Beads of sweat clung to the black man's forehead, face and neck. Justin gestured toward the water, unbuttoning the top two buttons of his shirt. "It was chilly out there before. Chasin' after them like that."

"No anchor on that boat, yet the guy's got an anchor ring and ball," Dean continued without taking his eyes off the tall ebony figure standing before him. "Odd."

Justin kept his trap shut, formulating a reply.

"We noticed some interesting marks along the gunwale," the detective persevered. "From galvanized chain and shackle, would be my guess. Know anything about that, Mr. Barnes?"

Now, it was Mr. Barnes.

"No," Justin answered abruptly.

"Anchor. Chain. Rope. Couple of clips, too, that the owner says were definitely on the boat. You know anything at *all* about any of that gear, Justin Barnes?" Nelson pressed in a tone that told Justin the proverbial shit was about to hit the fan.

"Knows lots 'bout *chains* and bein' 'eld down, mas'er," Justin confessed half-jokingly. "We folks been in 'em fo' 'better than five hundred years."

"You put that cocksucker overboard?" the cop asked straightforwardly. "Tell me. Wouldn't blame you if you did. Ain't that right, Brian?"

"They'd pin a medal on you if you did, Justin," Brian agreed.

Justin wanted to bolt. Oh, how he wished he could trust just *one* motherfuckin' white man, he told himself. *That's all. Just one.* Maybe Agent Andrew Miller. To a degree. For the two were in the thick of it. *Comrades in arms. Arms, for sure. Firepower directed at those fucking flunkies. Deserved everything they got.* He was sorry he had taken the agent's gun. Upset that he knocked him unconscious, too. *Down for the count.* What choice did he have? *None.* Not if he wanted to continue on his manhunt and find Monisha's killer. Not if he wanted to exact his revenge. Maybe they *would* pin a medal on him. *Yeah, right. A big one.* One that would sink his black ass to the bottom of the sea where Malcolm Columba lay. He stared at the two of them. Took them right into his eyes.

"Hell no, I didn't put no one overboard. Would have though if I'd caught up with 'im. Better believe that, man. Better believe I'd put that fucker down. With a bullet in his motherfuckin' brain. Then another for good measure." Justin formed a gun finger and jerked it forward twice, putting one make-believe bullet into each of their disbelieving heads.

Dean Nelson stared at Justin without any change of expression, staying with the one that read *guilty*—written across the black man's face. "I think you're lying to us," he stated evenly, which assuredly said in one fell swoop that Justin Barnes went from the status of an eyewitness to their prime suspect.

"Just like that." Justin laughed incredulously.

"The man you stole the boat from—"

"*Borrowed,*" Justin snapped.

"Least of your problems, Barnes," Nelson came back. "The man you swiped the boat from is a fucking fanatic with his toys. He says he had an anchor, chain, and two hundred feet of line aboard. Marked off every twenty-five feet with a colored tag. Claims there wasn't so much as a scratch on the boat. Not a single one. Starboard side of the hull now has metallic markings, along with a couple of nice chips and gouges in the gel coat."

"Yeah, well when people claim money or property loss, shit like that, they usually report a lot more missing or damaged than what actually is," Justin offered in reply. "Guy probably wants to make a few bucks off the insurance company. You blame 'im? So what else is new?"

"No significant saltwater crystallization accumulation on either side of the hull or stern," Dean remarked. "That tells me that most of the boat got a good hosing before you pulled in. Inside and out."

"I guess the guy gave it a good washin' fo' I borrowed it," Justin said lamely. "How the hell do I know? All I know is that you're tryin' to give *me* a hosin' here."

"You mean to tell us you didn't pick up any spray all the way from South Jamesport, Barnes?" Nelson questioned with a smirk, reaching for and feeling the front of Justin's flannel shirt. "You flyin' above the water or what? You told us you went after them. Fast. Remember? Forty plus knot boat you borrowed there," he posited, pointing over his shoulder with a thumb. The detective took out and opened up his notebook. "Quote. 'Like fuckin' lightnin' I went after those two motherfuckers.' End quote. Recall? If you were doin' *ten* knots, you'd have salt spray all over that boat with the way the wind was blowin' out there earlier."

Justin said nothing.

"Inside of that boat, for the most part, is spick-and-span, Barnes. Fresh water near the scuppers. Not salt. Only you missed a spot of blood underneath the combing near the bow. That's the padded vinyl strip below the rail. Another drop of blood along a corner of the cooler beneath the cushion seat. Cut yourself shaving? Or is the blood going to match Malcolm Columba's, Mr. Barnes? We'll know soon enough."

"Maybe it'll match some motherfuckin' gamefish, mate," Justin blew, making his fists into a ball.

Brian Archer stepped between the two men, turned and took Justin aside. "Look."

"Yeah, I'm lookin' and listenin' to a bunch o' horseshit." Justin boiled. "Doin' *your* fuckin' job, and this is the thanks I get. I found him for you! All right? Sorry he slipped the fuck away."

"All right. Just calm down."

"Calm down nothin'. Motherfuckin' partner o' yours been on my back from the minute Theo and Andrew took me in. Motherfucker's just jealous that *I* found 'im."

"Yeah, found him and lost him out there," Dean Nelson declared, leaving his neutral corner and walking back over to the pair while pointing toward the ocean. "Took 'im for a fuckin' sea trial is what you did. Became his judge, jury and executioner. I'd bet my pension on it, Bri. But let me tell you something, Barnes. We'll find him if you dropped him in a thousand feet of water out there. Believe you me."

Brian put his hand out for Dean to simmer down. "All we want here is the truth, Justin. Okay? You did good. All right? You really want to waste our time chasing a ghost when we should be moving on to other things?" He shot a glance past Justin to his partner for approval.

Dean drew in his lips, shrugged, then nodded.

"Things that concern *you*, Justin, to an even greater extent," Brian continued.

"What are you talkin' 'bout?"

"Miss Sloop, for one."

"Who?"

"The woman up in Connecticut."

"What woman?"

"The woman whose home you visited last night."

Ms. Slopbucket, Justin understood. "What about her?"

"She's dead," Brian said straightaway. "Murdered."

Justin looked like he had seen a ghost. Malcolm's. Monisha's. The other bodies up in Redding Ridge. "Murdered how?" he asked in a whisper. "When?"

"Your gun. Or one of them, anyhow," Brian answered. "When did you leave there?"

Justin sank to his ankles and took a seat, facing the end of the pier, placing his forehead upon his kneecaps. He shut his eyes tightly and slowly shook his head. "Where is Andrew Miller?" he demanded.

"Detective Archer just asked you when you left Thelma Sloop's home."

"Thelma Sloop," Justin spoke without lifting his head.

"Yes," Brian said.

"I never even had a chance to ask her name. Can you believe that?"

"What time did you leave there, Justin?" Brian asked again.

Justin raised his head. "You think I killed her. Don't you?"

"No, asshole," Dean announced. "We think you killed Malcolm Columba, and we need to know so that we don't go off on some wild-goose chase out there."

"We need to know so that we can put all our energies into finding Agent Andrew Miller," Brian said calmly. "He may be in grave danger. What time did you leave her home, Justin?"

Justin appeared disoriented. Distrustful. He was well-aware of the deceptive tactics police used to make suspects roll over. Was this one of them? *Themes* were the games detectives played, he knew first and foremost. The murders of prostitutes were downplayed. They were simply portrayed as lowlifes who somehow deserved what they got. A cagey cop helped nail serial killer Howard Mills with that one. Show *sympathy* toward the suspect. *Vilify* the victim: *"They had it coming to them, Howard,"* is what the team told the guy, the maverick heard through the grapevine. And as for Justin . . . *"They'd pin a medal on you if you did, Justin,"* Brian had said. *Yeah. J for jailbird. Pin a rap on my sorry black ass is what they're gonna pin. Pin me to the mat.* Only medal he would see were those metallic vertical bars, he entertained. *Their theme? 'Our hero! You rid the world of vermin for us, Justin. Justice for Justin. Just tell us how you did it and sign on the bottom line after you initial each and every page for us,* **Boy.'** *Justice? Maybe in the next life.*

He would not admit to anything in this one. No way. Nohow.

Like a steady current, his troubled state of mind carried him into the past.

Maybe it was payback time for killing a cop—a million years ago. A *dirty* cop. It seemed as though the incident happened in another lifetime. Maybe it had. He did not buy into the detectives' themes then, and he surely would not blow it now. He had told Monisha only half the truth. Made himself look like a big shot before her. Or so he thought, initially. Cop killer! Tough guy. Bad motherfuckin' dude. Made himself out to be real cool. *Had to kill that fucker, Monisha. Had to put him down.* The truth? Who wanted to hear the motherfucking truth? Not the man or his partner who came to arrest his ass a lifetime ago. *Not the motherfuckin' team of homicide dicks. Teams and themes. Not the D.A., either.* They would not believe his story if he took a series of lie detector tests and passed them all with flying colors, because they were *all* blindsided by black and white back then, as they surely were today. *Take one o' dem polygraphs?* The big problem being was that he would come up short when asked the sixty-four thousand dollar question:

Did you kill Police Officer Talbot?

Oh, how he would have loved to tell them *all* the truth. A full confession:

Yeah, I killed one of your vermin, man. Kill him over again, too, if he was standin' here before me. Reason? Oh, I got me a good reason. Reason is the motherfucker wanted to fuck my black ass. No, I don't mean in the figurative sense, Detectives. I mean he wanted to put his white pecker up my tight black butt. He wanted to take away my manhood, motherfucker. Said he wanted to teach me a motherfucking lesson. Wanted to de·grade me. Said no one gonna believe my story if or when I ever got to tell it. Told me if I did tell it, he'd find me, shoot me, then say that I tried to escape after he put me under arrest. So fucking scared I was. So very fucking scared. But no more scared of him doin' what he had in mind to do. He was a powerful dude. Took him by surprise like I did another flatfoot years before, before they grabbed my butt fo' Grand Theft Auto. Auto theft, my ass. Borrowed cousin Elmo's wheels was all. Messed up that copper's fuckin' face but good back then 'cause I had me the element of surprise. Never thought a skinny little nigger gonna whop his sorry ass. Truth was he never thought I'd have the nerve. But this skinny fuckin' nigger sittin' fo yo was bad and fast. Not so fast this last time out, though. Around the corner in a dark alley this horny honkey had me boxed in good.

"Gonna cornhole you, nigger; and you're gonna love it; then you're gonna beg for more. Now bend your black ass over that shit can and drop your pants and draws and spread 'em."

This here nigger started to do as he was told. But as I lowered my trousers to my ankles, I came up with a special surprise. A slug from a Saturday-night special caught him on an early Monday morning—right between his motherfuckin' eyes. I mean dead center, bro. I mean I watched the fucker bleed, and I felt . . . well . . . special!

But Justin never told a soul the *whole* story.

Couldn't tell Monisha. Wouldn't ever tell no po·lice·man dat.

"I don't know what the fuck yo' talkin' 'bout, motherfuckers," the youthful offender had told the law. *"I ain't crazy 'nough to kill no cop."*

And the beating he took from those two white interrogating detectives he would never ever forget. But they could not break him no matter what they did; and they did plenty. As a last resort, after none of their *themes* and *schemes* worked, came the final game of chance. One of them put the muzzle of a small caliber revolver in Justin's bad black mouth and told him to say a prayer. One bullet, they said, sat in a cylinder chamber. They were going to give him another opportunity to tell the truth, the pair went on to explain, or they would spill his brains on the bathroom floor of a Harlem precinct. The older German cop who held the revolver was dubbed the Spin-*Meister*, although the rookie got to spin the cylinder.

Justin's heart and head exploded each time the hammer fell. But he never once blinked his hateful, fearful eyes, nor took them off the single initial *B* engraved in the walnut handle of another weapon —a German pistol—which the young detective placed on the porcelain sink: the *Deutsche Werke* collector's piece ingrained in the prisoner's memory bank forever.

He promised himself he would kill those two bastards before the month was out. Though he never did, although he swore to himself that he would one day even the score. The pair hounded him for over a year. He thought seriously about killing their wives and children, too. He even followed several of them home from supermarkets and schools once or twice. Mothers. Their daughters. A crippled son. Shortly thereafter, the Spin-*Meister* was found shot to death outside a gay bar which he frequented, allegedly shaking down homosexuals, word had it. Word was also out that the Spin-*Meister* and the cop, who Justin was suspected of killing, had been lovers.

Justin hated everything white, including Christmas. Everything, that is, except his beautiful bright-white teeth, along with Monisha's winning smile. Through the years, he had to stand tough in order to keep all thirty-two in his head. Those sorrowful years. Most of the homeboys he hung with in the past had at least one or two teeth extracted for them—courtesy of rival gangs.

Brian Archer placed a hand on Justin's shoulder. "I asked what time you left Thelma Sloop's home."

"I left her last night around eight—alive—to go look for Columba," Justin told Nelson and Archer. "I found Columba and I lost him, guys. I didn't dump him or anybody overboard."

Dean Nelson smiled and shook his head slowly and patiently, taking a different tact. "I wouldn't be tellin' you some of the things forensics and I found down there—" he said, gesturing back toward the *borrowed* Boston Whaler "—that clearly says you *did* dump him, Barnes, if we were gonna build a case against you. Use your head. You wanna hear more? I'll give you more."

"Give it your best shot, Detective. But I didn't kill Columba."

"Fibers. Fibers from the line. The line you cut clean off the eye bolt in the anchor locker. You hosed the boat, but you didn't hose it well."

Justin looked at Nelson in the best bored expression that he could muster. "Maybe someone else did, mister. Me? All I did was find him and follow him for you."

Dean sighed and nodded sadly. "We found fibers locked between the blade and the handle of your pocketknife. They're consistent with the ones the lab fellows vacuumed up. We'll know shortly if we have a match. Want to hear more, shit-for-brains?"

Justin weighed the situation and his surroundings carefully, believing he could grab Brian's gun and deck Dean before the two knew what hit them. Brian stood just inches from his side. Handle of his handgun handy. Of course, he would have to kill at least one of them.

"I'll wager that our tool marks man is gonna tell us that the striations found on the stainless steel bolt—made when you sawed through the anchor rope—match your knife blade to a tee. And that's just for openers, bonehead," Nelson continued.

Two cops and one tech stood down at the end of the dock, talking with one another. Justin knew he would never make it to the boats before they would cut him down like a cornstalk. He knew, too, that if he did, the Coast Guard would have him in no time flat; that is, if he even made it out to the bay. Making a run toward the front of the house would prove fruitless as well, for at least a dozen law enforcement personnel would drill him in an instant. Only one thing left to do. Deny. Deny. Deny. *Name, rank and serial number, soldier,* he calmly told himself: *Justin Barnes. Bad ass motherfuckin' nigger.* Cell Block and ID numbers from days of old were as good as they were going to get. *Nothin' more. Not one syllable. 'Less they want to listen and learn their states and capitals.*

"Got more good stuff," Nelson went on. "So, you wanna talk to us now? Or do I hand over the rest of the findings to the D.A. in order to *make* a solid case? Be smart, Barnes, and cooperate."

The rest? Justin soured. *Any more evidence, and they won't need a fucking body or confession,* he knew.

Nelson hunched his shoulders indifferently. "Then I guess you'll hear the rest of the laundry list through your attorney at disclosure," the cop threatened. "Make that two attorneys in a capital case. Very costly, Justin Barnes. Unless the court appoints you Moe and Larry. Curly does their legwork from a barstool while you're waiting in the wings. Get the picture, Barnes? What wing you want me to reserve for you?"

Justin was getting the picture, all right; but not the one that the detective was trying to paint so bleakly. "Tell me about Agent Andrew Miller," Justin said abruptly.

"You listening to me, fella?" Dean blasted. "*I'm* askin' the questions. Got that straight?"

What Justin was getting straight in his mind was that the police probably had a mess on their hands in Connecticut, and no one was talking. Agent Andrew Miller was somehow out of the loop, unable to fill them in on many unanswered questions. Get this troublesome nigger to admit to Malcolm Columba's murder, and they would have him off the street, he figured was Nelson's and Archer's game plan— for the moment. Sort out the details concerning Redding Ridge later. *Where's Miller? And why would anyone want to kill the Sloop woman? Unless* . . . unless someone knew that he was going after Columba at all costs and wanted to stop him cold. *But who? Miller?* Then back again he drifted in wonder as to a reason *why? Unless Andrew is one of Columba's disciples. One of the federal agents in Charlotte's web, which she bragged about so openly. Were Charlotte and Austin Izzo part of some cult? No.* Their business was simply *family* business. Loyal to Don Ciccio, right up to the end. Don Ciccio was the 'boss of all bosses,' Justin firmly believed. The mobster's business was strictly about bucks. Not kicks or causes, he affirmed.

"Either I'm under arrest, or I walk, now, Detective Nelson," Justin said confidently and curtly.

"Then you'll walk right into the backseat of an unmarked vehicle waiting for you up at the house. And you'll answer our questions at headquarters. The choice is yours."

Justin frowned. "Yeah, some choice, fuck-face."

"Get movin', tough guy."

Chapter 79

"This landline secure?"

"Absolutely."

"We got big problems," the veteran cop confided in Federal Agent Andrew Miller. "Big problems," he repeated.

"The world is full of problems. That's probably why we went into law enforcement in the first place. Right? To solve those problems. We do that each and every day. We're problem solvers, you and I. This one will be no different. You'll see."

"With Columba gone?"

"*Father* Columba, if you please," Miller intoned against the mouthpiece. "Please show a little respect."

"Father Columba sleeps upon a seabed," Detective Dean Nelson made perfectly clear.

"Then at least extend your condolences for the dearly departed," Miller added rather cynically. "If I didn't know any better, I'd put the blame on Don Ciccio and the bad company he keeps."

"That's the way it was *supposed* to go down. So what the fuck happened?"

"You know damn well what happened, Dean. Justin Barnes happened on the scene. So, now you write him out of it—after he signs off with a confession."

"That's not going to be easy."

"Are you the lead detective on this, or not?"

"Yeah, but—"

"But nothing. You find a way. You solve the problem."

"It's not going to be easy."

"You just said that."

"There's a lot of talent on this case. And I do have a partner. Remember?"

"You'll find a way."

Dean Nelson took a deep breath before he spoke again. "I'd

like you to find someone else to do this." There was a long pause. "You there?"

"I'm here."

"Well, did you hear what I said?"

"Yes, Dean. I heard you."

"And?"

"And I'm waiting for you to come to your senses."

"Andy, listen—"

"There's no one else, Dean. I think you know that. No one," the man repeated firmly. "There's very little time."

Dean wanted to smash the receiver against the Lucite wall, wondering how things ever got this far. He was trapped. Psychologically as well as figuratively confined. Standing there all alone on the street corner. Boxed in a narrow claustrophobic phone booth with the door closed. Half a block away from his home. Pinned to the untenable situation. So close to retirement. He could *not* afford to blow it now. But there was no way out, short of plastering his brains beneath the aluminum roof, precisely where he stood. Then again, he could go back to the car, his home, or even headquarters and do it there.

"I'm going to need some time."

"Two days are all you've got, Dean. Know why?"

"I know."

"Tell me."

"I said, I know."

"Tell me, so I know you know," the agent insisted. "Humor me."

"Brian and Kim will be back from a Vegas weekend. I'm the one who twisted their arms to go. Recall?"

"Two days. That's it—before the Connecticut boys start to piece together what really happened up at Redding Ridge."

"All right."

"All right what?"

"It'll get done."

"It better."

"I said, it'll get done."

"Good, because that coon's a loose cannon and a loose end."

"Suppose the Connecticut authorities *do* figure it out."

491

"They won't. Not if you act now."

"Why's that?"

"Things have been set in place so that they won't look past their noses."

"What the hell is that supposed to mean?"

"It means, Dean, that they've latched onto the business at hand up there. They'll toss it around for a while, then come away satisfied. They'll hang their hats on it. Investigate it to death, they will not do. So. What did they find up there, Dean? Let me hear it."

"A prostitution ring."

"That's it. Plain and simple. It won't go beyond that. Know why?"

"No, why?"

"It's too complicated. Too bizarre. Not even Kim and Big Sister or Brian could figure it out."

"That I wouldn't bet on."

"No?"

"No."

"So it behooves you to put an end to this. Let Justin Barnes stand as the final chapter in this story. Then they'll all let sleeping dogs lie. He went berserk and killed *all* those people up there at Redding Ridge. Broke into my trunk and stole those weapons. I tried to stop him, but he bested me. True enough, in fact. He needed a safe house, and so he befriended, then betrayed Thelma Sloop, murdering the woman in cold blood. Motive? She'd connect him to the slaughter. And, of course, we *do* know he killed the Father of The Federation."

"The only problem is we have a witness who can place Barnes getting off a ferry back at Port Jefferson, *before* the time of Sloop's death."

"Witness was mistaken. Coroner, too. Time of death was two hours earlier than erroneously recorded. Coroner's a chronic alcoholic. And your eyewitness is seventy-seven years old with cataracts. It won't be too difficult to discredit either of them. No one will push the issue once Barnes is out of the picture. Permanently."

"What about Ciccio?"

"What about him?"

"Won't he squawk?"

"About what?"

"Charlotte Magni and Austin Izzo, for openers. He lost a few key people up there. Not to mention the chance to score *big*."

"Let me tell you something about Don Vincent Ciccio, Dean. Above all else, he's a businessman. If you want to know the truth, he was getting a little leery of Magni. Rumor has it she wanted to go out on her own with Izzo. It's one of the reasons why Ciccio kept a close eye on her of late. But those two certainly can and will be replaced. Ciccio gets paid very well to use part of his operation as a front. Prostitution as a cover for proselytizing. Who'd pick up on that? It usually works the other way around. Correct? Columba's people recruited some nineteen thousand last year alone, Dean. Over half a million strong to begin the new millennium. Along with a thousand luminaries and benefactors—like Evan Tamblin—spread across twenty countries. Some with their heads up their asses or in the clouds. Big business is blinding, Dean. The New Order is on solid ground. Don Ciccio has his thing. And *we*, thanks to Father Columba, God rest his sick fucking soul, have ours."

"What if you're exposed?"

"We *are* exposed, Dean. And that's the beauty of it. As naked as the day we were born. Parading in the light of truth. And do you know what that single truth is? We've infiltrated practically every known cult of significance in the Western Hemisphere. We figure twenty, maybe twenty-five percent of similar groups in the Mideast. We help keep America safe, Dean. The United States of America. People like you and me. It's not so much a nuclear attack we should be worried about as it is the explosion of brainwashed youth creating havoc in towns and cities throughout the world. But we're in there, Dean. Thick as thieves. Yet, they can't see us because we've blindsided them. Father Columba was a visionary. A genius."

"Father Columba was a nut. A self-proclaimed savior. A serial killer."

"He had his predilections, I suppose."

"You suppose," Nelson said sarcastically.

"Like any of us, Dean."

"Don't even begin to compare me—"

"To a summer's day? You're absolutely right. How can I compare thee—"

"Cut the crap, all right?"

"Just bear in mind that Father Columba, a lobsterman for all intents and porpoises," the agent funned, "created the brainchild of infiltrating virtually *every* organization—known and unknown, big and small—like nobody's agency has or ever will again. We've got more that just a foothold, Dean. We're in like Flynn. The likes of which has never been done before. From dubious cluster groups fostering their brand of fetishes, to extreme and dangerous circles of fanatics. From high-tech evangelism for profit, to the storefront criminal and on up through the ranks of organized crime's infrastructure, to its very core. Father Columba provided us with the who, why, where, when and how. The *how*, Dean. The how was the hard part. Eliminating for us, not minimizing, mind you, but essentially removing the risk of revealment of our undercover agents. That's a remarkable accomplishment. The only shame being in that we couldn't patent the package for ourselves," the federal agent admitted quite seriously. "But we sure learned how to mind the store. So, let's give credit where credit is due. Shall we?"

Nelson could envision the megalomaniac gloating satisfactorily on the other end of the line. "But at what price, Andy?"

Agent Andrew Miller snickered. "You can answer that better than I, Dean. I don't happen to have my abacus handy at the moment."

"Twelve innocent lives that lunatic took. Twelve lives that we know of. There came a point in this investigation that I believed he might have gone after my wife and daughter."

There was another pause.

"I see, Andy. All just casualties of war as far as you're concerned. Collateral damage. The end justifies the means. Is that it?"

"Tell you a little story, Dean. Shouldn't, but I shall. Last year we averted what would have been a mid-air disaster. The lives of over four hundred passengers and crew were an hour away from annihilation. No thank yous or even innocuous pats upon the back were given because we kept everything quiet. The public never knew a thing. Of course, the airline and its customers bitched over the inconvenience of having been brought back down to earth. Just imagine. Your *estranged* wife—who you really don't give two shits about—and daughter, who you love deeply, could have been on that flight, Dean. All right? Seven Middle Eastern terrorists, who *wear* their sheets to bed, are dead. That's just one story. I can't go into the other concerning Air Force One last month. Now. Our business is almost over, Dean."

"Why did you let him operate so long? You had the fucking formula for success."

"That formula varies with each new situation. The simple fact is we needed him right up to the end."

This time Dean Nelson did, indeed, smash the receiver into one of the wall panels.

"What was that, Dean?" Miller asked, although he knew well enough. "A childish display of anger?"

Dean put the instrument back up to his ear. "You were just going to allow him to continue to operate. Weren't you?"

"You know that's not true. Don't you?"

"I know nothing of the sort."

"We assisted you. Did we not? You would have gotten him. We would have gotten him. Or Ciccio's crew would have gotten him. He was out there hanging in the wind."

"What about the *variation* to that fucking formula of yours? Huh? Every new situation required *him*, you just said."

"Yes, but there finally came a point. East Point to be precise. He outwore his usefulness to us when he finished off Evan Tamblin."

"I don't get it."

"Of course, you don't, Dean. That's why you don't have to worry, because no one else is going to get it either. Not the Connecticut police. Not Kim, in conjunction with Big Sister. And not any of your other *talent*, as you put it. Including your partner, Brian Archer."

Dean Nelson's mind was whirling like a dervish. "What are you talking about?"

"Father Columba, I thought," Andrew answered.

"You going to tell me?"

"Sure. Why not, Dean?"

"I'm listening."

"Evan Tamblin was his contact."

"Whose contact?"

"Columba's."

"What are you saying?"

"You don't think a lobsterman operating by his lonesome can

infiltrate the corners of the world that Tamblin did, do you? Evan Tamblin literally walked Father Columba into those secret societies to which the industrialist belonged. Scores of them. Malcolm was trusted. He was treated with immeasurable respect. Tamblin, as you know, did business in practically every corner of the globe. Lived modestly for a multibillionaire. Ironic he should die in the home of a man of lesser means, but one who could still buy a small country if he wanted to."

"Was Tamblin aware of Columba's dealings with your agency as it concerns us?"

"Not whatsoever."

Amazing, Nelson thought.

"Tamblin was too busy raking in money hand over fist to make it his business to snoop—or to have anyone else do it, for that matter. Not on a grand scale. And, like I said, he trusted Columba implicitly. After Tamblin's daughter was murdered, Evan set up a meeting with Don Ciccio and people of the inner circle. One in city government. One of your own ilk, in fact—whose names shall remain anonymous. Ciccio suspected that Columba was the one who helped give us the heads of several organized crime figures on a platinum platter. From the intelligence we gathered, Vincent made a cool ten million off Tamblin, apart from the murder of that half-breed, Donald Bellport. Fact of the matter is Ciccio would have hunted down Columba for nothing save expenses if it came to that. Actually, he even offered to do so, but Tamblin wanted special attention to detail. The kind of detail that a few of Ciccio's people really enjoy doing and do so well."

"But you still would have let Columba operate if he hadn't killed Tamblin," Nelson said angrily. "Isn't that so, Andy?"

"No, that's not so."

"How so?"

"Because the sky is falling. Because people like Kim with Big Sister get closer to the truth every single day. Because the information highway is becoming a two-way street. That's why we end this business, now, with Barnes."

"But not because twelve serial murders were committed and that you had to draw the line in the sand someplace because enough was enough?"

"Those unfortunates, unwittingly and indirectly, of course, saved literally thousands of lives. You have no idea of the madness in the world, Dean."

"I don't, huh?"

"No, you really don't. Not even a fucking clue. Believe me when I tell you that. Malcolm Columba, as author and architect of the most successful covert operation any government agency in the world has ever known—making even the CIA's campaign in Afghanistan look like a game of checkers—will never be equaled.

"And now that both Columba and Tamblin are dead?"

Agent Andrew Miller considered the question carefully before he spoke. "Let's just say that we're going to have our hands full concerning a certain militant Islamic fundamentalist faction if we can't keep all our ducks in a row—if the lid is ever blown off Columba's deep-cover operation."

Homicide Detective Dean Nelson had nothing further to say.

"Two days, Dean. Let's complete the final chapter. And remember. We need that nigger's confession first and foremost."

Chapter 80

A dense fog bank gradually lifted as Brian and Kim drove toward the building in the distance. Police headquarters stood somberly situated at 30 Yaphank Avenue. Home away from home for the Suffolk County Homicide Squad. A few minutes later, the pair pulled into the parking lot, stepped out, then headed briskly for the rear entrance.

Justin Barnes stood alone in the infamous 8 x 8 foot interrogation room—a transient stopover for holdovers on their way to an earthly hell. His right foot was chained securely to a shackle in the floor, both wrists tightly bound in manacles.

Dean Nelson carefully opened the door to the confined space, clumsily balancing a towering white Styrofoam container, serving as a pedestal on which sat a small brown paper bag, clamped beneath the man's chin. Two pens were locked between his teeth. The other hand held a ruled pad of white paper. With a foot, he pushed the steel door closed.

"You're right, Barnes. You folks just can't seem to keep yourselves out of chains and trouble. Can you? No matter how hard you try," he said rather indistinctly, smiling broadly from behind the pair of black plastic pens sticking out from the sides of his mouth like thick whiskers. Dean set the items down upon a small table against the wall, just outside of Justin's reach, far enough away from the prisoner's free leg, just in case the detective's caged collar decided to vent. Over the years, several of them had. "I'm gonna give you some facts, Barnes. Know why we have the success rate in solving homicides like we do?"

"Sure. You railroad folks, like you doin' me, chump."

Nelson laughed lightly and shook his head. "I'll put it to you plain and simple-like. I know you're good with figures and smart enough to understand. As I'm sure you're well-aware, we've got three teams here at homicide. Twenty-five men investigating about forty murders a year, as opposed to some other areas of the country where they run roughly two hundred and fifty murders annually—with guess how many men? Ten on average. I shit you not. Now, you tell me how ten detectives can effectively investigate two hundred and fifty murders a year. Bet your ass some spooks and gooks and spics get railroaded. But here in Suffolk County, Barnes, we've got plenty of manpower. Plenty of resources, too. We have our own accredited DNA lab. What I'm sayin' here, Mr. Barnes, is that we got you dead to rights. All the evidence is in. And guess where it points? You cooperate now, and you'll see light at the end of the tunnel. Fuck with me, and I'll bury you forever. That's a promise. So. You ready to sign off and save your black ass?"

"Fuck you."

"Fuck me?"

"Yeah, fuck you."

"No, fuck you!"

"You have no right holding me here like this. You said you were bringing me in for questioning. I answered your questions. Only, not to your liking."

"What we questioned you about was the *truth*. But that word doesn't appear to be in your vocabulary. New, or old. Does it?"

"You can't hold me without food and water. You can't hold me here without letting me make a fucking phone call. I have rights."

"You have a bad attitude, if you ask me." Dean Nelson opened the bag, removed a stack of napkins, then unwrapped the greasy paper from around a juicy cheeseburger. Next, he lifted the lid from the container of rich coffee. The aromas pervaded the space and rose invitingly to Justin's nostrils.

"You gonna eat another fucking cheeseburger in front of me and drink more goddamn coffee?" Justin barked.

"I'm gonna *give you* this burger and coffee if you'll just cooperate and tell us the truth."

"Then the truth is you're gonna eat that burger and drink that java yourself, 'cause I ain't givin' you jack-shit, Jack. I ain't givin' you the time of day, but you can bet your motherfuckin' ass I'm tellin' it to the judge. A day-and-a-half, dickhead. A day-and-a-half without a meal except for an end of a slice of Sicilian pizza, along with half a cup of water that you *accidentally* spilled and did not bother to refill."

"Truth is my men grew tired of taking you to the bathroom twice a day. Which tells me you're no longer full of piss, shit and vinegar. Which also tells me you're gonna sign a confession to killing Malcolm Columba, in exchange for a pass for the murders you committed up in Redding Ridge—or you won't see a fucking crumb, 'cept maybe a mouthful of water from the porcelain throne, if your lucky." And with that declaration, Detective Dean Nelson sank his teeth into the greasy bun and burger before lifting the cup of coffee to his lips . . . paused . . . then toasted Justin with a subtle salute.

"Fuck you, you piece of white garbage. When I get out of here, you goin' down, honky."

"You just don't learn. Do you, Justin Barnes?"

"Learned all I need to know 'bout white man's law. Need all I need know 'bout yo' motherfuckin' daughter, too. Gonna do her good when I get outta here, cocksucker." Justin opened his fists and extended two gun-fingers—a short length of chain dangling from his braceleted wrists. "And then I'm gonna come for you."

Dean Nelson stopped chewing somewhere in the middle of Justin's threat. He put his coffee and burger down upon the table, then stood.

"That's right, motherfucker. Know all 'bout yo' broke up family and where they hang out in sunny ol' Florida," Justin swore. "And jus' in case I don't make it out o' here, I got me people on the outside who gonna take real good care of 'em." The veins in Justin's neck flared. "Hear me, coward? You ain't fuckin' 'round wif no janitor, motherfucker. You fuckin' 'round wif *moi*."

Oh, I hear you all right, Justin Barnes. I hear you loud and clear. You just made it so easy for me to do what I have to do to you. You'll make it out of here, all right. You'll make it to where I'm gonna break you into a thousand pieces. But first you'll write and sign a full confession. That I can assure you, nigger. Before the day is out, Dean Nelson swore inwardly.

The detective sat back down with feigned composure. Drinking the dark, rich coffee—eating the rare cheeseburger smothered with fried onions sandwiched between the meat and sesame seed bun. The sound of a thick, crunchy slice of raw onion, too, beneath the bottom half of the bun, kept beat with a masticating jaw. Like the Burger King slogan goes, Nelson would have it his way. He would have Justin Barnes' full confession with his signature on the bottom line. He would have him initial the top of every page. He would have him cryin' in his beer. Literally. For most of their confessors were rewarded a plastic cup filled to the brim with either beer or soda, followed by a cigarette, in exchange for their *true* crime stories, regardless of whether they were completely true or not. But if Justin Barnes was not careful, he would be wearing the Bud and Marlboro across his foul black mouth whether he drank, smoked or not, Dean Nelson promised himself. Then he would take his prisoner for a final ride.

Dean heard the door open behind him before abruptly and angrily turning around.

Chapter 81

Detective Brian Archer walked into the interrogation room, leaving the door wide open. The *interview* room, as it was euphemistically referred to by police when addressing the community at large, left many naive folks with a false impression that a question-and-answer session was to be conducted in a civil manner. Nothing could be further from the truth, as questions were virtually set forth as statements of fact, to which the suspect's answers had better match the preconceived notions of the *interviewer.* For once a prisoner passed beneath the sign above the doorway—the sign that read 𝕿𝖍𝖔𝖚 𝕾𝖍𝖆𝖑𝖙 𝕹𝖔𝖙 𝕶𝖎𝖑𝖑—crossing that threshold, he or she was presumed guilty. Suffolk County Homicide's success rate in acquiring written and/or signed confessions, along with the interrogating detective's John Hancock, signed, sealed and delivered to the district attorney's office, was ninety-eight percent.

Detective Dean Nelson looked up at his partner and scowled. "You're back early, buddy. Guess you can see I'm conducting an interview here, Bri."

"Theo asked me to step in," Brian put forth bluntly.

Dean's displeasure disappeared as the look of sheer surprise took its place. "Step in, like to say, hello? Or step in to interfere?" he questioned unabashedly. "Which is exactly what you're doing, guy," the lead detective stated matter-of-factly, with an edge to his voice that could cut glass.

"I guess a little of both," Brian answered uncomfortably.

Dean Nelson stared at his cohort. "You guess?"

"Theo—"

"I said, I'm conducting an interview, Brian," Dean repeated.

"Theo wants me to take over here. He wants to see you in his office."

"He does." It was not a question.

"Yes. Right now."

"Mr. Barnes and I are right in the middle of a little chat. Ain't that right, *boy*? Justin Barnes wants to bare his soul before me. *Now.*"

Brian glanced at Justin, then fixed his eyes firmly on Nelson. "I'm sorry, Dean."

"Sorry that you're interrupting? Or just a sorry shit?"

"There's no need to be—"

"Who the fuck do you think you are, fella? Huh?" Then, with a single swipe, Dean wiped the table's surface clean. The Styrofoam coffee container, nearly filled to its brim, along with the rest of the burger, flew against the wall, as did the pad, pens, napkins and sheet of greasy wrap. "Just where the fuck do you get off?"

Brian smiled sadly. "I'm afraid it's where you get off, Dean. You're off the case. I figured you'd rather hear it from me first than wait till you got upstairs."

Nelson looked at Archer like he had two heads. "Say what?"

Brian raised his eyes to a corner where the ceiling met the walls. "They just finished fishing Columba's body from the sea." He lowered his head and held Justin's gaze.

Dean got up, took one step closer to Justin, then forced a smile before he began his preamble. "So. I guess you're not going anywhere for a while, Barnes. And when you do, it'll be to your arraignment. Then off to Riverhead Jail. Not for boat theft," he clarified with a grin, "but to await trial for murder. From there you're goin' up to Dannemora, where you'll surely sink. Right along a river. For the rest of your natural life. That is, if you're lucky. Either way, *I* know people up there who I promise are gonna show ya a real nice time, pretty boy." The detective turned away, brushed past his partner, then angrily left the claustrophobic space, slamming the door closed behind him.

Chapter 82

Detective Brian Archer unlocked and removed the restraints from Justin's wrists and foot, soaked up most of the spilled coffee off the floor and table with a fistful of napkins, then took a seat against the wall, directing the prisoner to do the same.

Justin sat and rubbed his wrists, reached down and massaged his right ankle.

"Brave motherfucker; ain't ya, Brian?" Justin sounded off.

"How's that?"

"Sittin' here wif nothin' 'tween that door 'cept you an' me is what I mean."

"I don't think I have anything to worry about. Do you?"

"I could put yo' porch lights out 'fo you ever bat an eyelid, motherfucker."

"Justin. You ever listen to yourself? I mean *really* stop and listen to yourself. You sound like a black Fonzie with a foul mouth. Ever see those reruns? Henry Winkler. Fifties character. Only thing you're missing is the motorcycle jacket."

Justin wore a dumb expression.

"Not important," Brian said behind a friendly smile. "What *is* important is that you stop and think."

"I *been* thinkin', man. I'm thinkin' you fuckers are setting me up for the fall. That's what I'm thinkin', Mister De·tec·tive."

"You're playin' a role that doesn't quite become you, Justin. Tough guy. State prisons are full of them, as I know you know."

"And just what role *you* playin'? Huh? You playin' good cop after that bad motherfucker hit the door? I'm supposed to listen to yo' line of crap 'bout what's in my best interest, then roll over? Is that what you 'spect me to do? Huh?"

"No, Justin."

"Fuckin' A, 'No, Justin.' No way, José. And jus' like O. J., I got me the motherfuckin' juice to outlast ya all. How 'bout *dem* oranges, Dick Tracy?"

Brian laughed. "You talk the talk. But you don't really walk the walk."

"Whatchoo mean?"

"What I mean is that I never saw you with your pants down around your ass. Never saw you do a shuffle off to Buffalo sashay, where it would take two lifetimes to make it around the corner and back. That's what I mean. I saw you at your best doing police work alongside Miller, with those maps and Moose Lodge listings. It's a silly show you're putting on now, J. Nonproductive. Antagonistic. And what's worse—"

"Yeah, what's worse, Detective? You tell me."

"What's worse is that you're playing right into their hands."

"Ohhh, *their* hands. Tell me. Who is *they*? Like you ain't part of the equation? Like Detectives Dean Nelson and Brian Archer don't add up to two peas in the same pod? Well, when Miller has his say, you'll be singing my praises. And *then* maybe you'll help my po' black ass instead of kickin' it around."

Brian pulled his chair in half a foot closer to Justin's. "I want to help you right now."

"You do? Wow! Whatta I gotta do? I know." Justin reached down and picked up the coffee-soaked pad and a pen from a small puddle on the floor. He ripped off several pages, down to the driest section of sheets.

Two detectives, just outside the doorway, stood at the ready— peering through the two-way mirror in the wall.

Justin roughly set pen to paper and scribbled something down.

The pair behind the door relaxed and smiled satisfactorily to one another.

Justin pushed the page beneath Archer's nose. "There."

Brian looked amused. "That's good, J. Except for a few things."

"What's that?"

"Capital is spelled with an *a-l*, not *o-l*. Nevada has two *a*'s. Not three. N-*e*-v-a-d-a. And Carson City is with an s-o-n. Not s-u-n. Renamed after Kit Carson."

"Kit Carson, huh?" Justin said, averting the issue.

"Know who he was?"

"Sure I know who he was. White man who killed all dem Indians."

"Pretty much an unsettled and troubled young man like yourself. He ran away from his problems but later found himself, in his early thirties, as a famous guide—then went on to become a colonel in the army. Later, a brigadier general. In the last year of his life, he was named superintendent of Indian affairs."

Justin frowned. "Figures, don't it?"

Brian smiled amicably.

"Jus' why the spellin' and history lesson? Huh, Brian?"

"Well, we all know how hard you've been working at trying to improve yourself, J."

"Jus' *tryin'*, huh?"

"Doing a pretty good job of it until you decided to take the law into your own hands."

"Jus' doin' *your* job, Detective. Only difference bein' is dat you got da badge, which makes it *all* so *le·gal* like. Now, ain't dat right? But like I said, when Miller shows, he's gonna set things straight. You'll see."

"That's what I want to talk to you about. Andrew Miller."

Justin did not like the detective's tone or the look on his face.

"Andy says you went on a rampage up at Redding Ridge. A killing spree. That you shot a dozen people in cold blood, including Viola Johnson and her daughter, Virginia Dupree, while hunting for Malcolm Columba. Left no witnesses. Murdered the Sloop woman. Came back here to find and kill the man who murdered your kissing cousin, Monisha Washington." He let the information sink into Justin's head.

"Said all dat, did he?"

Brian nodded.

"Well, I don't fucking believe you. How's *that*?"

Brian pulled a copy of the report from his pocket and handed it over. "Read."

Justin stared at the papers vacantly. "You read it."

Brian fixed his eyes on Justin and took back the pages, leaving them faceup on the table. He did not have to read it. He and Kim knew Miller's half of the story by heart. Instead, without taking his eyes off the suspect, he told Justin in sum and substance what the undercover

506

federal agent had written in his five-page report.

"It says that when Andy arrived at the ranch, he found two men and a woman dead inside the house, upstairs. He said he located you in a parking field just north of the ranch. That you had broken into the trunk of his car and stolen several automatic weapons. He told you that you were under arrest, at which point a wounded male figure lying on the ground fired a shot in your direction from a tree line, catching Miller off guard. That's when you clobbered him, rendering him unconscious, then took his service weapon and handcuffs. When he came to, he discovered several more bodies in and around the area. Security people mostly. Ciccio's people. All licensed to carry firearms. All stone-cold dead. The authorities found Viola Washington. Shot in the back. Some distance away, the body of her daughter, Virginia, was discovered in a ditch. Shot in the back of the head with one of your handguns. Taurus Millennium Pro., 9-millimeter. One of the two pistols Miller said he confiscated from you. Then he tracked you to Sloop's home and found her murdered when he got there. The Connecticut police lifted your prints from the table in the living room, a water glass in the sink, toilet seat cover, doorknob, et cetera. She was shot in the side of the head, three times, at point-blank range. Ballistics matched those slugs to the three taken from the bodies found upstairs at the ranch: Austin Izzo, Charlotte Magni, and her nephew. A total of six 9-millimeter Kurz rounds that were fired from your AMT Backup —threaded with a silencer. Two additional slugs removed from two men in the parking field I mentioned. Again, they were fired from your Taurus. Both handguns were found in a Dumpster near you home. A Weatherby rifle that killed Viola Johnson was recovered in the woods, nearby. Prints wiped clean. What would you conclude from all that, Justin?"

Justin sounded like a deflated tire as he steadily let the air out of his lungs. "I'd conclude that yo' got yo'self a fox in da hen house if what you say is true. But it didn't go down like that at all, Brian." Justin shook his head. "Miller is gonna hav'ta tell me to my face that he wrote and signed that report."

"Before what? Before you tell me what really happened up there? Before someone takes you out of here and you wind up having a fatal accident, or that I'm told you were shot outright while trying to escape?"

"In *po·lice* custody, my man?"

"Yeah, in fucking police custody, asshole. Who'd know that better than a black man from the hood?"

Justin smirked. "Whitey in the woodpile, Brian."

"Meaning?"

"Meaning one of you's a lyin' motherfucker is what it means. And I ain't sayin' 'nother fuckin' word till I get me my mouthpiece."

"You mean that shyster who got you off the hook a couple of times on gunrunning charges across state lines, Justin? We're talking multiple murder charges here. You're going to need a team of experienced murder trial lawyers. You're going to need—I'll spell it out for you. C-a-p-i-t-a-l. Understand? Lots of greenbacks, fella."

Justin studied Brian Archer before he opened his mouth again. "So, why would I want to talk to you? Huh? Tell me. Anything I say can and will be used against me in a court of law. Right? I haven't even been charged with anything yet. Okay? That asshole partner of yours didn't even Mirandize me. You talkin' a whole lot o' shit here, but I ain't heard no fuckin' formal charge. You jus' unhappy 'cause you can't pin dis Columba shit on me, so you goin' off on one o' dem fishin' expeditions that yo' pricks are famous fo'. You ain't got squat, Dick Tracy. What you got are balls of brass, tryin' ta lay dis shit on me."

"What we got, Justin, is Columba's body."

"Got zip," Justin prayed. "You jus' blowin' smoke."

"Look at me. You hit the Man Overboard button on the GPS. Only you forgot or didn't know to cancel it. It gave us the coordinates. Columba is who we went fishing for because we know you drowned him back there. Just as sure as you live in Mastic/Shirley, Pearly. You bound his feet with nylon line. You cuffed him in back with Miller's bracelets, clipped one end of a twelve-inch piece of quarter-inch nylon line to the link between the manacles, the other end to the anchor chain, then threw him overboard into a hundred sixty-some feet of water southeast of the inlet. He had on a pair of beige latex gloves when they brought him to the top. That and a pair of underwear. That's why we didn't find his fingerprints on *Boy 'n Sea*. But Dean told you about his blood. It places him on that boat with you."

"If I had the fucking foresight to put latex gloves on Columba to conceal his fucking fingerprints, then why didn't *I* wear gloves at

Thelma Sloop's place if I planned on murdering her, instead of leaving my calling card on a water glass, toilet seat cover, or wherever the fuck else you found 'em? Huh?"

"That's one of the questions a colleague and I were asking ourselves. We thought maybe Columba had them on when he did Tamblin, but that wasn't the case. His prints were all over Eyler's place. That's the waterfront property you returned to in case you didn't know the owner's name. Malcolm Columba didn't need to hide his identity at that point. He knew we knew who he was by then. It's one of the smartest questions you've raised since we began this conversation."

"Yeah, well we're not havin' no conversation, Detective. I want to call my lawyer, *now*."

"Fine. That's the way you want it?"

"That's the way it's gotta be, Brian."

"Then I'm formally charging you with the murder of Malcolm Columba, for openers." Detective Brian Archer stood and pulled a rights card from a well-worn trifold and began reading:

"You have the right to remain silent.

Anything you say can and will be used in a court of law.

You have the right to talk to a lawyer right now and have him present with you while you are being questioned.

If you cannot afford a lawyer and want one, a lawyer will be appointed for you by the court before any questioning.

If you decide to answer questions now without a lawyer present, you will have the right to stop the questioning at any time until you talk to a lawyer."

Detective Brian Archer paused before he read the next three questions:

"Do you understand each of these rights that I have explained to you?"

Justin sat with his arms folded firmly across his chest, puckering his thick lips.

"Well, do you, Mr. Barnes?"

"Know I do, white boy," Justin sassed the cop.

"Do you wish to contact a lawyer?"

"Does a junky need a fix, Sherlock? Yeah, I want me my motherfuckin' mouthpiece. Already tol' ya dat."

"Having these rights in mind, do you wish to talk to me now without a lawyer?"

"Man, who writes this shit fo' yo'? Huh? If I answered *yes* to number two, why the fuck would I *wish* to talk to you now or ever? What I *wish* is that you'd get me some motherfuckin' chow, chump. That's what I wish."

Brian put the rights card down on the table in front of the accused. "Initial the top of the card, then next to each of the three questions. I'm sure you know the drill, J.B. Initials can double for Jail Bird, bro."

Justin did just that.

Brian and he were finished.

"Consider yourself Mirandized," the detective said. "Consider yourself fucked."

Fuck! Justin said to himself. *Motherfucker.*

Brian turned away and headed for the door.

Chapter 83

Detective Dean Nelson stepped into the hotel room and closed the door behind him.

Special Agent Andrew Miller blew sky high. "What the fuck do you mean, he's in protective custody?"

"Theo put him there, Andy," Dean explained, plopping himself into a seat against the wall.

Andrew Miller paced the floor. "Cryin' out loud! I give you one simple task to carry out, and you blow it."

"Brian and Kim came back early."

"Early? Early, Dean?

"I warned you about them. Didn't I?"

"And I warned *you*, very early on, about the consequences of failing to take care of Barnes, as well as the importance of his confession. And whether you secured it or you didn't, I told you to put an end to this business. I told you that with that nigger out of the picture, you boys and girls would move on. But no. You had to drag things out."

"I was about to take him to Hauppauge. Only he never would have made his arraignment."

"And now? Now he's had a chance to tell his side of the story. To Archer, no less."

"He didn't tell Archer anything."

"But maybe he said something to Theo. Certainly his lawyer."

"I don't think—"

"That's right. You don't *think*. You don't think because you don't *know*. You don't know because Theo took you off the case. Which tells me that he suspects something."

"It's your word against Barnes'."

Miller shook his head. "It's so much more than that now, Dean. It's my word against Barnes', coupled with Brian's and Kim's interference into the matter, along with Theo's suspicion—and God only knows what else. If Theo puts more people on this, and it launches into a full-scale investigation, the lid could come off this thing."

"So, what do you propose?"

Miller stopped pacing and smiled broadly. "Dean, I propose a toast." The agent stepped over to a liquor cabinet.

The detective followed his movements with anxious eyes. "A toast?"

"Yes."

"To what?"

"To all good things that must come to an end."

"Such as?"

Andrew turned around. "You, for one, Dean." From six feet away, the federal agent drew a handgun with a silencer pointed at the homicide detective's chest.

Dean Nelson did not seem surprised. "You don't think I came here without knowing that you had murder on your mind. Do you, Andy? I asked myself why you would even take a chance on us being seen together—unless it was absolutely necessary. This little conversation we're having, we could have had over a secure phone. But a face-to-face only meant one thing to me. My demise. In a sense, this moment *is* my death, Andrew. Far worse than the immediate kind, because it's a death I'll have to live with every day for the rest of my life. I think Columba taught some of us that lesson—if he taught us nothing else."

"I don't know what you're getting at, Dean."

"That's because you're still young yet, kid. Still wet behind the ears like your partner told you several times."

"So, if you knew what I had in store for you, why did you bother to come?"

"You can't figure that one out for yourself, Andy?"

"Afraid I can't."

"It's good to be afraid, fella," Dean shot back playfully, looking up at the killer calmly. "I guess I'll have to tell you so as to clear away the cobwebs. I came here to watch you die."

Andrew laughed incredulously. "You kidding me or what?"

"Wouldn't kid a kid, kid."

"What you're accomplishing here, I have to admit, is one of the great stall tactics of all time. You're good, Dean. Cool as a cucumber.

That's why I picked you. But now it's time to say goodbye."

Dean gave a depressing grin. "One quick question before we part company then," he said rather anxiously.

"Sure. Why not? Just one."

"Is this your decision or the agency's?"

"Mine alone, Dean."

"How about a drink before I go?"

"Sorry, Dean. I don't drink."

Andrew's thumb and forefinger moved merely a fraction when suddenly the side of his head exploded quietly in an upward rain of red. Blood and bone and tissue splashed against a stark-white wall. In an instant, the federal agent fell to the floor. Dead as a door knocker. Just not as cold.

"And just what the fuck were you waiting for?" Nelson snapped.

Detective Ed Hennesey opened wide the adjoining door between the connecting rooms, came forward, and with a footsweep, sent the agent's handgun away from the body. "Had to be sure he meant business, laddie. You wouldn't want me shootin' someone down in cold blood. Now would ya?" he questioned with a grin.

"He could have shot me in mid-sentence, Ed."

"He'd haveta 'ave taken the safety off first, Dean. I shot 'im when he started to do just that. So relax. Besides. You bought some time, and now you know you got no score to settle with the feds."

"I got plenty to settle with them bastards."

Ed studied Dean carefully and saw nothing but trouble in Nelson's dark brown eyes. "Let it go, Dean. I'm tellin' you here and now to let it go. Just like you're gonna let *all* this business go. It's done. Finished. Over with. Understand?"

Dean shook his head. "I'm turning in my badge and gun when I get back."

"Are like hell. Shoot you now myself if I haveta 'fore I'd ever let ya do a fool thing like that."

"It's all gonna come out, Ed. I just wanna wipe the slate clean beforehand."

"And lose your pension? You wanna do your retirement in a cell? Think of your family, if not yourself."

"D.A. may go easy on me if I cooperate fully with the

department now instead of later."

Hennesey shook his head. "D.A., huh? You know better than that. C'mon now. You know what you gotta do. You walk away from this. There's no disgrace in what you did. You pursued Malcolm Columba with a vengeance. We all did. In spite of them bastards, Dean."

"They could have had him anytime they wanted."

"Maybe yes, and maybe no."

"I could have blown the whistle on them."

"And in turn, they would've had someone outside the agency, sooner than later, blow up your home or car with you in it. Maybe even in that new and bigger boat you want so badly, which I'm gonna make sure you get so's I have a place to stay when I come down to visit you in sunny Florida during President's week—when you'll be well into retirement, good buddy. I sure as hell ain't gonna visit ya in the clink if you screw me out of this vacation I've got planned." The detective sergeant deliberately creased the corners of his mouth into a reproachful smile.

Dean sighed uneasily. "Listen to me. I've—"

"No, Dean. You listen to the voice of experience. You listen very carefully to what I have to say. Miller wasn't far from wrong when he told you to do Barnes and that certain folks were gonna look the other way. Now, I'm tellin' you that with Columba and this piece of work gone, certain people in both the bureau and the department *are* gonna look the other way." Hennesey looked down at the body. "This is the signal we're sending them. You open up a can of worms with your admissions, you're defeating what we're doing here today. And *we* is the operative word, lad. I put my neck out to save yours. Don't throw it all away thinkin' you're gonna clear your conscience, 'cause you're not. Innocent people got killed. No two ways about it, Dean. We did everything we could to try and catch that son of a bitch.

"Look at me, Dean. The feds got what they wanted in the interest of national security. We got what we want. Columba in a body bag. A wet one. But still a body bag. Personally, I liked it better when he was at the bottom of the sea. If I could, I *would* pin a medal on that fellow, Barnes. Way I see it, all he did was make a citizen's arrest," the big Irishman chaffed with a grin. "I don't know about that other business up at Redding Ridge. Don't really give a flyin' good fuck, either. All Ciccio's soldiers. Soldiers are expendable. Far as I'm concerned, Barnes did real good. And you was gonna take his black ass out and shoot it? Shame on you, Dean," Ed Hennesey chided his friend in a fatherly fashion.

Dean soughed sadly. "Truth is, Ed, I would have shot myself before I drew down on an innocent human being. I was just very angry at the time."

"Oh, this Justin Barnes ain't no saint, Dean. Suspected cop killer, mind you. Not an easy pill for any of us to swallow, until you get it straight in your head that the cop he presumably wasted was bad news bears, and that Barnes was just a victim of circumstance. Kim did her homework on that fag cop. Actually, we're all victims of circumstance here, Dean," Hennesey reflected sadly. "Like the victims whose lives Columba took. Eight innocent young women and that little Dawson girl, Becky. Freddie Dupree; his own flesh and blood. Along with Evan Tamblin and that lowlife second wife of his, Sally—for a grand total of twelve human beings."

"Twelve that we know of."

"That we know of," Ed agreed. "Not to mention the fallout with regard to Ciccio's soldiers, who bought the farm at Redding Ridge," he threw in for good measure. "But like I always told you. The mob's a necessary evil. It's one of the reasons why our government's found in bed with them from time to time. One hand washes the other, and both hands wash the face. All those victims, Dean? All casualties of war when you stop to think about it. Collateral damage. Columba's victims were as innocent as Donald Bellport, unknowingly thrust into the middle of a sick game of three-dimensional chess. The Federation's end game—mostly played with pawns. Virginia Dupree and Viola Johnson as well. Sacrifices, too, in a sense. One and all."

"You're sounding something like him," Dean said, staring down at Miller's body.

"Well, he's dead, Dean. I know you don't want to hear it, but he happened to be right. About everything. Like it or not. But it's the way he and other strategists in the war room went about things that turned out all wrong. I think they walked too fine a line. Miller crossed it when he took matters into his own hands. No different than Barnes. The question you should have asked Miller is whether or not the agency *would* have sanctioned his actions had he gone to them *first* for

515

permission to silence you. You might have learned something useful. He'd have gladly told you the truth, seeing as how he believed you were going to die anyhow."

"Madmen in charge of madmen is how I see this whole business, Ed."

"I guess it depends on which side of the desk you're sitting," the veteran detective sergeant replied knowingly.

"I don't know."

"Think if I went to Theo, he'd sanction this?" Ed questioned, glancing down at the bloody figure.

"Sure he would. It was either him or me."

"That's not what I mean, Dean."

"Then, what *do* you mean?"

"What if I just came here to kill him, period? Regardless of whether or not Miller pulled a gun on you."

"No, I don't think Theo would, Ed."

"No?"

"No."

"Interesting question, though."

"Guess we'll never know."

"You never know."

"Ed?"

"Yes, lad?"

"Ask you a question?"

"Shoot."

"How did you get a handle on this business in the first place? And how is it that you know so much about Miller and *his* people?"

"That's two questions, Dean. Miller only allowed you one," the detective sergeant answered with a wink.

"Miller told me the truth."

"That's because Miller thought you were a goner."

Dean Nelson stared curiously at the older, wiser man, but said nothing.

"You gonna commit political suicide or any other kind when you get back, Dean? Screw me out of my Florida vacation? I can take just so much of The Mick down there in Orlando, you know."

Dean put his head down and slowly shook it back and forth. "No."

"That's good to hear. I'm really not at liberty to answer your questions, laddie," Ed stated flatly. "But I'll tell you this much," he concluded, fixing his eyes on Miller. "Never trust a fellow who begrudges you a drink."

Dean smiled. "Thanks for everything," he said sincerely. "I owe you big time."

"Now get going."

"You sure I—"

"Scram. Out the back entrance and down the stairs."

Dean did an about-face and put his hands in the air in sweet surrender. "Any other instructions, Sergeant?"

"Yeah, I want you to start looking for a serious boat as soon as you get back, Detective."

"Aye aye, Captain."

"You're the captain, Dean."

"I'm not so sure about that, fella."

Detective Sergeant Edward Hennesey stood grinning from ear to ear.

Twenty minutes later, on the hour, several of Don Ciccio's crew showed up in uniform, wheeling two carts filled with cleaning equipment.

Ed Hennesey left the hotel room in very capable hands.

Chapter 84

Leaning against a barrier of shoulder-high, dusty, musty buff-colored boxes and gray cardboard file cabinets, stood a host of bristly brooms and cotton-topped mop heads, all crisscrossed helter-skelter. They stood like a series of discombobulated stick figures. Justin sat alone on a cot in the corner of the neighboring cage. The area served solely as temporary storage space, for there were no longer any official holding cells at police headquarters.

Just outside the threshold, situated several feet away, stood the source of an offensive acerbic odor emanating from a large yellow plastic bucket set upon four black wheels. Long, thick strands of green yarn clamped tightly in the crushing metal jaws of the wringer, locked the heavy-duty mop head securely in place. Earlier, Justin tried persistently but unsuccessfully to move the stench away from his airy abode by grabbing and utilizing the lengthiest of the long-handled implements found within the adjacent arsenal of metal and wooden poles. The attempt only made matters worse, for as he stretched his arm to its limit, maneuvering the head of a push broom forward of the bars at the base of the cell door, inching toward the loathsome liquid, he wound up spilling and splashing the slimy acrid contents upon the floor. The bucket of acidulous solution had been filled to its brim. The smell akin to rancid buttermilk pervaded the entire space.

There was no question that the putrid juices had been sitting for quite some time. In Justin's opinion, the pail had been intentionally and strategically positioned at that precise spot by someone into mind games—one of many games jailers enjoyed playing in order to *fuck* with a prisoner's head, the maverick smoldered.

Justin sat there, isolated and despondent. Thinking. Thinking of his predicament. Thinking about Virginia Dupree and Viola Johnson. Thinking of his beloved Monisha. Thinking of Ms. Thelma Sloop and the fact that she had jokingly called herself Ms. Slopbucket. Funny, because she was anything but that. Although dirt poor, she was actually a neat-freak. Why would anyone want to kill her? he asked himself again and again. *Why?* He wondered, too, if his lawyer would be successful in downgrading the charges of murder one to something that ran along the lines of self-defense. After finally being fed a decent meal, which Brian saw to personally, the maverick told his attorney the absolute truth about what had happened up at Redding Ridge. Still, Justin flatly denied any involvement in Malcolm Columba's murder. Then again, there was no question that the police found the serial killer's body—all because he pressed the MOB button on *Boy 'n' Sea*.

"Stupid, stupid, stupid," Justin seethed aloud. His thoughts were abruptly interrupted by the sound of footsteps coming down the hall. He slowly got to his feet.

"Hello, Justin."

"How much longer you gonna keep me here, clown?"

"What the hell is that smell?" Brian asked in distraction, wrinkling his nose.

"I asked, how much longer you gonna keep me here, motherfucker?"

"You're free to go."

"Say what?"

"I said, you're free to go."

"Go where?"

"Anyplace you like."

"You shittin' me or what?"

"We worked things out."

"Who's we?"

"We the people," Brian said in preamble. "Theo, Connecticut police, the district attorney's office, your mouthpiece."

"Ahhh, ran circles 'round your sorry ass, did he?" Justin sounded off with a satisfactory laugh.

"Oh, if you only knew the half of it."

"I gotta make any court appearances or anything?"

Brian shook his head. "It's all over. You can go home."

"Where's my lawyer now?" Justin asked suspiciously.

"Circling in a sea of self-conceit, along with all the other sharks, I suppose."

Justin beamed, knowing from the cop's face that whatever that meant, it had to be purely positive. "Did I tell you he'd spring my black ass, motherfucker? Did I tell you that, or not?"

"Oh, he'll take the credit along with a nice chunk out of your bank account for his time and trouble. That's for damn sure. But if you want to thank somebody, it was someone behind the scenes who saved your butt, if you really want to know the truth."

"Oh, yeah?"

"Yeah."

"Who?"

"My wife."

"Your wife? Who you jivin'? Thought you wasn't married, chump."

"Wasn't. Flew off to Vegas the other night to tie the knot. Cut our honeymoon short in New Hampshire because she smelled a rat. My bride went to work on your behalf immediately."

"You serious?"

Brian proudly displayed his golden wedding band.

"Suppose yo' be lookin' for a gift or somethin', chump."

"Just a thank you that I can pass along to her will do fine," the detective suggested.

"What'id you do? Put up bail money or somethin' 'cause you was feelin' guilty and not havin' any fun on your honeymoon, spoon? Knowin' I be's *in·no·cent.*"

"You know there was no bail attached to those murder charges. And as far as feeling guilty, guy, you also know as well as I that you're as guilty as sin itself."

Justin did not address the remark. "So, what'id this wifey of yours do fo' me, particularly, that I owe her a debt of thanks. Huh?"

"Worked her little fingers to the bone," Brian answered straightaway.

"That a fact?"

"That *is* a fact."

"So, what she do fo' a livin', chump, if I might ask."

"She's a detective, here, just like me."

"Oh, there ain't a detective here or anywhere like you in all o' Suffolk County, Brian. And you can bank on that."

"I'll take that as a compliment."

"You take it anyway yo' want."

"So, you going to stay in there all day, or you gonna move your ass on out of there?"

520

"Soon as you unlock this motherfuckin' door, champ."

Brian laughed at his absentmindedness and simply shook his head, selecting a single key from a silver ring—unlocking and pulling open the dusty, grating cell door.

"You so *pre·occ·u·pied,* spoon, you don't know what the fuck yo' doin'. Do you?"

"Guess not," Brian admitted.

Justin smiled. "Ask you somethin'?"

"Sure."

"She pretty?"

"You bet."

"She got a sister?" he baited, figuring to get a rise from the cop for a black dude even considering a white woman for sport.

"A Big Sister," Brian replied mischievously.

"Big meaning, big?" Justin tested, passing his palms slightly forward of his muscular chest. "Or is she just big across the beam," he teased, stepping forward and whacking Brian playfully on the butt.

"Wider than she is tall, I have to admit," Brian answered truthfully.

"Then scratch that idea," Justin said freely, crossing the threshold.

"Would you like to meet the bride, though, before you go?"

"Tell you the truth, I'd jus' rather go."

"Suit yourself."

It was the tone of disappointment in Brian's voice that made Justin stop and turn around.

"She here now?"

Brian nodded a smile.

"Then, lead the way, spoon."

Downstairs and around a narrow corridor the tall cop strode. Justin was a half a step behind him.

"Where you leading me, champ?" Justin was beginning to worry. "This ain't some kind o' trick is it . . . where next yo' tell me yo' gonna transfer my ass upstate?"

"Computer room. Not really a room. More like an alcove. It's off-limits to unauthorized personnel. Recall?"

"Vaguely. The sign I remember most is over that . . . never mind."

"I hear you. But where I'm leading you now, few civilians ever get to see. I'm serious."

The pair passed through two separate doors, one of which displayed the sign. Brian led Justin up to the computer maven, who was busy with her work.

"Honey. I'd like you to take a minute to say hello."

The woman detective immediately stopped what she was doing and swiveled around in her chair.

Justin Barnes' mouth fell open wide.

"Hello, J," Kim said warmly, extending her hand in welcome. "Brian told me the good news, so I made him promise me he'd go get you himself."

"Yes, ma'am," Justin said in shock.

"Is there anything the matter, J? You look like you've just seen a ghost," she remarked coyly.

"Been seein' a lot of ghosts of late, ma'am," Justin admitted openly. "It's just that you're the prettiest person I've seen in quite a spell, Detective . . . Archer. As a matter of fact, I remember seeing you shortly after I came here. 'Course you was Detective Booker then."

"Kim, Justin. Please call me Kim."

"Kim. I just didn't expect this detective here to have such good taste. What I mean is," Justin said awkwardly, "well, I just assumed you was white when he told me he took a wife."

"Well, I was white as white could be this past weekend, J," Kim stated candidly through a light laugh. "Covered from head to toe in white, I was. Why, I was so white I thought I was laden with snow. Ate white cake with vanilla filling. Shielded my face from a shower of rice; 'course this wise guy husband of mine had to throw in a little brown for good luck," she tattled with a giggle. "Climbed into a white limo, too. And talk about climbing—shoo. While you was sittin' 'round on your butt, six thousand two hundred and eighty-eight feet that man standing beside you had me climb. Mount Washington. And J —you don't mind if I call you J, do you? We honeymooned, get this, in the White Mountains in Franconia, New Hampshire. I'm not making this up," the pretty woman told all. "Know what he did when we reached the summit?"

Justin shook his head in awe of the friendly woman.

"Well, I'm gonna tell you. He takes this paper plane he made.

Paper and wood—"

"Balsa, actually," Brian interrupted.

"—from the case he's carrying. And he winds it up."

"Rubber band and prop," Brian clarified.

"And then he sends it off the mountain top. Know what he says to me?" Kim put the tip of a forefinger to her chin, pausing for the full effect. "He says, 'That's for Justin, come Monday morning when they're going to set him free.' That's when I made him promise me *he'd* be the one to open up your cell."

Justin looked between the newlyweds before staring down at the floor in embarrassment.

"Ah, Detective Archer says I have you to thank for helping get me out of there."

"Both me and Big Sister." Detective Kim Archer smiled amicably, swiveling halfway around to face the unit, then back about. "Couldn't have done it without her. Truth is, I have a few Big Sisters around these United States. One in New Hampshire," she added frankly. "And other places that even my dear husband doesn't know about. Anyhow, we *sisters* all keep in touch with one another. You see, we're very close-knit."

Justin looked at the wall of technology with the petite woman sitting in the midst of it. He laughed heartily and nodded discerningly, smiling brightly at Brian. "Big Sister, huh?"

"What's so funny?" the new bride wanted to know.

"Guy thing." Brian winked at Justin.

"Definitely a guy thing," Justin agreed.

"Anyhow, if you're smart, young man, you'll find yourself a special someone and settle down," Kim said rather seriously.

"Yeah, only problem is I keep losing 'em," was Justin's immediate reply.

Kim nodded both sadly and knowingly. "Well, when that special gal does come along, and I can assure you that she will, Brian and I are going to have you both over for dinner. Isn't that right, dear."

"But only if he can name the capital of New Hampshire in the next five seconds," Brian insisted.

"Concord," the free man answered in no time flat.

Brian was pleased, wanting to show him off. "He knows all fifty states and capitals. Tell Kim how you do it."

"Association," Justin said proudly. "My cousin, Monisha, taught me the method."

"How did you associate New Hampshire with Concord, J?" she asked, apparently impressed.

"That's an easy one." Justin closed his eyes and took a deep breath. "You see, the state's shaped just like the mountain, upon which I'm standing . . . in my mind."

"And?" Brian pressed.

"And?" Kim chimed in, too.

"And . . . and then . . . 'I came, I saw, I *con·quered*,'" Justin recited sheepishly, opening wide his eyes with a self-conscious smile.

"That you did," the homicide detective agreed. "That you did, indeed."

"Just don't ask me to spell it," Justin added with a grin. "*Conquered*, that is."

"I'll let you in on a little secret, J," Kim beckoned. "If it wasn't for Big Sister here, and spellcheck, I wouldn't be able to write either my maiden or married name," the new bride bantered playfully. "*He's* the speller," Kim said braggingly, pointing a finger and nodding fondly at her spouse.

"Oh, don't I just know it," Justin agreed. "Say, listen! Let me take you both out for dinner some night this week. Some place nice. My wedding present to the two of you. I insist. I know a great spot in the Hamptons area. West Tiana, actually. Italian. The very best. A Sicilian family runs it."

"Wouldn't happen to be the Bella Sera, would it?" Kim asked.

"That's exactly the place! Off Montauk Highway."

"The place is fabulous," Kim wholeheartedly agreed, lifting her eyebrows to the ceiling. "Pure heaven." She bunched the tips of her fingers together, kissed and raised them to the roof.

Brian looked somewhat surprised. "You've been there, Kim?"

"*Steak*out," she punned playfully.

"Stakeout?" Brian questioned, missing the humor. "You're here with computers; not in the field."

"Yeah. And every time I strike gold, all you guys ever buy me is a burger and beer, if I'm lucky. So, every once in a while I treat myself to a lunch or dinner at the Bella Sera. Expensive, but I'm worth it. But not so expensive when you think about what you get. I eat for three nights on what I take home in a doggy bag. *Steak* out. Lobster out. Pasta out. I pig-out once every few months when you fellows let me down. If you haven't had their steak with mushroom and onions, or pizzaiola style, J, you haven't lived. Or their veal—to die for."

"I knew it. She's going to get fat on me," Brian swore. "Once they get married, you hear what can happen. I can see it coming."

"Well, I'm not gonna get in the middle of this," Justin said wisely. "All I know is that I'm takin' you both out. My treat. My pleasure."

"We accept," Kim decided. "But only if you promise us you'll come to our home after we're settled in, and let me make you and a special friend one of the finest southern home-cooked meals you ever had this side of the Mason-Dixon line, homeboy."

Justin laughed uncomfortably. "Homeboy?"

"Promise me."

"I promise, but you don't know nothin' 'bout my home, girl," he said respectfully, yet with an edge to his voice.

Kim lowered her voice to a whisper, keeping the sharpness out but framing her words firmly. "J, I know everything about you from the time you were born, right up to the hour Detective Nelson put you in the clink. Got it? I know what you run. Where you pick up and drop-ship. Who you're associated with. What you eat and where you drink. What magazines you like to *look* at, 'cause you still can't read worth a shit. But all that is going to change after you let us help you. I'm getting way ahead of myself here, I know. I was going to broach the subject after we had our housewarming, but I more than sense a bit of that hostility of yours seeping out right now, so I want to set you straight from the start."

Justin looked disbelievingly at the new Mrs. Brian Archer. "And just who the hell are you?" Justin said evenly. "My mother?"

"A far cry from her and her madding crowd, fella. You just consider Brian and me your two saviors for now. Your soon-to-be mentors. Reading. Writing. Math. Police investigation, if you're good. Brian's going to work with you on history, geography and spelling— you can bet your boots. There you'll have better luck with him than me," she said quite candidly.

Justin was being thrown for a loop and put through the proverbial hoop. "Police investigation?"

"That will come a little later after you prove yourself in the areas that you're lacking."

"Well, I know my motherfu—I know my math," Justin said defensively, not knowing what else to say.

"Then I'm sure you can add things up and recognize a good deal when you see one. Yes? Yes," Kim answered for him in a single breath.

As if in a trance, Justin turned his head and stared at Detective Brian Archer.

"Listen to her, Justin. Everyone needs a little help."

"Little help?"

"We're offering you a second chance; not everyone gets one. As a matter of fact, few—"

"And what if I say thanks, but no thanks?"

"Then I'll still wind up serving you dinner like I said. Only it'll be right back here in this building instead of our home; back upstairs in that space that doubles as a file room and a broom closet—if you keep going the way you're going," Kim answered for her husband.

"Gettin' by jus' fine on my own, Ms. Detective," Justin drawled curtly.

"Suit yourself," the woman replied banally.

Justin smirked. "Same script as the spoon, here, I'm hearin'. You two have this *thang* rehearsed?"

"Chapter and verse, J," Kim admitted. "One-time offer. But I'll tell you what. We'll give you this week to think about it. It's going to be the most important decision of your *motherfuckin'* life, homeboy."

Brian stared at Kim in absolute surprise—if not shock—seeing a different side to the woman he thought he knew so well. Never had he heard her speak profanely. Never ever had he heard her utter a single curse.

Justin nodded. "I'll be givin' it my due *con·sid·er·a·tion,* Detective*sss* Archer," he sibilated, staring them down with a curious mix of indignation and respect.

"You do that, J," Kim replied crisply. "Friday night. Bella Sera. On you. Six o'clock sharp. Place fills up by seven. You let us know beforehand."

Justin drew his lips in and nodded. "I'll be sure to let you know."

When Justin left the space, Brian turned to his wife. "Why does he keep calling me spoon?"

Kim just smiled and shrugged her slender shoulders. "Guess you have to ask him yourself when we see him on Friday," she said quite confidently.

"How do you know he'll show?"

"He may be a bit angry right now, my love. But he's certainly not stupid. Trust me on that."

Chapter 85

Detective Lieutenant Theodore Groche and Justin Barnes were involved in a rapid-fire exchange of Q&A, working their way through the lengthy list.

"New Jersey?"

"Trenton."

"New Mexico?"

"Santa Fe.

"New York?"

"Albany."

"North Carolina?"

"Raleigh."

"Ohio?"

"Columbus."

Theo shook his head and smiled in mild amusement. "How do you keep them straight in your head, J?"

"Association," Justin answered up smartly.

"Yeah, I heard. But how? I mean, what do you associate with what? Take North Carolina, for instance. How do you make the connection to Raleigh?"

"The fact that I was born there," Justin put forth plainly.

Kim and Brian nodded appreciatively.

"Funny man, Barnes," Theo frowned.

"No, that's true, Theo," Kim jumped in. "Justin was born in Raleigh, before the family moved to Harlem. He's not joking."

"I didn't think he was. Which reminds me. Did you hear the one about the woman they found murdered in Central Park?"

Justin shook his head politely and raised a forkful of salad from his plate.

"Found her in the bushes. Faceup. Strawberry stuck in one ear. Banana sticking out of the other. An apple planted solidly in her mouth. Forensics carefully lifted the victim and, discovering a spoon and bowl beneath the body, suddenly realized they had a cereal killer on their hands," Theo deadpanned.

Both Kim and Brian shot dagger eyes Theo's way.

"What?" the lieutenant asked in mock confusion.

"You don't joke around like that," Kim scolded quietly, silently mouthing the name, *Mo·ni·sha.*

"Lighten up, folks," Theo ordered. "All right?"

Justin put down his fork and cracked a smile.

"See?" the lieutenant said satisfactorily. "The man knows from funny."

Kim shifted uncomfortably before turning her full attention back to the bowl of pasta fagioli before her.

Brian bowed his head and brought a tablespoonful of steaming minestrone to his mouth, glancing across at his bride, whose shoulders suddenly rose and fell in keeping with a titter. "What's so funny, honey?"

Justin fixed his attention on Brian, then suddenly guffawed, shaking his head back and forth uncontrollably, averting the man's eyes and ignoring his question altogether. It was not solely the lieutenant's silly joke, or that Brian's soupspoon cut a comic, caricatural image into the maverick's mind; that being the detective's beanstalk-like frame, slightly oversized balding head, and marginally concaved features. It was, in fact, the sudden release of six months of mounting tension bottled up inside each and every one of them— Justin's infectious laughter notwithstanding.

"See? It just takes a little time for the humor to sink in." Theo took the credit for their moment of mirth. "Hey, that bastard's finally off the street, so Justin can use a little laugh," he added, putting aside the civilian's atlas and focusing on the man.

It was the first time the lieutenant had addressed the man by his Christian name.

Justin was still hysterical with laughter. It was the best he had felt in a quite awhile.

"So, you going to offer our man of the hour here a deal?" Kim pressed Theo when she was finally able to compose herself. "It's one of the reasons why you're here," she reminded him. "Actually, it's the only reason," she jived.

"I said, I'd think about it," Theo replied with some annoyance, surprised that Kim would put him on the spot like that in public.

"Well, you have between now and dessert to decide," Kim decreed quite presumptuously.

Theo cast a look at Kim that carried with it a good five seconds of silence.

"After that, I'm going to make a bid that he sees someone in the D.A.'s office," Kim added unfazed.

"It's not enough that I'm picking up the check?" Theo tabled uncharacteristically.

"Hardly."

"I already told you guys, *I'm* taking care of the check," Justin chimed in. "Remember that *I* invited you."

"Yeah. That was before *deep pockets* here insisted he'd tag along," Kim jabbed, setting dark eyes back on her boss.

"Are you saying I'm cheap, Detective Kim *Archer*?" the detective lieutenant questioned sorely.

"Oh, I like the sound of that a lot," the newlywed replied happily, staring down conspicuously at her diamond wedding ring. Each fingernail depicted a series of diminutive tiny white bells ringed with pink ribbon.

Being in a playful if not mischievous mood, Theo made a suggestion. "I'll tell you what, Kim. Since you feel that I invited myself along, I'll ask the waitress for a separate check. How's that?"

"That's bullshit," she snapped. "You pull a stunt like that, and I'll pull the plug on Big Sister. Tell you she won't boot up. Tell you she has a virus. Tell you *I* have a fever and then call in sick tomorrow. How's *that*? You're picking up this tab, sport," Kim said decidedly.

"You're too quiet over there, Brian," the lieutenant sounded. "Please explain to your bride what insubordination is, or I'll insist that you leave the tip."

"Incorrigible," Kim groused.

Justin smiled. "I already took care of everything before you guys got here. *Gra·tu·ity* included. My new word for the day. I said I was takin' you folks out to dinner, and that's that."

"Well, thank God for that," Theo said with a sigh of relief, "because I'm a little low on cash, and I think my credit card is maxed out," he put forth with a straight face. "Now I know I can enjoy the rest of the meal."

"On second thought, I could *still* give the waitress a high sign to hand you a separate check," Justin said teasingly. "So you better listen to Kim."

Theo scowled. "That's blackmail, Barnes."

"But I *am* a black male," Justin bantered back playfully.

"Extortion is a very serious charge. Tell him, Bri."

"Just add it to my dirty laundry list," Justin retorted shamelessly.

Theo picked up Justin's travel atlas where the two left off.

"Oklahoma?"

"Oklahoma City."

"Oregon?"

"Salem."

"Pennsylvania?"

"Harrisburg."

"Rhode Island?"

"Providence."

"Damn." Theo perused the list. "I'll tell you what."

"What?"

"We'll finish the list. You miss one—just one—you tell the waitress, *one* check. Yours!"

"Theeooo," Kim whined.

"And if I don't miss any," Justin countered, "I get a *le·git·i·mate* assignment with you suits. Deal?"

"Deal."

Justin put out his hand.

Theo took and shook it firmly.

"Wyoming."

"Whoa! Hold you horses," Kim broke in. "That's like dealing from the bottom of the deck, cowboy."

"That's right," Brian offered in support. "You left off with Rhode Island."

"What's the damn difference? Unless, of course, he just knows them in a given order, which is exactly what I'm betting on." Theo smiled smugly.

"That's not fair," Kim balked.

"Wyoming, Mr. Barnes."

"Cheyenne."

"Wisconsin."

"Madison."

"West Virginia."

"Charleston."

"Washington."

"Olympia."

Theo seemed impressed.

"Hold on a second," Brian stayed the game by sweetening the pot. "I got a sawbuck on my man here," he decided, taking a ten spot from his wallet and placing it on the table.

Theo dipped into a front pocket and came up with a five dollar bill. "I want two-to-one odds."

"Why, you cheapskate!" Kim blared, going into her bag, then smacking a ten-dollar bill upon the table as customers all around them looked on with smiles and miles of curiosity. "I'll take a piece of that action. Now, put up or shut up."

"All right, already." Theo took out another five and placed it on top of the other bills. "There."

"Hey, hey, hey; what's goin' on here?" Phil Cancilla asked, walking over to the table with a frown. "There's no gambling allowed in this establishment. Cops come in and out of here all the time," he declared with a friendly wink.

Kim smiled warmly. "Evening, Phil. We're just making sure Theo has enough cash to pay the check."

"Oh, I see. Everything all right?"

"Everything is fine, Phil. How's the family?" Theo asked sincerely.

"Good, good. How's your mom doing?"

"Much better, thanks."

"How about some more wine?" Phil suggested.

"Absolutely," Justin agreed.

"Jackie tell you the specials?"

"Sure did," Brian affirmed.

"I have some nice fresh calamari just come in. I'm gonna bring some over. You gonna enjoy."

Kim closed her eyes, licked her lips, and beamed. "Wait till you taste. It's fabulous the way they do it here."

"I think you've been here more than you let on," Brian decided with a bobbing head.

"Excuse me for just a moment," Phil said pleasantly, then took his leave.

"Ready to continue, Justin?" Theo asked.

"Ready."

"Vermont."

"Monteplier."

"Utah."

"Salt Lake City."

"Texas."

"Austin."

"Tennessee."

"Nashville."

Theo paused and grinned. "Pierre?" he put forth flatly.

"What?" Brian puled. "That's not fair!"

"What's not fair?" Theo bristled, staring down greedily at the cash. "He has to name the states and capitals. Right? Why not the other way around? Match the capital to the state. Pierre, Justin," Theo repeated crisply.

"Pierre?" Kim echoed in confusion, searching her own mind.

"Yes, Pierre," Theo said as calmly as he could.

"You call me, monsieur?" Phil asked in a phony French accent, returning with a wide smile and carrying a full carafe of Montepulciano, red.

Kim was practically hanging off her chair.

Brian's forehead almost knocked the corner of the table.

Justin was slapping his thigh.

Theo was sitting there impatiently, eyeballing the money while Phil Cancilla topped off everyone's glass.

"Who's Pierre?" their host asked innocently as the three launched into a second fit of hysterics.

Phil and Theo looked on as the trio tried to catch their breaths.

"It's the big stall before I take the winnings off the table," Theo explained in part.

"Maybe I make a big mistake. *Too* much wine, perhaps," Phil voiced solely to himself, walking off gayly, glad that his patrons were having such a good time.

"Come on, come on now, Justin Barnes. Name the state, if you can."

"South Dakota," Justin answered up.

Theo double-checked the atlas, then slowly shook his head in mock defeat as Kim and Brian started to grab and divvy up the cash.

"Not so fast," Theo commanded. "He's got one more to go."

"What?" Brian snapped, grabbing and consulting the Contents page. "We went through the list. We're back to Providence, Rhode Island. We won!"

"There's one state and capital he didn't do yet," Theo repeated smugly.

"Oh, yeah?" Kim balked.

"No, he's right," Justin admitted. "The lieutenant left one out of order earlier—in order to try and trip me up."

"North Dakota?" the top cop challenged anxiously.

"Bismarck," Justin finished with a flair.

"Yes?" Brian questioned, though unsure.

"Correct," Theo murmured and nodded quietly in defeated.

Both husband and wife swooped up and divided the loot.

"How in hell did you link Pierre to South Dakota, J? I really thought I had you with that one. Tell me," Theo insisted.

"Easy. I picture a Frenchman sitting in an old Plymouth Dodge De Soto. Remember them?"

"De Soto? You weren't even born yet."

"No, but my uncle had one in *Mo·bile*, Alabama. Finest mechanic around. Still runnin' in fact. Not the 'ol man, but the machine," Justin clarified with a chuckle.

"But how do you keep things straight in your head? North Dakota. South Dakota. Easy enough to confuse. That's why I purposely skipped over North Dakota, to try and trip you up—just like you said—figuring you'd answer in their given order. How do you delineate? I mean, what's the connection to Pierre?"

Justin leaned across the table toward The Man. "Lieutenant. When I retire—which'll probably be before you—I plan to 'ave me a chauffeur-driven limousine somewhere down in the deep South. A cook, a butler and a gardener, too. And guess what I plan on namin' all four of 'em? Just so I don't mix them up in my mind," Justin questioned, grinning from ear to ear.

"Pierre."

"You got it."

"You forget the female housekeeper?" Theo shot back playfully.

"Fifi, if I don't find me a wife—first and foremost."

Kim Archer practically put a mouthful of Montepulciano in her husband's lap.

Theo studied Justin Barnes carefully and seriously before he spoke. "You know anything about the group Columba headed, J?"

"The Federation?"

Theo nodded.

"A little," Justin admitted.

"How?"

"I read one of the faxes."

"Which one?"

"The one . . . "

"Go on," Theo coaxed. "I won't ask you how you *acquired* it."

"The one that suggested Columba successfully placed federal agents within the ranks of extremist groups throughout the world."

"Thought you couldn't read."

"Not very well. I had to look up every other word, it seemed. Just to get the gist. But I'm getting there."

Theo nodded encouragingly. "Want to work on The Federation's case file with us?" he asked in a low voice.

Brian and Kim looked at one another in total disbelief.

"Yes, sir," Justin answered up incisively.

"Think you might do that before retirement?"

Justin brightened. "Oh, absolutely."

"Good. Now, would you be so kind as to pass me the pepper mill?"

Justin reached for the device. "Would you like me to grind it for you, too, Lieutenant?" he jested with sheer but guarded excitement.

"No, but I think you should inform the waitress before the end of the meal that there'll be *one* check. Mine." Their leader smiled, handing over Justin's credit card, still wrapped in a hundred-dollar bill.

"Ah, no *wonder* Phil is sending over a complimentary plate of calamari," Brian said decidedly.

"No, he takes care of his *good* customers. Even skinflints like me," Theo recouped quite nicely.

"Oh, my God!" Kim said, sitting completely upright in her

seat, gesturing toward the tray that was headed their way.

A large platter was set upon their table, piled high with truncated, translucent-white cones and light golden-battered rings of both grilled and fried calamari. "I brought both hot and medium sauce," Phil Cancilla said, setting down two bowls. "Enjoy. Jackie will take your order whenever you're ready."

"This could feed an army," Brian avowed.

"Gonna need one before we're finished with The Federation and the feds," Theo affirmed quietly as Phil headed back toward the kitchen.

Justin said nothing, his mind a jumble, inhaling the marvelous aroma of spicy tomato sauce, basil, olive oil and garlic.

Kim served a generous portion on everyone's plate. The new bride beamed brightly. "And this is just the appetizer, fellas."

"But I'm not leaving any hundred-dollar tip. I'll tell you that!" Theo swore, returning his thoughts to Justin's over-the-top gesture of generosity.

"Well, we all know that, Theo," Kim acknowledged, wrinkling her nose and loosely bunching the tips of her fingers, moving them ever so slightly before her bossman's face. "Don't we? So. *Mangia*; all right?"

"Kim's way of saying, 'shut up now and eat,'" Brian explained to their newest member of the team, raising his glass to toast Justin— and the beginning of a most unusual relationship.

"Oh, I read her loud and clear," the maverick made known, raising his glass high in *salute*. "Sign language I have no problem with," he added quite cheerfully.

Theo's *salute* to Kim ran more along the lines of a temporary truce.

Chapter 86

Justin stepped into Detective Lieutenant Groche's office and was immediately directed to take a seat opposite The Man. The commanding officer's desk was piled high with papers and reports. *Organized chaos*, the civilian realized as the head of homicide found what he needed in the center of an anonymous stack. Theo got right to the business at hand.

"I have an intelligence report here which states that Columba is believed to have kept a journal of his murderous dealings. Fine. Not unusual. Lots of nut cases do just that. The problem is that no one can find it. It's a problem because it's actually more than a journal, J. It's supposedly an encrypted blueprint of The Federation's entire operation. Code names of federal agents placed within secret societies. Their contacts. Lists of organizers and members' names; their phone numbers and addresses. Agendas. Timetables. Sources of revenue, and so on. Do you have any idea how explosive a package like that is in the wrong hands?"

Justin nodded his understanding.

"Good. Can you appreciate the fed's situation presently in not being able to move forward without putting certain agents at risk?"

"Yes, sir."

Theo studied Justin Barnes as if the recruit were under a microscope, which to a large extent he was. The lieutenant increased the magnification. "You and I both know you were the last person to see Malcolm Columba alive. The feds suspect it. You still deny it. *We* know it to be so. So. Where do we go from here?" Theo paused. "To my next question, I suppose. Ready?"

"Shoot."

"This is not a game of states and capitals, J. Although the wrong answer could topple several throughout the Free World. With me?"

Again, Justin nodded.

"Did Malcolm Columba mention, in any way, shape or form, a

journal or manuscript, before you deep-sixed him? Yes or no?"

Justin simply and slowly shook his head.

"So, why is it that I don't believe you, J?"

"I guess because the truth is sometimes blinding," he responded, as he could think of nothing else to say.

"No. I think it's because of my thirty-five years experience as a cop," Theo set forth without expression.

"What do you want to do here today, Theo?"

It was the first time the maverick had ever called The Man by his abbreviated given name. Perhaps in part because Justin believed that the meeting was going to be abbreviated as well.

Theo leaned back in his chair and set his eyes on the ceiling. "I really don't know, J. I truly don't."

"May I make a suggestion?"

"You may."

Justin smiled. "Suppose we just pretend for the moment that what you believe is true."

"Okay," Theo agreed without taking his eyes from the overhead.

"Suppose he did happen to mention a journal or manuscript. What could I possibly do with it?"

"Try and peddle it to the highest bidder, for openers. Governments. Tabloids. Talk shows. *60 Minutes*, for fifteen minutes of fame."

"That's assuming I didn't know it was a coded transcript that could jeopardize the well-being of federal agents in many corners of the world."

"And now that you do know, you know you couldn't just hawk it on the open market."

"Too dangerous."

"Too many hawks, ready to swoop."

Justin nodded knowingly. "So, if I wanted to turn it into profit, I'd have to be very careful who I approached."

"Very careful, indeed."

"I'd have to find someone who had the power and the proper contacts."

"Someone you could trust completely."

"Tall order."

"Even for someone who deals in contraband on a daily basis."

"Dealt in. Past tense. A promise is a promise. And I promised both Brian and Kim."

"But still reason enough to break that promise in order to cash in on one more *final* score. A score that could net you a bloody fortune; note that I didn't say future, J. Might, too, send you to an early grave."

It was now Justin who was studying The Man. "Let's take this scenario to the next level, Lieutenant," the felon put forth articulately. "Let's assume Columba told me a manuscript existed, but that he didn't tell me where. Where would I look?"

"I already told you. We, as well as others, have been looking *everywhere*. No one knows."

"Maybe it doesn't exist."

"I think it does."

"How so?"

"Because a source who knew Columba quite well has indicated that he always kept the manuscript close at hand."

"I don't understand."

"In that suitcase."

"The suitcase?"

"Yes, the suitcase, J. A broken down black leather valise. He was seen carrying it at times and places that coincide with the victims' deaths. We think he toted the manuscript around with him, along with the paraphernalia he needed to carry out his sadistic acts. Like the ice skates he used to cross the Peconic River, from Flanders to Riverhead, when he put Wendy Linden's body on the bow of that boat. Or the plastic spools and rubber tubing he used on Fern Rodman and Diane Nash. The gallon of hydraulic fluid he fed the latter. Items like that, J. Did you see or hear of such a suitcase? Yes? No? Maybe?"

Again, Justin shook his head.

"Strange he wouldn't tell you its whereabouts before he was about to die."

"Speaking hypothetically, of course."

"But of course," the lieutenant agreed with a tentative smile.

"Why do you think he would carry around such incriminating evidence? This manuscript, I mean."

"An insurance policy, perhaps. Something to bargain with, I

suppose."

"Bargain for what?"

"His life. His freedom."

"He's free now, Lieutenant. And we're free of him."

"Maybe in realizing that he was going to die anyhow, he wanted it found. Wanted the world to know. To know that he was The Founder and Father of The Federation."

Justin shrugged.

"He didn't mention any such manuscript? Didn't offer you a deal?"

"No."

"He didn't bait you? Torment you? Perhaps Columba happened to mention what he did to Monisha up there in Michigan. Maybe he told you that you could read it for yourself. It had to be something like that, J. Just had to be."

Justin put his head down and slowly shook it back and forth a final time.

"That's it, isn't it?"

Justin sat in silence.

"You both lost your cool. Columba knew he was going to die for what he had done to Monisha. He knew there could be no deal. So he told you where the suitcase was. Didn't he?"

Justin raised his eyes to meet Theo's but said nothing.

"That's the way it's going to be? Is it, J?"

A good half a minute passed between them.

Theo sighed. "All right. Our problem is that we didn't learn about the manuscript until after we released the crime scene and gave the Eylers back their home, their property, and their lives. In the interim, you or somebody else went back and found it. Had to be, because we, as well as others, covered every square inch of the house, grounds, outbuildings, boats and docks a second, third, and then a fourth time. You wouldn't want to see their home and grounds today, J."

"Maybe he had it close by, like you said, but not at East Point."

"Maybe. But I'll lay ten to one you have or know where that suitcase is, J. I just know you do. Have to," he repeated. "You. You'll be killed for it if you do. No two ways about it. Don Ciccio's henchmen will come after you. Along with a faction of federal agents conveniently off the payroll, so that nothing kicks back to the bureau and bites them in the ass. And then there's Columba's loyal followers themselves. Believe me when I tell you they're out there in droves. Or maybe there's some disenchanted soul who got wind that such a manuscript exists and that their beloved Father somehow double-crossed them. You're a marked man. It's just a matter of time."

"If I had such a book, don't you think that somebody would have gotten to me by now?"

"Oh, they have. It just happens to be Suffolk County's finest, giving you a chance to save your hide before word gets out that you iced the author and architect of modern day espionage."

"I thought you guys *ex·punged* my record and any involvement I had at East Point, as well as Redding Ridge."

"Did all that. But you think no one else knows? We've got a mole in our midst."

"Yeah, FBI Agent Andrew Miller."

"I'm talking about a cop."

"Nelson, if I had to take a guess."

Theo shook his head. "I know he's not lily-white from where you're sitting, but he's not the one we're looking for. Anyway, he's out. His paperwork went through two days ago. Early retirement package."

"Then who? I'm sure you have some idea."

"Not a clue."

"Just like I don't have a clue as to the manuscript's whereabouts. Can't tell you what I don't know," Justin said emphatically.

"Fine. Maybe you'll be more convincing to those who are sure to pay you a little visit."

"You got an assignment for me, Theo? Or is our little talk here what this meeting is all about?"

The lieutenant leaned well forward in his seat. "Oh, have I got an assignment for you, Justin Barnes. Believe you me."

Chapter 87

Justin wept silently as he put Malcolm Columba's journal back into the battered black valise after a second *read* that week. He could not decipher any sort of clandestine code. He did not, of course, possess the necessary skills. Nor did he need or want to. As a matter of fact, if Theo had not told him that there was such an encoded blueprint, he would never have known. Any kind of covert communication was lost on him, for he could barely make it through the lengthy chapter concerning Monisha without having to struggle with a multitude of words. There was no question in Justin's mind that Malcolm's was twisted. No question whatsoever that the brilliant boy's early childhood, as described in the author's preface, had a direct bearing on his sick behavior later on in life.

But Justin did not concern himself with Malcolm's mental illness, or any secret codes. Justin focused on the way in which the serial killer delighted in taking Monisha's life. There was nothing profound or beyond the bounds of common understanding that he could see as clandestine communication. Malcolm simply killed her—killed her in a climate of extreme cold—having suspended her from a bridge, exposed to the elements—after first going on forever about her cousin, Tyrone Phillips, dumping toxic chemicals out in Kansas.

Justin wished that he could bring Malcolm back to life just so that he could have the pleasure of killing him all over again. He prayed to God that he could bring Monisha back *into* his life. Yet, in a sense, up there at Redding Ridge, he felt he had. She was there watching over him, he wanted badly to believe. Even through his ordeal with the authorities, he felt her presence from time to time. He knew she knew he loved her and always would.

What should he do with the manuscript? he wondered. Return it to the sea with several bricks laden in the killer's suitcase as he had done with Malcolm's clothing before returning to the inlet? Or simply set the tome on Theo's desk and let the authorities have a field day? Or better yet, he could go straight to the feds and make an even exchange for Andrew Miller's head—not knowing that his enemy was already dead.

Where had the special agent disappeared to? No one seemed to know the answer. Probably went underground, Justin imagined. Or off to another country, perhaps. *Or maybe he's lurking just around the corner—searching for the manuscript along with the rest of the ship of fools.* Maybe the two would meet up one day in some distant city or state—now that he was *unofficially* an undercover civilian operative, covertly hired by Suffolk County Homicide's head honcho. Who would believe it? His target? A mole operating between the poles of the Mafia and police; or more specifically, Don Ciccio's second in command.

Hey, nigger.
Yeah, bro?
You done good.
Yeah?
Yeah.
Let you in on a little secret.
What?
You ain't seen nothin' yet.

Chapter 88

"**A**re you sure no one knows about this meeting or why you're here, Don Ciccio?" Phil Cancilla asked with assumed respect.

"You crazy? I'm gonna advertise a deal I'm making you like this? Who am I gonna tell? You tell me." The big man laughed. "I'm sure you heard by now that my two associates and confidants are dead. They had one of their last great meals here, you recall."

"What I heard was that you'd be crazy to go anywhere alone today with the company you been keeping."

Don Ciccio grinned cagily. "I have my driver waiting in the car, Philip. That's it. This business is strictly between you and me. No one else."

Phil looked about his restaurant uneasily. "All right then. How much it gonna cost me?"

"For you? Fifteen percent."

The owner of the Bella Sera shook his head. "Ten."

Vincent Ciccio raised his hands in mock surrender. "Okay, okay. I'm not even gonna haggle here. Ten percent. I'm gonna argue with a man who's kept me at arm's length, how many years?"

The owner shrugged.

"Ten percent the first year, Philip. Fifteen the next, after I double whatever you import now. Fair?"

"We'll see," Phil said anxiously.

"We'll see, he says. You'll see a fuckin' fortune is what you'll see, Philip. But okay. I got my beak part way in the basin. Next year, you gonna come and beg me to wet it back there in the double sink." Vincent laughed uproariously. "Know what I'm gonna say to you then, Philip?"

Phil Cancilla waited for the answer.

"*Twenty percent!*" the don bellowed and slapped Phil's knee. "But, hey. Like you say, we'll wait and see. Listen, how come you didn't send Jackie over to my table tonight? Huh? You send her home sick?"

"Jackie's no longer waitressing, Vincent."

"No kidding. She get smart and go into real estate with your eldest, Lucia?"

Phil Cancilla smiled. "No, Jackie is now managing the restaurant, Vincent."

"Good for her! After six long years, she finally woke up and told you to shit or get off the pot. Yes?" the don quizzically questioned the owner.

"No. She paid her dues. She made her bones, Vincent."

"Hey, watch that kind of talk, Philip," Vincent warned kiddingly. "Bones make me very nervous. I don't like to talk about bones."

Phil Cancilla smiled uncomfortably.

"Well, I'm glad it's simply that, Philip, and not some kind of slight. An insult, I can't forgive. *Capisci*? Anyhow, you tell her I'm happy for her. She around?"

"No, actually she and Tomas are off Mondays. We alternate. Gives me a chance to catch my breath. Weekends we're both here."

"I see. Anyhow, great meal as usual, Philip. I gotta run. I'm pleased we can finally do business."

"Like you really give me much of a choice."

"There're always choices, Philip. That's what life is all about. There's life, and there is death. Believe me when I tell you, you made the right one," Vincent assured the man. "Believe me."

"We'll see."

The two men got up from the table.

It was after midnight.

Vincent was heading out the back of the restaurant as a waitress came walking over to the table with the mobster's check.

Phil Cancilla raised his hand, then put a finger to his lips for silence. "Vincent's in a hurry, Gina. Let him go," he said, taking cash out of his own pocket and putting it on the table.

"You're too good to people," his youngest daughter frowned, stuffing the money back into her father's hand. "You should make him pay."

"Oh, he'll pay, all right," Phil Cancilla promised. "Believe me. One day he'll pay."

Don Ciccio's driver headed the Mercedes out the rear of the parking lot, turning south onto Bess Road. Vincent settled himself comfortably into the backseat, most pleased with himself.

"Go okay?" the big Irishman asked, already knowing the answer from the expression on Vincent's face reflected in the rearview mirror.

Vincent beamed. "Tonight is a very special night, Edward. Tonight we scored a *big* chip. In two years time, I'll be one-third owner of one of the most successful restaurants on the South Shore of Long Island. Three years, tops, it'll all be ours for the taking. Mark my words. Thirty years they've been in business, fella. And with me around, that restaurant will see thirty more. "We stood to gain a small fortune if we could only have delivered Columba to Tamblin in time," the don went on. "But we didn't. That *melanzana*, Justin Barnes, saw to that. In the meantime, we chip away here, and chip away there. Fill the coffers, partner. Ready the war chest. And when we find that nigger, 'cause you and I both know he's got that fuckin' book, we're gonna be top banana," the don concluded resoundingly. "Tamblin's billions will look like chicken feed. Yes, it's a wonderful country, Ed. Absolutely wonderful."

"Yeah, just take a look at that wonder up ahead, Vincent."

"Where?" the big man asked, straightening up and craning his thickset neck.

"On the bicycle." The driver flashed his high beams.

"Wow! What a figure."

"Tiny heinie." Ed Hennesey giggled and gawked.

"Whoa, slow down. I think I know whose buns those are. Yes, siree. Put the windows down."

The detective sergeant switched the headlights back to low beams, pulling alongside the beautiful woman—sending the tinted windows southward.

"Hey, gorgeous!" Vincent called out. "Hold up there a second, Ms. Big-a-Shot Manager, and say hello."

Jacqueline Rubino brought her bike to an abrupt halt.

"How you doin', Jackie?" The don brightened, moving his bulky frame closer to the door.

"*Zu* Vincent!" the handsome woman said with some surprise,

smiling ever so sweetly that she practically melted Vincent's heart on the spot.

"She called me Uncle Vincent," the mobster said with a sigh, curving up the corners of his mouth to form a most expansive grin. "This *is*, *indeed*, a very special night."

"Very special, indeed," Jacqueline agreed, reaching over the handlebars and pulling a 7.65 mm handgun from her wicker basket filled with loaves of crusty bread, swiftly and efficiently putting a bullet into the center of Detective Ed Hennesey's forehead at point-blank range.

"No! Oh, my G—"

Don Ciccio never got the last word completely out of his mouth, although Phil Cancilla's niece knew perfectly well the single fragmented syllable omitted from the man's retort, silencing the sound forever as she emptied the pistol into the mob boss's head, face and neck.

"May be *your* God, Vincent," she practically whispered to the doomed man. "Couldn't possibly be the same as mine." Unsmilingly, unflinchingly, unshamefully, Jacqueline Rubino let the firearm fall to the ground as instructed.

Chapter 89

A vehicle appeared out of nowhere, and in less than thirty seconds, Jacqueline and her bike and bread were off the block. The pair fled, speeding south along the dark and desolate road before heading west then north onto Montauk Highway. Her accomplice gradually reduced his speed, keeping the *borrowed* SUV to fifty miles per hour.

Jacqueline silently said her prayers, unconsciously lacing, then unlocking long and lovely glove-covered fingers.

"You okay?" the figure asked with genuine concern.

"Never better," she said, wiping a tear or two away from her pretty sea-green eyes.

"No, really."

"I'll be all right."

"You did good."

Jacqueline kept her tongue.

"I just wish we could have set things up differently," Justin said, signaling before moving over to the right lane.

"I know, but that's the route he always takes. Took," she breathed uneasily. "It had to be back there or no place. It had to be tonight or never."

"I just hope the police don't press your Uncle Phil with too many questions."

"Maybe they won't even connect Vincent to the restaurant."

"You shittin' me or what? A block away from the place? Ciccio's haunt? Get real, girl. When the M.E. unbags that pig, they won't even haveta gut 'em to figure out what and where he ate tonight," Justin put forth plainly.

"And why's that?"

"'Cause I ain't never seen the motherfucker stop to chew or swallow his food. That's why. All that eggplant and spaghetti's probably stuck right here." Justin pointed to his Adam's apple.

Jacqueline forced a smile.

"But not to worry," he added comfortingly. "Rough part's over with. We made it the hell out of there without being seen."

She nodded nervously.

"Think Phil or anyone in your family might suspect it was you?" Justin questioned anxiously.

Jacqueline shook her pretty head emphatically. "I'm the last one they'd *ever* suspect."

"How come so sure?"

"Because *I* can't even believe it was me," she answered in all seriousness.

"Got that right," Justin agreed. "And *that* was our ace in the hole."

"What are you going to do with the manuscript, J?"

"I already took care of it."

"How?"

"Burnt it. In the same fireplace where Columba stashed Tamblin before carting him over to East Point."

"Good for you."

"You know, I thought everything was over and done with when I put the bastard down," Justin jabbered, shaking his head slowly and sadly from side to side. "Then I realized that nothing's really ever over till people get what they want."

"And what is it that *you* want, J?"

"Peace."

"Me, too," Jacqueline said in total agreement.

"Amen to that."

"J?"

"What?"

"Ask you a question?"

"Fire away—in a manner of speaking, that is," he kidded, his eyes glued to the road ahead of them.

"How did you learn that Columba was the Father of the Federation, let alone locate him?"

"Kept my eyes and ears open. One day, I overheard Hennesey and Miller arguing about an author and architect. I thought they were talking about two professionals up there in South Jamesport, because there's an architect who happens to live next-door to Tamblin, and an author who just moved in on the other side of him. I didn't know at the time that they were referring to Malcolm Columba as the author and architect of the Federation. When I got back from Connecticut and learned that Evan Tamblin had suddenly disappeared, along with a neighbor's boat named *The Author*, which the guy keeps at a marina next to his property while his dock is being built, well, I borrowed the keys to *Boy 'n' Sea* and went-a-huntin'—just on a hunch. I really didn't know what or who I was gonna turn up. As it turned out, I found them both. Tamblin and Columba. You know the rest of the story."

"But how was Columba able to place federal agents into extremist groups in the first place, so that they wouldn't be discovered, I mean?"

"What little I learned from a source, whose name shall go unmentioned, Columba had a core of special agents he networked with around the world. A tightly knit group from which he personally handpicked and introduced to suspected heads of terrorist organizations that he made it his business to befriend beforehand through Tamblin's countless contacts. Many of those under suspicion were movers and shakers who couldn't live unless they had a *cause*— but not necessarily one to die for. These people form what are called cells: a loosely woven bunch of radicals like themselves who, in turn, would go out and recruit others to do their bidding, promising whatever it took to accomplish their goals. One guy or gal might fly from say Afghanistan to New York and enlist the services of a person or persons sympathetic to their movement here, give them instruction, then fly back home. Pretty much like how I picked, trained, and placed you. Only I didn't have so far to travel," he ribbed.

"What are you talking about? I picked you."

"No, no, no. I handpicked you, Jackie."

Jacqueline shook her head. "You were my customer. Remember?"

"What does that prove? You were my waitress—what—a dozen times before you got yourself promoted?"

"More like two dozen."

"Fine—which reminds me—every single time I asked you about any dish on the menu, you'd always say, 'Oh, that's *really* very good. Oh, that's a *very* good choice.' How could *everything*, *every time*, be so very friggin' good? No. I picked you as carefully as I picked out an entrée. You were my ace in the hole, like I said."

"No, J. You were *my* ace of spades."

"Excuse me?"

"That's not what I meant," she said through a giggle.

"Sounds to me like a form of racial profiling from where I'm sittin', girl," he chaffed.

She shook her pretty head. "Sorry. But *I* still picked you."

"Listen. If you remember correctly, I'd tell *you* certain things about that fat fuck and his friends sittin' in back at that favorite corner table of his. All *you'd* talk about was the food and how everything was 'oh, so *very* good.' Recall?"

"Yes, and *I'm* the one who overheard some threatening comments made concerning *you*, whispered at his table, then warned *you*. You remember that? I figured there was already bad blood between you two."

"But *I'm* the one who did some digging and found out exactly what he had in store for your family down the pike. Like the kind of stranglehold he was applying to Phil."

"Okay, so we both knew he had to go."

"Straight to hell."

Jacqueline nodded anxiously.

"It's gonna be all right, Jackie. Trust me."

"I hope so. I don't mind telling you I'm really scared."

"Hey. I read a bit of Columba's book before I burnt it," Justin said confidently. "Learned a few things, too, like how not to get caught," he boasted so as to put her mind at ease. "Not to worry."

"I thought you said you couldn't decode any of it."

"I made a bit of headway before I incinerated it," he outright lied.

Jacqueline smiled archly. "Wanna know something?"

"What?"

"I don't think you even know how to read."

Justin looked over at his accomplice queerly. "Now, where did you get an idea like that?"

"Oh, I could tell from the way you looked at the menu before you ordered," she tested.

"Oh, yeah?"

"Yeah."

"So, what was I holdin' it upside down or something?"

"Nooo," she said by way of a giggle once again, holding back a wall of laughter behind an elegantly sculpted, latex glove-covered hand. "You were trying to pronounce the words to yourself when you thought no one was looking."

"Is that so?"

"That and the fact you always pointed to a selection and asked me, 'How's that?' when you really meant, 'What's that?'"

"Again, to which you *always* answered, 'Oh, it's really *very* good.'"

"You really want to know what the giveaway was?"

"I'm sure you're about to tell me whether I want to hear it or not."

Jacqueline's slender shoulders shook from laughter. "It was the first time I ever laid eyes on you," she chortled.

"Well, go on. Have your little laugh."

"I handed you a wine list, and you ordered number 97 for a '97 Valpolicella, telling me you wanted it nice and moist and not dried out."

"The wine list, huh?" Justin echoed vacantly. "So then tell me. How come I got a veal and chicken dish instead of a bottle of wine?"

Jacqueline could not stop laughing.

"Go on," Justin pressed with some annoyance. "Tell me."

"Well, I figured you thought *val* somehow stood for veal, and *pol, pollo* for chicken," she tittered. "I don't know. Anyhow, you loved it."

"I did, huh?"

"Uh-huh."

"You sure it was me? Because I hear rumor that we all pretty much look alike," he needled.

"No, it was some time ago, but it was positively you, J."

"Yeah?"

"Yep."

"You sure?"

"Sure, I'm sure."

"How sure?"

"Come on, now."

"No, tell me. I wanna hear."

"All right," she said, deciding to play his silly game. "For one thing, you always sat alone, and you're the only single customer who ever left me a fifty-dollar tip. Each and every time. So there."

Justin nodded. "But you don't think I can read, huh?"

Jacqueline relaxed and shook her head. "No, I do not."

Justin reached quickly into the backseat and came up with a book. "Here."

"Here, what?"

"Pick a page."

Jacqueline took the book and put it near the dash light. "This? This is a book called *Book of Lists*."

"So?"

"You're going to read from a list?"

"Well, you said I didn't know a wine list from a menu, so I'm gonna prove you wrong. Turn to any list you like. Go ahead. French Authors. National Parks. U.S. Presidents."

"That won't prove *anything*."

"Why not?"

"Anyone could recite a list from memory."

"Oh, really?"

"Yes, really. I think you might recognize, say, most presidents' names if you could read even just a little bit."

"Oh, so now it's 'just a little bit,' is it?"

"Something like that," she hedged with a smile.

"How about French Authors?"

"I don't know whether *I'd* be able to read them correctly," she admitted, staring down the column filled with more than a few unfamiliar names.

"All right then. How about states and capitals? Think anyone could just recite *all* of them?"

Jacqueline thought for a moment, flipping through the pages to the lengthy list. "All right. But *I* get to point to the names—anywhere I choose."

"Anywhere you wish."

"Good."

"Well, show me the list."

"Not just yet."

"Why not?"

"Because you've got to keep your eyes on the road. That's why not."

"We're gonna catch that light up ahead."

"Fine. You read for me then."

"Fine."

Justin and Jacqueline caught the traffic light as it was turning amber. She put the page under his nose and held the book steadily.

"So, now read for me. From the bottom up. How's that, Mister Smarty Pants?"

Justin scrunched his face and wrinkled his brow.

"Just as I thought, Justin Barnes. Just as I thought."

Justin flicked on and adjusted the overhead map light. "There we go."

"There we go, what?" she mimicked, the slightest hint of a smirk creasing the corners of her pretty mouth.

"Wyoming, Cheyenne; Wisconsin, Madison; West Virginia, Charleston; Washington, Olympia; Virginia, Richmond; Vermont, Mont·pel·yer," Justin rattled off and pronounced the names with perfect diction.

"Jesus," Jacqueline groaned, running a slender, double-layered latex-finger on up the column. "Read."

"Utah, Salt Lake City; Texas, Austin; Tennessee, Nashville. Satisfied, Miss Smarty Pants?" he gave back in spades.

Jacqueline shook her head. "One more."

"Light's green."

"One more, I said," she ordered. "Pretty, please," she cooed like a dove. "Just one more?"

Justin stepped on the gas just as the car in back of them leaned on the horn. He glanced at the page and smiled mischievously. "South Dakota, Pe·âr," the trickster enunciated with perfect diction.

Jacqueline could not believe her ears. "So why did you lead me on like that, J?"

"'Cause I wanted you to think that you picked me," Justin answered with a wide grin.

Jacqueline playfully hit his shoulder with the book. "I still say I picked you," she insisted.

"Well, however it went down, it's like I said before. No one's gonna come lookin' for you. 'Cause the gun I gave you? It's a piece I got that's gonna kick back to a real piece of garbage who's connected to Ciccio's crew."

"Who?"

"*Who* is not important."

"Tell me."

"A high-ranking police official from Manhattan is all I'll say for now. I'm sure you'll read about his arrest real soon."

"Jesus, J. How did you happen to get his gun?"

"Through a collector friend of mine who made the necessary withdrawal from the cop's private collection."

"But I'm sure the owner of that gun will have an alibi for tonight. No?"

"No," Justin said with utmost assurance.

"How come?"

"Because he was sitting in an empty parking lot at a Thai restaurant several blocks away from Bella Sera, waiting for an anonymous snitch who never showed up with information about a certain manuscript, 'cause I was waiting off Bess Road for you. He was told I might be runnin' a little late and to wait for me there after the place closed. He's probably still waiting as we speak. He'll have some real explaining to do."

Jacqueline Rubino smiled and nodded. "You're very devious, Justin Barnes. Know that?"

"You don't know the half of it. Anyhow, I'm not half as devious as you."

"How do you mean?"

"Because the more I think about it, the more I'm beginning to believe that you *did*, in fact, pick me."

"Why do you say that now?"

"Sixth sense, you might say."

"I don't follow."

"I'm thinking maybe a certain member of your family *knew* that something might be going down tonight."

"Really?"

Justin nodded warily.

"How do you figure that, J?"

"It's just something I'm reading in your eyes."

Jacqueline gave up a smile that could light the distant stars behind the clouds. "You know, I think it's like you said a moment ago."

"What's that?"

"Everything's going to turn out all right."

Justin gave her a promising wink and a nod there in the dimly lit interior of the *borrowed*, Lincoln Navigator, a second family vehicle belonging and registered to—not unlike the cop's ***Deutsche Werke*** pistol—William Mattheson's paternal family from Bayside, Queens.

"It will, Jackie," he reassured the young woman, gently touching her cheek with glove-covered fingers before turning up the air conditioning, displaying his pearly whites for all they were worth. "It surely will."

Chapter 90

It was a late evening toward the end of June when Inspector William Mattheson of Manhattan's NYPD was being escorted from his home in Bayside, Queens, then lead toward an unmarked gray sedan by two arresting homicide detectives from Queens County. It took all the self-control the fifty-three-year-old veteran could muster to keep from lashing out at the young black reporter who had somehow broken rank and was on their heels. Mattheson desperately wished to turn around and kick the facile-tongued staff writer in the groin. He so wanted to thrash the newspaperman's foul mouth, if not for the pair of steel bracelets fashioned around two furious clenched fists at the small of his back.

Alan Jones, from *Newsday*, had driven all the way in from his Melville office, just to humiliate him further, was Mattheson's assessment of the situation. It was not Jones' single question, per se, that got to the inspector, but the way in which the reporter framed it. His tone. His arrogant demeanor. His stance when he caught up to them. Even the way in which he held his poison pen. Poised above his notepad. Venomous black ink was about to be put to paper that would, in turn, be set in print. Forever. Powerful words that would surely wound the veteran cop. Sentences that should sentence him to unspeakable hurt and horror. Paragraphs that promised to place him in the Hall of Shame.

The story could clobber them all.

BAD BOYS IN BLUE, ANEW he envisioned the morning headline to read.

William Mattheson ran the reporter's question through his mind again and again. *The unmitigated gall.* How the inspector wanted to respond in kind but knew that his lawyer—if not the Governor of the state himself—would murder him later if he opened his mouth now.

Glancing over his shoulder, he could see his wife crying hysterically from behind a downstairs, brightly lit window, her angry father standing alongside with a protective arm wrapped around his daughter's trembling shoulders. Where was his legal eagle? Matheson wondered. Probably still upstairs, enviously eyeing and just dying to handle the family's prized handgun collection, waiting patiently for both car and client to take their leave.

The collection.

His father's first and last true love. William was just its keeper. Like a curator in some museum. The handsome trove of weaponry dated back to the days when his paternal grandfather was a cop on the streets of Harlem. Like Bill and his father before him.

Simpler times, for sure.

"All right, let's go, inspector," one of the two detectives said, his hand atop the top cop's head as he carefully placed him into the backseat of the waiting sedan.

The other detective turned around quietly and put his refrigerator-like frame an inch away from the reporter's notepad.

Alan Jones looked up and smiled. "No need for a statement from you, Detective Quill. Your body language says it all," the five-and-a-half footer funned.

"Night, Al," the big detective said, standing steadfast.

"Ny-Quil—" Alan Jones punned "—which is what I think the inspector's going to need tonight if he's to get any sleep at all," he wisecracked.

"I wouldn't push it," the detective warned, his hand placed firmly upon the handle of the rear door.

"Well, it doesn't close by itself," Jones tormented, racing through his shorthand before putting a period at the end of his piece. "There," the writer concluded, known throughout the five boroughs for his vituperative tongue and pen.

"Stick it," the Bayside cop from the 111th Precinct snapped.

"If you'll just face about and spread 'em," the reporter sallied with a happy-go-lucky grin. "It's sure to conform. One size fits all, pal," he goaded, holding the pen out and upright.

Inspector William Mattheson sat staring straight ahead—the corrupt police official framed in profile for a final moment before several cameras flashed and the car sped off into the night.

How does Jones come off asking me such a question? Mattheson worried and wondered. *How could he or anyone possibly know . . . ?*

. . . Know, perhaps, that William once used that very weapon in an illegal shooting; hence, the cover-up . . . when he was a rookie working the streets of Harlem.

No one knew but Vincent Ciccio, and the don was dead.

In their reckless youth, Vincent had disposed of the body for his friend. It was *their* secret. William took care of the gun by simply putting it back in his father's collection of heirlooms, handed down through the course of years. One of the few handguns in the entire collection that could not be traced.

So how is it that particular gun gets stolen, now? William Matheson pondered his predicament. *Why the handgun with the letter 𝔇 for Deutsche emblazoned into its handle? Why not another more valuable piece? Why not the whole damn lot for that matter? Why that single, solitary weapon?*

Why had he kept the pistol in the first place? he blasted himself. Because his father was still alive at the time and would surely know—know that his son had shot and killed a man in cold blood.

That's why.

He was just a rookie the first time he removed the pistol from his father's collection and carried the piece into the precinct to impress his senior German partner. The Spin-*Miester*. The second time was when he used it in the fatal shooting, while still the impulsive hotheaded fledging that he was. He should have just tossed it out and told his father that it was stolen—stolen like that handgun and his black Lincoln Navigator that had been filched the week before.

In his troubled mind, Matheson kept mulling over the reporter's haunting questions:

"Care to comment on who shot and killed the Spin-Meister, inspector? Care to make a statement? Want to know where the bones are buried? Bet you'd just love to know my source."

How could the reporter possibly know? Oh, he was being set up so nicely now, he knew. *But by whom?*

Halfway out to the 112th Precinct in Forest Hills, Bill Mattheson believed he knew the answer, which raised the larger question. How much of the story did the *Newsday* reporter, Alan Jones, actually know?

By the time they reached the precinct, Inspector Mattheson

recalled the angry words of a young black buck who the Spin-*Meister* and he had brought in for questioning in connection with the murder of a cop—many a year ago. After which, the two had little choice but to release the maverick. Mattheson remembered the young man's words as he was being led from the car to the building:

"What goes around comes around—motherfuckers."

www.ingramcontent.com/pod-product-compliance
Lightning Source LLC
Chambersburg PA
CBHW071332020726
47502CB00001B/76